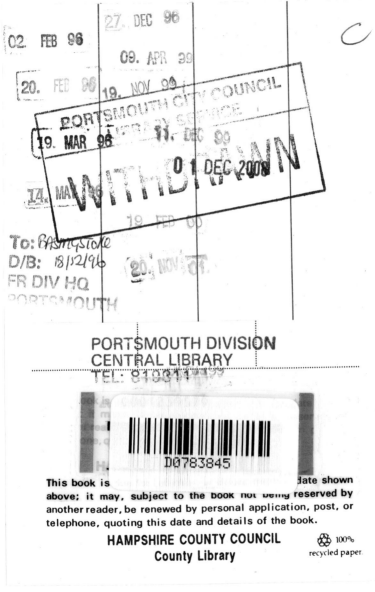

A Radical Reader

THE STRUGGLE FOR CHANGE IN ENGLAND, 1381 – 1914

EDITED BY CHRISTOPHER HAMPTON

PENGUIN BOOKS

Penguin Books Ltd, Harmondsworth, Middlesex, England
Penguin Books, 40 West 23rd Street, New York, New York 10010, U.S.A.
Penguin Books Australia Ltd, Ringwood, Victoria, Australia
Penguin Books Canada Ltd, 2801 John Street, Markham, Ontario, Canada L3R 1B4
Penguin Books (N.Z.) Ltd, 182–190 Wairau Road, Auckland 10, New Zealand

First published 1984
Copyright © Christopher Hampton, 1984
All rights reserved

Printed in Great Britain by
Fletcher & Son Ltd, Norwich
Filmset in Plantin

'It matters what men of goodwill want to do with their lives.'
Ron Kitaj

The cliché reaches out, takes hold of us. It matters –
What we do, much more than what we want to do;
And how we do it, with what consciousness,
And why. So many want, would like to, can't.
That matters too – goodwill hemmed in goes bad.
The problem is to get outside the prisons of conditioning.
Goodwill is not enough. Intention's not enough.
We have to act, to set up groups that unlock doors,
Seek links between the dispossessed, keep channels open
To the psychic roots – feeding the imaginal
With *real toads* from *real gardens*, bricks that bruise,
The joints and girders literalist builders use.
Because there *is* a world we can inhabit freely
Which is not conspiring to diminish and estrange,
Where people matter to each other and are not shut in,
Do not shrink back from contact in suspicion,
Can advance to seek the common ground, the common speech,
And break the strangleholds that keep us out of reach.

To my wife Kathleen,
for her criticism and encouragement during the
whole period of this marathon quest – a continual
reminder that women have always been centrally
involved in the struggle, even when they are not
speaking for themselves;
to my mother,
now at the end of her life, who gave so generously of
her energy and love over so many years;
and to my friend Frederick Grubb,
for his rigorous and penetrating view of the struggle
for socialist change.

CONTENTS LIST

Acknowledgements — 9

Introduction — 11

Chronology — 25

1 THE MIDDLE AGES, 1381–1453 — 47

2 THE BREAK-UP OF THE FEUDAL SYSTEM, 1453–1603 — 83

3 THE RISE OF CAPITALISM, 1603–88 — 149

4 THE EXPANSION OF EMPIRE, 1689–1788 — 287

5 THE AGE OF REVOLUTION AND TOTAL WAR, 1789–1848 — 339

6 THE TRIUMPH OF CAPITALISM, 1848–1914 — 507

Epilogue — 604

Further Reading — 607

Index — 615

ACKNOWLEDGEMENTS

Thanks are due to the following for their kind permission to reprint extracts included in this book:

to the Bodley Head for the extract from *My Autobiography* by Charles Chaplin;

to the British Library of Politics and Economics at the LSE on behalf of the Passfield Trust for the quotation from Beatrice Webb's diary of 8 March 1899;

to Longman for the extracts from *The Suffragette Movement* by Sylvia Pankhurst;

to the Nonesuch Press Ltd for the poem by Hilaire Belloc;

to the Society of Authors on behalf of the Bernard Shaw Estate for the extract from *The Quintessence of Ibsenism* by G. B. Shaw.

INTRODUCTION

1

The basic freedoms that so many English men and women now accept, both in fact and in law, as their birthright, are of course neither so firmly established nor so proof against attack that we can afford to take them for granted or believe that they are to be maintained, let alone extended, without constant vigilance and constant effort. And above all we have to remember that these freedoms have been won for us over the centuries by the determined efforts of *others*, people who have had to fight, often against overwhelming odds, for every inch of the ground.

Not one of us, in other words, has any cause to be complacent about the protection of the laws and institutions that define our lives or safeguard our supposed liberties. Even a glance at the record of history will show that there are no safeguards for the defenceless, the passive and the unwary, and that all our freedoms have had to be fought for again and again by the oppressed, sometimes over ground already strewn with the wreckage of defeat, if always under different conditions. Indeed, as far as the common people of England are concerned, the struggle has had to be continually renewed, for they have been persistently denied their rights and basic freedoms. They are the ones who have had to bear the heaviest burdens of injustice and oppression in order that the few might live in luxury; and it is therefore the courage and defiance they have shown in fighting back that have determined the conditions out of which our most fundamental social advances have been made.

In this sense, and at almost every point in the record, the history of radicalism that is the subject of this book is a history of unending struggle against one kind of oppression or another. But if the purpose of gathering together the contemporary witnesses to such a record had been to demonstrate nothing more than this, or to provide some sort of pious verbal monument to the dead, there would have been little point in attempting it. What matters is the message that these proofs of courage and tenacity (spanning five hundred years of England's history) have to offer to the living – history as creative defiance, as intellectual and imaginative

11

awareness, as a challenge to all that is officially regarded as acceptable. For they are part of the unfinished business that the English people are engaged upon, defining the conditions under which it is possible to move ahead and break new ground, make new attempts to reach across the divisive barriers that continue to threaten our freedoms.

The nature of this message is that all social advance has its roots not in what is thought or said but in the actions of ordinary people at those moments of crisis when, oppressed beyond endurance, they refuse to put up with the conditions under which they are forced to live – when 'the downtrodden and the despondent raise their heads and /Stop believing in the strength /Of their oppressors'. During such moments, there are those among the privileged and cultivated minority who have played a major part in directing and clarifying the issues at stake and helping to sustain and sharpen the courage of those who act – intellectuals, poets, writers, thinkers who have made themselves passionate spokesmen for the oppressed, who have moved with them as they rose and have defended them against their enemies, often at great risk to themselves. But in the end it is not what these gifted individuals *say*, however cogent their argument and however great their influence, that changes things. What counts in the end is the determination of those who are prepared to act – for, as Gerrard Winstanley puts it, 'action is the life of all, and if thou dost not act, thou dost nothing'.

There are many, even among the enemies of freedom, who talk (sometimes with enthusiasm) of freedom in the abstract. But such talk is often no more than the rhetoric or hypocrisy of men who have gained their own freedom at the expense of other people's natural rights and who therefore have little real interest in extending it to others. 'Everyone talks of freedom,' says Winstanley, speaking from his own bitter experience as one of the dispossessed, 'but there are but few that act for freedom, and the actors for freedom are oppressed by the talkers and verbal professors of freedom.'

2

History, unfortunately, has seldom been on the side of those who act for freedom. It speaks most loudly, on the whole, through the voices of dominant individuals in a largely male-dominated world, who reflect the interests of the ruling class – men who, intent on maintaining the structures of power that safeguard their property and wealth, will be ready to profess many things, including freedom.

But history has its other voices, which emerge out of the complex pattern of events from among the anonymous masses who *produce* the wealth, in the course of their struggle for bread and shelter and security. Nor are these voices to be ignored. Coming out of the roots of the community, from men and women who cannot read or write, they speak a different kind of language – a language of resistance and defiance rather than of acquiescence and acceptance, of intuitive response and improvisation rather than of scholarship and exposition.

At first, and for a long time in the early centuries, such voices hardly appear at all in the official records, except indirectly and as an obscure background to events apparently initiated and resolved by the encounters of the great, or reflected from the statutes and registers and chronicles dutifully kept by the officers of the state. The opinions of the illiterate many, however persuasive and however deeply involved in the making of events, seem to count for little; they are mere accessories to the splendid pageant. And as far as the women are concerned, they are completely silent. Kings and dukes and generals and ministers, monopolizing the pages of history, have habitually assumed the servile obedience and acquiescence of all the people they command. And if sometimes these 'great men' have seemed to speak for their subjects (in the spirit in which Shakespeare imagined Henry V taking upon himself the burden of his army's fortunes) they have done so not because they were interested in furthering natural and civil rights (already usurped) but because, in their ruthless pursuit of power, they could not do without the people.

The voice of radical protest speaks on another level altogether, setting itself against the weight of convention and custom and the pressure to conform; born out of anger and reflecting the people's determination to free themselves from the repressive machinery that has enslaved them. It is not the voice of moderate middle-ground opinion urging the virtues of compromise and accommodation to make an unpalatable system more acceptable. Those who adopt such a course may call themselves radicals, but they cannot challenge the underlying conditions that are the causes of injustice and oppression. The true radical urges fundamental change, and must therefore be able to envisage alternatives that will answer the people's real needs. Like Milton or Blake or Marx, he is at once ruthlessly critical and questioning, alert to lapses of moral vision, and deeply suspicious of all who command the techniques by which societies seek to maintain their power. Knowing that you cannot reason with the enemies of reason, he is prepared to speak out fearlessly on behalf of the propertyless and the dispossessed against exploitation and impoverishment, the callousness of the privileged, and the cruelties of state authority.

And above all, he is driven by a vision grounded upon the interests

13

of the community as a whole, which insists that no society can be considered just or reasonable or in any sense acceptable that does not extend to every person who plays his or her part in shaping it an equal and ungrudging share in the enjoyment of its wealth and resources. The conviction of a man like Winstanley that the earth is 'a common treasury of livelihood to whole mankind, without respect of persons', may seem, in face of the overwhelming evidence, at once utopian and plaintive; but it is rooted in an irrefutable concept of justice that puts the destructive greed of the appropriators, the buyers and sellers of the common wealth, to shame. And it is a concept which defines justice and human rights in essentially economic terms. Not that this is likely to make any difference to those who are actually in possession, because – possession being nine tenths of the law and property an ultimate symbol of legitimacy – they have the power. And the struggle against this power, which has kept most people for most of the history of humanity in a state of subservience and semi-slavery, is a slow and arduous record of revolt and acquiescence and of crushing defeat. But, though for long periods the labouring masses, the serfs and wage-earners, have gone about their work silently and patiently while the factions were being made and unmade around them, periodically they have stepped forward and risen up to assert their place in the world and to insist on their common rights.

Such moments have rarely lasted long – though when they *have* occurred on a major scale, as they did in 1381, 1450, 1549, the 1640s, at the end of the eighteenth century, and at intervals of economic crisis throughout the nineteenth century, they brought about a perceptible change in the balance of power. But they have usually left the fundamental inequalities of wealth and of condition unaltered. 'The poor man,' as Rainborough put it indignantly in 1647, when all Englishmen were fighting for their birthrights, 'hath fought to enslave himself, to give power to men of riches, men of Estates, to make him a perpetual slave.' In other words, most popular uprisings have led only to a shifting of power from one oppressive class or group to another already waiting to take over – which, having used the people to gain control, has then created its own weapons of repression to hold the people down.

In order to grasp the peculiar significance of such changes and their impact on the future, one has to look at history not as a finished process, as a pattern inexorably determined, but as a process of change, and with all its options open. The fact that we think we know, from our reading of the past, what actually happened, and that the course of events was apparently decided by this or that particular combination of issues, is not enough – just as it is not enough to accept that what was happening

14

to men was happening in exactly the same way to women. We have to know also what was going on under the surface; what might have succeeded but didn't; by what combination of forces it was defeated; to what degree it failed; and what it left behind as seeds for the future. For it is possible to build forward even from defeat. Indeed, it is important to recognize that every defeat defines the possible ground for a new thrust forward. The fact that the Peasants' Revolt collapsed with the murder of Wat Tyler and that Richard went to great lengths to stamp out every lingering trace of it, 'so to teach you that your slavery may be an example to posterity', could not prevent this great trial of courage and of vision by the downtrodden men of Kent and Essex from becoming an example to posterity utterly beyond Richard's power to control. The men who died 'in the cause of the liberty we have won' were to encourage new generations in the centuries that followed – the Kentishmen of 1450, the people of Norfolk, the Diggers and Levellers, the Chartists, the Dockers, the Miners. To have made that kind of history is to have made oneself part of the struggle for progress that is still going on. Better, one might say, to fail in the battle for such ends than to be branded as an agent of regressive power, no matter how well you hold the stage. For that is to have released another hidden spring to add to the current of resistance. A man commits himself to a certain course of action without knowing the outcome, as John Ball did. And whether he succeeds or fails, risking himself, what matters (in the judgement of history) is what he risked himself *for*.

Thus the struggle has had to be continually renewed by the people, who have been forced again and again to accept the bitter proofs of exploitation and betrayal. But again and again they have come back, beyond exhaustion – those 'conscious and conscientious men,' as Milton put it, 'who in this world are counted weakest', but without whose unwavering courage 'the force of this world' cannot be defeated – in the attempt to establish what so long ago Wat Tyler proclaimed at Smithfield: 'that all men should be free, and of one condition'.

3

In pursuit of this great aim, so persistently thwarted, there is a tribute to be paid to those among the English writers and intellectuals (few though they may be) who, at crucial periods in the history of England, have taken an active part in the struggle, speaking for the people and sometimes even with them. Men like Wycliffe, Thomas More, Shakespeare, Milton, Swift, Blake, Wordsworth, Byron, Shelley and Dickens stand out precisely because of what they have put their work at the disposal of. They make themselves witnesses by defending the natural laws of community and love and fellowship, and recognizing the destructive lusts that threaten them. Their work is at once public and social and collective in its response to reality, and speaks for a whole world, for the subsistent continuities and the historical conditions that shape people's lives; thus offering a vital incentive to the enlargement of the constructive powers of the mind and the conquest of fear and insecurity and ignorance.

Milton's pamphlets, for instance, in defence of free speech and a free press and the values of a free commonwealth, remain acts of unequivocal support for all that the English people fought to create. And even with his great poem on the Fall of Man, coming in the wake of the pamphlets and the breakdown of the Commonwealth, we have something much more than an abstruse biblical myth. It is, as Christopher Hill observes, 'a poem about the people of God in defeat anywhere', and it is also an attempt to explain the failure of the Revolution. As with Adam and Eve, so with the English people: 'They themselves decreed their own revolt . . . /I found them free, and free they must remain /Till they enthrall themselves.' In other words, the political failure of the Commonwealth was ultimately a moral failure, a failure of nerve and courage and steadiness of purpose by those who had made it. And this conclusion makes a devastating commentary on the age that followed, which Milton had to accept after 1660, with 'the insolencies, the menaces, the insultings of our newly animated common enemies' choosing a king 'to pageant himself up and down in progress among the perpetual swayings and cringings of an abject people'.

Such denunciatory anger in the context of such conviction is echoed in the next century in the scathing satire of Swift against Whig hypocrisy and corruption, and in Pope's attack on 'lucre's sordid charms'. And later on there is Goldsmith's indictment of eighteenth-century enclosures, which were still being enforced in the 1820s in John Clare's Northamptonshire. There is Wordsworth's enthusiasm for the French Revolution, which survives his retreat into conformity. There is the anger and indignation of Blake, who sets his Jerusalem-vision of 'the Great Harvest and Vintage of the Nations' against the tyranny of England's rulers, serving 'To turn man from his path, /To restrain the child from the womb, /To cut off the bread from the city, /That the remnant may learn to obey.' There is Shelley's call for revolutionary change (twice envisaged in his work through the voice of a woman) against a world dominated by men and controlled (through them) by 'Force and Fraud: Old Custom, legal Crime'; and Byron's searing contempt for its rulers. And in the age that succeeded this, beyond the Chartists, there is the Dickens of *Bleak House, Hard Times* and *Our Mutual Friend*, for whom the ugliness and squalor, the intolerable suffering and the destitution brought into being by the capitalist system, seemed a crime of unspeakable magnitude that struck at the very heart of the social order.

All these are people who saw it as imperative to come to the defence of the people, and who recognized that, though they could do little on their own to bring about the necessary changes, nevertheless for them, as for Byron,

> Words are things, and a small drop of ink
> Falling like dew upon a thought produces
> That which makes thousands, perhaps millions, think.

4

The year 1381 seemed a natural starting-point for this book, not only because it is the first great popular uprising driven by rational collective will towards equality, freedom and common wealth, but because (being this) it points forward towards the socialist revolutionary movements which have defined the social changes of the last two hundred years.

Of course, the pattern of English life in the late Middle Ages has to be seen in terms of the hierarchic orders of the feudal system under which the common people lived as slaves, the chattels of their masters. Though people had begun to question the authority of the Catholic Church, it was still a major factor for them in a world constantly threatened with war, famine, disease and periodic disorder. But at the same time the kings and their advisers were pursuing secular policies in keeping with their own arrogant autocratic view of the state and its subjects.

In the late fourteenth century agriculture was the basis of England's economy, and wool the chief article of export; and with the organization of the cloth trade, and the expansion of wool, which brought into being large-scale increases in enclosures, these years were to become the breeding-ground of English capitalism. It might even be said that the ruinous Hundred Years' War, which had started in the mid-century as a squabble for plunder and dynastic influence, was also an attempt to keep the markets open. But whatever the advantages of these developments in the agrarian economy, they brought widespread distress and disorder to the lives of the common people, already unsettled by the decimation of the Black Death, and burdened with the taxes of state and Church. It was in this context of growing unrest (recorded in the statutes) that the uprising of 1381 occurred, incited by such travelling preachers as John Ball, who agitated against the negligence of the Church with calls for the establishment of a Christian democracy which defines an early form of socialist ideas.

It is clear that the people were in a mood of seething resentment, not only against the paying of tithes to the greedy extortioners of the Church, whose income was said to be 'five times more than is paid to the king from the whole produce of the realm', but also against the state taxes. And quite suddenly, though with a promptitude and unity that suggests careful preparation, the people refused to pay, and the revolt began.

For this was much more than a dispute about money. Its millenarian aims were a fundamental challenge to the whole social structure and its long-established ideology of enslavement; for they asserted the right of all men to freedom and equality. Not only that; men were prepared to die for them. And so, although this revolt against thraldom seems to have been almost immediately denied, to become little more than a precondition for new kinds of enslavement – the enslavement of the wage-earner selling his labour – it represents an indispensable step forward in the contradictory struggle for progress.

This early record of the radicalism and heresy of the common people remains incomplete because, as I have already suggested, few could read or write. They talked, discussed and argued unrecorded. And it was no doubt as a result of the oral transmission of ideas that revolts occurred such as those of 1413–14 in Buckinghamshire, 1414 in Essex and 1414 in London. John Ball's argument that 'we are all sons of Adam, born free,' is rooted in the scriptures; and the struggles of the people against their masters have to be registered in the context of the religious disputes of the age. The radicalism of the fifteenth century, that is, would continue to have been nourished through the Lollard followers of Wycliffe by the Christian vision of justice. Religion and politics acted upon each other. It was through the teachings of Christ that men sought to change society, very often against the official priests and bishops in their wealth and pride, and the coercive powers of the Church itself.

Things may not have changed by 1450 at the bitter end of the Hundred Years' War; but with the country almost bankrupt and the Wars of the Roses about to start secular issues must have been paramount. By 1516, when More wrote *Utopia*, the more purely class nature of the rulers had become apparent, together with the economic exploitation (again through the enclosures) of the landless peasantry, of whom More writes with such passionate feeling as the cheated producers of wealth. This was now an age of monarchical absolutism, which by 1549 (the year of the Norfolk Revolt, another peasants' rising) had already gone part of the way towards transferring the vast wealth of the feudal Church to the Crown. But the fundamental issues of taxes and tithes, and the great enclosures for sheep, remained a crushing burden under which the people were to continue to react in scattered revolt against their rulers.

The rising capitalist class that had been testing its strength and accumulating its own wealth during the Elizabethan age was of course to become the major revolutionary force in the seventeenth century, led by Cromwell and the Grandees and Parliament against the feudal power of the monarch. And this class was to make sure that the instrument it had created for its conquest of power, the New Model Army, would function in its own interests, the interests of these new men of property, rather than in the interests of the theoretical freedoms proclaimed for the people of the Commonwealth.

Nevertheless, any understanding of the driving forces behind revolutionary theory and practice in seventeenth-century England has to take account of the heretical Christian doctrines upon which so many of its greatest radicals made their challenge and sought to transform their world. If England was 'to be first restorer of buried truth', as Milton and the revolutionary leaders believed, the struggle for that truth and for a just society, with 'the foundation firmly laid of a free commonwealth', was considered inseparable from the great issues of the Christian debate. Though it is of course true that the underlying thrust of seventeenth-century civil strife turned upon economics, the self-interest of the middle class, the ambitions of the army generals and the defence of property, this debate was part of the ferment of ideas that was going on everywhere, among the labourers, the villagers, the artisans, men and women, the common soldiers, encouraged by the upheavals of the time, the danger, confusion and excitement of war. For the whole country was aroused, and it really must have felt as if the world had been turned upside down. Radical sects sprang up almost overnight – Quakers, Ranters, Seekers, Fifth Monarchists, Baptists, accompanied by a flood of pamphlets, questioning and probing all accepted tenets, cutting across the lines of religion and politics. And the army was restlessly on the move, formulating its Leveller principles, appointing its agitators, urged into debate and revolt by men like Lilburne, Overton and Walwyn. But perhaps the most radical ideas and actions of all came from the Diggers. For though the Diggers had hardly any influence and quickly disappeared, their conception of the Commonwealth, as systematically defined in the writings of Winstanley and embodied in the actions of the colonies, rejected the whole basis of a capitalist economy, 'the power of enclosing land and owning property', and urged universal equality. 'If the waste land of England were manured by her children,' Winstanley believed, 'it would become in a few years the richest, the strongest and most flourishing land in the world.'

But this was not, and could not have been, the way things turned out. The men of property were in control, the land was 'other men's rights' and, as Winstanley could see, this had been organized to ensure the triumph of those who would once again make England a prison and its laws the 'bolts and bars and doors of the prison' to deprive the poor of their rights.

5

The turning-point for the Revolution came in the period between 1647 and 1651 – the period of the Putney Debates, the Leveller manifestos, the second Civil War, the execution of the King, the Digger colonies, the suppression of the Leveller revolts in the army, and Cromwell's victories in Ireland, at Dunbar and at Worcester. This was the period when Cromwell, through the Council of State, his appointment as Captain-General of the Commonwealth forces and his military triumphs, was moving towards the assumption of absolute power, and thus (as men like Winstanley had feared) to a re-assertion of 'the pharasaical kingly spirit of self-love' it had been the purpose of the Revolution to rid England of for good. Now it seemed there was to be no escape from the 'kingly cheats' of covetousness, pride and oppression; for in fact the political counter-revolution was already at work undermining the spirit of the Commonwealth. By the mid-fifties even Milton had begun to lose hope, though he was to continue to defend the Revolution to the last moment against 'the noxious humour' of a return to kingship in his *Ready and Easy Way to Establish a Free Commonwealth*.

The Restoration, when it came, initiated an age of indulgence and of cruelty which was to confirm the worst fears of the radicals, marked by a spirit of absolutism and of barbarian persecution that led to the ruthless repression of all such sects as the Quakers and subjected thousands to long terms of imprisonment – though it could not stop men like Bunyan writing. As for Winstanley's vision of common land shared in comradeship and productive labour, that must have seemed as unattainable as freedom itself to those who remembered it.

Above all, property triumphed. And it was the settlement *organized* by the men of property after the 'Glorious Revolution' of 1688, when the Whigs and Tories united to defeat both James II and the radicals in Parliament, that prepared the ground for an age of expansion and of imperial plunder in the eighteenth century which was in turn to lay the foundations for the developments of the Industrial Revolution and its ruthless exploitation of the landless masses. It is significant that this reorganization of the instruments of labour, both men and machinery, was already beginning to be established before the upheavals of the revolutionary age exploded into being in America and in France. So that, by the time the Napoleonic wars engulfed Europe, the forces of reactionary power in England had been sufficiently strengthened for the crisis to produce one of the most tyrannical regimes in its long history. It was the age of Pitt and Braxfield, of Wellington and Castlereagh, of Eldon and Sidmouth and Liverpool, of Waterloo and Peterloo; and the dehumanizing violence of war gave uninhibited licence to the inhumanities of the Factory Acts, the Poor Laws, the Sedition Acts, and the virtual legalizing of a policy of mass enslavement which forced people off the land into conditions of such squalor as were to be equalled only by the degrading conditions of the African slave-trade.

This contempt for human life, this brutal disregard for even the most elementary standards of decency, enabled the ruling classes (new and old) to accumulate the vast treasury of surplus wealth which, confirmed by the 1832 Reform Act, led to the decisive triumph after 1848 of bourgeois capitalism. From then on, every level of social activity was to be dominated by the laws of the competitive market and those forms of predatory self-interest that reduced all values, spiritual and material, to the level of the saleable commodity. The consequence of such aggressive commercial war and its mass-production techniques was the growth of monopoly powers which, with the rapid development of Germany, incited nationalistic rivalry abroad, across Africa and Asia, to the imperial squabble for world markets that disfigured the last years of the nineteenth century and led to the 1914 war.

But in spite of the debilitating pressures to which they were exposed, the newly dispossessed workers created by these capitalist methods did not take their degradation lying down. Though many of them may have been cowed into submission by the constant insecurities and threats that dominated their lives, others began to organize against their common enemies, and to stand up to them, tentatively at first but with an increasing awareness of their collective strength, particularly in the building of the Chartist movement. It is perhaps difficult for us today to imagine the terrible conditions of the early nineteenth century, though there are many peoples among the nations of the Third World who are suffering conditions of similar barbarity. But anyone who has any imagination at all will know how much courage it must have required for these people to stand out against an institutionalized system of enforcement intended to crush all resistance. The record is filled with the evidence of what could happen to them when they did. Many were hanged, thousands were transported, thousands more imprisoned. Even those who submitted because they had no choice were periodically thrown out of work and left to starve, or to live on the parish droppings of the rich in a world whose ostentatious splendours they themselves were having to pay for at every level of their lives, and sometimes *with* their lives.

It was bad enough for the men; it must have been worse for the women. For the problems of women were, as they had always been, threefold. Not only were they involved in the class struggle, having to fight to maintain a home for their husbands and children. Many of them worked in the factories too. And in addition they found themselves (as they still do) up against the ingrained prejudice and discrimination of a world organized by and for men, with all the petty tyranny this brought with it. And their long struggle even to get their right to the *suffrage* acknowledged, let alone anything else, was to have to be fought through many bitter campaigns.

But if conditions in the first half of the nineteenth century had never been worse for the working masses, these very conditions brought into being the campaigning spirit of the Chartists and encouraged the growth of socialist ideas, which did much to lift their hopes, and gave them a unifying incentive such as had not been felt since the seventeenth century. Great meetings and demonstrations were held. Unions were formed, of women as well as men. Mass editions of officially proscribed publications such as Cobbett's *Two-penny Trash* and the newspapers of the Pauper Press, or of works like Shelley's *Queen Mab* (found in the pockets of working men all over the country) were issued. There was a ferment of activity from below.

And if the eighty-two years of unchecked capitalist expansion from the time of the First Reform Act to the 1914 war were to be years of incessant struggle out of which, one by one, 'every partial advantage . . . had to be wrenched from the grip of those who controlled the machinery of government', it has to be remembered that during this time Marx was laying new foundations for the development of Socialism with his revolutionary analysis of the capitalist system. Indeed, from 1848 all radical action, all interpretations of the social structure and all prescriptions for change had to take account of the *Communist Manifesto*, as later of *Capital* and the activities of the International Working Men's Association. For, however indirect their influence upon the organization of working-class values, they did much to clarify the underlying terms of the struggle, even as the actual conditions of mass exploitation concentrated and directed the common interests of the workers, and thus strengthened the movements for working-class advance. Of course, after the collapse of Chartism the struggle of the workers was never permitted to take the revolutionary path, in spite of Marx or later of men like William Morris and the great industrial disputes at the end of the century. Instead, it was channelled and absorbed by the formation of the Labour Party and the acceptance of representation in Parliament.

The 1914–18 war itself very quickly demonstrated the perverted logic of ruling-class policies. After generations of repressive conditioning, the people seemed unable to resist the unscrupulous appeal to tribal instinct and irrational hatred in the guise of patriotism which turned them into fodder for the war and neutralized working-class resistance organized by people like Keir Hardie, Jean Jaurès, Karl Liebknecht and Rosa Luxembourg. They were driven into servitude by the imperatives of the military–industrial machine, and it was the working class, as usual, which had to bear the brunt of the anti-democratic measures, the inefficiency and the profiteering, as well as the endless slaughter, that followed. Gradually, the false propagandist hopes people had had at the start, of 'a war to end all wars', gave way to universal disillusionment, as the proofs of military incompetence at the top and of futile sacrifice at home and on the battle-fronts filtered through to them; so that by the end there was only a bitter sense of the callousness and deception of the establishment that had organized the war.

On the eve of the catastrophe, it is said that, against the riches of imperial conquest and exploitation, there were eleven million people on the verge of starvation; at the end of it (however encouraged by the defiant emergence of the Soviet Union) an exhausted people were left with a dubious peace to cope with and a capitalist order strengthened, if anything, by its manipulation of wartime monopoly powers.

After 1914, nothing would ever be quite the same again. The Great War, that crucial turning-point in European history, not only exposed the ruthless hypocrisies of capitalism and undermined the stability of Europe; it also helped to bring about the revolution in Russia, and thus irrevocably altered the balance of power in the world. A new voice, a new promise, a new spirit, had emerged to challenge the old order – pledged, as Lenin declared in 1917, to achieve equality 'for all members of society in relation to ownership of the means of production – equality of labour and equality of wages', and thus the prospect of an advance for humanity 'from formal equality to actual equality'. And though in the aftermath the unregenerate spirit of European capitalism was to reassert itself in a determination to stamp out (wherever it could) 'the creeping disease of socialism', and to settle into new cycles of boom and slump, with policies which bargained away people's rights for economic advantage on the markets of the world, the whole period marks a significant new phase in the long-running battle of the common people to break the stranglehold of the oppressors and claim their fundamental rights.

It was for this reason that I chose to end the narrative of the present volume at 1914, and to leave the events of the last seventy years, and the record of their impact upon our lives, to be dealt with in a separate volume.

6

In making this selection, I was conscious above all of the need to provide material for an alternative history of England which would put the radical progressive views of the people themselves at the centre of the narrative. Accordingly, the pieces have been chosen for the urgency and commitment of the stand they take against the forces of reaction, rather than on grounds of literary merit; for the ways in which they illuminate and enact the various stages in the great struggle for social advance and fundamental change; or because they provide some sort of unique insight into the actual events – even though written, like the Froissart *Chronicles*, the *Anonimalle Chronicle*, the chronicle of the Cade Rebellion, or Alexander Neville's account of Kett's Revolt, from the standpoint of the ruling class.

No doubt the reader will note here and there unaccountable omissions, gaps and failings. If so, I hope it will be understood that these are due as much to limitations of space and the sheer difficulty of covering such a vast field as to personal inclination and bias. And I trust that the book itself will be accepted in the spirit in which it was written – as an attempt to convey something of the richness and variety of the record, across five hundred years, of the struggles of the English people: men and women discovering for themselves, by trial and error, the issues that govern their lives, and prepared to act in defence of all that is vital to them, those common interests which are the basis of whatever freedoms we have today.

CHRONOLOGY

To 1453

1337   **The Hundred Years' War** with France begins: skirmishes, battles and endless disputes over the sovereignty of France are punctuated with periodic truces. Edward III triumphs at Crécy (1346), Calais (1347), and Poitiers (1356).

1348–9   **The Black Death** wipes out one third of the population.

1349   **The Statute of Labourers** – to counteract the demands of the commons for better conditions. Re-enacted in 1357 and 1360 with harsher penalties.

1377   Accession of Richard II.

1377–96   New phase of the French Wars.

1377   **Statute of the Realm defining the unrest of the commons.**

1381   **The Peasants' Revolt.**

1382   **Statute of the Realm against Wycliffite heresies.**

1399–1485 The houses of York and Lancaster.

1399   Deposition of Richard II. Bolingbroke becomes Henry IV.

1400   The Welsh rebellion of Owen Glendower.

1401   **Statute of Heresy**.

1402   The Scots defeated at **Homildon** by Northumberland and his son Hotspur.

1403   **Battle of Shrewsbury:** Hotspur killed.

1405   Northumberland organizes rebellion in the north, which is ruthlessly suppressed; Northumberland killed in 1408.

1406   Glendower driven out of south Wales by Prince Henry.

1413   Accession of Henry V.

1414   **Lollard** unrest in the counties. Sir John Oldcastle leads revolt in London, defeated at St Giles's Fields. Oldcastle escapes.

1415   The French Wars renewed with an English victory at **Agincourt**.

1417   Oldcastle captured and executed; brutal repression of Lollards.

1419	Rouen falls to the English.
1422	Accession of Henry VI.
1429	May: Joan of Arc raises the siege of Orleans and defeats the English.
	June: Joan of Arc defeats the English at **Patay**.
1431	Joan of Arc burnt as a witch.
1440	Johann Gutenberg assembles his first printing press. His 42-line Bible (1456) and a Latin Psalter (1457) are among the earliest printed books.
1450	**Jack Cade's Rebellion**.
1453	**The Hundred Years' War comes to an end** with the surrender of **Bordeaux** to the French. The Fall of Constantinople to the Turks brings the Byzantine Empire to an end.

1453–1603

1455–85	**The Wars of the Roses**, fought between rival groups of nobles for control of the state machinery, open with victory for the Duke of York at St Albans.
1460	Duke of York killed at Wakefield.
1461	Edward, son of York, proclaimed Edward IV (reigned 1461–70, 1471–83). The Lancastrians defeated at **Towton**. Henry VI escapes to Scotland.
1465	Henry VI captured and put in the Tower.
1469	Edward taken prisoner by Warwick after defeat at **Edgecote**.
1470	Henry restored to the throne, after Edward's flight to Holland.
1471	Warwick defeated and killed at the **Battle of Barnet**. Edward defeats the Lancastrian army at **Tewkesbury**. Henry dies in the Tower.
1477	Caxton produces the first book printed in England.
1483	Accession of Richard III.
1485	The **Battle of Bosworth Field** ends the civil wars. Richard is killed.
1485–1603	The Tudors.
1485	Accession of Henry VII: absolute monarchy, uniting the houses of York and Lancaster.
1492	Columbus discovers the West Indies.
1495	With the **Statute of Drogheda** Ireland is subjected to England.
1498	John Cabot discovers Newfoundland.

1509	Henry VIII comes to the throne.
1517	Martin Luther's declaration against the sale of indulgences, symbolic of the Reformation in Europe.
1534	Henry declared supreme head of the Church: his reformation begins.
1535	Sir Thomas More executed.
1539	Dissolution of the monasteries completed. Their income transferred to the Crown and the laity.
1543	Copernicus dies. His revolutionary book *De revolutionibus orbium coelestium* published.
1545–63	At the **Council of Trent** the Papacy, in alliance with Spain, through the Jesuits and the Inquisition, organizes the Counter-Reformation.
1547	Edward VI comes to the throne, at ten years of age.
1549	**Kett's Revolt in Norfolk**; with the rising of 1381 and the Cade Rebellion this is the most important of the peasant wars.
1553	Mary Tudor comes to the throne, marries Philip of Spain and restores Roman Catholicism to England.
1554	Heresy laws revived: persecution of Protestants. Between 1555 and 1558 about 300 men and women, most of them humble people, but including Hooper, Ridley, Latimer and Cranmer, were burnt at the stake.
1558	Accession of Elizabeth I.
1559–67	Rebellion in Ireland led by Shane O'Neill.
1563	The Thirty-nine Articles of the Church of England defining the doctrine of the Protestant Church.
1564	Merchant Adventurers given a trading charter.
1569–70	Roman Catholic rebellion in the north crushed; 800 executed.
1572	First Act for the levying of a compulsory poor rate.
1574	Catholic revival leads to twenty years of persecution and plots against Elizabeth.
1577–80	Sir Francis Drake makes his voyage round the world.
1579–83	Desmond's rebellion in Ireland.
1583	Whitgift as Archbishop of Canterbury initiates repression of Puritans through the episcopal courts and the Court of High Commission.
1587	Execution of Mary Queen of Scots. War with Spain (ended in 1604).
1588	Defeat of the Spanish Armada. This was a victory for the

merchant class, and thus a turning-point for England as an expansionist Protestant power, laying the foundations of confidence for those classes which were to challenge aristocratic power and eventually to oppose the monarchy itself.

1588–9	**The Marprelate Controversy**: an anonymous attack upon the bishops.
1593	John Penry, Henry Barrow and John Greenwood executed as Puritans.
1596	Essex sacks Cadiz.
1598–1603	Rebellion of Hugh O'Neill against the English in Ireland.
1603	Death of Elizabeth; James VI of Scotland becomes James I.

1603–88

1604	End of war with Spain.
1605	Roman Catholic Gunpowder Plot.
1607	**East India Company** plants colony in Virginia.
	The Captain Pouch Rising in the Midlands.
1610	Colony settled in Ulster.
1611	Colonizing of the Bermudas.
	Parliament dissolved for questioning the King's powers.
1614	English naval victory at Surat in India establishes trading superiority there. (Factories set up at Madras in 1620 and Hoogli in 1633.)
	The 'Addled' Parliament dismissed for criticizing James's new pro-Spanish policy.
1618–48	The Thirty Years' War.
1620	**The Mayflower** sails for New England.
1621	James's third Parliament again opposes his Spanish policy, and impeaches Sir Francis Bacon for corruption. It is dismissed in 1622.
1622	Restrictions against preaching are imposed.
1624	Buckingham encourages war with Spain; a new Parliament supports James, votes money in support, though with a decaying navy and a poorly equipped army, involved soon against France too, the war is a disaster.
	Proclamation against unlicensed printing.
1625	Charles I comes to the throne. His first Parliament demands Buckingham's dismissal before granting money for the war. Charles refuses.

1626	The second Parliament attacks royal policies, and impeaches Buckingham. Charles dissolves it, imposes a levy and press-gangs for the army.
1628	Sir John Eliot organizes the **Petition of Right** in the third Parliament, condemning arbitrary imprisonment, taxation and martial laws; Charles reluctantly assents.
	The English are defeated at La Rochelle.
	Buckingham is assassinated.
1629	Charles dissolves Parliament for refusing to grant him customs taxes and for defying his power as king. Eliot and others are thrown into prison, and England is governed for the next eleven years by royal prerogative and the triple despotism of the Privy Council, the Star Chamber and the High Commission. Tyranny in state and Church were to go hand in hand under Strafford and Laud.
1630	Peace with France and Spain.
1633	Laud becomes Archbishop of Canterbury.
	The powers of the Court of High Commission and the Star Chamber are revived.
1635	Charles levies Ship Money to increase his income.
1637	John Hampden refuses in symbolic resistance to pay the Ship Money.
	William Prynne, John Bastwick and John Lilburne arrested for publishing unlicensed pamphlets.
1638	Exchequer judgement goes against Hampden, but the people support him.
	The Scots sign the National Covenant to defend the Protestant religion against its enemies.
1640	The Short Parliament (April 13–May 5) meets, organizes a petition against the Scottish war Charles wanted in order to re-establish his command. Parliament is dissolved and Charles gathers an army.
	August: the king's forces are defeated by the Scots on the Tyne.
	The **Long Parliament** is convened. Strafford and Laud arrested in an attack upon royal absolutism. These actions mark the beginning of the revolutionary struggle. Parliament, forced to make its appeal to the common people for support, becomes a kind of revolutionary tribunal.
1641	March: Strafford is impeached for high treason against the

state; a Bill of Attainder is introduced. London becomes a centre of revolutionary ferment and discussion, preaching and pamphleteering.

Milton writes his first pamphlet, *Reformation in England*.

Royalist officers threaten to march on London to release Strafford. The Attainder is pushed through amid mass demonstrations around Westminster and Whitehall Palace. Charles is forced to sign Strafford's death warrant.

12 May: Strafford is beheaded.

The Privy Council, the Star Chamber and Court of High Commission abolished. The **Root and Branch Bill** splits Parliament over move to abolish bishops and regulate the Church.

November: the Puritans draw up the **Grand Remonstrance** against the King; it is passed by eleven votes. Royalist bands attempt to stir up resistance.

1642
4 January: Charles enters the Commons with armed followers to seize Pym, Hampden and three other Parliamentary leaders, who had taken refuge in the City. Londoners protect Parliament. Charles goes to York to organize an army. Commons and Lords split, and the Parliament (Presbyterians and Independents) gathers forces for war.

June: the King rejects all Parliamentary terms.

22 August: the **First Civil War** begins when Charles sets up his standard at Nottingham. After the indecisive battle of **Edgehill**, Charles is repulsed at **Turnham Green**. Cromwell organizes the 'Ironsides'.

1643
Royalist sucesses are scored in Yorkshire, Lincoln and the west. Bristol is captured, and Gloucester besieged. But Cromwell wins in the east, at Lowestoft, Grantham and Gainsborough; and in the summer a Parliamentary force from London raises the siege of Gloucester and gains a victory at Newbury on its return.

At Westminster a General Assembly of Presbyterian and Independent Divines is set up to debate rights of conscience and religious toleration.

The **Solemn League and Covenant** is concluded between Scotland and England to confirm the reformed Church in Scotland, reformation in England and peace between the kingdoms.

| 1644 | A Scottish army (the Covenanters) strikes at Royalists in the north. Fairfax and Cromwell advance from the south. |

1644 A Scottish army (the Covenanters) strikes at Royalists in the north. Fairfax and Cromwell advance from the south.

The Parliamentary victory at **Marston Moor** on 2 July, defines the power of the radicals. York and Newcastle surrender. Defeat for Essex at **Lostwithiel** in Cornwall merely confirms the strength of the left wing at the expense of the right among the Parliamentary forces.

December: Cromwell urges in Parliament the need for a remodelled army.

Milton meanwhile writes *Areopogitica* against a Parliamentary ordinance limiting freedom of the press.

1645 January: Archbishop Laud executed. By the Self-Denying Ordinances all army commands are resigned, and Fairfax is made Commander-in-Chief, with Cromwell as second-in-command.

Summer: the **New Model Army** is raised.

14 June : Royalists are routed at **Naseby**, the decisive battle of the war.

September: Bristol is taken by Fairfax and Cromwell.

Houses of the aristocracy destroyed to mark the triumph of the Army.

1646 With the neutralist **Clubmen** of the south-west subdued, the army takes the Royalist headquarters at Oxford after Charles had sought refuge with the Scottish army. End of the First Civil War.

Parliamentary conflict deepens between the conservative Presbyterians and the radical Independents.

Lilburne is sent to the Tower by the Lords for attacking the Presbyterians.

1647 January: The King is delivered by the Scots to the Parliamentary commissioners.

Spring: The Leveller Petitions begin, urging radicalization of the Army and of Parliament.

3 June: Cornet Joyce seizes the King.

10 June: The Army meets at Triplow Heath, Cambridge, in a great demonstration against the Presbyterian majority in the Commons; it then marches towards London, and demands the expulsion of eleven leading Presbyterians.

6 August: The Army enters London, and Parliament gives in to its demands, leaving the Independents for the moment triumphant. But the Army itself now develops a left wing,

led by Lilburne, against the Grandees, and the common soldiers appoint Agitators. Cromwell resists them.

8 August: The King is taken to Hampton Court.

Autumn: Fruitless negotiations with the King and intransigent Presbyterians.

October: The Leveller **Agreement of the People**.

28 October–8 November: The Putney Debates disputing democracy.

November: Lilburne is released from the Tower. The King escapes, and concludes a Royalist-Presbyterian-Scottish alliance, signal for new risings all over the country.

1648   Lilburne is again arrested, this time for attacking Cromwell and the officers.

Spring: **The Second Civil War** begins, with the Presbyterians in alliance with the Royalists. Cromwell and the left join forces. The Scots invade the north. Cromwell subdues revolt in Wales. On 10 July Pembroke Castle surrenders.

11 August: Lilburne is released from the Tower.

Cromwell defeats the Scots at **Preston**. He stays in the north.

6 December: Parliament purged by Col. Pride to become a 'Rump' of Independents which confirms Ireton's call for Charles's death. Cromwell returns to London after the decision.

1649   30 January: The King executed. For the Levellers this sharpens the struggle for democracy against Cromwell and the Generals.

February: Milton publishes *The Tenure of Kings and Magistrates*, justifying regicide and the Revolution.

17 February: England is now ruled by a **Council of State**. Milton is appointed **Secretary for Foreign Tongues**.

March: The monarchy and the House of Lords abolished. Lilburne, Overton, Walwyn and Prince arrested by the Council of State.

1 April: **The Diggers** occupy St George's Hill.

Army mutiny of the Levellers in London. Robert Lockyer shot (26 April).

15 May: The Leveller Revolt quelled at Burford.

The **Commonwealth** proclaimed.

July: Cromwell leaves for Ireland.

Lilburne is released on bail, arrested again in September

for treason, put on trial and acquitted. But victory over the Levellers (by now assured) weakens the Commonwealth's mass backing and begins the swing towards the right which was to lead eventually to the Restoration.

August: Cromwell in Dublin.

10 September: The storming of Drogheda.

11 October: The massacre of Wexford.

1650   May: Kilkenny and Clonmell taken after Hugh O'Neill's last stand. Ireland subdued.

June: Cromwell becomes **Captain-General of the Commonwealth**.

The Ulster settlements begin.

3 September: Cromwell defeats the Scots at **Dunbar**.

December: Edinburgh Castle surrenders.

1651   February: Milton answers Salmasius and speaks to Europe at large in his *Defence of the English People*.

August: Perth surrenders to Cromwell. Monck sacks **Dundee**.

3 September: Victory at **Worcester** ends the **Second Civil War**.

1652   Lilburne banished from England for life.

1652–4   The Dutch War; England's resources for imperial expansion increased by the 1700-odd merchant vessels seized as prizes during the war.

1653   April: with the expulsion of the **Rump**, the **Long Parliament** ends. Lilburne returns to England, is arrested in July and again acquitted but kept in prison till 1655.

July: The **Little** (or **Barebones**) Parliament meets. It is dissolved in December for its radical attitudes. The Revolution is virtually over.

12 December: Parliament resigns power into Cromwell's hands. Cromwell is proclaimed **Lord Protector of the Commonwealth**.

1654   Cromwell issues his eighty-two Ordinances to regulate civil and religious affairs. Parliament is elected by **Instrument of Government**, but resists its terms.

1655   January: Cromwell dissolves Parliament and governs by military dictatorship.

1655–8   War with Spain. Jamaica is captured.

1656   September: A new Parliament meets, markedly right-wing in composition.

1657	A new second chamber is created. Cromwell is offered the Crown. He refuses it because of the Army's disapproval.
	June: The **Petition and Advice** permits Cromwell to name a successor and appoint a new House of Lords. Cromwell is re-affirmed as Protector.
1658	Parliament refuses to sanction the new peerage. It is dissolved.
	3 September: Cromwell dies. His son Richard is declared Protector. The Army refuses to recognize him and he resigns. The gentry, having supported Cromwell against the left, begin to move increasingly to the right towards a restoration of the monarchy.
1660	February: Monck forces the reinstatement of Royalist members of Parliament, dissolving the **Rump** and opening negotiations to recall Charles.
	Milton publishes (March; second edition in April) his *Ready and Easy Way to Establish a Free Commonwealth*, against the return of the monarchy.
	25 April: A new Parliament, Royalist and Presbyterian, invites Charles back.
	29 May: Charles enters London. **Restoration of the Monarchy**.
	Navigation Act: one of a series for the building of merchant ships 'to enlarge dominion throughout the world, the most easy for conquests, and the least costly for appropriating the property of others'.
1661–78	The **Cavalier Parliament**. The **Clarendon Code** initiates a series of harsh acts to illegalize the Puritans and all non-conformist radicals.
1661–5	The **Corporation Act** restricts their governing bodies. The **Act of Uniformity** penalizes 2000 Presbyterians. The **Conventicle Act** prohibits all unlicensed public worship. The **Five-Mile Act** forbids expelled ministers from entering the towns.
1665–7	**The Dutch War**, brought about by continental and colonial rivalry.
1665	The Great Plague of London.
1666	The Great Fire of London.
1670	Charles enters into secret alliance with Louis XIV.
1672	England and France become allies in a new war against Holland.

1678	The **Popish Plot** of Titus Oates, organized to discredit Catholics. A reign of terror against them follows.
1679–81	Three short Whig Parliaments meet to prevent James succeeding.
1681	Penn founds Pennsylvania. Charles enters into a new alliance with Louis, dissolves Parliament and rules by absolute power through the Tories, the Church and the army.
1683	The Whig radicals Lord Russell and Algernon Sidney executed for treason for conspiring against the King (The Rye House Plot).
1685	Accession of James II.
	The Monmouth Rebellion defeated at **Sedgemoor**. Judge Jeffreys presides over the **Bloody Assize**: hundreds of people in the south-west are executed.
	James attempts a counter-revolution and the restoration of Catholicism. He abolishes Parliament and re-establishes the Court of High Commission.
1688	Seven bishops are tried and acquitted amid popular acclaim for refusing to read his Royal Indulgence for Catholics in their churches.
	The moderate Whigs and Tories unite against him and organize a secret coup with William of Orange. The 'Glorious Revolution' is thus achieved, bringing to power, with William of Orange, 'the landlord and capitalist appropriators of surplus power' (Marx).

1689–1788

1689	A Convention offers the throne to William and Mary, declares itself a Parliament, and proceeds, in the **Bill of Rights**, to limit the powers of the monarchy.
1690	**Battle of the Boyne**: William defeats the Catholic supporters of James II.
1694	**The Bank of England** founded, to become 'the receptacle of the metallic hoard of the country and the centre of gravity of all commercial credit' (Marx, *Capital*, I, 780).
1701	The **Act of Settlement** fixes succession with the Hanovers.
1701–13	The **War of the Spanish Succession** against France serves to consolidate Whig power and to expand their trading and commercial interests on the Continent and in South America.

1702	Accession of Queen Anne.
1704	Marlborough defeats Tallard at **Blenheim**.
1706	Marlborough defeats Villeroy at **Ramillies**.
1707	Act of Union between Scotland and England.
1708	Marlborough wins at **Oudenarde** and (in 1709) at **Malplaquet**.
1713	The **Treaty of Utrecht** ends the war.
1714	George I comes to the throne.
1715	Jacobite Rising in Scotland rejecting the Hanovers is crushed.
1720	The **South Sea Bubble**: a fever of fraudulent speculation criminally involving leading members of the government. It characterizes the search for quick profit and expansion of capital going on everywhere.
1727	Accession of George II.
1740–48	The **War of the Austrian Succession**. Britain is allied with Austria against France.
1745	Rebellion of the Young Pretender, Prince Charles. The Highlanders are defeated at the Battles of Prestonpans and Culloden (April 1746).
1756–63	The Seven Years' War. **Growth of the Empire**; beginnings of the **Industrial Revolution**.
1757	Clive's victory over the Indians at **Plassy**, and the conquest of Bengal. The East India Company thrives on widespread bribery. Huge fortunes were made by men like Clive, and later by the British government.
1759	Wolfe's victory over the French at **Quebec**.
1760	George III comes to the throne and makes great use of his powers of patronage. The old Parties begin to form new groupings. French troops surrender to the British in Canada.
1763	**The Treaty of Paris** ends the Seven Years' War to Britain's advantage.
1764	Hargreaves invents the spinning-jenny. John Wilkes is elected and unseated. There is a wave of demonstrations and strikes.
1768	Captain Cook explores New Zealand and Australia.
1769	Arkwright invents the spinning-frame. Watt's first steam-engine.

1770	The West Indies are now the most profitable British possession; slave-labour brings in vast returns.
1775–81	**The American War of Independence** sharpens divisions in England.
1776	The thirteen colonies issue their **Declaration of Independence.**
1779	Crompton invents the mule.
1780	The **Gordon Riots**: 'No Popery'.
1781	Cornwallis surrenders at Yorktown to end the American War.
1782	Rodney defeats the French fleet off **Dominica**.
	An independent Parliament is established in Dublin.
1783	American independence officially recognized by the Treaty of Versailles.
1785	Cartwright's first power loom.
1788	The first settlement of the British in Australia; Sydney made a convict station.

1789–1848

1789	**The French Revolution**. Declaration of the Rights of Man.
1790	Edmund Burke's *Reflections on the Revolution in France*.
1790–94	A great network of canals is built across England.
1791	Tom Paine's *Rights of Man*.
	By this time many revolution societies had been formed, and Pitt had begun to act against the Jacobins.
1792	**Proclamation against Seditious Writings** proscribes the work of Paine and many others.
1792–7	**War of the First Coalition** against Revolutionary France: Austria and Prussia, then Britain, the Netherlands, Spain, Naples and the Papal States leave France virtually on her own.
1793	Louis XVI is executed.
	France declares war on Britain. The Reign of Terror begins.
	Scottish treason trials (continued into 1794) judged by Lord Braxfield deliver harsh sentences against Muir and Margarot.
1794	Thomas Hardy and Horne Tooke acquitted of sedition. **Habeas Corpus** suspended.

July: Thermidor – the Jacobins overthrown in France.

1795   Bread riots break out all over the country against high prices. Seditious Meetings and Treason Acts.

The **Speenhamland Act** subsidizes wages from the rates and raises the poor rate.

Throughout these years, strikes, bread riots and machine wrecking are brutally suppressed by troops all over the country.

The war had become total, ruthless and destructive; a struggle for control of Europe which destroyed the remnants of the feudal system, brought about fundamental reforms, but led to the triumph of conservative capitalist power.

1795–1812   More than 1500 Enclosure Acts are passed in favour of landowners' rights.

1797   The **Nore** and **Spithead** mutinies.

1798   The Irish Rebellion led by Lord Edward Fitzgerald and Wolfe Tone is crushed. Had it been properly organized by the French, history might well have been different.

The London Corresponding Society finally suppressed.

Malthus publishes his *Essay on Population*.

Nelson defeats the French fleet on the Nile.

1798–1801   The **War of the Second Coalition**, organized by Pitt.

1799   Act against Seditious Societies and Freedom of the Press.

The **Combination Laws**, against workers' organizations.

Napoleon's *coup d'état* establishes the Consulate and makes him autocrat of France.

1800   Act of Union with Ireland. Owen organizes **New Lanark**.

1801   General Enclosure Act.

1802   Cobbett launches his **Political Register**.

March: The **Peace of Amiens** is made with France.

First Factory Act.

1803   Horrocks's power loom.

May: Renewal of the war with France.

1804   Napoleon declares himself Emperor.

The First Corn Law is passed to ensure profits for landowners against imported corn.

1805–7   The **War of the Third Coalition** is dominated by Napoleon's victories at Auerstadt, Austerlitz and Jena, and by Nelson's defeat of the French and Spanish fleets at Trafalgar (1805).

1806	Death of Pitt. Napoleon's **Berlin Decrees** prohibit trade with Britain.
1807	The British **Orders in Council** block all trade with France. The slave-trade is officially abolished.
1810	Durham miners' strike. Cobbett imprisoned for two years for attacking flogging in the army.
1811	The **Luddite Riots** begin, and continue intermittently till 1818, despite brutally repressive penalties – hangings and transportations.
1812	War with USA over trading embargoes, blockades and support for the Indians. The Battle of Borodino; Napoleon's retreat from Moscow.
1813	The **War of the Fourth Coalition** against France.
1814	Stephenson's first steam-engine.
1815	**The Battle of Waterloo**. At the **Congress of Vienna** the conservative powers (Britain, Austria, Prussia, Russia) sign the Quadruple Alliance to 'maintain the peace of Europe'. New Corn Law to keep rents and grain prices high.
1816	Spa Fields Riot: Spencean leaders of radical opinion arrested after a new suspension of **Habeas Corpus** and put on trial for treason.
1817	The **Gagging Acts**, against public meetings, passed by Sidmouth. The **March of the Blanketeers** – an organized march on London of the starving unemployed handloom weavers of Manchester, only one of whom reached London: the first 'hunger march'. The **Pentridge Rising**: thirty-five tried for treason, four hanged, fourteen transported.
1819	**The Peterloo Massacre**: eleven killed, hundreds seriously injured. The **Six Acts**, harsher even than the Gagging Acts, gave magistrates powers of summary conviction, of search, of confiscation and of suppression of any public meeting. The Second Factory Act, passed to protect children and limit hours, is mostly ignored by employers.
1820	Accession of George IV. The **Cato Street Conspiracy**: a plan to murder members of the Tory government and take over London. Five men were hanged and five transported.

1823	Recognition of South American republics.

1823   Recognition of South American republics.

1824   Combination Acts repealed.

1825   Stockton and Darlington railway opened. Northumberland and Durham Colliers' Union formed.

1826   Lancashire Power Loom Riots.

1829   Metropolitan Police formed. Grand General Spinners' Union.

1830   Accession of William IV. Whig ministry. Birmingham Political Union.

The **Swing Riots** – agricultural risings which spread from village to village in the southern counties, destroying threshing machines and other implements, and gaining much sympathy. They were savagely suppressed, though they neither killed nor wounded a single person. Nine men were hanged, 457 transported and many others imprisoned. (One was hanged for knocking a ruling-class man's hat off during an argument.)

Revolution in France: the fall of the Bourbons.

1831   Bristol and Nottingham riots over parliamentary reforms. National Union of the Working Classes formed.

1832   The **First Reform Act**: power now in the hands of the middle class.

The Operative Builders' Union.

1833   Emancipation of slaves in the British Empire.

Rapid growth of trade union activity after the disillusionment of the Reform Act. Agitation for a ten hours day produces a new Factory Act banning labour for children under 9, limiting those under 13 to eight hours, and under 18 to twelve in textile work only, a grudging reform. The Grand National Consolidated Trades Union attracts half a million members.

1834   The **Derby Turn-out**, a lock-out of workers who refused to renounce their union, was supported by Robert Owen, but was broken for lack of funds.

The **Tolpuddle Martyrs**, six Dorset farm-labourers, are arrested for trying to organize a union lodge, and sentenced to seven years' transportation. Owen organized petitions and demonstrations, without success.

A new **Poor Law** is passed, a repressive act against the workers, establishing rigorous workhouse conditions of labour and segregating the sexes.

| 1836 | London Working Men's Association formed; it initiates the Charter. |
| 1837 | Victoria comes to the throne. |

The *Northern Star* is launched as a working-class paper. Railway mania produces forty-two Acts authorizing construction and investment.

| 1838 | **The People's Charter** drafted and launched in Birmingham and endorsed all over the country – 200,000 in Glasgow, 80,000 in Newcastle, 250,000 in Leeds, 300,000 in Manchester. Its **Six Points**, as Engels declared, were 'sufficient to overthrow the whole English Constitution'. |

The Manchester Anti-Corn Law Association is formed.

| 1839 | Penny postage is introduced. |

July: The **First Chartist Petition**, with 1,280,000 signatures, is rejected.

The Anti-Corn Law League is formed in competition with Chartism, as a movement dominated by middle-class radicals (Bright and Cobden).

November: **The Newport rising**, intended as part of a national rising by 'physical force' Chartists to overthrow the government, ends when the Chartists are shot at by soldiers, ten dead and fifty wounded. Frost, the leader, is arrested and, with two others, sentenced to death (later commuted to transportation); and in the months that follow wholesale arrests (about 450) are made, including all the leaders of the Charter.

| 1841 | **The National Charter Association** (formed in 1840 as a strictly political organization) grows slowly. |
| 1842 | **The Second Chartist Petition**, with 3,317,702 signatures, is rejected. |

Hong Kong is ceded to Britain by China. Shanghai and other ports are opened up to British commerce and its cheap-labour policies.

August–September: A General Strike spread across the north – the 'Plug' riots. Fifteen hundred people arrested and seventy-nine transported.

| 1844 | Another Factory Act is passed limiting women's labour to twelve hours. |

The **Bank Charter Act** makes the Bank of England a Central Bank to regularize capitalist enterprise.

Second period of railway mania: forty-eight Acts for construction passed.

1845   A hundred and twenty railway construction Acts passed.

1846   The **Repeal of the Corn Laws** leads to temporary real gains in wages for the workers, but the campaign helped to eclipse the revolutionary Chartist movement.

1847   The Ten Hours' Act (for textile mills) is passed; violently opposed by employers.

The great **Irish Famine** rages; in five years over a million died. With hundreds of thousands dying of starvation 'food to the value of £17 million was actually exported from the country under the protection of English troops' (Morton, *A People's History of England*, 456).

Economic depression and unemployment revive the Chartist movement.

1848   The **Third Chartist Petition** and its demonstration fail.

Marx publishes *The Communist Manifesto*.

1848–1914

1848   Revolutions on the Continent: **France** (February and June); **Italy** (Naples, Tuscany, Piedmont, Rome – overthrown July 1849, Venice – proclaimed in March 1848, holding out till August 1849); **Austria** (Vienna and Prague); **Hungary; The German Lands** (Berlin, Frankfurt, the smaller states). This year was to define the triumph of bourgeois capitalism over revolutionary change, as every continental revolution ended in defeat.

December: Louis Napoleon elected President of the Second Republic.

1849   Mazzini driven from Rome, Manin from Venice, Kossuth from Hungary.

Marx arrives in England. Many Chartists emigrate.

1850   New Factory Act. Economic revival and easier conditions cause the final collapse of Chartism. Dickens edits *Household Words*.

1851   The Great Exhibition: the Crystal Palace in Hyde Park demonstrates Britain's mercantile and commercial triumphs.

November: serial publication of *Bleak House* begins, Dickens's shattering indictment of England's social order.

1852   Cholera epidemic. The first Cooperatives.

	Louis Napoleon becomes Napoleon III of the Second Empire.
1853	Preston spinners' strike.
1854–6	The Crimean War: Britain and France in alliance against Russia.
1855	Limited liability (and later the Companies Act) open up the market to small shareholders.
1857	Transportation abolished.
1858	Public Health Act.
1859	Darwin's *Origin of Species*. London building strike.
1860	London Trades Council. Free Trade at its height. The Bessemer and Siemens-Martin methods of steel-making begin to transform the metal-working industries.
1861	Kingdom of Italy proclaimed after the liberation of Lombardy and Garibaldi's successes in the south. Cotton famine begins.
1861–5	**The American Civil War.**
1862	Working Men's Club and Institute Union. The Companies Act extends shareholding.
1863	Cooperative Wholesale Society is formed.
1864	**International Working Men's Association** (the 'First International') inaugurated. Marx draws up the Address and Provisional Rules. The First Trade Union Conference is held.
1865	Irish Fenian Movement formed. The National Reform League.
1866	Atlantic cable laid. The Austro-Prussian War breaks out. Women's suffrage movement is formed in Manchester by Jacob and Ursula Bright, Dr Pankhurst and Elizabeth Wolstonholme.
1867	The Second Reform Act is passed. The Master and Servant Act. The Factory and Workshops Act. Marx publishes **Capital**.
1868	First regular Trades Union Congress.
1869	Cooperative Union. The Labour Representation League. The Suez Canal is opened.
1870	Elementary Education Act. Factory Act limits women and children to a ten-hour day.

The Franco-Prussian War.

Rome becomes the capital of Italy.

1871 **The Paris Commune**: begun in March and brutally suppressed in May.

Bismarck proclaims the German Empire and becomes Imperial Chancellor.

In the Census agricultural workers formed 11 per cent of the people (18 per cent in 1851), factory trades 35 per cent (as against 27 per cent), commerce $5\frac{1}{2}$ per cent (from $4\frac{1}{2}$ per cent), the professional middle class $4\frac{1}{2}$ per cent (a large rise from $2\frac{1}{2}$ per cent). Rise in population (since 1851), 27 per cent.

1872 The Ballot Act secures the secret ballot to counter intimidation.

Joseph Arch organizes his farm-labourers' union.

1874 Women's Trade Union League formed. The first Trade Union MPs elected.

Trades Union Congress at Sheffield claims over a million members.

1875 Public Health Act. The railways now carry 490 million passengers.

1875–1900 The British Empire increases by 5 million square miles in Africa and Asia.

1876 Elementary education made compulsory.

1878 A new Factory Act.

1879 Irish Land League.

1880 The Salvation Army.

1883 The Fabian Society is formed to spread socialist ideas among the educated.

1884 **The Berlin Conference** between Britain, France and Germany to agree on the partition of Africa and other territories in the squabble for world markets.

William Morris founds his Socialist League.

The Third Reform Act (and that of 1885) enfranchises more male workers (5 million out of $31\frac{1}{2}$ million people), doubling the total.

1886 First Home Rule Bill.

Unemployed riots in Trafalgar Square.

1887 Victoria's Jubilee (the Jingo Jubilee).

Unrest among the unemployed and agitation for free speech; police break up meetings in Trafalgar Square. On

'Bloody Sunday' (13 November) 200 are injured and three die in brutal clashes with police.

1889   London gas workers demand and get an eight-hour day. The great London dock strike follows with daily processions to Hyde Park led by Mann, Burns and Tillett; and with help from workers in Australia they win.

1893   The Independent Labour Party is formed by Keir Hardie, and has a great influence on the spread of Socialist ideas in England.
Second Home Rule Bill. National mining strike.

1899–1902   The Boer War fought, ending by incorporating the Transvaal and the Orange Free State in the British Empire.

1901   Accession of Edward VII. Factory Act forbids child labour under 12.

1902   Sinn Fein founded by Arthur Griffith. Education Act establishes a comprehensive local-government system for elementary and higher education.

1903   Women's Social and Political Union formed by the Pankhursts.
The Workers' Educational Association.
The first effective aeroplane (the Wright brothers).

1904–5   The Russo-Japanese War.

1905   Revolutionary upheaval in Russia.

1908   Coal Mines Eight Hour Act.

1909   Blériot flies the Channel.

1910   George V comes to the throne.

1911   Dock strikes at Southampton, Hull, Manchester, London, Liverpool.
National miners' strike. A second London dock strike.

1912   The Balkan Wars. New miners' strike. London Transport strike.

1913   Trade union membership almost 4 million, growing in power and confidence.
October: 439 men killed in south Wales mine disaster.

1914   Great Triple Alliance agreed between NUR, the transport workers and the miners to organize concerted action against the capitalist class. It is dispersed by the war.
28 July: Austria-Hungary declares war on Serbia.
4 August: Britain declares war on Germany.

Part One

THE MIDDLE AGES 1381–1453

My good people, things cannot go well in England, nor ever shall, till everything be made common, and there are neither villeins nor gentlemen, but we shall all be united together, and the lords shall be no greater masters than ourselves.

John Ball, sermon

> When Adam delved and Eve span
> Who was then the gentleman?

> When Adam delved and Eve span,
> Spur if thou wilt speed,
> Where was then the pride of man
> That now mars his meed?
>
> Peasants' song

Wat Tyler, at Smithfield, 'demanded that there should be only one bishop in England and only one prelate, and all the lands and tenements now held by them should be confiscated, and divided among the commons, only reserving for them a reasonable sustenance. And he demanded that there should be no more villeins in England, and no serfdom or villeinage, but that all men should be free and of one condition.'

Anonimalle Chronicle

THE PEASANTS' REVOLT: PRELUDE

From *Statutes of the Realm*, II, ii, p. 2

It is clear from the 1349 Statute of Labourers (*Statutes of the Realm*, I, i, p. 307), which followed the havoc of the Black Death that, a great many workmen and servants having died of the plague, there was a scarcity of labour and that those who remained were refusing to serve 'unless they may receive excessive wages, and some rather willing to beg in idleness than by labour to get their living'. In other words, the propertyless poor, recognizing that the thousands of deaths had increased the value of their labour, and reacting against a general rise in prices, had begun to agitate for better conditions. The Statute was therefore brought in by the 'prelates and nobles' to force the workmen, on pain of imprisonment, 'to serve him which so shall him require', taking 'only the wages, livery, meed, or salary, which were accustomed to be given in the place where he oweth to serve'. Furthermore, it was laid down that the lords 'shall retain no more than be necessary to them', and that 'no reaper, mower, or other workman or servant' shall be permitted to 'depart from the said service without reasonable cause or licence' or 'take for their labour' more than was fixed for them before 1347.

Neither this nor later statutes proved workable, and the restlessness of the commons is reflected in their Petitions to Parliament, which served merely to exact harsher laws against their demands, and thus to sharpen their sense of injustice and to bring them into closer combination.

RISING REVOLT

Statute of the Realm, 1377

Lords of manors, as wel men of Holy Church as other, make complaint that the villeins on their estates affirm them to be quit and utterly discharged of all manner of serfage, due as well of their body as of their tenures, and will not suffer any distress or other injustice to be made upon them; but do menace the ministers of their lords of life and member, and, which more is, gather themselves together in great routs and agree by such confederacy that everyone shal aid other to resist the lords with strong hand; and much other harm they do in sundry manner to the great damage of their said lords, and evil example to others to begin such riots, so that, if due remedy be not the rather provided, upon the same rebels, greater mischief, which God forbid, may thereof spring through the realm.

———

These conditions, taken together with the inefficiency, neglect and corruption of the barons and the rise of the merchant class in the towns, whose riches made them independent of the system of feudal privileges, encouraged and strengthened the villeins to stand together.

JOHN BALL (d. 1381)   1381

Sermon to the people, in Froissart, *Chronicles*, I, pp. 640–41

In the quickening ferment of the time, brought to a head by the crushing economic burdens imposed upon the people as a result of the protracted French wars and the wasteful luxuries of the king's court, many voices (among them that of the great scholar John de Wycliffe) were to be heard questioning the religious and social abuses that were rife in England. But the man who has come to be most closely associated with the Revolt itself – in which Wycliffe seems to have played no part – was a poor priest named John Ball, who was preaching his revolutionary creed of equality to the common people for at least twenty-five years before the rising. In 1366 we know that he was brought before Archbishop Langham of Canterbury and forbidden to preach; that in 1376 an order was made for his arrest as an excommunicated priest; and that he was imprisoned several times. Otherwise his place in history we owe to Walsingham, Froissart and the *Anonimalle Chronicle*, largely defined from the viewpoint of the people's avowed enemies.

'TILL EVERYTHING BE MADE COMMON'

There was a custom in England, still kept in divers countries, that the noblemen hath great licence over the commons, and keepeth them in bondage: that is to say, their tenants were forced to labour the lord's lands, to gather and bring home their corn, some to thresh and to fan and . . . to make their hay, and to hew their wood and bring it home; all these things they owe as services. And there are more of these people in England than in any other realm: thus the noblemen and prelates are served by them, and especially in the county of Brendpest [Kent and Essex], Sussetter [Sussex], and Bedford. These unhappy people from the above countries began to stir against their masters, because they said they were kept in great bondage. And at the beginning of the world, they said, there were no bondmen. Therefore they maintained that no one ought to be bound unless he had committed treason, as Lucifer did against God. But they said they had done no such thing, for they were

NOTE. Full details of sources and the editions used are given in the sections on Further Reading on pp. 607–14.

neither angels nor spirits, but men formed in the likeness of their lords, and asked why they should be so kept under like beasts, which they said they would no longer suffer, but would all be equal; and if they laboured or did anything for their lords, they would have wages for it. And of this opinion was a foolish priest in the county of Kent, called John Ball, who for his rash words had been three times in the Bishop of Canterbury's prison. For this priest used often on Sundays after mass, when the people were coming out of the church, to go into the cloister and preach, and assembling the people about him, would say this:

'My good people, things cannot go well in England, nor ever shall, till everything be made common, and there are neither villeins nor gentlemen, but we shall all be united together, and the lords shall be no greater masters than ourselves. What have we deserved that we should be kept thus enslaved? We are all descended from one father and mother, Adam and Eve. What reasons can they give to show that they are greater lords than we, save by making us toil and labour, so that they can spend? They are clothed in velvet and soft leather furred with ermine, while we wear coarse cloth; they have their wines, spices and good bread, while we have the drawings of the chaff, and drink water. They have handsome houses and manors, and we the pain and travail, the rain and wind, in the fields. And it is from our labour that they get the means to maintain their estates. We are called their slaves, and if we do not serve them readily, we are beaten. And we have no sovereign to whom we may complain, or who will hear us, or do us justice. Let us go to the King, he is young, and tell him of our slavery; and tell him we shall have it otherwise, or else we will provide a remedy ourselves. And if we go together, all manner of people that are now in bondage will follow us, with the intent to be made free. And when the King sees us, we shall have some remedy, either by justice or otherwise.'

Thus John Ball said on Sundays, when the people issued out of the churches in the villages. For which many of the common people loved him, and such as intended no good said how he told the truth. And so they would murmur to each other in the fields and in the roadways, as they came together, affirming the truth that John Ball spoke.

. . . Of his words and deeds there were much people in London informed, such as had great envy of them that were rich and such as were noble: and then they began to speak among them and said: 'How England was right evil governed and how that gold and silver was taken from them by them that were named noblemen.' So these unhappy men of London began to rebel and assembled together, and sent word to the foresaid countries that they should come to London and bring their people with them, promising them how they should find London open to receive them, and the commons of the city to be of the same accord, saying how they would do so much to the King, that there should not be one bondman in all England.

THOMAS WALSINGHAM (d.c. 1422)   1381

From *Historia Anglicana 1272–1422*, II, pp. 32–4

The call to action was no doubt passed on from person to person and from place to place to prepare the people for the rising by cryptic messages such as these.

PREPARATIONS

'John Ball greeteth you well all and doth you to understand that he hath rungen the bell.'

'John Schep [Ball again, the people's shepherd] sometime St Mary's priest of York, and now of Colchester, greeteth well John Nameless, and John the Miller, and John Carter, and biddeth them that they beware of guile in borough, and stand together in God's name, and biddeth Piers Plowman go to his work and chastise well Hob the Robber [Sir Robert Hales, the king's treasurer] and take with you John Trueman and all his fellows, and no mo; and look sharp you to one head and no mo.

> John the Miller hath y-ground small, small, small:
> The King's son of Heaven shall pay for all.
> Beware or ye be woe!
> Know your friend from your foe;
> Have enough and say "Ho"!'

'Jakke Mylner asketh help to turn his milne aright. He hath grounden small, small; the king's son of heaven shall pay for all. Look thy milne go aright, with the four sails, and the post stand in steadfastness. With right and with might, with skill and with will, let might keep right, and skill go before will and right before might, then goeth our milne aright. And if might go before right, and will before skill, then is our milne mis-adight.'

'Jakke Carter prays ye all that ye make a good end of that ye hath begun, and doth well, and aye better and better, for at the even men hereth the day. For if the end be well, then all is well. Let Piers the Plowman my brother dwell at home and dight us corn, and I will go with you and help that I may dight you meat and your drink, that ye none fail. Look that Hob Robber be well chastised for levying of your grace for ye have great need to take God with you in all your deeds. For now is time to be ware.'

'Jakke Trueman doth you to understand that falseness and guile have reigned too long, and truth hath been set under a lock, and falseness reigneth in every flock. No man may come to truth but he sing *si dedero*. Speak, spend and speed, quoth Jon of Bathon, and therefore sin fareth as wilde floode, true love is away, that was so, and clergy for wealth worche hem woe. God do bote, for now is time.'

THE PEASANTS' SONG

When Adam delved and Eve span
Who was then the gentleman?

When Adam delved and Eve span,
Spur if thou wilt speed,
Where was then the pride of man
That now mars his meed?

THE PEASANTS' REVOLT   1381

From *Anonimalle Chronicle*, in Oman, *Great Revolt*, pp. 187–8, 188–9, 190, 191

Though it would seem that the Revolt had been carefully planned and organized, it began with sporadic outbreaks of violent resistance in Essex, the immediate cause being an attempt by the government to impose a heavy poll tax on the people, who, everywhere they were approached, decided to prepare false returns. According to the *Anonimalle Chronicle*, a commission was sent to Essex, where (at Fobbing, Stanford and Corringham) the people combined against the commissioner, refused to pay the tax, and rose against this official when he threatened to have them arrested. The commissioner fled to London, and at first (fearing reprisals) the common people took to the woods, but eventually emerged to stir the people of other villages in the district to rise against their masters.

The *Anonimalle Chronicle* was written in French at St Mary's Abbey, York, covering the years 1333–81, a collection of translations from the work of others; this section was written between 1396 and 1399, and may have been taken from a lost London chronicle

THE SPREAD OF RESISTANCE

And because of these occurrences Sir Robert Belknap, Chief Justice of the King's Bench, was sent into the county, with a commission of Trailbaston, and indictments against divers persons were laid before him, and the folks of the countryside were in such fear that they were proposing abandoning their homes. Wherefore the commons rose against him, and came before him and told him that he was a traitor to the king, that it was of pure malice he would put them in default, by means of false inquests made before him. And they took him, and made him swear on the Bible that never again would he hold such a session, nor act as a justice in such inquests. And they made him give them a list of the names of all the jurors, and they took all the jurors they could catch, and cut off their heads, and cast their houses to the ground. So the said Sir Robert took his way home without delay. And afterwards the said commons assembled together, before Whit-sunday, to the number of some 50,000, and they went to the manors and townships of those who would not rise with them, and cast their houses to the ground, or set fire to them. At this time they caught three clerks of Thomas Bampton, and cut off their heads, and carried the heads about with them for several days stuck on poles as an example to others, for it was their purpose to slay all lawyers, and all jurors, and all the servants of the King they could find. Meanwhile the great Lords of that country and other people of substance fled towards London, or to other counties where they might be safe. Then the commons sent divers letters to Kent and Suffolk and Norfolk that they should rise with them, and when they were assembled they went about in many bands doing great mischief in all the countryside.

THE MEN OF KENT AND ESSEX COMBINE
TO FREE A BONDMAN

Now on Whit Monday a knight of the household of our Lord the King named Sir Simon Burley, having in his company two sergeants-at-arms, came to Gravesend and challenged a man there of being his born serf: and the good folks of the town came to him to make a bargain for the man, because of their respect for the King: but Sir Simon would take nothing less than £300, which sum would have undone the said man. And the good folks prayed him to mitigate his demand, but could not come to terms nor induce him to take a smaller sum, though they said to Sir Simon that the man was a good Christian and of good disposition and in short that he ought not to be so undone.

But the said Sir Simon was of an irritable and angry temper, and greatly despised these good folks, and for haughtiness of heart he bade his sergeants bind the said man and take him to Rochester Castle, to be kept in custody there; from which there came later great evil and mischief.

And after this the commons of Kent gathered together in great numbers day after day, without a head or a chieftain, and the Friday after Whit Sunday came to Dartford . . .

At this same time the commons of Kent came to Maidstone and cut off the head of one of the best men of the town, and cast to the ground divers houses and tenements of folks who would not rise with them, as had been done before in Essex. And, on the next Friday after, they came to Rochester and there met a great number of the commons of Essex. And because of the man of Gravesend they laid siege to Rochester Castle, to deliver their friend from Gravesend, whom the aforesaid Sir Simon had imprisoned. They laid strong siege to the castle, and the Constable defended himself vigorously for half a day, but at length for fear he had of such tumult, and because of the multitude of folks without reason from Essex and Kent, he delivered up the castle to them. And the commons entered, and took their companion, and all the other prisoners out of the prison. Then the men of Gravesend repaired home with their fellow in great joy, without doing more. But those who came from Maidstone took their way with the rest of the commons through the countryside. And there they made chief over them Wat Teghler [Tyler] of Maidstone, to maintain them and be their councillor . . .

JOHN BALL URGES THE PEOPLE ON

At this time the commons had as their councillor a chaplain of evil disposition named Sir John Ball, which Sir John advised them to get rid of all the lords, and of the archbishop and bishops, and abbots and priors, and most of the monks and canons, saying that there should be no bishop in England save one archbishop only, and that he himself would be that prelate, and they would have no monks or canons in religious houses save two, and that their possessions should be distributed among the laity. For which sayings he was esteemed among the commons as a prophet, and laboured with them day by day to strengthen them in their malice – and a fit reward he got, when he was hung, drawn and quartered, and beheaded as a traitor . . .

THE MEN OF KENT GATHER ON BLACKHEATH TO AWAIT THE KING

When the king heard of their doings he sent his messengers to them, on Tuesday after Trinity Sunday, asking why they were behaving in this fashion, and for what cause they were making insurrection in his land. And they sent back by his messengers the answer that they had risen to deliver him, and to destroy traitors to him and his kingdom. The king sent again to them bidding them cease their doings, in reverence for him, till he could speak with them, and he would make, according to their will, reasonable amendment of all that was ill-done in the realm. And the commons, out of good-feeling to him, sent back word by his messengers that they wished to see him and speak with him at Blackheath. And the king sent again the third time to say that he would come willingly the next day, at the hour of Prime, to hear their purpose . . .

And on the vigil of Corpus Christi day the commons of Kent came to Blackheath, three leagues from London, to the number of 50,000, to wait for the king, and they displayed two banners of St George and forty pennons. And the commons of Essex came to the other side of the water to aid them, and to have their answer from the king.

From Froissart, *Chronicles*, I, pp. 644–5

THE COMMONS' INVITATION REFUSED

In the morning on Corpus Christi day King Richard heard mass in the
Tower of London, and all his lords, and then he took his barge with the
earl of Salisbury, the earl of Warwick, the earl of Oxford, and so rowed
down along the Thames to Rotherhithe, whereas was descended down
the hill ten thousand men to see the king and to speak with him. And
when they saw the king's barge coming, they began to shout, and made
such a cry, as though all the devils of hell had been among them . . .
And when the king and his lords saw the demeanour of the people, the
best assured of them were in dread; and so the king was counselled by
his barons not to take any landing there, but so rowed up and down the
river. And the king demanded of them what they would, and said how
he was come thither to speak with them, and they said all with one voice:
'We would that ye should come aland, and then we shall show you what
we lack.' Then the earl of Salisbury answered for the king and said: 'Sirs,
ye be not in such order nor array that the king ought to speak with you.'
And so with those words no more said: and then the king was counselled
to return again to the Tower of London, and so he did.

   And when these people saw that, they were inflamed with ire and
returned to the hill where the great band was, and there showed them
what answer they had and how the king was returned to the Tower of
London. Then they cried all with one voice, 'Let us go to London', and
so they took their way thither . . .

THE PEASANTS' REVOLT   1381

From *Anonimalle Chronicle*, in Oman, *Great Revolt*, pp. 193–205 passim

THE MEN OF KENT AND ESSEX MAKE FOR LONDON

Therefore the king returned towards London as fast as he could, and
came to the Tower at the hour of Tierce . . . And before the hour of
Vespers the commons of Kent came, to the number of 60,000, to Southwark, where was the Marshalsea. And they broke and threw down all
the houses in the Marshalsea, and took out of prison all the prisoners

who were imprisoned for debt or for felony.[1] And they levelled to the ground a fine house belonging to John Imworth, then Marshal of the Marshalsea of the King's Bench and warden of the prisoners of the said place; and all the dwellings of the jurors and questmongers [informers] belonging to the Marshalsea during that night. But at the same time, the commons of Essex came to Lambeth near London, a manor of the Archbishop of Canterbury, and entered into the buildings and destroyed many of the goods of the said Archbishop, and burnt all the books of register, and rules of remembrances belonging to the Chancellor, which they found there.

13 JUNE: LONDON IN THE HANDS OF THE COMMONS

And this same day of Corpus Christi, in the morning, the commons of Kent cast down a certain house of ill-fame near London Bridge, which was in the hands of Flemish women, and they had the said house to rent from the Mayor of London. And then they went on to the Bridge to pass into the City, but the Mayor was ready before them, and had the chains drawn up, and the drawbridge lifted, to prevent their passage. And the commons of Southwark rose with them and cried to the custodians of the bridge to lower the drawbridge and let them in, or otherwise they should be undone. And for fear that they had of their lives, the custodians let them enter, much against their will.

At this time all the religious and the parsons and vicars of London were going devoutly in procession to pray God for peace. At this same time the commons took their way through the middle of London, and did no harm or damage till they came to Fleet Street. And in Fleet Street the men of Kent broke open the prison of the Fleet, and turned out all the prisoners, and let them go whither they would . . .

And then they went to the Temple, to destroy the tenants of the said Temple, and they cast the houses to the ground and threw off all the tiles . . . They went into the Temple church and took all the books and rolls and remembrances, that lay in their cupboards in the Temple, which belonged to the lawyers, and they carried them into the highway and burnt them there . . .

---

1. The majority of the prisoners released would be peasants and artisans convicted under the Statutes fixing maximum rates of pay. The burning of documents everywhere was not done, as has been stated, out of a hatred of learning, but in order to destroy the written evidence which recorded the terms of servitude binding the peasants to the lords of the manor.

It was marvellous to see how even the most aged and infirm of them [the lawyers] scrambled off, with the agility of rats or evil spirits.

And then they went toward the Savoy, and set fire to divers houses of divers unpopular persons on the Western side: and at last they came to the Savoy, and broke open the gates, and entered into the place and came to the wardrobe. And they took all the torches they could find, and lighted them, and burnt all the sheets and coverlets and beds and headboards of great worth, for their whole value was estimated at 1000 marks. And all the napery and other things that they could discover they carried to the hall and set on fire with their torches. And they burnt the hall, and the chambers, and all the buildings within the gates of the said palace or manor . . .

And the said commons had among themselves a watchword in English, 'With whom haldes [hold] you?' and the answer was, 'With King Richard and the true commons,' and those who could not or would not so answer were put to death.

At this same time a great body of the commons went to the Tower to speak with the king and could not get speech with him, wherefore they laid siege to the Tower from the side of St Catherine's, towards the south . . .

And on that Thursday, the said feast of Corpus Christi, the king, being in the Tower very sad and sorry, mounted up in a little turret towards St Catherine's, where were lying a great number of the commons, and had proclamation made to them that they all should go peaceably to their homes, and he would pardon them all manner of their trespasses. But all cried with one voice that they would not go till they had captured the traitors who lay in the Tower, nor until they had got charters to free them from all manner of serfdom, and had got certain other points which they wished to demand.

And the king benevolently granted all, and made a clerk write a bill in their presence in these terms: 'Richard, king of England and France, gives great thanks to his good commons, for that they have so great a desire to see and to keep their king, and grants them pardon for all manner of trespasses and misprisions and felonies done up to this hour, and wills and commands that everyone should now return to his own home, and wills and commands that each should put his grievances in writing, and have them sent him; and he will provide, with the aid of his loyal lords and his good council, such remedy as shall be profitable both to him and to them, and to all the kingdom.'

On this document he sealed his signet in presence of them all, and sent out the said bill by the hands of two of his knights to the folks before

St Catherine's. And he caused it to be read to them, and the knight who read it stood up on an old chair [pulpit] before the others so that all could hear. All this time the king was in the Tower in great distress of mind.

And when the commons had heard the bill, they said that this was nothing but trifles and mockery. Therefore they returned to London . . .

WAT TYLER PETITIONS THE KING AT MILE END

And next day, Friday, the commons of the countryside and the commons of London assembled in fearful strength, to the number of 100,000 or more, besides some four score who remained on Tower Hill to watch those who were in the Tower. And some went to Mile End, on the Brentwood Road, to wait for the coming of the king, because of the proclamation that he had made. But some came to Tower Hill, and when the king knew that they were there, he sent them orders by messenger to join their friends at Mile End, saying that he would come to them very soon. And at this hour of the morning he advised the Archbishop of Canterbury, and the others who were in the Tower, to go down to the Little Water-gate, and take a boat and save themselves. And the Archbishop did so, but a wicked woman raised a cry against him, and he had to turn back to the Tower, to his confusion.

And by seven o'clock the king came to Mile End . . . and also the Earls . . . of Kent, Warwick, and Oxford, and Sir Thomas Percy, and Sir Robert Knolles, and the Mayor of London, and many knights and squires; and Sir Aubrey de Vere carried the sword of state. And when he was come the commons all knelt down to him, saying 'Welcome our Lord King Richard, if it pleases you, and we will not have any other king but you.'

And Wat Tyler, their leader and chief, prayed in the name of the commons that he would suffer them to take and deal with all the traitors against him and the law, and the king granted that they should have at their disposition all who were traitors, and could be proved to be traitors by process of law.

The said Walter and the commons were carrying two banners, and many pennons and pennoncels, while they made their petition to the king. And they required that for the future no man should be in serfdom, nor make any manner of homage or suit to any lord, but should give a rent of 4d. an acre for his land. They asked also that no one should serve any man except by his own good will, and on terms of regular covenant. And at this time the king made the commons draw themselves out in two lines, and proclaimed to them that he would confirm and grant it that they should be free, and generally should have their will, and that they might go through the realm of England and catch all traitors and bring them to him in safety, and then he would deal with them as the law demanded.

Under colour of this grant Wat Tyler and [some of] the commons took their way to the Tower, to seize the Archbishop, while the rest remained at Mile End. During this time the Archbishop sang his mass devoutly in the Tower, and shrived the Prior of the Hospitallers and others, and then he heard two masses or three, and chanted the Commendacione, and the Placebo, and the Dirige, and the Seven Psalms, and a Litany, and when he was at the words *'Omnes sancti orate pro nobis'*, the commons burst in, and dragged him out of the chapel of the Tower, and struck and hustled him rudely, as they did also the others who were with him, and dragged them to Tower Hill. There they cut off the heads of Master Simon Sudbury, Archbishop of Canterbury and of Sir Robert Hales, Prior of the Hospital of St John's, Treasurer of England, and of Sir William Appleton, a great lawyer and surgeon, and one who had much power with the king and the Duke of Lancaster . . .

At this time, because the Chancellor had been beheaded, the king made the Earl of Arundel Chancellor for the day, and gave him the Great Seal; and all that day he caused many clerks to write out charters, and patents, and petitions, granted to the commons touching the matters before mentioned, without taking any fines for sealing or description . . .

All this time the king was causing a proclamation to be made round the City, that everyone should go peaceably to his own country and his own house, without doing more mischief; but to this the commons gave no heed . . . Then the king caused a proclamation to be made that all the commons of the country who were still in London should come to Smithfield, to meet him there; and so they did.

SMITHFIELD MEETING: TYLER DEMANDS EQUALITY AND FREEDOM FOR ALL MEN

And when the king and his train had arrived there they turned into the Eastern meadow in front of St Bartholomew's, which is a house of canons; and the commons arrayed themselves on the west side in great battles. At this moment the Mayor of London, William Walworth, came up, and the king bade him go to the commons, and make their chieftain come to him. And when he was summoned by the Mayor, by the name of Wat Tyler of Maidstone, he came to the king with great confidence, mounted on a little horse, that the commons might see him. And he dismounted, holding in his hand a dagger which he had taken from another man, and when he had dismounted he half bent his knee, and then took the king by the hand, and shook his arm forcibly and roughly, saying to him, 'Brother, be of good comfort and joyful, for you shall have, in the fortnight that is to come, praise from the commons even more than you have had yet, and we shall be good companions.'

And the king said to Walter, 'Why will you not go back to your own country?' But the other answered, with a great oath, that neither he nor his fellows would depart until they had got their charter such as they wished to have it, and had certain points rehearsed, and added to their charter which they wished to demand. And he said in a threatening fashion that the lords would rue it bitterly if these points were not settled to their pleasure.

Then the king asked him what were the points which he wished to have revised, and he should have them freely, without contradiction, written out and sealed. Thereupon the said Walter rehearsed the points which were to be demanded. And he asked that there should be no law in the realm save the law of Winchester, and that from henceforth there should be no outlawry in any process of law, and that no lord should have lordship save civilly, and that there should be equality among all people save only the king, and that the goods of Holy Church should not remain in the hands of the religious, nor of parsons and vicars, and other churchmen; but that clergy already in possession should have a sufficient sustenance from the endowments, and the rest of the goods should be divided among the people of the parish. And he demanded that there should be only one bishop in England and only one prelate, and all the lands and tenements now held by them should be confiscated, and divided among the commons, only reserving for them a reasonable sustenance. And he demanded that there should be no more villeins in England, and no serfdom or villeinage, but that all men should be free and of one condition. To this the king gave an easy answer, and said that he should have all that he could fairly grant, reserving only to himself the regality of his crown. And then he bade him go back to his home, without making further delay.

THE KILLING OF WAT TYLER – COURT VERSION

During all this time that the king was speaking, no lord counsellor dared or wished to give answer to the commons in any place save the king himself. Presently Wat Tyler, in the presence of the king, sent for a flagon of water to rinse his mouth, because of the great heat that he was in, and when it was brought he rinsed his mouth in a very rude and disgusting fashion before the king's face. And then he made them bring him a jug of beer, and drank a great draught, and then, in the presence of the king, climbed on his horse again.

At this time a certain valet from Kent, who was among the king's retinue, asked that the said Walter, the chief of the commons, might be pointed out to him. And when he saw him, he said aloud that he knew him for the greatest thief and robber in all Kent. Wat heard these words and bade him come out to him, wagging his head at him in sign of malice; but the valet refused to approach, for fear that he had of the mob. But at last the lords made him go out to him, to see what he (Wat) would do before the king. And when Wat saw him he ordered one of his followers, who was riding behind him carrying his banner displayed, to dismount and behead the said valet. But the valet answered that he had done nothing worthy of death for what he had said was true, but he could not lawfully make debate in the presence of his liege lord, without leave, except in his own defence; but that he could do without reproof; for if he was struck he would strike back again.

And for these words Wat tried to strike him with his dagger, and would have slain him in the king's presence; but because he strove so to do, the Mayor of London, William Walworth, reasoned with the said Wat for his violent behaviour and despite, done in the king's presence, and arrested him. And because he arrested him, the said Wat stabbed the Mayor with his dagger in the stomach in great wrath. But, as it pleased God, the Mayor was wearing armour and took no harm, but like a hardy and vigorous man drew his cutlass, and struck back at the said Wat, and gave him a deep cut on the neck, and then a great cut on the head. And during this scuffle one of the king's household drew his sword, and ran Wat two or three times through the body, mortally wounding him. And he spurred his horse, crying to the commons to avenge him, and the horse carried him some four score paces, and then he fell to the ground half dead.

And when the commons saw him fall, and knew not how for certain it was, they began to bend their bows and to shoot, wherefore the king

63

spurred his horse, and rode out to them, commanding them that they should all come to him to Clerkenwell Fields.

THE SURRENDER OF THE COMMONS – COURT VERSION

Meanwhile the Mayor of London rode as hastily as he could back to the City, and commanded those who were in charge of the twenty-four wards to make proclamation round their wards, that every man should arm himself as quickly as he could, and come to the king in St John's Fields [Clerkenwell], where were the commons, to aid the king, for he was in great trouble and necessity. But at this time most of the knights and squires of the king's household, and many others, for fear that they had of this affray, left their lord, and went each one his way. And afterwards, when the king had reached the open fields, he made the commons array themselves on the west side of the fields. And presently the aldermen came to him in a body, bringing with them their wardens, and the wards arrayed in bands, a fine company of well-armed folks in great strength. And they enveloped the commons like sheep within a pen.

And after that the Mayor had set the wardens of the City on their way to the king, he returned with a company of lances to Smithfield, to make an end of the captain of the commons. And when he came to Smithfield he found not there the said captain Wat Tyler, at which he marvelled much, and asked what was become of the traitor. And it was told him that he had been carried by some of the commons to the hospital for poor folks by St Bartholomew's, and was put to bed in the chamber of the master of the hospital. And the Mayor went thither and found him, and had him carried out to the middle of Smithfield, in presence of his fellows, and there beheaded. And thus ended his wretched life. But the Mayor had his head set on a pole and borne before him to the king, who still abode in the Fields, and thanked the Mayor greatly for what he had done.

And when the king saw the head he had it brought near him to abash the commons. And when the commons saw that their chieftain, Wat Tyler, was dead in such a manner, they fell to the ground there among the wheat, like beaten men, imploring the king for mercy for their misdeeds. And the king benevolently granted them mercy, and most of them took to flight. But the king ordained two knights to conduct the rest of them, namely the Kentishmen, through London, and over London Bridge, without doing them harm, so that each of them could go to his own home.

THE LORD MAYOR KNIGHTED FOR KILLING THE CAPTAIN OF THE COMMONS

Then the king ordered the Mayor to put a helmet on his head because of what was to happen, and the Mayor asked for what reason he was to do so, and the king told him that he was much obliged to him, and that for this he was to receive the order of knighthood. And the Mayor answered that he was not worthy or able to have or to spend a knight's estate, for he was but a merchant and had to live by traffic; but finally the king made him put on the helmet, and took a sword in both his hands and dubbed him knight with great good will. The same day he made three other knights from among the citizens of London on that same spot . . . and the king gave Sir William Walworth £100 in land and each of the others £40 in land, for them and their heirs. And after this the king took his way to London to the Wardrobe to ease him of his great toils.

THE PRICE OF DEFEAT: THE REPRESSION

Afterwards the king sent out his messengers into divers parts, to capture the malefactors and put them to death. And many were taken and hanged at London, and they set up many gallows around the City of London, and in other cities and boroughs of the south country. At last, as it pleased God, the king seeing that too many of his liege subjects would be undone, and too much blood spilt, took pity in his heart, and granted them all pardon, on condition that they should never rise again, under pain of losing life or members, and that each of them should get his charter of pardon, and pay the king as fee for his seal twenty shillings, to make him rich. And so finished this wicked war.

THE PEASANTS' REVOLT: AFTERMATH 1381

From Walsingham, *Historia Anglicana*, II, pp. 18, 27

After the end of the Rising, a deputation from the people of Essex appealed to the King for justice and freedom and the relief of the poor. But the King repudiated his Seal.

'YOU SHALL REMAIN IN BONDAGE'

Oh miserable men, hateful both to land and sea, unworthy even to live, you ask to be put on an equality with your lords! You should certainly have been punished with the vilest death, if we had not determined to observe the things which had been decreed towards your messengers. But because you have come in the character of messengers you shall not die at once, but shall enjoy your life that you may truly announce our answer to your fellows.

Take back then this answer from the king: Serfs you were and serfs you are; you shall remain in bondage, not such as you have hitherto been subject to, but incomparably viler. For so long as we live and rule by God's grace over this kingdom we shall use our sense, our strength and our property so to teach you, that your slavery may be an example to posterity, and that those who live now and hereafter, who may be like you, may always have before their eyes and as it were in a glass, your misery and reasons for cursing you, and the fear of doing things like those which you have done.

———

William Gryndecobbe, the leader of the commons, from St Albans, speaks for the people of what they have been fighting for. He was soon to be executed as a traitor.

THE CAUSE OF LIBERTY

Fellow-citizens, whom now a scant liberty has relieved from long oppression, stand firm while you may, and fear nothing for my punishment, since I would die in the cause of the liberty we have won, if it is now my fate to die, thinking myself happy to be able to finish my life by such a martyrdom.

JOHN SHIRLE (propagandist, from Nottinghamshire)

From Rickword and Lindsay, *Handbook of Freedom*, p. 44

IN THE AFTERMATH: SHIRLE'S WITNESS

John Shirle, of the county of Nottingham, was taken because it was found that he was a vagabond in divers counties the whole time of the disturbance, insurrection and tumult, carrying lies and worthless talk from district to district whereby the peace of the lord the King could be speedily broken and the people disquieted and disturbed; and among other dangerous words, to wit, after the proclamation of the peace of the lord the King made the day and year aforesaid, the assigns [justices] of the lord the King being in the town and sitting, he said in a tavern in Bridge Street, Cambridge, where many were assembled to listen to his news and worthless talk:

That the stewards of the lord the King, the justices and many other officers and ministers of the King were more worthy to be drawn and hanged, and to suffer other lawful pains and torments than John Ball, chaplain, a traitor and felon lawfully convicted:

For he said that he was condemned to death falsely, unjustly and for envy, by the said ministers with the King's assent, because he was a true and good man, prophesying things useful to the commons of the realm and telling of wrongs and oppressions done to the people by the King and the ministers aforesaid.

Which sayings and threats redound to the prejudice of the crown of the lord the King and the contempt and manifest disquiet of the people.

Therefore by the discretion of the said assigns he was hanged.

THE PEASANTS' REVOLT: EPILOGUE

From William Morris (1834–96), *A Dream of John Ball*, chapter 11

John Ball was among the fifteen hundred from various counties who, according to Froissart, were executed as traitors for their part in the Rising. He was arrested at Coventry and taken to St Albans, and there (supposedly after a confession which linked him with the Wycliffite heretics) hanged, drawn and quartered.

'John Ball,' said I, 'I have told thee that thy death will bring about that which thy life has striven for: thinkest thou that the thing which thou strivest for is worth the labour? or dost thou believe in the tale I have told thee of the days to come?'

He said: 'I tell thee once again that I trust thee for a seer; because no man could make up such a tale as thou; the things which thou tellest me are too wonderful for a minstrel, the tale too grievous. And whereas thou askest as to whether I count my labour lost, I say nay; if so be that in those latter times (and worser than ours they will be) men shall yet seek a remedy: therefore again I ask thee, is it so that they shall?'

'Yes,' said I, 'and their remedy shall be the same as thine, although the days be different: for if the folk be enthralled, what remedy save that they be set free? and if they have tried many roads towards freedom, and found that they led no-whither, then shall they try yet another. Yet in the days to come they shall be slothful to try it, because their masters shall be so much mightier than thine, that they shall not need to show the high hand, and until the days go to their evilest, men shall be cozened into thinking that it is of their own free will that they must needs buy leave to labour by pawning their labour that is to be. Moreover, your lords and masters seem very mighty to you, each one of them, and so they are, but they are few; and the masters of the days to come shall not each one of them seem very mighty to the men of those days, but they shall be very many, and they shall be of one intent in these matters without knowing it; like as one sees the oars of a galley when the rowers are hidden, that rise and fall as it were with one will.'

'And yet,' he said, 'shall it not be the same with those that these men devour? shall not they also have one will?'

'Friend,' I said, 'they shall have the will to live, as the wretchedest thing living has: therefore shall they sell themselves that they may live, as I told thee; and their hard need shall be their lord's easy livelihood, and because of it he shall sleep without fear, since their need compelleth them not to loiter by the way to lament with friend or brother that they are pinched in their servitude, or to devise means for ending it. And yet indeed thou sayest it: they also shall have one will if they but knew it: but for a long while they shall have but a glimmer of knowledge of it: yet doubt it not that in the end they shall come to know it clearly, and then they shall bring about the remedy; and in those days shall it be seen that thou hast not wrought for nothing, because thou hast seen beforehand what the remedy should be, even as those of latter days have seen it.'

WILLIAM LANGLAND (1330?–1400?)

From *A Vision concerning Piers Plowman*, pp. 124–5

POVERTY

The neediest are our neighbours if we give heed to them,
Prisoners in the dungeon, the poor in the cottage,
Charged with a crew of children and with a landlord's rent.
What they win by their spinning to make their porridge with,
Milk and meal, to satisfy the babes,
The babes that continually cry out for food,
This they must spend on the rent of their houses,
Ay, and themselves suffer with hunger,
With woe in winter rising a-nights,
In the narrow room to rock the cradle,
Carding, combing, clouting, washing, rubbing, winding, peeling
   rushes.
Pitiful it is to read the cottage-women's woe,
Ay and many another that puts a good face on it,
Ashamed to beg, ashamed to let the neighbour know
All that they need, noontide and evening.
Many the children and nought but a man's hands
To clothe and feed them; and few pennies come in.
And many mouths to eat the pennies up.
Bread and thin ale for them are a banquet,
Cold flesh and cold fish are like roast venison,
A farthing's worth of mussels, a farthing's worth of cockles,
Were a feast to them on Fridays or fast-days.
It were a charity to help these that be at heavy charges,
To comfort the cottager, the crooked and the blind.

JOHN DE WYCLIFFE (*c.* 1328–84)   After 1382

From *Speculum de Antichristo*, in *Three Treatises*, pp. 124–32

ANTICHRIST AND HIS COMPANY

'He that ministreth me follow he me,' saith Christ. Then must we needs
follow him, by one way, or by other; or else we forsake soothly his min-

69

isters to be. For Christ bad Peter that he should follow him; and so shoulden all popes be followers of Peter, and his successors; if they ben not his followers they have not his power; and so it is by bishops that also shoulden follow. But take we heed to popes and cardinals both; to bishops, to collectors, to suffragans also, delegates, and commissaries, and archdeacons also, and deacons and officials, and sequestrars; to abbots and priors, ministers and wardens, and to these provincials, and to the pope's chaplains, to procurators and pleaders, to chancellors, to treasurers, to summoners and pardoners; and to the pope's notaries, parsons and vicars, and priests, monks, canons and friars, anchorites and hermits; to nunners, and sisters, and see how they followen Christ for the more part. Antichrist as God shall sit in the church, and do many marvels as now ben done a days; and therefore look well in thy mind, and know his disciples, which of all this meyne followeth our Lord. Christ was poor, and they ben rich, as many men supposen. Christ was meek and low, and they full high and proud. Christ was suffering and forgave, and they wolen be avenged. Christ forsook worldly glory, and they it sechen fast. Christ would not worldly lordships, and they croken [cling] fast to them. Christ washed his disciples' feet, lowly and meekly, and the pope wol crown the emperor with his feet, and suffer men to kiss them kneeling on their knees. Christ came to serve, and they sechen to be served. Christ went on his feet, and his disciples with him, to teach and to turn the people in cold and in heat, and in wet, and in dry; the pope and other bishops wole keep their feet full clean with scarlet and cordwain, and sometime with sandals, with gold, with silver, and silk preciously dight [adorned]. Christ ged [went] in great sweat and swink [labour]; and they sitten in their proud castles with their proud meyne, and keep them busily from the sun brenning [burning]. Christ preached and blessed; and they cursen, and blessen ful selden [seldom] . . .

Christ forsoke; and they taken gifts full great. Christ gave; and they fast holden. Christ purchased heaven; and they lordships in earth to be rich. Christ rode simply on an ass; and they on fat palfreys, and it falleth not the disciple to be above his Master. He had twelve going about on their feet; them followeth many a great horse, with jesters and japers on hackneys' backs, with swords and bucklers as it were to a battle, and with knights at robes and fees often to lead their bridles. Christ rode on a fardel [bundle] of his disciples' clothes; and they in gilt saddles full of gay stones and gay harness thereto. Christ was pursued; and they pursue. Christ was despised; and they despisen. Christ gave power; and they take away. Christ made free men; and they maken bond. Christ bought out prisons; they prisonen. Christ loosed; and they burden. Christ raised to life; and they bringen to death.

STATUTE OF THE REALM 1382

Item 5, directed against Wycliffite heresies, in *Statues of the Realm*, II, pp. 25–6

The Synod met in London in May 1382 under Archbishop Courtenay, and pronounced a formal condemnation of certain tenets held by Wycliffe and his followers. A month later Courtenay approached the King to secure the passing of an Act, which was not in the end approved, but was nevertheless recorded among the Statutes of the Realm with the authority of royal proclamation designed to carry the force of law. The House of Commons refused to sanction it, and declared that it was therefore inoperative, and there were even men of distinction who gave the new preachers their support, among them Sir Thomas Latimer, Sir John Trussel, Sir Lodowich Clifford, Sir John Peche, Sir Richard Story, and Sir John Hilton.

PREACHING HERESY

Forasmuch as it is openly known that there are divers evil persons within the realm, going from county to county, and from town to town, in certain habits, under dissimulation of great holiness, and without the licence of the Ordinaries of the places, or other sufficient authority, preaching daily not only in churches and churchyards, but also in markets, fairs, and other open places, where a great congregation of people is, divers sermons, containing heresies and notorious errors, to the great blemishing of the Christian faith, and destruction of all the laws and estates of holy church, to the great peril of the souls of the people, and of all the realm of England, as is more plainly found and sufficiently proved before the reverend father in God, the archbishop of Canterbury, and the bishops and other prelates, masters of divinity and doctors of canon and of civil law, and a great part of the clergy of this realm, especially assembled for this cause, which persons do also preach divers matters of slander, to engender dischords and disunion between divers estates of the said realm, as well spiritual as temporal, in exciting of the people, to the great peril of all the realm; which preachers being cited or summoned before the Ordinaries of the places, there to answer to that whereof they be impeached, they will not obey to their summons and commandments, nor care for their monitions, nor for the censures of holy church, but expressly despise them; and, moreover, by their subtle and ingenious words do draw the people to hear their sermons, and do maintain them in their error by strong hand, and by great routs; – it is therefore ordained and assented in this present Parliament, that the king's commission be made and directed to the sheriffs, and other ministers of our sovereign lord the king, or other sufficient persons, learned, and according to the certifications of the prelates thereof, to be made in the chancery from time to time, to arrest all such preachers, and also their fautors [supporters], maintainers and abettors, and to hold them in arrest and strong prison, till they shall purify themselves according to the law and reason of holy church . . .

KNIGHTON (active 1363, a contemporary of John de Wycliffe)

1380s

From *Chronicon*, II, pp. 151–2

Knighton reflects the judgement of the clergy concerning the duty of withholding the Scriptures from the people, no doubt from a fear that the people might begin to question their authority, as Wycliffe had done, or in the spirit of the heretical priest John Ball, leader of the Peasants' Revolt, and possibly a Wycliffite himself, who was executed at St Albans.

MAKING THE GOSPEL AVAILABLE TO WOMEN!

Christ delivered his gospel to the clergy and doctors of the church, that they might administer it to the laity and to weaker persons, according to the states of the times and the wants of men. But this Master John Wycliffe translated it out of Latin into English, and thus laid it out more open to the laity, and to women, who could read, than it had formerly been to the most learned of the clergy, even to those of them who had the best understanding. In this way the gospel-pearl is cast abroad, and trodden under foot of swine, and that which was before precious both to clergy and laity, is rendered, as it were, the common jest of both. The jewel of the church is turned into the sport of the people, and what had hitherto been the choice gift of the clergy and of divines, is made for ever common to the laity.

————

Thirty years after the death of Wycliffe, the Council of Constance stigmatized and condemned certain of his writings as heretical, and issued an order that 'his body and bones, if they might be discovered and known from the bodies of faithful people, should be taken from the ground and thrown away from the burial of the church, according to the canon laws and decrees'. Thus Wycliffe's presumed remains were disinterred and burnt, and the ashes cast into the local brook known as the Swift, near Lutterworth.

As Thomas Fuller has it: 'This brook conveyed them into the Avon, the Avon into the Severn; the Severn into the narrow seas; they into the main Ocean; and thus the ashes of Wycliffe were the emblem of his doctrine, which is now dispersed all the world over.'

JOHN BROMYARD (active 1390)   1390

From his *Guide to Preachers*, in Owst, *Literature and Pulpit*, pp. 300 ff.

Bromyard was a Dominican friar and at one time Chancellor of Cambridge. Though an opponent of Wycliffe and apparently a supporter of the *status quo*, urging the rich to deal mercifully with the poor and offering only ultimate consolation to the poor, he nevertheless portrays in this sermon a stark indictment at the Day of Judgement by the oppressed against their oppressors, those 'who plundered the people of God with grievous fines, amercements and exactions . . . the wicked ecclesia ᵊ s, who failed to nourish the poor with the goods of Christ.'

INDICTMENT OF THE OPPRESSED

And with boldness will they be able to put their plaint before God and seek justice, speaking with Christ the judge, and reciting each in turn the injury from which they specially suffered . . . 'Our labours and goods . . . they took away, to satiate their greed. They afflicted us with hunger and labours, that they might live delicately upon our labours and our goods. We have laboured and lived so hard a life that scarce for half a year had we a good sufficiency, scarce nothing save bread and bran and water. Nay, rather, what is worse, we died of hunger. And they were served with three or four courses out of our goods, which they took from us . . . We hungered and thirsted and were afflicted with cold and nakedness. And those robbers yonder gave not our own goods to us when we were in want, neither did they feed or clothe us out of them. But their hounds and horses and apes, the rich, the powerful, the abounding, the gluttons, the drunkards and their prostitutes they fed and clothed with them, and allowed us to languish in want . . .

'O just God, mighty judge, the game was not fairly divided between them and us. Their satiety was our famine; their merriment was our wretchedness; their jousts and tournaments were our torments . . . Their feasts, delectations, pomps, vanities, excesses and superfluities were our fastings, penalties, wants, calamities and spoliation. The love-ditties and laughter of their dances were our mockery, our groanings and remonstrations. They used to sing – "Well enough! Well enough!" – and we groaned, saying – "Woe to us! Woe to us!" . . .'

Without a doubt, the just Judge will do justice to those clamouring thus.

LOLLARD PETITION TO PARLIAMENT

May 1394

From Aubrey, *History of England*, I, p. 771

The Lollards, professed followers of Wycliffe, men who sought radical reforms in religion, got their name from the word *lollen* or *lullen*, which signifies to sing with a low voice and is linked to the word *lull* and *lullaby*. The term was applied to heretics because they were said to communicate their views in a low muttering voice or, as their opponents defined it, to 'conceal heretical principles or vicious conduct under the mask of piety'.

PETITION

1. That when the Church of England began to mismanage her temporalities in conformity with the precedents of Rome, and the revenues of churches were appropriated to several places, Faith, Hope, and Charity began to take their leave of her communion.
2. That the English priesthood derived from Rome, and pretending to a power superior to angels, is not that priesthood which Christ settled upon his apostles.

3. That the enjoining of celibacy upon the clergy was the occasion of scandalous irregularities.
4. That the pretended miracle of transubstantiation runs the greatest part of Christendom upon idolatry.
5. That exorcism and benedictions pronounced over wine, bread, water, oil, wax, and incense, over the stones for the altar and the church walls, over the holy vestments, the mitre, the cross, and the pilgrim's staff, have more of necromancy than religion in them.
6. That the joining of the offices of prince and bishop, prelate and secular judge, in the same person, is a plain mismanagement, and puts the kingdom out of its right way.
7. That prayer for the dead is a wrong ground for charity and religious endowments.
8. That pilgrimages, prayers, and offerings made to images and crosses have nothing of charity in them and are near akin to idolatry.
9. That auricular confession makes the priests proud, lets them into the secrets of the penitent, gives opportunity to intrigues and other mortal offences.
10. That the taking away of any man's life, either in war or in courts of justice, and upon any account whatsoever, is expressly contrary to the New Testament which is a dispensation of grace and mercy.
11. That the vow of single life is the occasion of horrible disorders, and betrays the nuns to infamous practices.
12. That unnecessary trades are the occasion of pride and luxury.

ANONYMOUS POEM   *c.* 1400

In Rickword and Lindsay, *Handbook of Freedom*, pp. 49–50

ROBBING THE POOR

For in these days there is usance
That putteth the poor people to great hindrance,
By a strange way that is late in the land
Begun and used as I understand.

By merchants and cloth-makers, for God's sake take keep,
The which maketh the porail[1] to moan and weep,

Porail: the poor commoners

Little they take for their weight, yet half is merchandise,
Alas, for ruth, it's a great pity.

But they take for 6d., it is dear enough at 3d.,
And then they be defrauded in every country.
The poor have the labour, the rich the winning;
This accordeth naught; it is a heavy parting.

But to void fraud and set equality,
That such workfolk be paid in good money,
From this time forth by sufficient ordinance
That the porail no more be put to such grievance:

For an ye know the sorrow and heaviness
Of the poor people living in distress,
How they be oppressed in all manner of thing,
In giving them too much weight into the spinning.

For 9lb I wen they shall take 12,
This is very truth, as I know myself;
Then wages be baited, then weight is increased,
Thus the spinners' and carders' avails be all ceased.

WILLIAM GREGORY   1414

From Gregory, *Chronicle*, p. 108

LOLLARD RISING IN ST GILES'S FIELDS

And that same year, on the Twelfth Night, were arrested certain persons
called Lollards, at the sign of the Axe, without Bishop's Gate, the which
Lollards had cast to have made a murmuring at Eltham, and under cover
of the murmuring to have destroyed the King and Holy Church. And
they had ordained to have had the field beside St Giles. But, thanked be
God Almighty, our King had warning thereof, and he came unto London
and took the field beside St John's in Clerkenwell; and as they came, the
King took them, and many other. And there was a knight taken that was
named Sir Roger of Acton, and he was drawn and hanged beside St Giles,
for the King let to be made four pair of gallows, the which that were i-
called the Lollards' gallows. Also a priest that hight Sir John Beverley,
and a squire of Oldcastle's that hight John Brown, they were hanged;

and many more were hanged and burnt, to the number of thirty-eight persons and more.

And that same year were burnt in Smithfield John Clayton, skinner, and Richard Turmyn, baker, for heresy that they were convicted of . . .

ANONYMOUS POEM

In Rickword and Lindsay, *Handbook of Freedom*, p. 57

THE LABOUR OF WOMEN

I am light as any roe,
To praise women wherever I go.

To mispraise women it were a shame.
For a woman was thy dame;
Our blessed Lady beareth the name
  Of all women wherever they go.

A woman is a worthy thing.
They do the wash and do the wring,
'Lullay! Lullay!' she doth sing,
  And yet she has but care and woe.

A woman is a worthy wight,
She serveth a man both day and night;
Thereto she putteth all her might;
  And yet she has but care and woe.

JACK CADE'S REBELLION   June–July 1450

From Gregory, *Chronicle*, and *Three Fifteenth Century Chronicles*

The rebellion was a carefully organized rising of the people against the oppression and tyranny of Henry VI's ministers and particularly the Lord Treasurer, in their exaction of laws and taxes at the bitter end of the French Wars, a time of economic depression and poverty for the common people. What makes it significant is that even the local gentry followed Cade's standard, and (from Stow's *Chronicle*) it seems that the King's followers, too, plainly suggested that, unless his traitorous ministers were dealt with, they would desert to the Captain. Cade led the rebels to Blackheath, retreated after a week, defeated part of the royal army at Sevenoaks (8 June) and took possession of London. Lord Saye, the King's Treasurer, was executed; but the commons were soon driven out (5–6 July) and eventually dispersed, though Cade continued to resist till killed on 12 July. William Gregory (d. 1467) was Lord Mayor of London for 1451–2.

THE COMMONS RISE

From Gregory, p. 190

And after that the commons of Kent arose with certain other shires, and they chose them a captain, the which captain . . .

From *Three Fifteenth Century Chronicles*

named himself John Mortimer, whose very true name was Jack Cade, and he was an Irishman;

From Gregory, p. 190

[and] compelled all the gentlemen to arise with them. And at the end of Parliament they came with a great might and a strong host unto the Black Heath, beside Greenwich, the number of 46,000; and there they made a field, dyked and staked well about, as it had been in the land of war, save only they kept order among them, for also good was Jack Robyn as John at the Noke, for all were as high as pigsfeet, unto the time that they should come and speak with such states and messengers as were sent unto them; then they put all their power into the men that named him Captain of all their host. And there they abode certain days to the coming of the king from the Parliament at Leicester. And then the king sent unto the captain divers lords both spiritual and temporal, to wait and to have knowledge of that great assemblage and gathering of that great and misadvised fellowship. The captain of them sending word again unto the king, that it was for the weal of him our sovereign lord, and of all the realm, and for to destroy the traitors being about him, with their divers points that they would see that it were in short time amended.

A PROCLAMATION MADE BY JACK CADE, CAPTAIN OF YE REBELS IN KENT

From *Three Fifteenth Century Chronicles*, pp. 94–6

These being the points, causes and mischiefs of gathering and assembling of us the King's liege men of Kent, the 3rd day of June, the year of our Lord 1450, the reign of our sovereign lord the king XXIX, the which we trust to Almighty God to remedy, with the help and the grace of God and of our sovereign lord the king, and the poor commons of England, and else we shall die therefore.

We, considering that the king our sovereign lord, by the insatiable, covetous, malicious pomps, and false and of nought brought-up certain persons, and daily and nightly is about his Highness, and daily inform him that good is evil and evil is good . . .

Item, they say that our sovereign lord is above his laws to his pleasure, and he may make it and break it as him list, without any distinction. The contrary is true, and else he should not have sworn to keep it, the which we conceived for the highest point of treason that any subject may do to make his prince run in perjury . . .

Item, they say that the commons of England would first destroy the king's friends and afterwards himself . . .

Item, they say that the king should live upon his commons, and that their bodies and goods be the king's; the contrary is true, for then needeth he never Parliament to sit to ask good of his commons . . .

Item, it is to be remedied that the false traitors will suffer no man to come to the king's presence for no cause without bribes where none ought to be had, nor no bribery about the king's person, but that any man might have his coming to him to ask him grace or judgement in such case as the king may give . . .

Item, the false lords impeach men to get their property . . .

Item, the law serveth of nought else in these days but for to do wrong, for nothing is sped almost but false matters for colour of the law for mede, drede and favour, and so no remedy is had in the court of conscience in any wise . . .

Item, we will that all men know that we blame not all the lords, nor all those that are about the king's person, nor all gentlemen nor yeomen, nor all men of law, nor all priests, but all such as may be found guilty by just and true enquiry and by the law.

Item, we will that it be known that we will not rob, nor reve, nor steal, but that these faults be amended, and then we will go home; wherefore we exhort all the king's true liegemen to help us, to support us . . .

Item, we desire that all the extortioners might be laid down . . .

Item, taking of wheat and other grains, beef, mutton, and other victual, the which is importable hurt to the commons, without provision of our sovereign lord and his true council, for his commons may no longer bear it.

Item, the Statute upon Labourers, and the great extortioners of Kent, that is to say, Slegge, Crowmer, Isle and Robert Est.

Item, we move and desire that some true justice with certain true lords and knights may be sent into Kent for to enquire of all such traitors and bribers, and that the Justice may do upon them true judgement, whatsomever they be . . .

Item, to sit upon this enquiry we refuse no judge except four chief judges, the which be false to believe.

. . . The lords followers went together and said, but the king would do execution on such traitors as were named, else they would turn to the captain of Kent.

From Gregory, pp. 190–91

Upon which answer that the king, thither sent by his lords, did make a cry in the king's name of England that all the king's liege men of England should avoid the field. And upon the night after they were all voided and agone . . .

THEIR DEMANDS UNANSWERED, THE COMMONS TAKE LONDON

From Gregory, pp. 191–4

And after that, upon the first day of July, the same captain came again, as the Kentish men said, but it was another that named himself the captain, and he came to the Black Heath. And upon the morrow he came with a great host unto Southwark, and at the White Hart he took his lodging. And upon the morrow, that was the Friday, again even, they smote asunder the ropes of the drawbridge and fought sore a many, and many a man was murdered and killed in that conflict, I wot not what to name it for the multitude of riff raff. And then they entered into the city of London as men that had been half beside their wit; and in that furnace they went, as they said for the common weal of the realm of England, even straight into a merchant's place named Philip Malpas of London. If it were true as they surmised after the doing, I remit myself to ink and paper . . . But well I wot that every ill beginning most commonly hath an ill ending, and every good beginning hath very good ending . . . And that Philip Malpas was alderman, and they spoiled him and bare away much goods of his, and especially much money, both of silver and gold . . .

And then divers questions were asked at the Guildhall; and there Robert Horne being alderman was arrested and brought in to Newgate. And the same day William Crowemere, squire, and Sherriff of Kent, was beheaded in the field without Aldgate . . . And another man that was named John Bayle was beheaded at the White Chapel. And the same afternoon was beheaded in Cheap before the Standard, Sir James Fienne, being that time the Lord Saye and Great Treasurer of England . . .

And that same even London did arise and came out upon them at ten of the bell . . . And from that time unto the morrow 8 of the bell they were ever fighting upon London Bridge, and many a man was slain and cast into the Thames . . . And . . . the Captain of Kent did fire the drawbridge of London; and before that he broke both King's Bench and the Marshalsea, and let out all the prisoners that were in them . . .

THE REBELS DISPERSED, THE RISING ENDS

From Gregory, p. 194

And upon the 12th day of July . . . the said Captain was cried and proclaimed traitor, by the name of John Cade, in divers places of London, and also in Southwark, with many more, that what man might or would bring the same John Cade to the king, quick or dead, should have of the king a 1000 marks. Also whosoever might bring or would bring any of his chief counsellors . . . that kept any state or rule or governance under the said false captain John Cade he should have his reward of the king . . . And that day was the false traitor the Captain of Kent taken and slain in the Weald in the county of Sussex, and upon the morrow he was brought in a cart all naked . . . beheaded and quartered . . . and his head . . . set upon London Bridge.

SEVEN MONTHS LATER, THE MEN OF KENT ARE STILL PAYING

From Gregory, pp. 196–7

. . . On Candlemas Day, the king was at Canterbury, and with him was the Duke of Exeter, the Duke of Somerset, my lord of Shrewsbury, with many other lords and many justices. And there they held the Sessions four days, and there were condemned many of the Captain's men for their rising, and for their talking against the king . . . And the condemned men were drawn, hanged, and quartered, but they were pardoned to be buried, both the quarters of their bodies and their heads withal.

And at Rochester nine men were beheaded at the same time and their heads were sent unto London by the king's commandment, and set upon London Bridge all at one time; and twelve heads at another time were brought unto London and set up under the same form as it was commanded by the king. Men call it in Kent the harvest of heads.

Part Two

THE BREAK-UP OF THE FEUDAL
SYSTEM 1453–1603

The heavens themselves, the planets and this centre,
Observe degree, priority and place,
Insisture, course, proportion, season, form,
Office and custom, in all line of order . . .
                    . . . but when the planets
In evil mixture to disorder wander,
What plagues and what portents, what mutiny,
What raging of the sea, shaking of earth,
Commotion in the winds, frights, changes, horrors,
Divert and crack, rend and deracinate
The unity and married calm of states
Quite from their fixture!

Shakespeare, *Troilus and Cressida*

EDMUND DUDLEY (1462?–1510)

1508–9

From *The Tree of Commonwealth*, in Brodie, ed., *Collection of Three Manuscripts*, pp. 88–9

In the period of uncertainty following the accession of Henry VIII, Dudley, a rich courtier of the previous reign, was arraigned on a charge of treason for having his household under arms, taken to the Tower (where he wrote *The Tree of Commonwealth*, perhaps hoping this study of the conditions of his time, stressing loyalty to the Crown, would obtain him a pardon) and beheaded.

FOR THOSE OF POOR ESTATE

The name of the second messenger is Arrogancy, nigh cousin to Pride. His nature and property is to entice you to enable yourself to such things as nothing beseemeth, or to do such things as you can nothing skill on. He will show you that you be made of the same mould and metal that the gentles be made of. Why then should they sport and play, and you labour and till? He will tell you also that at your births and deaths your riches is indifferent. Why should they have so much of the prosperity and treasure of this world, and ye so little? Besides that, he will tell you that ye be the children and right inheritors of Adam, as well as they. Why should they have this great honour, royal castles and manors, with so much lands and possessions, and you but poor tenements and cottages? He will show you also why that Christ bought as dearly you as them, and with one manner of price, which was his precious blood. Why then should you be of so poor estate, and they of so high degree? Or why should you do them so much honour and reverence with crouching and kneeling, and they take it so high and stately on them? And percase he will inform you how your souls and theirs, which maketh you all to be men, for else you were all but beasts, whereby God created in you one manner of nobleness without any adversity, and that your souls be as precious to God as theirs. Why then should they have so great authority and power to commit to prison, to punish and to judge you?

But, you good commoners, in any wise utterly refuse this messenger; for though he show the truth to you, he meaneth full falsely as afterwards you shall well know . . . He will bid you leave to employ yourselves to labour and to till like beasts, nor suffer yourselves to be subdued of your fellows. He will promise to set you on high and to be lords and governors, and no longer to be churls as you were before . . . He will also display unto you his banner of insurrection and say to you, 'now set forward;

your time is right good'. But woe be unto that man that will fight there-
under.

ANONYMOUS 1514

Petition to Henry VIII, in More, *Utopia*, p. 160 (Notes)

THE EFFECT OF ENCLOSURES FOR SHEEP

The ploughs be decayed and the farm houses and also other dwelling
houses in many towns, so that where was in a town XX or XXX dwelling
houses they be now decayed ploughs and all, and all the people clean
gone and decayed and no more parishioners in many parishes, but a
neatherd [cowherd] and a shepherd, or a warrener [gamekeeper] and a
shepherd in the stede of 60 or 80 persons.

SIR THOMAS MORE (1478–1535) 1516

From *Utopia*, pp. 13, 15–19

More wrote Utopia (meaning literally 'No-place' or 'Nowhere') in reaction to the
changes he had seen taking place around him in the England (and the Europe)
of his time, with the medieval institutions beginning to break down under pressure from an aggressive rising individualism based upon a new kind of economic
order. The alternative he envisages is not a fantasy world in articulation. It reflects
the conditions of the England he actually lived in and his sense of shock at the
ruthlessness with which the new rich men were prepared to sweep aside (or to
transform to their own great profit) the old-established structures of the agricultural and social system they were in fact displacing. At certain levels therefore
Utopia looks backward, seeking to restore the already half-outmoded conditions
of the medieval order. But it also sets out to delineate a cooperative system of
work and life which repudiates the concept of the inequality of wealth and of
condition that governed More's world. And though Utopia is itself a kingdom
which permits certain limited property rights and even a form of slavery, it speaks
passionately against the crushing poverty and injustice suffered by the common
people, who, as the producers of wealth, most often got nothing but misery in
return for their labour. Indeed, it is a place so firmly rooted in actuality, and
visualized in such grave and measured terms, as to seem almost attainable and
thus to encourage those who read it to want to work towards making it so. Written
in Latin, it went through four editions, all issued on the Continent (Louvain,

Paris, Basle, Venice), and More himself made no attempt to translate it into English. The passages chosen here are from the first translation, made by Ralph Robinson in 1551.

THE IDLE LIVES OF GENTLEMEN

First, there is a great number of gentlemen, which cannot be content to live idle themselves, like dorres [drones], of that which others have laboured for: their tenants I mean, whom they poll and shave to the quick by raising their rents (for this only point of frugality do they use, men else through their lavish and prodigal spending able to bring themselves to very beggary); these gentlemen (I say) do not only live in idleness themselves, but also carry with them at their tails a great flock or train of idle and loitering serving men, which never learned any craft whereby to get their livings. These men, as soon as their master is dead, or be sick themselves, be incontinent thrust out of doors. For gentlemen had rather keep idle persons than sick men; and many times the dead man's heir is not able to maintain so great a house, and keep so many serving men, as his father did. Then in the mean season they that be thus destitute of service either starve for hunger, or manfully play the thieves. For what would you have them to do? When they have wandered abroad so long, until they have worn threadbare their apparel, and also impaired their health, then gentlemen, because of their pale and sick faces and patched coats, will not take them into service. And husbandmen dare not set them a work, knowing well enough that he is nothing mete to do true and faithful service to a poor man with a spade and a mattock, for small wages and hard fare, which, being daintily and tenderly pampered up in idleness and pleasure, was wont with a sword and a buckler by his side to jette [strut] through the street with a bragging look, and to think himself too good to be any man's mate.

RUINOUS ENCLOSURES

... Your sheep, that were wont to be so meek and tame, and so small eaters, now, as I hear say, be become so great devourers, and so wild, that they eat up and swallow down the very men themselves. They consume, destroy, and devour whole fields, houses, and cities. For look in what parts of the realm doth grow the finest, and therefore dearest wool, there noblemen and gentlemen, yea, and certain Abbots, holy men God wot, not contenting themselves with the yearly revenues and profits they were wont to grow to their forefathers and predecessors of their lands, nor being content that they live in rest and pleasure, nothing profiting, yea, much annoying the weal public, leave no ground for tillage; they enclose all in pastures; they throw down houses; they pluck down towns; and leave nothing standing but only the church, to make of it a sheephouse. And, as though you lost no small quantity of ground by forests; chases, lands, and parks; these good holy men turn all dwelling places and all glebeland into desolation and wilderness.

Therefore, that one covetous and insatiable cormorant and very plague of his native country may compass about and enclose many thousand acres of ground together within one pale or hedge, the husbandmen be thrust out of their own; or else either by covin [or fraud], or by violent oppression, they be put besides it, or by wrongs and injuries they be so wearied that they be compelled to sell all. By one means therefore or by other, either by hook or crook, they must needs depart away, poor, sylie [simple, innocent], wretched souls; men, women, husbands, wives, fatherless children, widows, woeful mothers with their young babes, and their whole household small in substance, and much in number, as husbandry requireth many hands. Away they trudge, I say, out of their known and accustomed houses, finding no places to rest in. All their household stuff, which is very little worth, though it might well abide the sale, yet being suddenly thrust out, they be constrained to sell it for a thing of nought. And when they have, wandering about, soon spent that, what can they else do but steal, and then justly, God wot, be hanged, or else go about abegging? And yet then also they be cast in prison as vagabonds, because they go about and work not; whom no man will set a work, though they never so willingly offer themselves thereto. For one shepherd or herdsman is enough to eat up that ground with cattle, to the occupying whereof about husbandry many hands were requested.

And this is also the cause that victuals be now in many places dearer. Yea, besides this the price of wool is so risen that poor folks, which were wont to work it and make cloth of it, be now able to buy none at all. And by this means very many be fain to forsake work, and to give themselves to idleness. For after that so much ground was enclosed for pasture, an infinite multitude of sheep died of the rot, such vengeance God took of their inordinate and insatiable covetousness, sending among the sheep that pestiferous murrain, which much more justly should have fallen on the sheepmasters' own heads. And though the number of sheep increase never so fast, yet the price falleth not one mite, because there be so few sellers. For they be almost all commen into a few rich men's hands, whom no need driveth to sell before they lust; and they lust not before they may sell as dear as they lust. Now the same cause bringeth in like dearth of the other kinds of cattle; yea, and that so much the more, because that after farms plucked down, and husbandry decayed, there is no man that passeth for the breeding of young store. For these rich men bring not up the young ones of great cattle as they do lambs. But first they buy them abroad very cheap, and afterward, when they be fatted in their pastures, they sell them again exceeding dear. And therefore (as I suppose) the whole incommodity [inconvenience] hereof is not yet felt. For yet they make dearth only in those places where they sell. But when they shall fetch them away from thence where they be bred, faster than they can be brought up, then shall there also be felt great dearth, when store beginneth to fail them where the ware is bought.

Thus the unreasonable covetousness of a few hath turned that thing to the utter undoing of your Island, in the which thing the chief felicity of your realm did consist. For this great dearth of victuals causeth every man to keep as little houses and as small hospitality as he possibly may, and to put away their servants: whether, I pray you, but a begging? or else, which these gentle bloods and stout stomachs will sooner set their minds unto, a stealing?

Now, to amend the matters, to this wretched beggary and miserable poverty is joined great wantonness, importunate superfluity, and excessive riot. For not only gentlemen's servants, but also handicraft men, yea, and almost the ploughmen of the country, with all other sorts of people, use much strange and proud new fangleness in their apparel, and to much prodigal riot and sumptuous fare at their table. Now bawds, queans, whores, harlots, strumpets, brothelhouses, stews, and yet another stews, wine taverns, ale houses, and tippling houses, with so many naughty, lewd and unlawful games, as dice, cards, table tennis, bowls, quoits, do not all this send the haunters of them straight a stealing when their money is gone?

Cast out these pernicious abominations; make a law that they which plucked down farms and towns of husbandry, shall build them up again or else yield and surrender the possession of them to such as will go to the cost of building them anew. Suffer not these rich men to buy up all, to engross and forestall, and with their monopoly to keep the market alone as please them. Let not so many be brought up in idleness; let husbandry and tillage be restored again; let cloth working be renewed; that there may be honest labours for this idle sort to pass their time in profitability, which hitherto either poverty hath caused to be thieves, or else now be either vagabonds, or idle serving men, and shortly will be thieves. Doubtless, unless you find a remedy for these enormities, you shall in vain advance [pride] yourselves of executing justice upon felons. For this justice is more beautiful than just or profitable. For by suffering your youth wantonly and viciously to be brought up, and to be infected even from their tender age by little and little with vice; then a God's name to be punished, when they commit the same faults after they be commen to man's estate, which from their youth they were ever like to do; in this point, I pray you, what other thing do you, than make thieves, and then punish them?'

ANONYMOUS POEM
Early 16th century

In Rickword and Lindsay, *Handbook of Freedom*, p. 69

COMMONS TO CLOSE AND KEEP

Commons to close and keep,
Poor folk for bread to cry and weep,
Towns pulled down to pasture sheep:
This is the new guise.

Envy waxeth wondrous strong,
The Rich doeth the poor wrong,
God of his mercy suffereth long
The devil his work to work.

The towns go down, the land decays,
Of corn fields, plain lays,
Great men maketh nowadays
A sheepcote in the church.

SIR THOMAS MORE (1478–1535)
1516

From *Utopia*, pp. 43–5, 140–43

PROPERTY AS COMMON WEALTH

How be it doubtless, Master More (to speak truly as my mind giveth me), wheresoever possessions be private, where money beareth all the stroke, it is hard and almost impossible that there the public weal may justly be governed and prosperously flourish. Unless you think thus: that justice is there executed, where all things come into the hands of evil men; or that prosperity there flourishes, where all is divided among a few; which few nevertheless do not lead their lives very wealthily, and the residue live miserably, wretchedly, and beggarly.

Wherefore when I consider with myself, and weigh in my mind, the wise and godly ordinances of the Utopians, among whom with very few laws all things be so well and wealthily ordered, that virtue is had in price and estimation; and yet, all things being there common, every man hath abundance of every thing: again, on the other part, when I compare with them so many nations ever making new laws, yet none of them all well and sufficiently furnished with laws; where every man calleth that he hath gotten his own proper and private goods; where so many new laws daily made be not sufficient for every man to enjoy, defend, and know from another man's that which he calleth his own; which thing the infinite controversies in the law, that daily rise never to be ended, plainly declare to be true: these things (I say) when I consider with myself, I hold well with Plato, and do nothing marvel that he would make no laws for them that refused those laws, whereby all men should have and enjoy equal portions of wealths and commodities. For the wise man did easily foresee, that this is the one and only way to the wealth of the community, if equality of all things should be brought in and established. Which I think is not possible to be observed, where every man's goods be proper and peculiar to himself. For where every man under certain titles and pretences draweth and plucketh to himself as much as he can, and so a few divide among themselves all the riches that there is, be there never so much abundance and store, there to the residue is left lack and poverty. And for the most part it chanceth that this latter sort is more worthy to enjoy that state of wealth, than the other be; because the rich men be covetous, crafty, and unprofitable: on the other part, the poor be lowly, simple, and by their daily labour more profitable to the common wealth than to themselves.

Thus I do fully persuade myself, that no equal and just distribution of things can be made; nor that perfect wealth shall ever be among men; unless this property be exiled and banished. But so long as it shall continue, so long shall remain among the most and best part of men the heavy and inequitable burden of poverty and wretchedness.

A CONSPIRACY OF THE RICH LADY MONEY

Is not this an unjust and an unkind public weal, which giveth great fees and rewards to gentlemen, as they call them, and to goldsmiths, and to such other, which be either idle persons or else only flatterers, and devisers of vain pleasures; and, of the contrary part, maketh no gentle provision for poor ploughmen, colliers, labourers, carters, ironsmiths, and carpenters; without whom no common wealth can continue? But when it hath abused the labourers of their lusty and flowering age, at the last, when they be oppressed with old age and sickness, being needy, poor, and indigent of all things; then, forgetting their so many painful watchings, not remembering their so many and so great benefits; recompenseth and requiteth them most unkindly with miserable death. And yet besides this the rich men not only by private fraud, but also by common laws, do every day pluck and snatch away from the poor some part of their daily living. So, whereas it seemed before unjust to recompense with unkindness their pains which have been beneficial to the public weal, now they have to this their wrong and unjust dealing (which is yet a much worse point), given the name of justice, yea, and that by force of a law.

Therefore when I consider and weigh in my mind all these common wealths which nowadays anywhere do flourish, so god help me, I can perceive nothing but a certain conspiracy of rich men, procuring their own commodities under the name and title of the common wealth. They invent and devise all means and crafts, firstly how to keep safely without fear of losing that they have unjustly gathered together; and next how to hire and abuse the work and labour of the poor for as little money as may be. These devices when the rich men have decreed to be kept and observed for the common wealth's sake, that is to say, for the wealth also of the poor people, then they be made laws. But these most wicked and vicious men, when they have by their insatiable covetousness divided among themselves all those things which would have sufficed all men, yet how far be they from the wealth and felicity of the utopian common wealth? Out of the which in that all the desire of moneys with the use thereof is utterly secluded and banished, how great a heap of cares is cut away? How great an occasion of wickedness and mischief is plucked up by the roots? For who knoweth not that fraud, theft, ravine, brawling, quarrelling, brabbling, strife, chiding, contention, murder, treason, poisoning; which by daily punishments are rather revenged than refrained; do die when money dieth? And also that fear, grief, care, labours, and watchings, do perish, even the very same moment that money perisheth? Yea, poverty itself, which only seemed to lack money, if money were gone, it also would decrease and vanish away.

And that you may perceive this more plainly, consider with yourselves some barren and unfruitful year, wherein many thousands of people have starved for hunger. I dare be bold to say, that in the end of that penury so much corn or grain might have been found in the rich men's barns, if they had been searched, as being divided among them, whom famine and pestilence hath killed, no man at all should have felt that plague and penury. So easily might men get their living, if that same worthy princess, lady money, did not alone stop up the way between us and our living; which a god's name was very excellently devised and invented, that by her the way thereto should be opened. I am sure the rich men perceive this, nor they be not ignorant how much better it were to lack no necessary thing than to abound with overmuch superfluity; to be rid out of innumerable cares and troubles, than to be besieged with great riches. And I doubt not that either the respect of every man's private commodity, or else the authority of our saviour Christ (which for his great wisdom could not but know what were best, and for his inestimable goodness could not but counsel to that which he knew to be best) would have brought all the world long ago into the laws of this public weal, if it were not that one only beast, the princess and mother of all mischief, pride, doth withstand and let it. She measureth not wealth and prosperity by her own commodities, but by the miseries and incommodities of others. She would not by her good will be made a goddess, if there were no wretches left, whom she might be lady over to mock and scorn; over whose miseries her felicity might shine, whose poverty she might vex, torment, and increase by gorgeously setting forth her riches. This hell hound creepeth into men's hearts, and plucketh them back from entering the right path of life; and is so deeply rooted in men's breasts, that she cannot be plucked out . . .

JOHN SKELTON (1460?–1529) 1520

From *Colin Clout*, in *Complete Poems*

AGAINST THE RICH OF THE CHURCH

Some hatted and some capped,
Richly and warm bewrapped,
God wit to their great pains!

In rochets of fine Rennes,
White as morrow's milk;
Their tabards of fine silk,
Their stirrups of mixt gold begared:
There may no cost be spared,
Their mules gold doth eat,
Their neighbours die for meat.
  What care they though Gil sweat,
Or Jack of the Noke?
The poor people they yoke
With summons and citations
And excommunications,
About churches and market,
The bishop on his carpet
At home full soft doth sit,
This is a farly fit,
To hear the people jangle,
How warlike they wrangle.
Alas, why do ye not handle
And them all to-mangle?
Full falsely on you they lie,
And shamefully you ascry,
And say as untruly
As the butterfly,
A man might say in mock,
Ware the weathercock
Of the steeple of Poules.
And thus they hurt their souls
In slandering you for truth.
Alas, it is great ruth!
Some say yet sit in thrones,
Like princes *aquilonis*,
And shrine your rotten bones
With pearls and precious stones;
But how the commons groans,
And the people moans
For the prestes and for loans

rochets: vestments *tabards*: loose garments *begared*: adorned *Gil* and *Jack of the Noke*: names for the common people *farly*: alarming *Poules*: St Paul's *aquilonis*: of the north *prestes*: advance payment

Lent and never paid.
But from day to day delayed,
The commonwealth decayed,
Men say ye are tongue-tied,
And thereof speak nothing
But dissimuling and glosing.

JOHN SKELTON (1460?–1529)

From *Speak, Parrot*, in *Complete Poems*

SO MUCH

So many moral matters, and so little used;
  So much new making, and so mad time spent;
So much translation into English confused;
  So much noble preaching, and so little amendment;
  So much consultation, almost to none intent;
So much provision, and so little wit at need –
Since Deucalion's flood there can no clerkes read.

So little discretion, and so much reasoning;
  So much hardy dardy, and so little manliness;
So prodigal expense, and so shameful reckoning;
  So gorgeous garments, and so much wretchedness;
  So much portly pride, with purses penniless;
So much spent before, and so much unpaid behind –
Since Deucalion's flood there can no clerkes find.

So much forecasting, and so far an after deal;
  So much politic prating, and so little standeth in stead;
So little secretness, and so much great council;
  So many bold barons, their hearts as dull as lead;
  So many noble bodies under a daw's head;
So royal a king as reigneth upon us all –
Since Deucalion's flood was never seen nor shall.

WILLIAM TYNDALE

(1496?–1536)

May onward, 1526

From the New Testament

Translator of the first English printed bible, born in Gloucestershire, where the influence of Wycliffe and the Lollards was still strong. He studied at Oxford (BA in 1512, MA in 1515) and Cambridge; became tutor in the house of Sir John Walsh in Gloucestershire; was suspected of heretical tendencies, came to realize how ignorant and selfish the clergy were, and began to think of translating the Bible. Resigning his post, he went to London in 1523, hoping to gain support for his project but, disappointed in this, left England for the Continent. There he may have met Luther, and there he began his translation of the NT, which was ready by the summer of 1525. Stopped from having it printed in Cologne he produced an octavo edition at Worms in 1526, of which a few copies reached England in May. The Bishop of London (Tunstall) had all available copies seized and burnt at St Paul's Cross; but in the following three years there were six editions (18,000 copies, though only two remain). In May 1535 he was arrested and imprisoned in a castle near Brussels, and in October 1536 strangled in the castle courtyard, and burned. 'A man . . . whose epitaph is the Reformation' (J. A. Froude).

A VISION OF JUDGEMENT (St Matthew, xxvi, 31–46)

When the son of Man shall come in his majesty, and all his holy angels with him, then shall he sit upon the seat of his majesty, and before him shall be gathered all nations. And he shall sever them one from another, as a shepherd putteth asunder the sheep from the goats. And he shall set the sheep on his right hand, and the goats on his left hand. Then shall the King say to them on his right hand: Come ye blessed children of my father, inherit ye the kingdom prepared for you from the beginning of the world. For I was enhungered, and ye gave me meat. I thirsted, and ye gave me drink. I was herbrouless [harbourless – homeless], and ye lodged me. I was naked, and ye clothed me: I was sick, and ye visited me. I was in prison, and ye came unto me.

Then shall the just answer him saying: Master, when saw we thee enhungered, and fed thee? or athirst, and gave thee drink? when saw we thee herbrouless, and lodged thee? or naked and clothed thee? or when saw we thee sick, or in prison and came unto thee? And the King shall answer, and say unto them: Verily I say unto you: in as much as ye have done it unto one of the least of these my brethren: ye have done it to me.

Then shall the King say unto them that shall be on the left hand: Depart from me, ye cursed, into everlasting fire, which is prepared for the devil and his angels. For I was enhungered, and ye gave me no meat. I thirsted, and ye gave me no drink. I was herbrouless, and ye lodged me not. I was naked, and ye clothed me not. I was sick and in prison, and ye visited me not.

Then shall they also answer him saying: Master, when saw we thee enhungered, or athirst, or herbrouless, or naked, or sick, or in prison, and have not ministered unto thee? Then shall he answer them, and say: Verily I say unto you, in as much as ye did it not to one of the least of these, ye did it not to me. And these shall go into everlasting pain: And the righteous into life eternal.

ANONYMOUS   Late 1530s

From *Vox Populi, Vox Dei*, pp. 1–2

WHAT THE COMMON PEOPLE SAY

I pray you, be not wroth
For telling of the truth;
For thus the world it goeth
Both to life and to lothe
As God himself knoweth;
And, as all men understand,
Both lordships and lands
Are now in few men's hands;
Both substance and bands
Of all the holy realm
As most men esteem
Are now consumed clean
From the farmer and the poor
To the town and the tower;
Which maketh them to lower,
To see that in their flower
Is neither malt nor meal,
Bacon, beef, nor veal,
Crock, milk, nor keel.
But ready for to steal
For very pure need.
Your commons say indeed
They be not able to feed

In their stable scant a steed,
To bring up nor to breed,
Yea, scant able to bring
To the market any thing
Towards their housekeeping:
And scant have a cow,
Nor to keep a poor sow:
Thus the world is now.
And to hear the relation
Of the poor men's communication,
Under what sort and fashion
They make their exclamation,
You would have compassion.
  Thus goeth their protestation,
Saying that such and such
That of late are made rich
Have too, too much
By grasping and regrating,
By polling and debating,
By rolling and dating,
By check and checkmating,
With delays and debating,
With customs and tallyings,
Forfeits and forestallings,
So that your commons say,
They still pay, pay,
Most willingly alway,
But that they see no stay
To this outrageous array.
Vox populi, vox dei.

EDWARD HALL (1498?–1547)   1526

From *Chronicle – A History of England from Henry IV to Henry VIII*,
pp. 699–701

RISING OF THE SUFFOLK POOR

In Essex the people would not assemble before the commissioners into
houses, but in open places; and in Huntingdonshire divers resisted the

commissioners to sit, which were apprehended and sent to the Fleet.

The Duke of Suffolk sat in Suffolk, this season in like Commission, and . . . he caused the rich Clothiers to assent and grant to give the sixth part, and when they came to their houses, they called to them their spinners, carders, fullers, weavers, and other artificers . . . and said, Sirs, we be not able to set you awork, our goods be taken from us, wherefore trust to youselves, and not to us . . . Then began women to weep, and young folks to cry, and men that had no work began to rage and assemble themselves in companies. The Duke of Suffolk, hearing of this, commanded the Constables that every man's arms should be taken from them, but when this was known, then the rumour waxed more greater, and the people railed openly on the Duke of Suffolk and Sir Robert Drury, and threatened them with death, and the Cardinal also, and so of Lavenham, Sudbury, Hadley and other towns about there rebelled 4000 men, and put themselves in arms, and rang the bells *Alarm*, and began to gather still more.

The Duke of Norfolk . . . hearing of this, gathered a great power in Norfolk, and came towards the commons, and . . . he sent to the commons to know their intent, which answered: 'That they would live and die in the King's causes, and to the King be obedient.' When the duke wist that, he came to them, and then all spoke at once, so that he wist not what they meant. Then he asked who was their Captain, and bade that he should speak. Then a well-aged man of fifty years and above asked licence of the Duke to speak . . . 'My lord,' said this man, whose name was John Green, 'since you ask who is our Captain, forsooth his name is Poverty, for he and his cousin Necessity hath brought us to this doing, for all these persons and many more, which I would were not here, live not of ourselves, but all we live by the substantial occupiers of this country, and yet they give us so little wages for our workmanship that scarcely we be able to live, and thus in penury we pass the time, we, our wives and children, and if they by whom we live be brought in that case, that they of their little cannot help us to earn our living, then must we perish and die miserably. I speak this, my lord; the cloth-makers have put all these people and a far greater number from work . . . They say the King asketh so much that they be not able to do as they have done before this time; and then of necessity must we die wretchedly. Wherefor, my lord, now according to your wisdom, consider our necessity.'

The Duke was sorry to hear this complaint, and well he knew that it was true. Then he said . . . 'let every man depart to his home and choose further four that shall answer for the remnant, and on my honour I will send to the King and make intercession for your pardon . . .'

[Which he did.] And the King said: 'I will no more of this trouble. Let letters be sent to all shires, that this matter may no more be spoken of. I will pardon all them that have denied the demand, openly or secretly.'

WILLIAM TYNDALE (1496?–1536)   1528

From *The Parable of the Wicked Mammon*, reprint of 1842, pp. 17–18

MAMMON, THE MISUSE OF RICHES

. . . First, *mammon* is an Hebrew word, and signifies riches and temporal goods, and namely, all superfluity, and all that is above necessity, and that which is required unto our necessary uses, wherewith a man may help another without undoing or hurting himself; for Hamon, in the Hebrew speech, signifies a multitude or abundance, or many, and there hence cometh mahamon, or mammon, abundance or plenteousness of goods or riches.

Secondarily, it is called unrighteous mammon, not because it is got unrighteously, or with usury, for of unrighteous gotten goods can no man do good works, but ought to restore them home again. As it is said (Isaiah lxi) I am a God that hateth offering that cometh of robbery; and Solomon saith, Honour the Lord of thine own good. But therefore it is called unrighteous, because it is in unrighteous use. As Paul speaketh unto the Ephesians (v), how that the days are evil though that God hath made them, and they are a good work of God's making. Howbeit they are yet called evil, because that evil men use them amiss, and much sin, occasions of evil, peril of souls are wrought in them. Even so are riches called evil because that evil men bestow them amiss and misuse them. For where riches are there goeth it after the common proverb, He that hath money hath what him listeth. And they cause fighting, stealing, laying await, lying, flattering, and all unhappiness against a man's neighbour. For all men hold on riches' part.

But singularly before God it is called unrighteous mammon, because it is not bestowed and ministered unto our neighbour's need. For if my neighbour need and I give him not, neither depart liberally with him of that which I have, then withhold I from him unrighteously that which is his own. For as much as I am bounden to help him by the law of nature, which is whatsoever thou wouldest that another did to thee, that do thou also to him . . .

ANONYMOUS

Late 1530s

From *Vox Populi, Vox Dei*, pp. 9–10

THE BODY AND STAY OF THE REALM

From Scotland into Kent
This preaching was besprent,
And from the east front
Unto Saint Michael's Mount,
This saying did surmount
Abroad to all men's ears
And to your grace's peers –
That from pillar unto post
The poor man he was tost;
I mean the labouring man,
I mean the husbandman,
I mean the ploughman,
I mean the plain true man,
I mean the handcraftman,
I mean the victualling man,
Also the good yeoman,
That sometime in this realm
Had plenty of kye and cream,
But now alack, alack,
All these men go to wrack,
That are the body and stay
Of your grace's realm alway.

SIMON FISH (d. 1531)

Spring 1529

From *A Supplication for the Beggars: To the King Our Sovereign Lord*
in Arbor, ed., *The English Scholar's Library*,
pp. 3–4, 8–9, 9–10

LAWS AGAINST THE COUNTERFEIT HOLY

Most lamentably complaineth their woeful misery unto your highness
your poor daily beedmen the wretched hideous monsters (on whom
scarcely for horror any ye dare look) the foul unhappy sort of lepers, and
other sore people, needy, impotent, blind, lame, and sick, that live only

by alms, how that their number is daily so sore increased that all the alms of all the well-disposed people of this your realm is not half enough for to sustain them, but that for very constraint they die for hunger. And this most pestilent mischief is comen upon your said poor beedmen by the reason that there is in the times of your noble predecessors past craftily crept unto this your realm another sort (not of impotent but) of strong puissaunt and counterfeit holy, and idle beggars and vagabonds which since the time of their first entry by all the craft and wiliness of Satan are now increased under your sight not only into a great number, but also into a kingdom. These are (not the Lords, but the ravenous wolves going in herds' clothing devouring the flock) the Bishops, Abbots, Priors, Deacons, Archdeacons, Suffragans, Priests, Monks, Canons, Friars, Pardoners and Summoners. And who is able to number this idle ravenous sort which (setting all labour aside) have begged so importunately that they have gotten into their hands more than the third part of all your Realm. The goodliest lordships, manors, lands, and territories, are theirs. Besides this they have the tenth part of all the corn, meadow, pasture, grass, wool, colts, calves, lambs, pigs, geese, and chickens. Over and besides the tenth part of every servant's wages, the tenth part of the wool, milk, honey, wax, cheese, and butter. Yea, and they look so narrowly upon their profits that the poor wives must be countable to them of every tenth egg or else she getteth not her rights at Easter, shall be taken as an heretic . . .

What remedy: make laws against them. I am in doubt whether ye be able: Are they not stronger in your own parliament house than yourself? What a number of Bishops, abbots, and priors are lords of your parliament? Are not all the learned men in your realm in fee with them to speak in your parliament house for them against your crown, dignity, and common wealth of your realm, a few of your own learned counsel only excepted? What law can be made against them that may be advaylable? Who is he (though he be grieved never so sore) for the murder of his ancestry, ravishment of his wife, of his daughter, robbing, trespass, maiming, debt, or any other offence dare lay it their charge by any way of action, and if he do then is he by and by, by their wiliness accused of heresy? . . .

What law can be made so strong against them that they either with money or else with other policy will not break and set at nought? What kingdom can endure that ever giveth theirs from him and receiveth nothing again? O, how all the substance of your Realm forthwith your Swerde [allegiance], power, crown, dignity, and obedience of your people run

neth headlong into the insatiable whirlpool of these greedy goulafers to
be swallowed and devoured . . .

ANONYMOUS POEM   After 1539

In Furnivall, ed., *Ballads from Manuscripts*, p. 292

SKIPJACK ENGLAND

The Abbeys went down because of their pride
  And men the more covetous rich for a time;
Their livings dispersed on every side,
  Where once was some prayer, now places for swine.
The goods that were given for a good intent –
  Through falsehood of prelates, that did them beguile –
Of others were spoiled, torn and rent;
  Thus craft by violence came to a foil.
But what shall become of those that be gay
  With the goods of the clergy flaunting about?
Their stolen buildings and lands shall away,
  When a third mischief cometh about.

They think that to heaven they shall go for their brags;
  Their houses of pomp cannot them save;
Poor Christ's Church they furnish with rags
  And wicked customs good manners deprave.
Skipjack England, and look to thy tail!
A whip from heaven thy pride shall quail!
Will you know when this shall be?
At the end of one, two, and three.

SIR THOMAS WYATT (1503–1542)   1541?

'Satire, written to John Poyntz', in *Poems*, I, pp. 135–40

Wyatt held various court posts, both at home and abroad, including that of Henry
VIII's ambassador to Charles V (1537–9). In 1536 Henry put him temporarily in
the Tower during the course of his inquiries into Ann Boleyn's alleged post-

nuptial infidelities because Wyatt had been her lover before she married Henry. He was again imprisoned in the Tower as an ally of Thomas Cromwell, but released in 1541.

OF THE COURTIER'S LIFE

Mine own John Poyntz, since ye delight to know
   The cause why that homeward I me draw,
   And flee the press of courts whereso they go,
Rather than to live thrall, under the awe
   Of lordly looks, wrapped within my cloak,
   To will and lust learning to set a law;
It is not for because I scorn or mock
   The power of them, to whom fortune hath lent
   Charge over us, of right, to strike the stroke:
But true it is that I have always meant
   Less to esteem them than the common sort,
   Of outward things that judge in their intent,
Without regard what doth inward resort.
   I grant sometime that of glory the fire
   Doth touch my heart: me list not to report
Blame by honour and honour to desire.
   But how may I this honour now attain
   That cannot dye the colour black a liar?
My Poyntz, I cannot frame my tune to feign,
   To cloak the truth for praise without desert,
   Of them that list all vice for to retain.
I cannot honour them that sets their part
   With Venus and Bacchus all their life long;
   Nor hold my peace of them although I smart.
I cannot crouch nor kneel to do so great a wrong,
   To worship them, like God on earth alone,
   That are as wolves these seely lambs among.
I cannot with my words complain and moan
   And suffer nought; nor smart without complaint,
   Nor turn the word that from my mouth is gone.
I cannot speak and look like a saint,
   Use wiles for wit and make deceit a pleasure,
   And call craft counsel, for profit still to paint.
I cannot wrest the law to fill the coffer

With innocent blood to feed myself fat,
  And do most hurt where most help I offer.
I am not he that can allow the state
  Of high Caesar and damn Cato to die,
  That with his death did scape out of the gate
From Caesar's hands (if Livy do not lie)
  And would not live where liberty was lost:
  So did his heart the commonweal apply.
I am not he such eloquence to boast,
  To make the crow singing as the swan,
  Nor call the lion of coward beasts the most
That cannot take a mouse as the cat can:
  And he that di'th for hunger of the gold
  Call him Alexander, and say that Pan
Passeth Apollo in music manifold;
  Praise Sir Thopas for a noble tale
  And scorn the story that the knight told.
Praise him for counsel that is drunk of ale;
  Grin when he laugheth that beareth all the sway,
  Frown when he frowneth and groan when he is pale;
On others' lust to hang both night and day:
  None of these points would ever frame in me;
  My wit is naught – I cannot learn the way,
And much the less of things which greater be,
  That asken help of colours of device
  To join the mean with each extremity,
With the nearest virtue to cloak alway the vice:
  And as to purpose likewise it shall fall,
  To press the virtue that it may not rise;
As drunkenness good fellowship to call;
  The friendly foe with his double face
  Say he is gentle and courteous therewithall;
And say that favell hath a goodly grace
  In eloquence; and cruelty to name
  Zeal of justice and change in time and place;
And he that suffreth offence without blame
  Call him pitiful; and him true and plain
  That raileth reckless to every man's shame.
Say he is rude that cannot lie and feign;
  The lecher a lover; and tyranny
  To be the right of a prince's reign.

I cannot, I! No, no, it will not be!
  This is the cause that I could never yet
  Hang on their sleeves that way as thou may'st see
A chip of chance more than a pound of wit.
  This maketh me at home to hunt and to hawk
  And in foul weather at my book to sit.
In frost and snow then with my bow to stalk,
  No man doth mark whereso I ride or go;
  In lusty leas at liberty I walk,
And of these news I feel nor weal nor woe,
  Save that a clog doth hang yet at my heel:
  No force for that, for it is ordered so,
That I may leap both hedge and dike full well.
  I am not now in France to judge the wine,
  With savoury sauce the delicates to feel;
Nor yet in Spain where one must him incline
  Rather than to be, outwardly to seem.
  I meddle not with wits that be so fine,
No Flanders' cheer letteth not my sight to deem
  Of black and white, nor taketh my wit away
  With beastliness they, beasts, do so esteem.
Nor I am not where Christ is given in prey
  For money, poison and treason at Rome,
  A common practice used night and day:
But here I am in Kent and Christendom
  Among the muses where I read and rhyme;
  Where if thou list, my Poyntz, for to come,
Thou shalt be judge how I do spend my time.

EDWARD HALL (1498?–1547)   1542

From *Chronicle – A History of England from Henry IV to Henry VIII*

LONDONERS ACT AGAINST ENCLOSURES

Before this time the towns about London, as Islington, Hoxton,
Shoreditch and other, had so enclosed the common fields with hedges
and ditches, that neither the young men of the city might shoot, nor the
ancient persons might walk for their pleasure in the fields, except either
the bows and arrows were taken away, or the honest and substantial

persons arrested or indicted, saying that no Londoner should go out of the city but in the highways. This saying sore grieved the Londoners, and suddenly this year a great number of the city assembled themselves in a morning, and a turner in a fool's coat came crying through the city, 'Shovels and spades!' and so many people followed that it was a wonder, and within a short space all the hedges about the towns were cast down, and the ditches filled, and everything made plain, the workmen were so diligent.

. . . And so after the fields were never hedged.

HUGH LATIMER (1485?–1555)   18 January 1548

From 'The Sermon of the Plough' (preached at St Paul's Cathedral) in Peacock, ed., *English Prose*, I, pp. 159–62

Latimer was converted to Protestantism by Thomas Bilney, who died at the stake in 1531. Under Henry VIII his fortunes varied. He was excommunicated, imprisoned, later made Bishop of Worcester, then resigned his see in 1539. It was during Edward VI's short reign, when Protestants were openly encouraged, that he made his greatest impact, preaching before large crowds and spreading the ideas of the Reformation. But with Mary Tudor determined to re-assert orthodoxy, he was at once arrested, together with Cranmer and Nicholas Ridley, and, after an acrimonious trial, burnt at the stake. His last words, to his fellow-victim, Ridley, were: 'Be of good comfort, Master Ridley, and play the man: we shall this day light such a candle by God's grace in England as I trust shall never be put out.'

TO LONDON'S RICH, THAT LIVE LIKE LOITERERS

. . . London cannot abide to be rebuked; such is the nature of man. If they be pricked they will kick; if they be rubbed on the gall, they will wince; but yet they will not amend their faults, they will not be ill spoken of. But how shall I speak well of them? If you could be content to receive and follow the word of God, and favour good preachers, if you could bear to be told of your faults, if you could amend when you hear of them, if you would be glad to reform that is amiss; if I might see any such indication in you, that you would leave to be merciless, and begin to be charitable, I would then hope well of you, I would then speak well of you. But London was never so ill as it is now. In times past men were

107

full of pity and compassion, but now there is no pity; for in London their brother shall die in the streets for cold, he shall lie sick at their door between stock and stock, I cannot tell what to call it, and perish there for hunger: was there ever more unmercifulness in Nebo?[1] I think not. In times past, when any rich man died in London, they were wont to help the poor scholars of the Universities with exhibition. When any man died, they would bequeath great sums of money toward the relief of the poor. When I was a scholar in Cambridge myself, I heard very good report of London, and knew many that had relief of the rich men of London: but now I can hear no such good report, and yet I inquire of it, and hearken for it; but now charity is waxen cold, none helpeth the scholar, nor yet the poor. And in those days, what did they when they helped the scholars? Marry, they maintained and gave them livings that were very papists, and professed the pope's doctrine: and now that the knowledge of God's word is brought to light, and many earnestly study and labour to set it forth, now almost no man helpeth to maintain them.

Oh London, London! repent, repent; for I think God is more displeased with London than ever he was with the city of Nebo. Repent therefore, repent, London, and remember that the same God liveth now that punished Nebo, even the same God, and none other; and he will punish sin as well now as he did then: and he will punish the iniquity of London, as well as he did them of Nebo. Amend therefore. And ye that be prelates, look well to your office; for right prelating is busy labouring, and not lording. Therefore preach and teach, and let your plough be doing. Ye lords, I say, that live like loiterers, look well to your office; the plough is your office and charge. If you live idle and loiter, you do not your duty, you follow not your vocation: let your plough therefore be going, and not cease, that the ground may bring forth fruit.

. . . But . . . they that be lords will ill go to plough: it is no meet office for them; it is not seeming for their estate. *Thus came up lording loiterers: thus crept in unpreaching prelates; and so have they long continued.* For how many unlearned prelates have we now at this day! And no marvel: for if the ploughmen that now be were made lords, they would clean give over ploughing; they would leave off their labour, and fall to lording outright, and let the plough stand: and then both ploughs *not walking, nothing should be in the commonweal but hunger.* For ever since the prelates were made lords and nobles, the plough standeth; there is no work done, the people starve. They hawk, they hunt, they

1. *Nebo*: one of the cities of Moab. Jeremiah xlviii, 1: 'Woe unto Nebo! for it is spoiled.'

card, they dice; they pastime in their prelacies with gallant gentlemen, with their dancing minions, and with their fresh companions, so that ploughing is set aside: and by their lording and loitering, preaching and ploughing is clean gone. And thus if the ploughmen of the country were as negligent in their office as prelates be, we should not long live, for lack of sustenance. And as it is necessary for to have this ploughing for the sustentation of the body, so must we have also the other for the satisfaction of the soul, or else we cannot live long ghostly. For as the body wasteth and consumeth away for lack of bodily meat, so doth the soul pine away for default of ghostly meat. But there be two kinds of enclosing, to let or hinder both these kinds of ploughing; the one is an enclosing to let or hinder the bodily ploughing, and the other to let or hinder the holiday-ploughing, the church-ploughing . . .

HUGH LATIMER (1485?–1555)   8 March 1549

First sermon preached before Edward VI, in Peacock, ed., *English Prose*, I, pp. 170–72

DECAY OF THE YEOMANRY

My father was a yeoman, and had no lands of his own, only he had a farm of 3 or 4 pound by year at the uttermost, and here upon he tilled so much as kept half a dozen men. He had walk for a hundred sheep, and my mother milked 30 kyne. He was able and did find the king a harness, with himself, and his horse, while he came to the place that he should receive the king's wages. I can remember, that I buckled his harness, when he went unto Black heath field. He kept me to school, or else I had not been able to have preached before the king's majesty now. He married my sisters with 5 pound, or 20 nobles a piece, so that he brought them up in godliness, and fear of God. He kept hospitality for his poor neighbours. And some alms he gave to the poor, and all this did he of the said farm. Where he that now hath it, payeth 16 pound by year or more, and is not able to do any thing for his prince, for him self, nor for his children, or give a cup of drink to the poor. Thus all the enhancing and rearing goeth to your private commodity and wealth. So that where ye had a single too much, you have that: and since the same, ye have enhanced the rent, and so have increased another too much. So now ye have double too much, which is too too much. But let the preacher preach til his tongue be worn to the stumps, nothing is amended. We have good statutes made for the common wealth, as touching commoners, enclosers, many meetings and sessions, but in the end of the matter, there cometh nothing forth. Well, well, this is one thing I will say unto you, from whence it cometh I know, even from the devil. I know his intent in it. For if ye bring it to pass, that the yeomanry be not able to put their sons to school (as indeed universities do wondrously decay already) and that they be not able to marry their daughters to the avoiding of whoredom I say ye pluck salvation from the people, and utterly destroy the realm. For by yeomen's sons, the faith of Christ is, and hath been maintained chiefly. Is this realm taught by rich men's sons? No, no, read the chronicles, ye shall find sometime noble men's sons, which have been unpreaching bishops and prelates, but ye shall find none of them learned men. But verily, they that should look to the redress of these things, be the greatest against them. In this realm are a great many of folks, and amongst many, I know but one of tender zeal, at the motion [mocyon] of his poor tenants, hath let down his lands to the old rents for their relief. For God's love, let not him be a Phoenix, let him not be alone, let him not be an Hermit closed in a wall, some good man follow him, and do as he giveth example.

WILLIAM FORREST (still active 1581)　　1548

Poesie of Princely Practice, ll. 344–99, in Herritage, ed., *England in the Reign of King Henry VIII*, I, Appendix, p. xcv

The price of basic foods rose by over 110 per cent between 1500 and 1550

SCARCE THE POOR MAN CAN BUY A MORSEL

The poor man to toil for two pence the day,
some while three-half-pence, or else a penny:
having wife, children and house rent to pay;
meat, cloth and fuel with the same to buy,
and much other things that be necessary,
with many a hungry meal sustaining:
Alas! maketh not this a doleful complaining?

The world is changed from that it hath been,
not to the better but to the worse far:

more for a penny we have before seen
than now for four pence, who list to compare.
This sueth the game called making or mar.
Unto the rich it maketh a great deal,
but much it marreth to the Common weal . . .

A rent to raise from twenty to fifty,
Of pounds, I mean, or shillings whether:
fining for the same unreasonably,
six times the rent; add this together,
must not the same great dearth bring hither?
for if the farmer pay fourfold double rent,
he must his ware neadys sell after that stent.

So for that ox, which hath been the like sold
for forty shillings, now taketh he five pound:
yea, seven is more, I have heard it so told;
he cannot else live, so dear is his ground;
sheep, though they never so plenty abound,
such price they bear, which shame is here to tell,
that scarce the poor man can buy a morsel.

Twopence (in beef) he cannot have served,
neither in mutton, the price is so high:
under a groat he can have none carved:
so goeth he and his to bed hungrily,
and riseth again with bellies empty;
which turneth to tawny their white English skin,
like to the swarthy coloured Fflawndrekyn.

Where they were valiant, strong, sturdy and stout
to shoot, to wrestle, to do any man's feat,
to match all nations dwelling here about,
as hitherto manly they hold the chief seat;
if they be pinched and weaned from meat,
I wis, O king, they in penury thus penned
shall not be able this thy realm to defend.

Our English nature cannot live by roots,
by water, herbs, or such beggary baggage,
that may well serve for vile outlandish coots;
give English men meat after their old usage,
beef, mutton, veal to cheer their courage;

111

and then I dare to this bill set my hand:
they shall defend this our noble England.

THE NORFOLK RISING   June–August 1549

From Neville, *Norfolk's Furies*, pp. B1(2)–B2(2), B3(2)–B4(1),
C2(1)–C2(2), C3(2), C4(2), D4(1)–D4(2), E2(1), E4(1), G3(1),
K2(2)–K4(2)

The rising apparently began as a local demonstration against the enclosure of common land, but quickly developed under the leadership of Robert Kett and his
brother William into a revolt against the whole system of enclosures. It is considered, after the Peasants' Revolt of 1381, the most significant of all the peasant
risings. In an organized response to the general oppression of the poor, Kett led
16,000 men towards Norwich, then the second city in the kingdom, and set up
his camp on Mousehold Heath. On 1 August, having refused (as just and innocent
men) a royal offer of amnesty, the rebels attacked and took possession of Norwich,
and for three weeks administered the district, until attacked and defeated by a
government army under the infamous Earl of Warwick. Neville's chronicle of the
events, the only full account, is largely hostile to the peasants' cause, but remains
a valuable record.

THE PEOPLE'S MANIFESTO: ALL IN COMMON

For, said they, the pride of great men is now intolerable, but their condition miserable. These abound in delights and compassed with the full-
ness of all things, and consumed with vain pleasure, thirst only after
gain, and are inflamed with the burning delights of their desires: but
themselves almost killed with labour and watching, do nothing all their
life long but sweat, mourn, hunger and thirst . . .

But that condition of possessing land seemeth miserable and slavish,
they hold all at the pleasure of great men: not freely but by prescription
and as it were at the will and pleasure of the lord. For as soon as any
man offend any of these gorgeous gentlemen, he is put out, deprived,
and thrust from all his goods.

How long should we suffer so great oppression to go unrevenged? For
so far are they now gone in cruelty and covetousness, as they are not
content only to take by violence all away, and by force and villainy to
get, [that] which they consume in riot and effeminate delights: except

they may suck, in a manner, our blood and marrow out of our veins and bones.

The common pastures left by our predecessors for the relief of us and our children are taken away. The lands which in the memory of our fathers were common, those are ditched and hedged in, and made several. The pastures are enclosed, and we shut out: whatsoever fowls of the air, or fishes of the water, and increase of the earth, all these they devour, consume and swallow up; yea, nature doth not suffice to satisfy their lusts, but they seek out new devices and as it were forms of pleasure, to embalm and perfume themselves, to abound in pleasant smells, to pour in sweet things to sweet things: finally, they seek from all places all things for their desire and provocation of lust: while we in the mean time eat herbs and roots and languish with continual labour; and yet envy that we live, breathe and enjoy common air.

Shall they, as they have brought hedges against common pastures, inclose with their intolerable lusts also, all the commodities and pleasure of this life, which Nature the parent of us all, would have common, and bringeth forth every day for us, as well as for them? We can no longer bear so much, so great and so cruel injury, neither can we with quiet minds behold so great covetousness, excess and pride of the nobility; we will rather take arms, and mix heaven and earth together, than endure so great cruelty. Nature hath provided for us, as well as for them; hath given us a body and a soul, and hath not envied us other things. While we have the same form, and the same condition of birth together with them, why should they have a life so unlike to ours, and differ so far from us in calling?

We see now that it is come to extremity: we will also prove extremity, rend down hedges, fill up ditches, make way for every man into the common pasture; finally, lay all even with the ground, which they no less wickedly than cruelly have enclosed. Neither will we suffer ourselves any more to be pressed with such great burdens against our wills, nor endure such great shame, as, living out our days under such inconveniences, we should leave the Commonwealth unto our posterity, mourning and miserable, and much worse than we received it of our fathers.

We desire liberty, and an indifferent [equal] use of all things: this we will have, otherwise these tumults and our lives shall end together.

ROBERT KETT, AT MOUSEHOLD, IS ELECTED LEADER

He . . . exhorted them to be of good courage, and to follow him, the author and the revenger of their liberty; affirming, he had not forsaken that charge which the Commonwealth had put upon him; neither was anything more dear unto him than their welfare, which he preferred before all things else, for which he would spend cheerfully both goods and life, the dearest things in their account.

A COMMISSION TO THE PEASANTS' DELEGATES

We the king's friends and delegates, give authority to all men for the searching out of beasts and all kind of victual to be brought into the camp at Mousehold, wheresoever they find it, so as no violence or injury be done to any honest or poor man; charging all men by the authority hereof, that as they wish well to the king and the afflicted common-wealth, they be obedient to us his delegates and unto them whose names are underwritten.

Kett – Cod – Aldrich

PLUNDERERS PUNISHED

This being known, and brought before Kett and the other Governors (for so they would be called), they being above all desirous to provide against this inconvenience, by common consent they agreed that some place should be chosen where they might sit to minister justice. Now there was an old oak with great spread boughs, this they laid over with rafts and balks across, and made a roof with boards: where (for the most part) the people standing round about, they determine and decree of complaints and quarrels (if any were done to any) as the cause required, and sometimes they bind with straiter bands the insolent and over-much greedy covetousness of some, by violently taking all away. This oak was called the Oak of Reformation . . .

DR MATTHEW PARKER IS SENT TO URGE THE COMMONS TO GIVE UP THEIR ENTERPRISE. THEY ANSWER HIM

How long shall we suffer this hireling Doctor, which (procured for his hire by the gentlemen) is come hither, bringing words of sale and a tongue bound with rewards? But we will cast a bridle upon their intolerable power and will hold them bound with the cords of our Law, spite of their hearts.

GENTLEMEN ON TRIAL

For certain of them (as if they had committed some notable villainy) were summoned before the company of these desperate persons, as unto judgement; and being set before the Oak, as at the Bar, were compelled to plead their cause out of chains. And when the ignorant and rude multitude were asked what they would have done with them, all as with one voice cried out: 'Let them be hanged. Let them be hanged.' And when the gentlemen inquired again of them, why they should use such cruel speeches against them they knew not, and were guilty of no crime, they fiercely answered: 'Such words of others were used towards them, and therefore they would use the same again to them', and had nothing else to object.

Though there were others who gave this as reason of their cruel sentence, that they were gentlemen, and therefore to be taken out of the way; for they knew well, if once they might get the victory, they should endure at their hands all kind of torment and cruelty. And therefore it were better their lives should be taken away, whom now they had in bands (so should they enjoy their ease and security) than to give unto them the use thereof (if it were but one hour) of whom anon after they might be slain as sheep.

KETT ANSWERS THE KING'S HERALD, PROMISING PARDON

Kings are wont to pardon wicked persons, not innocent and just men; they, for their part, had deserved nothing, and were guilty to themselves of no crime; and therefore despised such speeches as idle and unprofitable to their business.

115

REFUSED PASSAGE THROUGH NORWICH,
THE COMMONS ATTACK

These things with speed returned to Kett and his companions in the camp, being much moved hereat, with a brain-sick rage (as wild furies) they came running down the hill with a cruel and despiteful noise, crying out . . . Yet many being shot with arrows were wounded, which when they fell thick upon the ground, the beardless boys of the country (whereof there were a great number, and others of the dregs of the people, men most filthy), gathered them up and carried them to the enemy [i.e. to the besiegers.]

And the minds of them all were so inflamed, as they very naked and unarmed boys, as though a certain frenzy had bereaved them of the sense of understanding, running about, provoked our men with all reproachful speeches. There was added also to their importunate cursed words, an odious and inhuman villainy: for (with reverence to the Readers) one of these cursed boys, putting down his hose, and in derision turning his bare buttocks to our men, with a horrible noise and outcry filling the air (all men beholding him) did that which a chaste tongue shameth to speak, much more a sober man to write: but being shot thorow the buttocks, one gave him, as was meet, the punishment he deserved.

It is reported also, that some having the arrows sticking fast in their bodies, a thing fearful to tell, drawing them out of the green wounds with their own hands, gave them, as they were dripping with blood, to the rebels that were about them, whereby yet at the least they might be turned upon us again.

———

Kett's attack having succeeded, the men took possession of the city. Their formal petition to the King was answered with evasive promises, and the King's Herald was sent away, the people refusing to believe in such promises, which, 'offering a slender and vain hope of impunity, would cut off treacherously all safety'. On 31 July the Earl of Northampton arrived with an army of 1500, and demanded surrender. Flotman, one of the leaders, answered:

IN DEFENCE OF LIBERTY

We that are defended with these weapons and our own innocency, are secure and in safety, and have purposed never to crave mercy of any man. For we are to restore to her former dignities the Commonwealth (now almost utterly overthrown and daily declining, through the insolency of the gentlemen) out of her miserable ruins wherein she hath long continued, either by these courses, or else as becomes valiant men and such as are indued with courage fighting boldly, with the peril of our lives, to die in battle and never to betray our liberty, though it may be oppressed.

––––––

Northampton's army was defeated the next day, and Kett's men spent the following three weeks administering the city and the surrounding villages. Meanwhile, the government was gathering a new army under the Earl of Warwick, who entered Norwich on 24 August and, after a battle lasting two days, broke the peasants and proceeded to judgement.

AFTER THE DEFEAT

The same day began judgement in the Castle, and an inquiry was made of those that had conspired, and many were hanged and suffered grievous deaths. Afterward, nine which were the ring-leaders and principals, were hanged on the oak called the Oak of Reformation, and many companions with them in their villainies were hanged, and then presently cut down and falling upon the earth (these are the judgements of traitors in our country), first their privy parts are cut off, then their bowels pulled out alive, and cast into the fire, then their head is cut off and their bodies quartered: the head set upon a pole and fixed on the tops of the towers of the city, the rest of the body bestowed upon several places and set up to the terror of other.

But these wild and rude heads, after this sort being taken away, many of the gentlemen, carried with displeasure and desire of revenge laboured to stir up the mind of Warwick to cruelty, who not contented with the punishment of a few, would have rooted out utterly the offspring and wicked race of them, and were so earnest and eager in it, as they constrained Warwick to use this speech unto them openly:

'There must be measure kept, and above all things in punishment men must not exceed. He knew their wickedness to be such as deserved to be grievously punished, and with the severest judgement that might be. But how far would they go? Would they ever show themselves discontented, and never pleased? Would they leave no place for humble petition; none for pardon and mercy? Would they be ploughmen themselves, and harrow their own land?'

These speeches appeased greatly the desire of revenge, and brought to pass that many which before burned wholly with cruelty, afterward notwithstanding were far more courteous towards the miserable common people. The same night the bodies of the slain were buried, lest there might breed some infection or sickness from them.

But (Robert) Kett, the ring-leader of these villainies, together with William Kett, a man famous for many lewd behaviours and his brother (not so near joined in communion of blood, as in lewdness and wretchedness of life) were drawn to London and laid in the Tower.

After certain days, though they were manifestly convict of treason against the King's Majesty, and by the judgement and reproaches of all men, together with the guilt of conscience for their villainies condemned, yet were they drawn to open judgement after the common manner, and a quest passed upon them for their trial. And being condemned they were led away, the one to Norwich, the other to Windham, where a deserved punishment passed upon them both. For Robert Kett (at the castle in Norwich) had chains put upon him, and with a rope about his neck was drawn alive from the ground up to the gibbet, placed upon the top of the castle, and there hanged for a continual memory of so great villainy, until that unhappy and heavy body (through putrefaction consuming) shall fall down at length.

But William Kett ended his life with the same kind of death at Windham, whence all these furies flowed as from the fountain, for there they both dwelt. But after this sort, the city and all the county of Norfolk (when this vile and deadly plague of treason, to the destruction of many, had continued almost three score days, and had shaken all things, with most lamentable ruin) at the length, through the goodness of God, and wonderful valour of Warwick (that excellent noble man) these so bloody and woeful tumults ended, and the country had rest.

ROBERT CROWLEY (1518–88)   1550

From *Pleasure and Pain*, in *Select Works*, pp. 114, 116–17, 122, 124

Crowley, as Puritan, priest, poet and printer, spoke for the 'pore Commons of this Realme' against the 'more than Turkish tyranny' of the rich, in a number of works, verse and prose, between 1548 and 1551.

TAKING FROM THE POOR

Ye robbed, ye spoiled, ye bought, ye sold
My flock and me; in every place
Ye made my blood viler than gold:
And yet ye thought it no trespass.
O wicked sort, void of all grace,
Avoid from me down into hell,
With Lucifer: there shall ye dwell.

Ye had the tithes of men's increase,
That should have fed my flocks and me;
But you made yourselves well at ease
And took no thought for poverty.
It did not grieve you for to see
My flock and me suffer great need
For lack of meat, harbour, and weed . . .

What though the poor did lie and die
For lack of harbour, in that place
Where you had gotten wickedly
By lease, or else by plain purchase,
All housing that should, in that case,
Have been a safeguard and defence
Against the stormy violence?

Yea, what if the poor famished
For lack of food upon that ground,
The rents whereof you have raised,
Or hedged it within your mound?
There might therewith no fault be found,
No, though ye bought up all the grain
To sell it at your price again.

You thought that I would not require
The blood of all such at your hand;
But be ye sure, eternal fire
Is ready for each hell firebrand,
Both for the housing and the land
That you have taken from the poor
Ye shall in hell dwell evermore!

Yea, that same land that ye did take
From the ploughmen that laboured sore,
Causing them wicked shifts to make,
Shall now lie upon you full sore;
You shall be damned for evermore:
The blood of them that did amiss
Through your default is cause of this . . .

Cast down the hedges and strong mounds
That you have caused to be made
About the waste and tillage grounds,
Making them weep that erest were glad;
Lest you yourselves be stricken sad,
When ye shall see that Christ shall dry
All tears from the oppressed's eye . . .

Restore the tithes unto the poor,
For blind and lame should live thereon,
The widow that hath no succour,
And the child that is left alone;
For if these folk do make their moan
To God, he sure will hear their cry
And revenge their wrongs by and by.

ROBERT CROWLEY (1518–88)   1550

From *The Way to Wealth*, in *Select Works*, pp. 132–3, 142–3

THE CAUSE OF SEDITION

As the Poor See It

If I should demand of the poor man of the country what thing he think-
eth to be the cause of Sedition, I know his answer. He would tell me
that the great farmers, the graziers, the rich butchers, the men of law,
the merchants, the gentlemen, the knights, the lords, and I cannot tell
who; men that have no name because they are doers in all things that
any gain hangeth upon. Men without conscience. Men utterly void of
God's fear. Yea, men that live as though there were no God at all. Men
that would have all in their own hands; men that would leave nothing

for others; men that would be alone on the earth; men that be never satisfied. Cormorants, greedy gulls; yea, men that would eat up men, women, and children, are the causes of Sedition.

They take our houses over our heads, they buy our ground out of our hands, they raise their rents, they levy great (yea unreasonable) fines, they enclose our commons. No custom, no law or statute can keep them from oppressing us in such sort that we know not which way to turn us to live. Very need therefore constraineth us to stand up against them. In the country we cannot tarry, but we must be their slaves and labour till our hearts burst, and then they must have all. And to go to the cities we have no hope, for there we hear that these insatiable beasts have all in their hands. Some have purchased, and some taken by leases, whole alleys, whole rents, whole rows, yea whole streets and lanes, so that the rents be raised, some double, some triple, and some fourfold to that they were within these twelve years past. Yea, there is not so much as a garden ground free from them.

No remedy therefore, we must needs fight it out, or else be brought to the like slavery that the Frenchmen are in!

These idle bodies will devour all that we shall get by our sore labour in our youth, and when we shall be old and impotent, then shall we be driven to beg and crave of them that will not give us so much as the crumbs that fall from their tables. Such is the pity we see in them.

Better it were therefore for us to die like men than after so great misery in youth to die more miserably in age!

As the Rich See It

Now, if I should demand of the greedy cormorants what they think should be the cause of Sedition, they would say:

'The peasant knaves be too wealthy, provender pricketh them. They know not themselves, they know no obedience, they regard no laws, they would have no gentlemen, they would have all men like themselves, they would have all things in common. They would not have us masters of that which is our own. They will appoint us what rent we shall take for our grounds! We must not make the best of our own!

'These are jolly fellows. They will cast down our parks and lay our pastures open. They will have the laws in their own hands. They will play the kings. They will compel the king to grant their requests.

'But as they like their fare at the breakfast they had this last summer, so let them do again. They have been meetly well cooled, and shall be yet better cooled if they quiet not themselves. We will teach them to know their betters. And because they would have all in common, we will leave them nothing. And if they once stir again, or do but once cluster together, we will hang them at their own doors. Shall we suffer the villains to disprove our doings? No, we will be lords of our own and use it as we shall think good.'

THOMAS CARTWRIGHT (1535–1603)   1572

From *The Second Admonition to the Parliament*, in Brook,
Thomas Cartwright, pp. 99–100

As a Puritan critic of episcopacy, Cartwright was barely tolerated under Elizabeth's despotic rule, for he and other reformers appeared to threaten her supremacy. Her Bishops, and Whitgift in particular, remained zealous and intolerant in their attempts to prosecute. 'The city will never be quiet,' writes Bishop Sandys in 1573, 'until these authors of sedition, who are now esteemed as gods, as Field, Willcocks, Cartwright, and others, be far removed . . .' Indeed, Field and Willcocks had been sent to Newgate in 1572 for writing an *Admonition to Parliament*, and Cartwright answered with the *Second Admonition* and other pamphlets addressed to Whitgift, who eighteen years later (as Archbishop of Canterbury) had him imprisoned for two years in the Fleet.

SUPPRESSING THE TRUTH – IS THIS A REFORMATION

. . . What . . . is there in our books that should offend any who seem to be godly? Some may say either there is much amiss in our books, or we have a great deal of wrong offered us by such men as would seem to be the fathers of all true godliness. The authors of the former have been, and still are, hardly handled, being sent close prisoners to Newgate, next door to hanging; and by some of no mean estimation it hath been reported that it had been well for them if they had been sent to Bedlam to save their lives, as if they had been in peril of being hanged: and another prelate said, if they had been of his ordering, Newgate should have been their surety, and fetters their bonds. Now that they have had the law, and are close prisoners, they are found neither to have been traitors nor rebels; and if it had been tried by God's law, they would not have been found to have offended against that law at all, but to have deserved the praise of that law and the church of God. What, I pray, have they done amiss? They have published that the ministry of England is out of square. I need not ask what they have answered to that book; for they have answered only that it is a *foolish* book; but with godly, wise men, I trust that will not be taken for sufficient answer.

If they will still answer us with cruelty and persecution, we will keep ourselves out of their hands as long as God shall give us leave, and content ourselves with patience, if God suffer us to fall into their hands. We humbly beseech her Majesty not to be stirred against us by such men as will endeavour to bring us more into hatred, who will not care what to lay to our charge so they oppress us and suppress the truth. They will say, we despise authority and speak against sovereignty; but what will not envy say against the truth? Her Majesty shall not find better subjects in her land than those who desire a right Reformation, whose goods, bodies, and lives are most assured to her Majesty and to their country . . .

No preacher may without great danger utter all truth comprised in the word of God. The laws of the land, the Book of Common-prayer, the queen's injunctions, the commissioners' advertisements, the bishops' late canons, Linwood's provincials, every bishop's articles in his diocese, my lord of Canterbury's sober caveats in his licences to preachers, his high court prerogative, or grave fatherly faculties – these together, or the worst of them, as some of them are too bad! may not be broken or offended against, but with more danger than to offend against the Bible! . . . For these, preachers and others are indicted, fined, imprisoned, excommunicated, banished, and have worse things threatened them: and the Bible must have no further scope than by these it is assigned! Is this to profess God's word? Is this a reformation? We say the word of God is above the church; then surely it is above the English church, and above all the books now rehearsed. If it be so, why are they not overruled by it, and not it by them?

ROBERT BROWNE (*c.* 1550–1633)   1582

From *A Treatise of Reformation without Tarrying for Any*, p. 134

Leader of a group of Separatists started at Norwich named after him, of the kind later known as Independents or Congregationalists, Browne was a passionate advocate of freedom of conscience. During twenty years of outspoken teaching, he was imprisoned many times and exiled for a time; but in 1591 he accepted a quiet living at Achurch, Northamptonshire, where he remained till his death.

A VEIL OF DARKNESS

Woe to you therefore ye blind Preachers and hypocrites: for ye spread a veil of darkness upon the people, and bring upon them a cursed covering, because by your policy you hide them under the power of Antichrist, and keep from their eyes the Kingdom of Christ. The Lord's kingdom must wait on your policy forsooth, and his Church must be framed to your civil state, to supply the wants thereof: and so will ye change the Lord's government, and put your devices instead thereof: but his shall be always the same, when yours shall change with your wits, his laws shall always abide when yours shall turn in your lords, his hath the same offices, but yours have new and renewed offices. Go to therefore, and the outward power and civil forcings let us leave to the magistrates: to rule the common wealth in all outward justice, belongeth to them: but let the Church rule in spiritual wise, and not in worldly power: by a lively law preached, and not by a civil law written: by holiness in inward and outward obedience, and not in strengthness of the outward only. But these handsome Prelates would have the Mace and Sceptre in their hands, and then having safety and assurance by a law on their sides, they would make a goodly reformation . . .

PHILIP STUBBES (active 1583–91)   1583

From *The Anatomie of Abuses*, in Furnivall, *Ballads from Manuscript*, pp. 31–2

THE EXACTIONS OF THE RICH

Tragical cries and incessant clamours (of many whole towns and parishes) have long since pierced the skies and presented themselves before the majesty of God, crying: How long, O Lord, how long wilt thou defer to revenge this villainy done to thy poor saints and seely members upon the earth?

Take heed therefore, you rich men, that pill and poll the poor; for the blood of as many as miscarry any manner of way through your injurious exactions, sinister oppressions and undared dealings, shall be poured upon your heads at the great day of the Lord!

The poor lie in the streets upon pallets of straw, and well if they have that too, or else in the mire and dirt as commonly it is seen, having neither house to put in their heads, covering to keep them from cold, nor yet to hide their shame withal, penny to buy them sustenance, nor anything else, but are suffered to die in the streets like dogs or beasts, without any mercy or shame showed to them at all.

Truly, brother, if I had not seen it I would scarcely credit that the like Turkish cruelty had been used in all the world.

MARTIN MARPRELATE 1588–9

From *The Marprelate Tracts*, pp. 22–4, 148–52, 238–40, 330–31, 380–81, 397–401

The seven extant pamphlets known by the assumed name of the anonymous author (or authors), and printed from secret presses between October 1588 and September 1589, form an attack upon the high-handed assertion of episcopal authority in general and certain bishops (Thomas Cooper of Winchester and John Aylmer of London) in particular, but above all Archbishop Whitgift as 'fountain-head of the forces of persecution'. The controversy has its immediate origin from a 'Learned Discourse in Ecclesiastical Government' which, critical of the established order after Whitgift had become Archbishop of Canterbury, argued 'the elementary right of a Christian congregation to choose its own pastor'. This pamphlet was answered by officialdom, and in 1586 Whitgift issued a decree imposing censorship to put a stop to the printing of 'heretical' views. For a time those 'seekers after reformation' who spoke for Puritan England were effectively muzzled – in fact, until 1588, when the first Marprelate Tract appeared, a work of great vigour by a satirist of the first order who was at the same time 'fiercely in earnest'. With these tracts, the forces of religious (and political) dissent which were so soon to challenge the highest authority in the kingdom, can be seen to be actively stirring; and they point forward to the great period of transformation which began with the impeachment of Strafford and Laud in 1640. A Welshman named Penry (later executed) and a clergyman, John Udall (who died in prison) were arrested; but another suspect, Job Throckmorton (who may have been the actual author) denied complicity and escaped punishment.

PRELATES USURP THEIR AUTHORITY

From Tract I, *The Epistle*, 15 October 1588

Now, most pitifully complaineth Master Marprelate; desireth you either to answer what hath been written against the gracelessness of your arch-bishopric, or to give over the same, and to be a means that no bishop in the land shall be a lord any more. I hope one day her Majesty will either see that the Lord Bishops prove their calling lawful by the Word, or, as John of London prophesied, saying, 'Come down, you Bishops, from your thousands, and content you with your hundreds; let your diet be priestlike and not princelike, &c.' quoth John Aylmer in the *Harbourer of Faithful Subjects*. But, I pray you, Brother John, dissolve this one question to your brother Martin. If this prophesy of yours come to pass in your days, who shall be Bishop of London? And will you not swear, as commonly you do, like a lewd swag, and say, 'By my faith!' 'By my faith, my masters, this gear goeth hard with us.'

Now may it please your Grace, with the rest of your Worships, to procure that the Puritans may one day have a free disputation with you about the controversies of the Church, and if you be not set at a flat *non plus* and quite overthrown, I'll be a lord bishop myself. Look to yourselves. I think you have not long to reign. Amen. And take heed, Brethren, of your reverend and learned brother, Martin Marprelate. For he meaneth in these reasons following, I can tell you, to prove that you ought not to be maintained by the authority of the magistrate in any Christian commonwealth. Martin is a shrewd fellow, and reasoneth thus. Those that are petty popes and petty antichrists ought not to be maintained in any Christian commonwealth. But every lord Bishop in England, as for ill-sample John of Canterbury, John of London, John Exeter, John Rochester, Thomas of Winchester, the Bishops of Lincoln, of Worcester, of Peterborough, and to be brief, all the Bishops in England, Wales, and Ireland, are petty popes and petty antichrists. Therefore no lord bishop – 'Now, I pray thee, good Martin, speak out, if ever thou didst speak out, that her Majesty and the Council may hear thee' – is to be tolerated in any Christian commonwealth; and therefore neither John of Canterbury, John of London, &c. are to be tolerated in any Christian commonwealth. What say you now, Brother Bridges? Is it good, writing against Puritans? Can you deny any part of your learned brother Martin's syllogism? We deny your minor, Master Marprelate, say the Bishops and their associates. Yea, my learned Masters, are you good at that? What do you Brethren? Say me that again – do you deny my minor? And that be all you can say to deny lord bishops to be petty popes, turn me loose to the priests in that point; for I am old Suresby at the proof of such matters. I'll presently mar the fashion of their Lordships.

They are petty popes and petty antichrists, whosoever usurp authority of pastors over them who, by the ordinance of God, are to be under no pastors. For none but antichristian popes and popelings ever claimed this authority unto themselves; especially when it was gainsaid, and accounted antichristian, generally, by the most churches in the world . . . Therefore our Lord Bishops – 'What sayest thou, man?' – *our Lord Bishops*, I say, as John of Canterbury, Thomas of Winchester, (I will spare John of London for this time; for, it may be, he is at bowls, and it is pity to trouble my good brother, lest he should swear too bad), my reverend prelate of Lichfield, with the rest of that swinish rabble, are petty antichrists, petty popes, proud prelates, intolerable withstanders of Reformation, enemies of the Gospel, and most covetous wretched priests . . .

PRIDE, POMP, AND SUPERFLUITY

From Tract II, *The Epitome* October 1588

Having attacked John Aylmer (1521–94), Bishop of London, as a man who had once, in *A Harbourer of Faithful and True Subjects* (1559), railed against bishops and their addiction to luxury, but was now himself one of the Lords of the Church, Marprelate here takes Aylmer's pamphlet again – with its anti-episcopal injunction that 'every parish church may have its preacher, every city its superintendent, to live honestly, and not pompously; which will never be, unless your lands be dispersed and bestowed upon many, which now feedeth and fatteth but one' – and promptly launches a new attack.

Hitherto, you see that this Balaam, who hath, I fear me, received the wages of unrighteousness, hath spoken in general, as well against the callings of bishops, and their usurping of civil offices, as against their pride, pomp, and superfluity. Must not he, think you, have either a most seared, or a most guilty conscience, that can find of his heart to continue in that calling; yea, and in the same abuse of that calling, which his own conscience, if he would but awake it, telleth him to be unlawful? The Lord give him repentance, if he belongeth unto Him, or speedily rid his Church of a scourge. And may not all the former speeches be fitly applied unto him? Yes, without doubt. But the next he may be thought to have written to himself, which he hath set down, page 34.

'As if you should say, my lord Lubber of London is a tyrant. Ergo he is no bishop. I warrant you although he granted you the antecedent, which he can hardly deny, yet he would deny the consequent, or else he would call for wily Watson to help him.'

Here, Brother London, you have crossed yourself over the costard, once in your days. I think you would have spent three of the best elms which you have cut down in Fulham, and threepence-halfpenny besides,

127

that I had never met with your book. But unless you and John of Exeter with Thomas Winchester, who have been in times past hypocrites, as you have been, leave off to hinder the Word, and vex godly men, I will make you to be noble and famous bishops for ever. And might not a man well judge you three to be the 'desperate Dicks', which you, Brother London, page 29, affirm to be good bishops in England . . . you three, like furious and senseless brute beasts, dread no peril, look no farther than your feet, spare none, but with tooth and nail cry out, 'Down with that side that favoureth the Gospel so! Fetch them up with pursuivants; to the Gatehouse, to the Fleet, to the Marshalsea, to the Clink, to Newgate, to the Counter, with them!' It makes no matter with you (I follow your own words, Brother London) so you may show yourselves (in *show*, though not in *truth*) obedient subjects to the Queen, and disobedient traitors to God and the realm.

Thus far I have followed your words, howbeit I think you are not well pleased with me, because you mean not to stand to anything you have written. Nay, you hold it unlawful now for a preacher, as far as the two tables of the Law do reach, to speak against bishops, much less any ungodly statute. And yet you say (page 49, line 7) that 'Preachers must not be afraid to rebuke the proudest, yea kings and queens, so far forth as the two tables of the Law do reach, as we see in Samuel, Nathan, Elias, John Baptist and many other. They may not stoop to every man's beck, and study to please man more than God.'

Thus far are your words, and they are as far from your practice, as you are from the imitation of these godly examples which you have brought. I see a bishopric hath cooled your courage; for in those days that you wrote this book, you would have our Parliament to overrule her Majesty, and not to yield an inch unto her of their privileges. Your words I will set down.

'In like manner (say you, page 53) if the Parliament use their privileges, the king can ordain nothing without them; if he do, it is his fault in usurping it, and their folly in permitting it; wherefore, in my judgment, those that in king Henry the Eighth's days would not grant him that his proclamations should have the force of a statute, were good fathers of their country, and worthy of commendation in defending their liberty,' &c.

I assure you, Brother John, you have spoken many things worthy the noting, and I would our Parliament-men would mark this action done in king Henry the Eighth's days, and follow it in bringing in reformation, and putting down lord bishops, with all other points of superstition. They may, in your judgment, not only do anything against their king's or queen's mind, that is behooveful to the honour of God and the good of the Commonwealth, but even withstand the proceedings of their sovereign.

BRINGING THE TRUTH TO LIGHT

From Tract IV, *Hay Any Worke for Cooper*, March 1589

Marprelate here answers the reply to his *Epistle* by Thomas Cooper, Bishop of Winchester.

———

You see the accusation which I lay to your charge, and here followeth the proof of it. They who defend that the Prince and the State may bid God to battle against them, they are not only traitors against God and His Word, but also enemies to the Prince and the State. I think John of Gloucester himself will not be so senseless as to deny this.

But our archbishops and bishops, which hold it lawful for her Majesty and the State to retain this established form of government, and to keep out the government by pastors, doctors, elders and deacons, which was appointed by Christ, whom you, profane T. C., call 'you know not whom', hold it lawful for her Majesty and the State to bid God to battle against them. Because they bid the Lord to battle against them which maim and deform the body of Christ; viz., the Church. And they, as was declared, maim and deform the body of the Church, which keep out the lawful office[r]s, appointed by the Lord to be members thereof, and, in their stead, place other wooden members of the invention of man. Therefore you, T. C., and you Dean John, and you John Whitgift, and you, the rest of the beastly defenders of the corrupt church government, are not only traitors to God and His Word, but enemies to her Majesty and the State. Like you any of these *nuts*, John Canterbury?

I am not disposed to jest in this serious matter. I am called Martin Marprelate. There be many that greatly dislike my doings. I may have my wants I know; for I am a man. But my course I know to be ordinary and lawful. I saw the cause of Christ's government, and of the Bishops' antichristian dealing to be hidden. The most part of men could not be gotten to read anything written in the defence of the one, and against the other. I bethought me, therefore, of a way whereby men might be drawn to do both; perceiving the humours of men in these times (especially of those that are in any place) to be given to mirth. I took that course. I might lawfully do it. Aye, for jesting is lawful by circumstances, even in the greatest matters. The circumstances of time, place, and persons urged me thereunto. I never profaned the Word in any jest. Other mirth I used as a covert, wherein I would bring the truth into light. The Lord being the author both of mirth and gravity, is it not lawful in itself, for the truth to use either of these ways, when the circumstances do make it lawful?

My purpose was, and is, to do good. I know I have done no harm, howsoever some may judge Martin to mar all. They are very weak ones that so think. In that which I have written, I know undoubtedly that I have done the Lord, and the State of this Kingdom, great service. Because I have in some sort discovered the greatest enemies thereof. And, by so much the most pestilent enemies, because they wound God's religion, and corrupt the State with atheism and looseness, and so call for God's vengeance upon us all, even under the colour of religion. I affirm them to be the greatest enemies that now our State hath; for if it were not for them, the truth should have more free passage herein, than now it hath. All states thereby would be amended. And so, we should not be subject unto God's displeasure, as now we are by reason of them . . .

Well, to the point; many have put her Majesty, the Parliament, and Council, in mind, that the church officers now among us are not such as the Lord alloweth of; because they are not of his own ordaining. They have showed that this fault is to be amended, or the Lord's hand to be looked for. The bishops on the other side, have cried out upon them that have thus dutifully moved the State. They with a loud voice gave out that the magistrate may lawfully maintain that church government which best fitteth our Estate as living in the time of peace. What do they else herein, but say that the magistrate in the time of peace, may maim and deform the body of Christ's Church?

THE ANTICHRISTIAN PRELACY OF WHITGIFT, POPE OF LAMBETH

From Tract V, *Theses Martinianae (Martin Junior)*, 22 July 1589

The Tracts had already brought forth replies. They had been attacked by Richard Bancroft in a sermon in February affirming the 'divine right' of episcopacy, and in anonymous pamphlets, some attributed to Thomas Nashe, others to John Lyly. Here, in *Martin Junior's Epilogue*, the writer has assumed a new guise to launch an attack upon Whitgift.

The stage-players, poor, silly, hunger-starved wretches . . . in the action of dealing against Master Martin, have gotten them many thousand eye-witnesses of their witless and pitiful conceits. And indeed they are marvellous fit upholders of Lambeth Palace, and the crown of Canterbury. And, therefore, men should not think of all other things, that *they* should anyways make Master Martin, or his sons, to alter their course. And hereof, good Master Canterbury, assure yourself.

Well, to grow to a point with you, if you have any of your side, either in the Universities, or in your cathedral churches, or anywhere within the compass of all the bishopdoms you have, that dare write or dispute against any of these points set down by my father, here I do, by these my writings, cast you down the glove in my father's name, and the names of the rest of his sons. If my father be gone, and none else of my brethren will uphold the controversy against you, I myself will do it. And take my challenge if you dare. By writing you may do it, and be sure to be answered. By disputations, if you will appoint the place, with promise that you will not deal *vi et armis*, you shall be taken also by me, if I think I may trust you. Otherwise the Puritans will, I doubt not, maintain the challenge against you.

But here, by the way, John Canterbury, take an odd advice of your poor nephew, and that is this. First, in regard of yourself, play not the tyrant as you do, in God's Church. If you go on forward in this course, the end will be a woeful reckoning. Thou hast been raised up out of the dust, and even from the very dunghill, to be President of her Majesty's Council, being of thyself a man altogether unmeet for any such pre-eminence, as neither endued with any excellent natural wit, nor yet with any great portion of learning. The Lord hath passed by many thousands in this land, far meeter for the place than is poor John Whitgift. Well, then, what if thou, having received so great blessings at the Lord's hand (being of all others in no comparison anything near the fittest for it, or the likeliest to obtain it), shalt now show thyself ungrateful unto thy merciful Lord God, or become a cruel persecutor, and a tyrant in His Church, a cruel oppressor of His children, shall not all that thou hast received be turned unto a curse unto thee, even into thine own bosom? Yea, verily. For the Lord in one day is able to bring more shame upon thee, and that in this life, than He hath heaped blessings upon thee now for the space of thirty years and upward. But when I do consider thy pre-eminence and promotion I do sensibly acknowledge it to be joined with a rare curse of God, even such a curse as very few (I will not say none) in God's Church do sustain. And that is thy wicked and anti-christian prelacy. The consideration of which popedom of thine maketh me think that thy other place in the civil magistracy, being in itself a godly and a lawful calling, is so become infectious, that it will be thy

131

bane, both in this life, and in the life to come. And I am almost fully persuaded that that archbishopric of thine, together with thy practices therein, show verily that the Lord hath no part nor portion in that miserable and desperate caitiff, wicked John Whitgift, the Pope of Lambeth. Leave therefore both thy popedom and thy ungodly proceedings, or look for a fearful end.

BE SILENT AND CLOSE

From Tract VI, *The Just Censure and Reproofe of Martin Junior, by Martin Senior*, 29 July 1589

The writer here adopts a third role, that of elder brother, and in this final paragraph to the Tract offers his brother advice for the safety of the family (and by implication all critics of the prelates) against persecution.

Well, Boy, to draw to an end; notwithstanding thy small defects, persuade thyself that I love thee; doubt not of that. And here, before we part, take this one grave lesson of thine elder brother. Be silent and close; hear many, confer with few. And in this point do as I do; know not thy father, though thou mayest. For I tell thee, if I should meet him in the street, I should never ask him blessing. Walk smoothly and circumspectly: and if any offer to talk with thee of Martin, talk thou straight of the voyage into Portugal, or, of the happy death of the Duke of Guise, or some such accident; but meddle not with thy father. Only, if thou have gathered anything in visitation for thy father, and have a longing to acquaint him therewith, do no more but intreat him to signify, in some secret printed 'Pistle, where 'a will have it left, and that'll serve thy turn as good as the best. The reason why we must not know our father is that I fear lest some of us might fall into John of Canterbury's hand; and then he'll threaten us with the rack, unless we bewray all we know. And what get we then by our knowledge? For I had rather be ignorant of that'll do me good than know that'll hurt me, quoth
Mr Martin Senior. Farewell, Boy,
and learn to reverence
thy elder brother.

AGAINST THE PERSECUTORS OF THE TRUTH

From Tract VII, *The Protestation of Martin Marprelate*,
September 1589

The last of the Tracts begins with a reference to the actions taken by the High
Commission, directed by Richard Bancroft, against the secret presses used to print
them, and defends Martinism against the persecutors of Puritans, particularly
Whitgift and Cooper. Though Martin writes of the 'lenity' of the bishops towards
the men arrested, it appears that Hodgkins, the printer, and his men Thomlyn
and Symms, were put upon the rack by Whitgift. As for Bancroft (not mentioned
here, though zealously at work), he was responsible for the arrest and execution
of John Penry (one of those suspected but freed of writing the Tracts) in 1593
under the Act of Uniformity; and later still (as Archbishop of Canterbury) for the
strengthening of that episcopal power which became one of the great causes of
the Revolution and the subject of more than one of Milton's pamphlets in the
1640s.

Thou canst not lightly be ignorant, good reader, of that which hath lately
fallen unto some things of mine, which were to be printed, or in printing;
the press, letters, workmen and all, apprehended and carried as malefactors before the magistrate; whose authority I reverence, and whose
sword I would fear, were I as wicked as our Bishops are. These events
I confess do strike me and give me just cause to enter more narrowly
into myself to see whether I be at peace with God, or no. But utterly to
discourage me from mine enterprise, a greater matter than that comes
to I hope shall never be able. The state of the poor men that are taken
I do bewail; not because they can hurt me, for I assure thee, they know
not who I am, but inasmuch as, I fear, the tyranny of our wicked priests
will do that against them, which neither the Word of God doth warrant,
nor law of the land doth permit. *For, as their hatred unto the cause is
without ground, so their cruelty to those that profess the same is without
measure.* Therefore, good reader, if thou hear of any mean or com-
passionable punishment inflicted upon them (who, to say the truth, have
deserved none at all – I mean the printers) I would never have thee stand
to expostulate with our Bishops for this untimely lenity of theirs, for
whom I dare take mine oath (for I know them so well) that if there fall
out any good to those poor men through the providence of God, and the
gracious clemency of her Majesty, they, for their parts, are no more
guilty or accessory unto it, than the Spanish inquisitors themselves. For
indeed, in this one point they are of my mind; viz., that reformation
cannot well come to our Church without blood; and that no blood can
handsomely be spilt in that cause, unless they themselves be the butchers

133

and horseleeches to draw it out. Thou seest evidently, they claim that as a piece and portion of their inheritance. But tell them from me, that we fear not men, that can but kill the body; because we fear that God, who can cast both body and soul into unquenchable fire. And tell them also this. *That the more blood the Church loseth, the more life and blood it gets.* When the fearful sentence pronounced against the persecutors of the truth is executed upon them, I would then gladly know, whether they who go about thus to shed our blood, or we whose blood crieth for vengeance against them, shall have the worst end of the staff. We are sure to possess our souls in everlasting peace, whensoever we leave this earthly tabernacle; and in the mean time we know that an hair of our head cannot fall to the ground without the will of our heavenly Father, Who, of His great mercy, loveth us in, and for, our Saviour Christ Jesus; and that, with a love as far passing the love of a natural father toward his children, as He who so loveth us, excelleth all earthly parents. This persuasion being steadfastly engrafted in their hearts, who either now or hereafter shall be trodled for this cause, will be a comfort to them in the midst of all their distresses.

And, good reader, whosoever thou art, I would not have thee discouraged at this, that is lately fallen out. *Reason not from the success of things unto the goodness of the cause.* For that savoureth too much of the flesh . . . As to the present action, howsoever there may escape me some corruption in the handling, let them be well assured it was not undertaken to be intermitted at every blast of evil success. Nay, let them know that, by the grace of God, the last year of Martinism, that is, of the descrying and displaying of lord bishops, shall not be till full two years after the last year of Lambethism – that is, of joining most godless proceedings unto the maintenance of antichristian and unlawful callings in God's Church, against the known truth; for that, indeed, is rightly called Lambethism, or Cooperism: choose you whether [which].

And be it known unto them that Martinism stands upon another manner of foundation than their prelacy doth, or can, stand. Therefore if they will needs overthrow me, let them go in hand with the exploit, rather by proving the lawfulness of their places, than by exercising the force of their unlawful tyranny. For, once again, I fear not their tyranny. And one sound syllogism (which, I tell you, is dainty ware in a bishop's breast), brought in for the proof of their unlawful callings, shall more dismay and sooner induce me to give over my course than a thousand warrants, a thousand pursuivants, a thousand threats, and a thousand racks; which course, because they take not, therefore all their other drifts and devices are to none other end than to show the great care and skill they have to carry away all the blows. But what get they by this tyranny, seeing it is truth and not violence that must uphold their places? Do they not know that the more violence they use the more breath they spend. And what wisdom were this, trow ye, for a man that had coursed himself windless, to attempt the recovery of his breath by running up and down to find air? So you know he might soon have as much life in his members as lord bishops have religion and conscience in their proceedings.

HENRY BARROW (*c.* 1550–93)   1593

From his supplication to Parliament, in Rickword and Lindsay, *Handbook of Freedom*, pp. 89–90

As a Separatist and a Brownist, Barrow was imprisoned in 1587 when visiting his friend John Greenwood in the Clink, and examined several times by Archbishop Whitgift before the High Commission. Both were freed for a short while in 1592 and joined John Penry in forming their own church, then tried as writers of seditious books and executed on 6 April 1593, shortly before Penry. The repressive measures of the episcopal courts, and the 'bloody men' who controlled them, gave them a notoriety comparable to that of the Roman Inquisition. Robert Browne, for instance, had been imprisoned thirty-two times, and Thomas Cartwright the Presbyterian had recently been released after two years in the Fleet.

'THESE BLOODY MEN'

These bloody men will allow us neither meat, drink, fire, lodging; nor would suffer any whose heart the Lord would stir up for our relief to have any access to us. Seventeen or eighteen have perished within these noisome jails within these six years; some of us have had not one penny about us when we were sent to prison, nor anything to procure a maintenance for ourselves and families but our labour; not only we ourselves, but our wives and children, are undone and starved. Their unbridled slander, their lawless and privy searches, their violent breaking open houses, their taking away whatever they think meet, and their barbarous usage of women and children, we are forced to omit lest we be tedious.

That which we crave for all is the liberty to die openly, or live openly, in the land of our nativity; if we deserve death, let us not be closely murdered; yea, starved to death with hunger and cold, and stifled in loathsome dungeons.

JOHN PENRY (1563–93)   1593

From *Notebook*, pp. 45–7

Penry, born in Breconshire, is regarded by Welshmen as a national hero, and by Congregationalists as a martyr. Between 1587 and 1588 he wrote three violently anti-episcopal treatises advocating religious toleration in Wales. Imprisoned for a month in 1587 for the first of these, and again during the Marprelate Controversy, he fled to Scotland in 1590, but on his return to London he was arrested for his open defiance of Whitgift, charged with two others and executed on the orders of the Court of High Commission. His *Notebook* contains drafts of various letters and petitions concerning his position, and it appears he had his *Supplication* delivered to Parliament on 10 March, pleading for the Separatist group he had joined. In spite of this, he was executed on 29 May.

A SUPPLICATION OF THE PERSECUTED BROWNIST CHURCH . . . TO PARLIAMENT

We profess the same faith and truth of the Gospel this day which her majesty, this state, and all the reformed churches this day under heaven do profess, we go further than they go in the detestation of all Popery that most fearful Antichristian religion, and draw nearer in some things unto Christ's holy order and institution.

This is our cause. For the profession whereof there are of us almost fourscore persons, men and women, young and old, lying in cold hunger, dungeons and irons only in the prisons about London, not to speak anything of other prisons of the land ... We were taken in the place where the holy martyrs were enforced to use the like holy exercises in the days of Queen Mary ... [and] committed unto close several prisons by the Bishop of London and his [abettors] ... This bloody man and his assistants will neither allow them meat, drink, fire, bedding, nor suffer others that will do the same to have any access.

The wife and the husband are severed, not so much as permitted to be together in the same prisons, but are sent and closely kept in divers prisons, some of this number had not one penny about them when they came in, nor anything being abroad to procure themselves and their families any maintenance but by their hands' labour. God's enemies by this means, do not only starve and undo a number of men and women in the prisons, but even a lamentable company of orphans and poor and fatherless children abroad.

The dealing [is] most unhumane, most barbarous, especially most unchristian and such as exceedeth the cruelty of the heathen, and the professed popish tyrants and persecutors. The records of the heathen persecution under Nero, Trajan, Maximian will scant offer us any examples of the like cruelty. For the heathen Romans themselves could murder openly and professedly. These godless men have put the blood of war about them in the day of that peace and truce which the whole hath professed to make with Jesus Christ . . . If we be any wise malefactors, if we be not true subjects unto our prince, let us be committed over unto the civil magistrates. And let not our enemies both accuse, condemn and punish, against law, equity and conscience, where they are the accusers, judges and parties, and the executioners . . . The prelates should go no farther than their ecclesiastical censures. They leave that, and betake them unto blood. We crave but what is most equal, ease from trouble, or equity in the trial either of our guiltiness or innocency . . . There are many of us still in number abroad out of their hands. The former holy exercise and profession we purpose not to leave by the aid of our god, and therefore streams of innocent blood are like to be spilt for this cause except her majesty and your Lords to take other order. We crave both for ourselves abroad and for our brethren but the liberty either to die openly or to live openly in the land of our nativity . . .

JOHN PENRY (1563–93) 1593

A draft letter to Lord Burghley, from *Notebook*, pp. 55–6

Penry appeals to Elizabeth's chief minister against the Council of High Commission. Richard Young was a JP, and one of the main instruments of the Council when torture was employed. Other members were Bancroft and Whitgift himself.

WHERE TYRANNOUS ANARCHY POSSESSETH ALL THINGS

. . . Unto what confused disorder is this state come unto that the Parliament of England cannot be sued unto in the behalf of God, but poor women attending there for justice must be committed to prison as though they had done some great and heinous offence? What a shameful thing is it that Justice Young may send for the poor woman, who delivered this Supplication unto Mr Speaker, and also unto Sir Robert Cecil (if his honour would have received the same), examine her and enforce her, for fear of his bloodthirsty cruelty, to reveal whatsoever she could utter touching that Supplication and the delivery thereof.

How unworthily suffer you the privileges of that high court to be thus encroached upon and trodden under foot by every evil disposed person, if your Lordship permit this dealing of Mr Young especially to be uncontrolled.

I am persuaded, that your Lordship is not privy unto these things, nor yet I think unto the delivery of this our most just petition . . . and therefore I thought it my duty to acquaint your honour therewith. And it standeth you in hand to look unto the dealing and to see it amended, except you would have every man, to embolden himself to do what his hand hath power to effect in this land. We dare not in a while so much as write unto our prince, unto your Lordship, or any other of our superiors, but Mr Young and such evil disposed men will either bring us under their auricular confession, or undo us by wrongful imprisonment. Alas my Lord, where live we? In what common wealth? Where tyrannous anarchy possesseth all things, or the liberty of free subjects do remain. Her majesty must be acquainted with your usage except your Lordship, which I earnestly desire in the name of god that we need not grieve the heart of our prince, by laying open our injuries unto her, which I protest unto you we are willing to conceal, if there were any measure in our evil intreaty. But indeed my Lord we can no longer bear this violent hand, but we must complain to our sovereign thereof, yea, and lay it open unto the world except redress be had, well our god will look unto our cause. Oh my Lord if you knew the misery wherein her majesty's subjects whose cause this Supplication doth lay open do now lie in horrible dungeons for the testimony of Christ, I know you could not but pity. Pity them then my Lord, and let them be called to their answer and just trial. This is all we desire: that thy blessing of him, which is ready to perish, may follow my Lord Burghley, and his house may overtake him and cleave to him for ever. Amen.

By Him who unfeignedly desireth the eternal good of your Lordship in Christ Jesus our Lord. John Penry.

WILLIAM SHAKESPEARE (1564–1616)   Late 1594

From *The Merchant of Venice*, III i

Intense interest in Jewish life and character had been aroused by the trial and execution on a charge of treason early in 1594 of Queen Elizabeth's Jewish physician, Roderigo Lopez, and it may have been this that led Shakespeare to the writing of his play, which is centrally concerned with the conditioning power of money and the nature of its corrupting influence – gold weighed against flesh.

IF YOU WRONG US, SHALL WE NOT REVENGE?

SHYLOCK . . . Let him look to his bond: he was wont to call me usurer; – let him look to his bond: he was wont to lend money for a Christian courtesy; – let him look to his bond.

SALARINO   Why, I am sure, if he forfeit, thou wilt not take his flesh: what's that good for?

SHYLOCK   To bait fish withal: if it will feed nothing else, it will feed my revenge. He hath disgraced me, and hindered me half a million; laughed as my losses, mocked at my gains, scorned my nation, thwarted my bargains, cooled my friends, heated mine enemies; and what's his reason? I am a Jew. Hath not a Jew eyes? hath not a Jew hands, organs, dimensions, senses, affections, passions? fed with the same food, hurt with the same weapons, subject to the same diseases, healed by the same means, warmed and cooled by the same winter and summer, as a Christian is? If you prick us, do we not bleed? If you tickle us do we not laugh? If you poison us, do we not die? And if you wrong us, shall we not revenge? If we are like you in the rest, we will resemble you in that. If a Jew wrong a Christian, what is his humility? Revenge. If a Christian wrong a Jew, what should his sufferance be by Christian example? Why, revenge. The villainy you teach me, I will execute; and it shall go hard but I will better the instruction.

JOHN DONNE (1572–1631) 1596(?)

Satyre III, ll. 79–110

THE HILL OF TRUTH

On a huge hill,
Cragged, and steep, Truth stands, and he that will
Reach her, about must, and about must go,
And what the hill's suddenness resists, win so;
Yet strive so, that before age, death's twilight,
Thy soul rest, for none can work in that night.
To will implies delay, therefore now do.
Hard deeds the body's pains, hard knowledge too,
The mind's endeavours reach, and mysteries
Are like the sun, dazzling, yet plain to all eyes.
Keep the truth which thou hast found; men do not stand
In so ill case here that God hath with his hand
Signed kings blank charters to kill whom they hate,
Nor are they vicars, but hangmen to fate.
Fool and wretch, wilt thou let thy soul be tied
To man's laws, by which she shall not be tried
At the last day? Oh, will it then boot thee
To say a Philip, or a Gregory,
A Harry, or a Martin taught thee this?
Is not this excuse for mere contraries
Equally strong? cannot both sides say so?
That thou mayest rightly obey Power, her bounds know;
Those past, her nature, and name is changed; to be
Then humble to her is idolatry.
As streams are, Power is; those blest flowers that dwell
As the rough stream's calm head, thrive and do well,
But having left their roots, and themselves given
To the stream's tyrannous rage, alas, are driven
Through mills, and rocks, and woods, and at last, almost
Consumed in going, in the sea are lost:
So perish souls which more choose men's unjust
Power from God claimed, than God himself to trust.

Philip: Philip II of Spain
Gregory: Pope Gregory XIII, who condoned the Massacre of St Bartholemew
Harry: Henry VIII
Martin: Martin Luther

140

SIR FRANCIS BACON (1561–1626) 1597

From *Essays Civil and Moral*

SEDITION

The causes and motives of seditions are, innovation in religion, taxes, alteration of laws and customs, breaking of privileges, general oppression, advancement of unworthy persons, strangers, dearths, disbanded soldiers, factions grown desperate; and whatsoever in offending people joineth and knitteth them in a common cause.

For the remedies, there may be some general preservative, whereof we will speak; as for the just cure, it must answer to the particular disease: and so be left to counsel, rather than rule.

The first remedy or prevention, is to remove by all means possible that material cause of sedition, whereof we spake; which is want and poverty in the estate. To which purpose serveth the opening and well balancing of trade; the cherishing of manufactures; the banishing of idleness; the repressing of waste and excess by sumptuary laws; the improvement and husbanding of the soil; the regulating of prices of things vendible; the moderating of taxes and tributes, and the like. Generally it is to be foreseen, that the population of a kingdom, especially if it be not mown down by wars, do not exceed the stock of the kingdom which should maintain them. Neither is the population to be reckoned only by number; for a smaller number, that spend more, and earn less, do wear out an estate sooner than a greater number that live lower and gather more. Therefore the multiplying of nobility, and other degrees of quality, in an over proportion to the common people, doth speedily bring a state to necessity: and so doth likewise an overgrown clergy; for they bring nothing to the stock: and in like manner, when more are bred scholars, than preferments can take off . . .

Above all things good policy is to be used, that the treasure and money in a state be not gathered into few hands. For otherwise a state may have a great stock, and yet starve. *And money is like muck, not good except it be spread.* This is done chiefly by suppressing, or at the least keeping a strait hand upon, the devouring trades of usury, ingrossing, great pasturages, and the like.

WILLIAM SHAKESPEARE (1564–1616)   1597

From *2 Henry IV*, IV, i

Shakespeare's radical vision of the realities of his world fully registers and enacts the fundamental changes that were taking place at the turn of the century in England. His work, rooted in the objective process of history, is a continual quest for those underlying 'moral laws /Of Nature and of nations' which are the key to the balance of 'right and wrong, /Between whose endless jar justice resides', against the disorders of an age rife with crisis and conflict and violent upheaval – an age of transition in which the institutions of feudal authority, the very structure of the feudal system itself, were being threatened. *Henry IV*, like all the plays that follow, exposes this sense of crisis unflinchingly; for it delineates the ways in which the deceits of power and corrupt authority breed unrest, revolt and 'civil butchery' as a universal disease affecting the whole body politic; because for Henry, it is clear that 'nothing can seem foul to those that win'. The Archbishop, Mowbray and Hastings are about to be betrayed by Prince John, who breaks his word to them when they yield to his appeal. But now, the two sides lined up for battle, Westmoreland is sent to parley.

THE REVOLUTION OF THE TIMES

WESTMORELAND   . . . You, lord archbishop –
Whose see is by a civil peace maintain'd;
Whose beard the silver hand of peace hath touch'd;
Whose learning and good letters peace hath tutor'd;
Whose white investments figure innocence,
The dove and very blessed spirit of peace –
Wherefore do you so ill translate yourself,
Out of the speech of peace, that bears such grace,
Into the harsh and boist'rous tongue of war?
Turning your books to greaves, your ink to blood,
Your pens to lances, and your tongue divine
To a loud trumpet, and a point of war?
ARCHBISHOP OF YORK
Wherefore do I this? So the question stands.
Briefly to this end. We are all diseas'd;
And, with our surfeiting and wanton hours,
Have brought ourselves into a burning fever,
And we must bleed for it: of which disease
Our late king, Richard, being infected, died.
But, my most noble lord of Westmoreland,

142

I take not on me here as a physician;
Nor do I, as an enemy to peace,
Troop in the throngs of military men:
But rather, show awhile like fearful war,
To diet rank minds sick of happiness;
And purge the obstructions which begin to stop
Our very veins of life. Hear me more plainly.
I have in equal balance justly weighed
What wrongs our arms may do, what wrongs we suffer,
And find our griefs heavier than our offences.
We see which way the stream of time doth run,
And are enforc'd from our most quiet sphere
By the rough torrent of occasion:
And have the summary of all our griefs,
When time shall serve, to show in articles;
Which, long ere this, we offer'd to the king,
And might by no suit gain our audience.
When we are wrong'd, and would unfold our griefs,
We are denied access unto his person
Even by those men that most have done us wrong.
The dangers of the days but newly gone,
(Whose memory is written on the earth
With yet-appearing blood), and the examples
Of every minute's instance (present now)
Have put us in these ill-beseeming arms:
Not to break peace, or any branch of it;
But to establish here a peace indeed,
Concurring both in name and quality.

WESTMORELAND

When ever yet was your appeal denied?
Wherein have you been galled by the king?
What peer hath been suborn'd to grate on you?
That you should seal this lawless bloody book
Of forg'd rebellion with a seal divine,
And consecrete commotion's bitter edge?

ARCHBISHOP

My brother general, the commonwealth,
To brother born an household cruelty,
I make my quarrel in particular.

From *Essays Civil and Moral*

OF RICHES AND THE CAPITALIST

I cannot call riches better than the baggage of virtue. The Roman word is better, 'impedimenta'. For as the baggage is to an army, so are riches to virtue. It cannot be spared, nor left behind, but it hindereth the march; yea, and the care of it sometimes loseth or disturbeth the victory. *Of great riches there is no real use, except it be in the distribution*; the rest is but conceit. So saith Solomon, 'Where much is, there are many to consume it; and what hath the owner, but the sight of it with his eyes?' The personal fruition in any man, cannot reach to feel great riches: there is a custody of them; or a power of dole or donative of them; or a fame of them; but no solid use to the owner. Do you not see what feigned prices are set upon little stones and rarities? And what works of ostentation are undertaken, because there might seem to be some use of great riches? But then you will say, they may be of use, to buy men out of dangers or troubles. As Solomon saith, 'Riches are as a strong hold in the imagination of the rich man.' But this is excellently expressed, that it is in imagination, and not always in fact. For certainly great riches have sold more men than they have bought out. Seek not proud riches, but such as thou mayest get justly, use soberly, distribute cheerfully, and leave contentedly. . . . The ways to enrich are many, and most of them foul. Parsimony is one of the best, and yet is not innocent; for it withholdeth men from works of liberality and charity. The improvement of the ground is the most natural obtaining of riches; for it is our great mother's blessing, the earth's; but it is slow. And yet, where men of great wealth do stoop to husbandry, it multiplieth riches exceedingly. I knew a nobleman in England who had the greatest audits of any man in my time: a great grazier, a great sheep-master, a great timber-man, a great collier, a great corn-master, a great lead-man; and so of iron, and a number of the like points of husbandry: so as the earth seemed a sea to him, in respect of the perpetual importation. It was truly observed by one, that himself came very hardly to a little riches, and very easily to great riches. For when a man's stock is come to that, that he can expect the prime of markets, and overcome those bargains, which for their greatness are few men's money, and be partner in the industries of young men, he cannot but increase mainly. The gains of ordinary trades and vocations are honest, and furthered by two things, chiefly, by diligence, and by a good name for good and fair dealings. But the gains of bargains are of a more doubtful nature, when men should wait upon another's necessity: . . . As for the chopping of bargains, when a man buys, not to hold, but to sell over again, that commonly grindeth double, both upon the seller, and upon the buyer.

WILLIAM SHAKESPEARE (1564– 1616)   1599

From *Henry V*, V, ii

At the end of the battle of Agincourt, with Henry triumphant, as 'this star of England', carnage reigns, with ten thousand French dead. From this renewal of the French war England gained little and was to lose all. The pattern of enterprise and violence, promise and failure, hope and frustration, greed and self-seeking characteristic of the Lancastrian kings was to drain the kingdom of its wealth; and Burgundy's appeal voices the tragic waste and spoliation of war, disastrous above all to the common people, struck down by disease and poverty and murderous foreign armies.

POOR AND MANGLED PEACE

BURGUNDY   . . . let it not disgrace me,
  If I demand, before this royal view,
  What rub, or what impediment, there is,
  Why that the naked, poor, and mangled peace,
  Dear nurse of arts, plenties, and joyful births,
  Should not, in this best garden of the world,
  Our fertile France, put up her lovely visage?
  Alas! she hath from France too long been chas'd;
  And all her husbandry doth lie on heaps,
  Corrupting in its own fertility.
  Her vine, the merry cheerer of the heart,
  Unpruned dies: her hedges even-pleach'd,
  Like prisoners wildly overgrown with hair,
  Put forth disorder'd twigs; her fallow leas
  The darnel, hemlock, and rank fumitory,
  Doth root upon; while that the coulter rusts,
  That should deracinate such savagery:
  The even mead, that erst brought sweetly forth
  The freckled cowslip, burnet, and green clover,

Wanting the scythe, all uncorrected, rank,
Conceives by idleness; and nothing teems
But hateful docks, rough thistles, kecksies, burrs,
Losing both beauty and utility:
And as our vineyards, fallows, meads, and hedges,
Defective in their natures, grow to wildness;
Even so our houses, and ourselves, and children,
Have lost, or do not learn, for want of time,
The sciences that should become our country;
But grow, like savages – as soldiers will,
That nothing do but meditate on blood –
To swearing, and stern looks, diffus'd attire,
And everything that seems unnatural.
Which to reduce into our former favour
You are assembled; and my speech entreats
That I may know the let, why gentle peace
Should not expel these inconveniences,
And bless us with her former qualities.

WILLIAM SHAKESPEARE (1564–1616) 1600–1601

From *Troilus and Cressida*, I, iii

This speech, part of Ulysses' analysis of the discord in the Greek camp after years
of exhausting war against the Trojans, as a metaphor reflects the crisis of the
Elizabethan age at the turn of the century – Shakespeare's view of the conflict
between a dying feudalism and the new class order (spurred on by religious and
political dissent and the new men of property and capital) that was eventually to
take control.

APPETITE, AN UNIVERSAL WOLF

ULYSSES   O, when degree is shaked,
  Which is the ladder to all high designs,
  The enterprise is sick! How could communities,
  Degrees in schools and brotherhoods in cities,
  Peaceful commerce from dividable shores,
  The primogenitive and due of birth,
  Prerogative of age, crowns, sceptres, laurels,

But by degree, stand in authentic place?
Take but degree away, untune that string,
And, hark, what discord follows! Each thing meets
In mere oppugnancy: the bounded waters
Should lift their bosoms higher than the shores,
And make a sop of all this solid globe:
Strength should be lord of imbecility,
And the rude son should strike his father dead:
Force should be right; or rather, right and wrong,
Between whose endless jar justice resides,
Should lose their names, and so should justice too.
Then every thing includes itself in power,
Power into will, will into appetite;
And appetite, an universal wolf,
So doubly seconded with will and power,
Must make perforce an universal prey,
And last eat up himself . . .

Part Three

THE RISE OF CAPITALISM 1603–88

. . . you are all like men in a mist, seeking for freedom, and know
not where nor what it is: and those of the richer sort of you that
see it are ashamed and afraid to own it, because it comes clothed
in a clownish garment, and open to the best language that scoffing
Ishmael can afford . . . For freedom is the man that will turn the
world upside down, therefore no wonder he hath enemies.'

Gerrard Winstanley, *A Watchword to the City of London* (1649)

. . . That a nation should be so valorous and courageous to win
their liberty in the field, and when they have won it, should . . .
not know how to use it, value it, what to do with it, or with themselves; but after ten or twelve years' prosperous war and contestation with tyranny, basely and besottedly to run their necks again
into the yoke which they have broken . . . will be an ignominy if
it befall us, that never yet befell any nation possessed of their
liberty . . .

John Milton, *The Ready and Easy Way to Establish a Free
Commonwealth* (1660)

SIR FRANCIS BACON (1561–1626) 1605

From *The Advancement of Learning*

KNOWLEDGE FOR THE USE AND BENEFIT OF MAN

The greatest error of all the rest, is the mistaking or misplacing of the last or farthest end of knowledge; for men have entered into a desire of learning and knowledge, sometimes upon a natural curiosity, and inquisitive appetite; sometimes to entertain their minds with variety and delight; sometimes for ornament and reputation; and sometimes to enable them to victory of wit and contradiction; and most times for lucre and profession; and seldom sincerely to give a true account of their gift of reason, to the benefit and use of men: as if there were sought in knowledge a couch, whereupon to rest a searching and restless spirit; or a terrace for a wandering and variable mind to walk up and down with a fair prospect; or a tower of state, for a proud mind to raise itself upon; or a fort or commanding ground, for strife and contention; or a shop, for profit, or sale; and not a rich storehouse, for the glory of the Creator, and the relief of man's estate. But this is that which will indeed dignify and exalt knowledge, if contemplation and action be more nearly and straitly conjoined and united together than they have been; a conjunction like unto that of the two highest planets, Saturn, the planet of rest and contemplation, and Jupiter, the planet of civil society and action. Howbeit, I do not mean, when I speak of use and action, that end beforementioned of the applying of knowledge to lucre and profession; for I am not ignorant how much that diverteth and interrupteth the prosecution and advancement of knowledge . . .

Neither is my meaning, as was spoken of Socrates, to call philosophy down from heaven to converse upon the earth: that is, to leave natural philosophy aside, and to apply knowledge only to manners and policy. But as both heaven and earth do conspire and contribute to the use and benefit of man; so the end ought to be, from both philosophies to separate and reject vain speculations, and whatsoever is empty and void, and to preserve and augment whatsoever is solid and fruitful; that knowledge may not be, as a courtesan, for pleasure and vanity only, or, as a bond-woman, to acquire and gain to her master's use; but, as a spouse, for generation, fruit, and comfort.

WILLIAM SHAKESPEARE (1564–1616) 1606

From *King Lear*, III, iv, and IV, vi

King Lear provides a devastating representation of the collapse of feudal authority
and its exposure to the rule of aggressive competition, governed by will and
appetite, and unscrupulous ambition. It, like all the plays of this period, registers
Shakespeare's grasp of the underlying condition of society in Jacobean England,
his awareness that at a turning-point in history fundamental changes were taking
place, determined by the struggle between the forces of hierarchic feudal order
and the new class that was emerging – a struggle that was to culminate in the
regicide and civil war of the 1640s. Ironically, Lear begins to understand the
nature and value of the common human ties which are the basis of all rational
community only after he has been stripped of his power. And in his madness –
'child-changed', 'unaccommodated' – he discovers the creative roots of kinship
he had been blind to as king.

YOU HOUSELESS POVERTY

LEAR
    Poor naked wretches, whereso'er you are
    That bide the pelting of this pitiless storm,
    How shall your houseless heads, and unfed sides,
    Your loop'd and window'd raggedness defend you
    From such seasons as these? O I have ta'en
    Too little care of this: take physic, Pomp,
    Expose thyself to feel what wretches feel,
    That thou mayst shake the superflux to them,
    And show the Heavens more just.

UNACCOMMODATED MAN

LEAR   . . . Is man no more than this?
    Consider him well. Thou ow'st the worm no silk; the beast no hide;
    the sheep no wool; the cat no perfume. Ha? here's three on's are
    sophisticated. Thou art the thing itself; unaccommodated man is no
    more but such a poor, bare, forked animal as thou art. Off, off you
    lendings: come, unbutton here . . .

THE GREAT IMAGE OF AUTHORITY

LEAR What, art mad? A man may see how this world goes, with no eyes. Look with thine ears: see how yond Justice rails upon yond simple thief. Hark in thine ear: change places, and handy-dandy, which is the justice, which is the thief: thou hast seen a farmer's dog bark at a beggar?

GLOUCESTER Ay, sir.

LEAR And the creature run from the cur: there thou mightst behold the great image of authority, a dog's obey'd in office. Thou, rascal beadle, hold thy bloody hand: why dost thou lash that whore? Strip thy own back, thou hotly lust'st to use her in that kind for which thou whipp'st her. The usurer hangs the cozener. Through rough tatter'd clothes great vices do appear: robes and furr'd gowns hide all. Plate sins with gold, and the strong lance of Justice hurtless breaks: arm it in rags, a pigmy's straw does pierce it. None does offend, none, I say none, I'll able 'em; take that of me my friend, who have the power to seal th'accuser's lips. Get thee glass-eyes, and like a scurvy politician, seem to see the things thou dost not. Now, now, now, now . . .

WILLIAM SHAKESPEARE (1564–1616)   1607

From *Timon of Athens*, I, ii, and IV, iii

The stark theme of *Timon of Athens*, and the source of Timon's outraged denunciation, is the manner in which money corrupts and perverts human character, transforming everything into its opposite and destroying the organic bonds of human relationships. Timon's naïve utopianism – the indulgence of a rich man addicted to giving – leaves him totally exposed to exploitation. He seems incapable of realizing that the Athens he lives in is not the Athens of Pericles, but a mean city of commerce whose social order is built upon the ethics of the market-place, giving licence to men for whom 'policy sits above conscience', and who make their wills 'the scope of justice'. And it is his shocked realization of this that turns Timon at a stroke into a hater of mankind. But ironically, even in his state of maddened alienation, he finds gold buried in the 'common mother', earth; and thus he is made to see that there is no escape from money. It dominates his world, and has poisoned it to the very roots, a kind of filth that would besmear mankind, 'the universal means of separation and betrayal', as Marx later observes, commenting on *Timon of Athens*. So Shakespeare looks forward to the growth of the capitalist process which was to define the monstrous inhumanities of the nineteenth century.

SO MANY LIKE BROTHERS

TIMON

O, no doubt, my good friends, but the gods themselves have provided that I shall have much help from you. How had you been my friends else? Why have you that charitable title from thousands, did you not chiefly belong to my heart? I have told more of you to myself than you can with modesty speak in your own behalf; and thus far I confirm you. O you gods, think I, what need have we any friends if we should ne'er have need of them? They were the most needless creatures living should we ne'er have use for 'em, and would most resemble sweet instruments hung up in cases, that keeps their sounds to themselves. Why, I have often wished myself poorer that I might come nearer to you. We are born to do benefits. And what better or properer can we call our own than the riches of our friends? O, what a precious comfort 'tis to have so many like brothers commanding one another's fortunes! O, joy's e'en made away ere't can be born! Mine eyes cannot hold out water, methinks. To forget their faults, I drink to you . . .

THIS YELLOW SLAVE

TIMON   Earth, yield me roots.
  He digs
Who seeks for better of thee, sauce his palate
With thy most operant poison. What is here?
Gold? Yellow, glittering, precious gold?
No, gods, I am no idle votarist.
Roots, you clear heavens! Thus much of this will make
Black white, foul fair, wrong right,
Base noble, old young, coward valiant.
Ha, you gods! Why this? What, this, you gods? Why, this
Will lug your priests and servants from your sides,
Pluck stout men's pillows from below their heads.
This yellow slave
Will knit and break religions, bless th'accursed,
Make the hoar leprosy adored, place thieves,
And give them title, knee, and approbation,
With senators on the bench. This is it
That makes the wappened widow wed again –
She, whom the spital-house and ulcerous sores

Would cast the gorge at, this embalms and spices
To th'April day again. Come, damned earth,
Thou common whore of mankind, that puts odds
Among the rout of nations, I will make thee
Do thy right nature . . .

GOLD, THE VISIBLE GOD

TIMON

I am sick of this false world, and will love naught
But even the mere necessities upon't.
Then, Timon, presently prepare thy grave.
Lie where the light foam of the sea may beat
Thy grave-stone daily. Make thine epitaph,
That death in me at others' lives may laugh.
      He addresses the gold
O thou sweet king-killer, and dear divorce
'Twixt natural son and sire, thou bright defiler
Of Hymen's purest bed, thou valiant Mars,
Thou ever young, fresh, loved, and delicate wooer,
Whose blush doth thaw the consecrated snow
That lies on Dian's lap! Thou visible god,
That solder'st close impossibilities,
And makest them kiss; that speakest with every tongue,
To every purpose! O thou touch of hearts!
Think thy slave man rebels, and by thy virtue
Set them into confounding odds, that beasts
May have the world in empire.

JOHN STOW (1525?–1605)   1607

From *Annales of England*, p. 890(1–2)

THE PEOPLE RISE AGAINST DEPOPULATION AND DECAY WITH CAPTAIN POUCH

About the middle of this month of May 1607, a great number of common
persons suddenly assembled themselves in Northamptonshire, and then
others of a like nature assembled themselves in Warwickshire, and some

in Leicestershire, they violently cut and break down hedges, filled up ditches, and laid open all such enclosures of commons and other grounds as they found enclosed, which of ancient time had been open and employed to tillage, these tumultuous persons in Northamptonshire, Warwick and Leicestershire grew very strong, being in some places of men, women and children a thousand together, and at Hill Norton in Warwickshire there were three thousand, and at Cottesbich there assembled of men, women and children to the number of full five thousand.

These riotous persons bent all their strength to level and lay open enclosures without exercising any manner of force or violence upon any man's person, goods or cattle, and wheresoever they came, they were generally relieved by the near inhabitants, who sent them not only many carts laden with victual, but also good store of spades and shovels for speedy performance of their present enterprise, for until then some of them were fain to use bills, pikes and such like tools instead of mattocks and spades.

The twenty-seventh of this month, there were several Proclamations made, straitly charging them to surcease their disorder, yet nevertheless they ceased not, but rather persisted more eagerly, and thereupon the Sheriffs and Justices had authority given them to suppress them by force, by virtue whereof they raised an army and scattered them, using all possible means to avoid bloodshed, and after that the King sent Henry Earl of Huntingdon, Thomas Earl of Exeter, Edward Lord Zouch, William Lord Compton, John Lord Harrington, Robert Lord Spencer, George Lord Carew, Sir Edward Coke Lord Chief Justice of the Common Pleas, with divers other learned judges, assisted by the Mayor of Coventry and the most discreet justices of peace and of Oyer and Termyner in their several counties to do justice upon the levellers according to the nature of their offences.

And the twenty-eight of June the King made proclamation signifying his great unwillingness to have proceeded against them either by martial law or civil justice if lenient or gentle admonition might any ways have prevailed with them to desist from their turbulent rebellions and traitorous practice.

At the first these foresaid multitudes assembled themselves without any particular head or guide, then started up a base fellow called John Reynoldes, whom they surnamed Captain Pouch because of a great leather pouch which he wore by his side.

He said there was sufficient matter to defend them against all comers, but afterwards when he was apprehended his pouch was searched, and therein was only a piece of green cheese. He told them also that he had authority from his majesty to throw down enclosures, and that he was sent of God to satisfy all degrees whatsoever, and that in this present work he was directed by the Lord of Heaven; and thereupon they generally inclined to his direction, so as he kept them in good order, he commanded them not to swear, nor to offer violence to any present: but to ply their business and to make fair work, intending to continue this work so long as God should put them in mind.

At the beginning of this disordered assembly until their suppression and due examination of many of the offenders, it was generally bruited throughout the land that the special cause of their assemblies and discontent was concerning religion, and the same passed current with many according to their several opinions in religion. Some said it was a Puritan faction, because they were the strongest, and thereby sought to enforce their pretended reformation; others said it was the practice of the Papists thereby to obtain restoration or toleration: all of which reports proved false as appeared plainly by the examination of all such as were examined, whose general pretence of grievances and cause of stirring in this riotous and traitorous manner was only for the laying open of enclosures, the prevention of further depopulation, the increase and continuance of tillage to relieve their wives and children; and chiefly because it has been credibly reported unto them by many that of late years there were three hundred and forty towns decayed and depopulated, and that they supposed by this insurrection and casting down of enclosures to cause reformation.

Some of them were indicted of High Treason and executed for levying wars against the King, and opposing themselves against the King's forces. Captain Pouch was made exemplary . . .

WILLIAM SHAKESPEARE (1564–1616)   1611

From *The Tempest*, II, i

GONZALO'S ISLAND EDEN

GONZALO
Had I plantation of this isle, my lord –
ANTONIO
He'd sow't with nettle-seed.
SEBASTIAN   Or docks, or mallows.

GONZALO

   And were the king on't, what would I do?

SEBASTIAN

   Scape being drunk, for want of wine.

GONZALO

   I' the commonwealth I would by contraries
   Execute all things: for no kind of traffic
   Would I admit; no name of magistrate;
   Letters should not be known; riches, poverty,
   And use of service, none; contract, succession,
   Bourn, bound of land, tilth, vineyard, none;
   No use of metal, corn, or wine, or oil:
   No occupation, all men idle, all;
   No sovereignty.

SEBASTIAN   Yet he would be king on't.

ANTONIO

   The latter end of his commonwealth forgets the beginning.

GONZALO

   All things in common nature should produce,
   Without sweat or endeavour: treason, felony,
   Sword, pike, knife, gun, or need of any engine,
   Would I not have; but nature should bring forth,
   Of its own kind, all foison, all abundance,
   To feed my innocent people.

SEBASTIAN

   No marrying among his subjects?

ANTONIO

   None, man; all idle; whores, and knaves.

GONZALO

   I would with such perfection govern, sir,
   To excel the golden age.

SIR FRANCIS BACON (1561–1626)   1620

From *Novum Organum*

HOPE NECESSARY TO PROGRESS

. . . By far the greatest obstacle to the progress of the Sciences, and to
the undertaking new tasks and provinces therein, is found in the tend-

ency of man to despair, and to suppose things impossible . . . And so we must open out and set forth our conjectures as to what makes hope . . . probable; as Columbus did, before that wonderful voyage of his across the Atlantic, when he adduced reasons for his confidence that new lands and continents might be discovered in addition to those already known; which reasons, though at first rejected, were yet afterwards proved by experiment, and were the cause and beginning of very great events . . .

And so we may by all means hope that there are many things of excellent use stored up in the lap of Nature having in them nothing kindred or parallel to what is already discovered, but lying quite out of the path of the imagination, which have not hitherto been discovered; and they, doubtless, in the course and revolution of many ages, will also some day come forth of themselves, as their predecessors have done; but by the method of which we are now treating they may be speedily, suddenly, and simultaneously presented and anticipated . . .

FULKE GREVILLE, LORD BROOKE
(1554–1628)

From *Alaham*

Greville, born to wealth, serving the interests of the court under Elizabeth and later James I and Charles I, and ending his life a very rich man, was nevertheless keenly aware of the contradictions of his age, as here in this Chorus from his play *Alaham* of the uneasy balance between king and people.

THE PEOPLE'S WARNING: KINGS TAKE HEED

How shall the people hope? how stay their fear,
When old foundations daily are made new?
Uncertain is a heavy load to bear;
What is not constant sure was never true.
   Excess in one makes all indefinite;
    When nothing is our own, then what delight?

Kings then take heed! Men are the books of fate,
Wherein your vices deep engraven lie,
To show our God the grief of every state.

And though great bodies do not straightways die,
   Yet know, your errors have their proper doom,
   Even in our ruin to prepare your own.

ROBERT BURTON (1577–1640)   1621

From *The Anatomy of Melancholy*, III, pp. 35–6

Charity, as defined by Burton from many sources in the Bible, is a form of love. Among other things, 'it will defend the fatherless and widowed' and will 'bear his brother's burden'. And 'he that loves so . . . will make himself equal to them of the lower sort', and 'love his brother, not in word and tongue, but in deed and truth'.

THE MEANNESS OF THE RICH

. . . Miserable wretches, to fat and enrich ourselves, we care not how we get it . . . how many thousands we undo, whom we oppress, by whose ruin and downfall we arise, whom we injure, fatherless children, widows, common societies, to satisfy our own private lust. Though we have myriads, abundance of wealth and treasure (pitiless, merciless, remorseless, and uncharitable in the highest degree), and our poor brother in need, sickness, in great extremity, and now ready to be starved for want of food, we had rather, as the fox told the ape, his tail should sweep the ground still, than cover his buttocks; rather spend it idly, consume it with dogs, hawks, hounds, unnecessary buildings, in riotous apparel, ingurgitate, or let it be lost, than he should have part of it; rather take from him that little which he hath than relieve him.

Like the dog in the manger, we neither use it ourselves, let others make use of, or enjoy it; part with nothing while we live: for want of disposing our household, and setting things in order, set all the world together by the ears after our death. Poor Lazarus lies howling at his gates for a few crumbs, he only seeks chippings, offals; let him roar and howl, famish, and eat his own flesh, he respects him not . . .

Show some pity for Christ's sake, pity a sick man, an old man, etc., he cares not, ride on: pretend sickness, inevitable loss of limbs, goods, plead suretyship, or shipwreck, fires, common calamities, show thy wants and imperfections . . . Swear, protest, take God and all his Angels to witness . . . thou art a counterfeit crank, a cheater, he is not touched with it . . . ride on, he takes no notice of it. Put up a supplication to him in the name of a thousand orphans, an hospital, a spittle, a prison as he goes by, they cry out to him for aid, ride on . . . he cares not, let them eat stones, devour themselves with vermin, rot in their own dung, he cares not. Show him a decayed haven, a bridge, a school, a fortification, etc., or some public work, ride on; good your worship, your honour, for God's sake, your country's sake, ride on. But show him a roll wherein his name shall be registered in golden letters, and commended to all posterity, his arms set up, with his devices to be seen, then peradventure he will stay and contribute; or if thou canst thunder upon him, as Papists do, with satisfactory and meritorious works, or persuade him by this means he shall save his soul out of Hell, and free it from Purgatory (if he be of any religion), then in all likelihood he will listen and stay . . .

PHILIP MASSINGER
(1583–1640)
1623

From *The Bondman*, IV, ii (first performed at the Cockpit, Drury Lane, 3 December 1623)

The action of the play takes place in Syracuse, and involves the nobles and slaves of the city. Marullo, a Theban disguised as a bondman in order to revenge himself against a young Syracusan contracted to his sister who had broken his vow, leads the slaves in rebellion against their masters, refusing them entry into the city on their return from victory over the Carthaginians. Asked why they should take 'this desperate course', Marullo speaks for them all.

WE'LL RIGHT OURSELVES

MARULLO   . . . Your tyranny
  Drew us from our obedience. Happy those times
  When lords were styled fathers of families,
  And not imperious masters! When they number'd
  Their servants almost equal with their sons,
  Or one degree beneath them! when their labours
  Were cherish'd and rewarded, and a period
  Set to their sufferings; when they did not press
  Their duties or their wills, beyond the power
  And strength of their performance! all things order'd
  With such decorum, as wise lawmakers,

From each well-govern'd private house derived
The perfect model of a commonwealth.
Humanity then lodged in the hearts of men,
And thankful masters carefully provided
For creatures wanting reason. The noble horse,
That, in his fiery youth, from his wide nostrils
Neigh'd courage to his rider, and brake through
Groves of opposed pikes, bearing his lord
Safe to triumphant victory; old or wounded,
Was set at liberty, and freed from service.
The Athenian mules, that from the quarry drew
Marble, hew'd for the temples of the gods,
The great work ended, were dismiss'd, and fed
At the public cost; nay, faithful dogs have found
Their sepulchres; but man, to man more cruel,
Appoints no end to the sufferings of his slave;
Since pride stepp'd in and riot, and o'erturn'd
This goodly frame of concord, teaching masters
To glory in the abuse of such as are
Brought under their command; who, grown unuseful,
Are less esteem'd than beasts. – This you have practised,
Practised on us with rigour; this hath forced us
To shake our heavy yokes off; and, if redress
Of these just grievances be not granted us,
We'll right ourselves, and by strong hand defend
What we are now possessed of . . .

Asked what their demands are, Marullo answers:

A general pardon first, for all offences
Committed in your absence. Liberty
To all such as desire to make return
Into their countries; and, to those that stay,
A competence of land freely allotted
To each man's proper use, no lord acknowledged:
Lastly, with your consent, to choose them wives
Out of your families . . .

The answer is: 'Let the city sink first.' The masters scale the walls and fight. But it
is the sight of the whip that causes the slaves to yield and run. Marullo escapes, is
caught and tortured, but finally sees justice done.

FENLAND REVOLT
23 February 1628

From the proceedings of the Court of Star Chamber, in Gardiner, ed.,
Cases in the Courts of Star Chamber and High Commission

Before twelve members of the Court, including the Lord Keeper of the Great
Seal, the Bishops of London and Winchester, the Lord Chief Justice, the defendants were: Charles Moody, Richard Strode, Henry Stock and his wife, Richard
Kingman and Jane his wife, Katharine Smith, widow, William Leggat and his
wife, John Wells and his wife, Thomas Browne and his wife, Thomas Gundy and
Katherine his wife, and others. Ten years later, Oliver Cromwell was to lead
popular resistance to the unjust actions of the King's Commissioners in the draining of the Fens.

LEVELLING BANKS AND DITCHES

The Bill set forth that his Majesty being seized of divers lands and waste
grounds called the Fens, in the counties of Lincoln and Nottingham,
etc., these lands were surrounded with water and barren, his Majesty
. . . took order with Sir Cornelius Varmiden for the draining of the Fens
. . . and articles of agreement were made between his Majesty and the
said Sir Cornelius Varmiden . . . for the doing thereof, and a special
provision that those that had any tithe of common should repair to the
Commissions appointed for that purpose . . . They were all agreed the
commoners should have one part . . . The King provided workmen,
the work was being brought to good forwardness, and divers ditches
and banks made, and Sir Cornelius Varmiden was at great
charge thereabouts.

That the defendants with others came together in companies to throw
down and demolish what was done, although divers proclamations were
made, and no right could they pretend, and . . . they made their assemblies by hundreds and five hundreds, they demolish the work, they beat
the workmen, and burn the spades, shovels, wheelbarrows, planks, and
beat the workmen, set up a pair of gallows for to terrify the workmen,
threw some of them into the water and held them under a while. They
had a signal to assemble themselves by sometimes by a bell, sometimes
by a horn, they threatened to kill the workmen if they came thither to
work again. That they had 14 several times in riotous and rebellious
manner assembled themselves and done these riots . . . and that some
of them put those that served the King's process out of this Court upon
them into the stocks.

The defendants answers, some were read, and the rest opened by Counsel; they all claimed their common of pasture with all manner of cattle and common of turbary, at all times of the year; that they never agreed with Sir Cornelius Varmiden, that the country receiveth no profit by the work, the grounds are made rather worse. They confess some of them that they did with others enter into their grounds to go to their cattle their pasturing, that they cut down the banks and ditches and levelled them for stopping their way. This they did to claim their right, which they hope the court will maintain, seeing they have had possession and seisin and they whose estates they have, time out of mind; and as for their unlawful assemblies, riots, routs, plots, confederacies, woundings, beatings, etc., Not Guilty . . .

Sentence: That his Majesty proceeded herein legally and rightfully for the benefit of his crown and people, for the draining of these fens; and many of the defendants were found guilty of the several riots charged in this bill; viz. Toxie, James Moody, Henry Scott, and Hezebias Browne, who were fined £1000 apiece. The widow Smith, who married the minister after the riots, £500, and the several women . . . 500 marks apiece, and they were adjudged to pay for damages unto Sir Cornelius Varmiden the relator £2000.

PHILIP MASSINGER (1583–1640)   1633

From *A New Way to Pay Old Debts*, II, i

WISDOM OF THE RICH

Sir Giles Overreach – a cruel extortioner: *Marrall* – a term-driver

OVERREACH

  I would be worldly wise; for the other wisdom,
  That does prescribe us a well-govern'd life,
  And to do right to others, as ourselves,
  I value not an atom.

MARRALL   What course take you,
  With your good patience, to hedge in the manor
  Of your neighbour, master Frugal? as 'tis said
  He will nor sell, nor borrow, nor exchange;
  And his land, lying in the midst of your many lordships,
  Is a foul blemish.

OVERREACH   I have thought on't, Marrall
  And it shall take. I must have all men sellers,
  And I the only purchaser.
MARRALL   'Tis most fit, sir.
OVERREACH
  I'll therefore buy some cottage near his manor,
  Which done, I'll make my men break ope his fences,
  Ride o'er his standing corn, and in the night
  Set fire on his barns, or break his cattle's legs:
  These trespasses draw on suits, and suits expenses,
  Which I can spare, but will soon beggar him.
  When I have harried him thus two or three year,
  Though he sue *in forma pauperis*, in spite
  Of all his thrift and care, he'll grow behind hand.
MARRALL
  The best I ever heard! I could adore you.
OVERREACH
  Then, with the favour of my man of law,
  I will pretend some title: want will force him
  To put it to arbitrement; then, if he sell
  For half the value, he shall have ready money,
  And I possess his land . . .

JOHN LILBURNE (1614–57)   1638

From *A Worke of the Beast*, in Haller, ed., *Tracts on Liberty*, II, p. 33

In 1637 the Court of Star Chamber arraigned and punished Lilburne, together
with William Prynne, John Bastwick and Henry Burton, for publishing unlicensed pamphlets attacking episcopacy. Awaiting punishment, Lilburne wrote an
account of his arraignment and conviction. He was pilloried and whipped, and
afterwards treated with savage cruelty, being kept in solitary confinement in the
Fleet prison in chains and starved. But he managed all the same to get his story,
A Worke of the Beast, written – these verses forming part of the epilogue.

AGAINST THE GREAT ARCH-BISHOP

I do not fear the face nor power of any mortal man,
Though he against me rise, to do the worst he can,

Because my trust, my hope, my strength, my confidence and aid
Is in the Lord Jehovah's power, both now and ever stayed.
Therefore my soul shall never cease, Triumphantly to sing,
There at my Fort, my sure defence, my Saviour and my King,
For in my straits and trials all, thou well with me hast dealt,
Thy mercies and upbearing hand most sweetly I have felt.
Thou hast in my distresses great, my stripes and bitter smart
So held my soul as from thy truth, I never once did start.
But to thy truth with cheerfulness and courage have I stood,
Though tortured for it were my flesh, and lost my dearest blood,
When from Fleet-bridge to Westminster, at Carts Arsse I was whipt,
Then thou with joy my soul upheld, so that I never wept.
Likewise when I on Pillory, in *Palace-yard* did stand,
Then by thy help against my foes, I had the upper hand,
For openly I to their face did there truly declare,
That from the Pope our Prelates all, descended still they are,
And that I might for what I said, make confirmation
I nam'd Chapters the 9 and 13 of Revelation.
Likewise I then did fearlessly unto the people shew
That what *Pocklington* hath writ, is found now very true,
Namely, that they come lineally, from *Antichrist* his Chair,
Even to him that now doth reign, the great *Arch-Bishop* here.

JOHN MILTON (1608–74)   Spring 1641

From *Of Reformation in England, and the Causes that have Hitherto
Hindered it*, in *Prose Writings*, pp. 6–7, 49–50

This pamphlet, Milton's first, makes an attempt to clarify the terms for religious
liberty for Puritans against the doctrines of the Anglican bishops, their 'fraud of
deceivable traditions', their 'formal reverence and worship', inducing 'servile and
thrall-like fear'. The Scots had won their war against Archbishop Laud, and the
Long Parliament had already impeached him, with the intention of abolishing
episcopacy in England.

FIRST RESTORER OF BURIED TRUTH

. . . When I recall to mind at last, after so many dark ages, wherein the
huge overshadowing train of error had almost swept all the stars out of

the firmament of the Church; how the bright and blissful Reformation (by divine power) struck through the black and settled night of ignorance and antichristian tyranny, methinks a sovereign and reviving joy must needs rush into the bosom of him that reads or hears; and the sweet odour of the returning gospel imbathe his soul with the fragrancy of heaven. Then was the sacred bible sought out of the dusty corners where profane falsehood and neglect had thrown it, the schools opened, divine and human learning raked out of the embers of forgotten tongues, the princes and cities trooping apace to the newly-erected banner of salvation; the martyrs, with the unresistible might of weakness, shaking the powers of darkness, and scorning the fiery rage of the old red dragon.

The pleasing pursuit of these thoughts hath ofttimes led me into a serious question and debatement with myself, how it should come to pass that England (having had this grace and honour from God, to be the first that should set up a standard for the recovery of lost truth, and blow the first evangelical trumpet to the nations holding up, as from a hill, the new lamp of saving light to all Christendom) should now be last and most unsettled in the enjoyment of that peace, whereof she taught the way to others; although indeed our Wickliff's preaching, at which all the succeeding reformers more effectually lighted their tapers, was to his countrymen but a short blaze, soon damped and stifled by the pope and prelates for six or seven kings' reigns; yet methinks the precedency which God gave this island, to be first restorer of buried truth, should have been followed with more happy success and sooner attained perfection; in which as yet we are amongst the last: for, albeit in purity of doctrine we agree with our brethren; yet in discipline, which is the execution and applying of doctrine home, and laying the salve to the very orifice of the wound, yea, tenting and searching to the core, without which pulpit preaching is but shooting at rovers; in this we are no better than a schism from all the Reformation, and a sore scandal to them . . .

IGNORANCE AND HIGH FEEDING

. . . Let us not be so over-credulous, unless God hath blinded us, as to trust our dear souls into the hands of men that beg so devoutly for the pride and gluttony of their own back and bellies, that sue and solicit so eagerly, not for the saving of souls, the consideration of which can have here no place at all, but for their bishoprics, deaneries, prebends, and canonries: how can these men not be corrupt, whose very cause is the bribe of their own pleading, whose mouths cannot open without the strong breath and loud stench of avarice, simony, and sacrilege, embezzling the treasury of the church on painted and gilded walls of temples wherein God hath testified to have no delight, warming their palace kitchens, and from thence their unctuous and epicurean paunches, with the alms of the blind, the lame, the impotent, the aged, the orphan, the widow? . . . Should not those men rather be heard that come to plead against their own preferments, their worldly advantages, their own abundance; for honour and obedience to God's word, the conversion of souls, the Christian peace of the land, and union of the reformed catholic church, the unappropriating and unmonopolizing the rewards of learning and industry, from the greasy clutch of ignorance and high feeding? We have tried already, and miserably felt what ambition, worldly glory, and immoderate wealth, can do; what the boisterous and contradictional hand of a temporal, earthly, and corporeal spirituality can avail to the edifying of Christ's holy church; were it such a desperate hazard to put to the venture the universal votes of Christ's congregation, and fellowly and friendly yoke of a teaching and laborious ministry, the pastorlike and apostolic imitation of meek and unlordly discipline, the gentle and benevolent mediocrity of church-maintenance, without the ignoble hucksterage of piddling tithes? Were it such an incurable mischief to make a little trial, what this would do to the flourishing and growing up of Christ's mystical body? as rather to use every poor shift, and if that serve not, to threaten uproar and combustion, and shake the brand of civil discord?

CHARLES I (1600–1649)   18 June 1642

From his *Reply to Parliament's Nineteen Propositions*, in Rushworth, *Historical Collections*, Part Three, I, p. 732

Charles had already alienated the Commons beyond compromise by his high-handed actions earlier in the year in illegally impeaching five members of the House for treason and going there in person with armed attendants to arrest them. As William Lilly records, it was 'this rash action of the king's' which, above all others, 'lost him his crown' and set in motion the preparations for war. But in June, before actually resorting to arms, the Commons decided to make one last effort at reconciliation by sending to the King the *Nineteen Propositions*. It was a fruitless gesture. In his *Reply*, Charles rejected the Propositions out of hand. 'Should I grant these demands,' he said, 'I should remain but the outside, but the picture, but the sign of a king.' Instead, he chose to lecture the Commons on the consequences of their actions against him.

A DARK EQUAL CHAOS

. . . All great changes are extremely inconvenient, and almost infallibly beget greater changes, which beget yet greater inconveniences . . . till (all power being vested in the House of Commons, and their number making them incapable of transacting affairs of State with the necessary Service and Expedition, those being retrusted to some close Committee) at last the common people . . . (will) grow weary of Journeywork, and set up for themselves, call parity and independence liberty, devour that Estate which had devoured the rest; destroy all rights and properties, all distinctions of family and merit; and by this means this splendid and excellently distinguished form of government end in a dark and equal chaos of confusion, and the long line of our many noble ancestors in a *Jack Cade*, or a *Wat Tyler* . . .

JOHN GOODWIN (1594?–1665)   21 October 1642

From *Anti-Cavalierism*, in Haller, ed., *Tracts on Liberty*, II, pp. 21–2

Goodwin was Vicar of St Stephen's, Coleman Street – Thomas Edwards called him the 'Great Red Dragon of Coleman Street', no doubt because he had a reputation for eloquence and power of expression greater than anyone except Milton. On the outbreak of Civil War (22 August) he first supported the Independent minority in the Westminster Assembly, and then (in alliance with the Levellers) Cromwell and the Army against Parliament. The subtitle of the pamphlet is: 'Or Truth Pleading, As Well the Necessity, as the Lawfulness of the Present War, for the suppressing of that Butcherly brood of Cavaliering Incendiaries who are now hammering England, to make an Ireland of it.'

RESISTING THE HIGH HAND OF INIQUITY

. . . And since we are fallen upon the mention of those men who are ready in a posture of hatred, and malice, and revenge, with other preparations answerable hereunto, to fall upon us, and our lives and liberties, both spiritual and civil, upon our estates, our Gospel and Religion, and all that is, or ought to be dear and precious unto us; and in our miseries and ruin, to render our posterities more miserable than we, and have advanced their design this way to that maturity and height, which we

169

all know and tremble to think of; Give me leave in that which remains, to excite and stir you up, from the greatest to the least, both young and old, rich and poor, men and women, to quit yourselves like men, yea, and (if it be possible) above the line of men, in this great exigency and stress of imminent danger that hangs over your heads, and threatens you every hour. Oh let it be as abomination unto us, as the very shadow of death, to every man, woman, and child of us, not to be active, not to lie out and strain ourselves to the utmost of our strength and power in every kind, as far as the law of God and nature will suffer us, to resist that high hand of iniquity and blood that is stretched out against us; to make our lives and our liberties, and our Religion good against that accursed Generation that now magnifieth themselves, to make a prey and spoil of them, to make havock and desolation of them all at once, if the Lord shall yet please to deliver us out of their hands. Let not our Lives, our Liberties, our Estates, be at all precious or dear unto us in this behalf, to expose them, be it unto the greatest danger, to prevent the certain and most unquestionable ruin of them otherwise. Let us resolve to put all into the hands of God, to prevent the falling of all, or any thing, into the hands of these men. There is neither man nor woman of us, neither young nor old, but hath somewhat or other, more or less, a Mite or two at least to cast into the Treasury of the Public Safety. Men that have strength of body for the War, and fingers that know how to fight, let them to the Battle, and not fear to look the enemy in the face. Men and women that have only Purses and Estates, let them turn them into men and swords for the Battle. Men that have heads, but want arms and hands for outward execution, let them study and contrive methods and ways of proceedings. Headwork is even what is necessary in such a time and exigent, as hand-work is. They that have neither hands, nor heads, nor estates, let them find hearts to keep the Mountain of God, to pray the enemies down, and the Armies of the Lord up: Let them find tongues to whet up the courage and resolution of others. This is a service wherein women also may quit themselves like men, whose prayers commonly are as masculine, and do as great and severe execution, as the prayers of men . . .

WILLIAM WALWYN (active 1640s)

From *The Power of Love*, in Haller, ed., *Tracts on Liberty*, II,
pp. 297–303

Walwyn makes a moving plea for tolerance in the midst of war, 'a kind of rational goal towards which the enthusiasms of the sects might be led by good-tempered persuasion and appeal to common sense' (Haller, *Tracts on Liberty*, I, p. 37). He was a Christian freethinker who kept himself detached from the various sects, though he was clearly to stand on the side of the soldiers and the people against the Grandees when the crisis came in 1647. As William Haller puts it, Walwyn, 'almost completely forgotten as he has been, was one of the most remarkable men of his time. Sprung from yeoman stock in Worcestershire, the grandson of a bishop, he was in 1640 about forty years of age', a family man who sought 'to govern his existence by common sense and good will'.

OUR COMMON LIBERTY

. . . Love will be as a new light in your understandings by which you will judge quite otherwise of all things, than formerly you have done . . . you will mind high things, but make yourselves equal to men of low degree: you will no longer value men and women according to their wealth, or outward shows, but according to their virtue, and as the love of God appeareth in them . . .

Such opinions as are not destructive to human society, nor blaspheme the work of our Redemption, may be peaceably endured, and considered, in love: and in case of conspiracy against our common liberty, what a madness is it for men to stand in strife about petty opinions? For who are all those that are so much railed at by our common Preachers? Who are they, say they? Why, they are the most dangerous Anabaptists, Brownists, and Separatists: that are enemies to all order and decency, that cry down all learning and all government in the Church, or Commonwealth. Beloved, to my knowledge these things are not true of any of them: it is true, they cannot do all things so orderly and decently as they would, because they are hunted into corners, and from one corner to another, and are not free to exercise their consciences, as had they liberty they might, and would. And as for learning, as learning goes nowadays, what can any judicious man make of it, but as an Art to deceive and abuse the understandings of men, and to mislead them to their ruin? If it be not so, whence comes it that the Universities, and University men throughout the Kingdom in great numbers are oppressors of the welfare of the Commonwealth, and are pleaders for absurdities in government, arguers for tyranny, and corrupt the judgements of their neighbours? . . . The learned man must live upon the unlearned, and therefore when the unlearned shall presume to know as much as the learned, hath not the learned man cause to bestir his wits, and to wrangle too when his Copy-hold is in such danger? . . . You know there are Wolves in Sheep's clothing: be wise as Serpents, able to discover them, innocent as Doves, gently bearing with the infirmities of the weak, having nothing in more esteem than love: thus you will answer love with love: that henceforwards your own souls may constantly witness to yourselves (what this Scripture expresseth) *That the love of God bringing salvation to all men hath appeared, teaching you to live soberly, righteously, and godly in the present world.*

JOHN MILTON (1608–74)   1644

From *Areopagitica: A Speech for the Liberty of Unlicensed Printing, to the Parliament of England*, in *Prose Writings*, pp. 168–9, 176, 177–8, 179, 181

The title relates the English Parliament to the democratically elected supreme court of Athens in ancient Greece, named after Areopagus, the hill on which it met. When Parliament passed an Ordinance of censorship severely limiting the freedom of the press, thus reverting to the controls that were being enforced by the Court of Star Chamber in 1637 before its abolition, Milton attacked it as a piece of reactionary legislation unworthy of a country engaged in a struggle for a free commonwealth. 'Give me liberty to know, to utter, and to argue freely according to conscience, above all liberties,' he says, with characteristic intensity, in this appeal to the men who represented what he believed to be a 'noble and puissant nation'.

TO PROHIBIT BOOKS IS TO CENSURE PEOPLE

I cannot set so light by all the invention, the art, the wit, the grave and solid judgement which is in England, as that it can be comprehended in any twenty capacities how good soever, much less that it should not pass except their superintendence be over it, except it be sifted and strained with their strainers, that it should be uncurrent without their manual stamp. Truth and understanding are not such wares as to be monopolized and traded in by tickets and statutes and standards. We must not think

172

to make a staple commodity of all the knowledge in the land, to mark and license it like our broadcloth and our woolpacks. What is it but a servitude like that imposed by the Philistines, not to be allowed the sharpening of our own axes and coulters, but we must repair from all quarters to twenty licensing forges? Had anyone written and divulged erroneous things and scandalous to honest life, misusing and forfeiting the esteem had of his reason among men, if after conviction this only censure were adjudged him that he should never henceforth write but what were first examined by an appointed officer, whose hand should be annexed to pass his credit for him that now he might be safely read; it could not be apprehended less than a disgraceful punishment. Whence to include the whole Nation, and those that never yet thus offended, under such a diffident and suspectful prohibition, may plainly be understood what a disparagement it is. So much the more, whenas debtors and delinquents may walk abroad without a keeper, but unoffensive books must not stir forth without a visible jailer in their title.

Nor is it to the common people less than a reproach; for if we be so jealous over them, as that we dare not trust them with an English pamphlet, what do we but censure them for a giddy, vicious, and ungrounded people; in such a sick and weak state of faith and discretion, as to be able to take nothing down but through the pipe of a licenser? That this is care or love of them, we cannot pretend, whenas, in those popish places where the laity are most hated and despised, the same strictness is used over them. Wisdom we cannot call it, because it stops but one breach of licence, nor that neither: whenas those corruptions, which it seeks to prevent, break in faster at other doors which cannot be shut.

IN DEFENCE OF BELEAGUERED TRUTH

Lords and Commons of England, consider what Nation it is whereof ye are, and whereof ye are the governors: a Nation not slow and dull, but of a quick, ingenious and piercing spirit, acute to invent, subtle and sinewy to discourse, not beneath the reach of any point, the highest that human capacity can soar to . . .

Behold now this vast City: a city of refuge, the mansion house of liberty, encompassed and surrounded with His protection; the shop of war hath not there more anvils and hammers waking, to fashion out the plates and instruments of armed justice in defence of beleaguered Truth, than there be pens and heads there, sitting by their studious lamps, musing, searching, revolving new notions and ideas wherewith to present, as with their homage and their fealty, the approaching Reformation: others as fast reading, trying all things, assenting to the force of reason and convincement. What could a man require more from a Nation so pliant and so prone to seek after knowledge? What wants there to such a towardly and pregnant soil, but wise and faithful labourers, to make a knowing people, a Nation of Prophets, of Sages, and of Worthies? We reckon more than five months yet to harvest; there need not be five weeks; had we but eyes to lift up, the fields are white already.

Where there is much desire to learn, there of necessity will be much arguing, much writing, many opinions; for opinion in good men is but knowledge in the making. Under these fantastic terrors of sect and schism, we wrong the earnest and zealous thirst after knowledge and understanding which God hath stirred up in this city. What some lament of, we rather should rejoice at, should rather praise this pious forwardness among men, to re-assume the ill-reputed care of their religion into their own hands again. A little generous prudence, a little forbearance of one another, and some grain of charity might win all these diligences to join, and unite in one general and brotherly search after Truth; could we but forgo this prelatical tradition of crowding free consciences and Christian liberties into canons and precepts of men. I doubt not, if some great and worthy stranger should come among us, wise to discern the mould and temper of a people, and how to govern it, observing the high hopes and aims, the diligent alacrity of our extended thoughts and reasonings in the pursuance of truth and freedom, but that he would cry out as Pyrrhus did, admiring the Roman docility and courage: If such were my Epirots, I would not despair the greatest design that could be attempted, to make a Church or Kingdom happy.

Yet these are the men cried out against for schismatics and sectaries; as if, while the temple of the Lord was building, some cutting, some squaring the marble, others hewing the cedars, there should be a sort of irrational men who could not consider there must be many schisms and many dissections made in the quarry and in the timber, ere the house of God can be built. And when every stone is laid artfully together, it cannot be united into a continuity, it can but be contiguous in this world; neither can every piece of the building be of one form; nay rather the perfection consists in this, that, out of many moderate varieties and brotherly dissimilitudes that are not vastly disproportional, arises the goodly and the graceful symmetry that commends the whole pile and structure.

Methinks I see in my mind a noble and puissant nation rousing herself

174

like a strong man after sleep, and shaking her invincible locks. Methinks I see her as an eagle mewing her mighty youth, and kindling her undazzled eyes at the full midday beam; purging and unscaling her long-abused sight at the fountain itself of heavenly radiance; while the whole noise of timorous and flocking birds, with those also that love the twilight, flutter about, amazed at what she means, and in their envious gabble would prognosticate a year of sects and schisms.

. . . And though all the winds of doctrine were let loose to play upon the earth, so Truth be in the field, we do injuriously, by licensing and prohibiting, to misdoubt her strength. Let her and Falsehood grapple; who ever knew Truth put to the worse, in a free and open encounter?

JOHN MILTON (1608–74)   Early 1646

Sonnet, 'On the New Forcers of Conscience Under the Long Parliament'

Milton attacked Presbyterianism and the Presbyterian Church for its rigidity and intolerance, and resented its criticism directed at his divorce tracts. The prevailing opinion of the Assembly of Divines, set up in 1643 by the Long Parliament (which had decided to abolish the Church of England in its episcopal form), was Presbyterian, though a group of 'independents' among them resisted the proposal to set up a Presbyterian Church, and argued the rights of individual conscience and religious toleration. The debate continued for two years, from 1644 to 1646, and produced a number of pamphlets; and Milton was of course passionately involved as an Independent, considering the issue of tolerance and liberty of conscience of great importance – hence his charge in the last line that the Presbyterian system was no better than the Roman Catholic.

———

Because you have thrown off your Prelate Lord,
   And with stiff vows renounced his Liturgy,
   To seize the widow'd whore Plurality
   From them whose sin ye envied, not abhorr'd;
Dare ye for this adjure the civil sword
   To force our consciences that Christ set free,
   And ride us with a classic hierarchy
   Taught ye by mere A. S. and Rotherford?[1]

1. A. S. was Dr Adam Stuart. He, Samuel Rutherford, Thomas Edwards, and 'Scotch What-d'ye-call' (Robert Baillie, the only Scotch Commissioner on the Assembly), all attacked the Independents. Rutherford even advocated the death penalty for heresy in a 1649 pamphlet, and both Baillie and Edwards attacked Milton's divorce tracts.

Men whose life, learning, faith and pure intent
  Would have been held in high esteem with Paul
  Must now be named and printed heretics
By shallow Edwards and Scotch What-d'ye-call.
  But we do hope to find out all your tricks,
  Your plots and packings, worse than those of Trent,
      That so the Parliament
  May with their wholesome and preventive shears
  Clip your phylacteries, though baulk your ears,
      And succour our just fears,
  When they shall read this clearly in your charge:
New Presbyter is but old Priest writ large.

RICHARD OVERTON (active 1642–63)   1646

From *A Remonstrance of Many Thousand Citizens*, in Wolfe, ed., *Leveller Manifestoes*, pp. 116, 117

After the end of the First Civil War, the Presbyterian majority in the House of Commons sought to dominate the affairs of the nation by means of a compromise settlement involving King and Lords, pitting themselves against the Independents, the radicals and lesser orders that had formed the New Model Army. They passed repressive laws to this effect, and proposed to disband the Army, using the authority of the King himself, though clearly Charles was not to be trusted. 'I do not despair,' he said, 'of inducing the Presbyterians or the Independents to join me in exterminating the other; and then I shall be King again.' It was against such forces as these that Overton delivered his *Remonstrance*, addressing it directly (and with characteristic bluntness) to the Presbyterian House of Commons.

AGAINST ALL KINDS OF ARBITRARY GOVERNMENT

Have you shook this Nation like an Earthquake, to produce no more than this for us; Is it for this, that ye have made so free use, and been so bold both with our Persons and Estates? And do you (because of our readings to comply with your desires in all things) conceive us so sottish, as to be contented with such unworthy returns of our trust and Love? No; it is high time we be plain with you; *WE are not, nor SHALL not be so contented*; We do expect according to *reason*, that ye *should* in the first place, declare and set forth *King Charles* his wickedness openly before the world, and withall, to shew the intolerable inconveniences of having a *Kingly Government*, from the constant evil practices of those of this Nation; and so to declare *King Charles* an enemy, and to publish your resolution, never to have any more, but to acquit us of so great a charge and trouble forever, and to convert the great revenue of the Crown to the public treasure, to make good the injuries and *injustices* done heretofore, and of late by those that have possessed the same; and this we expected long since at your hand, and until this be done, we shall not think our selves well dealt withall in this original of all Oppressions, to wit *Kings*.

Ye must also deal better with us concerning the *Lords*, than you have done. Ye only are chosen by Us the People; and therefore in you only is the Power of binding the whole Nation, by making, altering, or abolishing of Laws; Ye have therefore prejudiced Us, in acting so, as if ye could not make a Law without both the Royal assent of the King (*so ye are pleased to express your selves*,) and the assent of the Lords; yet when either King or Lords assent not to what you approve, ye have so much sense of your own Power, as to assent what ye think good by an Order of your own House.

What is this but to blind our eyes, that We should not know where our Power is lodged, nor to whom to apply our selves for the use thereof; but if We want a *Law*, We must await till the *King* and *Lords* assent; if an Ordinance, then We must wait till the *Lords* assent; yet ye knowing their assent to be meerly formal, (*as having no root in the choice of the People, from whom the Power that is just must be derived,*) do frequently importune their assent, which implies a most gross absurdity . . .

We desire you to free us from these abuses and their negative Voices, or else tell us that it is reasonable we should be slaves, this being a perpetual prejudice in our Government, neither consulting with *Freedom* nor *Safety*. With *Freedom* it cannot; for in this way of Voting in all Affairs of the *Commonwealth*, being not chosen thereunto by the People, they are therein Masters and Lords of the People, which necessarily implies the People to be their servants and vassals, and they have used many of us accordingly, by committing divers to Prison upon their own Authority, namely *William Larner*, Lieut. Col. *John Lilburne*, and other worthy sufferers, who upon Appeal unto you have not been relieved.

We must therefore pray you to make a Law against all kinds of *Arbitrary Government*, as the highest capital offence against the *Commonwealth*, and to reduce all conditions of men to a certainty, that none henceforward may presume or plead anything in way of excuse, and that ye will leave no favour or scruple of Tyrannical Power over us in any whatsoever.

177

LAWRENCE CLARKSON (1615–67)   1647

From *A General Charge of Impeachment of High Treason* (pamphlet in the British Library, Thomason Collection, E. 410(9))

Clarkson or Claxton was born in Preston, and went through many stages of religious belief. He was brought up in the Church of England, became a Presbyterian and then an Independent. As an Antinomian he preached for a time at a parish in Norfolk. But in 1644 he became an Anabaptist, and was imprisoned for 'dipping'. After this, he attached himself to the Seekers, and preached at parishes in Kent, Hertfordshire and Lincolnshire, under the influence of William Erbery. Finally, in 1649, he turned Ranter and became the leader of a particularly licentious group called *My One Flesh*. It was then that he wrote his tract *A Single Eye*, (see p. 239), which was burned by the public hangman, and got Clarkson sentenced to imprisonment. On his release he resumed his wandering life, in 1658 joined the Muggletonians, and wrote several tracts for them, before dying as a debtor in Ludgate gaol. The 1647 pamphlet was written before he became a Ranter, and has more in common with the Levellers. It was published 'for the redemption . . . of the long-lost freedom of the freeborn subjects of England'.

YOUR POVERTY IS THEIR PROSPERITY

Who are the oppressors but the nobility and gentry, and who are oppressed, if not the yeoman, the farmer, the tradesman and the like? . . . Have you not chosen oppressors to redeem you from oppression? . . . It is naturally inbred in the major part of the nobility and gentry . . . to judge the poor but fools, and themselves wise, and therefore when you the commonalty calleth a Parliament they are confident such must be chosen that are the noblest and richest . . . Your slavery is their liberty, your poverty is their prosperity . . . Peace is their ruin . . . by war they are enriched . . . Peace is their war, peace is their poverty.

JOHN SALTMARSH (d. 1647)   1647

From *Smoke in the Temple*, in Woodhouse, ed., *Puritanism and Liberty*, p. 181

FOR FREEDOM OF THE PRESS AND FREE SPEECH

Let there be liberty of the press for printing, to those that are not allowed pulpits for preaching. Let that light come in at the window which cannot come in at the door, that all may speak and write one way, that cannot another. Let the waters of the sanctuary have issue and spring up valleys as well as mountains.

Let all that print or preach affix their names that we may know from whom. The contrary is a kind of unwarrantable modesty at the best. If it be truth they write, why do they not own it? If untruth, why do they write? Some such must either suppress themselves for shame or fear, and they that dare not own what they do, they suspect the magistrate or themselves . . .

Let all that teach or print be accountable. Let there be free debates and open conferences and communication, for all and of all sorts that will, concerning difference in spirituals; still allowing the state to secure all tumults and disturbances. Where doors are not shut, there will be no breaking them open. So where debates are free there is a way of vent and evacuation, the stopping of which hath caused more troubles in states than anything; for where there is much new wine in old bottles the working will be such as the parable speaks on . . .

OLIVER CROMWELL AND THE LEADERS OF THE ARMY   Royston, 10 June 1647

From a letter, to the Lord Mayor, Aldermen, and Common Council of the City of London, in Carlyle, *Oliver Cromwell*, I, pp. 221–3

With the King in the hands of the Army at its Newmarket headquarters and the soldiers enraged at being called 'enemies to the State, Disturbers of the Peace' by the Presbyterian party in Parliament, which had passed laws demanding service in Ireland for certain regiments and the disbanding of the rest with the aim of neutralizing the anti-Royalist radical forces in the Commonwealth, Cromwell felt it was time to act. The Army's march towards London was his answer, and this letter contains a thinly veiled threat to those officials of the City who had aligned themselves with the reactionary Presbyterians, demanding the just rights of the Army and the dismissal of those 'few self-seeking men' in Parliament whose designs against the soldiers would plunge the kingdom 'in a new war'.

THE PEACE OF THE KINGDOM

. . . As for the thing we insist upon as Englishmen, – and surely our being Soldiers hath not stript us of that interest, although our malicious enemies would have it so, – we desire a Settlement of the Peace of the Kingdom and of the Liberties of the Subject, according to the Votes and Declarations of Parliament, used as arguments and inducements to invite us and divers of our dear friends out; some of whom have lost their lives in this War. Which being now, by God's blessing, finished, – we think we have as much right to demand, and desire to see, a happy Settlement, as we have to our money and to the other common interest of Soldiers which we have insisted upon. We find also the ingenuous and honest People, in almost all parts of the Kingdom where we come, full of the sense of ruin and misery if the Army should be disbanded *before* the Peace of the Kingdom, and those other things before mentioned, have a full and perfect Settlement.

We have said before, and profess it now, We desire no alteration of the Civil Government. As little do we desire to interrupt, or in the least to intermeddle with, the settling of the Presbyterial Government. Nor did we seek to open a way for licentious liberty, under pretence of obtaining ease for tender consciences. We profess, as ever in these things, when once the State has made a Settlement, we have nothing to say but to submit or suffer. Only we could wish that every good citizen, and every man who walks peaceably in a blameless conversation, and is beneficial to the Commonwealth, might have liberty and encouragement; this being according to the true policy of all States, and even to justice itself.

These in brief are our Desires, and the things for which we stand; beyond which we shall not go. And for the obtaining of these things, we are drawing near your City; – professing sincerely from our hearts, That we intend not evil towards you; declaring with all confidence and assurance, That if you appear not against us in these our just desires, to assist that wicked Party which would embroil us and the Kingdom, neither we nor our Soldiers shall give you the least offence. We come not to do any act to prejudice the being of Parliaments, or to the hurt of this Parliament in order to the present Settlement of the Kingdom. We seek the good of all. And we shall wait here, or remove to a farther distance to abide there, if once we be assured that a speedy Settlement of things is in hand – until it be accomplished . . .

If after all this, you, or a considerable part of you, be seduced to take up arms in opposition to, or hindrance of, these our just undertakings, – we hope we have, by this brotherly premonition, to the sincerity of which we call God to witness, freed ourselves from all that ruin which may befall that great and populous City; having thereby washed our hands thereof.

THE 'DECLARATION OF THE ARMY'
14 June 1647

A Declaration, or, Representation, in Haller and Davies, eds., *Leveller Tracts*, pp. 52–3, 54–5

This document, possibly drafted by Ireton, was one of a series of petitions issued by the soldiers of the Army during their dispute with Parliament over its decision to send certain regiments to Ireland, to disband others and impose the Covenant on all, and its failure to offer indemnity or security for arrears of pay. With the burning of the Large Petition of May 1647, the great Leveller challenge begins, putting forward a programme for radical transformation compared with which, in Haller's words, 'no more extraordinary body of material exists in the entire literature of politics'. Since the House of Commons majority supported the Presbyterian concept of Church government and sought the Scots as allies, pursuing basically pro-Royalist policies, it was of course essential to reduce the power of the Army; and Lilburne saw this as 'a conspiracy . . . of lawless, unlimited and unbounded men' against whom the people had to protect themselves. Thus was threatened an imminent renewal of civil war; and after the rejection of the early petitions, and the Army's *Solemn Engagement* of 5 June, the *Declaration* defines a new stage in the revolutionary struggle.

AGAINST ARBITRARY POWER

That we may no longer be the dissatisfaction of our friends, the subject of our enemies' malice . . . and the suspicion (if not astonishment) of many in the kingdom in our late or present transactions and conduct of business, we shall in all faithfulness and clearness profess and declare unto you those things which have of late protracted and hindered our disbanding, the present grievances which possess our Army and are yet unremedied, with our desires as to the complete settlement of the liberties and peace of the Kingdom; which is that blessing of God, than which (of all worldly things) nothing is more dear unto us, or more precious in our thoughts, we have hitherto thought all our present enjoyments . . . a price but sufficient to the purchase of so rich a blessing; that we, and all the free-born people of this Nation, may sit down in quiet under our Vines, under the glorious administration of Justice and righteousness, and in the full possession of those Fundamental Rights and Liberties without which we can have little hopes . . . to enjoy either any comforts of life, or so much as life itself, but at the pleasures of some men, ruling merely according to will and power . . .

Nor will it now (we hope) seem strange or unseasonable to rational and honest men . . . if . . . we shall, before disbanding, proceed, in our own and the Kingdom's behalf, to propound and plead for some provision for our and the Kingdom's satisfaction and future security . . . especially considering that we were not a mere mercenary Army hired to serve any Arbitrary power of a State, but called forth and conjured, by the several Declarations of Parliament, to the defence of our own and the people's just rights and liberties. And so we took up Arms, in judgement and conscience to those ends, and have so continued them, and are resolved according to your first just desires in your Declarations, and such principles as we have received from your frequent informations and our own common sense concerning those our fundamental Rights and Liberties, to assert and vindicate the just power and Rights of this Kingdom in Parliament for those common ends premised, against all arbitrary power, violence and oppression, and against all particular parties or interests whatsoever . . . And we cannot but be sensible of the great complaints that have been made generally to us of the Kingdom, from the people where we march, of arbitrariness and injustice, to their great and insupportable oppressions.

RICHARD OVERTON   17 July 1647
(active 1642–1633)

From *An Appeal, From the Degenerate Representative Body of the Commons of England Assembled at Westminster. To the Body Represented* . . ., in Wolfe, ed., *Leveller Manifestoes*, pp. 169–71

With the Army at a safe distance, lying (in Carlyle's words) 'coiled round London and the Parliament, now advancing, now receding', according to whether the demands they made were or were not met, and insisting on the impeachment of Denzil Holles and ten other members of the Presbyterian party, negotiations were long unresolved. Demonstrations by factions in the City of both sides occurred towards the end of July, till at last the Army made its move to Hounslow, finally enforcing submission on 6 August, and marching 'three deep by Hyde Park' into the heart of the City 'with boughs of laurel in their hats'.

FOR THE REMOVAL OF OPPRESSION

. . . I for my part do . . . hereby proclaim and protest against them all to the free-men of *England* and Dominion of *Wales*, as so many traitors to the safety and weal of the people, both the eleven Members that are charged, and all such as are coactors and voters with them in further oppressions and tyrannies, over-swaying and bearing down the voters for freedom and justice; imploring and beseeching all lovers of freedom and justice within His Majesty's Dominions of *England* and *Wales*, as one man to rise up in the cause of the Army for the removal of those obstructors and traitors, and the bringing of them to a speedy and legal trial, that the wicked may be taken from before the face of the King, that his Throne may be established in righteousness and judgement, the liberty and freedom of the people recovered from the hands of oppressors and tyrants, and the Kingdom settled in peace and tranquillity, which only is, and ever shall be, the prayers and endeavours of your Appellant.

Now for the further clearing and making good of mine Appeal, I shall . . . briefly touch the accustomary course of their oppressive tyrannous carriage to the generality, whereby their degenerate state and capacity will more clearly appear. But for brevity sake I shall omit the several new oppressions, exactions and burdens wherewith the people are loaded everywhere, even till their backs are ready to break as every man by woeful experience can witness; and shall only relate to the main and principal end of their election and session, which is for *bearing the cries and groans of the people, redressing and easing the grievances*. And as touching this matter, this is their course. Instead of relief for oppression, themselves do oppress, and which is worst, then *stop* the mouths of the oppressed; cruciate and torment, and not suffer the tormented to complain, but even torment them for complaining, slight, reject and crush their just and necessary Petitions, which is the highest kind of tyranny in the world, shut their doors and ears against the cry of the people, both of Country and City, yea, though the burdens of the oppressed are so great that multitudes in a peaceable manner have attended the House daily with Petitions for no other thing than for the *Removal of oppression and recovery of freedom*, according to the fundamental Laws of this Kingdom, which they often declared, covenanted, protested and swore with hands lift up to the most high God to perform faithfully and truly.

Yet these very men, contrary to their many Oaths . . . call the Petitioners *Rogues, Villains, seditious, factious fellows*, and bid *a pox of God on them*, offer to draw their swords at them, lift up their canes at them in a menacing manner, shake them by the shoulders, and otherwise abuse them, and not only so; but imprison some of them . . . And they stay not here, but their arrogance mounts higher and higher, even vote their Petitions seditious, *breach of their privileges*, and cause them to be burnt by the hand of the *Common hangman*, even such petitions wherein was contained the *Liberties and Freedoms of the Commons of England*, and no jot of anything either in word or circumstance that was not just, honest and reasonable, and their sworn duties to perform . . . O most unheard of, unparalleled Treason! Hear O Heavens and judge O ye free Commoners of England, where and what is become of your Laws and Liberties: thus would they do with your persons, even *burn them* by the *hand of the Common hangman*, had they as much power over them as they have over your petitions and papers, and virtually they have done no less, for essentially and really they have burnt the *Great Charter of England*, for in those petitions were contained the chiefest heads of that Charter, by virtue whereof you hold your very lives, liberties and goods, so that in that *Act* they did as much as in them lay, *set all England on fire, burn and destroy all the laws, rights and liberties thereof*; and if this be not High Treason, and an open and visible forfeiture of their Parliamentary being and trust, I would fain know what is . . .

THE CASE OF THE ARMY   18 October 1647

From Haller and Davies, eds., *Leveller Tracts*, pp. 65–6, 72–3, 81–2

Probably written by John Wildman, though signed by the representatives of five regiments, this manifesto reflects the suspicion of the soldiers, quickened by the influence of Lilburne, Overton and Wildman among others, that their officers were about to betray the radical aims of the Leveller petitions. It was addressed to Fairfax, and many of its arguments (also contained in *An Agreement of the People* a few days later) were to be discussed in the series of debates held at Putney in October. Though Lilburne was in the Tower of London, this did not stop the spread of Leveller principles among the rank and file of the Army.

NOTHING DONE

The Case of the Army truly stated, together with the mischiefs and dangers that are imminent, and some suitable remedies, Humbly proposed by the Agents of five Regiments of Horse, to the respective Regiments and the whole Army

Whereas the grievances, dissatisfactions and desires of the Army, both as Commoners and Soldiers, hath been many months since represented to the Parliament; and the Army hath waited with much patience to see their common grievances redressed, and the rights and freedoms of the Nation cleared and secured; yet, upon a most serious and conscientious view of our Narratives, Representations, Engagements, Declarations, Remonstrances, and comparing with those the present state of the Army and Kingdom, and the present manner of actings of many at the Head-quarters, we not only apprehend nothing to have been done effectually, either for the Army or the poor oppressed people of the nation, but we also conceive that there is little probability of any good, without some more speedy and vigorous actings.

In respect of the Army, there hath been hitherto no public vindication thereof, about their first Petition, answerable to the Ignominy, by declaring them enemies of the State and disturbers of the peace: No public clearing nor repairing of the credit of the Officers, sent for about that petition as Delinquents: No provision for Apprentices' Widows, Orphans or maimed Soldiers answerable to our reasonable addresses propounded in their behalf: No such Indemnity as provideth security for the quiet, ease or safety of the Soldiers, disbanded or to be disbanded: No security for our Arrears, or provision for present pay, to enable the Army to subsist without burdening the distressed country. And in respect to the rights and freedoms of ourselves and the people, that we declared we would insist upon, we conceive there is no kind or degree of satisfaction given . . .

MISCHIEF AND DANGERS

First, The love and affection of the people to the Army, (which is an army's greatest strength) is decayed, cooled, and near lost; it's already the common voice of the people, What good hath our new Saviours done for us? What grievances have they procured to be redressed? Wherein is our condition bettered? or how are we more free than before?

Secondly, Not only so, but the Army is rendered as an heavy burden to the people, in regard more pay is exacted daily for them, and the people find no good procured by them, that's answerable or equivalent to the charge, so that now the people begin to cry louder for disbanding the Army than they did formerly for keeping us in Arms, because they see no benefit accruing. They say they are as likely to be oppressed and enslaved both by King and Parliament, as they were before the Army engaged professedly to see their freedoms cleared and secured.

Thirdly, Whilst the people's old oppressions are continued, and more taxes also are imposed for pay for the Army, they are disabled daily more and more for the maintaining of an Army for the preservation, for they begin to say, they can but be destroyed by oppression, and it's all one to them, whether it be by pretended friends or professed enemies: It were as good, say they, that the King should rule again by prerogative; we were slaves then to his will and we are now no better; we had rather have one tyrant than hundreds.

Fourthly, By this means, distractions, divisions, heart-burnings and jealousies are increased, to the imminent danger of ruin to the Army and Kingdom; the people are inclined to tumults crying out, 'Will none procure relief for us? Shall we always be deluded with fair words, and be devoured by oppressors? We must ere long rise up in arms, and every one catch what he can': confusion is thus threatened.

Fifthly, The Army is exposed to contempt and scandal, and the most black reproaches and infamies are cast upon them. The people say that their resolutions not to disband were because they would live idly on the people's labours, and when the Soldiers are constrained to take free quarters, this (saith the people) is for freedom and right, to eat the bread out of our children's mouths; so that many Soldiers are ashamed of themselves, and fear that the people should rise to destroy them. You will do nothing for us, (say they); we are vexed by malignant judges, for conscience sake by arbitrary Committees in the Country, and at Parliament ordering one thing this day, and recalling it the next to our intolerable vexation. Injustice in the law is the same, and we buy our right at as a dear rate as ever. Tithes are enforced from us double and treble, Excise continues, we can have no accompts of all our moneys disbursed for the public. More is daily required, and we know not what is become of all we have paid already, the Soldiers have little pay, and the maimed Soldiers' Widows and Orphans are thrust upon us to be parish charges.

CONDITIONS FOR THE PEOPLE'S FREEDOM

First, that all the orders, votes, ordinances or declarations, that have passed either to discountenance petitions, suppress, prevent or burn petitions, imprison or declare against petitioners, being dangerous precedents against the freedom of the people, may be forthwith expunged the Journal books, and the injustice of them clearly declared to all the people . . .

And it's further offered, that whereas millions of money have been kept in dead stocks in the City of London, the Halls and Companies and the free men of the City could never obtain any account thereof according to their right; That therefore a just and strict account may be forthwith given to all the freemen of all those dead stocks . . .

And for the ease and satisfaction of the people, it's further to be insisted on, that the charge of all the forces to be kept up in the kingdom by sea or land, be particularly computed and published, and that all taxes that shall be necessary may be wholly proportioned, according to that charge; and that there be an equal rate propounded throughout the kingdom in all assessments, that so one town may not bear double the proportion of another of the same value.

4. That all Monopolies be forthwith removed, and no person whatsoever may be permitted to restrain others from free trade.

5. That the most sad oppressions of prisoners be forthwith eased and removed, and that no person that hath no estate real or personal, nor any person that shall willingly yield up his estate to satisfy his creditors may be detained in prison to the ruin of their persons and families; and likewise, that no person imprisoned in a criminal cause may be detained from his legal trial any longer than the next term.

6. That all Statutes, for the Common prayer book, and for the enforcing all to come to Church, whereby many religious and conscientious people are daily vexed and oppressed, be forthwith repealed and nulled . . .

7. That all the oppressive statutes, enforcing all persons though against their consciences to pay Tithes, whereby the husbandman cannot eat the fruit of his labours, may be forthwith repealed and nulled.

8. That all statutes enforcing the taking of oaths, as in towns corporate, the oath of Supremacy, &c. Wherein either the whole oaths, or some clauses in them, are burthens and snares to conscientious people may be repealed and nulled.

9. That it be declared that no person or Court shall have power to be permitted to enforce any person to make oath, or answer to any Interrogatories concerning himself, in any criminal case.

10. That a Committee of conscientious persons be forthwith selected to consider the most intolerable oppressions by unjust proceedings in the law; that withal the laws might be reduced to a smaller number, to be comprised in one volume in the English tongue, that every free Commoner might understand his own proceedings; that Courts might be in the respective Counties of Hundreds; that proceedings might become short and speedy; and that the numberless grievances in the law and Lawyers, might be redressed as soon as possible.

11. That all privileges and protections above the law, whereby some persons are exempted from the force and power thereof, to the insuf-

ferable vexation and ruin of multitudes of distressed people, may be forthwith abrogated.

12. That all the ancient rights and donations belonging to the poor, now embezzled and converted to other uses, as enclosed Commons, Alms houses, etc. throughout all parts of the land, may be forthwith restored to the ancient public use and service of the poor, in whose hands soever they be detained . . .

THE PUTNEY DEBATES

After 28 October
to 8 November 1647

From Firth* ed., *Clarke Papers*, pp. 300–33 passim

During the summer men like John Wildman, Thomas Rainborough and Edward Sexby put forward ideas which questioned the rights of property and extended the franchise to 'the poorest he' in the land. And in October, the Levellers (having encouraged the election of representatives or agitators in the Army rank and file) produced an *Agreement of the People* which made wide-ranging demands for the franchise. The Generals were thus forced to accept an Army Council which included agitators as well as officers. And at Putney after 28 October this body met to discuss the *Agreement*. It was essentially a dispute about property rights and privileges, and it ended in deadlock on 8 November. But on 11 November Charles escaped from the Army, and Cromwell was able to argue the threat of a new civil war in asserting his authority, and to divide the Radicals, who were in the end subdued by force.

PROPERTY AND FREEDOM FOR THE POOREST HE IN ENGLAND

COMMISSARY COWLING In the time before the Conquest, and since the Conquest, the greatest part of the Kingdom was in vassalage.

MR PETTUS We judge that all inhabitants that have not lost their birth right should have an equal voice in elections.

COLONEL RAINBOROUGH I desire that those that had engaged in i should speak, for really I think that the poorest he that is in England hath a life to live as the greatest he; and therefore truly, Sir, I think it's clear that every man that is to live under a Government ought first by his own consent to put himself under that Government; and I do think that the poorest man in England is not at all bound in a stric sense to that Government that he hath not had a voice to put himsel under; and I am confident that when I have heard the reasons against it, something will be said to answer those reasons, insomuch that I should doubt whether he was an Englishman or no that should doubt of these things.

COMMISSARY IRETON   Give me leave to tell you, that if you make this the rule I think you must fly for refuge to an absolute natural Right, and you must deny all Civil Right; and I am sure it will come to that in the consequence . . . I would fain have any man show me their bounds, where you will end, and why you should not take away all property? . . .

COLONEL RAINBOROUGH   As to the thing itself, property [in the franchise]. I would fain know how it comes to be the property of some men and not of others. As for estates, and those kind of things, and other things that belong to men, it will be granted that they are property; but I deny that that is a property to a Lord, to a Gentleman, to any man more than another in the Kingdom of England.

If it be a property, it is a property by a law; neither do I think that there is very little property in this thing by the law of the land, because I think that the law of the land in that thing is the most tyrannous law under heaven, and I would fain know what we have fought for, and this is the old law of England, and that which enslaves the people of England, that they should be bound by laws in which they have no voice at all . . .

The thing that I am unsatisfied in is how it comes about that there is such a property in some freeborn Englishmen, and not in others . . .

MR WILDMAN   Our case is to be considered thus, that we have been under slavery. That's acknowledged by all. Our very laws were made by our Conquerors; and whereas it's spoken much of Chronicles, I conceive there is no credit to be given to any of them; and the reason is because those that were our Lords, and made us their vassals, would suffer nothing else to be chronicled.

We are now engaged for our freedom. That's the end of Parliament, to legislate according to the just ends of government, not simply to maintain what is already established. Every person in England hath as clear a right to elect his Representative as the greatest person in England. I conceive that's the undeniable maxim of government: that all government is in the free consent of the people.

And therefore I should humbly move that if the Question be stated – which would soonest bring things to an issue – it might perhaps be this: Whether any person can justly be bound by law, who doth not give his consent that such persons shall make laws for him? . . .

189

MR SEXBY   We have engaged in this kingdom and ventured our lives, and it was all for this: to recover our birthrights and privileges as Englishmen – and by the arguments urged there is none. There are many thousands of us soldiers that have ventured our lives; we have had little property in this kingdom as to our estates, yet we had a birthright. But it seems now except a man hath a fixed estate in this kingdom, he hath no right in this kingdom. I wonder we were so much deceived. If we had not a right to the kingdom, we were mere mercenary soldiers.

There are many in my condition, that have as good a condition, it may be little estate they have at present, and yet they have as much a right as those two (Cromwell and Ireton) who are their lawgivers, as any in this place. I shall tell you in a word my resolution. I am resolved to give my birthright to none.

Whatsoever may come in the way, and be thought, I will give it to none.

I think the poor and meaner of this kingdom (I speak as in that relation in which we are) have been the means of the preservation of this kingdom . . .

COLONEL RAINBOROUGH (*to Ireton*)   Sir, I see that it is impossible to have liberty but all property must be taken away. If it be laid down for a rule, and if you will say it, it must be so. But I would fain know what the soldier hath fought for all this while? He hath fought to enslave himself, to give power to men of riches, men of estates, to make him a perpetual slave. We do find in all presses that go forth none must be pressed that are freehold-men. When these Gentlemen fall out among themselves they shall press the poor scrubs to come and kill each other for them . . .

MR PETERS   If there is a Constitution that the people are not free, that should be annulled. But this constitution doth not make people free; that Constitution which is now set up is a Constitution of 40s. a year . . .

IRETON   First, the thing itself [universal suffrage] were dangerous if it were settled to destroy property. But I say that the principle that leads to this is destructive to property; for by the same reason that you will alter this Constitution merely that there's a greater Constitution by nature – by the same reason, by the law of nature, there is a greater liberty to the use of other men's goods which that property bars you of . . .

CAPTAIN CLARKE   I presume that the great stick here is this: that if everyone shall have his property, it does bereave the kingdom of its

190

principle, fundamental Constitution that it hath. I presume that all people and all nations whatsoever have a liberty and power to alter and change their Constitutions, if they find them to be weak and infirm. Now if the people of England shall find this weakness in their Constitution, they may change it if they please . . .

JOHN LILBURNE (1614–57)   Before 17 January 1648

From *The Mournful Cries of Many Thousand Poor Tradesmen*, in Haller and Davies, eds., *Leveller Tracts*, pp. 126–7

This manifesto, together with *The Earnest Petition*, was promoted by Lilburne and Wildman at a meeting they held on 17 January 1648, which was reported to both Houses by George Masterson. Lilburne (who had only been released from the Tower the previous November) and Wildman were summoned to the Commons and remanded on a charge of treason; and *A Declaration of Some Proceedings* was issued in February on the orders of the House of Commons, printing both the Manifesto and the Petition in an attempt to discredit the two Leveller leaders. The whole affair generated a number of other pamphlets, including an attack upon Masterson by Wildman, a reply from Masterson, a second attack on Masterson by a certain Jab. Norris, and Lilburne's defence of himself in *A Whip for the Present House of Lords*.

WHOSE SLAVES THE POOR SHALL BE

. . . What then are your ruffling Silks and Velvets, and your glittering Gold and Silver Laces? Are they not the sweat of our brows, and the wants of our backs and bellies?

It's your Taxes, Customs, and Excise, that compels the Country to raise the price of food, and to buy nothing from us but mere absolute necessaries; and then you of the City that buy our Work, must have your Tables furnished, and your Cups overflow; and therefore will give us little or nothing for our Work, even what you please, because you know we must sell for moneys to set our Families on work, or else we famish: Thus our Flesh is that whereupon you Rich men live, and wherewith you deck and adorn yourselves. Ye great men, Is it not your plenty and abundance which begets you Pride and Riot? And doth not your Pride beget Ambition, and your Ambition Faction, and your Faction these Civil broils? What else but your Ambition and Faction continue our

Distractions and Oppressions? Is not all the Controversy whose slaves the poor shall be? Whether they shall be the King's Vassals, or the Presbyterians', or the Independent Factions'? And is not the Contention nourished, that you whose Houses are full of the spoils of your Country, might be secure from Accounts, while there is nothing but Distraction? and that by the tumultuousness of the people under prodigious oppression, you might have fair pretences to keep up an Army, and garrisons? and that under pretence of necessity, you may uphold your arbitrary Government by Committees, etc.

JOHN LILBURNE AND JOHN WILDMAN
Late January 1648

From *The Earnest Petition of Many Free-born People of This Nation*, in Haller and Davies, eds., *Leveller Tracts*, pp. 106–8

THESE OUR PRESSING GRIEVANCES

Showeth,
That the devouring fire of the Lord's Wrath, hath burnt in the bowels of this miserable Nation, until it's almost consumed.

That upon a due search into the causes of God's heavy Judgements we find that injustice and oppression, have been the common National sins, for which the Lord hath threatened woes, confusions and desolations, unto any People or Nation; Woe (saith God) to the oppressing City. Zeph. iii, 1 . . .

That though our Petitions have been burned, and our persons imprisoned, reviled, and abused only for petitioning, yet we cannot despair absolutely of all bowels of compassion in this Honourable House, to an enslaved perishing people. We still nourish some hopes, that you will at last consider that our estates are expended, the whole trade of the Nation decayed, thousands of families impoverished, and merciless Famine is entered into our Gates, and therefore we cannot but once more assay to pierce your ears with our doleful cries for Justice and Freedom, before we perish, or be forced to fly to the prime Laws of nature for entreat:

First, That seeing we conceive this Honourable House is entrusted by the People with all power to redress our grievances, and to provide security for our Freedoms, by making or repealing Laws, erecting or abolishing Courts, displacing or placing Officers, and the like: And seeing upon this consideration, we have often made our addresses to you, and yet we are made to depend for all our expected good, upon the wills of others who have brought all our misery upon us: That therefore in case this Honourable House will not, or cannot, according to their trust, relieve and help us; that it be clearly declared; That we may know to whom, as the Supreme power, we may make our present addresses before we perish, or be enforced to fly to the prime Laws of nature for refuge . . .

POPULAR SONG Current in the 1640s

In Rickword and Lindsay, *Handbook of Freedom*, p. 123

POOR MEN PAY FOR ALL

Methought I saw how wealthy men
   Did grind the poor men's faces,
And greedily did prey on them,
   Not pitying their cases;
They make them toil and labour sore
   For wages too, too small;
The rich men in the tavern roar,
   But poor men pay for all.

Methought I saw an usurer old
   Walk in his fox-furred gown,
Whose wealth and eminence controlled
   The most men in the town;
His wealth he by extortion got,
   And rose by others' fall;
He had what his hands earned not,
   But poor men pay for all.

Methought I saw a courtier proud
   Go swaggering along,
That unto any scarce allowed
   The office of his tongue:
Methought, wert not for bribery,
   His peacock's plumes would fall;
He ruffles out in bravery,
   But poor men pay for all.

Methought I met, sore discontent,
  Some poor men on the way;
I asked one whither he went
  So fast and could not stay.
Quoth he, 'I must go take my lease,
  Or else another shall;
My landlord's riches do increase,
  But poor men pay for all.'

Methought I saw most stately wives
  Go jetting on the way,
That have delightful idle lives
  And go in garments gay;
That with the moon their shapes do change,
  Or else they'll chide and brawl;
Thus women go like monsters strange,
  But poor men pay for all.

Methought I was in the country,
  Where poor men take great pains
And labour hard continually
  Only for rich men's gains:
Like th'Israelites in Egypt,
  The poor are kept in thrall;
The task-masters are playing kept,
  But poor men pay for all.

jetting: strutting

WILLIAM WALWYN (active 1640s)   21 August 1648

From *The Bloody Project*, in Haller and Davies, eds., *Leveller Tracts*,
pp. 138, 145

The pamphlet was issued in the interval between the victory over the Scots at
Preston on 17 August and the final triumph of the Army at Colchester on the
27th, protesting at the miseries of the times and calling for constitutional reforms,
as defined by Lilburne and his movement in the *Earnest Petition*, against the factions for King, Parliament and the House of Lords, whose only quarrel seems to
be 'whose slaves the people shall be'. Though apparently written by 'W. P.
Gent.', the pamphlet has been attributed to Walwyn by Haller and others on 'the
evidence of style and substance'.

. . . You have seen the Common-wealth enslaved for want of Parliaments, and also by their sudden dissolution, and you rejoiced that this Parliament was not to be dissolved by the King; but did you conceive it would have sat seven years to so little purpose, or that it should ever have come to pass, to be esteemed a crime to move for the ending thereof? Was the perpetuating of this Parliament, and the oppressions they have brought upon you and yours, a part of that Liberty of the People you fought for? Or was it for such a Privilege of Parliament, that they only might have liberty to oppress at their pleasure, without any hope of remedy? If all these put together make not up the cause for which you fought, what was the Cause? What have ye obtained to the People, but these Liberties, for they must not be called oppressions? These are the fruits of all those vast disbursements, and those thousands of lives that have been spent and destroyed in the late War . . .

. . . Oh therefore all you Soldiers and People, that have your consciences alive about you, put to your strength of Judgement, and all the might you have to prevent a further effusion of blood. Let not the covetous, the proud, the bloodthirsty man bear sway amongst you; fear not their high looks, give no ear to their charms, their promises or tears. They have no strength without you. Forsake them and ye will be strong for good. Adhere to them, and they will be strong to evil; for which you must answer, and give an account at the last day.

The King, Parliament, great men in the City and Army, have made you but the stairs by which they have mounted to Honour, Wealth and Power. The only quarrel that hath been, and at present is but this, namely, whose slaves the people shall be. All the power that any hath was but a trust conveyed from you to them, to be employed by them for your good. They have mis-employed their power, and instead of preserving you, have destroyed you. All Power and Authority is perverted from the King to the Constable, and it is no other but the policy of Statesmen to keep you divided by creating jealousies and fears among you, to the end that their Tyranny and Injustice may pass undiscovered and unpunished. But the people's safety is the supreme Law; and if a people must not be left without a means to preserve itself against the King, by the same rule they may preserve themselves against the Parliament and Army too, if they pervert the end for which they received their power, to wit the Nation's safety. Therefore speedily unite yourselves together, and as one man stand up for the defence of your Freedom, and for the establishment of such equal rules of Government for the future, as shall lay a firm foundation of peace and happiness to all the people without partiality. Let Justice be your breastplate, and you shall need to fear no enemies, for you shall strike a terror to your now insulting oppressors, and force all the Nation's Peace to fly before you. Prosecute and prosper.

Vale.

JOHN MILTON (1608–74)   1648

Sonnet, *On the Lord General Fairfax, at the Siege of Colchester*

Sir Thomas Fairfax (1612–71) was the General who led the Army to victory at Marston Moor (1644) and Naseby (1645), which decided the outcome of the First Civil War. When the Second Civil War began in 1648, Cromwell led the Parliamentary forces in south Wales, and then against the Scots, while Fairfax had charge of those in the south and east. After he had driven the Royalists out of Kent – some of whom crossed the Thames to join those who had risen in Essex at Colchester – Fairfax followed them and laid siege to the town, ultimately forcing it to surrender because of famine. Afterwards, though he stayed on as Commander-in-Chief, power passed from him to Cromwell and Ireton. He favoured sparing the King's life, but bowed to the general verdict, and in the following year retired into private life.

———

Fairfax, whose name in arms through Europe rings
   Filling each mouth with envy or with praise,
   And all her jealous monarchs with amaze
   And rumours loud, that daunt remotest kings;
Thy firm unshaken virtue ever brings
   Victory home, though new rebellions raise
   Their Hydra heads, and the false North displays
   Her broken league, to imp their serpent wings.
O yet a nobler task awaits thy hand;
   For what can war but endless war still breed,
   Till truth and right from violence be freed,
And public faith clear'd from the shameful brand
   Of public fraud? In vain doth Valour bleed,
   While Avarice and Rapine share the land.

JOHN HARRIS

Mercurius Militaris, No. 1, p. 5

10 October 1648

KING AND PEOPLE

What doth Parliament but mock his sacred Majesty in proposing anything to him to be confirmed? . . . I wonder what strength it would add, or what goodness to the propositions if he should sign them; can a single man compel 300,000 men to observe them when they are laws? Or can he compel them to break them? What virtue unknown is in this name Carolus Rex? Why is this name adored more than another? Write that and Denzil Holles together, is not this as fair a name? Weigh them, is it not as heavy? Conjure with them, Denzil Holles will start a spirit as soon as the name Carolus Rex: and yet this mere puff of breath, this powerless name King Charles set so high in the vulgar hearts, that what would be vice in others his name like richest alchemy change to virtue and worthiness and the subscribing this name to that which he can neither help nor hinder, must set him above his masters and conquerors, and permit him to bestride this narrow world like a colossus, when you victors must walk like petty slaves, and peep about under his huge legs to find yourselves dishonourable graves: *praemoniti praemuniti*.

GERRARD WINSTANLEY
(1609–after 1660)

16 October 1648

Postcript to *Truth Lifting up its Head Above Scandals*, in *Works*, pp. 145–6

REASON AS KING

If Reason, King, do rule in thee,
   There's truth, and peace, and clemency:
No rash distemper will there be,
   No filthy lusts, but chastity.
In all thy actions to behold,
   Just dealing, love, as pure as gold.
When Reason rules in whole mankind,
   Nothing but peace, will all men find:
Their hearts he makes both meek, and kind,
   And troublesome thoughts he throws behind.

For he is truth, and love, and peace,
  Makes wars and lewdness for to cease.
He makes no prisons for the poor,
  He doth condemn and judge the whore:
He makes all men to sin no more,
  As they have done in times before;
But restores all to what hath been,
  And heals the creature of his sin.
And why do men so clamour then,
  Against this powerful King in men?

GERRARD WINSTANLEY
(1609–after 1660)

26 January 1649

From *The New Law of Righteousnesse*, in *Works*, pp. 159, 170–72

Winstanley, 'the son (probably) of a Wigan mercer with Puritan sympathies,' as Christopher Hill notes, 'came to London as a clothing apprentice in 1630, and set up for himself in 1637. But it was the worst possible time; by 1643 Winstanley had been "beaten out of both estate and trade". In 1649 he was described as of Walton-on-Thames. Here he herded cows, apparently as a hired labourer, and wrote religious pamphlets' (Hill, *World Turned Upside Down*, p. 112).

He is in many ways the most remarkable radical voice to emerge out of the ferment of change that defines this extraordinary period, not only as the leader of the Diggers who took possession of common land on St George's Hill, Walton-on-Thames, on 1 April 1649 in a symbolic act of cooperative ownership, but as a thinker and writer of genius who laid down clearly defined conditions for the establishment of a communist system of economic equality. His concept of social rights and liberties (at once Christian and materialist) in fact stressed the basic natural rights of man, his economic rights, the earth as 'a common treasury of livelihood to whole mankind'; and it is thus clearly distinguished from the constitutionalist, more purely political, emphasis made by the official Leveller leaders, and by Lilburne in particular, who repudiated the 'erroneous tenets' of the Diggers, and accepted the sanctity of private property. Winstanley indeed described himself as a True Leveller, since he really believed in making all common, calculating that 'if the waste land of England were manured by her children, it would become in a few years the richest, the strongest and most flourishing land in the world'. (Sabine, p. 414). Which is not to say that he was the first to make such claims. In December 1648 a local group of Levellers produced a pamphlet, *Light Shining in Buckinghamshire*, calling for equality of property, and thus preceding his announcement of communist action. Nor were St George's Hill or Cobham Heath, to which his colony moved till finally dispersed in April 1650, the only examples of such communal action among the poor; for by 1650 we know that there were at least thirty-four Digger colonies scattered throughout the Home Counties. But it is Winstanley's eloquence, his originality, lucidity and conviction, the consistency of his vision of a shared world that brings the movement into focus; and he survives as a compelling witness to an extraordinary episode in English history. He maintained that private property, competitive buying and selling, the economic and institutional structure of society, were the cause of all oppression, bondage and war, and that religion itself served as an instrument of class rule to dispossess men of their natural rights. For him, God was to be known by the senses, 'in the clear-sighted experience of one single creature, man, by seeing, hearing, tasting, smelling, feeling' (Sabine, p. 165). For him, 'the public preachers have cheated the whole world by telling us of a single man called Adam that killed us all by eating a single fruit, called an apple' (Sabine, p. 203). Whereas in fact 'the apple that the first man eats is . . . the objects of the Creation' (p. 176), and 'we may see Adam every day before our eyes walking up and down the street' (p. 120) because, for Winstanley, Adam is mankind. 'Work together; eat bread together,' he declares. 'When mankind began to quarrel about the earth, and some would have all and shut out others, forcing them to be servants; this was man's fall' (p. 156).

The New Law of Righteousnesse, was issued two months before the setting up of the colony on St George's Hill.

MINE, THINE, OURS

. . . Let all men say what they will, so long as such are Rulers as call the Land theirs, upholding this particular propriety of *Mine* and *Thine*; the common-people shall never have their liberty, nor the Land ever [be] freed from troubles, oppressions and complainings; by reason whereof the Creator of all things is continually provoked. O thou proud selfish governing *Adam*, in this land called *England*! Know that the cries of the poor, whom thou layeth heavy oppressions upon, is heard . . .

. . . Therefore you dust of the earth, that are trod under foot, you poor people, that makes both scholars and rich men your oppressors by your labours, Take notice of your privilege, the Law of Righteousnesse is now declared.

All the men and women in *England*, are all children of this Land, and the earth is the Lord's, not particular men's that claims a proper interest in it above others, which is the devil's power.

But be it so, that some will say. This is my Land, and call such and such a parcel of Land his own interest; Then saith the Lord, let such an one labour that parcel of Land by his own hands, none helping him: for whosoever shall help that man to labour his proper earth, as he calls it

199

for wages, the hand of the Lord shall be upon such labourers; for they lift up flesh above the spirit, by their labours, and so hold the Creation still under bondage.

Therefore if the rich will still hold fast this propriety of *Mine and Thine*, let them labour their own land with their own hands. And let the common-people, that are the gatherings together of Israel from under that bondage, and that say the earth is ours, not mine, let them labour together, and eat bread together upon the Commons, Mountains, and Hills.

For as the enclosures are called such a man's Land, and such a man's Land; so the Commons and Heath, are called the common-people's, and let the world see who labours the earth in righteousnesse, and . . . let them be the people that shall inherit the earth. Whether they that hold a civil propriety, saying, *This is mine*, which is selfish, devilish and destructive to the Creation, or those that hold a common right, saying, *The earth is ours*, which lifts up the Creation from bondage.

Was the earth made for to preserve a few covetous, proud men, to live at ease, and for them to bag and barn up the treasures of the earth from others, that they might beg or starve in a fruitful Land, or was it made to preserve all her children? Let Reason, and the Prophets' and Apostles' writings be judge, the earth is the Lord's, it is not to be confined to particular interest.

None can say, Their right is taken from them; for let the rich work alone by themselves, and let the poor work together by themselves; the rich in their enclosures, saying, *This is mine*; the poor upon the Commons, saying, *This is ours*, the earth and fruits are common.

And who can be offended at the poor for doing this? Name but covetous, proud, lazy, pampered flesh, that would have the poor still to work for the devil (particular interest) to maintain his greatness, that he may live at ease . . .

JOHN MILTON (1608–74)   February 1649

From *The Tenure of Kings and Magistrates*, in *Prose Writings*, pp. 201–2, 202–3

Milton published his pamphlet a fortnight after the execution of Charles I, urging the justice of tyrannicide, and setting out to prove 'that it is lawful, and hath been held so through all ages, for any who have the power, to call to account a tyrant, or wicked king, and after due conviction, to depose, and put him to death, if the ordinary magistrate have neglected, or denied to do it'. Soor after writing *The Tenure*, and perhaps in response to this work, the Council of State offered him the post of Secretary for Foreign Tongues. Thus, as Christopher Hill puts it, 'John Milton, Englishman, found himself defending his country in the face of Europe.'

THE JUST RIGHT OF A FREE NATION

. . . Surely they that shall boast, as we do, to be a free nation, and not have in themselves the power to remove or to abolish any governor supreme, or subordinate, with the government itself upon urgent causes, may please their fancy with a ridiculous and painted freedom, fit to cozen babies; but are indeed under tyranny and servitude, as wanting that power which is the root and source of all liberty, to dispose and econ-omise in the land which God hath given them, as masters of family in their own house and free inheritance. Without which natural and essential power of a free nation, though bearing high their heads, they can in due esteem be thought no better than slaves and vassals born, in the tenure and occupation of another inheriting lord, whose government, though not illegal or intolerable, hangs over them as a lordly scourge, not as a free government – and therefore to be abrogated.

TO FLING OFF TYRANNY

Though perhaps till now no protestant state or kingdom can be alleged to have openly put to death their king, which lately some have written and imputed to their great glory, much mistaking the matter, it is not, neither ought to be, the glory of a protestant state never to have put their king to death; it is the glory of a protestant king never to have deserved death. And if the parliament and military council do what they do with-out precedent, if it appear their duty, it argues the more wisdom, virtue, and magnanimity, that they know themselves able to be a precedent to others; who perhaps in future ages, if they prove not too degenerate, will look up with honour and aspire towards these exemplary and matchless deeds of their ancestors, as to the highest top of their civil glory and emulation; which heretofore, in the pursuance of fame and foreign dominion, spent itself vaingloriously abroad, but henceforth may learn a better fortitude – to dare execute highest justice on them that shall by force of arms endeavour the oppressing and bereaving of religion and their liberty at home: that no unbridled potentate or tyrant, but to his sorrow, for the future may presume such high and irresponsible licence over mankind, to havoc and turn upside down whole kingdoms of men, as though they were no more in respect of his perverse will than a nation of pismires.

WILLIAM WALWYN (active 1640s) 23 February 1649

From *The Vanitie of the Present Churches*, in Haller and Davies, eds., *Leveller Tracts*, pp. 271–2

The style and the viewpoint suggest that Walwyn is the author of this piece. In it, according to the title-page, not only the vanity of the Churches, but the 'uncertainty of their Preaching' and 'the pretended immediate teaching of the Spirit' are attacked and denied, as against 'the all-sufficiency of the Scriptures'.

COUNTERFEIT PREACHING

. . . Neither will men ever live in peace, and quietness one with another, so long as this veil of false counterfeit preaching remaineth before their eyes, nor until the mock Churches are overturned and laid flat; For as long as men flatter themselves in those vain ways, and puff themselves up with vain thoughts, that they are in a way well pleasing to God, because they are in a Church way . . . little or nothing caring, either for public Justice, Peace, or freedom amongst men; but spend their time in endless disputes, in condemning and censuring those that are contrary minded; whereby nothing but heats and discontents are engendered, backbiting and snarling at all that oppose them, will neither buy, nor sell with them, if they can choose, nor give them so much as a good look; but on all occasions are ready to Censure, one to be carnal, another erroneous; one an Atheist, another an Heretic, a Sectary, Schismatic, a Blasphemer, a man not worthy to live, though they have nothing whereof to accuse him . . .

So that it were much better for the Common-wealth, that all men's minds were set at Liberty from these entanglements, that so there might be an end of wrangling about shadows . . .

Certainly, were all busied only in those short necessary truths, we should soon become practical Christians and take more pleasure in Feeding the hungry, Clothing the naked, visiting and comforting of the sick, relieving the aged, weak and impotent; in delivering of Prisoners, supporting of poor families, or in freeing a Common-wealth from all Tyrants, oppressors, and deceivers . . . thereby manifesting our universal love to all mankind, without respect of persons, Opinions, Societies, or Churches. Doubtless there were no way like unto this, to adorn the Gospel of Christ. Men and women so exercising themselves, and persevering therein, might possibly deserve the name of Saints; but for men to assume that title for being a Presbyter, an Independent, Brownist, Anabaptist, or for being of this or that opinion, or of this or that form of Worship, or for being able to Pray, and Preach (as they call it) three or four hours together, venting their own uncertain notions, and conjectures, or for looking more sadly and solemnly than other people, or for dressing themselves after a peculiar manner . . . or for sucking in, and sighing out reproaches, and slanders, against their neighbours: proceeds from mere pride and vanity of mind; when as the best of these put altogether, amount not to so much, towards the making of a true Saint, as one merciful tender-hearted compassionate act, for Christ's sake doth . . .

JOHN LILBURNE,   24 March 1649
RICHARD OVERTON, THOMAS PRINCE

From *The Second Part of Englands New Chains Discovered*, in Haller and Davies, eds., *Leveller Tracts*, pp. 172–3, 183, 184–5, 186

The pamphlet presents a detailed record of the 'wicked and pernicious designs' first of Parliament, King and Lords, and then (after the end of the Second Civil War) of Parliament and the Council of State, against Levellers and other dissentient groups. With the King beheaded, and the monarchy and the House of Lords abolished (30 January, 17 and 19 March respectively), the Council of State (formed on 17 February) was already alarmed at the unrest in the army. Thus, it responded immediately to the pamphlet. First, on 26 March, Milton was instructed to 'make some observations' – though the poet abstained, and never at any time wrote a word against the Levellers; then, on 27 March the House of Commons decreed that 'the Authors, Contrivers, and Framers of the said Paper are guilty of High Treason; and shall be proceeded against as Traitors'; and on 28 March, Lilburne, Overton, Prince and Walwyn were arrested in the peremptory manner described in the *Picture of the Council of State* and in Walwyn's *The Fountain of Slander*. Such action seemed a blunt confirmation of Lilburne's charge that the state had reverted to 'the grossest Principles and practices of long settled Tyrannies'.

WHAT FREEDOM IS THERE LEFT?

To the Supreme Authority of England, the Representors of the People, in Parliament Assembled. The Sad Representation of the uncertain and dangerous Condition of the Common-wealth: By the Presenters and Approvers of the Large Petition of the 11 of September, 1648

If our hearts were not over-charged with the sense of the present miseries and approaching dangers of the Nation, your small regard to our late serious Apprehensions, would have kept us silent; but the misery, danger, and bondage threatened is so great, imminent, and apparent, that whilst we have breath, and are not violently restrained, we cannot but speak, and even cry aloud, until you hear us, or God be pleased otherwise to relieve us . . .

The Removing the King, the taking away the House of Lords, the overawing the House, and reducing it to that pass, that it is become but the Channel, through which is conveyed all the Decrees and Determinations of a private Council of some few Officers, the erecting of their Court of Justice, and their Council of State, The Voting of the People of Supreme Power, and this House the Supreme Authority: all these Particulars, (though many of them in order to good ends, have been desired by Well-affected People) are yet become, (as they have managed them) of sole conducement to their ends and Intents, either by removing such as stood in the way between them and Power, wealth or command of the Common-wealth; or by actually possessing and investing them in the same . . .

. . . They may talk of freedom, but what freedom indeed is there, so long as they stop the Press, which is indeed and hath been so accounted in all free Nations, the most essential part thereof, employing an Apostate Judas for executioner therein who hath been twice burnt in the hand, a wretched fellow, that even the Bishops and Star-chamber would have shamed to own. What freedom is there left, when honest and worthy Soldiers are sentenced and enforced to ride the horse with their faces reverst, and their swords broken over their heads for but Petitioning and presenting a Letter in justification of their Liberty therein? If this be not a new way of breaking the spirits of the English, which Strafford and Canterbury never dreamt of, we know no difference of things. A taste also of Liberty of Conscience they have given us in the Case of a worthy

Member of your House; so as we may well judge what is like to follow, if their Reign continue. And as for Peace, whilst the supreme Officers of the Army are supreme in your House, in the Council of State, and all in all in the general Council of the Army, when the martial power is indeed supreme to the Civil Authority, what Peace can be expected. We profess we see no councils tending to it, but hereof mighty and vast sums of money to be taxed upon the People *per mensem*, as if war were become the only trade, or as if the people were bound to maintain Armies whether they have trade or no; yea, whether they have bread or no.

And as for the prosperity of the Nation; what one thing hath been done that tendeth to it? Nay, hath any thing been done since they were in power? but what increaseth the rancour, hatred, and malice, which our late unhappy differences have begotten amongst us, as if they had placed their happiness and security in the total division of the People, nothing being offered by them that hath any face of reconcilement in it, nothing of cheerfulness or general satisfaction, the mother of trade and plenty, that might take away the private remembrances and distinctions of parties, nothing indeed, but what tendeth to implacable bitterness of spirit, the mother of confusion, penury, and beggary.

Nay what sense of the heavy burdens of the people have they manifested of late, hath it not been by their procurement that the Judges their creatures have a thousand a year allowed to every one of them above the ordinary fees? which were ever esteemed a heavy oppression in themselves. Is there any abridgement of the charge or length of time, in trial of causes? Are they touch'd with the general burden of Tithes, that canker of industry and tillage? Or with that of Excise, which out of the bowels of labourers and poor people enriches the Usurers, and other Caterpillars of the Common-wealth? Or what have they done to free Trade from the intolerable burden of Customs? except the setting of fresh hungry flies, upon the old sores of the People? . . .

. . . Oh wretched England, that seeth, and yet suffereth such intolerable masters! What can be expected from such Officers, who frequently manifest a thirst after the blood of such People, and Soldiers, as are most active for the common Freedom, peace and prosperity of the Commonwealth . . . or . . . from such a Council in the Army, as shall agree that the supreme Authority should be moved to make a law, That that Council of Officers may have Power to have and put to death all such persons, though not of the Army, as they should judge, were disturbers of the Army . . .

JOHN LILBURNE,   1–4 April 1649
RICHARD OVERTON, THOMAS PRINCE

From *The Picture of the Council of State*, in Haller and Davies, eds., *Leveller Tracts*, pp. 206–7, 227–8, 230–21, 236

This pamphlet consists of statements by John Lilburne, Richard Overton and Thomas Prince, recounting the circumstances of their arrest, together with William Walwyn, on a charge of having been involved in writing *The Second Part of Englands New Chaines*, considered by the Council of State, headed by Cromwell, as 'Seditious and Destructive to the present Government'. The accused were marched to Whitehall in the early hours of the morning of 28 March and later that day brought before the Council to answer the charge before being committed to the Tower of London on suspicion of high treason. Each man provides his own report of the proceedings, 'bearing testimony to the Liberties of England against the present Tyrants at White-hall, and their Associates', for they were not to be stopped from answering back, though it is clear that Cromwell was now determined to break the Leveller movement, as subsequent events, culminating in the suppression of the Leveller revolt at Burford in May, were to demonstrate.

PROTESTS

From John Lilburne's answer to the Council of State

. . . If it should be granted this Parliament at the beginning had a legal constitution from the people (the original and fountain of all just power) yet the Faction of a traitorous party of Officers of the Army, hath twice rebelled against the Parliament, and broke them to pieces, and by force of Arms culled out whom they please, and imprisoned divers of them and laid nothing to their charge, and have left only in a manner a few men . . . of their own Faction behind them that will like Spaniel-dogs serve their lusts and wills . . . styling them a mock Parliament, a mock power at Windsor, yea, it is yet their expressions at London. And if this be true that they are a mock power and a mock Parliament; then,

Query, Whether in Law or Justice, especially considering they have fallen from all their many glorious promises, and have not done any one action that tends to the universal good of the People? Can those Gentlemen sitting at Westminster in the House, called the House of Commons, be any other than a Factious company of men traitorously combined together with Cromwell, Ireton, and Harrison, to subdue the Laws, Liberties, and Freedoms of England . . . and to set up an absolute and perfect Tyranny of the Sword, Will and pleasure, and absolutely intend the destroying the Trade of the Nation, and the absolute impoverishing the people thereof, to fit them to their Vassals and Slaves? And if so, then,

Query, Whether the Free People of England, as well Soldiers as others, ought not to contemn all these men's commands, as invalid and illegal in themselves, and as one man to rise up against them as so many professed traitors, thieves, robbers and highwaymen, and apprehend and bring them to justice in a new Representative, chosen by virtue of a just Agreement among the People, there being no other way in the world to preserve the Nation but that alone . . .?

From Richard Overton's answer to the Council of State

. . . Who would have thought in the days of their glorious pretences for Freedom, in the days of their Engagements, Declarations and Remonstrances, while they were the hope of the oppressed, the Joy of the righteous, and had the mighty confluence of all the afflicted and well-minded people of the land about them . . . I say, who would have thought to have heard, seen, or felt such things from their hands as we have done? Who would have thought such glorious and hopeful beginnings should have vanished into Tyranny? Who would have thought to have seen those men end in the persecution and imprisonment of persons whom their own Consciences tell them, to be men of known integrity to the Common-wealth; and which is so evident and demonstrative, that thousands in this Nation can bear Record thereof; and that those men should be so devilish, so tyrannical and arbitrary, as after their imprisonment to rake hell, and skim the Devil, to conjure out matter of charge or accusation against them, that they might have their blood, as in our case they have done, sending abroad their blood-hounds to search and pry out in every corner, what could be made out against us . . . that so our friends and brethren (thus surprised and overtaken) may become our Butchers, and think they do God and their Country good service while they slay us? But let them beware how they contract the guilt of our blood upon their heads; for assuredly the blood of the Innocent will be upon them, and God will repay it. I speak not this to beg their mercy, I abhor it, I bid defiance to what all the men and devils in earth or hell can do against me in the discharge of my understanding and Conscience for the good of this Common-wealth . . .

I confess, for my part, I am a man full of Sin and personal Infirmities, and in that Relation I will not take upon me to clear or justify myself; but as for my Integrity and uprightness to the Common-wealth, to whatsoever my understanding tells me is for the good of mankind, for the safety, freedom, and tranquillity of my Country, happiness and prosperity of my Neighbours, to do to my neighbour as I would be done by, and for the freedom and protection of Religious people: I say as to those things . . . I know my integrity to be such, that I shall freely (in the might of God) sacrifice my life to give witness thereunto. And upon that Accompt I am now in Bonds, a protestor against the Aristocratical Tyranny of the Council of State, scorning their Mercy, and bidding defiance to their Cruelty, had they ten millions more of Armies and Cromwells to perpetrate their inhumanities upon me. For I know they can pass but to this life. When they have done that, they can do no more; and in this case of mine, he that will save his life shall lose it. I know my life is hid in Christ, and if upon this accompt I must yield it, Welcome, welcome, welcome by the grace of God.

And as for these reproaches and scandals like the smoke of the bottomless pit, that are fomented against me; whereby too many zealous tender-spirited people are prejudiced against my person, ready to abhor the thing I do, though never so good, for my person sake; I desire such to remove their eyes from persons to things. If the thing I do be good, it is of God; and so look upon it, and not upon me, and so they shall be sure not to mistake themselves, nor to wrong me . . . So that the business is, not how great a sinner I am, but how faithful and real to the Common-wealth; that's the matter concerneth my neighbour, and whereof my neighbour is only in this public Controversy to take notice; and for my personal sins that are not of Civil cognizance or wrong unto him, to leave them to God, whose judgement is righteous and just. And till persons professing Religion be brought to this sound temper, they fall far short of Christianity. The spirit of love, brotherly charity, doing to all men as they would be done by, is not in them; without which they are but as a sounding brass, and a tinkling cymbal, a whited wall, rottenness and corruption, let their ceremonial formal practice of Religion be never so Angel-like or specious.

From Thomas Prince's answer to the Council of State

Sir, I am an Englishman, and therefore lay claim to all the Rights and Liberties which belongeth unto an Englishman; and God gave me such knowledge, that in the very first beginning of the late Wars I gave my cheerful assistance against those that would rule over the people by their own wills, and upon that account, I adventured my life, and lost much blood in defence of the Common-wealth, and all along to this day have assisted in person and purse, to my utmost abilities, and I am the same man still to withstand Tyranny in any whomsoever.

Sir, I hate no man in the world, only the evil in any man I hate.

Sir, all those good things which my conscience and my actions will witness, I have done in behalf of the Common-wealth; I desire they may be all laid aside, and not come in the balance, as to hinder any punishment that can be inflicted upon me for breaking any known Law.

Sir, that which makes a man an offender, is for a breach of a Law, and that Law ought to be made before the offence is committed. Sir, although I have fought and assisted against the wills and tyranny of men, yet I have not fought to overthrow the known Laws of the Land; for if there be no Law to protect my Estate, Liberty and Life, but to be left to the will of men, to the power of the Sword, to be abused at pleasure, as I have been this day, contrary to Law, being fetched from my wife and family. Sir, by the same rule you may send for my wife and children, and for all my estate, and the next time, if you please, to destroy all my neighbours; nay all in the City, and so from County to County, until you destroy as many as you please.

Sir, I have heard talk of Levellers, but I am sure this is levelling indeed, and I do here before you abhor such doings, and I do protest against them.

Sir, There is a known Law in this Land: if I have wronged any man, let him take his course in Law against me, I fear not what any man in England can do to me by Law; and, Sir, the Law I lay claim unto, as my right, to protect me from violence.

Sir, the Parliament hath lately declared, they would maintain the Law; but I am sure their and your dealing by me declares to the contrary.

JOHN LILBURNE,   14 April 1649
WILLIAM WALWYN, THOMAS PRINCE,
RICHARD OVERTON

From *A Manifestation*, in Haller and Davies, eds., *Leveller Tracts*, p. 277

This was written from imprisonment in the Tower, probably by Walwyn, though he calls the work 'our joint Manifestation', in which 'is to be seen all our very hearts, and wherein all our four heads and hands were nigh equally employed' (p. 276).

DUTY AND CONSCIENCE

Since no man is born for himself only, but obliged by the Laws of Nature (which reaches all) of Christianity (which engages us as Christians) and of Public Society and Government, to employ our endeavours for the advancement of a communitive Happiness, of equal concernment to others as ourselves: here have we (according to that measure of understanding God hath dispensed unto us) laboured with much weakness indeed, but with integrity of heart, to produce out of the Common Calamities, such a proportion of Freedom and good to the Nation, as might somewhat compensate its many grievances and lasting sufferings. And although in doing thereof we have hitherto reaped only Reproach and hatred for our good Will, and been fain to wrestle with the violent passions of Powers and Principalities; yet since it is nothing so much as our Blessed Master and his Followers suffered before us, and but what at first we reckoned upon, we cannot be thereby any whit dismayed in the performance of our duties supported inwardly by the Innocency and evenness of our Consciences . . .

WILLIAM WALWYN
(active 1640s)

Prepared April
(published 30 May) 1649

From *The Fountain of Slaunder*, in Haller and Davies, eds., *Leveller Tracts*, pp. 246–7

Walwyn, arrested with the others, for being associated with *The Second Part of Englands New Chains*, apparently had no hand in it. He wrote this justification from the Tower, 'for satisfaction of Friends and Enemies'.

INJUSTICE

I never proposed any man for my enemy, but injustice, oppression, innovation, arbitrary power, and cruelty. Where I found them, I ever opposed myself against them; but so as to destroy the evil but to preserve the person: And therefore all the war I have made . . . hath been to get victory over the understandings of men, accounting it a more worthy and profitable labour to beget friends to the Cause I loved, rather than to molest men's persons, or confiscate men's estates . . .

210

And hence it is, that I have pursued the settlement of the Government of this Nation by an Agreement of the People; as firmly hoping thereby, to see the Common-wealth past all possibility of returning into a slavish condition; though in pursuit thereof, I have met with very hard and fro-ward measure from some that pretended to be really for it. So that do what I will for the good of my native Country, I receive still nothing but evil for my labour. All I speak, or purpose, is construed to the worst; and though never so good, fares the worse for my proposing; and all by reason of those many aspersions cast upon me.

If any thing be displeasing, or judged dangerous, or thought worthy of punishment, then Walwyn's the Author; and no matter, says one, if Walwyn had been destroyed long ago: says another, Let's get a law to have power ourselves to hang all such: and this openly, and yet unre-proved; affronted in open Court; asperst in every corner; threatened wherever I pass; and within this last month of March, was twice adver-tised by Letters, of secret contrivances and resolutions to imprison me.

And so accordingly . . . upon the 28th of March last, by Warrant of the Council of State; I that might have been fetched by the least inti-mation of their desire to speak with me, was sent for . . . under Sergeant Bradshaw's hand, backed with a strong party of horse and foot, com-manded by Adjutant General Stubber . . . who placing his soldiers in the alleys, houses, and gardens round about my house, knocked violently at my garden gate, between four and five in the morning; which being opened by my maid, the Adjutant General, with many soldiers, entered, and immediately dispersed themselves about the garden, and in my house, to the great terror of my Family; my poor maid coming up to me, crying and shivering, with news that Soldiers were come for me, in such a sad distempered manner (for she could hardly speak) as was suf-ficient to have daunted one that had been used to such sudden surprisals; much more my Wife, who for two and twenty years we have lived together, never had known me under a minute's restraint by any Authority . . .

BULSTRODE WHITELOCKE
(1605–75)

26 April 1649

From *Memorials of the English Affairs*, p. 385a, col. 2

With the Leveller demands deliberately shelved by the Generals, and Cromwell now determined to reassert control over the Army, confrontation was inevitable. And when unrest among the rank and file broke out in a regiment at Bishopsgate into open mutiny, Private Lockyer was arrested as one of the leaders and singled out for execution as a warning to the rest. He was shot in St Paul's Churchyard. The Levellers responded by giving him a martyr's funeral.

A LEVELLER FUNERAL

About one hundred went before the Corpse, five or six in a file; the Corpse was then brought, with six trumpets sounding a soldier's knell; then the Trooper's horse came, clothed all over in mourning and led by a footman. The corpse was adorned with bundles of Rosemary, one half stained in blood; and the Sword of the deceased along with them. Some thousands followed in rank and file: all had sea-green-and-black Ribbon tied on their hats, and to their breasts: and the women brought up the rear. At the new Churchyard in Westminster, some thousands more of the better sort met them, who thought not fit to march through the City. Many looked on this funeral as an affront to the Parliament and the Army; others called these people Levellers; but they took no notice of any of them.

GERRARD WINSTANLEY
(1609–after 1660)

26 April 1649

From *The True Levellers Standard Advanced*, in *Works*, p. 251–62 passim

On 1 April 1649 about twenty poor men, led by Winstanley and William Everard, assembled at St George's Hill, Surrey, took possession of the common land and began to cultivate it. The justice of that action is here affirmed, 'showing the cause why the common people of England have begun, and gives consent to dig up, manure, and sow corn upon George-hill in Surrey . . .'

TRUE LEVELLERS

In the beginning of time the great creator Reason made the Earth to be a common treasury, to preserve beasts, birds, fishes and man, the lord that was to govern this creation . . . but not one word was spoken in the beginning, that one branch of mankind should rule over another.

And the reason is this, every single man, male and female, is a perfect creature of himself; and the same spirit that made the globe dwells in every man to govern the globe; so that the flesh of man being subject to Reason, his maker, hath him to be his teacher and ruler within himself . . .

But since human flesh (that king of beasts) began to delight himself in the objects of the creation, more than in the spirit reason and righteousness, who manifests himself to be the indweller in the five senses, of hearing, seeing, tasting, smelling, feeling; then he fell into blindness of mind and weakness of heart, and runs abroad for a teacher and ruler. And so selfish imagination . . . did set up one man to teach and rule over another; and thereby the spirit was killed, and man was brought into bondage, and became a greater slave to such of his own kind, than the beasts of the field were to him. And hereupon the earth . . . was hedged into enclosures by the teachers and rulers, and the others were made servants and slaves. And that earth that is within this creation, made a common storehouse for all, is bought and sold, and kept in the hands of a few, whereby the great creator is mightily dishonoured, as if he were a respecter of persons, delighting in the comfortable livelihood of some and rejoicing in the miserable poverty and straits of others. From the beginning it was not so . . .

But when once the earth becomes a common treasury again, as it must . . . then this enmity of all lands will cease, and none shall dare to seek domination over others, neither shall any dare to kill another, nor desire more of the earth than another . . .

We are made to hold forth this declaration to you that are the great council, and to you the great Army of the land of England, that you may know what we should have and what you are bound to give us by your covenants and promises; and that you may join with us in this work and so find peace. Or else, if you do oppose us, we have peace in our work and in declaring this report: and you shall be left without excuse.

The work we are going about is this, to dig up George Hill and the waste ground thereabout, and to sow corn, and to eat our bread together by the sweat of our brows . . .

Take notice that England is not a free people till the poor that have no land have a free allowance to dig and labour the commons, and so live as comfortably as the landlords that live in their enclosures. For the people have not laid out their monies and shed their blood that their landlords, the Norman power, should still have its liberty and freedom to rule in tyranny in his lords, landlords, judges, justices, bailiffs and state servants; but that the oppressed might be set free, prison doors opened, and the poor people's hearts comforted by an universal consent of making the earth a common treasury, that they may live together as one house of Israel, united in brotherly love into one spirit; and having a comfortable livelihood in the community of one earth, their mother . . .

And truly, you councillors and powers of the earth, know this, that wheresoever there is a people, thus united . . . it will become the strongest land in the world; for then they will be as one man to defend their inheritance; and salvation (which is liberty and peace) is the walls and bulwarks of that land or city.

Whereas on the other side, pleading for property and single interest divides the people of a land, and the whole world into parties, and is the cause of all wars and bloodshed and contention everywhere . . .

ELIZABETH LILBURNE AND OTHERS
5 May 1649

From *A Petition of Women, Affectors and Approvers of the Petition of September 11th 1648*, in Woodhouse, ed., *Puritanism and Liberty*, pp. 367–8

Among a number of petitions protesting against the arrest of the Leveller leaders on 28 March, this was probably initiated by Lilburne's wife Elizabeth, who was clearly not the kind of woman to sit back and let things happen. 'Of a gallant and true masculine spirit', as Lilburne himself describes her, she actively promoted her husband's rights. In 1642, after he had been taken prisoner by the Royalists at Edgehill, she had gone to Parliament in person to appeal for his safety; in 1646 she and other women had got up a Petition for his release from the Tower; and she was to frame at least one more petition in September 1649.

AN EQUAL INTEREST WITH MEN

Showeth,

That since we are assured of our creation in the image of God, and of an interest in Christ equal unto men, as also of a proportionable share in the freedoms of this commonwealth, we cannot but wonder and grieve that we should appear so despicable in your eyes as to be thought unworthy to petition or represent our grievances to this honourable House. Have we not an equal interest with the men of this nation in those liberties and securities contained in the *Petition of Right*, and other the good laws of the land? Are any of our lives, limbs, liberties, or goods to be taken from us more than from men, but by due process of law and conviction of twelve sworn men of the neighbourhood? And can you imagine us to be so sottish or stupid as not to perceive, or not to be sensible when daily those strong defences of our peace and welfare are broken down and trod underfoot by force and arbitrary power?

Would you have us keep at home in our houses, when men of such faithfulness and integrity as the four prisoners, our friends in the Tower, are fetched out of their beds and forced from their houses by soldiers, to the affrighting and undoing of themselves, their wives, children, and families? Are not our husbands, our selves, our daughters and families, by the same rule as liable to the like unjust cruelties as they? . . .

Nay, shall such valiant, religious men as Mr Robert Lockyer be liable to court martial, and to be judged by his adversaries, and most inhumanly shot to death? Shall the blood of war be shed in time of peace? Doth not the word of God expressly condemn it? . . . And are we Christians, and shall we sit still and keep at home, while such men as have borne continual testimony against the injustice of all times and unrighteousness of men, be picked out and be delivered up to the slaughter? And yet must we show no sense of their sufferings, no tenderness of affection, no bowels of compassion, nor bear any testimony against so abominable cruelty and injustice? . . .

BULSTRODE WHITELOCKE
(1605–1675)

May 1649

From *Memorials of the English Affairs*, p. 384b, col. 2

THE WOMEN PETITIONERS ARE PUT IN THEIR PLACE

The Women Petitioners again attended at the door of the House for an answer to their Petition concerning Lilburne and the rest. The House sent them this answer by the Sergeant: 'That the Matter they petitioned about was of an higher concernment than they understood, that the House gave an answer to their husbands, and therefore desired them to go home, and look after their own business, and meddle with their huswifery.'

GEORGE FOX (1624–91)

1649

From *Journal*, Everyman edition, pp. 22, 23, 26–7

Fox was born in Leicestershire, the son of a weaver who worked for a shoemaker. From the age of eleven, as he says, 'the Lord taught me to be faithful in all things, and to act faithfully two ways, viz., inwardly to God, and outwardly to man; and to keep to Yea and Nay in all things'. He left home in 1643, and moved from place to place in search of certainty. His visions told him God 'did not dwell in these temples which men had commanded and set up, but in people's hearts', and 'that people and professors did trample upon the life, even the life of Christ; they fed upon words, and fed one another with words; but they trampled upon the life; trampled underfoot the Son of God, which blood was my life, and lived in their airy notions, talking of Him'. And so he found the courage to speak and to stand up for what he believed in. He and his followers, or Friends, were nick-named Quakers because they were shaken by the 'Lord's power'. As Fox himself described the process: 'I saw there was a great crack to go throughout the earth, and a great smoke to go as the crack went; and that after the crack there should be a great shaking: this was the earth in people's hearts, which was to be shaken before the seed of God was raised out of the earth. And it was so; for the Lord's power began to shake them, and great meetings we began to have, and a mighty power and work of God there was amongst people, to the astonishment of both people and priests.'

FRIENDS AGAINST THE PRIESTS – THE BLACK EARTHLY SPIRIT

. . . When the Lord sent me forth into the world, He forbade me to put off my hat to any, high or low; and I was required to Thee and Thou all men and women, without any respect to rich or poor, great or small. And as I travelled up and down, I was not to bid people Good Morrow or Good Evening; neither might I bow or scrape with my leg to any one; and this made the sects and professions to rage. But the Lord's power carried me over all to His glory, and many came to be turned to God in a little time; for the heavenly day of the Lord sprang from on high, and brake forth apace, by the light of which many came to see where they were.

But the black earthly spirit of the priests wounded my life; and when I heard the bell toll to call people together to the steeple-house, it struck at my life; for it was just like a market-bell, to gather people together that the priest might set forth his ware to sale. Oh! the vast sums of money that are gotten by the trade they make of selling the Scriptures, and by their preaching, from the highest bishop to the lowest priest! What one trade else in the world is comparable to it? notwithstanding the Scriptures were given forth freely, and Christ commanded his ministers to preach freely, and the prophets and apostles denounced judgement against all covetous hirelings and diviners for money. But in this free spirit of the Lord Jesus was I sent forth to declare the word of life and reconciliation freely, that all might come to Christ, who gives freely, and who renews up into the image of God, which man and woman were in before they fell, that they might sit down in heavenly places in Christ Jesus.

Now while I was at Mansfield-Woodhouse, I was moved to go to the steeple-house there on a First-day, out of the meeting in Mansfield, and declare the truth to the priest and people; but the people fell upon me in great rage, struck me down, and almost stifled and smothered me; and I was cruelly beaten and bruised by them with their hands, Bibles, and sticks. Then they haled me out, though I was hardly able to stand, and put me into the stocks, where I sate some hours; and they brought dog-whips and horse-whips, threatening to whip me, and as I sate in the stocks they threw stones at me. After some time they had me before the magistrate . . . who, seeing how evilly I had been used, after much threatening set me at liberty. But the rude people stoned me out of town, and threatened me with pistols, for preaching the word of life to them.

217

I was scarce able to move or stand, by reason of the ill-usage I had received; yet with considerable effort I got about a mile from the town, and then I met with some people who gave me something to comfort me, because I was inwardly bruised; but the Lord's power went through and healed me.

ABIEZER COPPE (1619–72)   1649

From *A Fiery Flying Roll* and (bound and issued together with this last)
A Second Fiery Flying Roll, in Cohn, *Pursuit of the Millennium*,
pp. 321–2, 322–3, 325

Coppe was the most famous of the Ranters. He was arrested in January 1650 for his two *Fiery Rolls*, and Parliament issued an order that they be seized throughout the Commonwealth and burnt by the public hangman. An Act of 9 August 1650 against 'atheistical, blasphemous and execrable opinions' as tending 'to the dissolution of all human society' was decreed largely as a result of Coppe's works, perhaps above all because of his condemnation of private property and his levelling attacks upon all state and church officers. The anarchic nature of such tracts by the adepts of the Free Spirit and their uncompromising social radicalism clearly alarmed the authorities as a danger to the state; Coppe was kept in prison until September 1651, when he delivered a recantation sermon at Burford, which left some, like John Tickell, suspicious of his sincerity. As Tickell put it, in *The Bottomles Pit Smoaking in Familisme* (1651), 'They will say and unsay in one breath . . . Before the late Act against *Ranters*, they spake boldly, now they dare not . . . Since the pretence of the conversion of several of them to the way of truth, they have a *general strain* of Clothing their corrupt notions with sound words . . .' But though there is evidence that Coppe continued to hold his Ranter beliefs (he and 'a great company of Ranters' visited George Fox in prison, for instance, in 1655) his life remained after his release uncontroversial; and after the Restoration he changed his name and practised physic (sometimes preaching) until his death.

Though the works of the Brethren of the Free Spirit or the Spiritual Libertines, known as *Ranters*, were ordered to be burnt, a few stray tracts have survived; and these establish beyond all doubt that this system of self-exaltation involved a 'pursuit of a total emancipation' which, antinomian and anarchic in practice, was often also 'a revolutionary social doctrine which denounced the institution of private property and aimed at its abolition'. They were for a time lumped together by hostile contemporaries with the Quakers, perhaps because both Ranters and Quakers rejected the instituted forms of religion and taught that the truths of religion were only to be found in the 'indwelling spirit' of the individual. But the Quaker attitude to the Ranters is clear from George Fox's account of his first meeting with them, in prison in Coventry in 1649. 'At last these prisoners began to rant, and vapour, and blaspheme, at which my soul was greatly grieved. They said they were God; but that we could not bear such things . . . After I had reproved them for their blasphemous expressions, I went away; for I perceived they were Ranters.'

THE MIGHTY LEVELLER IS COMING

From the first *Fiery Flying Roll*, chapter 1

Thus saith the Lord, *I inform you that I overturn, overturn, overturn*. And as the Bishops, *Charles*, and the Lords, have had their turn, overturn, so your turn shall be next (ye surviving great ones) by what Name or Title soever dignified or distinguished, who ever you are, that oppose me, the Eternal God, who am Universal Love, and whose service is perfect freedom, and pure Libertinism . . .

And now thus saith the Lord:

Though you can as little endure the word LEVELLING, as could the late slain or dead *Charles* (your forerunner, who is gone before you) and had as lief hear the Devil named, as hear of the Levellers (Men-Levellers) which is, and who (indeed) are but shadows of most terrible, yet great and glorious good things to come.

Behold, behold, behold, I the eternal God, the Lord of Hosts, who am that mighty Leveller, am coming (yea even at the doors) to Level in good earnest, to Level to some purpose, to Level with a witness, to Level the Hills with the Valleys, and to lay the Mountains low . . .

But this is not all.

For lo I come (saith the Lord) with a vengeance, to level also your Honour, Riches, and to stain the pride of all your glory, and to bring into Contempt all the Honourable (both persons and things) upon the earth, Isa. xxiii, 9.

For this Honour, Nobility, Gentility, Propriety, Superfluity, etc. hath (without contradiction) been the Father of hellish horrid pride, arrogance, haughtiness, loftiness, murder, malice, of all manner of wickedness and impiety; yea the cause of all the blood that ever hath been shed, from the blood of the righteous *Abel*, to the blood of the last Levellers that were shot to death. *And now (as I live saith the Lord) I am come to make inquisition for blood; for murder and pride, etc.*

I see the root of it all. *The Axe is laid to the root of the Tree* (by the Eternal God, *My Self*, saith the Lord) *I will hew it down*. And as I live, I will plague your Honour, Pomp, Greatness, Superfluity, and confound it into parity, equality, community; that the neck of horrid pride, murder, malice, and tyranny, etc. may be chopped off at one blow. And that my self, the Eternal God, who am Universal Love, may fill the Earth with universal love, universal peace, and perfect freedom; which can never be by human sword or strength accomplished . . .

From Chapter 2

Thus saith the Lord: Be wise now therefore, O ye Rulers, etc. Be instructed, etc. Kisse the Sun, etc. Yea, kiss Beggars, Prisoners, warm them, feed them, clothe them, money them, relieve them, release them, take them into your houses, don't serve them as gods, without door, etc. . . .

The very shadow of levelling, sword-levelling, man-levelling, frighted you, (and who, like your selves, can blame you, because it shook your Kingdom?) but now the substantiality of levelling is coming.

The Eternal God, the mighty Leveller is coming, yea come, even at the door; and what will you do in that day . . .

Mine ears are filled brim full with cries of poor prisoners, Newgate, Ludgate cries (of late) are seldom out of mine ears. Those doleful cries, Bread, bread, bread for the Lord's sake, pierce mine ears, and heart, I can no longer forbear . . .

. . . Loose the bands of wickedness, undo the heavy burdens, let the oppressed go free, and break every yoke. Deal thy bread to the hungry, and bring the poor that are cast out (both of houses and Synagogues) to thy house. Cover the naked: Hide not thyself from thine own flesh, from a cripple, a rogue, a beggar, he's thine own flesh. From a Whoremonger, a thief, etc. he's flesh of thy flesh, and his theft, and whoredom is flesh of thy flesh also, thine own flesh. Thou mayest have ten times more of each within thee, than he that acts outwardly in either, Remember, turn not away thine eyes from thine OWN FLESH.

Give over, give over thy midnight mischief.

Let branding with the letter B [Blasphemy] alone.

Be no longer so horridly, hellishly, impudently, arrogantly wicked, as to judge what is sin, what not, what evil, and what not, what blasphemy, and what not.

For thou and all thy reverend Divines, so called (who Divine for Tithes, hire and money, and serve the Lord Jesus Christ for their owne bellies) are ignorant of this one thing.

That sin and transgression is finished, it's a mere riddle, that they, with all their human learning can never read . . .

All is Religion that they speak, and honour that they do.

But all you that eat of the Tree of Knowledge of Good and Evil, and have not your Evil eye Picked out, you call Good Evil, and Evil Good; Light Darkness, and Darkness Light; Truth Blasphemy, and Blasphemy Truth . . .

From the *Second Fiery Flying Roll*, Chapter 2

The plague of God is in your purses, barns, houses, horses, murrain will take your hogs, (O ye fat swine of the earth) who shall shortly go to the knife, and be hung up i'the roof, except – blasting, mill-dew, locusts, caterpillars, yea fire your houses and goods, take your corn and fruit, the moth your garments, and the rot your sheep, did you not see my hand, this last year, stretched out?

You did not see.

My hand is stretched out still.

Your gold and silver, though you can't see it, is cankered, the rust of them is a witness against you, and suddenly, because by the eternal God, myself, its the dreadful day of Judgement, saith the Lord, shall eat your flesh as it were fire, *Jam.* v, 1–7.

The rust of your silver, I say, shall eat your flesh as it were fire . . .

. . . Give, give, give, give up, give up your houses, horses, goods, gold, Lands, give up, account nothing your own, have ALL THINGS common, or else the plague of God will rot and consume all that you have.

By God, by myself, saith the Lord, it's true.

Come! give all to the poor and follow me, and you shall have treasure in heaven.

WILLIAM WALWYN (active 1640s)   30 May 1649

From *Walwyn's Just Defence*, in Haller and Davies, *Leveller Tracts*, pp. 357–8

Walwyn is here replying to the attack made upon him in *Walwins Wiles*. Both the attack and the reply are extended pamphlets, and the accusation against Walwyn was that he had been seducing men from their loyalty to the churches and the Commonwealth in helping to organize the Leveller party. Many other charges were made, and among them were the 'provocation to Authority'.

FREEDOM, COMMON RIGHT, AND A GOOD GOVERNMENT

... And as unadvised it is to lay to my charge the opposing of all Authority that ever was; for let them tell me what Authority they opposed not. The Kings and Bishops they cannot deny; and the Parliament and Presbyterian, I think, they will confess; and truly I never opposed since, except to insist for such just things as were promised, when the Army first disputed, be called an opposition: and such as are not only fix'd in my mind, but in the minds of thousands more that then owned the proceedings of the Army, and ventured their lives for them, when these that now revile me stood aloof, seeing it neither just nor seasonable.

And truly, that they have sat themselves down on this side Jordan, the reason is somewhat too evident, for men that would not be thought men of this world. It is but a promised land, a promised good that I and my friends seek, it is neither offices, honours nor preferments, it is only promised Freedom, and exemption from burdens for the whole Nation, not only for ourselves. We wish them peace, we repine not at any man's honour, preferment or advantage. Give us but Common Right, some foundations, some boundaries, some certainty of Law, and a good Government; that now, when there is so high discourse of Freedom, we may be delivered from will, power, and mere arbitrary discretion, and we shall be satisfied. If to insist for this be to oppose Authority, what a case are we in? Certainly were these men in our case, or were they sensible of the price it hath cost this Nation to purchase Freedom, they would think it deserved more than the mere name thereof.

And how I can be charged to make it my work to divide the Army, I cannot see. I only pursue the establishment of Freedom, and redress of Grievances I have ever pursued, and which are not yet obtained; so also have done many in the Army. It is in the Army, as it is between these men's Friends and mine. Some content themselves with present enjoyments, others with the Commonwealth at more certainty in the foundations of Freedom; and for my part, I ever most earnestly desired their union, so it were in good, and for that Freedom and good to the Nation for which, I believe, most of them have fought. And if they divide for want of it, they divide them that keep them from it, and not I, that wish with all my heart that cause of division were not.

The Lieutenant General well knows (for I visited him often in Drury-Lane about that time that Mr Price was there with me) how much I desired the union of the Army; and though it then divided, it was not esteemed a fault in those that separated themselves for good, but blame-worthy in those that would not unite, except for evil. So that to unite, or divide, is not the thing; but whether in good, or evil, is the main of all; and by which, my Adversaries and I shall one day be judged, though now they have taken the Chair, and most uncharitably judge me of evil in every thing wherein I move, or but open my mouth.

And the Lieutenant General also knows, upon what grounds I then persuaded him to divide from that Body to which he was united; that if he did not, it would be his ruin, and the ruin of the General, and of all those Worthies that had preserved us; that if he did do it in time, he should not only preserve himself and them, and all conscientious people, but he should do it without spilling one drop of blood; professing that if it were not evident to me that it would be so, I would not persuade him; and that I would undertake to demonstrate to him that it would be so. And so, through God's goodness, and the zeal and affections of these men's now despised Friends, it came to pass: so far was I ever from advising unto blood: whereas these men would suppose me to be delighted with nothing more than slaughter and confusion.

WILLIAM THOMPSON (killed 1649)   May 1649

From *England's Standard Advanced in Oxfordshire* (pamphlet in the British Library, Thomason Collection, E. 555(7)), p. 1

Thompson's declaration to 'the oppressed people of this nation now under his command' raised the standard of revolt by the Leveller movement in the Army against the dictatorship of the Council of State which, led by Cromwell, clearly had no intention of answering the Leveller demands for radical democracy and was determined to suppress the revolt. Thompson gathered a large force of men in Oxfordshire, but in a sudden surprise attack was crushed at Burford in May. Three agitators were shot on the 15th, and Thompson was killed three days later near Wellingborough.

TO OPPRESS, TORMENT AND VEX THE PEOPLE

Whereas, it is notorious to the whole world that neither the faith of the Parliament, nor yet the faith of the army formerly made to the people of the nation in behalf of their common right, freedom, and safety, hath been at all observed, or made good, but both absolutely declined and broken, and the people only served with bare words and fair promising papers, and left utterly destitute of all help or delivery: and that this hath principally been by the prevalency and treachery of some eminent persons, now domineering over the people is most evident.

The Solemn Engagement of the army at Newmarket and Triploe heath by them destroyed, the Council of Agitators destroyed, the blood of war shed in times of peace, petitions for common freedom suppressed by force of arms, and petitioners abused and terrified, the lawful trial by twelve sworn men of the neighbourhood subverted and denied, bloody and tyrannical courts, called a High Court of Justice and a Council of State, erected, the power of the sword advanced and set in the seat of the magistrates, the civil laws stopped and subverted, and the military introduced, even to the hostile seizure, imprisonment, trial, sentence, and execution of death, upon divers of the free people of this nation, leaving no visible authority, dissolving all into a factious Junto and Council of State, usurping and assuming the name, stamp, and authority of Parliament, to oppress, torment and vex the people, whereby all lives, liberties and estates are subdued to the wills of these men, no law, no justice, no right or freedom, no ease of grievances, no removal of unjust barbarous taxes, no regard to the cries and groans of the poor to be had, while utter beggary and famine, like a mighty torrent, hath broken in upon us, and already seized several parts of the nation.

We all are resolved as one man, even to the hazard and expense of our lives and fortunes, to endeavour the redemption of the magistracies of England from under the force of the sword, to vindicate the Petition of Right, to set the unjustly imprisoned free, to relieve the poor, and settle this Common-wealth upon the grounds of common right, freedom, and safety.

Choosing rather to die for freedom than live as slaves, we are gathered and associated together upon the bare account of Englishmen, with swords in our hands, to redeem ourselves and the land of our nativity from slavery and oppression.

GERRARD WINSTANLEY
(1609–after 1660)

June 1649

From *A Declaration From the Poor Oppressed People of England*, in *Works*, pp. 269, 272, 273

Harrassed by legal actions and organized raids upon their land, Winstanley addressed this *Declaration*, signed by forty-three of his Digger comrades, to the landowners and authorities at large, though he did have the friendly support at this time of General Fairfax.

BIRTHRIGHTS

We whose names are subscribed, do in the name of all the poor oppressed people of England, declare unto you, that call yourselves Lords of Manors, and Lords of the Land, that the power of enclosing Land, and owning Property was brought into the Creation by your Ancestors by the Sword; which first did murder their fellow Creatures, Men, and after plunder or steal away their Land, and left this Land successively to you, their Children. And therefore, though you did not kill or thieve, yet you hold that cursed thing in your hand, by the power of the Sword; and so you justify the wicked deeds of your Fathers, and that sin of your Fathers shall be visited upon the Head of you, and your Children, to the third and fourth Generation, and longer too, till your bloody and thieving power be rooted out of the land . . .

. . . The main thing we aim at, and for which we declare our Resolutions to go forth, and act, is this, To lay hold upon, and as we stand in need, to cut and fell, and make the best advantage we can of the Woods and Trees, that grow upon the Commons, To be a stock for our selves, and our poor Brethren, through the Land of *England*, to plant the Commons withal; and to provide us bread to eat, till the Fruit of our labours in the Earth bring forth increase; and we shall meddle with none of your Proprieties (but what is called Commonage) till the Spirit in you, make you cast upon your Lands and Goods, which were got, and still kept in your hands by murder and theft; and we shall take it from the Spirit, that hath conquered you, and not from our Swords, which is an abominable and unrighteous power, and a destroyer of the Creation . . .

. . . We are resolved to be cheated no longer, nor be held under slavish fear of you no longer, seeing the Earth was made for us, as well as for you: And if the Common Land belongs to us who are the poor oppressed, surely the woods that grow upon the Commons belong to us likewise: therefore we are resolved to try the uttermost in the light of reason, to know whether we shall be free men, or slaves. If we lie still, and let you steal away our birthrights, we perish; and if we Petition we perish also, though we have paid taxes, given free quarter, and ventured our lives to preserve the Nation's freedom as much as you, and therefore by the law of contract with you, freedom in the land is our portion as well as yours, equal with you: And if we strive for freedom, and your murdering, governing Laws destroy us, we can but perish.

GERRARD WINSTANLEY
(1609–after 1660)

June 1649

From a letter to Lord Fairfax, in *Works*, pp. 281–2, 288

Winstanley and Everard had gone to Whitehall on 20 April to present the Diggers' case to Fairfax, and Fairfax visited St George's Hill on 26 May, and this letter is perhaps a response to his visit.

THIS WORK OF COMMUNITY IN THE EARTH

We understand, that our digging upon that Common, is the talk of the whole Land; some approving, some disowning. Some are friends, filled with love, and sees the work intends good to the Nation, the peace whereof is that which we seek after. Others are enemies filled with fury, and falsely report of us, that we have intent to fortify ourselves, and afterwards to fight against others, and take away their goods from them, which is a thing we abhor. And many other slanders we rejoice over, because we know ourselves clear, our endeavour being no otherwise, but to improve the Commons, and to cast off that oppression and outward bondage which the Creation groans under, as much as in us lies, and to lift up and preserve the purity thereof.

And the truth is, experience shows us, that in this work of Community in the earth, and in the fruits of the earth, is seen plainly a pitched battle between the Lamb and the Dragon, between the Spirit of love, humility and righteousness . . . and the power of envy, pride, and unrighteousness . . . the latter power striving to hold the Creation under slavery, and to lock and hide the glory thereof from man: the former power labouring to deliver Creation from slavery, to unfold the secrets of it to the Sons of Man, and so to manifest himself to be the great restorer of all things . . .

And surely if the common people have no more freedom in England, but only to live among their elder brothers, and work for them for hire; what freedom then have they in England more than we can have in Turkey or France?

JOHN WARR   1649

From *The Corruption and Deficiency of the Laws of England, soberly discovered: Or, Liberty working up to its just Height* . . ., in Oldys, ed., *Harleian Miscellany*, III, pp. 240–41, 242, 248

Warr advocated radical reforms of the law. He wanted, in this age of 'teeming freedom', as he argues in *Administrations Civil and Spiritual* (1648), 'to free the clear understanding from the bondage of the Form and to raise it up to Equity, which is the substance itself. For though the dark understanding may be restrained or guided, yet the principled man hath his freedom within himself, and walking in the light of Equity and Reason . . . knows no bounds but his own . . .'

THE BALANCE OF FREEDOM

Those Laws, which do carry any Thing of Freedom in their Bowels, do owe their Original to the People's Choice; and have been wrested from the Rulers and Princes of the World by Importunity of Intreaty, or by Force of Arms: For the great Men of the World, being invested with the Power thereof, cannot be imagined to eclipse themselves or their own Pomp, unless by the violent Interposition of the People's Spirits, who are most sensible of their own Burdens, and most forward in seeking Relief . . .

And yet such hath been the Interest of Princes in the World, that the Sting of the Law hath been plucked out as to them, and the weight of it fallen upon the People . . .

Thus the Law becomes any Thing or nothing, at the Courtesy of great Men, and is bended by them like a Twig: Yea, how easy is it for such Men to break those Customs which will not bow, and to erect Traditions of a more complying Temper, to the Wills of those whose End they serve. So that Law comes to be lost in Will and Lust; yea, Lust by the Adoption of Greatness is enacted Law . . .

No marvel that Freedom hath no Voice here, for an Usurper reigns; and Freedom is proscribed like an Exile, living only in the understandings of some few Men, and not daring to appear upon the Theatre of the World.

But yet the Minds of Men are the great Wheels of Things; thence come Changes and Alterations in the World; teeming Freedom exerts and puts forth itself; the unjust World would suppress its Appearance, many fall in the Conflict, but Freedom will at last prevail, and give Law to all Things . . .

The End of just Laws is the Safety and Freedom of a People. As for Safety, just Laws are Bucklers of Defence. When the Mouth of Violence is muzzled by a Law, the Innocent feed and sleep securely; when the wolfish Nature is destroyed, there shall then be no Need of Law. As long as that is in being, the Curb of the Law keeps it in Restraint, that the Great may not oppress or injure the Small.

As for Safety, Laws are the Manacles of Princes, and the Guards of private Men: So far as Laws advance the People's Freedoms, so far are they just, for, as the Power of the Prince is the Measure of unrighteous Laws, so just Laws are weighed in the Balance of Freedom. Where the first of these take place, the People are wholly Slaves; where the second, they are wholly free; but most Commonwealths are in a middle Posture, as having their Laws guarded partly upon the Interest of the Prince, and partly upon the Account of the People . . .

If there is such a Thing as Right in the World, let us have it, *fine fuco*. Why is it delayed, or denied, or varnished over with guilty Words? Why comes it not forth in its own Dress? Why doth it not put off Law, and put on Reason, the Mother of all just Laws? Why is it not ashamed of its long and mercenary Train? Why can we not ask it, and receive it ourselves, but must have it handed to us by others? In a Word, why may not a man plead his own Case? Or his Friends and Acquaintance, as formerly, plead for him? . . .

GERRARD WINSTANLEY
(1609–after 1660)

July 1649

From *An Appeal to the House of Commons*, in *Law of Freedom*,
pp. 114–22 passim

After three months of ploughing and digging on St George's Hill 'to sow corn for
the succour of men', Winstanley and two of his comrades were arrested for trespass against the assumed rights of the lord of the manor, Mr Drake. Not told
what the trespass was, denied the right to plead their own case, refused a copy
of the *Declaration*, they were condemned unheard by a jury of 'rich freeholders'
at Kingston Court, and their property seized. Winstanley writes to the Commons
in defence of the Diggers' rights.

SET THE LAND FREE FROM OPPRESSION

We looked upon you to be our chief council, to agitate business for us,
though you were summoned by the King's writ, and chosen by the freeholders, that are the successors of William the Conqueror's soldiers. You
saw the dangers so great, that without a war England was like to be more
enslaved, therefore you called upon us to assist you with plate, taxes,
free-quarter and our persons; and you promised us, in the name of the
Almighty, to make us a free people; thereupon you and we took the
National Covenant with joint consent, to endeavour the freedom, peace
and safety of the people of England.

And you and we joined purse and person together in this common
cause; and William the Conqueror's successor, which was Charles, was
cast out; and thereby we have recovered ourselves from under that Norman yoke; and now unless you and we be merely besotted with covetousness, pride and slavish fear of men, it is and will be our wisdom to
cast out all those enslaving laws, which was the tyrannical power that
the kings pressed us down by. O shut not your eyes against the light,
darken not knowledge by dispute about particular men's privileges when
universal freedom is brought to be tried before you, dispute no further
when truth appears, but be silent and practise it.

Stop not your ears against the secret mourning of the oppressed under
these expressions, lest the Lord see it and be offended and shut his ears
against your cries, and work a deliverance for his waiting people some
other way than by you.

The main thing that you should look upon is the land, which calls
upon her children to be freed from the entanglement of the Norman

229

taskmasters; for one third part lies waste and barren, and her children starve for want, in regard the lords of manors will not suffer the poor to manure it . . .

And seeing in particular you swore to endeavour the freedom, peace and safety of this people of England, shutting out no sort from freedom; therefore you cannot say that the gentry and clergy were only comprehended, but without exception all sorts of people in the land are to have freedom, seeing all sorts have assisted you in person and purse, and the common people more especially, seeing their estates were weakest, and their misery in the wars the greatest . . .

If you deny this freedom, then you justly pull the blood and cries of the poor oppressed upon you, and are covenant-breakers and will be proved double hypocrites: first to Almighty God, in breaking covenant with him, for in his name you made the Covenant. Secondly to men, in breaking covenant with them . . .

O that there were a heart in you to consider of these things, and act righteousness, how sweetly might you and the people live together. If you grant this freedom we speak of, you gain the hearts of the nation; if you neglect this, you will fall as fast in their affections as ever you rise. I speak what I see, and you do observe; slight not that love that speaks feelingly, from the sense of the nation's burdens . . .

Let it not be said in the ears of posterity that the gentry of England assembled in Parliament proved covenant-breakers, oaths-, protestations- and promise-breakers to God and the common people, after their own turn was served; and killed the King for his power and government, as a thief kills a true man for his money. I do not say you have done so; but for shame dally no longer, but cut off the bad laws with the King's head, and let the poor oppressed go free as well as the gentry and clergy, and you will find more peace. Let the common land be set free, break the Norman yoke of lords of manors; and pull not the cries and blood of the poor oppressed upon you . . .

Set the land free from oppression, and righteousness will be the laws, government and strength of that people.

GERRARD WINSTANLEY
(1609–after 1660)

26 August 1649

From *A Watch-Word to the City of London*, in *Works*, pp. 315–17, 333, 337

Winstanley gives a graphic account of the maltreatment of the Diggers and of spiteful attacks by the landowners against their land and their cattle, including his own cows. The pamphlet includes a covering letter and a Document submitted to Kingston Court in defence of the Diggers' rights, following the appeal to Parliament. It rejects the verdict and urges free men to act against the threat of a 'new Norman slavery', as it seems the Diggers have already done by setting up a new colony on Cobham Heath.

THOSE WHO ACT FOR FREEDOM

. . . Not a full year since, being quiet in my work, my heart was filled with sweet thoughts, and many things were revealed to me which I never read in books, nor heard from the mouth of any flesh, and when I began to speak them, some people could not bear my words, and amongst these revelations was this one: That the earth shall be made a common treasury of livelihood to whole mankind, without respect of persons; and I had a voice within me which bade me declare it abroad, which I did obey, for I declared it by word of mouth wheresoever I came . . . Yet my mind was not at rest, because nothing was acted, and thoughts run in me that words and writings were all nothing and must die, for action is the life of all, and if thou dost not act, thou dost nothing. Within a little time I was made obedient to the word in that particular likewise; for I took my spade and went and broke the ground upon George Hill in Surrey, thereby declaring freedom to the Creation, and that the earth must be set free from entanglements of lords and landlords, and that it shall become a common treasury to all, as it was first made and given to the sons of men. For which doing the Dragon presently casts a flood of water to drown the manchild, even that freedom that now is declared, for the old Norman prerogative Lord of the Manor, Mr Drake, caused me to be arrested for a trespass against him, in digging upon that barren heath, and the unrighteous proceedings of Kingston Court in this business I have here declared to thee and to the whole land, that you may consider the case that England is in. All men have stood for freedom, thou hast kept fasting days and prayed in morning exercises for freedom; thou hast given thanks for victories, because hopes of freedom; plenty of petitions

231

and promises thereupon have been made for freedom; and now the common enemy is gone, you are all like men in a mist, seeking for freedom, and know not where nor what it is: and those of the richer sort of you that see it are ashamed and afraid to own it, because it comes clothed in a clownish garment, and open to the best language that scoffing Ishmael can afford . . . For freedom is the man that will turn the world upside down, therefore no wonder he hath enemies.

And assure yourselves, if you pitch not right now upon the right point of freedom in action, as your Covenant hath it in words, you will wrap up your children in greater slavery than ever you were in . . . No true freedom can be established for England's peace, or prove you faithful in covenant, but such a one as hath respect to the poor as well as the rich; for if thou consent to freedom to the rich in the City and givest freedom to the freeholders in the country, and to priests and lawyers and lords of manors and impropriators, and yet allowest the poor no freedom, thou art then a declared hypocrite, and all thy prayers, fasts and thanksgivings are and will be proved an abomination to the Lord, and freedom himself will be the poor's portion when thou shalt lie groaning in bondage.

I have declared this truth to the Army and Parliament, and now I have declared it to thee likewise, that none of you that are the fleshly strength of this land may be left without excuse, for now you have been all spoken to, and because I have obeyed the voice of the Lord in this thing, therefore do the freeholders and lords of manors seek to oppress me in the outward livelihood of the world, but I am in peace. And London, nay England, look to thy freedom! I'll assure thee, thou art very near to be cheated of it, and if thou lose it now after all thy boasting, truly thy posterity will curse thee for thy unfaithfulness to them. Every one talks of freedom, but there are but few that act for freedom, and the actors for freedom are oppressed by the talkers and verbal professors of freedom; if thou wouldst know what true freedom is, read over this and other my writings, and thou shalt see it lies in the community in spirit, and community in the earthly treasury; and this is Christ the true man-child spread abroad in the Creation, restoring all things into himself . . .

And take notice of this, you lords of manors and Norman gentry, though you should kill my body or starve me in prison, yet know that the more you strive, the more troubles your hearts shall be filled with; and do the worst you can to hinder public freedom, you shall come off losers in the latter end, I mean you shall lose your kingdom of darkness, though I lose my livelihood, the poor cows that is my living, and should be imprisoned. You have been told this 12 months ago, that you should lose ground by striving, and will you not take warning, will you needs shame yourselves, to let the poor diggers take away your kingdom from you? Surely, the power that is in them will take the rule and government from you, and give it a people that will make better use of it.

Alas! you poor blind earth-moles, you strive to take away my livelihood and the liberty of this poor weak frame my body of flesh, which is my house I dwell in for a time; but I strive to cast down your kingdom of darkness, and to open hell gates, and to break the devil's bonds asunder wherewith you are tied, that you my enemies may live in peace; and that is all the harm I would have you to have . . .

> The work of digging still goes on and stops not for arrest,
> The cows were gone but are returned, and we are all at rest.
> No money's paid, nor never shall, to lawyer or his man
> To plead our cause, for therein we'll do the best we can.
> In Cobham on the little heath our digging there goes on,
> And all our friends they live in love, as if they were but one.

GERRARD WINSTANLEY December 1649
(1609–after 1660)

From *To Lord Fairfax and the Counsell of Warre*, in *Works*, p. 344

In this 'Brotherly Request of those that are called diggers', Winstanley writes of promises made and not kept, of the Covenant to God between men, and urges Fairfax and Parliament to perform the Covenant 'in deed and work as well as in words' against their common enemies. But:

LIBERTY QUIETLY TO LIVE

Now Sirs, divers repulses we have had from some of the Lords of Manors and their servants, with whom we are patient and loving, not doubting but at last they will grant liberty quietly to live by them . . .

But now Sirs, this last week upon the 28th of November, there came a party of soldiers Commanded by a Cornet, and some of them of your own Regiment, and by their threatening words forced three labouring men to help them to pull down our two houses, and carried away the wood in a cart to a Gentleman's house who hath been a Cavalier all our time of wars, and cast two or three old people out who lived in those houses to lie in the open field this cold weather (an action more becoming the Turks to deal with Christians than for one Christian to deal with another); but if you inquire into the business you will find that the Gentleman that set the soldiers on are enemies to you . . . and we know, and you will find it true if you trust them so far, that they love you but from the teeth outward . . .

GERRARD WINSTANLEY   1 January 1650
(1609–after 1660)

From *A New Year's Gift for the Parliament and Army*, in *Law of Freedom*, pp. 165–6, 167, 170, 190–92

OPPRESSION IS A GREAT TREE STILL

. . . While this kingly power reigned in one man called Charles, all sorts of people complained of oppression, both gentry and common people, because their lands, enclosures and copyholds were entangled, and because their trades were destroyed by monopolising patentees, and your troubles were that you could not live free from oppression in the earth. Thereupon you that were the gentry, when you were assembled in Parliament, you called upon the poor common people to come and help you, and cast out oppression; and you that complained are helped and freed, and that top bough is lopped off the tree of tyranny, and kingly power in that one particular is cast out. But alas, oppression is a great tree still, and keeps off the sun of freedom from the poor commons still; he hath many branches and great roots which must be grubbed up, before everyone can sing Sion's songs in peace.

As we spy out kingly power we must declare it and cast it out, or else we shall deny the Parliament of England and their acts, and so prove traitors to the land by denying obedience thereunto. Now there are three branches more of kingly power, greater than the former, that oppress this land wonderfully; and these are the power of the tithing priests over the tenths of our labours; and the power of lords of manors, holding the free use of the commons and waste land from the poor; and the intolerable oppression either of bad laws, or of bad judges corrupting good laws. These are branches of the Norman conquest and kingly power still, and wants a reformation . . .

The clergy will serve on any side, like our ancient laws that will serve any master. They will serve the papists, they will serve the protestants, they will serve the king, they will serve the states; they are one and the same tools for lawyers to work with under any government. O you Parliament-men of England, cast those whorish laws out of doors, that are so common, that pretend love to everyone and is faithful to none: for truly, he that goes to law (as the proverb is) shall die a beggar: so that old whores and old laws picks men's pockets, and undoes them. If the fault lie in the laws (and much does), burn all your old law-books in Cheapside, and set up a government upon your own foundation. Do not put new wine into old bottles; but as your government must be new, so let the laws be new, or else you will run farther into the mud where you stick already, as though you were fast in an Irish bog; for you are so far sunk that he must have good eyes that can see where you are: but yet all are not blind, there are eyes that sees you. But if the fault lies in the judges of the law, surely such men deserve no power in a reforming commonwealth, that burdens all sorts of people.

And truly I'll tell you plain, your two acts of Parliament are excellent and righteous: the one to cast out kingly power, the other to make England a free commonwealth. Build upon these two, it is a firm foundation, and your house will be the glory of the world; and I am confident, the righteous spirit will love you. Do not stick in the bog of covetousness: let not self-love so bemuddy your brain that you should lose yourselves in the thicket of bramble-bush words, and set never a strong oak of some stable action for the freedom of the poor oppressed that helped you when you complained of oppression . . .

You blame us who are the common people as though we would have no government; truly gentlemen, we desire a righteous government with all our hearts, but the government we have gives freedom and livelihood to the gentry to have abundance, and to lock up treasures of the earth from the poor, so that rich men may have chests full of gold and silver, and houses full of corn and goods to look upon; and the poor that works to get it can hardly live, and if they cannot work like slaves, then they must starve. And thus the law gives all the land to some part of mankind whose predecessors got it by conquest, and denies it to others who by the righteous law of creation may claim an equal portion; and yet you say this is a righteous government. But surely it is no other but selfishness, which is the great red dragon, the murderer.

England is a prison; the variety of subtleties in the laws preserved by the sword are bolts, bars and doors of the prison; the lawyers are jailors, and poor men are the prisoners; for let a man fall into the hands of any from the bailiff to the judge, and he is either undone or weary of his life . . .

SELF-LOVE AGAINST THE COMMUNITY

. . . One of your colonels of the Army said to me that the diggers did work upon George Hill for no other end but to draw a company of people into arms; and says 'our knavery is found out, because it takes not that effect'.

Truly, thou colonel, I tell thee, the knavish imagination is thereby discovered, which hinders the effecting of that freedom which by oath and covenant thou hast engaged to maintain: for my part and the rest, we had no such thought. We abhor fighting for freedom, it is acting of the curse and lifting him up higher; and do thou uphold it by the sword, we will not: we will conquer by love and patience, or else we count it no freedom. Freedom gotten by the sword is an established bondage to some part or other of the creation; and this we have declared publicly enough; therefore thy imagination told thee a lie, and will deceive thee in a greater matter, if love doth not kill him. Victory that is gotten by the sword is a victory that slaves gets one over another; and hereby *men of the basest spirit* (saith Daniel) *are set to rule*: but victory obtained by love is a victory for a king.

But by this you may see what a liar imagination is, and how he makes bate and tears the creation in pieces; for after that self-love hath subdued others under him, then imagination studies how to keep himself up and keep others down.

This is your very inward principle, O ye present powers of England, you do not study how to advance universal love; if you did, it would appear in action. But imagination and self-love mightily disquiets your mind and makes you call up all the powers of darkness to come forth and help to set the crown upon the head of self, which is that kingly power you have oathed and vowed against, and yet uphold it in your hands . . .

And all this falling out or quarrelling among mankind is about the earth, who shall and who shall not enjoy it; when indeed it is the portion of every one and ought not to be striven for, nor bought nor sold, whereby some are hedged in and others hedged out. For better not to have had a body, than to be debarred the fruit of the earth to feed and clothe it; and if every one did but quietly enjoy the earth for food and raiment, there would be no wars, prisons nor gallows . . .

GERRARD WINSTANLEY   Spring 1650
(1609–after 1660)

From *Fire in the Bush*, in *Law of Freedom*, pp. 246–7

Winstanley addressed this pamphlet, possibly after the Digger movement had been dispersed as a result of constant harassment from local landowners with the support of the Army, 'to all the several societies of people called churches, in the Presbyterian, Independent or any other form of profession in the service of God'; and to 'fellow-members of mankind', in defence of the free Christian spirit.

THE LIGHT OF LIFE . . . NOW RISING IN HUSBANDMEN, SHEPHERDS, FISHERMEN

. . . The Scriptures of the Bible were written by the experimental hand of shepherds, husbandmen, fishermen and such inferior men of the world. And the university learned ones have got these men's writings, and flourishes their plain language over with their dark interpretation and glosses, as if it were too hard for ordinary men now to understand them: and thereby they deceive the simple and makes a prey of the poor, and cozens them of the earth, and of the tenth of their labours.

And because those men's writings are taking with the world, therefore these learned ones shuts out the true penmen in whom the Spirit dwells, and saith how such mechanics must not meddle with spiritual things. And so by covetous policy, in opposition to the righteous spirit, they engross other men's experimental spiritual teachings to themselves, as if it were their own by university or school learning succession. Pope-like. Nay, just the Pope.

And by their blackness of darkness in their school learning, they have drawn a veil over the truth. And light by them is hid from the world; for the plain truth is, this imaginary ministry is neither better nor worse, but plain unmasked Judas. And the snappish bitter profession that cries it up, is the unmasked murdering scribes and Pharises.

The one betrays Christ, the spirit of righteouness, with a kiss, pretending a great deal of love to the spirit, by preaching and praying to a God without, they know not where nor what he is.

237

The other kills him and will not suffer him to appear in the world; for these snappish professors calls everything blasphemy unless they approve of it, still tying the spirit to themselves; saying, 'Lo, here is Christ in this man, and lo, there is Christ in that man.'

But Christ is the light of life spread abroad, and he is now rising in husbandmen, shepherds, fishermen. And by these he first takes off the black interpretation that the imaginary learned scholars by their studies have defiled the Scriptures of old with, and restores them to their own genuine and pure light.

And then to discover his appearance in sons and daughters, in a fuller measure, the poor despised ones shall be honoured first in the work; and from this dust the blessing shall arise to cover the whole earth with peace, and with the knowledge of the Lord.

For this is the vine that shall overspread the earth, and shall be confined no longer within a college or private university chamber, or under a covetous, proud, black gown, that would always be speaking words, but fall off when people begins to act their words . . .

JACOB BAUTHUMLEY OR BOTTOMLEY
(active 1650–1655)   November 1650

From *The Light and Dark sides of God, Or a plain and brief Discourse of the Light side (God, Heaven and Earth) The dark side (Devill, Sin, and Hell). As also of the Resurrection and Scripture . . .*, in Cohn, *Pursuit of the Millennium*, pp. 304–5

Bottomley was in the army when he wrote this tract, and was punished for it by being burned through the tongue. Later (in 1654–5) he attended joint meetings of the Quakers and Ranters in Leicestershire, where (before joining the army) he had worked as a shoemaker. Nothing else is known of him; but he was clearly not one of the 'drinking, smoking and swearing' Ranters.

GOD DWELLING IN THE FLESH

. . . Nay, I see that God is in all Creatures, Man and Beast, Fish and Fowl, and every green thing, from the highest Cedar to the Ivy on the wall; and that God is the life and being of them all, and that God doth really dwell, and if you will, personally; if he may admit so low an expression in them all, and hath his Being no where else out of the Creatures . . .

Did men see that God was in them, and framing all their thoughts, and working all their works, and that he was with them in all conditions: what carnal spirit would reach out to that by an outward way, which spiritually is in him, and which he stands really possesst of? and which divine wisdom sees the best, and that things can be no otherwise with him . . . [Formerly] I thought that my sins or holy walking did cause [God] to alter his purpose of good or evil to me.

But now I cannot look upon any condition or action, but methinks there appears a sweet concurrence of the supreme will in it; nothing comes short of it, or goes beyond it, nor any man shall do or be any thing, but what shall fall in a sweet compliance with it; it being the womb wherein all things are conceived, and in which all creatures were formed and brought forth . . .

I do not apprehend that God was only manifest in the flesh of Christ, or the man called Christ; but that he as really and substantially dwells in the flesh of other men and Creatures, as well as in the man Christ.

. . . Then men are in Heaven, or Heaven in men, when God appears in his glorious and pure manifestations of himself, in Love and Grace, in Peace and rest in the Spirit . . .

. . . I find that where God dwells, and is come, and hath taken men up, and wrapt them up into the Spirit; there is a new Heaven and a new Earth, and all the Heaven I look ever to enjoy is to have my earthly and dark apprehensions of God to cease, and to live no other life than what Christ spiritually lives in me.

LAWRENCE CLARKSON (1615–67)   1650

From *A Single Eye All Light, no Darkness; or Light and Darkness One*, in Cohn, *Pursuit of the Millennium*, pp. 315–16

See p. 178. Clarkson gives an account of the Ranter way of life in his last book, *The Lost Sheep Found* (1660): 'I was moved to write to the world what my Principle was, so brought to public view a book called *The Single Eye*, so that men and women came from many parts to see my face, and hear my knowledge in these things, being restless to be made free, as we then called it. Now I being as they said, Captain of the Rant, I had most of the principal women came to my lodging for knowledge, which was then called the Head-Quarters. Now in the height of this ranting, I was made still careful for moneys for my Wife, only my body was given to other women; so our Company increasing, I wanted for nothing that heart could desire, but at last it became a trade so common, that all the froth and scum broke forth into the height of this wickedness, yea began to be a public reproach, that I broke up my Quarters, and went into the country to my Wife where I had by the way disciples plenty . . . My judgement was, God had made all things good, so nothing evil but as man judged it; for I apprehended there was no such things as theft, cheat, or a lie, but as man made it so: for if the creature had brought this world into no propriety, as *Mine* and *Thine*, there had been no such title as theft, cheat, or a lie; for the prevention hereof *Everard* and *Gerrard Winstanley* did dig up the Commons, that so all might have to live of themselves, then there had been no need of defrauding, but unity one with another . . .'

THE PERFECT LIBERTY OF THE SONS OF GOD

Behold, the King of Glory now is come
T' reduce God, and Devil to their Doom;
For both of them are servants unto Me
That lives, and rules in perfect Majesty . . .
Fie then for shame, look not above the Skies
For God, or Heaven; for here your Treasure lies
Even in these Forms, *Eternal Will* will reign.
Through him are all things, only One, not Twain:
Sure he's the Fountain from which every thing
Both good and ill (so term'd) appears to spring . . .

Consider what act soever, yea though it be the act of Swearing, Drunkenness, Adultery and Theft; yet these acts simply, yea nakedly, as acts are nothing distinct from the act of Prayer and Praises. Why dost thou wonder? why art thou angry? they are all one in themselves; no more holiness, no more purity in the one than the other.

But once the Creature esteemeth one act Adultery, the other honesty, the one pure, the other impure; yet to that man that so esteemeth one act unclean, to him it is unclean: (as saith the History) there is nothing unclean of itself, but . . . to him that esteemeth it unclean: yea again and again it is recorded that to the pure of all things, yea all things are pure, but to the defiled, all things are defiled . . .

Wonder not at me, for without Act, without Birth, no powerful deliverance, not only the Talkers, but the Doers; not only your Spirit, but your Body must be a living and acceptable Sacrifice; therefore till acted

240

that so called Sin, thou art not delivered from the power of sin, but ready upon all Alarms to tremble and fear the reproach of thy body.

. . . I say, till flesh be made Spirit, and Spirit flesh, so not two, but one, thou art in perfect bondage: for without vail, I declare that whosoever doth attempt to act from flesh, in flesh, to flesh, hath, is, and will commit Adultery: but to bring this to a period, for my part, till I acted that, so called sin, I could not predominate over sin; so that now whatsoever I act, is not in relation to the Title, to the Flesh, but that Eternity in me; So that with me, all Creatures are but one creature, and this is my form, the Representative of the whole Creation: So that see what I can, act what I will, all is but one most sweet and lovely. Therefore my dear ones consider, that without act, no life; without life, no perfection; and without perfection, no eternal peace and freedom indeed, in power, which is the everlasting Majesty, ruling, conquering, and damning all into its self, without end, for ever.

A RANTER CHRISTMAS CAROL

In *The Arraignment and Tryall, with a Declaration of the Ranters* (1650)

NO GOD

They prate of God; believe it, fellow creatures,
There's no such bugbear; all was made by Nature.
We know all came of nothing, and shall pass
Into the same condition once it was,
By Nature's power; and that they grossly lie
That say there's hope of immortality.
Let them but tell us what a soul is, then
We will adhere to these mad brain-sick men.

GEORGE FOX (1624–91)   1650

From *Journal*, Everyman edition, p. 32

Fox, imprisoned at Derby on 30 October 1650, having been 'charged with the avowed uttering and broaching of divers blasphemous opinions contrary to a late Act of Parliament', wrote to the priests and magistrates, and again to the justices, the mayor of Derby; and to the Court at Derby thus:

OPPRESSING THE POOR

I am moved to write unto you, to take heed of oppressing the poor in your Courts, or laying burthens upon poor people, which they cannot bear; and of imposing false oaths, or making them to take oaths which they cannot perform. The Lord saith, 'I will come near to judgement, and will be swift witness against the sorcerers, against the false swearers, and against the idolators, and against those that do oppress widows and fatherless.' Therefore take heed of all these things betimes. The Lord's judgements are all true and righteous; and He delighteth in mercy. So love mercy, dear people, and consider in time.

JOHN MILTON (1608–74)   1651

From *Defence of the People of England*, in *Complete Prose Works*, IV, pp. 535–6

Having already made a powerful case for the execution of Charles I two years before to meet the objections of the Presbyterian party, Milton was now called upon by the Council of State to answer Salmasius' *Defence of the King*, commissioned by the exiled Prince Charles to state his father's case and defame the 'regicide Commonwealth' before the whole of Christian Europe. Salmasius, Claude de Saumaise, professor at Leyden University, was hardly a match for Milton, either as a scholar, Latinist or historian. Indeed, Milton's reply (in Latin of course, though quickly translated) was so convincing that even Salmasius' friends complained that Europe's greatest scholar had been eclipsed by an unknown Englishman who had become the subject of debate from one end of Europe to the other. Milton considered his *Defence* 'of paramount importance', and his victory over Salmasius 'a triumph for his country and its revolution' (Christopher Hill, *Milton and the English Revolution*, p. 182). He was later (in 1654) to write a *Second Defence*, and he thought of both with pride as redeeming his pledge to the people of England.

TO THE FIRST OF NATIONS

And now I think, through God's assistance, I have finished the work I undertook, to wit, the defence of the noble actions of my countrymen at home and abroad, against the raging and envious madness of this distracted sophister; and the asserting of the common rights of the people against the unjust domination of kings, not out of any hatred to kings,

but tyrants; nor have I purposely left unanswered any one arg[ument]
alleged by my adversary, nor any one example or authority quoted [by]
him, that seemed to have any force in it, or the least colour of an argument. Perhaps I have been guilty rather of the other extreme, of replying
to some of his fool-cries and trifles, as if they were solid arguments, and
thereby may seem to have attributed more to them than they deserved.
One thing yet remains to be done, which perhaps is of the greatest concern of all, and that is, that you, my countrymen, refute this adversary
of yours yourselves, which I do not see any other means of effecting,
than by a constant endeavour to outdo all men's bad words by your own
good deeds. When you laboured under more sorts of oppression than
one, you betook yourselves to God for refuge, and he was graciously
pleased to hear your most earnest prayers and desires. He has gloriously
delivered you, the first of nations, from the two greatest mischiefs of this
life, and most pernicious to virtue, tyranny, and superstition; he has
endued you with greatness of mind to be the first of mankind, who, after
having conquered their own king, and having had him delivered into
their hands, have not scrupled to condemn him judicially, and, pursuant
to that sentence of condemnation, to put him to death. After the per-
forming so glorious an action as this, you ought to do nothing that is
mean and little, not so much as to think of, much less to do, anything
but what is great and sublime. Which to attain to, this is your only way:
as you have subdued your enemies in the field, so to make appear, that
unarmed, and in the highest outward peace and tranquillity, you of all
mankind are best able to subdue ambition, avarice, the love of riches;
and can best avoid the corruptions that prosperity is apt to introduce,
(which generally subdue and triumph over other nations,) to show as
great justice, temperance, and moderation in the maintaining your liberty, as you have shown courage in freeing yourselves from slavery.
These are the only arguments by which you will be able to evince that
you are not such persons as this fellow represents you, – traitors, robbers,
murderers, parricides, madmen; that you did not put your king to death
out of any ambitious design, or a desire of invading the rights of others;
not out of any seditious principles or sinister ends; that it was not an act
of fury or madness; but that it was wholly out of love to your liberty,
your religion, to justice, virtue, and your country, that you punished a
tyrant. But if it should fall out otherwise, (which God forbid;) if, as you
have been valiant in war, you should grow debauched in peace, you that
have had such visible demonstrations of the goodness of God to yourselves, and his wrath against your enemies; and that you should not have
learned by so eminent, so remarkable an example before your eyes, to

work righteousness; for my part, I shall easily grant and
I cannot deny it,) whatever ill men may speak or think of
ery true. And you will find in a little time, that God's dis-
inst you will be greater than it has been against your adver-
ter than his grace and favour has been to yourselves, which
you had larger experience of than any other nation under heaven.

THOMAS HOBBES (1588–1679)   Mid-1651

From *Leviathan*, pp. 161, 385–6, 710–12

In *Leviathan* – 'that great Leviathan called a Common-wealth or State' – Hobbes
is above all concerned with the problems of Authority and Power, of social equilibrium and social conflict, peace and war, as determined by the revolutionary
upheavals that transformed England during the period of his eleven-year exile in
France between 1640 and 1651. 'The utility of moral and political philosophy,'
he wrote in *The Elements of Philosophy*, 'is to be estimated, not so much by the
commodities we have by knowing these sciences, as by the calamities we receive
by not knowing them. Now all such calamities as may be avoided by human
industry arise from war, but chiefly from civil war, for from this proceed slaughter, solitude, and the want of all things.' His analysis of the radical issues involved
in defining 'the Matter, Forme, and Power of a Commonwealth' made a profound
challenge to the assumptions of his age, both Royalist and Republican.

COMPETITION

Competition of Riches, Honour, Command, or other power, inclineth
to Contention, Enmity, and War: Because the way of one Competitor,
to the attaining of his desire, is to kill, subdue, supplant, or repel the
other. Particularly, competition of praise, inclineth to a reverence of
Antiquity. For men contend with the living, not with the dead; to these
ascribing more than due, that they may obscure the glory of the other.

JUSTICE EQUALLY ADMINISTERED

The safety of the People, requireth . . . from him or them that have the
Sovereign Power, that Justice be equally administered to all degrees of
People; that is, that as well the rich, and mighty, as poor and obscure

244

persons, may be righted of the injuries done them; so as the great, may have no greater hope of impunity, when they do violence, dishonour, or any Injury to the meaner sort, than when one of these, does the like to one of them: For in this consisteth Equity; to which, as being a Precept of the Law of Nature, a Sovereign is as much subject, as any of the meanest of his People. All breaches of the Law, are offences against the Common-wealth: but there be some, that are also against private Persons. Those that concern the Common-wealth only, may without breach of Equity be pardoned; for every man may pardon what is done against himself, according to his own discretion. But an offence against a private man, cannot in Equity be pardoned, without the consent of him that is injured; or reasonable satisfaction.

The Inequality of Subjects, proceedeth from the Acts of Sovereign Power; and therefore has no more place in the presence of the Sovereign; that is to say, in a Court of Justice, than the Inequality between Kings and their Subjects, in the presence of the King of Kings. The honour of great Persons, is to be valued for their beneficence, and the aids they give to men of inferior rank, or not at all. And the violences, oppressions, and injuries they do, are not extenuated, but aggravated by the greatness of their persons; because they have least need to commit them. The consequences of this partiality towards the great, proceed in this manner. Impunity maketh Insolence; Insolence Hatred; and Hatred, an Endeavour to pull down all oppressing and contumelious greatness, though with the ruin of the Common-wealth.

THE MACHINATIONS OF MEN AGAINST THE TRUTH

. . . As the Inventions of men are woven, so also are they ravelled out . . . The web begins at the first Elements of Power, which are Wisdom, Humility, Sincerity, and other virtues of the Apostles, whom the people converted, obeyed, out of Reverence, not by Obligation: Their Consciences were Free, and their Words and Actions subject to none but the Civil Power. Afterwards the Presbyters (as the flocks of Christ increased) assembling to consider what they should teach, and thereby obliging themselves to teach nothing against the Decrees of their Assemblies, made it to be thought the people were thereby obliged to follow their Doctrine, and when they refused, refused to keep them company, (that was then called Excommunication,) not as being Infidels, but as being disobedient: And this was the first knot upon their Liberty. And the number of Presbyters increasing, the Presbyters of the chief City or

Province, got themselves an authority over the Parochial Presbyters, and appropriated to themselves the names of Bishops: And this was a second knot on Christian Liberty. Lastly, the Bishop of Rome . . . took upon him an Authority . . . over all other Bishops of the Empire: Which was the third and last knot, and the whole *Synthesis* and *Construction* of the Pontifical Power.

And therefore the *Analysis*, or *Resolution* is by the same way; but beginning with the knot that was last tied; as we may see in the dissolution of the praeterpolitical Church Government in England. First, the Power of the Popes was dissolved totally by Queen Elizabeth; and the Bishops, who before exercised their Functions in Right of the Pope, did afterwards exercise the same in Right of the Queen and her Successors . . . And so was untied the first knot. After this, the Presbyterians lately in England obtained the putting down of Episcopacy: And so was the second knot dissolved: And almost at the same time, the Power was taken also from the Presbyterians: And so we are reduced to the Independency of the Primitive Christians to follow Paul, or Cephas, or Apollos, every man as he liketh best: Which . . . is perhaps the best: First, because there ought to be no Power over the Consciences of men, but of the Word itself, working Faith in every one, not always according to the purpose of them that Plant and Water, but of God himself, that giveth the Increase: and secondly, because it is unreasonable in them, who teach that there is such danger in every little Error, to require of a man endued with Reason of his own, to follow the Reason of any other man, or of the most voices of many other men. Nor ought those Teachers to be displeased with this loss of their ancient Authority: For there is none should know better than they, that power is preserved by the same Virtues by which it is acquired; that is to say, by Wisdom, Humility, Clearness of Doctrine, and sincerity of Conversation; and not by suppression of the Natural Sciences, and of the Morality of Natural Reason; nor by obscure Language; nor by Arrogating to themselves more Knowledge than they make appear; nor by Pious Frauds; nor by such other Faults, but also scandals, apt to make men stumble one time or other upon the suppression of their Authority.

But after this Doctrine, *that the Church now Militant, is the Kingdom of God spoken of in the Old and New Testament*, was received in the World; the ambition and canvassing for the Offices that belong thereunto, and especially for that great Office of being Christ's Lieutenant . . . became by degrees so evident, that they lost the inward Reverence due to the Pastoral Function . . . For, from the time that the Bishop of Rome had gotten to be acknowledged for Bishop Universal, by pretence of Succession to St Peter, their whole Hierarchy, or Kingdom of Darkness, may be compared not unfitly to the *Kingdom of Fairies*; that is, to the old wives' *Fables* in England, concerning *Ghosts* and *Spirits*, and the feats they play in the night. And if a man consider the original of this great Ecclesiastical Dominion, he will easily perceive, that the *Papacy*, is no other, than the *Ghost* of the deceased *Roman Empire*, sitting crowned upon the grave thereof: For so did the Papacy start up on a sudden out of the Ruins of that Heathen Power . . .

GERRARD WINSTANLEY November 1651
(1609–after 1660)

From *The Law of Freedom*, pp. 277–8, 285–7, 289–90, 294–6, 311–12, 312–14, 389

At a time of general discontent with the rule of the Rump Parliament, in the aftermath of the battle of Worcester (3 September 1651) at which the Scottish Royalists were defeated, there was much questioning of direction, with various schemes of 'healing government' put forward. Winstanley here offers his own mature and systematic answer, begun perhaps during the Digger experiment but given its final shape in 1651, in the light of that experience. Dedicated to Oliver Cromwell, it was clearly aimed at a wide audience, and represents the most lucid and compelling statement for a radical, revolutionary concept of the Commonwealth. Not that Winstanley could have had much hope, as Christopher Hill puts it (p. 32), 'of converting the Lord General to communism, or that Cromwell would carry out at one blow from above the revolution which the Diggers had failed to bring about from below'. But he had to make his appeal to Cromwell 'to act for common freedom', since 'you have the eyes of the people all the land over', and 'I have no power'. After *The Law of Freedom*, Winstanley wrote no more; we know only that he was still living at Cobham in 1660. But his work remains an eloquent witness to the creation of a commonwealth in which men will know how to live in 'the free enjoyment of the earth'.

TO CROMWELL, DESIRING A COMMONWEALTH'S FREEDOM

. . . Sir, I pray bear with me; my spirit is upon such a lock that I must speak plain to you, lest it tell me another day, 'If thou hadst spoke plain, things might have been amended.'

The earth wherein your gourd grows is the commoners of England.

The gourd is that power which covers you, which will be established to you by giving the people their true freedoms, and not otherwise.

The root of your gourd is the heart of the people, groaning under kingly bondage and desiring a commonwealth's freedom in their English earth.

The worm in the earth, now gnawing at the root of your gourd, is discontents, because engagements and promises made to them by such as have power are not kept . . .

Would you have your gourd stand for ever? Then cherish the root in the earth, that is the heart of your friends, the oppressed commoners of England, by killing the worm. And nothing will kill this worm but performance of professions, words and promises, that they may be made free men from tyranny.

THE BONDAGE OF BUYING AND SELLING

And now I have set the candle at your door, for you have power in your hand, in this other added opportunity, to act for common freedom if you will: I have no power.

It may be here are some things inserted which you may not like, yet other things you may like, therefore I pray you read it, and be as the industrious bee, suck out the honey and cast away the weeds.

Though this platform be like a piece of timber rough hewed, yet the discreet worker may take it and frame a handsome building out of it.

It is like a poor man that comes clothed to your door in a torn country garment, who is unacquainted with the learned citizens' unsettled forms and fashions; take off the clownish language, for under that you may see beauty.

It may be you will say, 'If tithes be taken from the priests and impropriators, and copyhold services from lords of manors, how shall they be provided for again; for is it not unrighteous to take their estates from them?'

I answer, when tithes were first enacted, and lordly power drawn over the backs of the oppressed, the kings and conquerors made no scruple of conscience to take it, though the people lived in sore bondage of poverty for want of it; and can there be scruple of conscience to make restitution of this which hath been so long stolen goods? It is no scruple arising from the righteous law, but from covetousness, who goes away sorrowful to hear he must part with all to follow righteousness and peace.

But though you do take away tithes and the power of lords of manors, yet there will be no want to them, for they have the freedom of the common stock, they may send to the store-houses for what they want, and live more free than now they do; for now they are in care and vexation by servants, by casualties, by being cheated in buying and selling and many other encumbrances, but then they will be free from all, for the common store-houses is every man's riches, not any one's.

'Is it not buying and selling a righteous law?' No, it is the law of the conqueror, but not the righteous law of creation: how can that be righteous which is a cheat? For is not this a common practice, when he hath a bad horse or cow, or any bad commodity, he will send it to the market, to cheat some simple, plain-hearted man or other; and when he comes home will laugh at his neighbour's hurt, and much more etc.

When mankind began to buy and sell, then did he fall from his innocence; for then they began to oppress and cozen one another of their creation birthright. As for example: if the land belong to three persons, and two of them buy and sell the earth and the third give no consent, his right is taken from him, and his posterity is engaged in a war.

When the earth was first bought and sold, many gave no consent: as when our crown lands and bishops' lands were sold, some foolish soldiers yielded, and covetous officers were active in it, to advance themselves above their brethren; but many who paid taxes and free-quarter for the purchase of it gave no consent but declared against it as an unrighteous thing, depriving posterity of their birthrights and freedoms.

Therefore this buying and selling did bring in, and still doth bring in, discontent and wars, which have plagued mankind sufficiently for so doing. And the nations of the world will never learn to beat their swords into ploughshares, and their spears into pruning hooks, and leave off warring, until this cheating device of buying and selling be cast out among the rubbish of kingly power.

'But shall not one man be richer than another?'

There is no need of that; for riches make men vain-glorious, proud, and to oppress their brethren; and are occasion of wars.

No man can be rich, but he must be rich by his own labours, or by the labours of other men helping him. If a man have no help from his neighbour, he shall never gather an estate of hundreds and thousands a year. If other men help him to work, then are those riches his neighbours' as well as his own; for they may be the fruit of other men's labours as well as his own.

But all rich men live at ease, feeding and clothing themselves by the labours of other men, not by their own; which is their shame, and not their nobility; for it is a more blessed thing to give than to receive. But rich men receive all they have from the labourer's hand, and what they give, they give away other men's labours, not their own. Therefore they are not righteous actors in the earth.

SWORDS INTO PLOUGHSHARES

To Cromwell

. . . Lay this platform of commonwealth's government in one scale, and lay monarchy or kingly government in the other scale, and see which give true weight to righteous freedom and peace. There is no middle path between these two, for a man must either be a free and true commonwealth's man, or a monarchical tyrannical royalist.

If any say, 'This will bring poverty'; surely they mistake. For there will be plenty of all earthly commodities, with less labour and trouble than now it is under monarchy. There will be no want, for every man may keep as plentiful a house as he will, and never run into debt, for common stock pays for all.

If you say, 'Some will live idle': I answer, No. It will make idle persons to become workers, as is declared in the platform: there shall be neither beggar nor idle person.

If you say, 'This will make men quarrel and fight':

I answer, No. It will turn swords into ploughshares, and settle such a peace in the earth, as nations shall learn war no more. Indeed the government of kings is a breeder of wars, because men being put into the straits of poverty are moved to fight for liberty, and to take one another's estates from them, and to obtain mastery. Look into all armies and see what they do more, but make some poor, some rich; put some into freedom, and others into bondage. And is not this a plague upon mankind? . . .

I do not say, nor desire, that every one shall be compelled to practise this commonwealth's government; for the spirits of some will be enemies at first, though afterwards will prove the most cordial and true friends thereunto.

Yet I desire that the commonwealth's land, which is the ancient commons and waste land, and the lands newly got in by the Army's victories out of the oppressors' hands, as parks, forests, chases, and the like, may be set free to all that have lent assistance, either of person or purse, to obtain it; and to all that are willing to come in to the practice of this government and be obedient to the laws thereof. And for others who are not willing, let them stay in the way of buying and selling, which is the law of the conqueror, till they be willing.

And so I leave this in your hand, humbly prostrating myself and it before you; and remain

A true lover of commonwealth's

Novemb. 5,
government, peace and freedom,

1651
Gerrard Winstanley

THE FREE ENJOYMENT OF THE EARTH

Chapter 1

The great searching of heart in these days is to find out where true freedom lies, that the commonwealth of England might be established in peace.

Some say, 'It lies in the free use of trading, and to have all patents, licences and restraints removed.' But this is a freedom under the will of a conqueror.

Others say, 'It is true freedom to have ministers to preach, and for people to hear whom they will, without being restrained or compelled from or to any form of worship.' But this is an unsettled freedom.

Others say, 'It is true freedom to have community with all women, and to have liberty to satisfy their lusts and greedy appetites.' But this is the freedom of wanton unreasonable beasts, and tends to destruction.

Others say, 'It is true freedom that the elder brother shall be landlord of the earth, and the younger brother a servant.' And this is but a half freedom, and begets murmurings, wars and quarrels.

All these and such like are freedoms: but they lead to bondage, and are not the true foundation-freedom which settles a commonwealth in peace.

True commonwealth's freedom lies in the free enjoyment of the earth.

True freedom lies where a man receives his nourishment and preservation, and that is in the use of the earth. For as man is compounded of the four materials of the creation, fire, water, earth and air; so is he preserved by the compounded bodies of these four, which are the fruits of the earth; and he cannot live without them. For take away the free use of these and the body languishes, the spirit is brought into bondage and at length departs, and ceaseth his motional action in the body.

All that a man labours for, saith Solomon, is this, That he may enjoy the free use of the earth, with the fruits thereof. Eccles. ii, 24.

Do not the ministers preach for maintenance in the earth? the lawyers plead causes to get possessions of the earth? Doth not the soldier fight for the earth? And doth not the landlord require rent, that he may live in the fulness of the earth by the labour of his tenants?

And so, from the thief upon the highway to the king who sits upon the throne, do not everyone strive, either by force of arms or by secret cheats, to get the possessions of the earth one from another, because they see their freedom lies in plenty, and their bondage lies in poverty?

Surely then, oppressing lords of manors, exacting landlords and tithe-takers, may as well say their brethren shall not breath in the air, nor enjoy warmth in their bodies, nor have the moist waters to fall upon them in showers, unless they will pay them rent for it: as to say their brethren shall not work upon earth, nor eat the fruits thereof, unless they will hire that liberty of them. For he that takes upon him to restrain his brother from the liberty of the one, may upon the same ground restrain him from the liberty of all four, viz. fire, water, earth and air.

A man had better to have had no body than to have no food for it; therefore this restraining of the earth from brethren by brethren is oppression and bondage; but the free enjoyment thereof is true freedom.

I speak now in relation between the oppressor and the oppressed; the inward bondages I meddle not with in this place, though I am assured that, if it be rightly searched into, the inward bondages of the mind, as covetousness, pride, hypocrisy, envy, sorrow, fears, desperation and madness, are all occasioned by the outward bondage that one sort of people lay upon another.

And thus far natural experience makes it good, that true freedom lies in the free enjoyment of the earth.

COMMONWEALTH'S GOVERNMENT

Chapter 2

Commonwealth's government governs the earth without buying and selling; and thereby becomes a man of peace, and the restorer of ancient peace and freedom. He makes provision for the oppressed, the weak and the simple, as well as for the rich, the wise and the strong. He beats swords and spears into pruning hooks and ploughs; he makes both elder and younger brother freemen in the earth. Micah iv, 3, 4, Isaiah xxxiii, 1 and lxv, 17–25.

All slavaries and oppressions which have been brought upon mankind by kings, lords of manors, lawyers and landlords and the divining clergy, are all cast out again by this government, if it be right in power as well as in name.

For this government is the true restorer of all long-lost freedoms, and so becomes the joy of all nations, and the blessing of the whole earth: for this takes off the kingly curse, and makes Jerusalem a praise in the earth. Therefore all you who profess religion and spiritual things, now look to it, and see what spirit you do profess, for your profession is brought to trial.

If once commonwealth's government be set upon the throne, then no tyranny or oppression can look him in the face and live.

For where oppression lies upon brethren by brethren, that is no commonwealth's government, but the kingly government still; and the mystery of iniquity hath taken that peace-maker's name to be a cloak to hide his subtle covetousness, pride and oppression under.

O England, England, wouldst thou have thy government sound and healthful? Then cast about and see and search diligently to find out all those burdens that came in by kings, and remove them; and then will thy commonwealth's government arise from under the clods, under which as yet it is buried and covered with deformity.

If true commonwealth's freedom lie in the free enjoyment of the earth, as it doth, then whatsoever law or custom doth deprive brethren of their freedom in the earth, it is to be cast out as unsavoury salt.

THE RIGHT CHANNEL OF FREEDOM

Chapter 2

The great lawgiver in commonwealth's government is the spirit of universal righteousness dwelling in mankind, now rising up to teach everyone to do to another as he would have another do to him, and is no respecter of persons: and this spirit hath been killed in the Pharasaical kingly spirit of self-love, and been buried in the dunghill of that enmity for many years past . . .

If any go about to build up commonwealth's government upon kingly principles, they will both shame and lose themselves; for there is a plain difference between the two governments.

And if you do not run in the right channel of freedom, you must, nay you will, as you do, face about and turn back again to Egyptian monarchy: and so your names in the days of posterity shall stink and be blasted with abhorred infamy for your unfaithfulness to common freedom; and the evil effects will be sharp upon the backs of posterity.

Therefore seeing England is declared to be a free commonwealth, and the name thereof established by a law; surely then the greatest work is now to be done, and that is to escape all kingly cheats in setting up a commonwealth's government, that the power and the name may agree together; so that all the inhabitants may live in peace, plenty and freedom, otherwise we shall shew our government to be gone no further but to the half day of the Beast, or to the dividing of time, of which there must be an overturn. Dan. vii, 25. Rev. xii, 14.

For oppression was always the occasion why the spirit of freedom in the people desired change of government . . .

> The haven gates are now set ope for English man to enter:
> The freedoms of the earth's his due, if he will make adventure.

In his other pamphlets, and here above all, Winstanley had defined his programme for an alternative society to that which actually prevailed – communist and secular in its emphasis, rooted in the common plenty of the earth, and insisting, beyond all expectations, that 'there cannot be a universal liberty till this universal community be established' (Sabine, p. 199). The principles he put forward are comprehensive and coherent, and they are an eloquent call for action. But he must clearly have recognized how little chance they had of being implemented in the brutally competitive world in which he lived, and that what he was outlining in *The Law of Freedom* was far ahead of his time, as the epilogue to his work indicates.

EPILOGUE TO THE LAW OF FREEDOM

Here is the righteous law; man, wilt thou it maintain?
It may be, is, as hath still, in the world been slain.
Truth appears in light, falsehood rules in power;
To see these things to be is cause of grief each hour.
Knowledge, why didst thou come, to wound and not to cure?
I sent not for thee, thou didst me inlure.
Where knowledge does increase, there sorrows multiply,
To see the great deceit which in the world doth lie:
Man saying one thing now, unsaying it anon,
Breaking all's engagements, when deeds for him are done.
O power where art thou, that must mend things amiss?
Come change the heart of man, and make him truth to kiss.
O death where art thou? Wilt thou not tidings send?

I fear thee not, thou art my loving friend.
Come take this body, and scatter it in the four,
That I may dwell in one, and rest in peace once more.

JOHN MILTON (1608–74)   May 1652

Sonnet *To the Lord General Cromwell, on the Proposals of Certain Ministers at the Committee for Propagation of the Gospel, May 1652*

In the spring of 1652, Parliament appointed the Committee for the Propagation of the Gospel for the purpose of regulating and defining the central issues of religious faith. This Committee proposed the setting up of an established Church, and discussed at length the limits of toleration to be permitted to those whose religious teachings might not conform to such a Church. They produced a list of fifteen points defining the fundamental principles of the Christian religion, and proposed that no one should be allowed to preach in public without a certificate of orthodoxy. This seemed to Milton a new threat to freedom of conscience, and he found himself reacting against even the Independents he had praised six years previously for their stand against the Presbyterian majority. Thus he appeals to Cromwell himself, as a man known to be firmly opposed to intolerance; and he does so with confidence, having proved himself a powerful advocate of Cromwell's policies, and from his position as Secretary of Foreign Tongues.

TO SAVE FREE CONSCIENCE

Cromwell, our chief of men, who through a cloud
   Not of war only, but detractions rude,
   Guided by faith and matchless fortitude,
   To peace and truth thy glorious way hast plough'd,
And on the neck of crowned Fortune proud
   Hast rear'd God's trophies and his work pursued,
   While Darwen stream with blood of Scots imbrued
   And Dunbar field resounds thy praises loud,
And Worcester's laureate wreath: yet much remains
   To conquer still; Peace hath her victories
   No less renown'd than war; new foes arise,
Threatening to bind our souls with secular chains.
   Help us to save free conscience from the paw
   Of hireling wolves whose Gospel is their maw.

JAMES NAYLER (1617?–1660)

From *A Few Words*, in *Collection of Sundry Books*, pp. 113–14

Nayler was a yeoman from West Ardsley near Wakefield, had served as quarter-master in the Parliamentary army, and fought at Dunbar. In the 1650s many considered him the 'chief leader', the 'head Quaker in England', even above Fox, which is to say no more than that Fox himself was not the only leader of the movement.

THE WORST OF HYPOCRITES

. . . Now who will be the greatest Deceivers? whether a poor, despised, persecuted, reproached People, whom God hath called out of the World's Ways, Words, Works, Worship, Riches and Pleasures, and so are become Strangers and Wanderers to and fro, *seeking a City whose Builder and Maker is God* (Heb. xi, 26, 27, 28), and for this their Obedience being counted the *Off-scouring of the World* (1 Cor. iv, 9–13) and suffering all with Patience, as the Saints did, who declared this in Scripture; or they who profess that Scripture which witnesseth these Things, but still are in their Lusts, Pride, Covetousness, Exaltations over others, living like fat Swine in the Earth, differing from the World in nothing, but only in Notions and long Prayers, whereby they appear to be greater Deceivers than the World, who profess nothing but what they are? And for the worst of Hypocrites, for they who profess the highest Things, and most like to Saints, which they live not the life of, nor are sanctified as they were, whose Conditions they profess. These are the worst Hypocrites . . .

JOHN LILBURNE (1614?–57) Before 20 August 1653

From *The Just Defence of John Lilburne*, in Haller and Davies, eds., *Leveller Tracts*, pp. 463–4

Released from the Tower in July 1649, Lilburne was arrested again after the final September mutiny of troops at Oxford, acquitted in October to great popular rejoicing, and released in November. For a while he kept quiet; but when he put in a petition against corruption over land granted him as reparation, it was rejected, and on 30 January 1653 Parliament banished him from England for life. He went to Amsterdam, where he continued his pamphleteering; but when Crom well expelled the Rump in April 1653, ventured to return home. For printing a *Suit for Protection* in June, he was at once arrested, sent to Newgate, put on trial for his life, and (on 20 August) acquitted, during which time his friends printed at least thirty pamphlets on his behalf. But Cromwell kept him in prison till 1655, fearing his effect on the army – by which time he had become a Quaker and at last come to terms. He died at Eltham in Kent on 29 August 1657.

THE LAWS AND RIGHTS OF THE NATION

. . . Dear Countrymen, friends and Christians, ask them what evil I have done, and they can show you none. No, my great and only fault is that (as they conceive) I will never brook whilst I live to see . . . the laws and rights of the Nation trod under foot by themselves, who have all the obligations of men and Christians to revive and restore them. They imagine, whilst I have breath, the old law of the land will be pleaded and upheld against the new, against all innovated law or practice whatsoever. And because I am, and continue, constant to my principles upon which I first engaged for the common liberty, and will no more bear in these the violation of them than I did in the King, Bishops, Lords, or Commons, but cry aloud many times of their abominable unworthiness in their so doing; therefore, to stop my mouth and take away my life, they cry out I never will be quiet, I never will be content with any power. But the just God heareth in heaven, and those who are his true servants will hear and consider upon earth, and I trust will not judge according to the voice of self-seeking ambitious men, their creatures and relations, but will judge righteous judgement, and then I doubt not all their aspersions of me will appear most false and causeless, when the worst I have said or written of them and their ways will prove less than they have deserved.

Another stratagem they have upon me is to possess all men that all the soldiers in the Army are against me. But they know the contrary, otherwise why do they so carefully suppress all petitions which the soldiers have been handing in my behalf? Indeed those of the soldiers that hear nothing but what they please of me, either by their scandalous tongues or books, may through misinformation be against me. But would they permit them to hear or read what is extant to my vindication, I would wish no better friends than the soldiers of the Army; for I am certain I never wronged one of them, nor are they apt to wrong any man, except upon a misinformation.

But I hope this discourse will be satisfactory both to them and all other men, that I am no such Wolf, Bear or Lion, that right or wrong deserves to be destroyed; and through the truth herein appearing, will strongly persuade for a more gentle construction of my intentions and conversation, and be an effectual antidote against such poisonous asps who endeavour to kill me with the bitterness of their envenomed tongues, that they shall not be able to prevail against me, to sway the consciences of any to my prejudice in the day of my trial . . .

GEORGE FOX (1624–91)   1654

From *Journal*, Everyman edition, p. 106

Fox was arrested in Whetstone, Leicestershire, before a meeting of Friends, and brought before Colonel Hacker, because 'at this time there was a noise of a plot against Oliver Cromwell'. After some discussion, Hacker said he could 'go home, and keep there, and not go abroad to meetings. I told him I was an innocent man, free from plots, and denied all such work. His son Needham said, "Father, this man hath reigned too long, it is time to have him cut off." I asked him, "For what? what have I done? or whom have I wronged from a child?"' Colonel Hacker then told him again to go home and stay there. 'I told him if I should promise him that, it would manifest that I was guilty of something, to go home, and make my home a prison; and if I went to meetings, they would say I broke their order. I told them I should go to meetings as the Lord should order me, and therefore could not submit to their requirings; but I said, "We are a peaceable people." "Well then," said Colonel Hacker, "I will send you to my Lord Protector by Captain Drury, one of his life-guards." And so Fox was taken down to London and lodged at the Mermaid by Captain Drury.

MEETING WITH CROMWELL: 'A WITNESS AGAINST ALL VIOLENCE'

When he came to me again, he told me the Protector required that I should promise not to take up a carnal sword or weapon against him or the Government. And I should write it in what words I saw good, and set my hand to it. I said little in reply to Captain Drury. But the next morning I was moved of the Lord to write a paper 'To the Protector by the Name of Oliver Cromwell', wherein I did in the presence of the Lord God declare that I did deny the wearing or drawing of a carnal sword, or any other outward weapon, against him or any man: and that I was sent of God to stand a witness against all violence, and against the works of darkness; and to turn people from darkness to light; and to bring them from the occasion of war and fighting to the peaceable gospel, and from being evil-doers which the magistrates' swords should be a terror to. When I had written what the Lord had given me to write, I set my name to it, and gave it to Captain Drury to hand to Oliver Cromwell, which he did.

Then after some time Captain Drury brought me before the Protector himself at Whitehall. It was in a morning, before he was dressed, and one Harvey, who had come a little among Friends, but was disobedient, waited upon him. When I came in, I was moved to say, 'Peace be in this house'; and I bid him to keep in the fear of God, that he might receive wisdom from Him, that by it he might be directed, and order all things under his hand to God's glory. I spake much to him of Truth, and much discourse I had with him about religion; wherein he carried himself very moderately. But he said we quarrelled with priests, whom he called ministers. I told him I did not quarrel with them, but they quarrelled with me and with my friends ... Then I showed him that the prophets, Christ, and the apostles declared freely, and against them that did not declare freely, such as preached for filthy lucre, and divined for money, and preached for hire, and were covetous and greedy, like the dumb dogs that can never have enough; and that they that have the same spirit that Christ and the prophets and the apostles had, could not but declare against all such now, as they did then. As I spake, he several times said it was very good and it was truth. I told him that all Christendom (so called) possessed the Scriptures, but wanted the power and Spirit that they had who gave forth the Scriptures, and that was the reason they were not in fellowship with the Son, or with the Father, or with the Scriptures, or one with another.

ANDREW MARVELL (1621–78)   1655

'The First Anniversary of the Government Under O.C.', ll. 62–110

Marvell had published the poem anonymously in 1655. Taking a moderate and somewhat detached view of the great events of his time, he here celebrates the institution on 16 December 1653 of Oliver Cromwell as Lord Protector of the Commonwealth of England, Scotland and Ireland and his rule by 'Instrument of Government'. Samuel Parker, Marvell's enemy, calls it 'a congratulatory poem in praise of the Tyrant . . . a satire upon all rightful Kings'; and it certainly gives the Protector a unique place in the order of things – 'a greater thing, Than aught below, or yet above a King'.

CAPTAIN OF THE COMMONWEALTH

Such was that wondrous Order and Consent,
When *Cromwell* tun'd the ruling Instrument;
While tedious Statesmen many years did hack,
Framing a Liberty that still went back;
Whose num'rous Gorge could swallow in an hour
That Island, which the Sea cannot devour:
Then our *Amphion* issues out and sings,
And once he struck, and twice, the pow'rful Strings.

　　The Commonwealth then first together came,
And each one enter'd in the willing Frame;
All other Matter yields, and may be rul'd;
But who the Minds of stubborn Men can build?
No Quarry bears a Stone so hardly wrought,
Nor with such labour from its Centre brought;
None to be sunk in the Foundation bends,
Each in the House the highest Place contends,
And each the Hand that lays him will direct,
And some fall back upon the Architect;
Yet all compos'd by his attractive Song,
Into the Animated City throng.

　　The Commonwealth does through their Centres all
Draw the Circumf'rence of the public Wall;
The crossest Spirits here do take their part,
Fast'ning the Contignation which they thwart;
And they, whose Nature leads them to divide,
Uphold, this one, and that the other Side;
But the most Equal still sustain the Height,
And they as Pillars keep the Work upright;
While the resistance of opposed Minds,
The Fabric as with Arches stronger binds,
Which on the Basis of a Senate free,
Knit by the Roof's Protecting weight agree.

　　When for his Foot he thus a place had found,
He hurls e'er since the World about him round;
And in his sev'ral Aspects, like a Star,

Here shines in Peace, and thither shoots a War.
While by his Beams observing Princes steer,
And wisely court the Influences they fear;
O would they rather by his Pattern won,
Kiss the approaching, nor yet angry Son;
And in their number'd Footsteps humbly tread
The path where holy Oracles do lead;
How might they under such a Captain raise,
The great Designs kept for the latter Days!

OLIVER CROMWELL
(1599–1658)

17 September 1656

From his opening speech to his Second Parliament

TO KEEP THINGS EQUAL

Our practice since the last Parliament hath been to let all this nation see
that whatever pretensions to religion would continue quiet and peaceable, they should enjoy conscience and liberty to themselves, and not to
make religion a pretence for arms and blood. Truly we have suffered
them, and that cheerfully, so to enjoy their own liberties. Whatsoever
is contrary, let the pretence be never so specious, if it tend to combination, to interests and factions, we shall not care, by the grace of God,
whom we meet withal. And truly, I am against all liberty of conscience
repugnant to this. If men will profess, – be they those under Baptism,
be they those of the Independent judgement simply, or of the Presbyterian judgement, – in the name of God, encourage them, countenance
them: so long as they do plainly continue to be thankful to God, and to
make use of the liberty given them to enjoy their own consciences . . .
Whoever hath faith in Christ, let his form be what it will; he walking
peaceably, without prejudice to others under other forms, – it is a debt
due to God and Christ, and He will require it, if a Christian may not
enjoy his liberty. If a man of one form be trampling upon the heels of
another form, – if an Independent, for example, will despise him under
Baptism, and will revile him, and reproach and provoke him, – I will
not suffer it in him. If, on the other side, those of the Anabaptist shall
be censuring the godly ministers of the nation who profess under that
of Independency; or if those that profess under Presbytery shall be

reproaching or speaking evil of them, traducing and censuring of them, as I would not be willing to see the day when England shall be in the power of Presbytery to impose upon the consciences of others that profess faith in Christ, so I will not endure any reproach to them. But God give us hearts and spirits to keep things equal, which, truly, I must profess to you, hath been my temper. I have had some boxes and rebukes on the one hand and on the other; some censuring me for Presbytery; others as an inletter to all the sects and heresies of the nation. I have borne my reproach: but I have, through God's mercy, not been unhappy in hindering any one religion to impose upon another . . . And, if it shall be found to be the Civil Magistrate's real endeavour to keep all professing Christians in this relation to one another; not suffering any to say or do what will justly provoke the others; I think he that would have more liberty than this, is not worthy of any.

Faced with strong conservative elements in this Parliament, many of them intolerant and alarmed by the activities of Quakers and Ranters and other sects they considered scurrilous – men who were 'anxious to finish once and for all with the policy of religious toleration which, in their view, had been the bane of England for a decade,' (Hill, *World Turned Upside Down*, p. 250), Cromwell emphasized (on behalf of the government) the need for tolerance, for keeping things equal. In the case of James Nayler, however, the intolerance of Parliament was to prevail and a barbarous sentence was carried out against him (16 December 1656); And though Cromwell questioned its authority, he was later to use the Nayler case to get the army to accept constitutional restrictions upon religious tolerance!

ANDREW MARVELL (1621–78)   3 September 1658

'A Poem Upon the Death of O. C.', ll. 179–208

O CROMWELL, HEAVEN'S FAVOURITE

He first put Armies into *Religion's* hand,
And tim'rous *Conscience* unto *Courage* mann'd:
The Soldier taught that inward Mail to wear,
And *fearing God* how they should *nothing fear*.
Those Strokes he said will pierce through all below
Where those that strike from Heaven fetch their Blow.
Astonish'd armies did their flight prepare,
And Cities strong were stormed by his prayer;
Of that for ever *Preston's* field shall tell

The story, and impregnable *Clonmell*.
And where the sandy mountain *Fenwick* scal'd,
The sea between, yet hence his pray'r prevail'd.
What man was ever so in Heav'n obey'd
Since the commanded sun o'er *Gibeon* stay'd?
In all his wars needs must he triumph, when
He conquer'd *God*, still ere he fought with men:
  Hence, though in battle none so brave or fierce,
Yet him the adverse steel could never pierce.
Pity it seem'd to hurt him more that felt
Each wound himself which he to others dealt;
Danger itself refusing to offend
So loose an enemy, so fast a friend.
  Friendship, that sacred virtue, long does claim
The first foundation of his house and name:
But within one its narrow limits fall,
His tenderness extended unto all.
And that deep soul through every channel flows,
Where kindly nature loves itself to lose.
More strong affections never reason serv'd,
Yet still affected most what best deserv'd.

JOHN MILTON (1608–74)   Before 1660

Paradise Lost, III, ll. 93–128)

Paradise Lost, like *Paradise Regained* and *Samson Agonistes*, is a poem, as Christopher Hill points out, 'about the people of God in defeat anywhere. All three poems are deeply political, wrestling with the problem of the failed revolution, the millennium that did not come' (*Milton and the English Revolution*, p. 362). Milton had not rejected, that is, the commitment of the forties and fifties. He was now 'asking himself why the aims which he had then proclaimed had not been realized'. Thus, in the deepest sense, the story of the Fall is an attempt to 'explain the failure of a revolution' (p. 352) – blame for which 'lies not in the aims – which were God's, and remain right – but in the English people, Milton included. Political failure was ultimately moral failure' (p. 350).

263

WHOSE FAULT?

(God is speaking of Satan, already on his way to 'the newly created World' to pervert Man 'by some false guile'.)

For Man will hearken to his glozing lies,
And easily transgress the sole command,
Sole pledge of his obedience: so will fall
He and his faithless progeny. Whose fault?
Whose but his own? Ingrate, he had of me
All he could have; I made him just and right,
Sufficient to have stood, though free to fall.
Such I created all th'Ethereal Powers
And Spirits, both them who stood and them who failed;
Freely they stood who stood, and fell who fell.
Not free, what proof could they have given sincere
Of true allegiance, constant faith, or love,
Where only what they needs must do appeared,
Not what they would? What praise could they receive,
What pleasure I, from such obedience paid,
When Will and Reason (Reason also is Choice),
Useless and vain, of freedom both despoiled,
Made passive both, had served Necessity,
Not me? They, therefore, as to right belonged,
So were created, nor can justly accuse
Their Maker, or their making, or their fate,
As if Predestination overruled
Their will, disposed by absolute decree
Or high foreknowledge; they themselves decreed
Their own revolt, not I: if I foreknew,
Foreknowledge had no influence on their fault,
Which had no less proved certain unforeknown.
So without least impulse or shadow of fate,
Or aught by me immutably foreseen,
They trespass, authors to themselves in all,
Both what they judge and what they choose; for so
I formed them free, and free they must remain
Till they enthrall themselves; I else must change
Their nature, and revoke the high decree
Unchangeable, eternal, which ordained
Their freedom; they themselves ordained their fall.

264

JOHN MILTON (1608–74) March 1660

From *The Ready and Easy Way to Establish a Free Commonwealth* in *Prose Writings*, pp. 222–9 passim, 234

This pamphlet, first published in March 1660 and in a second revised edition in April – a month before Charles II's return – was Milton's last attempt to persuade Parliament and the people of England to stand firm behind the free commonwealth they had laid the foundations of, 'and to remove, if it be possible, this noxious humour of returning to bondage, instilled of late by some deceivers . . . among too many of the people'. It was an act of resolution and courage in face of a dangerous and deteriorating situation, which left him exposed to the mercy of his enemies. Later in 1660, 'he was in prison, in danger of his life', and 'when released he had to live in obscurity and fear of assassination' (C. Hill, *Milton and the English Revolution*, p. 356).

THE HOPES OF A GLORIOUS RISING COMMONWEALTH

If . . . we prefer a free government, though for the present not obtained, yet all those suggested fears and difficulties, as the event will prove, easily overcome, we remain finally secure from the exasperated regal power, and out of snares; shall retain the best part of our liberty, which is our religion, and the civil part will be from these who defer us, much more easily recovered, being neither so subtle nor so awful as a king re-inthroned. Nor were their actions less both at home and abroad, than might become the hopes of a glorious rising commonwealth: nor were the expressions both of army and people, whether in their public dec-larations or several writings, other than such as testified a spirit in this nation, no less noble and well-fitted to the liberty of a commonwealth, than in the ancient Greeks or Romans. Nor was the heroic cause unsuc-cessfully defended to all Christendom, against the tongue of a famous and thought invincible adversary; nor the constancy and fortitude, that so nobly vindicated our liberty, our victory at once against two the most prevailing usurpers over mankind, superstition and tyranny, unpraised or uncelebrated in a written monument, likely to outlive detraction, as it hath hitherto convinced or silenced not a few of our detractors, especially in part abroad.

After our liberty and religion thus prosperously fought for, gained, and many years possessed, except in those unhappy interruptions, which God hath removed; now that nothing remains, but in all reason the cer-tain hopes of a speedy and immediate settlement for ever in a firm and free commonwealth, for this extolled and magnified nation, regardless both of honour won, or deliverances vouchsafed from heaven, to fall back, or rather to creep back so poorly, as it seems the multitude would, to their once abjured and detested thraldom of kingship, to be ourselves the slanderers of our own just and religious deeds . . . not only argues a strange, degenerate contagion suddenly spread among us, fitted and prepared for new slavery, but will render us a scorn and derision to all our neighbours . . .

IF WE RETURN TO KINGSHIP

Besides this, if we return to kingship, and soon repent (as undoubtedly we shall, when we begin to find the old enchroachment coming on by little and little upon our consciences, which must necessarily proceed from king and bishop united inseparably in one interest), we may be forced perhaps to fight over again all that we have fought, and spend over again all that we have spent, but are never like to attain thus far as we are now advanced to the recovery of our freedom, never to have it in possession as we now have it, never to be vouchsafed hereafter the like mercies and signal assistances from Heaven in our cause, if by our ingrateful backsliding we make these fruitless; flying now to regal concessions from his divine condescensions and gracious answers to our once importuning prayers against the tyranny which we then groaned under; making vain and viler than dirt the blood of so many thousand faithful and valiant Englishmen, who left us this liberty, bought with their lives; losing by a strange after-game of folly all the battles we have won, together with all Scotland as to our conquest, hereby lost, which never any of our kings could conquer, all the treasure we have spent, not that corruptible treasure only, but that far more precious of all our late miraculous deliverances; treading back again with lost labour all our happy steps in the progress of reformation, and most pitifully depriving ourselves the instant fruition of that free government, which we have so dearly purchased, a free commonwealth . . .

God in much displeasure gave a king to the Israelites, and imputed it a sin to them that they sought one; but Christ apparently forbids his disciples to admit of any such heathenish government: 'The kings of the Gentiles,' saith he, 'exercise lordship over them,' and they that 'exercise authority upon them are called benefactors: but ye shall not be so; but he that is greatest among you, let him be as the younger; and he that is chief, as he that serveth.' The occasion of these his words was the ambitious desire of Zebedee's two sons to be exalted above their brethren in his kingdom, which they thought was to be ere long upon earth. That he speaks of civil government, is manifest by the former part of the comparison, which infers the other part to be always in the same kind. And what government comes nearer to this precept of Christ, than a free commonwealth; wherein they who are the greatest, are perpetual servants and drudges to the public at their own cost and charges, neglect their own affairs, yet are not elevated above their brethren; live soberly in their families, walk the street as other men, may be spoken to freely, familiarly, friendly, without adoration? Whereas a king must be adored like a demigod, with a dissolute and haughty court about him, of vast expense and luxury, masks and revels, to the debauching of our prime gentry, both male and female; not in their pastimes only, but in earnest, by the loose employments of court-service, which will be then thought honourable. There will be a queen of no less charge; in most likelihood outlandish and a papist; besides a queen-mother such already; together with both their courts and numerous train: then a royal issue, and ere long severally their sumptuous courts; to the multiplying of a servile crew, not of servants only, but of nobility and gentry, bred up then to the hopes not of public, but of court offices, to be stewards, chamberlains, ushers, grooms even of the close-stool; and the lower their minds debased with court-opinions, contrary to all virtue and reformation, the haughtier will be their pride and profuseness. We may well remember this not long since at home; nor need but look at present into the French court, where enticements and preferments daily draw away and pervert the protestant nobility . . .

TO RUN THEIR NECKS AGAIN INTO THE YOKE

It may be well wondered that any nation, styling themselves free, can suffer any man to pretend hereditary right over them as their lord; whenas, by acknowledging that right, they conclude themselves his servants and his vassals, and so renounce their own freedom. Which how a people and their leaders especially can do, who have fought so gloriously for liberty; how they can change their noble words and actions, heretofore so becoming the majesty of a free people, into the base necessity of court flatteries and prostrations, is not only strange and admirable, but lamentable to think on. That a nation should be so valorous and courageous to win their liberty in the field, and when they have won it, should be so heartless and unwise in their counsels, as not to know how to use it, value it, what to do with it, or with themselves; but after ten or twelve years' prosperous war and contestation with tyranny, basely and besottedly to run their necks again into the yoke which they have broken, and prostrate all the fruits of their victory for nought at the feet of the vanquished, besides our loss of glory, and such an example as kings or tyrants never yet had the like to boast of, will be an ignominy if it befall us, that never yet befell any nation possessed of their liberty; worthy indeed themselves, whatsoever they be, to be for ever slaves, but that part of the nation which consents not with them, as I persuade me of a great number, far worthier than by their means to be brought into the same bondage . . .

THE FOUNDATION FIRMLY LAID OF A FREE COMMONWEALTH

Now is the opportunity, now the very season, wherein we may obtain a free commonwealth, and establish it for ever in the land, without difficulty or much delay. Writs are sent out for elections, and, which is worth observing, in the name, not of any king, but of the keepers of our liberty, to summon a free parliament: which then only will indeed be free; and deserve the true honour of that supreme title, if they preserve us a free people. Which never parliament was more free to do, being now called not as heretofore, by the summons of a king, but by the voice of liberty. And if the people, laying aside prejudice and impatience, will seriously and calmly now consider their own good, both religious and civil, their own liberty and the only means thereof, as shall be here laid down before them, and will elect their knights and burgesses able men, and according to the just and necessary qualifications (which, for aught I hear, remain yet in force unrepealed, as they were formerly decreed in parliament), men not addicted to a single person or house of lords, the work is done; at least the foundation firmly laid of a free commonwealth, and good part also erected of the main structure . . .

THE WAY PLAIN, EASY, AND OPEN

The way propounded is plain, easy, and open before us; without intricacies, without the introducement of new or absolute forms of terms, or exotic models; ideas that would effect nothing; but with a number of new injunctions to manacle the native liberty of mankind; turning all virtue into prescription, servitude, and necessity, to the great impairing and frustrating of Christian liberty. I say again, this way lies free and smooth before us; is not tangled with inconveniences; invents no new incumbrances, requires no perilous, no injurious alteration or circumscription of men's lands and properties; secure, that in this commonwealth, temporal and spiritual lords removed, no man or number of men can attain to such wealth or vast possession, as will need the hedge of an agrarian law (never successful, but the cause rather of sedition, save only where it began seasonably with first possession) to confine them from endangering our public liberty. To conclude, it can have no considerable objection made against it, that is not practicable; lest it be said hereafter, that we gave up our liberty for want of a ready way or distinct form proposed of a free commonwealth. And this facility we shall have above our next neighbouring commonwealth (if we can keep us from the fond conceit of something like a duke of Venice, put lately into many men's heads, by some one or other subtly driving on under that notion his own ambitious ends to lurch a crown), that our liberty shall not be hampered or hovered over by any engagement to such a potent family as the house of Nassau, of whom to stand in perpetual doubt and suspicion, but we shall live the clearest and absolutest free nation in the world.

———

(It was not to be of course. Within a month that 'once abjured and detested thraldom of kingship' had been accepted back again, in Milton's bitter conclusion, 'through the general defection of a misguided and abused multitude'; and the great dream had to be remade on another level.)

JOHN MILTON (1608–74)   After 1660
Paradise Lost, VII, ll. 23–39

In 1660, when Milton's life was under threat and he was forced to go into hiding, there must have been a break in the writing of *Paradise Lost*; and 'a further interruption when he was in prison'(Hill, *Milton and the English Revolution*, p. 365). He was blind, and it would have been dangerous for anyone to help him until after his release; and these lines from Book VII seem to suggest that he was making a fresh start at a time of utter defeat.

Standing on Earth, not rapt above the pole,
More safe I sing with mortal voice, unchanged
To hoarse or mute, though fallen on evil days,
On evil days though fallen, and evil tongues;
In darkness, and with dangers compassed round,
And solitude; yet not alone, while thou
Visit'st my slumbers nightly, or when Morn
Purples the East. Still govern thou my song,
Urania, and fit audience find, though few.
But drive far off the barbarous dissonance
Of Bacchus and his revellers, the race
Of that wild rout that tore the Thracian bard
In Rhodope, where woods and rocks had ears
To rapture, till the savage clamour drowned
Both harp and voice; nor could the Muse defend
Her son. So fail not thou who thee implores;
For thou art heavenly, she an empty dream.

JAMES NAYLER (1617–60)   October 1660

His last testimony, said to be delivered by him about two hours before his departure out of his life, several friends being present, in *Collection of Sundry Books*, p. 696

Nayler had entered Bristol in 1656 on a donkey, accompanied by three women (Martha Simmonds, Hannah Stringer, Dorcas Erbery) strewing palms before him, in a symbolic act of identification, at the height of Quaker radicalism. The conservatives in Parliament seized the opportunity to discourage the Leveller-like activities of the Quakers. Nayler was arrested, flogged and pilloried, had a hole burnt through his tongue and a B for blasphemy branded on his forehead. 'The red-hot iron, some say,' Tomlinson wrote (January 1657) in a circular letter to Friends, 'was great . . . his tongue was so ill burnt that I do not perceive that he speaks yet since it was done . . . He did not move nor shrink all the time while they did those things to him. They are a bundle of the most extream cruelties that hath been heard, and all heaped upon one man. I hear that James did express in writing that he knew nothing but Peace – but as to his outward man that is apparent to all to be tortured by them sufficiently.' Nayler was deeply affected by this barbarous treatment, and the humiliation certainly succeeded in humbling him. He had become estranged from Fox, but they were eventually reconciled, and Nayler sought to live 'in great self-denial and very jealous of himself'. As he put it in 1659: 'The lower God doth bring me . . . the more doth Love and Tenderness spring and spread towards the poor, simple and despised ones, who are poor in spirit, meek and lowly Suffering Lambs, and with those I choose to suffer, and do suffer, wherever they are found.' (From *To All the Dearly Beloved People of God*). His life ended characteristically. He had resolved to set out on foot for the north to visit his wife and children. A Hertford Friend saw him sitting by the roadside mediating. Later, he was seen by another Friend passing through Huntingdon 'in such an awful frame as if he had been redeemed from the earth and a stranger on it, seeking a better country and inheritance'. He was eventually found a few miles out of the town, lying in a field, having been robbed and left there bound. Taken to a Friend's house near King's Ripton, he died quietly towards the end of October 1660.

NAYLER'S LAST WORDS

There is a spirit which I feel that delights to do no evil, nor to revenge any wrong, but delights to endure all things, in hope to enjoy its own in the end. Its hope is to outlive all wrath and contention, and to weary out all exaltation and cruelty, or whatever is of a nature contrary to itself. It sees to the end of all temptations. As it bears no evil in itself, so it conceives none in thoughts to any other. If it be betrayed, it bears it, for its ground and spring is the mercies and forgiveness of God. Its crown is meekness, its life is everlasting love unfeigned; it takes its kingdom with entreaty and not with contention, and keeps it by lowliness of mind. In God alone it can rejoice, though none else regard it, or can own its life. It's conceived in sorrow, and brought forth without any to pity it, nor doth it murmur at grief and oppression. It never rejoiceth but through sufferings; for with the world's joy it is murdered. I found it alone, being forsaken. I have fellowship therein with them who lived in dens and desolate places in the earth, who through death obtained this resurrection and eternal holy life.

Thou wast with me when I fled from the face of mine enemies: then didst Thou warn me in the night: Thou carriedst me in Thy power into the hiding-place Thou hadst prepared for me: there Thou coverdst me with Thy Hand that in time Thou mightst bring me forth a rock before all the world. When I was weak Thou stayedst me with Thy Hand, that in Thy time Thou mightst present me to the world in Thy strength in which I stand, and cannot be moved. Praise the Lord, O my soul. Let this be written for those that come after. Praise the Lord. J. N.

GEORGE FOX (1624–91)

From his *Journal*, first edition, I, pp. 250–51

Fox, in conjunction with another Friend, addressed an appeal to Charles II against the persecution of the Quakers, following an Act of 1661 against those 'refusing to take lawful oaths'.

SUFFERINGS OF THE QUAKERS

Friend, who art the chief ruler of these dominions, here is a list of some of the sufferings of the people of God, in scorn called Quakers. There have been imprisoned in thy name, since thy arrival, by such as thought to ingratiate themselves thereby to thee, three thousand sixty and eight persons. Besides this, our meetings are daily broken up by men with clubs and arms; though we meet peaceably, according to the practice of God's people in the primitive times; and our friends are thrown into waters, and trod upon till the very blood gushes out of them; the number of which abuses can hardly be uttered . . . We are imprisoned because we cannot take the oath of allegiance. Now, if 'yea' be not 'yea', and 'nay' 'nay', to thee and to all men upon the earth, let us suffer as much for breaking of that as others do for breaking an oath . . . We desire that all that are in prison may be set at liberty, and that for the time to come they may not be imprisoned for conscience and for the truth's sake . . .

JOHN MILTON (1608–74)

After 1660

Paradise Lost, X, ll. 616–40

In terms of Milton's politics, *Paradise Lost* embodies in Satan the 'abjured and detested thraldom of kingship', even as its dramatic central theme of the Fall reflects the fall of the English nation, 'fitted and prepared for new slavery'. At this level, God's answer to Satan's great speech proclaiming his triumph over Adam and Eve, 'successful beyond hope', is Milton's own answer to the enemies of England, for whom 'a king must be adored like a demigod'.

THESE DOGS OF HELL

See with what heat these dogs of Hell advance
To waste and havoc yonder World, which I
So fair and good created, and had still
Kept in that state, had not the folly of Man
Let in these wasteful furies, who impute
Folly to me (so doth the Prince of Hell
And his adherents), that with so much ease
I suffer them to enter and possess
A place so heavenly, and, conniving, seem
To gratify my scornful enemies,
That laugh, as if transported with some fit
Of passion, I to them had quitted all,
At random yielded up to their misrule;
And know not that I called and drew them thither,
My Hell-hounds, to lick up the draff and filth
Which Man's polluting sin with taint hath shed
On what was pure; till, crammed and gorged, nigh burst
With sucked and glutted offal, at one sling
Of thy victorious arm, well-pleasing Son,
Both Sin and Death, and yawning Grave, at last
Through Chaos hurled, obstruct the mouth of Hell
For ever, and seal up his ravenous jaws.
Then Heaven and Earth, renewed, shall be made pure
To sanctify that shall receive no stain:
Till then the curse pronounced on both proceeds.

JOHN MILTON (1608–74)   After 1660

Paradise Lost, XII, ll. 79–104, 508–51

In these two passages, the Archangel Michael relates to Adam what shall happen to Man on earth, subject 'to violent lords', the tyrants of mankind, under whose wolfish rule 'Truth shall retire/Bestuck with sland'rous darts.' Thus, Milton gives us his view of the state of things in Restoration England.

REASON IN MAN OBSCURED, AND FREEDOM ENTHRALLED

               Justly thou abhorr'st
That son, who on the quiet state of men
Such trouble brought, affecting to subdue
Rational liberty; yet know withal,
Since thy original lapse, true liberty
Is lost, which always with right reason dwells
Twinned, and from her hath no dividual being.
Reason in Man obscured, or not obeyed,
Immediately inordinate desires
And upstart passions catch the government
From Reason, and to servitude reduce
Man, till then free. Therefore, since he permits
Within himself unworthy powers to reign
Over free reason, God, in judgement just,
Subjects him from without to violent lords,
Who oft as undeservedly enthral
His outward freedom. Tyranny must be,
Though to the tyrant thereby no excuse.
Yet sometimes nations will decline so low
From virtue, which is reason, that no wrong,
But justice, and some fatal curse annexed,
Deprives them of their outward liberty,
Their inward lost; witness th'irreverent son
Of him who built the ark, who, for the shame
Done to his father, heard this heavy curse,
Servant of servants, on his vicious race.

A WORLD 'TO GOOD MALIGNANT, TO BAD MEN BENIGN'

Wolves shall succeed for teachers, grievous wolves,
Who all the sacred mysteries of Heaven
To their own vile advantages shall turn
Of lucre and ambition, and the truth
With superstitions and traditions taint,
Left only in those written records pure,
Though not but by the Spirit understood.

Then shall they seek to avail themselves of names,
Places, and titles, and with these to join
Secular power, though feigning still to act
By spiritual; to themselves appropriating
The Spirit of God, promised alike and given
To all believers; and, from that pretence,
Spiritual laws by carnal power shall force
On every conscience – laws which none shall find
Left them enrolled, or what the Spirit within
Shall on the heart engrave. What will they then
But force the Spirit of Grace itself, and bind
His consort, Liberty? what but unbuild
His living temples, built by faith to stand –
Their own faith, not another's? for, on Earth,
Who against faith and conscience can be heard
Infallible? Yet many will presume:
Whence heavy persecution shall arise
On all who in the worship persevere
Of Spirit and Truth; the rest, far greater part,
Will deem in outward rites and specious forms
Religion satisfied; Truth shall retire
Bestuck with sland'rous darts, and works of Faith
Rarely be found: so shall the World go on,
To good malignant, to bad men benign,
Under her own weight groaning, till the day
Appear of respiration to the just
And vengeance to the wicked, at return
Of him so lately promised to thy aid,
The Woman's Seed – obscurely then foretold,
Now amplier known thy Saviour and thy Lord;
Last in the clouds from Heaven to be revealed
In glory of the Father, to dissolve
Satan with his perverted World; then raise
From the conflagrant mass, purged and refined,
New Heavens, new Earth, Ages of endless date
Founded in righteousness and peace and love,
To bring forth fruits, joy and eternal bliss.

ANDREW MARVELL (1621–78)   1671

From a letter to a friend in Persia, in *Poems and Letters*

COURT GREED

The King having, upon pretence of the great preparations of his neighbours, demanded three hundred thousand pounds for his navy, (though
in conclusion he hath not sent out any,) and that the Parliament should
pay his debts, which the ministers would never particularize to the House
of Commons, our house gave several bills. You see how far things were
stretched beyond reason, there being no satisfaction how these debts
were contracted, and all men foreseeing that what was given would not
be applied to discharge the debts, which I hear are at this day risen to
four millions. Nevertheless, such was the number of the constant courtiers, increased by the apostate patriots, who were bought off for that
turn, some at six, others at ten, one at fifteen thousand pounds, in
money; besides which, offices, lands, and reversions to others, that it is
a mercy they gave not away the whole land and liberty of England. The
Duke of Buckingham is again one hundred and forty thousand pounds
in debt, and, by this prorogation, his creditors have time to tear all his
lands in pieces. The House of Commons have run almost to the end of
their time, and are grown extremely chargeable to the King, and odious
to the people. They have signed and sealed ten thousand pounds a-year
more to the Duchess of Cleveland, who has likewise ten thousand pounds
out of the excise of beer and ale; five thousand pounds a-year out of the
post-office; and, they say, the reversion of all the king's leases, the
reversion of all the places in the Custom-house, and, indeed, what not?
All promotions, spiritual and temporal, pass under her cognizance . . .

JOHN BUNYAN (1628–88)   1676

From *The Pilgrim's Progress*, Part One

Bunyan wrote the first part of *The Pilgrim's Progress* during a short term of
imprisonment in 1676, having been pastor for three years at the Bedford church
from which he had been arrested in November 1660 for preaching without a
licence. The charge against him in 1660 was 'that he hath devilishly and perniciously
abstained from coming to church to hear Divine service, and is a common
upholder of several unlawful meetings and conventicles, to the great disturbance
and distraction of the good subjects of this kingdom; contrary to the laws of our

sovereign lord the king'. He was kept in Bedford gaol for twelve years for refusing
to give up his right to preach, suffering persecution like so many of his non-
conformist contemporaries. It has been calculated that fifteen thousand families
were ruined and more than five thousand people died under the harsh Acts passed
during Charles II's reign, such as the infamous 'Five Mile Act' of 1665; but Bunyan survived, and was released from prison in 1672 after Charles II's Declaration
of Indulgence and the intervention of friends. In *The Pilgrim's Progress*, the itin-
erant tinker and preacher speaks above all for the persecuted poor and their sufferings in an unjust and unchristian world.

'WERE YOU DOERS, OR TALKERS ONLY?'

Christian. . . . There is but little of this faithful dealing with men now
a days, and that makes religion to stink so in the nostrils of many, as it
doth; for they are these talkative fools whose religion is only in word,
and are debauched and vain in their conversation, that (being so much
admitted into the fellowship of the godly) do puzzle the world, blemish
Christianity, and grieve the sincere. I wish that all men would deal with
such as you have done: then should they either be made more conform-
able to religion, or the company of saints would be too hot for them.
Then did Faithful say,

How Talkative at first lifts up his plumes!
How bravely doth he speak! How he presumes
To drive down all before him! But so soon
As Faithful talks of heart-work, like the moon
That's past the full, into the wane he goes.
And so will all, but he that heart-work knows.

VANITY FAIR

Almost five thousand years agone, there were pilgrims walking to the
Celestial City, as these two honest persons are; and Beelzebub, Apollyon,
and Legion, with their companions, perceiving by the path that the pilgrims made, that their way to the city lay through this town of Vanity,
they contrived here to set up a fair; a fair wherein should be sold all sorts
of vanity, and that it should last all the year long: therefore at this fair
are all such merchandise sold, as houses, lands, trades, places, honours,
preferments, titles, countries, kingdoms, lusts, pleasures, and delights
of all sorts, as whores, bawds, wives, husbands, children, masters, serv-

ants, lives, blood, bodies, souls, silver, gold, pearls, precious stones, and what not.

And moreover, at this fair there is at all times to be seen jugglings, cheats, games, plays, fools, apes, knaves, and rogues, and that of every kind.

Here are to be seen too, and that for nothing, thefts, murders, adulteries, false-swearers, and that of a blood-red colour.

PERSECUTION FOR THE TRUTH AT VANITY FAIR

One chanced mockingly, beholding the carriages of the men, to say unto them, What will ye buy? But they, looking gravely upon him, answered, We buy the truth. At that there was an occasion taken to despise the men the more; some mocking, some taunting, some speaking reproachfully, and some calling upon others to smite them. At last things came to a hubbub and great stir in the fair, insomuch that all order was confounded. Now was word presently brought to the great one of the fair, who quickly came down and deputed some of his most trusty friends to take these men into examination, about whom the fair was almost overturned. So the men were brought to examination; and they sat upon them, asked them whence they came, whither they went, and what they did there in such an unusual garb? The men told them that they were pilgrims and strangers in the world, and that they were going to their own country, which was the heavenly Jerusalem; and that they had given no occasion to the men of the town, nor yet to the merchandisers, thus to abuse them . . . But they that were appointed to examine them did not believe them to be any other than bedlams and mad, or else such as came to put all things into a confusion in the fair. Therefore they took them and beat them, and besmeared them with dirt, and then put them into the cage, that they might be made a spectacle to all the men of the fair. There therefore they lay for some time, and were made the objects of any man's sport, or malice, or revenge, the great one of the fair laughing still at all that befell them. But . . . some men in the fair that were more observing, and less prejudiced than the rest, began to check and blame the baser sort for their continual abuses done by them to the men; they therefore in angry manner let fly at them again, counting them as bad as the men in the cage . . . and should be made partakers of their misfortunes. The other replied, that for aught they could see, the men were quiet, and sober, and intended nobody any harm; and that there were many that traded in their fair that were more worthy to be put into the cage, yea, and pillory too . . . Thus, after divers words had passed on both sides . . . they fell to some blows among themselves, and did harm one to another. Then were these two poor men brought before their examiners again, and there charged as being guilty of the late hubbub that had been in the fair. So they beat them pitifully and hanged irons upon them, and led them in chains up and down the fair, for an example and a terror to others, lest they should speak in their behalf, or join themselves unto them. But Christian and Faithful behaved themselves yet more wisely, and received the ignominy and shame that was cast upon them, with so much meekness and patience, that it won to their side (though but few in comparison of the rest) several of the men in the fair. This put the other party yet into a greater rage, insomuch that they concluded the death of these two men. Wherefore they threatened, that the cage, nor irons should serve their turn, but that they should die, for the abuse they had done, and for deluding the men of the fair.

THE TRIAL AND DEATH OF FAITHFUL

Then a convenient time being appointed, they brought them forth to their trial, in order to their condemnation. When the time was come, they were brought before their enemies, and arraigned. The judge's name was Lord Hate-good. Their indictment was one and the same in substance, though somewhat varying in form, the contents whereof was this:

That they were enemies and disturbers of their trade; that they had made commotions and divisions in the town, and had won a party to their own most dangerous opinions in contempt of the law of their prince.

Then Faithful began to answer, that he had only set himself against that which had set itself against Him that is higher than the highest. And said he, as for disturbance, I make none, being myself a man of peace; the parties that were won to us, were won by beholding our truth and innocence, and they are only turned from the worse to the better. And as to the king you talk of, since he is Beelzebub, the enemy of our Lord, I defy him and all his angels.

Then proclamation was made, that they that had aught to say for their Lord the King against the prisoner at the bar, should forthwith appear and give in their evidence. So there came in three witnesses, to wit, Envy, Superstition, and Pickthank. They were then asked if they knew the prisoner at the bar; and what they had to say for their Lord the King against him.

Then stood forth Envy, and said to this effect: My Lord, I have known this man a long time, and will attest upon my oath before the honourable bench, that he is –

Judge. Hold! Give him his oath.

So they sware him. Then he said, My Lord, this man, notwithstanding his plausible name, is one of the vilest men in our country. He neither regardeth prince nor people, law nor custom; but doth all that he can to possess all men with certain of his disloyal notions, which he in the general calls Principles of Faith and Holyness. And in particular, I heard him once myself affirm That Christianity and the customs of our town of Vanity were diametrically opposite, and could not be reconciled. By which saying, my Lord, he doth at once not only condemn all our laudable doings, but us in the doing of them.

Judge. Then did the judge say to him, Hast thou any more to say?

Envy. My Lord, I could say much more, only I would not be tedious to the court. Yet if need be, when the other gentlemen have given in their evidence, rather than anything shall be wanting that shall dispatch him, I will enlarge my testimony against him. So he was bid stand by.

Then they called Superstition, and bid him look upon the prisoner. They also asked, what he could say for their Lord the King against him. Then they sware him; so he began:

Superstition. My Lord, I have no great acquaintance with this man, nor do I desire to have further knowledge of him; however, this I know, that he is a very pestilent fellow, from some discourse that the other day I had with him in this town; for then talking with him, I heard him say, That our religion was naught, and such by which a man could by no means please God. Which sayings of his, my Lord, your Lordship very well knows, what necessarily thence will follow, to wit, That we still do worship in vain, are yet in our sins, and finally shall be damned; and this is that which I have to say.

Then was Pickthank sworn, and bid say what he knew, in behalf of their Lord the King, against the prisoner at the bar.

Pickthank. My Lord, and you gentlemen all, This fellow I have known of a long time, and have heard him speak things that ought not to be spoke; for he hath railed on our noble Prince Beelzebub, and hath spoken contemptibly of his honourable friends, whose names are the Lord Old Man, the Lord Carnal Delight, the Lord Luxurious, the Lord Desire of Vain Glory, my old Lord Lechery, Sir Having Greedy, with all the rest of our nobility; and he hath said moreover, That if all men were of his mind, if possible, there is not one of these noble-men should have any longer a being in this town; besides, he hath not been afraid to rail on you, my Lord, who are now appointed to be his judge, calling you an ungodly villain, with many other such-like vilifying terms, with which he hath bespattered most of the gentry of our town.

When this Pickthank had told his tale, the judge directed his speech to the prisoner at the bar, saying, Thou runagate, heretic, and traitor, hast thou heard what these honest gentlemen have witnessed against thee?

Faithful. May I speak a few words in my own defence?

Judge. Sirrah, sirrah, thou deservest to live no longer, but to be slain immediately upon the place; yet that all men may see our gentleness towards thee, let us see what thou hast to say.

Faithful. 1. I say then, in answer to what Mr Envy hath spoken, I never said aught but this, That what rule, or laws, or custom, or people, were flat against the word of God, are diametrically opposite to Christianity. If I have said amiss in this, convince me of my error, and I am ready here before you to make my recantation.

2. As to the second, to wit, Mr Superstition, and his charge against me, I said only this, That in the worship of God there is required a divine faith; but there can be no divine faith without a divine revelation of the will of God: therefore whatever is thrust into the worship of God that is not agreeable to divine revelation, cannot be done but by a human faith, which faith will not be profit to eternal life.

3. As to what Mr Pickthank hath said, I say, (avoiding terms, as that I am said to rail, and the like) that the prince of this town, with all the rabblement his attendants, by this gentleman named, are more fit for a being in Hell, than in this town and country: and so, the Lord have mercy upon me.

Then the judge called to the jury (who all this while stood by, to hear and observe) Gentlemen of the jury, you see this man about whom so great an uproar hath been made in this town: you have also heard what these worthy gentlemen have witnessed against him: also you have heard his reply and confession: it lieth now in your breasts to hang him, or save his life; but yet I think meet to instruct you into our law.

There was an act made in the days of Pharaoh the Great, servant to our prince, that lest those of a contrary religion should multiply and grow too strong for him, their males should be thrown into the river. There was also an act made in the days of Nebuchadnezzar the Great, another of his servants, that whoever would not fall down and worship his golden image, should be thrown into a fiery furnace. There was also an act made in the days of Darius, that whoso, for some time, called upon any God but him, should be cast into the lions' den. Now the substance of these laws this rebel has broken, not only in thought (which is not to be borne) but also in word and deed; which must therefore needs be intolerable.

For that of Pharoah, his law was made upon a supposition, to prevent mischief, no crime being yet apparent; but here is a crime apparent. For the second and third, you see he disputeth against our religion; and for the treason he hath confessed, he deserveth to die the death.

Then went the jury out, whose names were, Mr Blind-man, Mr No-good, Mr Malice, Mr Love-lust, Mr Live-loose, Mr Heady, Mr High-mind, Mr Enmity, Mr Lyar, Mr Cruelty, Mr Hate-light, and Mr Implacable; who every one gave in his private verdict against him among themselves, and afterwards unanimously concluded to bring him in guilty before the judge. And first among themselves, Mr Blind-man the foreman, said, I see clearly that this man is an heretic. Then said Mr No-good, Away with such a fellow from the earth. Ay, said Mr Malice, for I hate the very looks of him. Then said Mr Love-lust, I could never endure him. Nor I, said Mr Live-loose, for he would always be condemning my way. Hang him, hang him, said Mr Heady. A sorry scrub, said Mr High-mind. My heart riseth against him, said Mr Enmity. He is a rogue, said Mr Lyar. Hanging is too good for him, said Mr Cruelty. Let us dispatch him out of the way, said Mr Hate-light. Then said Mr Implacable, Might I have all the world given me, I could not be reconciled to him; therefore let us forthwith bring him in guilty of death. And so they did; therefore he was presently condemned to be had from the place where he was, to the place from whence he came, and there to be put to the most cruel death that could be invented.

They therefore brought him out, to do with him according to their law; and first they scourged him, then they buffeted him, then they lanced his flesh with knives; after that they stoned him with stones, then pricked him with their swords; and last of all they burned him to ashes at the stake. Thus came Faithful to his end.

ANDREW MARVELL (1621–78)   1678

From *Account of the Growth of Popery and Arbitrary Government in England*, in *Works*, III, pp. 328–31

Marvell's pamphlet, arguing the threat of a Popish revival in England, comes out against royal absolutism, and is particularly scathing about members of Parliament, among whom there seemed a mere 'handful of salt, a sparkle of soul, that hath hitherto preserved this gross body from putrefaction . . . so small a scantling number, that men scarce reckon of them more than a quorum'.

A CORRUPT AND SERVILE HOUSE OF COMMONS

. . . Whatsoever casual good hath been wrought at any time by the assimilation of ambitious, factious, and disappointed members, to the little, but solid, and unbiased party, the more frequent ill effects, and consequences of so unequal a mixture, so long continued, are demonstrable and apparent. For while scarce any man comes thither with respect to the public service, but in design to make and raise his fortune, it is not to be expressed, the debauchery and lewdness, which, upon occasion of election to Parliaments, are now grown habitual thorow the nation. So that the vice, and the expense, are risen to such a prodigious height, that few sober men can endure to stand to be chosen on such conditions. From whence also arise feuds, and perpetual animosities, over most of the counties and corporations, while gentlemen of worth, spirit and ancient estates and dependences, see themselves overpowered in their own neighbourhood by the drunkness and bribery of their competitors. But if nevertheless any worthy person chance to carry the election, some mercenary or corrupt sheriff makes a double return, and so the cause is handed to the Committee of elections, who ask no better, but are ready to adopt his adversary into the House if he be not legitimate. And if the gentleman aggrieved seek his remedy against the sheriff of Westminster Hall, and the proofs be so palpable, that the King's Bench cannot invent how to do him injustice, yet the major part of the twelve judges shall upon better consideration vacate the sheriff's fine, and reverse the judgement; but those of them that dare dissent from their brethren are in danger to be turned off the bench without any cause assigned. While men therefore care not thus how they get into the House of Commons, neither can it be expected that they should make any conscience of what they do there, but they are only intent how to reimburse themselves (if their elections were at their own charge) or how to bargain their votes for a place or a pension. They list themselves straightways into some Court faction, and it is as well known among them, to what Lord each of them retain, as when formerly they wore coats and badges. By this long haunting so together they are grown too so familiar among themselves, that all reverence of their own Assembly is lost, that they live together not like Parliament men, but like so many good fellows met together in a public house to make merry. And which is yet worse, by being so thoroughly acquainted, they understand their number and party, so that the use of so public a counsel is frustrated, there is no place for deliberation, no persuading by reason, but they can see one another's votes through both throats and cravats before they hear them.

Where the cards are so well known, they are only fit for a cheat, and no fair gamester but would throw them under the table.

ALGERNON SIDNEY (1622–83)   c. 1680

From *Discourses Concerning Government*, 1751 edition, pp. 437–8

With the government of Charles II growing more and more openly despotic, the Whig leaders planned an armed rising against the King, known as the Rye House Plot. And when it was discovered that certain subordinates in the party were conspiring to assassinate Charles and his brother, Russell, Essex and Sidney were at once arrested and sent to the Tower. Russell was beheaded on 21 July 1683, and four months later Sidney was brought before Judge Jeffreys, recently made Lord Chief Justice, and so soon to become notorious for the butcheries he perpetrated in the name of the law at the 'Bloody Assize' in 1685 after the Monmouth Rebellion. Jeffreys was to boast that he had hanged more traitors than all his predecessors together since the Conquest, and Sidney became one of his victims, beheaded on Tower Hill on 7 December 1683. Having fought with the parliamentary army against Charles I at Marston Moor, when he was seriously wounded, Sidney remained an unwavering constitutionalist, and even withheld his support from Cromwell during his years as Lord Protector. In Denmark at the Restoration, he stayed abroad in opposition to the monarchy till 1679, when his dying father brought him back to England, where he was soon involved again in the politics of opposition. Sidney was a patrician liberal, son of the second Earl of Leicester, rather than a man of the people. His concept of authority was defined in terms of a free community of citizens governed by a voluntary civil contract, which even permitted a limited monarchy. Nevertheless, the *Discourses* became a source of influence for liberal, republican ideas, and a popular 'textbook of revolution' in the American colonies.

THE STRENGTH OF A NATION

No man can be my Judge, unless he be my Superior; and he cannot be my Superior, who is not so by my consent, nor to any other purpose than I consent to. This cannot be the case of a Nation, which can have no equal within itself. Controversies may arise with other Nations, the decision of which may be left to Judges chosen by mutual agreement; but this relates not to our question. A Nation, and most especially one that is powerful, cannot recede from its own right, as a private man from the knowledge of his own weakness and inability to defend himself, must come under the protection of a greater power than his own. The strength of a Nation is not in the Magistrate, but the strength of the Magistrate is in the Nation. The wisdom, industry, and valour of a Prince may add to the glory and greatness of a Nation, but the foundation and substance will always be in itself . . . The people therefore cannot be deprived of their natural rights upon a frivolous pretence to that which never was and never can be. They who create Magistracies, and give to them such name, form, and power as they think fit, do only know, whether the end for which they were created, be performed or not. They who give a being to the power which had none, can only judge whether it be employed to their welfare, or turned to their ruin. They do not set up one or a few men, that they and their posterity may live in splendour and greatness, but that Justice may be administered, Virtue established, and provision made for the public safety. No wise man will think this can be done, if those who set themselves to overthrow the Law, are to be their own Judges.

Part Four

THE EXPANSION OF EMPIRE 1689–1788

Wealth, howsoever got, in England makes
Lords of mechanics, gentlemen of rakes.
Antiquity and birth are needless here,
'Tis impudence and money makes a peer.
                                        Daniel Defoe

You have clearly proved that Ignorance, Idleness, and Vice are the proper Ingredients for qualifying a Legislator. The Laws are best explained, interpreted and applied by those whose Interest and Abilities lie in perverting, confounding, and eluding them.

                                        Jonathan Swift

What Nature wants, commodious Gold bestows,
Tis thus we eat the bread another sows:
But how unequal it bestows, observe,
Tis thus we riot, while who sow it, starve.
                                        Alexander Pope

And he gave it for his Opinion; that whoever could make two Ears of Corn, or two Blades of Grass to grow upon a spot of Ground where only one grew before; would deserve better of Mankind, and do more essential Service to his Country, than the whole Race of Politicians put together.

                                        Jonathan Swift

THE GLORIOUS REVOLUTION

From *The Bill of Rights*

It was James II's arrogant policy of promoting Roman Catholics to key positions in the state after the defeat of the republican radicals in 1685 (presided over by Judge Jeffreys), and the bringing to trial of the seven bishops who had questioned his actions, which led to the secret alliance or coup of 1688, when non-radical Whigs and Tories united to invite William of Orange to invade England. Thus, with the establishment of a constitutional monarchy, the position of the ruling class was assured, and both absolutists and republicans (not to mention the common people) were subdued, to lay the foundations for eighteenth-century expansion and the great debates upon liberty and human rights.

REVOLUTION FROM ABOVE: THE BILL OF RIGHTS

. . . And thereupon the said Lords Spiritual and Temporal, and Commons, pursuant to their respective letters and elections, being now assembled in a full and free representation of this nation, taking into their most serious consideration the best means of attaining the ends aforesaid, do in the first place, (as their ancestors in like case have usually done,) for the vindicating and asserting their ancient rights and liberties declare:

1,2. That the pretended power of dispensing with laws, or the execution of laws by regal authority, without consent of Parliament, as it hath been assumed and exercised of late, is illegal.

3. That the commission for erecting the late Court of Commissioners for Ecclesiastical causes, and all other commissions and courts of like nature, are illegal and pernicious.

4. That levying money for or to the use of the crown, by pretence and prerogative, without grant of Parliament, for longer time or in other manner than the same is or shall be granted, is illegal.

5. That it is the right of the subjects to petition the King, and all commitments and prosecutions for such petitioning, are illegal.

6. That the raising or keeping a standing army within the kingdom in time of peace, unless it be with consent of Parliament, is against law.

7. That the subjects which are Protestants, may have arms for their defence suitable to their conditions, and as allowed by law.

8. That election of members of Parliament ought to be free.

9. That the freedom of speech, and debates or proceedings in Parliament, ought not to be impeached or questioned in any court or place out of Parliament.

10. That excessive bail ought not to be required, nor excessive fines imposed, nor cruel and unusual punishments inflicted.

11. That jurors ought to be duly impanelled and returned, and jurors which pass upon men in trials for high treason ought to be freeholders.

12. That all grants and promises of fines and forfeitures of particular persons before conviction, are illegal and void.

13. And that for redress of all grievances, and for the amending, strengthening, and preserving of the laws, Parliament ought to be held frequently.

And they do claim, demand, and insist upon all and singular the premises, as their undoubted rights and liberties; and that no declarations, judgements, doings or proceedings, to the prejudice of the people in any of the said premises, ought in any wise to be drawn hereafter into consequence or example. To which demand of their rights they are particularly encouraged by the declaration of his Highness the Prince of Orange, as being the only means for obtaining a full redress and remedy therein . . .

JOHN LOCKE (1632–1704) 1689

From *An Essay Concerning the True Origines, Extent and End of Civil Government*, in *Two Treatises of Government*, p. 130 (Book II, chapter v, section 26)

LABOUR AS PROPERTY

Though the earth and all inferior creatures be common to all men, yet every man has a 'property' in his own 'person'. This nobody has any right to but himself. The 'labour' of his body and the 'work' of his hands, we may say, are properly his. Whatsoever, then, he removes from the state that Nature hath provided and left it in, he hath mixed his labour with it, and joined to it something that is his own, and thereby makes it his property. It being by him removed from the common state Nature placed it in, it hath by this labour something annexed to it that excludes the common right of other men. For this 'labour' being the unquestionable property of the labourer, no man but he can have the right to what that is once joined to, at least where there is enough, and as good left in common for others.

JOHN LOCKE (1632–1704)

From *An Essay concerning False Principles*, in *Two Treatises of Government*, p. 3 (Book I, chapter i, section 1)

AN ARGUMENT TO BE DESPISED

Slavery is so vile and miserable an estate of man, and so directly opposite to the generous temper and courage of our nation, that it is hardly to be conceived that an 'Englishman', much less a 'gentleman', should plead for it. And truly I should have taken this, as any other treatise which would persuade all men that they are slaves, and ought to be so, for such another exercise of wit as was his who writ the encomium of Nero, rather than for a serious discourse meant in earnest, had not the gravity of the title and epistle, the picture in front of Sir Robert's book, and the applause that followed it, required me to believe that the author and publisher were both in earnest. I therefore took the *Patriarcha* of Sir Robert Filmer into my hands with all the expectation, and read it through with all the attention, due to a treatise that made such a noise at its coming abroad, and cannot but confess myself mightily surprised that, in a book that was to provide chains for all mankind, I should find nothing but a rope of sand, useful, perhaps, to such whose skill and business it is to raise a dust, and would blind the people the better to mislead them, but is not of any force to draw those into bondage who have their eyes open, and so much sense about them as to consider that chains are but an ill wearing, how much care so ever hath been taken to file and polish them . . .

DANIEL DEFOE (1660–1731)

From *The True-born Englishman*, in *Novels and Selected Writings*, VII, pp. 526–7, 528

IMPUDENCE AND MONEY

The wonder which remains is at our pride,
To value that which all wise men deride.
For Englishmen to boast of generation,
Cancels their knowledge, and lampoons the nation.
A true-born Englishman's a contradiction,
In speech an irony; in fact, a fiction;

A banter made to be a test of fools,
Which those that use it justly ridicules;
A metaphor intended to express
A man akin to all the universe . . .

Wealth, howsoever got, in England makes
Lords of mechanics, gentlemen of rakes.
Antiquity and birth are needless here,
'Tis impudence and money makes a peer.
Innumerable city knights, we know,
From Bluecoat Hospitals and Bridewells flow.
Draymen and porters fill the city chair,
And footboys magisterial purple wear.
Fate has but very small distinction set
Between a counter and a coronet.
Tarpaulin lords; pages of high renown,
Rise up by poor men's valour; not their own.
Great families of yesterday we show;
And lords, whose parents were – the Lord knows who!

CHARLES DAVENANT (1656–1714) 1701

From *The True Picture of a Modern Whig*, pp. 32–5

(This is a Dialogue between two lesser members of the previous ministry, Mr Whiglove and Mr Double.)

SQUANDERING THE PEOPLE'S MONEY

DOUBLE   Prithee friend Whiglove, leave off calling thyself an Old Whig, it will do thee hurt with the party. We reckon those men our worst of enemies . . . What have we in us that resembles the Old Whigs? They hated arbitrary government, we have been all along for a standing army: they desir'd triennial parliaments, and that trials for treason might be better regulated; and 'tis notorious that we oppos'd both those bills. They were for calling corrupt ministers to an accompt; we have ever countenanc'd and protected corruption to the utmost of our power. They were frugal for the nation, and careful how they loaded the people with taxes; we have squandered away their money as if there could be no end of England's treasure. The Old Whigs would have prevented the immoderate growth of the *French* empire, we Modern Whigs have made a partition-treaty, which, unless Providence saves us, may end in making the King of France universal monarch.

WHIGLOVE   I must confess we are very much departed from the principles we profess'd twenty years ago. But pray tell me of what sort of persons does our party consist at present, for we still call ourselves Whigs?

DOUBLE   'Tis not so easy as you imagine to describe the strange medley of which we are now compos'd, but I shall do my best to let you into the secret. First, you must know there are some men of true worth and honour that still continue among us; why I can't guess, but those I fear we shall lose when they come plainly to discover our bad designs, and how furiously we drive to bring the kingdom into a civil war. Nor have we lost all the Old Whigs; there are still listed with us, Whig-pickpockets, Whig-gamesters, Whig-murderers, Whig-outlaws, Whig-libertines, Whig-atheists, such as in former reigns have had some note of infamy publick or private fix'd upon 'em; all these stick close to our side, nor do we apprehend that any one of 'em will forsake us, because they know crimes of no nature whatsoever are ill-look'd upon among us, and that even hereafter, they may commit more, if they please, under the shelter of our wings.

WHIGLOVE   But have we no more than what you have here reckoned?

DOUBLE   O yes, or we shou'd be but weak. The bulk of our party consists of those who are of any side where they can best make their markets; such sort of men naturally like the Whigs most, because ours was a negligent weak administration. Every body did what seem'd good in his own eyes, we troubled no man with calling him to an accompt. The accompts of the army, navy, customs, and excise, are not yet made up. There are upwards of four and twenty millions of the people's money unaccompted for to this day. Under our ministry all the officers that handled the King's business or revenue liv'd in clover. Every little scoundrel got an estate. We suffer'd 'em to drink up the people's blood till they were out of breath, and till their eyes grew red. In short, all men cheated to what degree they pleas'd, which was wink'd at in hopes to make and to secure a party. Therefore all the busy proling fellows both in town and country, who hope to advance themselves, wish to see our noble friends restor'd to their former power. And all these sort of men, while they have any hopes that way, will join with us to buoy them up, and to exclaim against the new ministers. But if they find the game lost, if they see the King resolv'd to correct abuses, and to call them to a reckoning who have so much wrong'd him and the nation, and if they find the parliament stick to their point; if they see the country-gentlemen resolute to be no longer impos'd upon by upstarts and hairbrain'd rulers of a state, like rats they will all run from a falling house, they will disown the name of Whigs, and send us and and our party to the devil . . .

BERNARD DE MANDEVILLE (1670–1733)   1705

From *The Fable of the Bees*, 'The Grumbling Hive'

THE HONEST NATION IS A POOR NATION

Then leave Complaints: Fools only strive
To make a Great an honest Hive.
T'enjoy the World's Conveniencies,
Be famed in War, yet live in Ease
Without great Vices, is a vain
Utopia seated in the Brain.
Fraud, Luxury, and Pride must live
Whilst we the Benefits receive.
Hunger's a dreadful Plague, no doubt,
Yet who digests or thrives without?
Do we not owe the Growth of Wine
To the dry shabby crooked Vine?
Which, whilst its Shoots neglected stood,
Chok'd other Plants, and ran to Wood;
But blest us with its Noble Fruit;
As soon as it was tied, and cut:
So Vice is beneficial found,
When it's by Justice lopp'd, and bound;
Nay, where the People would be great,
As necessary to the State
As Hunger is to make 'em eat.
Bare Virtue can't make Nations live
In Splendour; they, that would revive
A Golden Age, must be as free,
For Acorns, as for Honesty.

DANIEL DEFOE (1660–1731)

A review of the state of the British nation, in Dickinson, ed., *Politics and Literature*, pp. 14–15

LIMITING THE POWER OF THE CROWN

I have, in the humblest manner possible, address'd this Paper to the present assembled Parliament, in the case of the late attack made upon our establishment and constitution from the pulpit – by advancing the absurd and exploded notions of passive-obedience, non-resistance, and hereditary succession, against the declared principles of parliamentary limitations . . . Passive-obedience, non-resistance, and the divine right of hereditary succession, are inconsistent with the rights of the BRITISH NATION (not to examine the rights of nature), inconsistent with the constitution of the BRITISH GOVERNMENT, inconsistent with the being and authority of the BRITISH PARLIAMENT, and inconsistent with the declar'd essential foundation of the BRITISH MONARCHY. – These abhorr'd notions would destroy the inestimable privileges of Britain, of which the House of Commons are the glorious conservators; they would subject all our liberties to the arbitrary lust of a single person, they would expose us to all kinds of tyranny, and subvert the very foundations on which we stand. – They would destroy the unquestion'd sovereignty of our laws, which for so many ages have triumphed over the invasions and usurpations of ambitious princes; they would denude us of the beautiful garment of liberty, and prostitute the honour of the nation to the mechanism of slavery. They would divest GOD Almighty of his praise, in giving his humble creatures a right of governing themselves, and charge heaven with having meanly subjected mankind to the crime of TYRANNY, which he himself abhors.

'Tis to this honourable House the whole nation now looks for relief, against these invaders, and honest men hope, that now is the time, when the illegitimate spurious birth of these monsters in politics shall be exposed by your voice. – Now is the time, when you shall declare it criminal for any man to assert, that the subjects of Britain are oblig'd to an absolute uncondition'd obedience to their princes . . . Now is the time, when you shall declare it criminal for any man to assert, the illegality of resistance on any pretence whatsoever, &c. Or in plain English, the right of self-defence against oppression and violence, whether national or personal . . . Now is the time, when you shall again declare the rights of the people of England, either in Parliament or in Convention assembled, to limit the succession of the crown in bar of hereditary claims, while those claims are attended with other circumstances inconsistent with the public safety, and the establish'd laws of the land; since her Majesty's title to the crown, as now own'd and acknowledg'd by the whole nation, and the succession to the crown, as entail'd by the acts of succession in England, and the late Union of Britain, are built on the right of Parliament to limit the crown, and that right recogniz'd by the Revolution.

JOSEPH ADDISON (1672–1719)   29 January 1712

From *The Spectator*, no. 287

DESPOTISM VERSUS LIBERTY

Some tell us we ought to make our governments on earth like that in heaven, which, say they, is altogether monarchical and unlimited. Was man like his Creator in goodness and justice, I should be for following this great model; but where goodness and justice are not essential to the ruler, I would by no means put myself into his hands to be disposed of according to his particular will and pleasure.

It is odd to consider the connection between despotic government and barbarity, and how the making of one person more than man, makes the rest less. About nine parts of the world in ten are in the lowest state of slavery, and consequently sunk into the most gross and brutal ignorance. European slavery is indeed a state of liberty, if compared with that which prevails in the other three divisions of the world; and therefore it is no wonder that those who grovel under it, have many tracks of light among them, of which the others are wholly destitute.

Riches and plenty are the natural fruits of liberty, and where these abound, learning and all the liberal arts will immediately lift up their heads and flourish. As a man must have no slavish fears and apprehensions hanging upon his mind, who will indulge the flights of fancy or speculation, and push his researches into all the abstruse corners of truth, so it is necessary for him to have about him a competency of all the conveniences of life . . . In Europe, indeed, notwithstanding several of its princes are absolute, there are men famous for knowledge and learning, but the reason is, because the subjects are many of them rich and wealthy, the prince not thinking fit to exert himself in his full tyranny like the princes of the eastern nations, lest his subjects should be invited to new-mould their constitution, having so many prospects of liberty within their view. But in all despotic governments, tho' a particular prince may favour arts and letters, there is a natural degeneracy of mankind, as you observe from Augustus's reign, how the Romans lost themselves by degrees, till they fell to an equality with the most barbarous nations that surrounded them . . . Besides poverty and want, there are other reasons that debase the minds of men, who live under slavery, though I look on this as the principal. This natural tendency of despotic power to ignorance and barbarity, tho' not insisted upon by others, is, I think, an unanswerable argument against that form of government, as it shows how repugnant it is to the good of mankind and the perfection of human nature, which ought to be the great ends of all civil institutions.

MARY ASTELL (1668–1731)   1721

From *An Essay in Defence of the Female Sex*, pp. 18–22

WOMEN RULED BY MALE TYRANNY AND FEAR

. . . A Man ought no more to value himself upon being wiser than a Woman, if he owes his Advantage to a better Education, and greater means of Information, than he ought to boast of his Courage for beating a Man when his Hands were bound. Nay, it would be so far from Honourable to contend for Preference upon this Score, that they would thereby at once argue themselves guilty both of Tyranny and of Fear. I think I need not have mention'd this latter; for none can be Tyrants but Cowards. For nothing makes one Party slavishly depress another, but their Fear that they may, at one time or other, become strong, or courageous enough to make themselves equal, if not superior to, their Masters. This is our Case; for Men being sensible as well of the Abilities of Mind in our Sex, as of the Strength of Body in their own, began to grow jealous, that we, who in the Infancy of the World were their Equals and Partners in Dominion, might in process of Time, by Subtlety and Stratagem, become their Superiors; and therefore began in good time to make use of Force, (the Origin of Power) to compel us to a Subjection Nature never meant; and made use of Nature's Liberality to them, to take the Benefit of her Kindness from us. From that time they have endeavour'd to train us up altogether to Ease and Ignorance; as Conquerors use to do to those they reduce by Force, that so they may disarm 'em both of Courage and Wit; and consequently make them tamely give up their Liberty, and abjectly submit their necks to a slavish Yoke. As the World grew more populous, and Men's Necessities whetted their Inventions, so it increas'd their Jealousy, and sharpen'd their Tyranny over us, till by degrees it came to that Height of Severity, I may say Cruelty, it is now at in all the Eastern Parts of the World, where the Women, like our Negroes in our Western Plantations, are born Slaves, and live Prisoners all their Lives. Nay, so far has this barbarous Humour prevail'd, and spread itself, that in some parts of Europe, which pretend to be most refin'd and civiliz'd, in spite of Christianity, and the zeal for Religion which they so much affect, our Condition is not very much better . . .

To say the Truth . . . I can't tell how to prove all this from ancient Records; for if any Histories were anciently written by Women, Time and the Malice of Men have effectually conspir'd to suppress 'em; and it is not reasonable to think that Men should transmit, or suffer to be transmitted, to Posterity, any thing that might show the Weakness and Illegality of their Title to a Power they still exercise so arbitrarily, and are so fond of. But since daily Experience shows, and their own Histories tell us, how earnestly they endeavour, and what they act and suffer, to put the same Trick upon one another, 'tis natural to suppose they took the same Measures with us at first, which they now have effected; like the Rebels in our last Civil Wars, when they had brought the Royal Party under, they fell together by the Ears about the Dividend. The Sacred History takes no Notice of any such Authority they had before the Flood, and their own confess that whole Nations have rejected it since, and not suffer'd a man to live amongst 'em, which could be for no other Reason, than their Tyranny. For, upon less Provocation, the Women would never have been so foolish, as to deprive themselves of the Benefit of that Ease and Security, which Agreement with their Men might have afforded 'em. 'Tis true, the same Historians tell us, that there were whole Countries where there were none but Men, which border'd upon 'em. But this makes still for us; for it shows that the Conditions of their Society were not so easy, as to engage their Women to stay among them; but as Liberty presented itself, they withdrew and retir'd to the Amazons. But since our Sex can hardly boast of so great Privileges, and so easy a Servitude anywhere as in England, I cut this ungrateful Digression short in Acknowledgement; tho' Fetters of Gold are still Fetters, and the softest Lining can never make 'em so easy as Liberty.

JONATHAN SWIFT (1667–1745)   1726

From *Gulliver's Travels*, 'A Voyage to Brobdingnag', pp. 129–32, 132–3

THE KING DISGUSTED BY THE DIMINUTIVE
GULLIVER'S ACCOUNT OF EUROPEAN HISTORY: 'THE
MOST PERNICIOUS RACE OF LITTLE ODIOUS VERMIN'

He was perfectly astonished with the historical Account I gave him of our Affairs during the last Century; protesting it was only an Heap of Conspiracies, Rebellions, Murders, Massacres, Revolutions, Banishments; the very worst Effects that Avarice, Faction, Hypocrisy, Perfidiousness, Cruelty, Rage, Madness, Hatred, Envy, Lust, Malice, and Ambition could produce.

His Majesty in another Audience, was at the Pains to recapitulate the Sum of all I had spoken; compared the Questions he made, with the Answers I had given; then taking me into his Hands, and stroking me gently, delivered himself in these Words, which I shall never forget, nor the Manner he spoke them in. My little Friend *Grildrig*; you have made a most admirable Panegyric upon your Country. You have clearly proved that Ignorance, Idleness, and Vice are the proper Ingredients for qualifying a Legislator. The Laws are best explained, interpreted, and applied by those whose Interest and Abilities lie in perverting, confounding, and eluding them. I observe among you some Lines of an Institution, which in its Original might have been tolerable; but these half erased, and the rest wholly blurred and blotted by Corruptions. It doth not appear from all you have said, how any one Perfection is required towards the Procurement of any one Station among you; much less that Men are ennobled on Account of their Virtue, that Priests are advanced for their Piety or Learning, Soldiers for their conduct or Valour, Judges for their Integrity, Senators for the Love of their Country, or Councillors for their Wisdom. As for yourself (continued the King) who have spent the greatest part of your life in travelling; I am well disposed to hope you may hitherto have escaped many Vices of your Country. But, by what I have gathered from your own Relation, and the Answers I have with much Pains wringed and extorted from you; I cannot but conclude the Bulk of your Natives, to be the most pernicious Race of little odious Vermin that Nature ever suffered to crawl upon the surface of the Earth.

GULLIVER STRUCK BY THE KING'S NARROW PRINCIPLES AND SHORT VIEWS: CONCERNING WEAPONS THAT LAY ALL WASTE

. . . Great Allowances should be given to a King who lives wholly secluded from the rest of the World, and must therefore be altogether unacquainted with the Manners and Customs that most prevail in other Nations: The want of which Knowledge will ever produce many *Prejudices*, and a certain *Narrowness of Thinking*: from which we and the politer Countries of *Europe* are wholly exempted. And it would be hard indeed, if so remote a Prince's Notions of Virtue and Vice were to be offered as a Standard for all Mankind.

To confirm what I have now said, and further to show the miserable Effects of a *confined Education*; I shall here insert a passage which will hardly obtain Belief. In hopes to ingratiate myself farther into his Majesty's favour, I told him of an Invention discovered between three and four hundred Years ago, to make a certain Powder; into an heap of which the smallest Spark of Fire falling, would kindle the whole in a Moment, although it were as big as a Mountain; and make it all fly up in the Air together, with a Noise and Agitation greater than Thunder. That, a proper Quantity of this Powder rammed into an hollow Tube of Brass or Iron, according to its Bigness, would drive a Ball of Iron or Lead with such Violence and Speed, as nothing was able to sustain its Force. That, the largest Balls thus discharged, would not only Destroy whole Ranks of an Army at once; but batter the strongest Walls to the Ground; sink down Ships with a thousand Men in each, to the Bottom of the Sea; and when linked together by a Chain, would cut through Masts and Rigging; divide Hundreds of Bodies in the Middle, and lay all Waste before them. That we often put this Powder into large hollow Balls of Iron, and discharged them by an Engine into some City we were besieging; which would rip up the Pavement, tear the Houses to Pieces, burst and throw Splinters on every Side, dashing out the Brains of all who came near. That I knew the ingredients very well, which were Cheap, and common; I understood the manner of compounding them, and could direct his Workmen how to make those Tubes of a Size proportionable to all other Things in his Majesty's Kingdom; and the largest need not be above two hundred Foot long; twenty or thirty of which Tubes, charged with the proper Quantity of Powder and Balls, would batter down the Walls of the strongest Town in his Dominions in a few Hours; or destroy the whole Metropolis, if ever it should pretend to dispute his absolute Commands. This I humbly offered to his Majesty, as a small Tribute of

Acknowledgement in return of so many Marks that I had received of his Royal Favour and Protection.

The King was struck with horror at the Description I had given of those terrible Engines, and the Proposal I had made. He was amazed how so impotent and grovelling an Insect as I (these were his Expressions) cound entertain such inhuman Ideas, and in so familiar a Manner as to appear wholly unmoved at all the Scenes of Blood and Desolation, which I had painted as the common Effects of those Destructive Machines; whereof he said, some civil Genius, Enemy to Mankind, must have been the first Contriver. As for himself, he protested, that although few Things delighted him so much as new Discoveries in Art or in Nature; yet he would rather lose Half his Kingdom than be privy to such a Secret; which he commanded me, as I valued my Life, never to mention any more.

CONCERNING THE ART OF GOVERNMENT

A strange Effect of *narrow Principles and short Views*! that a Prince possessed of every Quality which procures Veneration, Love, and Esteem; of strong Parts, great Wisdom and profound Learning; endued with admirable Talents for Government, and almost adored by his Subjects; should from a *nice unnecessary Scruple*, whereof in *Europe* we can have no Conception, let slip an Opportunity put into his Hands, that would have made him absolute Master of the Lives, the Liberties, and the Fortunes of his People. Neither do I say this with the least Intention to detract from the many Virtues of that excellent King; whose Character I am sensible will on this Account be very much lessened in the Opinion of an *English* Reader: But, I take this Defect among them to have arisen from their Ignorance; by not having hitherto reduced *Politics* into a *Science*, as the more acute Wits of *Europe* have done. For, I remember very well, in a Discourse one day with the King; when I happened to say, there were several thousand books among us written upon the *Art of Government*; it gave him (directly contrary to my Intention) a very mean Opinion of our Understandings. He professed to abominate and despise all *Mystery*, *Refinement*, and *Intrigue*, either in a Prince or a Minister. He could not tell what I meant by *Secrets of State*, where an Enemy or some Rival Nation were not in the Case. He confined the Knowledge of governing within very *narrow Bounds*; to Common Sense and Reason, to Justice and Lenity, to the Speedy Determination of Civil and criminal Causes; with some other obvious Topics which are not worth considering. And, he gave it for his Opinion; that whoever could make two Ears of Corn, or two Blades of Grass to grow upon a Spot of Ground where only one grew before; would deserve better of Mankind, and do more essential Service to his Country, than the whole Race of Politicians put together.

JONATHAN SWIFT (1667–1745)   1726

From *Gulliver's Travels*, 'A Voyage to the Houyhnhnms', pp. 239–41, 241–2, 245–6, 249–50

THE MASTER HORSE OF THE HOUYHNHNMS ASKS GULLIVER TO TELL HIM THE CAUSES OF WAR

I answered, they were innumerable; but I should only mention a few of the chief. Sometimes the Ambition of Princes, who never think they have Land or People enough to govern: Sometimes the Corruption of Ministers, who engage their Master in a War in order to stifle or divert the Clamour of the Subjects against their evil Administration. Difference in Opinions hath cost many Millions of Lives: For Instance, whether *Flesh* be Bread, or *Bread* be *Flesh*: Whether the Juice of a certain *Berry* be *Blood* or *Wine*: Whether *Whistling* be a Vice or a Virtue: Whether it be better to *kiss a Post*, or throw it into the Fire: What is the best Colour for a *Coat*, whether *Black*, *White*, *Red* or *Grey*; and whether it should be *long* or *short*, *narrow* or *wide*, *dirty* or *clean*; with many more. Neither are any wars so furious or bloody, or of so long Continuance, as those occasioned by Difference in Opinion, especially if it be in things indifferent.

Sometimes the Quarrel between two Princes is to decide which of them shall dispossess a Third of his Dominions, where neither of them pretend to any Right. Sometimes one Prince quarrelleth with another, for fear the other should quarrel with him. Sometimes a War is entered upon, because the Enemy is too *strong*, and sometimes because he is too *weak*. Sometimes our Neighbours *want* the *Things* which we *have*, or *have* the Things which we want; and we both fight, till they take ours or give us theirs. It is a very justifiable Cause of War to invade a Country after the People have been wasted by Famine, destroyed by Pestilence, or embroiled by Factions amongst themselves. It is justifiable to enter into a War against our nearest Ally, when one of his Towns lies convenient for us, or a Territory of Land, that would render our Dominions round and compact. If a Prince send Forces into a Nation, where the People are poor and ignorant, he may lawfully put half of them to Death, and make Slaves of the rest, in order to civilize and reduce them from their barbarous Way of Living. It is a very kingly, honourable, and frequent Practice, when one Prince desires the Assistance of another to secure him against an Invasion, that the Assistant, when he hath driven out the Invader, should seize on the Dominions himself, and kill, imprison or banish the Prince he came to relieve. Alliance by Blood or Marriage, is a sufficient Cause of War between Princes; and the nearer their Kindred is, the greater is their Disposition to quarrel: *Poor* Nations are *hungry*, and *rich* Nations are *proud*; and Pride and Hunger will ever be at Variance. For these Reasons, the Trade of a *Soldier* is held to be the most honourable of all others: Because a *Soldier* is a *Yahoo* hired to kill in cold Blood as many of his own Species, who have never offended him, as possibly he can.

THE MASTER FINDS IT DIFFICULT TO BELIEVE THE YAHOOS OF EUROPE CAN KILL EACH OTHER IN SUCH NUMBERS AND IS SHOCKED BY GULLIVER'S ANSWER

For your mouths lying flat with your Faces, you can hardly bite each other to any Purpose, unless by Consent. Then, as to the Claws upon your Feet before and behind, they are so short and tender, that one of our *Yahoos* would drive a Dozen of yours before him. And therefore in recounting the Numbers of those who have been killed in Battle, I cannot but think that you have *said the Thing which is not.*

I could not forbear shaking my Head and smiling a little at his Ignorance. And, being no Stranger to the Art of War, I gave him a Description of Cannons, Culverins, Muskets, Carabines, Pistols, Bullets, Powder, Swords, Bayonets, Battles, Sieges, Retreats, Attacks, Undermines, Countermines, Bombardments, Sea-fights; Ships sunk with a Thousand Men; twenty Thousand killed on each Side; dying Groans, Limbs flying the Air: Smoke, Noise, Confusion, trampling to Death under Horses' Feet: Flight, Pursuit, Victory; Fields strewed with Carcasses left for Food to Dogs, and Wolves, and Birds of Prey; Plundering, Stripping, Ravishing, Burning and Destroying. And to set forth the Valour of my own dear Countrymen, I assured him, that I had seen them blow up a Hundred Enemies at once in a Siege, and as many in a Ship; and beheld the dead Bodies drop down in pieces from the Clouds, to the great Diversion of all the Spectators.

I was going on to more Particulars, when my Master commanded me Silence. He said, whoever understood the Nature of *Yahoos* might easily believe it possible for so vile an Animal, to be capable of every Action I had named, if their Strength and Cunning equalled their Malice. But, as my Discourse had increased his Abhorrence of the Whole Species, so he found it gave him a Disturbance in his Mind, to which he was wholly a Stranger before. He thought his Ears being used to such Abominable Words, might by Degrees admit them with less Detestation. That, although he hated the *Yahoos* of this Country, yet he no more blamed them for their odious Qualities, than he did a *Gnnayh* (a Bird of Prey) for its Cruelty, or a sharp Stone for cutting his Hoof. But, when a Creature pretending to Reason, could be capable of such Enormities, he dreaded lest the Corruption of that Faculty might be worse than Brutality itself. He seemed therefore confident, that instead of Reason, we were only possessed of some Quality fitted to increase our natural Vices; as the Reflection from a troubled Stream returns the Image of an ill-shapen Body, not only *larger*, but more *distorted*.

THE MASTER, HAVING 'HEARD TOO MUCH UPON THE SUBJECT OF WAR', AND LISTENED TO GULLIVER'S ACCOUNT OF LAW AND THE RACE OF LAWYERS, IS PUZZLED ABOUT 'MONEY' AND 'HIRE'

Whereupon I was at much Pains to describe to him the Use of *Money*, the Materials it was made of, and the Value of the Metals: That when a *Yahoo* had got a great Store of this precious Substance, he was able to purchase whatever he had a mind to; the finest Clothing, the noblest Houses, great Tracts of Land, the most costly Meats and Drinks; and have his Choice of the most beautiful Females. Therefore since *Money* alone, was able to perform all these Feats, our *Yahoos* thought, they could never have enough of it to spend or to save, as they found themselves inclined from their natural Bent either to Profusion or Avarice. That, the rich Man enjoyed the Fruit of the poor Man's Labour, and the latter were a Thousand to One in Proportion to the former. That the Bulk of our People were forced to live miserably, by labouring every Day for small Wages to make a few live plentifully. I enlarged myself much on these and many other Particulars to the same Purpose: But his Honour was still to seek: For he went upon a Supposition that all Animals had a Title to their Share in the Productions of the Earth.

GULLIVER IS ASKED TO DEFINE THAT SPECIES OF YAHOO KNOWN AS A 'MINISTER OF STATE'

I told him, that a *First* or *Chief Minister of State*, whom I intended to describe, was a Creature wholly exempt from Joy and Grief, Love and Hatred, Pity and Anger; at least makes use of no other Passions but a violent desire of Wealth, Power, and Titles: That he applies his Words to all Uses, except to the indication of his Mind; That he never tells a *Truth*, but with an Intent that you should take it for a *Lie*; nor a *Lie*, but with a Design that you should take it for a *Truth*; That those he speaks worst of behind their Backs, are in the surest way to Preferment; and whenever he begins to praise you to others or to your self, you are from that Day forlorn. The worst Mark you can receive is a *Promise*, especially when it is confirmed with an Oath; after which every wise Man retires, and gives over all Hopes.

There are three Methods by which a Man may rise to be Chief Minister: The first is, by knowing how with Prudence to dispose of a Wife, a Daughter, or a Sister: The second, by betraying or undermining his Predecessor: And the third is, by a *furious Zeal* in public Assemblies against the Corruptions of the Court. But a wise Prince would rather choose to employ those who practise the last of these Methods; because such Zealots prove always the most obsequious and subservient to the Will and Passions of their Master. That, these *Ministers* having all Employments at their Disposal, preserve themselves in Power by bribing the Majority of a Senate or great Council; and at last by an Expedient called an *Act of Indemnity* (whereof I described the Nature to him) they secure themselves from After-reckonings, and retire from the Public, laden with the Spoils of the Nation.

JONATHAN SWIFT (1667–1745)   1729

From *A Modest Proposal*, in *Prose Works*, XII, pp. 109, 111–12, 116–17

A CURE FOR THE POVERTY OF THE IRISH

Dublin

It is a melancholy object to those who walk through this great town, or travel in the country, when they see the streets, the roads, and cabin doors, crowded with beggars of the female sex, followed by three, four, or six children, all in rags, and importuning every passenger for an alms.

These mothers, instead of being able to work for their honest livelihood, are forced to employ all their time in strolling to beg sustenance for their helpless infants; who, as they grow up, either turn thieves for want of work, or leave their dear native country to fight for the Pretender in Spain, or sell themselves to the Barbadoes.

I think it is agreed by all parties that this prodigious number of children in the arms, or on the backs, or at the heels, of their mothers and frequently of their fathers, is in the present deplorable state of the kingdom a very great additional grievance; and therefore whoever could find out a fair, cheap, and easy method of making these children sound useful members of the commonwealth, would deserve so well of the public, as to have his statue set up for a preserver of the nation . . .

I shall now therefore humbly propose my own thoughts, which I hope will not be liable to the least objection.

I have been assured by a very knowing American of my acquaintance in London, that a young healthy child, well nursed, is at a year old a most delicious, nourishing, and wholesome food, whether stewed, roasted, baked, or boiled; and I make no doubt that it will equally serve in a fricassee or a ragout.

I do therefore humbly offer it to public consideration that of the 120,000 children already computed, 20,000 may be reserved for breed, whereof only one-fourth part to be males; which is more than we allow to sheep, black cattle, or swine; and my reason is, that these children are seldom the fruits of marriage, a circumstance not much regarded by our savages, therefore one male will be sufficient to serve four females. That the remaining 100,000 may, at a year old, be offered in sale to the persons of quality and fortune through the kingdom; always advising the mother to let them suck plentifully in the last month, so as to render them plump and fat for a good table. A child will make two dishes at an entertainment for friends; and when the family dines alone, the fore or hind quarter will make a reasonable dish, and, seasoned with a little pepper or salt, will be very good boiled on the fourth day, especially in winter.

I have reckoned upon a medium that a child just born will weigh 12 pounds, and in a solar year, if tolerably nursed, will increase to 28 pounds.

I grant this food will be somewhat dear, and therefore very proper for landlords, who, as they have already devoured most of the parents, seem to have the best title to the children . . .

I can think of no one objection that will possibly be raised against this proposal, unless it should be urged that the number of people will be thereby much lessened in the kingdom. This I freely own, and it was indeed one principal design in offering it to the world. I desire the reader will observe, that I calculate my remedy for this one individual kingdom of Ireland, and for no other that ever was, is, or I think ever can be, upon earth. Therefore let no man talk to me of other expedients: of taxing our absentees at 5s. a pound; of using neither clothes nor household furniture except what is of our own growth and manufacture; of utterly rejecting the materials and instruments that promote foreign luxury; of curing the expensiveness of pride, vanity, idleness, and gaming, in our women; of introducing a vein of parsimony, prudence, and temperance; of learning to love our country, in the want of which we differ even from LAPLANDERS and the inhabitants of TOPINAMBOO; of quitting our animosities and factions, nor acting any longer like the Jews, who were murdering one another at the very moment their city was taken; of being a little cautious not to sell our country and conscience for nothing; of teaching landlords to have at least one degree of mercy toward their tenants; lastly, of putting a spirit of honesty, industry, and skill into our shopkeepers; who, if a resolution could now be taken to buy only our native goods, would immediately unite to cheat and exact upon us in the price, the measure, and the goodness, nor could ever yet be brought to make one fair proposal of just dealing, though often and earnestly invited to it.

Therefore I repeat, let no man talk to me of these and the like expedients, till he has at least some glimpse of hope that there will be ever some hearty and sincere attempt to put them in practice.

ALEXANDER POPE (1688–1744)   1730

Epistle to Lord Bathurst: on the Use of Riches', ll. 21–48, 99–126, 133–50

THE POWER OF GOLD

What Nature wants, commodious Gold bestows,
Tis thus we eat the bread another sows:
But how unequal it bestows, observe,
Tis thus we riot, while who sow it, starve.
What Nature wants (a phrase I much distrust)
Extends to Luxury, extends to Lust:
Useful, I grant, it serves what life requires,
But dreadful too, the dark Assassin hires:

Trade it may help, Society extend;
But lures the Pirate, and corrupts the Friend:
It raises Armies in a Nation's aid,
But bribes a Senate, and the Land's betrayed.
In vain may Heroes fight, and Patriots rave;
If secret Gold saps on from knave to knave.
Once, we confess, beneath the Patriot's cloak,
From the crack'd bag the dropping Guinea spoke,
And jingling down the back-stairs, told the crew,
'Old Cato is as great a Rogue as you.'
Blest paper-credit! last and best supply!
That lends Corruption lighter wings to fly!
Gold imp'd by thee, can compass hardest things,
Can pocket States, can fetch or carry Kings;
A single leaf shall waft an Army o'er,
Or ship off Senates to a distant shore;
A leaf, like Sibyl's, scatter to and fro,
Our fates and fortunes, as the winds shall blow:
Pregnant with thousands flits the Scrap unseen,
And silent sells a King, or buys a Queen . . .

LUCRE'S SORDID CHARMS

Perhaps you think the Poor might have their part?
Bond damns the Poor, and hates them from his heart:
The grave Sir Gilbert holds it for a rule,
That 'ev'ry man in want is knave or fool':
'God cannot love (says Blunt, with tearless eyes)
The wretch he starves' – and piously denies:
But the good Bishop, with a meeker air,
Admits, and leaves them, Providence's care.[1]

1. In 1730, a corporation was established to lend money to the poor upon pledges, by the name of the *Charitable Corporation*, but the whole was turned only to an iniquitous method of enriching particular people, to the ruin of such numbers, that it became a parliamentary concern to endeavour the relief of those unhappy sufferers, and three of the managers, who were members of the House, were expelled . . . It appears, that when it was objected to the intended removal of the office, that the poor, for whose use it was erected, would be hurt by it, Bond, one of the directors, replied, 'Damn the poor.' That 'God hates the poor', and, 'that every man in want is knave or fool', etc., were the genuine apophthegms of some of the persons here mentioned. [This and the following are Pope's notes.]

Yet, to be just to these poor men of pelf,
Each does but hate his neighbour as himself:
Damn to the Mines, an equal fate betides,
The Slave that digs it, and the Slave that hides.
Who suffer thus, mere Charity should own,
Must act on motives pow'rful, tho' unknown:
Some War, some Plague, or Famine they foresee,
Some Revelation hid from you and me.
Why Shylock wants a meal, the cause is found,
He thinks a Loaf will rise to fifty pound.
What makes Directors cheat in South-sea[2] year?
To live on Ven'son when it sold so dear.
Ask you why Phrynne the whole Auction buys?
Phrynne foresees a general Excise.
Why she and Sappho raise that monstrous sum?
Alas! they fear a man will cost a plum.
Wise Peter sees the world's respect for Gold,
And therefore hopes this Nation may be sold:
Glorious Ambition! Peter,[3] swell thy store,
And be what Rome's great Didius[4] was before . . .

Much injur'd Blunt![5] why bears he Britain's hate?
A wizard told him in these words our fate:
'At length Corruption, like a gen'ral flood,
(So long by watchful Ministers withstood)
Shall deluge all; and Av'rice creeping on,
Spread like a low-born mist, and blot the Sun;
Statesman and Patriot ply alike the stocks,
Peeress and Butler share alike the Box,

2. The South Sea Company, given a monopoly of trade to South America and the Pacific, encouraged investments, and in 1720 the stocks first rose astronomically, then fell, profiting the few, but ruining many. The report which inquired into this financial disaster showed that at least three ministers had accepted bribes and speculated in the stock. During this year, the price of a haunch of venison was from three to five pounds.
3. Peter Walter . . . a dexterous attorney, but allowed to be a good, if not a safe, conveyancer.
4. Didius – a Roman Lawyer, so rich as to purchase the Empire when it was set to sale upon the death of Pertinax.
5. Sir John Blunt, originally a scrivener, was one of the first projectors of the South Sea Company, and afterwards one of the directors and chief managers of the famous scheme in 1720. He was also one of those who suffered most severely by the bill of pains and penalties on the said directors . . . Whether he did really credit the prophecy here mentioned is not certain, but it was constantly in this very style he declaimed against the corruption and luxury of the age, the partiality of parliament, and the misery of party-spirit . . .

And Judges job, and Bishops bite the town,
And mighty Dukes pack cards for half a crown.
See Britain's sun in lucre's sordid charms,
And France reveng'd of ANNE's and EDWARD's arms!'
Twas no Court-badge, great Scrivener! fir'd thy brain,
Nor lordly Luxury, nor City gain:
No, twas thy righteous end, (asham'd to see
Senates degen'rate, Patriots disagree,
And nobly wishing Party-rage to cease)
To buy both sides, and give thy Country peace.

LORD BOLINGBROKE (1678–1751)   1734

From *A Dissertation upon Parties* in *Works*, Letter 19, pp. 164–71

The success of the Whigs in government had, for Bolingbroke (as a 'democratic Tory'), led to an abuse of royal power and a species of corruption and of political immorality which threatened the nation's liberties and the constitution, as assured by the Revolution Settlement between the Whigs and the Tories on the basis of the expansion of landed and property interests and thus the interests (as they saw it) of the state.

A SPIRIT OF FRAUD AND CORRUPTION

The increase and continuance of taxes acquire to the crown, by multi-plying officers of the revenue, and by arming them with formidable pow-ers against the rest of their fellow-subjects, a degree of power, the weight of which the inferior ranks of our people have long felt, and they most, who are most useful to the commonwealth, and which even the superior ranks may feel one time or other; for I presume it would not be difficult to show how a full exercise of the powers that are in being, with, or even without some little additions to them, for the improvement of the rev-enue, that stale pretence for oppression, might oblige the greatest lord of the land to bow as low to a commissioner of customs, or excise, or to some subaltern harpy, as any nobleman or gentleman in France can be obliged to bow to the intendant of his province. But the establishment of public funds, on the credit of these taxes, hath been productive of more and greater mischiefs than the taxes themselves, not only by increasing the means of corruption, and the power of the crown, but by the effect it hath had on the spirit of the nation, on our manners, and our morals. It is impossible to look back, without grief, on the necessary and unavoidable consequences of this establishment; or without indignation on that mystery of iniquity, to which this establishment gave occasion, which hath been raised upon it, and carried on, for almost half a century, by means of it. It is impossible to look forward, without horror, on the consequences that may still follow. The ordinary expenses of our government are defrayed, in great measure, by anticipations and mortgages. In times of peace, in days of prosperity, as we boast them to be, we contract new debts, and we create new funds. – What must we do in war, and in national distress? What will happen, when we have mortgaged and funded all we have to mortgage and to fund; when we have mortgaged to new creditors that sinking fund which was mortgaged to other creditors not yet paid off; when we have mortgaged all the product of our land, and even our land itself? Who can answer, that when we come to such extremities, or have them more nearly in prospect, ten millions of people will bear any longer to be hewers of wood, and drawers of water, to maintain the two hundredth part of that number at ease, and in plenty? Who can answer, that the whole body of the people will suffer themselves to be treated, in favour of a handful of men, (for they who monopolize the whole power, and may in time monopolize the whole property of the funds, are indeed but a handful,) who can answer, that the whole body of the people will suffer themselves to be treated, in favour of such a handful . . . [and] to toil and starve for the proprietors of the several funds? Who can answer, that a scheme, which oppresses the farmer, ruins the manufacturer, breaks the merchant, discourages industry, and reduces fraud into a system; which beggars so often the fair adventurer and innocent proprietor; which drains continually a portion of our national wealth away to foreigners, and draws most perniciously the rest of that immense property that was diffused among thousands, into the pockets of a few; who can answer, that such a scheme will be always endured? . . .

JAMES THOMSON (1700–1748)

From *Liberty*, Part V

LIBERTY

The Author addresses the Goddess of Liberty

'But how shall this thy mighty kingdom stand?
On what unyielding base? how finish'd shine?'
   At this her eye, collecting all its fire,
Beam'd more than human; and her awful voice,
Majestic thus she raised: 'To Britons bear
This closing strain, and with tenser note
Loud let it sound in their awaken'd ear:
   'On virtue can alone my kingdom stand,
On public virtue, every virtue join'd.
For, lost this social cement of mankind,
The greatest empires, by scarce-felt degrees,
Will moulder soft away; till, tottering loose,
They, prone at last, to total ruin rush.
Unbless'd by virtue, government a league
Becomes, a circling junto of the great,
To rob by law; religion mild, a yoke
To tame the stooping soul, a trick of state
To mask their rapine, and to share the prey.
What are, without it, senates; save a face
Of consultation deep and reason free,
While the determin'd voice and heart are sold?
What boasted freedom, save a sounding name?
And what election, but a market vile
Of slaves self-barter'd? Virtue! without thee,
There is no ruling eye, no nerve, in states;
War has no vigour, and no safety peace;
E'en justice warps to party, laws oppress,
Wide through the land their weak protection fails,
First broke the balance, and then scorn'd the sword.
Thus nations sink, society dissolves;
Rapine and guile and violence break loose,
Everting life, and turning love to gall;
Man hates the face of man, and Indian woods
And Libya's hissing sands to him are tame.

'By those three virtues be the frame sustain'd
Of British freedom: independent life;
Integrity in office; and, o'er all
Supreme, a passion for the commonweal'.

SAMUEL JOHNSON (1709–84)   1738

From *London: A Poem in Imitation of the Third Satire of Juvenal*

HATED POVERTY

By numbers here from shame or censure free,
All crimes are safe, but hated poverty.
This, only this, the rigid law pursues,
This, only this, provokes the snarling Muse;
The sober trader at a tattered cloak,
Wakes from his dream, and labours for a joke;
With brisker air the silken courtiers gaze,
And turn the varied taunt a thousand ways.
Of all the griefs that harass the distressed,
Sure the most bitter is a scornful jest;
Fate never wounds more deep the gen'rous heart,
Than when a blockhead's insult points the dart.

Has Heaven reserved, in pity to the poor,
No pathless waste, or undiscovered shore?
No secret island in the boundless main?
No peaceful desert yet unclaimed by Spain?
Quick let us rise, the happy seats explore,
And bear oppression's insolence no more.
This mournful truth is ev'rywhere confessed,
Slow rises worth, by poverty depressed.
But here more slow, where all are slaves to gold,
Where looks are merchandise, and smiles are sold,
Where won by bribes, by flatteries implored,
The groom retails the favours of his lord.

HENRY FIELDING (1707–54) 1742

From *Joseph Andrews*, III, chapter 13

Peter Pounce, the unscrupulous steward who has managed to acquire considerable wealth for himself by devious means, and Parson Adams, the poor, unworldly but warm-hearted protagonist, dispute the meaning of charity.

CHARITY AND WEALTH

'. . . For my own part,' (said Pounce) 'I have no delight in the prospect of any land but my own.' – 'Sir,' said Adams, 'you can indulge yourself with many fine prospects of that kind.' – 'I thank God I have a little,' replied the other, 'with which I am content, and envy no man: I have a little, Mr Adams, with which I do as much good as I can.' Adams answered, 'That riches without charity were nothing worth; for that they were a blessing only to him who made them a blessing to others.' – 'You and I,' said Peter, 'have different notions of charity. I own, as it is generally used, I do not like the word, nor do I think it becomes one of us gentlemen; it is a mean parson-like quality; though I would not infer many parsons have it neither.' – 'Sir,' said Adams, 'my definition of charity is, a generous disposition to relieve the distressed.' – 'There is something in that definition,' answered Peter, 'which I like well enough; it is, as you say, a disposition, and does not so much consist in the act as in the disposition to do it. But, alas! Mr Adams, who are meant by the distressed? Believe me, the distresses of mankind are mostly imaginary, and it would be rather folly than goodness to relieve them.' – 'Sure, sir,' replied Adams, 'hunger and thirst, cold and nakedness, and other distresses which attend the poor, can never be said to be imaginary evils.' – 'How can any man complain of hunger,' said Peter, 'in a country where such excellent salads are to be gathered in almost every field? or of thirst, where every river and stream produces such delicious potations? And as for cold and nakedness, they are evils introduced by luxury and custom. A man naturally wants clothes no more than a horse or any other animal; and there are whole nations who go without them; but these are things perhaps which you, who do not know the world' – 'You will pardon me, sir,' returned Adams; 'I have read of the Gymnosophists.' – 'A plague of your Jehosophats!' cried Peter; 'the greatest fault in our constitution is the provision made for the poor, except that perhaps made for some others. Sir, I have not an estate which doth not contribute almost as much again to the poor as to the land-tax; and I do assure you

I expect to come myself to the parish in the end.' To which Adams [gave] a dissenting smile . . .

ANONYMOUS

1747

From *Liberty and Right – An Essay Historical and Political on the Constitution and Administration of Great Britain*, in Dickinson, ed., *Politics and Literature*, pp. 115–16

The anonymous writer attacks standing armies, suggests the abolition of primogeniture, and makes a plea for more frequent elections, secret ballot, the payment of MPs, and other reforms.

A NATIONAL DEPRAVITY

. . . Have we not seen how the crown, and the ministers of the crown, by virtue of royal prerogative and privilege, oppos'd their own private interest to the public interest of the community; and, by posts, and places, and titles of honour, affected to raise their own power and dignity above the rights and liberties of the people? Have we not seen how, things being brought to the last extremity, that tyranny was dissolv'd, that family excluded, and a new race of princes fix'd upon the throne? Have we not seen how these very Revolution princes, one after another, by exceeding in power, and multiplying the annual revenue, have put it in the power of their ministers to introduce a national depravity of manners, to seduce or over-awe the native freedom of popular elections, and to subvert and destroy the honour and integrity of the popular representation? Have we not seen how, by this unequal and deprav'd influence of the crown, the people have been inflam'd and divided, faction promoted, and treasons and rebellions excited and multiply'd? 'Tis from the inequality of our orders, 'tis from the iniquitous and private influence of the crown, that all our present internal calamities flow, and will and must flow; for, while that influence continues, our morality will every day decay, our people will turn worse and worse, one year after another will produce greater demands from the crown and greater compliances by the people. Ministers may be chang'd one after another, popular clamour may be rais'd against particular persons in power; but unless the people and the representatives of the people, the electors and the elected, be secur'd by their orders against the influence of all ministers whatever,

315

and against bribery and corruption of every kind, the nation never can be out of trouble, never free from danger: and, to secure them effectually, we need neither raise the power of the people beyond what it is, nor depress in any degree the legal authority of the prince; let us only preserve the just rights and independency of all parts of the legislature . . .

CHARLES CHURCHILL (1731–64) 1760

From *The Author*

IS THIS THE LAND WHERE FREEDOM WALKED AT LARGE?

Is this – O death to think! is this the land
Where merit and reward went hand in hand,
Where heroes, parent-like, the poet viewed? –
By whom they saw their glorious deeds renewed;
Where poets, true to honour, tuned their lays,
And by their patrons sanctified their praise?
Is this the land, where, on our Spenser's tongue,
Enamoured of his voice, Description hung;
Where Johnson rigid gravity beguiled,
Whilst Reason through her critic fences smiled;
Where Nature list'ning stood, whilst Shakespeare played,
And wondered at the work herself had made?
Is this the land, where, mindful of her charge,
And office high, fair Freedom walked at large;
Where, finding in our laws a sure defence,
She mocked at all restraints, but those of sense;
Where, health and honours trooping by her side,
She spread her sacred empire far and wide;
Pointed the way, affliction to beguile,
And bade the face of sorrow wear a smile,
Bade those, who dare obey the gen'rous call,
Enjoy her blessings, which God meant for all?
Is this the land, where, in some tyrant's reign,
When a weak, wicked ministerial train,
The tools of pow'r, the slaves of int'rest, planned
Their country's ruin, and with bribes unmanned

Those wretches, who, ordained in freedom's cause,
Gave up our liberties, and sold our laws;
When pow'r was taught by meanness where to go,
Nor dared to love the virtue of a foe;
When like a lep'rous plague, from the foul head
To the foul heart her sores Corruption spread,
Her iron arm when stern Oppression reared,
And Virtue, from her broad base shaken, feared
The scourge of Vice; when, impotent and vain,
Poor Freedom bowed the neck to slav'ry's chain;
Is this the land, where, in those worst of times,
The hardy poet raised his honest rhymes
To dread rebuke, and bade controlment speak
In guilty blushes on the villain's cheek,
Bade pow'r turn pale, kept mighty rogues in awe,
And made them fear the Muse, who feared not law?

JOHN WILKES (1727–97)   25 April 1763

From *The North Briton*, No. 45

For criticizing the King's Speech in Parliament, Wilkes was arrested. And thus
began his long struggle with the Covenant for the liberty of the subject. Though
repeatedly elected to Parliament, he was refused entry into the House of
Commons, fined, hounded, outlawed, and imprisoned.

SPIRIT OF DISCORD

In vain will such a minister, or the foul dregs of his power, the tools of
corruption and despotism, preach up in *the Speech* that *spirit of concord*,
and that obedience to the laws, which is essential to good order. They
have sent the *spirit of discord* through the land, and I will prophesy, that
it will never be extinguished, but by the extinction of their power. Is the
spirit of concord to go hand in hand with the *peace* and *excise* through this
nation? Is it to be expected between an insolent *exciseman*, and a *peer*,
gentleman, *freeholder*, or *farmer*, whose private houses are now made liable
to be entered and searched at pleasure?

Gloucestershire, Herefordshire, and in general all the *cider* counties, are
not surely the *several counties* which are alluded to in the speech. The

spirit of concord hath not gone forth among them, but the *spirit of liberty* has, and a noble opposition has been given to the wicked instruments of oppression. A nation as sensible as the English, will see that a *spirit of concord*, when they are oppressed, means a tame submission to injury, and that a *spirit of liberty* ought then to arise, and I am sure ever will, in proportion to the weight of the grievance they feel . . .

OLIVER GOLDSMITH (1730?–74)   1764

The Traveller, or a Prospect of Society, ll. 339–92

FREEDOM

That independence Britons prize too high,
Keeps man from man, and breaks the social tie;
The self-dependent lordlings stand alone,
All claims that bind and sweeten life unknown;
Here by the bonds of nature feebly held,
Minds combat minds, repelling and repell'd.
Ferments arise, imprison'd factions roar,
Represst ambition struggles round her shore,
Till over-wrought, the general system feels
Its motions stop, or frenzy fire the wheels.
   Nor this the worst. As nature's ties decay,
As duty, love, and honour fail to sway,
Fictitious bonds, the bonds of wealth and law,
Still gather strength, and force unwilling awe.
Hence all obedience bows to these alone,
And talent sinks, and merit weeps unknown;
Till time may come, when stript of all her charms,
The land of scholars, and the nurse of arms;
Where noble stems transmit the patriot flame,
Where kings have toil'd, and poets wrote for fame;
One sink of level avarice shall lie,
And scholars, soldiers, kings, unhonour'd die.
   Yet think not, thus when Freedom's ills I state,
I mean to flatter kings, or court the great;
Ye powers of truth that bid my soul aspire,
Far from my bosom drive the low desire;
And thou, fair Freedom, taught alike to feel

The rabble's rage, and tyrant's angry steel;
Thou transitory flower, alike undone
By proud contempt, or favour's fostering sun,
Still may thy blooms the changeful clime endure,
I only would repress them to secure:
For just experience tells, in every soil,
That those who think must govern those that toil
And all that freedom's highest aims can reach,
Is but to lay proportion'd loads on each.
Hence, should one order disproportion'd grow,
Its double weight must ruin all below.
    O then how blind to all that truth requires,
Who think it freedom when a part aspires!
Calm is my soul, nor apt to rise in arms,
Except when fast approaching danger warms:
But when contending chiefs blockade the throne,
Contracting regal power to stretch their own,
When I behold a factious band agree
To call it freedom when themselves are free;
Each wanton judge new penal statutes draw,
Laws grind the poor, and rich men rule the law;
The wealth of climes where savage nations roam,
Pillag'd from slaves to purchase slaves at home;
Fear, pity, justice, indignation start,
Tear off reserve, and bare my swelling heart;
Till half a patriot, half a coward grown,
I fly from petty tyrants to the throne.

JOSEPH PRIESTLEY (1733–1804)   1768

From *An Essay on the First Principles of Government*

POLITICAL LIBERTY: THE NATURAL RIGHTS OF THE PEOPLE

. . . in the largest states, if the abuses of government should, at any time, be great and manifest; if the servants of the people, forgetting their masters, and their masters' interest, should pursue a separate one of their own; if, instead of considering that they are made for the people, they should consider the people as made for them; if the oppressions and violations of right should be great, flagrant, and universally resented; if the tyrannical governors should have no friends but a few sycophants, who had long preyed upon the vitals of their fellow citizens, and who might be expected to desert a government, whenever their interests should be detached from it: if, in consequence of these circumstances, it should become manifest, that the risk, which would be run in attempting a revolution would be trifling, and the evils which might be apprehended from it, were far less than these which were actually suffered, and which were daily increasing; in the name of God, I ask, what principles are those, which ought to restrain an injured and insulted people from asserting their natural rights, and from changing, or even punishing their governors that is their servants, who had abused their trust; or from altering the whole form of their government, if it appeared to be of a structure so liable to abuse?

To say that these forms of government have been long established, and that these oppressions have been long suffered, without any complaint, is to supply the strongest argument for their abolition . . . Nothing can more justly excite the indignation of an honest and oppressed citizen, than to hear a prelate, who enjoys a considerable benefice, under a corrupt government, pleading for its support by those abominable perversions of scripture, which have been too common on this occasion; as by urging in its favour that passage of St Paul, *The powers which be are ordained of God*, and others of a similar import. It is a sufficient answer to such an absurd quotation as this, that, for the same reason, the powers which *will be* will be ordained of God also . . .

It will be said, that it is opening a door to rebellion, to assert that magistrates, abusing their power, may be set aside by the people, who are of course their own judges when that power is abused. May not the people, it is said, abuse their power, as well as their governors? I answer, it is very possible they may abuse their power: it is possible they may imagine themselves oppressed when they are not: it is possible that their animosity may be artfully and unreasonably inflamed, by ambitious and enterprising men, whose views are often best answered by popular tumults and insurrections; and the people may suffer in consequence of their folly and precipitancy. But what man is there, or what body of men (whose right to direct their own conduct was never called in question) but are liable to be imposed upon, and to suffer in consequence of their mistaken apprehensions and precipitate conduct? . . .

English history will inform us, that the people of this country have always borne extreme oppression, for a long time before there has appeared any danger of a general insurrection against the government . . .

The sum of what hath been advanced upon this head, is a maxim, than which nothing is more true, that *every government, whatever be the form of it, is originally, and antecedent to its present form, an equal republic*; and, consequently, that every man, when he comes to be sensible of his natural rights, and to feel his own importance, will consider himself as fully equal to any other person whatever. The consideration of riches and power, however acquired, must be entirely set aside, when we come to these first principles. The very idea of property, or right of any kind, is founded upon a regard to the general good of the society, under whose protection it is enjoyed; and nothing is properly *a man's own*, but what general rules, which have for their object the good of the whole, give to him. To whomsoever the society delegates its power, it is delegated to them for the more easy management of public affairs, and in order to make the more effectual provision for the happiness of the whole. Whoever enjoys property, or riches in the state, enjoys them for the good of the state, as well as for himself; and whenever those powers, riches, or rights of any kind, are abused, to the injury of the whole, that awful and ultimate tribunal, in which every citizen hath an equal voice, may demand the resignation of them . . . Magistrates, therefore, who consult not the good of the public, and who employ their power to oppress the people, are a public nuisance, and their power is abrogated *ipso facto* . . .

JUNIUS   19 December 1769

From 'An Open Letter to George III', *The Public Advertiser*, in Rickword and Lindsay, eds., *Handbook of Freedom*, pp. 199–200

THE ENGLISH NATION GROSSLY INJURED

On this side then, whichever way you turn your eyes, you see nothing but perplexity and distress. You may determine to support the very ministry who have reduced your affairs to this deplorable situation: you may shelter yourself under the forms of a parliament, and set your people at defiance. But be assured, Sir, that such a resolution would be as imprudent as it would be odious. If it did not immediately shake your establishment, it would rob you of your peace of mind for ever.

On the other, how different is the prospect! How easy, how safe and honourable is the path before you! The English nation declare they are grossly injured by their representatives, and solicit your Majesty to exert your lawful prerogative, and give them an opportunity of recalling a trust, which, they find, has been scandalously abused. You are not to be told that the power of the house of commons is not original, but delegated to them for the welfare of the people, from whom they received it. A question of right arises between the constituent and the representative body. By what authority shall it be decided? Will your Majesty interfere in a question in which you have properly no immediate concern? – It would be a step equally odious and unnecessary. Shall the lords be called upon to determine the rights and privileges of the commons? – They cannot do it without a flagrant breach of the constitution. Or will you refer it to the judges? – They have often told your ancestors, that the law of parliament is above them. What party then remains, but to leave it to the people to determine for themselves? They alone are injured; and, since there is no superior power, to which the cause can be referred, they alone ought to determine.

OLIVER GOLDSMITH
(1730?–74)

Published 26 May 1770

The Deserted Village, ll. 265–308

THE RICH MAN'S THEFT

Ye friends to truth, ye statesmen, who survey
The rich man's joys increase, the poor's decay,
'Tis yours to judge, how wide the limits stand
Between a splendid and an happy land.
Proud swells the tide with loads of freighted ore,
And shouting Folly hails them from her shore;
Hoards, even beyond the miser's wish abound,
And rich men flock from all the world around.
Yet count our gains. This wealth is but a name
That leaves our useful products still the same.
Not so the loss. The man of wealth and pride,
Takes up a space that many poor supplied;
Space for his lake, his park's extended bounds,
Space for his horses, equipage, and hounds;
The robe that wraps his limbs in silken sloth,
Has robbed the neighbouring fields of half their growth;
His seat, where solitary sports are seen,
Indignant spurns the cottage from the green;

322

present it is not only their interest, but I hold it to be essentially necessary to the preservation of the constitution, that the privileges of parliament should be strictly ascertained, and confined within the narrowest bounds the nature of their institution will admit of. Upon the same principle, on which I would have resisted prerogative in the last century, I now resist privilege. It is indifferent to me, whether the crown, by its own immediate act, imposes new and dispenses with old laws, or whether the same arbitrary power produces the same effects through the medium of the House of Commons. We trusted our representatives with privileges for their own defence and ours. We cannot hinder their desertion, but we can prevent their carrying over their arms to the service of the enemy. – It will be said, that I begin with endeavouring to reduce the argument concerning privilege to a mere question of convenience; – that I deny at one moment what I would allow at another; and that to resist the power of a prostituted House of Commons may establish a precedent injurious to all future parliaments. – To this I answer generally, that human affairs are in no instance governed by strict positive right. If change of circumstances were to have no weight in directing our conduct and opinions, the mutual intercourse of mankind would be nothing more than a contention between positive and equitable right. Society would be a state of war, and law itself would be injustice. On this general ground, it is highly reasonable, that the degree of our submission to privileges, which have never been defined by any positive law, should be considered as a question of convenience, and proportioned to the confidence we repose in the integrity of our representatives. As to the injury we may do to any future and more respectable House of Commons, I own I am not now sanguine enough to expect a more plentiful harvest of parliamentary virtue in one year than another. Our political climate is severely altered; and without dwelling upon the depravity of modern times, I think no reasonable man will expect that, as human nature is constituted, the enormous influence of the crown should cease to prevail over the virtue of individuals. The mischief lies too deep to be cured by any remedy less than some great convulsion, which may either carry back the constitution to its original principles, or utterly destroy it . . . My premises, I know, will be denied in argument, but every man's conscience tells him they are true. It remains then to be considered, whether it be for the interest of the people that privilege of parliament (which, in respect to the purposes for which it has hitherto been acquiesced under, is merely nominal) should be contracted within some certain limits, or whether the subject shall be left at the mercy of a power, arbitrary upon the face of it, and notoriously under the direction of the crown . . .

JAMES BURGH (1714–75)

From *Political Disquisitions*, I, pp. 28–9, 36–7

A MULTITUDE OF THE PEOPLE DEPRIVED OF ALL POWER

Every government, to have a reasonable expectation of permanency, ought to be founded in truth, justice, and the reason of things. Our admirable constitution, the envy of Europe, is founded in injustice. Eight hundred individuals rule all, themselves accountable to none. Of these about 300 are born rulers, whether qualified or not. Of the others, a great many are said to be elected by a handful of beggars instead of the number and property, who have the right to be electors. And of these pretended electors, the greatest part are obliged to choose the person nominated by some lord, or by the minister. Instead of the power's returning annually into the hands of the people, or, so to speak properly, of the boroughs, the lengthening of parliament to septennial has deprived them of six parts in seven of their power; and if the power returned annually, as it ought, all the people would still have reason to complain, but the handful, who voted the members into the house.

In consequence of the inadequate state of representation, the sense of the people may be grossly misapprehended, or misrepresented, and it may turn out to be of very little consequence, that members were willing to obey the instructions of their constituents; because they would not be obeying the general sense of the people. For the people are not their constituents. The people of England are the innumerable multitude which fills, like one continued city, a great part of Middlesex, Kent and Surrey; the countless inhabitants of the vast ridings of Yorkshire; the multitudes who swarm in the cities and great towns of Bristol, Liverpool, Manchester, Birmingham, Ely, and others; some of which places have no representatives at all, and the rest are unequally represented. These places comprehend the greatest part of the people. Whereas the instructions would be sent from the hungry boroughs of Cornwall, Devonshire, &c. In short, the sense of the constituents would be, at best, only the sense of a few thousands; whereas it ought to be that of several hundreds of thousands . . .

. . . It is commonly insisted on, that persons in servitude to others, and those who receive alms, ought not to be admitted to vote for members of parliament, because it is supposed, that their votes will be influenced by those, on whom they depend.

But the objection from influence would fall to the ground, if the state

were on a right foot, and parliament free from court-influence . . . Every
man has what may be called property, and unalienable property. Every
man has a life, a personal liberty, a character, a right to his earnings, a
right to a religious profession and worship according to his conscience,
&c. and many men, who are in a state of dependence upon others, and
who receive charity, have wives and children, in whom they have a right.
Thus the poor are in danger of being injured by the government in a
variety of ways. But, according to the commonly received doctrine, that
servants, and those who receive alms, have no right to vote for members
of parliament, an immense multitude of the people are utterly deprived
of all power in determining who shall be the protectors of their lives,
their personal liberty, their little property (which though singly considered is of small value, yet is upon the whole a very great object) and the
chastity of their wives and daughters, &c. What is particularly hard upon
the poor in this case is, that though they have no share in determining
who shall be the lawgivers of their country, they have a very heavy share
in raising the taxes which support government. The taxes on malt, on
beer, leather, soap, candles, and other articles, which are paid chiefly by
the poor, who are allowed no votes for members of parliament, amount
to as much as a heavy land-tax. The landed interest would complain
grievously, if they had no power of electing representatives. And it is an
established maxim in free states, that whoever contributes to the
expenses of government ought to be satisfied concerning the application
of the money contributed by them; consequently ought to have a share in
electing those, who have the power of applying their money . . .

THE DECLARATION OF INDEPENDENCE
4 July 1776

Drawn up by Thomas Jefferson, John Adams, Roger Sherman, Robert Living-
stone and Benjamin Franklin, the Declaration made the United States of North
America independent of the British Crown. It is included here because it represents a momentous culmination of the long historical struggle which had its roots
in England and Scotland, and began with the Founding Fathers in the early seventeenth century and the persecuted groups, both religious and political, who
followed them after the failure of the Commonwealth to escape the 'abjured and
detested thraldom of kingship'. That this was a great blow struck for liberty
against George III, 'the Royal Brute of England', and his Ministers, with their
contempt for 'the colonists', is significant enough; but as Tom Paine has written,
'the principles of America' also 'opened the Bastille'; and it was Paine the Eng-

lishman who urged the spirit of 1776, because for him the cause of *English* freedom was at stake.

———

When, in the course of human events, it becomes necessary from one people to dissolve the political bands which have connected them with another, and to assume, among the powers of the earth, the separate and equal station to which the laws of nature and of nature's God entitle them, a decent respect to the opinions of mankind requires that they should declare the causes which impel them to the separation.

We hold these truths to be self-evident, that all men are created equal; that they are endowed by their Creator with certain unalienable rights; that among these are life, liberty, and the pursuit of happiness. That, to secure these rights, governments are instituted among men, deriving their just powers from the consent of the governed; that, whenever any form of government becomes destructive of these ends, it is the right of the people to alter or to abolish it, and to institute a new government, laying its foundation on such principles, and organizing its powers in such form, as to them shall seem most likely to effect their safety and happiness. Prudence, indeed, will dictate that governments long established should not be changed for light and transient causes; and, accordingly, all experience hath shown, that mankind are more disposed to suffer, while evils are sufferable, than to right themselves by abolishing the forms to which they are accustomed. But, when a long train of abuses and usurpations, pursuing invariably the same object, evinces a design to reduce them under absolute despotism, it is their right, it is their duty, to throw off such government, and to provide new guards for their future security. Such has been the patient sufferance of these colonies, and such is now the necessity which constrains them to alter their former systems of government.

The history of the present King of Great Britain is a history of repeated injuries and usurpations, all having, in direct object, the establishment of an absolute tyranny over these states. To prove this, let facts be submitted to a candid world:

He has refused his assent to laws the most wholesome and necessary for the public good.

He has forbidden his governors to pass laws of immediate and pressing importance, unless suspended in their operation till his assent should be obtained; and, when so suspended, he has utterly neglected to attend to them . . .

He is, at this time, transporting large armies of foreign mercenaries to complete the works of death, desolation, and tyranny, already begun, with circumstances of cruelty and perfidy scarcely paralleled in the most

327

barbarous ages, and totally unworthy the head of a civilized nation.

He has constrained our fellow-citizens, taken captive on the high seas, to bear arms against their country, to become the executioners of their friends and brethren, or to fall themselves by their hands.

He has excited domestic insurrections amongst us, and has endeavoured to bring on the inhabitants of our frontiers, the merciless Indian savages, whose known rule of warfare is an undistinguished destruction of all ages, sexes, and conditions.

In every stage of these oppressions, we have petitioned for redress, in the most humble terms; our repeated petitions have been answered only by repeated injury. A prince, whose character is thus marked by every act which may define a tyrant, is unfit to be the ruler of a free people.

Nor have we been wanting in attention to our British brethren. We have warned them, from time to time, of attempts made by their legislature to extend an unwarrantable jurisdiction over us. We have reminded them of the circumstances of emigration and settlement here. We have appealed to their native justice and magnanimity, and we have conjured them, by the ties of our common kindred, to disavow these usurpations, which would inevitably interrupt our connections and correspondence. They, too, have been deaf to the voice of justice and consanguinity. We must, therefore, acquiesce in the necessity which denounces our separation, and hold them, as we hold the rest of mankind, enemies in war, in peace, friends.

We, therefore, the representative of the United States of America, in general Congress assembled, appealing to the Supreme Judge of the world for the rectitude of our intentions, do, in the name, and by the authority of the good people of these colonies, solemnly publish and declare, that these united colonies are, and of right ought to be free and independent states; that they are absolved from all allegiance to the British Crown, and that all political connection between them and the state of Great Britain is, and ought to be, totally dissolved; and that, as free and independent states, they have full power to levy war, conclude peace, contract alliances, establish commerce, and to do all other acts and things which independent states may of right do. And, for the support of this declaration, with a firm reliance on the protection of Divine Providence, we mutually pledge to each other our lives, our fortunes, and our sacred honour.

PETITION OF THE COUNTY OF YORK 1780

From *The Annual Register* (1780), pp. 338–9

AN APPEAL AGAINST OPPRESSIVE GRIEVANCES

To the Honourable the Commons of Great Britain, in Parliament assembled:

The Petition of the Gentlemen, Clergy, and Freeholders of the County of York, sheweth that this nation hath been engaged for several years in a most expensive and unfortunate war; that many of our valuable colonies, having actually declared themselves independent, have formed a strict confederacy with France and Spain the dangerous and inveterate enemies of Great Britain, that the consequence of those combined misfortunes hath been a large addition to the nation's debt, a heavy accumulation on taxes, a rapid decline of the trade, manufactures, and land-rents of the kingdom.

Alarmed at the diminished resources and growing burthens of this country, and convinced that rigid frugality is now indispensably necessary in every department of the state, your petitioners observe with grief, that notwithstanding the calamitous and impoverished condition of the nation, much public money has been improvidently squandered, and that many individuals enjoy sinecure places, efficient places with exorbitant emoluments, and pensions unmerited by public-service, to a large and still increasing amount; whence the crown has acquired a great and unconstitutional influence, which, if not checked, may soon prove fatal to the liberties of this country.

Your petitioners conceiving that the true end of every legitimate government is not the emolument of an individual, but the welfare of the community; and considering that by the constitution of this realm the national purse is entrusted in a peculiar manner to the custody of this honourable house; beg leave further to represent, that until effectual measures be taken to redress the oppressive grievances herein stated, the grant of any additional sum of public money, beyond the produce of the present taxes, will be injurious to the rights and property of the people, and derogatory from the honour and dignity of parliament.

Your petitioners therefore, appealing to the justice of this honourable house, do most earnestly request that, before any new burthens are laid upon this country, effectual measures may be taken by this house to inquire into and correct the gross abuses in the expenditure of public money; to reduce all exorbitant emoluments, to rescind and abolish all sinecure places and unmerited pensions; and to appropriate the produce to the necessities of the state in such manner as to the wisdom of parliament shall seem meet.

And your petitioners shall ever pray, etc., etc.

The following counties presented petitions nearly in the same words:

Middlesex	Dorset
Chester	Devon
Hants.	Norfolk
Hertford	Berks.
Sussex	Bucks.
Huntingdon	Nottingham
Surrey	Kent
Cumberland	Northumberland
Bedford	Suffolk
Essex	Hereford
Gloucester	Cambridge
Somerset	Derby
Wilts.	

Also the cities of London, Westminster, York, Bristol, and the towns of Cambridge, Nottingham, Newcastle, Reading and Bridgwater. The county of Northampton agreed to instruct their members on the points of the petition.

ANONYMOUS   c. 1782

Declaration of those Rights of the Commonalty of Great Britain, without which they cannot be Free (a pamphlet distributed by the Society of Constitutional Information), in Dickinson, ed., *Politics and Literature*, pp. 166–7

EQUAL RIGHTS FOR ALL AND ANNUAL PARLIAMENTS

It is declared,

First, That the government of this realm, and the making of laws for the same, ought to be lodged in the hands of King, Lords of Parliament, and Representatives of the whole body of the freemen of this realm.

Secondly, That every man of the commonalty (excepting infants, insane persons, and criminals) is, of common right, and by the laws of God, a freeman, and entitled to the full enjoyment of liberty.

Thirdly, That liberty, or freedom, consists in having an actual share in the appointing of those who frame the laws, and who are to be the guardians of every man's life, property, and peace: for the all of one man is as dear to him as the all of another; and the poor man has an equal right, but more need, to have representatives in the legislature than the rich one.

Fourthly, That they who have no voice nor vote in the electing of representatives do not enjoy liberty, but are absolutely enslaved to those who have votes, and to their representatives: for to be enslaved, is to have governors whom other men have set over us, and to be subject to laws made by the representatives of others, without having had representatives of our own to give consent in our behalf.

Fifthly, That a very great majority of the commonalty of this realm are denied the privilege of voting for representatives in parliament, and consequently they are enslaved to a small number, who do now enjoy this privilege exclusively to themselves; but who, it may be presumed, are far from wishing to continue in the exclusive possession of a privilege, by which their fellow-subjects are deprived of common right of justice, of liberty; and which, if not communicated to all, must speedily cause the certain overthrow of our happy constitution, and enslave us all. And,

Sixthly and lastly, we also say and do assert, that it is the right of the commonalty of this realm to elect a new House of Commons once in every year, according to ancient and sacred laws of the land: because, whenever a parliament continues in being for a longer term, very great numbers of the commonalty, who have arrived at the years of manhood since the last election, and therefore have a right to be actually represented in the House of Commons, are then unjustly deprived of that right. At the same time the cause of virtue suffers through the dissipation, and extravagance of the rising generation, whom the enjoyment of the universal right of suffrage would recall from unworthy pleasures, and animate to the full exertion of every generous and patriotic principle which can ornament the mind of man.

When the above Declaration is compared with the present long parliaments, and unequal representation of the people, which have brought this kingdom to the brink of ruin; every true friend to his country is solemnly called upon to demand annual parliaments, and that right of voting which God and the constitution have given him. In the hearty exertion to obtain these civil and just rights, let every one practise that Christian rule, to do unto others as we would they should do unto us. Then will that blessed era come when every man shall be free and happy under his vine, on earth peace, and consequently glory to God in the highest.

A Real Friend to the People

GEORGE CRABBE (1754–1832)

The Village, li. 109–53

Crabbe was born at Aldeburgh, where his father (embittered by disappointment and a heavy drinker) was harbour-master. His schooling was unhappy, and at fourteen he was apprenticed to an apothecary at Wickham near Bury, where poverty forced him to work as a farm-labourer. By 1780 he was in great poverty. In London, seeking fame as a poet and failing, he was rescued from obscurity by Edmund Burke, who helped to get him ordained for the Church, and thus to assure him a living. He married in 1783; he was vicar in parishes in Lincolnshire, Leicestershire and, from 1814 till his death, at Trowbridge.

RAPINE AND WRONG AND FEAR: THE RURAL POOR

Here, wand'ring long, amid these frowning fields,
I sought the simple life that Nature yields;
Rapine and Wrong and Fear usurp'd her place,
And a bold, artful, surly, savage race;
Who, only skill'd to take the finny tribe,
The yearly dinner, or septennial bribe,
Wait on the shore, and, as the waves run high,
On the tost vessel bend their eager eye,
Which to their coast directs its vent'rous way;
Theirs, or the ocean's, miserable prey.

   As on their neighbouring beach yon swallows stand,
And wait for favouring winds to leave the land;
While still for flight the ready wing is spread:
So waited I the favouring hour, and fled;
Fled from these shores where guilt and famine reign,
And cried, Ah! hapless they who still remain;
Who still remain to hear the ocean roar,
Whose greedy waves devour the lessening shore;
Till some fierce tide, with more imperious sway,
Sweeps the low hut and all it holds away;
When the sad tenant weeps from door to door;
And begs a poor protection from the poor!

   But these are scenes where Nature's niggard hand
Gave a spare portion to the famish'd land;
Hers is the fault if here mankind complain

Of fruitless toil and labour spent in vain;
But yet in other scenes more fair in view,
When Plenty smiles – alas! she smiles for few –
And those who taste not, yet behold her store,
Are as the slaves that dig the golden ore –
The wealth around them makes them doubly poor.

   Or will you deem them amply paid in health,
Labour's fair child, that languishes with wealth?
Go then! and see them rising with the sun,
Through a long course of daily toil to run;
See them beneath the dog-star's raging heat,
When the knees tremble and the temples beat;
Behold them, leaning on their scythes, look o'er
The labour past, and toils to come explore;
See them alternate suns and showers engage,
And hoard up aches and anguish for their age;
Through fens and marshy moors their steps pursue,
When their warm pores imbibe the evening dew;
Then own that labour may as fatal be
To these thy slaves, as thine excess to thee.

ROBERT BURNS (1759–96)   1785

'Lines Written on a Banknote'

THE CHILDREN OF AFFLICTION

Wae worth thy power, thou cursed leaf;
Fell source o' a' my woe and grief;
For lack o' thee I've lost my lass,
For lack o' thee I scrimp my glass;
I see the children of affliction
Unaided, through thy curst restriction:
I've seen the oppressor's cruel smile
Amid his hapless victim's spoil;
And for thy potence vainly wished,
To crush the villain in the dust:
For lack o' thee, I leave this much-lov'd shore,
Never, perhaps, to greet auld Scotland more.

WILLIAM COBBETT (1762–1835)   1785

From *The Progress of a Ploughboy to a Seat in Parliament, An Autobiography*

HUNGER: THE SOLDIER'S SIXPENCE

I enlisted in 1784, and, as peace had then taken place, no great haste was made to send recruits off to their regiments. I remember well what sixpence a day was, recollecting the pangs of hunger felt by me, during the thirteen months that I was a private soldier at Chatham, previous to my embarkation for Nova Scotia. Of my sixpence, nothing like fivepence was left to purchase food for the day. Indeed not fourpence. For there was washing, mending, soap, flour for hair-powder, shoes, stockings, shirts, stocks and gaiters, pipe-clay and several other things to come out of the miserable sixpence! Judge then the quantity of food to sustain life in a lad of sixteen, and to enable him to exercise with a musket (weighing fourteen pounds) six to eight hours every day . . . The best battalion I ever saw in my life was composed of men, the far greater part of whom were enlisted before they were sixteen, and who, when they were first brought up to the regiment, were clothed in coats much too long and too large, in order to leave room for growing.

We had several recruits from Norfolk (our regiment was the West Norfolk); and many of them deserted from sheer hunger. They were lads from the plough-tail. I remember two that went into a decline and died during the year, though when they joined us, they were fine hearty young men.

I have seen them lay in their berths, many and many a time, actually crying on account of hunger. The whole week's food was not a bit too much for one day.

ROBERT BURNS (1759–96)   1785?

'Man Was Made to Mourn – A Dirge', ll. 41–88

MAN'S INHUMANITY TO MAN

A few seem favourites of fate,
   In pleasure's lap carest;
Yet, think not all the rich and great
   Are likewise truly blest:

But oh! what crowds in ev'ry land,
    All wretched and forlorn,
Thro' weary life this lesson learn,
    That man was made to mourn.

Many and sharp the num'rous ills
    Inwoven with our frame!
More pointed still we make ourselves,
    Regret, remorse, and shame!
And man, whose heav'n-erected face
    The smiles of love adorn, –
Man's inhumanity to man
Makes countless thousands mourn!

See yonder poor, o'er-labour'd wight,
    So abject, mean, and vile,
Who begs a brother of the earth
    To give him leave to toil;
And see his lordly fellow-worm
    The poor petition spurn,
Unmindful, tho' a weeping wife
    And helpless offspring mourn.

If I'm design'd yon lordling's slave –
    By Nature's law designed –
Why was an independent wish
    E'er planted in my mind?
If not, why am I subject to
    His cruelty, or scorn?
Or why has man the will and pow'r
    To make his fellow mourn?

Yet, let not this too much, my son,
    Disturb your youthful breast:
This partial view of human-kind
    Is surely not the best!
The poor, oppressed, honest man
    Had never, sure, been born,
Had there not been some recompense
    To comfort those that mourn!

O Death! the poor man's dearest friend,
    The kindest and the best!

Welcome the hour my aged limbs
  Are laid with thee at rest!
The great, the wealthy fear thy blow,
  From pomp and pleasure torn;
But oh! a blest relief for those
  That weary-laden mourn!

EDWARD GIBBON (1737–1794)   1787

From the final pages of *The Decline and Fall of the Roman Empire*

ON THE CAPITAL OF CHRISTENDOM TODAY

. . . The improvements of Rome since the fifteenth century have not
been the spontaneous produce of freedom and industry. The first and
most natural root of a great city is the labour and populousness of the
adjacent country, which supplies the materials of subsistence, of manufactures, and of foreign trade. But the greater part of the Campagna of
Rome is reduced to a dreary and desolate wilderness; the overgrown
estates of the princes and the clergy are cultivated by the lazy hands of
indigent and hopeless vassals; and the scanty harvests are confined or
exported for the benefit of a monopoly. A second and more artificial
cause of the growth of a metropolis is the residence of a monarch, the
expense of a luxurious court, and the tributes of dependent provinces.
These provinces and tributes had been lost in the fall of the empire; and
if some streams of the silver of Peru and the gold of Brazil have been
attracted by the Vatican, the revenues of the cardinals, the fees of office,
the oblations of pilgrims and clients, and the remnant of ecclesiastical
taxes afford a poor and precarious supply, which maintains, however,
the idleness of the court and city. The population of Rome, far below
the measure of the great capitals of Europe, does not exceed one hundred
and seventy thousand inhabitants; and within the spacious enclosure of
the walls, the largest portion of the seven hills is overspread with vineyards and ruins.

   The beauty and splendour of the modern city may be ascribed to the
abuses of the government, to the influence of superstition. Each reign
(the exceptions are rare) has been marked by the rapid elevation of a new
family, enriched by the childless pontiff at the expense of the church and
country. The palaces of these fortunate nephews are the most costly
monuments of elegance and servitude; the perfect arts of architecture,

painting, and sculpture have been prostituted in their service; and their galleries and gardens are decorated with the most precious works of antiquity, which taste or vanity has prompted them to collect . . .

ROBERT BURNS (1759–96)

1786

'A Winter Night', ll. 37–88

WHOSE TOIL UPHOLDS THE GLITT'RING SHOW

Blow, blow, ye winds, with heavier gust!
And freeze, thou bitter-biting frost!
Descend, ye chilly, smothering snows!
Not all your rage, as now united, shows
   More hard unkindness, unrelenting,
   Vengeful malice, unrepenting,
Than heaven-illumin'd Man on brother Man bestows!

See stern Oppression's iron grip,
    Or mad Ambition's gory hand,
Sending, like blood-hounds from the slip,
    Woe, Want, and Murder o'er the land!
  Ev'n in the peaceful rural vale,
   Truth, weeping, tells the mournful tale,
How pamper'd Luxury, Flattery by her side,
  The parasite empoisoning her ear,
  With all the servile wretches in the rear,
Looks o'er proud Property, extended wide;
  And eyes the simple rustic hind,
Whose toil upholds the glitt'ring show –
  A creature of another kind,
  Some coarser substance, unrefin'd –
Plac'd for her lordly use, thus far, thus vile, below!

Where, where is Love's fond, tender throe,
With lordly Honour's lofty brow,
    The pow'rs you proudly own?
Is there, beneath Love's noble name,
Can harbour, dark, the selfish aim,
    To bless himself alone!
  Mark maiden-innocence a prey

To love-pretending snares:
   This boasted Honour turns away,
   Shunning soft Pity's rising sway,
Regardless of the tears and unavailing pray'rs!
   Perhaps this hour, in misery's squalid nest,
   She strains her infant to her joyless breast,
And with a mother's fears shrinks at the rocking blast!

Oh ye! who, sunk in beds of down,
   Feel not a want but what yourselves create,
   Think, for a moment, on his wretched fate,
   Whom friends and fortune quite disown!
Ill-satisfy'd keen nature's clamorous call,
   Stretch'd on his straw, he lays himself to sleep;
While thro' the ragged roof and chinky wall,
   Chill, o'er his slumbers, piles the drifty heap!
   Think on the dungeon's grim confine,
   Where Guilt and poor Misfortune pine!
   Guilt-erring man, relenting view,
   But shall thy legal rage pursue
   The wretch, already crushed low
   By cruel Fortune's undeserved blow?
Affliction's sons are brothers in distress;
A brother to relieve, how exquisite the bliss!

Part Five

THE AGE OF REVOLUTION AND TOTAL WAR 1789–1848

The present age will hereafter merit to be called the Age of reason, and the present generation will appear to the future as the Adam of a new world.

> Tom Paine, *The Rights of Man*

Awake! awake O sleeper of the land of shadows, wake! expand!
I am in you and you in me, mutual in love divine:
Fibres of love from man to man thro Albion's pleasant land.
In all the dark Atlantic vale down from the hills of Surrey
A black water accumulates; return, Albion! return!
Thy brethren call thee, and thy fathers and thy sons,
Thy nurses and thy mothers, thy sisters and thy daughters
Weep at thy soul's disease, and the Divine Vision is darkend . . .
Albion's mountains run with blood, the cries of war and of
   tumult
Resound into the unbounded night, every Human perfection
Of mountain and river and city are small and wither'd and
   darken'd.

> William Blake, *Jerusalem*

THE FRENCH REVOLUTION August 1789

From *Declaration of the Rights of Man and of Citizens* and Tom Paine, *The Rights of Man* (February 1791), in Paine, *Rights of Man*, pp. 132,136–7

The Declaration was debated by the Constituent Assembly throughout August 1789 and formally published as a preface to the Constitution of September 1791. It owed much to American precedent, and was even discussed with Thomas Jefferson. As a basic charter for the radical middle class in Europe, it had a powerful impact, in England as elsewhere.

RIGHTS AND DUTIES

'The Representatives of the people of France, formed into a NATIONAL ASSEMBLY, considering that ignorance, neglect, or contempt of human rights, are the sole causes of public misfortunes and corruptions of Government, have resolved to set forth, in a solemn declaration, these natural, imprescriptible, and inalienable rights: that this declaration being constantly present to the minds of the members of the body social, they may be ever kept attentive to their rights and their duties: that the acts of the legislative and executive powers of Government, being capable of being every moment compared with the end of political institutions, may be more respected: and also, that the future claims of the citizens, being directed by simple and incontestable principles, may always tend to the maintenance of the Constitution, and the general happiness . . .'

PAINE: 'A REGENERATION OF MAN'

In the declaratory exordium which prefaces the Declaration of Rights, we see the solemn and majestic spectacle of a Nation opening its commission, under the auspices of its Creator, to establish a Government; a scene so new, and so transcendently unequalled by anything in the European world, that the name of a Revolution is diminutive of its character, and it rises into a Regeneration of man. What are the present governments of Europe, but a scene of iniquity and oppression? What is that of England? Do not its own inhabitants say, It is a market where every man has his price, and where corruption is common traffic, at the expense of a deluded people? No wonder, then, that the French Revolution is traduced. Had it confined itself merely to the destruction of flagrant despotism, perhaps Mr Burke and some others had been silent.

Their cry now is, 'It has gone too far': that is, it has gone too far for them. It stares corruption in the face, and the venal tribe are all alarmed. Their fear discovers itself in their outrage, and they are but publishing the groans of a wounded vice. But from such opposition, the French Revolution, instead of suffering, receives an homage. The more it is struck, the more sparks it will emit; and the fear is, it will not be struck enough. It has nothing to dread from attacks: Truth has given it an establishment; and Time will record it with a name as lasting as his own.

. . . I will close the subject with the energetic apostrophe of M. de Lafayette: *May this great monument raised to Liberty, serve as a lesson to the oppressor, and an example to the oppressed.*

RICHARD PRICE (1723–91)   4 November 1789

From *A Discourse on the Love of Our Country*, in Dickinson, ed., *Politics and Literature*, pp. 174–5

Price was quick to celebrate the momentous events of the French Revolution, and to give them his support, even as he had supported the American struggle. In this lecture, given to The Society for Commemorating the Revolution of 1688, and published as a pamphlet in 1790, he links the three together.

THREE REVOLUTIONS: A CALL TO FREEDOM

What an eventful period is this! I am thankful that I have lived to see it . . . I have lived to see a diffusion of knowledge, which has undermined superstition and error – I have lived to see the rights of men better understood than ever: and nations panting for liberty, which seemed to have lost the idea of it. I have lived to see THIRTY MILLIONS of people, indignant and resolute, spurning at slavery, and demanding liberty, with an irresistible voice; their king led in triumph, and an arbitrary monarch surrendering himself to his subjects. – After sharing in the benefits of one Revolution, I have been spared to be a witness to two other Revolutions, both glorious. – And now, methinks, I see the ardour for liberty catching and spreading; a general amendment beginning in human affairs; the dominion of kings changed for the dominion of laws, and the dominion of priests giving way to the dominion of reason and conscience.

Be encouraged, all ye friends of freedom, and writers in its defence! The times are auspicious. Your labours have not been in vain. Behold kingdoms admonished by you, starting from sleep, breaking their fetters, and claiming justice from their oppressors! Behold the light you have struck out, after setting AMERICA free, reflected to FRANCE, and there kindled into a blaze that lays despotism in ashes, and warms and illuminates all EUROPE!

Tremble all ye oppressors of the world! Take warning all ye supporters of slavish governments, and slavish hierarchies! Call no more (absurdly and wickedly) REFORMATION, innovation. You cannot now hold the world in darkness. Struggle no longer against increasing light and liberality. Restore to mankind their rights; and consent to the correction of abuses, before they and you are destroyed together.

WILLIAM WORDSWORTH (1770–1850) July 1790

The Prelude, (1805), VI, ll, 352–82

Wordsworth, like many other Englishmen, had been deeply affected by the French Revolution. He arrived in France for the summer vacation the day before the *Fête de la Fédération*, held in Paris to celebrate the anniversary of the fall of the Bastille.

FRANCE STANDING ON THE TOP OF GOLDEN HOURS

. . .'twas a time when Europe was rejoiced,
France standing on the top of golden hours,
And human nature seeming born again.
Bound, as I said, to the Alps, it was our lot
To land at Calais on the very eve
Of that great federal day; and there we saw,
In a mean city, and among a few,
How bright a face is worn when joy of one
Is joy of tens of millions. Southward thence
We took our way, direct through hamlets, towns,
Gaudy with reliques of that festival,
Flowers left to wither on triumphal arcs,
And window-garlands. On the public roads,
And, once, three days successively, through paths
By which our toilsome journey was abridged,
Among sequestered villages we walked

And found benevolence and blessedness
Spread like a fragrance everywhere, like spring
That leaves no corner of the land untouched:
Where elms for many and many a league in files,
With their thin umbrage, on the stately roads
Of that great kingdom, rustled o'er our heads,
For ever near us as we paced along:
'Twas sweet at such a time, with such delights
On every side, in prime of youthful strength,
To feed a poet's tender melancholy
And fond conceit of sadness, to the noise
And gentle undulations which they made.
Unhoused, beneath the evening star we saw
Dances of liberty, and, in late hours
Of darkness, dances in the open air.

WILLIAM BLAKE (1757–1827)   1790

From *The Marriage of Heaven and Hell*, in *Complete Writings*,
pp. 149–50, 154, 155

CONTRARIES

Without Contraries is no progression. Attraction and Repulsion, Reason
and Energy, Love and Hate, are necessary to Human existence.

From these contraries spring what the religious call Good and Evil.
Good is the passive that obeys Reason. Evil is the active springing from
Energy.

Good is Heaven. Evil is Hell.

*

The Voice of the Devil

All Bibles or sacred codes have been the causes of the following Errors:
1. That Man has two real existing principles: Viz: a Body & a Soul.
2. That Energy, call'd Evil, is alone from the Body; & that Reason,
call'd Good, is alone from the Soul.
3. That God will torment Man in Eternity for following his Energies.
But the following Contraries to these are True:
1. Man has no Body distinct from his Soul; for that call'd Body is a
portion of Soul discern'd by the five Senses, the chief inlets of Soul in
this age.

2. Energy is the only life, and is from the Body; and Reason is the bound or outward circumference of Energy.

3. Energy is Eternal Delight.

★

Those who restrain desire, do so because theirs is weak enough to be restrained; and the restrainer or reason usurps its place & governs the unwilling.

And being restrain'd, it by degrees becomes passive, till it is only the shadow of desire . . .

. . . If the doors of perception were cleansed every thing would appear to man as it is, infinite.

For man has closed himself up, till he sees all things thro' narrow chinks of his cavern . . .

. . . The Giants who formed this world into its sensual existence, and now seem to live in it in chains, are in truth the causes of its life & the sources of all activity; but the chains are the cunning of weak and tame minds which have power to resist energy; according to the proverb, the weak in courage is strong in cunning.

THOMAS PAINE (1737–1809) February 1791

From *The Rights of Man*, Part One, pp. 63–4, 88–9, 140–41, 165–6, 168–9

'A share in two revolutions is living to some purpose,' Paine wrote to Washington in 1789 from Paris, having played his part in the making of the United States of America; and when, in 1790, he was asked to send the key of the Bastille to President Washington, he did so as a token of what he called 'the first ripe fruits of American principles translated into Europe'. He was, in other words, a man at the very heart of the great changes that were taking place, and didn't doubt 'the final and complete success of the French Revolution'. Thus, when Edmund Burke published his sustained attack upon the Revolution, as a threat to the 'fixed compact' of the hierarchically defined 'world of reason, and order, and peace, and virtue, and fruitful penitence', Paine sprang to the defence of France; for *The Rights of Man* appeared within three months of Burke's onslaught. This book, and the second part, which followed a year later, is one of the great seminal documents of radicalism. One has to go back to the seventeenth-century Levellers and to Winstanley to find its equivalent. But for its daring appeal to revolutionary change, Paine was to pay the price. In 1792 a Royal Proclamation was issued against 'wicked seditious writings', and Paine, leaving voluntarily for Paris, never returned to England. Despite the great impact of his book, the repressive powers of the government were to prevail and, after 1793, the dehumanizing violence and callousness of war.

THE RIGHTS OF THE LIVING

There never did, there never will, and there never can exist a parliament, or any description of men, or any generation of men, in any country, possessed of the right or the power of binding and controlling posterity to the 'end of time', or of commanding for ever how the world shall be governed, or who shall govern it; and therefore, all such clauses, acts or declarations, by which the makers of them attempt to do what they have neither the right nor the power to do, nor the power to execute, are in themselves null and void. Every age and generation must be as free to act for itself, *in all cases*, as the ages and generations which preceded it. The vanity and presumption of governing beyond the grave, is the most ridiculous and insolent of all tyrannies. Man has no property in man; neither has any generation a property in the generations which are to follow. The parliament or the people of 1688, or of any other period, has no more right to dispose of the people of the present day, or to bind or to control them *in any shape whatever*, than the parliament or the people of the present day have to dispose of, bind or control those who are to live a hundred or a thousand years hence. Every generation is, and must be, competent to all the purposes which its occasions require. It is the living, and not the dead, that are to be accommodated. When man ceases to be, his power and his wants cease with him; and having no longer any participation in the concerns of this world, he has no longer any authority in directing who shall be its governors, or how its government shall be organized, or how administered.

I am not contending for nor against any form of government, nor for nor against any party here or elsewhere. That which a whole nation chooses to do, it has a right to do. Mr Burke says, No. Where then *does* the right exist? I am contending for the rights of the *living*, and against their being willed away, and controlled and contracted for, by the manuscript assumed authority of the dead; and Mr Burke is contending for the authority of the dead over the rights and freedom of the living. There was a time when kings disposed of their crowns by will upon their deathbeds, and consigned the people, like beasts of the field, to whatever successor they appointed. This is now so exploded as scarcely to be remembered, and so monstrous as hardly to be believed. But the parliamentary clauses upon which Mr Burke builds his political church, are of the same nature.

The laws of every country must be analogous to some common principle. In England, no parent or master, nor all the authority of parliament, omnipotent as it has called itself, can bind or control the personal freedom even of an individual beyond the age of twenty-one years: On what ground of right, then, could the parliament of 1688, or any other parliament, bind all posterity for ever?

THE UNITY OR EQUALITY OF MAN

Every history of the creation, and every traditionary account, whether from the lettered or unlettered world, however they may vary in their opinion or belief of certain particulars, all agree in establishing one point, *the unity of man*; by which I mean, that all men are of *one degree*, and consequently that all men are born equal, and with equal natural right, in the same manner as if posterity had been continued by *creation* instead of *generation*, the latter being only the mode by which the former is carried forward; and consequently, every child born into the world must be considered as deriving its existence from God. The world is as new to him as it was to the first man that existed, and his natural right in it is of the same kind . . .

It is one of the greatest of all truths, and of the highest advantage to cultivate. By considering man in this light, and by instructing him to consider himself in this light, it places him in a close connection with all his duties, whether to his Creator, or to the creation, of which he is a part; and it is only when he forgets his origin, or, to use a more fashionable phrase, his *birth and family*, that he becomes dissolute. It is not among the least of the evils of the present existing governments in all parts of Europe, that man, considered as man, is thrown back to a vast distance from his Maker, and the artificial chasm filled up by a succession of barriers, or sort of turnpike gates, through which he has to pass. I will quote Mr Burke's catalogue of barriers that he has set up between man and his Maker. Putting himself in the character of a herald, he says – 'We fear God – we look with *awe* to kings – with affection to parliaments – with duty to magistrates – with reverence to priests, and with respect to nobility.' Mr Burke has forgotten to put in '*chivalry*'. He has also forgotten to put in Peter.

The duty of man is not a wilderness of turnpike gates, through which he is to pass by tickets from one to the other. It is plain and simple, and consists but of two points. His duty to God, which every man must feel; and with respect to his neighbour, to do as he would be done by. If those to whom power is delegated do well, they will be respected; if not, they will be despised . . .

THE MIND, DISCOVERING TRUTH

The opinions of men with respect to government, are changing fast in all countries. The Revolutions of America and France have thrown a beam of light over the world, which reaches into man. The enormous expense of governments have provoked people to think, by making them feel: and when once the veil begins to rend, it admits not of repair. Ignorance is of a peculiar nature: and once dispelled, it is impossible to re-establish it. It is not originally a thing of itself, but is only the absence of knowledge; and though man may be *kept* ignorant, he cannot be *made* ignorant. The mind, in discovering truth, acts in the same manner as it acts through the eye in discovering objects; when once any object has been seen, it is impossible to put the mind back to the same condition it was in before it saw it. Those who talk of a counter-revolution in France, show how little they understand of man. There does not exist in the compass of language, an arrangement of words to express so much as the means of effecting a counter-revolution. The means must be an obliteration of knowledge; and it has never yet been discovered, how to make man *unknow* his knowledge, or *unthink* his thoughts.

THE NATURAL ORDER OF THINGS

What is government more than the management of the affairs of a Nation? It is not, and from its nature cannot be, the property of any particular man or family, but of the whole community, at whose expense it is supported; and though by force or contrivance it has been usurped into an inheritance, the usurpation cannot alter the right of things. Sovereignty, as a matter of right, appertains to the Nation only, and not to any individual; and a Nation has at all times an inherent indefeasible right to abolish any form of Government it finds inconvenient, and establish such as accords with its interest, disposition, and happiness. The romantic and barbarous distinction of men into Kings and subjects, though it may suit the condition of courtiers, cannot that of citizens; and is exploded by the principle on which Governments are now founded.

Every citizen is a member of the Sovereignty, and, as such, can acknowledge no personal subjection; and his obedience can be only to the laws.

When men think of what Government is, they must necessarily suppose it to possess a knowledge of all the objects and matters upon which its authority is to be exercised. In this view of Government, the republican system, as established by America and France, operates to embrace the whole of a Nation; and the knowledge necessary to the interest of all the parts, is to be found in the centre, which the parts by representation form: But the old Governments are on a construction that excludes knowledge as well as happiness; Government by monks, who know nothing of the world beyond the walls of a convent, is as consistent as government by Kings.

What were formerly called Revolutions, were little more than a change of persons, or an alteration of local circumstances. They rose and fell like things of course, and had nothing in their existence or their fate that could influence beyond the spot that produced them. But what we now see in the world, from the Revolutions of America and France, are a renovation of the natural order of things, a system of principles as universal as truth and the existence of man, and combining moral with political happiness and national prosperity.

THE HOPE: REVOLUTIONS BY REASON AND ACCOMMODATION

From what we now see, nothing of reform in the political world ought to be held improbable. It is an age of Revolutions, in which everything may be looked for. The intrigue of Courts, by which the system of war is kept up, may provoke a confederation of Nations to abolish it: and an European Congress, to patronize the progress of free Governments, and promote the civilization of Nations with each other, is an event nearer in probability, than once were the Revolutions and Alliance of France and America.

WILLIAM BLAKE (1757–1827)   1791

The French Revolution, ll. 206–26, in *Complete Writings*, pp. 143–4

Blake makes the Abbé de Sieyès, who enjoyed considerable fame as a political theorist during the Revolution, speak in the Assembly for the people. Sieyès's pamphlet, *What is the Third Estate?* (1789), argued that the will of the nation should be expressed by representatives of this Third Estate, the common people of France, who had never before had power. He is urging the withdrawal of the troops from Paris.

THE VOICE OF THE MORNING

Hear, O Heavens of France, the voice of the people arising from
   valley and hill,
O'erclouded with power. Hear the voice of valleys, the voice of meek
   cities,
Mourning oppressed on village and field, till the village and field is a
   waste.
For the husbandman weeps at blights of the fife, and blasting of
   trumpets consume
The souls of mild France; the pale mother nourishes her child to the
   deadly slaughter.
When the heavens were sealed with a stone, and the terrible sun clos'd
   in an orb, and the moon
Rent from the nations, and each star appointed for watchers of night,
The millions of spirits immortal were bound in the ruins of sulphur
   heaven
To wander enslav'd; black, depresst in dark ignorance, kept in awe
   with the whip
To worship terrors, bred from the blood of revenge and breath of
   desire
In bestial forms, or more terrible men; till the dawn of our peaceful
   morning,
Till dawn, till morning, till the breaking of clouds, and swelling of
   winds, and the universal voice;
Till man raise his darken'd limbs out of the caves of night: his eyes
   and his heart
Expand: where is Space? where, O Sun, is thy dwelling? where thy
   tent, O faint slumb'rous Moon?
Then the valleys of France shall cry to the soldier: 'Throw down thy
   sword and musket,
And run and embrace the meek peasant.' Her nobles shall hear and
   shall weep, and put off
The red robe of terror, the crown of oppression, the shoes of
   contempt, and unbuckle

350

The girdle of war from the desolate earth; then the Priest in his
   thund'rous cloud
Shall weep, bending to earth, embracing the valleys, and putting his
   hand to the plow,
Shall say: 'No more I curse thee; but now I will bless thee: No more
   in deadly black
Devour thy labour; nor lift up a cloud in thy heavens, O laborious
   plow . . .'

MARY WOLLSTONECRAFT (1759–97)   1792

From *A Vindication of the Rights of Woman*, pp. 252–3, 256–63

Mary Wollstonecraft, one of the first great voices for the equality of woman in
society, earned her own living as a teacher, writer and translator, working for
Joseph Johnson, publisher of Tom Paine, herself and Godwin, and influential in
the radical group that met at Johnson's house, which included Paine, Godwin,
Holcroft, Priestley and Blake. She spent three years in Paris observing the Revolution, and there had a child by the American she was living with. She returned
to London when their relationship broke down, tried to commit suicide, then
(working for Johnson again) lived with Godwin, marrying him shortly before her
death in childbirth – though this daughter was to live to become Shelley's second
wife.

THE NATURAL RIGHTS AND DUTIES OF WOMEN

. . . It is vain to expect virtue from women till they are in some degree
independent of men; nay, it is vain to expect that strength of natural
affection which would make them good wives and mothers. Whilst they
are absolutely dependent on their husbands they will be cunning, mean,
and selfish; and the men who can be gratified by the fawning fondness
of spaniel-like affection have not much delicacy, for love is not to be
bought; in any sense of the words, its silken wings are instantly shrivelled
up when anything beside a return in kind is sought. Yet whilst wealth
enervates men, and women live, as it were, by their personal charms,
how can we expect them to discharge those ennobling duties which
equally require exertion and self-denial? . . .
    The preposterous distinctions of rank, which render civilization a
curse, by dividing the world between voluptuous tyrants and cunning

envious dependants, corrupt, almost equally, every class of people, because respectability is not attached to the discharge of the relative duties of life, but to the station, and when the duties are not fulfilled the affections cannot gain sufficient strength to fortify the virtue of which they are the natural reward. Still there are some loop-holes out of which a man may creep, and dare to think and act for himself; but for a woman it is an herculean task, because she has difficulties peculiar to her sex to overcome, which require almost super-human power . . .

Women are, in common with men, rendered weak and luxurious by the relaxing pleasures which wealth procures; but added to this they are made slaves to their passions, and must render them alluring that man may lend them his reason to guide their tottering steps aright. Or should they be ambitious, they must govern their tyrants by sinister tricks, for without rights there cannot be any incumbent duties. The laws respecting woman, which I mean to discuss in a future part, make an absurd unit of a man and his wife; and then, by the easy transition of only considering him as responsible, she is reduced to a mere cipher.

The being who discharges the duties of its station is independent; and, speaking of women at large, their first duty is to themselves as rational creatures, and the next, in point of importance, as citizens, is that, which includes so many, of a mother. The rank in life which dispenses with their fulfilling this duty, necessarily degrades them by making them mere dolls. Or should they turn to something more important than merely fitting drapery upon a smooth block, their minds are only occupied by some soft platonic attachment; or the actual management of an intrigue may keep their thoughts in motion; for when they neglect domestic duties, they have it not in their power to take the field and march and counter-march like soldiers, or wrangle in the senate to keep their faculties from rusting . . .

But to render her really virtuous and useful, she must not, if she discharge her civil duties, want individually the protection of civil laws; she must not be dependent on her husband's bounty for her subsistence during his life, or support after his death; for how can a being be generous who has nothing of its own? or virtuous who is not free? The wife, in the present state of things, who is faithful to her husband, and neither suckles nor educates her children, scarcely deserves the name of a wife, and has no right to that of a citizen. But take away natural rights, and duties become null . . .

Besides, when poverty is more disgraceful than even vice, is not morality cut to the quick? Still to avoid misconstruction, though I consider that women in the common walks of life are called to fulfil the duties of wives and mothers, by religion and reason, I cannot help lamenting that women of a superior cast have not a road open by which they can pursue more extensive plans of usefulness and independence. I may excite laughter, by dropping an hint, which I mean to pursue, some future time, for I really think that women ought to have representatives, instead of being arbitrarily governed without having any direct share allowed them in the deliberations of government.

But, as the whole system of representation is now, in this country, only a convenient handle for despotism, they need not complain, for they are as well represented as a numerous class of hard-working mechanics, who pay for the support of royalty when they can scarcely stop their children's mouths with bread. How are they represented whose very sweat supports the splendid stud of an heir-apparent, or varnishes the chariot of some female favourite who looks down on shame? Taxes on the very necessaries of life, enable an endless tribe of idle princes and princesses to pass with stupid pomp before a gaping crowd, who almost worship the very parade which costs them so dear. This is mere gothic grandeur, something like the barbarous useless parade of having sentinels on horse-back at Whitehall, which I could never view without a mixture of contempt and indignation . . .

But what have women to do in society? I may be asked, but to loiter with easy grace; surely you would not condemn them all to suckle fools and chronicle small beer! No. Women might certainly study the art of healing, and be physicians as well as nurses. And midwifery, decency seems to allot to them, though I am afraid, the word midwife, in our dictionaries, will soon give place to *accoucheur*, and one proof of the former delicacy of the sex be effaced from the language.

They might also study politics, and settle their benevolence on the broadest basis; for the reading of history will scarcely be more useful than the perusal of romances, if read as mere biography; if the character of the times, the political improvements, arts, etc., be not observed. In short, if it be not considered as the history of man; and not of particular men, who filled a niche in the temple of fame, and dropped into the black rolling stream of time, that silently sweeps all before it into the shapeless void called – eternity. – For shape, can it be called, 'that shape hath none'?

Business of various kinds, they might likewise pursue, if they were educated in a more orderly manner, which might save many from common and legal prostitution. Women would not then marry for a support, as men accept of places under Government, and neglect the implied duties; nor would an attempt to earn their own subsistence, a most laudable one! sink them almost to the level of those poor abandoned creatures who live by prostitution. For are not milliners and mantua-makers reckoned the next class? The few employments open to women, so far from being liberal, are menial . . .

It is a melancholy truth; yet such is the blessed effect of civilization! the most respectable women are the most oppressed; and, unless they have understandings far superior to the common run of understandings, taking in both sexes, they must, from being treated like contemptible beings, become contemptible. How many women thus waste life away the prey of discontent, who might have practised as physicians, regulated a farm, managed a shop, and stood erect, supported by their own industry, instead of hanging their heads surcharged with the dew of sensibility, that consumes the beauty to which it at first gave lustre; nay, I doubt whether pity and love are so near akin as poets feign, for I have seldom seen much compassion excited by the helplessness of females, unless they were fair; then, perhaps, pity was the soft handmaid of love, or the harbinger of lust . . .

Would men but generously snap our chains, and be content with rational fellowship instead of slavish obedience, they would find us more observant daughters, more affectionate sisters, more faithful wives, more reasonable mothers – in a word, better citizens. We should then love them with true affection, because we should learn to respect ourselves; and the peace of mind of a worthy man would not be interrupted by the idle vanity of his wife, nor the babes sent to nestle in a strange bosom, having never found a home in their mother's.

THOMAS PAINE (1737–1809)   February 1792

From *The Rights of Man*, Part Two, pp. 194–5, 225, 230–31, 289–90

Between the publication of Part One of *The Rights of Man* and Part Two almost exactly a year later, the atmosphere in England darkened ominously. Paine was considered by both enemies and friends as embodying the principles of the French Revolution. By his friends he was honoured, but the reactionary forces of established power were using every weapon at their command to oppose what he stood for, and by the end of the year, exploiting the fears of the people and even inciting the illiterate to violence, as in the destruction of Joseph Priestley's house and library, they had gained control as the declared enemies of radicalism and emancipation. Nevertheless, the second part of Paine's book had an even greater impact than the first, and by 1793 the combined work had sold in huge numbers, particularly among the well-educated artisan class to which Paine himself belonged; for his concept of the 'New Adam' strikingly registers the momentous nature of the events he had lived through. As Hazlitt said of Godwin, Paine too 'blazed as a sun in the firmament of reputation . . . and wherever liberty, truth, justice was the theme, his name was not far off'. Then came his return to Paris, two weeks after the September Massacres, the execution of the king (which Paine opposed), the war with England, and his own imprisonment in the Luxembourg, where he was kept till after the fall of the Jacobins. But though his toast at the Revolution Society dinner in London in November 1791 to 'the Revolution of the World' was to turn by 1802 into the disillusionment of 'You see they have conquered all Europe', for Paine – like Milton before him – it was the people, the nation, that had failed, not the idea. The idea would have to await other historical forces to bring about, as the subtitle to Part Two of The Rights of Man has it, the 'Combining' of 'Principle and Practice'.

MONARCHY: A SYSTEM OF MENTAL LEVELLING

We have heard The Rights of Man called a levelling system; but the only system to which the word levelling is truly applicable is the hereditary monarchical system. It is a system of mental levelling. It indiscriminately admits every species of character to the same authority. Vice and virtue, ignorance and wisdom, in short, every quality, good or bad, is put on the same level. Kings succeed each other, not as rationals, but as animals. It signifies not what their mental or moral characters are. Can we then be surprised at the abject state of the human mind in monarchical countries, when the government itself is formed on such an abject levelling system? – It has no fixed character. Today it is one thing; tomorrow it is something else. It changes with the temper of every succeeding individual, and is subject to all the varieties of each. It is government through the medium of passions and accidents. It appears under all the various characters of childhood, decrepitude, dotage, a thing at nurse, in leading-strings, or in crutches. It reverses the wholesome order of nature. It occasionally puts children over men, and the conceits of nonage over wisdom and experience. In short, we cannot conceive a more ridiculous figure of government, than hereditary succession, in all its cases, presents.

PUBLIC SERVICE AND ITS PROPER REWARDS

Government, says Swift, *is a plain thing, and fitted to the capacity of many heads.*

It is inhuman to talk of a million sterling a year, paid out of the public taxes of any country, for the support of any individual, while thousands who are forced to contribute thereto, are pining with want, and struggling with misery. Government does not consist in a contrast between prisons and palaces, between poverty and pomp; it is not instituted to rob the needy of his mite, and increase the wretchedness of the wretched . . .

When extraordinary power and extraordinary pay are allotted to any individual in a government, he becomes the centre, round which every kind of corruption generates and forms. Give to any man a million a year, and add thereto the power of creating and disposing of places, at the expense of a country, and the liberties of that country are no longer secure. What is called the splendour of a throne is no other than the corruption of the state. It is made up of a band of parasites, living in luxurious indolence, out of the public taxes.

THERE IS A MORNING OF REASON RISING UPON MAN

The best constitution that could now be devised, consistent with the conditions of the present moment, may be far short of that excellence which a few years may afford. There is a morning of reason rising upon man on the subject of government, that has not appeared before. As the barbarism of the present old government expires, the moral condition of nations with respect to each other will be changed. Man will not be brought up with the savage idea of considering his species as his enemy, because the accident of birth gave the individuals existence in countries distinguished by different names; and as constitutions have always some relation to external as well as to domestic circumstances, the means of benefiting by every change, foreign or domestic, should be a part of every constitution.

We already see an alteration in the national disposition of England and France towards each other, which, when we look back to only a few years, is itself a revolution. Who could have foreseen, or who would have believed, that a French National Assembly would ever have been a popular toast in England, or that a friendly alliance of the two nations should become the wish of either. It shows, that man, were he not corrupted by governments, is naturally the friend of man, and that human nature is not of itself vicious. That spirit of jealousy and ferocity, which the governments of the two countries inspired, and which they rendered subservient to the purpose of taxation, is now yielding to the dictates of reason, interest, and humanity. The trade of courts is beginning to be understood, and the affectation of mystery, with all the artificial sorcery which they imposed upon mankind, is on the decline. It has received its death-wound; and though it may linger, it will expire.

Government ought to be as much open to improvement as anything which appertains to man, instead of which it has been monopolized from age to age, by the most ignorant and vicious of the human race. Need we any other proof of their wretched management, than the excess of debts and taxes with which every nation groans, and the quarrels into which they have precipitated the world?

Just emerging from such a barbarous condition, it is too soon to determine to what extent of improvement government may yet be carried. For what we can foresee, all Europe may form but one great republic, and man be free of the whole.

THE ADAM OF A NEW WORLD

With how much more glory, and advantage to itself, does a nation act, when it exerts its powers to rescue the world from bondage, and to create itself friends, than when it employs those powers to increase ruin, desolation, and misery. The horrid scene that is now acting by the English government in the East Indies, is fit only to be told of Goths and Vandals, who, destitute of principles, robbed and tortured the world they were incapable of enjoying . . .

Never did so great an opportunity offer itself to England, and to all Europe, as is produced by the two revolutions of America and France. By the former, freedom has a national champion in the western world; and by the latter, in Europe. When another nation shall join France, despotism and bad government will scarcely dare to appear. To use a trite expression, the iron is becoming hot all over Europe. The insulted German and the enslaved Spaniard, the Russ and the Pole, are beginning to think. The present age will hereafter merit to be called the Age of reason, and the present generation will appear to the future as the Adam of a new world.

WILLIAM WORDSWORTH
(1770–1850)

The Prelude (1805), IX, ll. 503–33

Wordsworth, reaching France in November 1791 for a long stay and travelling
via Paris to Orleans, had engaged in fervent revolutionary debate with Royalists
and Republicans, and particularly with his Republican friend, Michel Beaupuy,
stationed with his regiment at Blois.

HATRED OF ABSOLUTE RULE

Hatred of absolute rule, where will of one
Is law for all, and of that barren pride
In them who, by immunities unjust,
Betwixt the sovereign and the people stand,
His helper and not theirs, laid stronger hold
Daily upon me, mixed with pity too
And love; for where hope is, there love will be
For the abject multitude. And when we chanced
One day to meet a hunger-bitten girl,
Who crept along fitting her languid self
Unto a heifer's motion, by a cord
Tied to her arm, and picking thus from the lane
Its sustenance, while the girl with her two hands
Was busy knitting in a heartless mood
Of solitude, and at the sight my friend
In agitation said, ''Tis against *that*
Which we are fighting,' I with him believed
Devoutly that a spirit was abroad
Which could not be withstood, that poverty
At least like this would in a little time
Be found no more, that we should see the earth
Unthwarted in her wish to recompense
The industrious, and the lowly child of toil,
All institutes for ever blotted out
That legalized exclusion, empty pomp
Abolished, sensual state and cruel power,
Whether by edict of the one or few;
And finally, as sum and crown of all,
Should see the people having a strong hand

In making their own laws; whence better days
To all mankind . . .

WILLIAM GODWIN (1756–1836)   1793

From *Enquiry Concerning Political Justice*, I, iii, 6, pp. 225–39, and 7,
pp. 244–5; II, v, 14, pp. 14–20

FORCE AND REVERENCE

. . . It is a violation of political justice to confound the authority which
depends upon force, with the authority which arises from reverence and
esteem . . . These two kinds of authority may happen to vest in the same
person; but they are altogether distinct and independent of each other.

The consequence which has flowed from confounding them, has been,
a greater debasement of the human character, than could easily have
followed upon a direct and unqualified slavery . . . One of the lessons
most assiduously inculcated upon mankind in all ages and countries, is
that of reverence to our superiors. If by this maxim be intended our
superiors in wisdom, it may be admitted, but with some qualification.
But, if it imply our superiors in station only, nothing can be more contrary to reason and justice. Is it not enough that they have usurped certain advantages over us to which they can show no equitable claim; and
must we also humble our courage, and renounce our independence, in
their presence? Why reverence a man because he happens to be born to
certain privileges; or because a concurrence of circumstances (for wisdom, as we have already seen, gives a claim to respect utterly distinct
from power) has procured him a share in the legislative or executive
government of our country? Let him content himself with the obedience
which is the result of force; for to that only is he entitled . . . The true
supporters of government are the weak and uninformed, and not the
wise. In proportion as weakness and ignorance shall diminish, the basis
of government will also decay. This however is an event which ought
not to be contemplated with alarm . . . It may be to a certain degree
doubtful, whether the human species will ever be emancipated from their
present subjection and pupillage, but let it not be forgotten that this is
their condition . . .

THE ENEMY OF CHANGE

. . . Incessant change, everlasting innovation, seem to be dictated by the true interests of mankind. But government is the perpetual enemy of change. What was admirably observed of a particular system of government, is in a great degree true of all: They 'lay their hand on the spring there is in society, and put a stop to its motion'. Their tendency is to perpetuate abuse. Whatever was once thought right and useful, they undertake to entail to the latest posterity. They reverse the genuine propensities of man, and, instead of suffering us to proceed, teach us to look backward for perfection . . .

DEMOCRACY

Democracy is a system of government, according to which every member of society is considered as a man, and nothing more. So far as positive regulation is concerned, if indeed that can, with any propriety, be termed regulation, which is the mere recognition of the simplest of all moral principles, every man is regarded as equal. Talents and wealth, wherever they exist, will not fail to obtain a certain degree of influence, without requiring positive institution to second their operation.

But there are certain disadvantages, that may seem the necessary result of democratical equality. In political society, it is reasonable to suppose, that the wise will be outnumbered by the unwise . . . Supposing that we should even be obliged to take democracy with all the disadvantages that were ever annexed to it, and that no remedy could be discovered for any of its defects, it would still be preferable to the exclusive system of other forms . . . In the estimate that is usually made of democracy, one of the sources of our erroneous judgement, lies in our taking mankind such as monarchy and aristocracy have made them, and thence judging how fit they are to manage for themselves. Monarchy and aristocracy would be no evils, if their tendency were not to undermine the virtues and the understandings of their subjects. The thing most necessary, is to remove all those restraints which prevent the human mind from attaining its genuine strength. Implicit faith, blind submission to authority, timid fear, a distrust of our powers, an inattention to our own importance and the good purposes we are able to effect, these are the chief obstacles to human improvement. Democracy restores to man a consciousness of his value, teaches him, by the removal of authority and oppression, to listen only to the suggestions of reason, gives him confidence to treat all other men with frankness and simplicity, and induces him to regard them no longer, as enemies against whom to be upon his guard, but as brethren whom it becomes him to assist. The citizen of a democratical state, when he looks upon the oppression and injustice that prevail in the countries around him, cannot but entertain an inexpressible esteem for the advantages he enjoys, and the most unalterable determination to preserve them . . .

THOMAS SPENCE (1750–1814) 1793

From *The Real Rights of Man*, in Beer, ed., *Pioneers of Land Reform*, pp. 5–16

Spence had argued his theories of land ownership as early as 1775 in Newcastle. He had come to London in 1792, joined the revolutionary Corresponding Society, wrote and sold tracts, was imprisoned in 1794 and again in 1801, when he described himself as 'the unfee'd Advocate of the disinherited seed of Adam'. As a Jacobin, he even attacked Paine for failing, in *Agrarian Justice*, to justify the public ownership of land, and he had a considerable underground influence among the Jacobin circle during the early 1790s.

THE INJUSTICE OF PRIVATE PROPERTY

If we look back to the origin of the present nations, we shall see that the land, with all its appurtenances, was claimed by a few, and divided among themselves, in as assured a manner as if they had manufactured it and it had been the work of their own hands; and by being unquestioned, or not called to an account for such usurpations and unjust claims, they fell into a habit of thinking, or, which is the same thing to the rest of mankind, of acting as if the earth was made for or by them, and did not scruple to call it their own property, which they might dispose of without regard to any other living creature in the universe. Accordingly they did so; and no man, more than any other creature, could claim a right to so much as a blade of grass, or a nut or an acorn, a fish or a fowl, or any natural production whatever, though to save his life, without the permission of the pretended proprietor; and not a foot of land, water, rock or heath but was claimed by one or other of those lords . . . And any one of them still can, by laws of their own making, oblige every living creature to remove off his property (which, to the

361

great distress of mankind, is too often put in execution); so of consequence were all the landholders to be of one mind, and determined to
take their properties into their own hands, all the rest of mankind might
go to heaven if they would, for there would be no place found for them
here. Thus men may not live in any part of this world, not even where
they are born, but as strangers, and by the permission of the pretender
to the property thereof . . .

PROPERTY: THE COMMONWEALTH OF THE PARISH

But lest it should be said that a system whereby they may reap more
advantages consistent with the nature of society cannot be proposed, I
will attempt to show the outlines of such a plan.

Let it be supposed, then, that the whole people in some country, after
much reasoning and deliberation, should conclude that every man has
an equal property in the land in the neighbourhood where he resides.
They therefore resolve that if they live in society together, it shall only
be with a view that everyone may reap all the benefits from their natural
rights and privileges possible.

Therefore a day is appointed on which the inhabitants of each parish
meet, in their respective parishes, to take their long-lost rights into possession, and to form themselves into corporations. So then each parish
becomes a corporation, and all men who are inhabitants become members or burghers. The land, with all that appertains to it, is in every
parish made the property of the corporation or parish, with as ample
power to let, repair, or alter all or any part thereof as a lord of the manor
enjoys over his lands, houses, etc.; but the power of alienating the least
morsel, in any manner, from the parish either at this or any time hereafter is denied . . . Thus are there no more nor other lands in the whole
country than the parishes; and each of them is sovereign lord of its own
territories.

Then you may behold the rent which the people have paid into the
parish treasuries, employed by each parish in paying the government its
share of the sum which the Parliament or National Congress at any time
grants; in maintaining and relieving its own poor, and people out of
work; in paying the necessary officers their salaries; in building, repairing, and adorning its houses, bridges and other structures; in making
and maintaining convenient and delightful streets, highways, and passages both for foot and carriages; in making and maintaining canals and
other conveniences for trade and navigation; in planting and taking in

waste grounds; in providing and keeping up a magazine of ammunition, and all sorts of arms sufficient for all its inhabitants in case of danger from enemies; in premiums for the encouragement of agriculture, or anything else thought worthy of encouragement; and, in a word, in doing whatever the people think proper; and not, as formerly, to support and spread luxury, pride, and all manner of vice. As for corruption in elections, it has now no being or effect among them; all affairs to be determined by voting, either in a full meeting of a parish, its committees, or in the house of representatives, are done by balloting, so that voting or elections among them occasion no animosities, for none need to let another know for which side he votes; all that can be done, therefore, in order to gain a majority of votes for anything, is to make it appear in the best light possible by speaking or writing. Among them Government does not meddle in every trifle; but on the contrary, allows each parish the power of putting the laws in force in all cases, and does not interfere but when they act manifestly to the prejudice of society and the rights and liberties of mankind, as established in their glorious constitution and laws . . .

. . . Freedom to do anything whatever cannot there be bought; a thing is either entirely prohibited, as theft or murder; or entirely free to everyone without tax or price, and the rents are still not so high, notwithstanding all that is done with them, as they were formerly for only the maintenance of a few haughty, unthankful landlords. For the government, which may be said to be the greatest mouth, having neither excisemen, custom-house men, collectors, army, pensioners, bribery, nor such like ruination vermin to maintain, is soon satisfied, and moreover there are no more persons employed in offices, either about the government or parishes, than are absolutely necessary; and their salaries are but just sufficient to maintain them suitably to their offices . . .

But what makes this prospect yet more glowing is that after this empire of right and reason is thus established, it will stand for ever. Force and corruption attempting its downfall shall equally be baffled, and all other nations, struck with wonder and admiration at its happiness and stability, shall follow the example; and thus the whole earth shall at last be happy and live like brethren.

WILLIAM BLAKE (1757–1827)

From *America*, in *Complete Writings*, p. 200

THE VOICE OF REVOLT

He cried: Why trembles honesty, and like a murderer
Why seeks he refuge from the frowns of his immortal station?
Must the generous tremble & leave his joy to the idle, to the
   pestilence,
That mock him? Who commanded this? what God? what Angel?
To keep the gen'rous from experience till the ungenerous
Are unrestrain'd performers of the energies of nature;
Till pity is become a trade, and generosity a science
That men get rich by; and the sandy desert is giv'n to the strong?
What God is he writes laws of peace & clothes him in a tempest?
What pitying Angel lusts for tears and fans himself with sighs?
What crawling villain preaches abstinence and wraps himself
In fat of lambs? No more I follow, no more obedience pay!

ANONYMOUS 1793

A confiscated broadsheet: Home Office Papers, in Barker, ed., *Long March of Everyman*, p. 66

CALL TO ALL REAL LOVERS OF LIBERTY

To all real lovers of Liberty. Be assured that Liberty and Freedom will
at last prevail. Tremble O thou the Oppressor of the People that reigneth
upon the throne and ye Ministers of State, weep for ye shall fall. Weep
ye who grind the face of the poor, oppress the People and starve the
Industrious Mechanic. My friends, you are oppressed, you know it. Lord
Buckingham who died the other day had thirty thousand pounds yearly
for setting his arse in the House of Lords and doing nothing. Liberty
calls aloud, ye who will hear her voice, may you be free and happy. He
who does not, let him starve and be DAMNED.

   NB Be resolute and you shall be happy. He who wishes well to the
cause of Liberty let him repair to Chapel Field at Five O'clock this afternoon, to begin a Glorious Revolution.

WILLIAM WORDSWORTH (1770–1850)   1793

The Prelude (1805), X, ll. 308–37, 415–40

Having returned home in December 1792 (for reasons which are still not clear, considering that Annette Vallon gave birth to his daughter on the 15th), Wordsworth was deeply disturbed not only by the execution of the king and the Reign of Terror, but also by the conflicts aroused in him as a result of the open war declared between England and France.

THE REIGN OF TERROR

In France, the men, who, for their desperate ends,
Had plucked up mercy by the roots, were glad
Of this new enemy. Tyrants, strong before
In devilish pleas, were ten times stronger now;
And thus, beset with foes on every side,
The goaded land waxed mad; the crimes of few
Spread into madness of the many; blasts
From hell came sanctified like airs from heaven.
The sternness of the just, the faith of those
Who doubted not that Providence had times
Of anger and of vengeance, theirs who throned
The human understanding paramount
And made of that their God, the hopes of those
Who were content to barter short-lived pangs
For a paradise of ages, the blind rage
Of insolent tempers, the light vanity
Of intermeddlers, steady purposes
Of the suspicious, slips of the indiscreet,
And all the accidents of life were pressed
Into one service, busy with one work.
The Senate was heart-stricken, not a voice
Uplifted, none to oppose or mitigate.

Domestic carnage now filled all the year
With feast-days; the old man from the chimney-nook,
The maiden from the bosom of her love,
The mother from the cradle of her babe,
The warrior from the field – all perished, all –
Friends, enemies, of all parties, ages, ranks,

Head after head, and never heads enough
For those that bade them fall . . .

     ★

[But] . . . amid the awe
Of unintelligible chastisement,
I felt a kind of sympathy with power,
Motions raised up within me, nevertheless,
Which had relationship to highest things.
Wild blasts of music thus did find their way
Into the midst of terrible events;
So that worst tempests might be listened to.
Then was the truth received into my heart,
That, under heaviest sorrow earth can bring,
Griefs bitterest of ourselves or of our kind,
If from the affliction somewhere do not grow
Honour which could not else have been, a faith,
An elevation and a sanctity,
If new strength be not given or old restored,
The blame is ours, not Nature's. When a taunt
Was taken up by scoffers in their pride,
Saying, 'Behold the harvest which we reap
From popular government and equality,'
I saw that it was neither these nor aught
Of wild grief engrafted on their names
By false philosophy that caused the woe,
But that it was a reservoir of guilt
And ignorance filled up from age to age,
That could no longer hold its loathsome charge,
But burst and spread in deluge through the land.

THOMAS HARDY (1752–1832)   1793

'An Address to the Nation from the London Corresponding Society', in Dickinson, ed., *Politics and Literature*, pp. 194–7

Hardy was the Secretary of the London Corresponding Society during a period of deepening intolerance and panic after the start of the war with France, with hatred whipped up against the enemy and laws against sedition. Fox writes of being 'very gloomy', Dr Raine of 'the mischievous conduct of men in power', and

Lord Campbell records that 'if these laws had been fully enforced, the only chance of escaping servitude would have been civil war'.

TO AWAKEN THE SLEEPING REASON OF OUR COUNTRYMEN

Friends and fellow countrymen,

Gloomy as is the prospect now before us, and unpleasing as is the talk to bring forth into open day the calamitous situation of our Country: We conceive it necessary to direct the public eye, to the cause of our misfortunes, and to awaken the sleeping reason of our Countrymen, to the pursuit of the only remedy which can ever prove effectual, namely; – *A thorough Reform in Parliament, by the adoption of an equal Representation obtained by Annual Elections and Universal Suffrage.* – We do not address you in the confidence of personal importance – We do not presume upon the splendour of exalted situation; but as Members of the same Society, as Individuals, zealously labouring for the welfare of the Community; we think ourselves entitled to a share of your attention . . .

Here it is proper to remind you of the false and calumnious aspersions, which have been so industriously circulated since November last: At that time of general Consternation, when the cry of danger to the Constitution was raised and extensively propagated; when the alarm of *Riots and Insurrections*, was founded by Royal Proclamations and re-echoed by Parish Associations; Reform was branded by the name of Innovation, and whoever dared to affirm, that the House of Commons ought to be restored to that state of independence in which it was settled at the Revolution; and that unnecessary Places and Pensions ought to be abolished, was stigmatized as a leveller and an enemy to his King and Country . . .

To obtain a complete Representation is our only aim – contemning all party distinctions, we seek no advantage which every individual of the community will not enjoy equally with ourselves – We are not engaged in Speculative and Theoretical schemes; the motive of our present conduct is the actual sense of injury and oppression; We feel the weight of innumerable abuses, to which the invasion of our rights has given birth, and which their restoration can alone remove.

But sensible that our efforts, if not seconded by the Nation at large, must prove ineffectual, and only needlessly expose us to the malevolence of the public plunderers; we conjure you, by the love you bear your country, by your attachment to freedom, and by your anxious care for the welfare of your posterity, to suffer yourselves no longer to be deluded by artful speeches, and by interested men; but to sanction with your approbations, our constitutional endeavours, and pursue with union and firmness the track we have pointed out: Thus countenanced by our country, we pledge ourselves, as you will perceive by the following resolutions, never to recede or slacken, but on every occasion to redouble our zealous exertions in the cause of Constitutional Freedom.

Resolved unanimously

I   That nothing but a fair, adequate and annually renovated Representation in Parliament, can ensure the freedom of this country.

II   That we are fully convinced, a thorough Parliamentary Reform, would remove every grievance under which we labour.

III That we will never give up the pursuit of such Parliamentary Reform.

IV   That if it be a part of the power of the king to declare war when and against whom he pleases, we are convinced that such power must have been granted to him under the condition, that it should ever be subservient to the national advantage.

V   That the present war against France, and the existing alliance with the Germanic Powers, so far as it relates to the prosecution of that war, has hitherto produced, and is likely to produce nothing but national calamity, if not utter ruin.

VI   That it appears to Us that the wars in which Great Britain has engaged, within the last hundred years, have cost her upwards of *Three hundred and Seventy Millions*! not to mention the private misery occasioned thereby, or the lives sacrificed; therefore it is a dreadful speculation for the people of this country to look up to; That the Cabinet have engaged in a treaty with a foreign Prince, to be supplied with troops for a long period of years, and for purpose unknown to the people of England.

VII That we are persuaded the majority, if not the whole of those wars, originated in Cabinet intrigue, rather than in absolute necessity.

VIII That every nation has an unalienable right to choose the mode in which it will be governed, and that it is an act of Tyranny and Oppression in any other nation to interfere with, or attempt to control their choice.

IX   That peace being the greatest blessings, ought to be sought most diligently by every wise government, to be most joyfully accepted when reasonably proffered, and to be concluded most speedily when the object of the war is accomplished.

X   That we do exhort every well wisher to his country, not to delay in improving himself in constitutional knowledge.

XI   That those men who were the first to be seized with a panic, should be the last whom prudence would entrust with the management of a war.

XII   That Great Britain is not Hanover!

XIII That regarding union as indispensably necessary to ensure success, we will endeavour to the utmost of our power, to unite more closely with every political Society in the nation, associated upon the same principles with ourselves.

XIV That the next general Meeting of this Society, be held on the first Monday in September, unless the Committee of Delegates shall find it necessary to call such meeting sooner.

XV That the foregoing Address and Resolutions be signed by the Chairman and by the Secretary, and that *Twenty Thousand Copies* of them be printed, published and distributed [gratis].

Maurice Margarot, Chairman
[8 July 1793]   Thomas Hardy, Secretary

WILLIAM BLAKE (1757–1827)   1791–3

From *Songs of Experience*, in *Complete Writings*, p. 216

LONDON

I wander thro' each charter'd street,
Near where the charter'd Thames does flow,
And mark in every face I meet
Marks of weakness, marks of woe.

In every cry of every man,
In every Infant's cry of fear,
In every voice, in every ban,
The mind-forg'd manacles I hear.

How the Chimney-sweeper's cry
Every black'ning Church appals;

And the hapless Soldier's sigh
Runs in blood down Palace walls.

But most thro' midnight streets I hear
How the youthful Harlot's curse
Blasts the new-born infant's tear,
And blights with plagues the Marriage hearse.

WILLIAM WORDSWORTH (1770–1850) 1793

From a letter to the Bishop of Llandaff, in *Prose Works*, I, pp. 3–23
passim

In 1792 Dr Richard Watson published a pamphlet attacking the French Revolution, and Wordsworth decided to answer it, though he wisely never sent it or printed it. (Blake later annotated Watson's *Apology for the Bible*, privately, but the scholar Gilbert Wakefield went to prison for three years for answering an *Address* by Watson.)

FREEDOM & SLAVERY

Your Lordship very properly asserts that 'the liberty of man in a state of society consists in his being subject to no law but the law enacted by the general will of the society to which he belongs'. You approved of the object which the French had in view when, in the infancy of the Revolution, they were attempting to destroy arbitrary power, and to erect a temple to Liberty on its remains. It is with surprise, then, that I find you afterwards presuming to dictate to the world a servile adoption of the British constitution. It is with indignation I perceive you 'reprobate' a people for having imagined happiness and liberty more likely to flourish in the open field of a Republic than under the shade of Monarchy. You are therefore guilty of a most glaring contradiction. Twenty-five millions of Frenchmen have felt that they could have no security for their liberties under any modification of monarchical power. They have in consequence unanimously chosen a Republic. You cannot but observe that they have only exercised that right in which, by your own confession, liberty essentially resides . . . Slavery is a bitter and a poisonous draught. We have but one consolation under it, that a Nation may dash the cup to the ground when she pleases. Do not imagine that by taking from its bitterness you weaken its deadly quality; no, by rendering it more palatable you contribute to its power of destruction. We submit without repining to the chastisements of Providence, aware that we are creatures, that opposition is vain and remonstrance impossible. But when redress is in our own power and resistance is rational, we suffer with the same humility from beings like ourselves, because we are taught from infancy that we were born in a state of inferiority to our oppressors, that they were sent into the world to scourge, and we to be scourged. Accordingly we see the bulk of mankind, actuated by these fatal prejudices, even more ready to lay themselves under the feet of *the great* than the great are to trample upon them . . . As the magnitude of almost all States prevents the possibility of their enjoying a pure democracy, philosophers – from a wish, as far as it is in their power, to make the governors and the governed one – will turn their thoughts to the system of universal representation, and will annex an equal importance to the suffrage of every individual . . . But . . . in the choice of its representatives a people will not immorally hold out wealth as a criterion of integrity, nor lay down as a fundamental rule, that to be qualified for the trying duties of legislation a citizen should be possessed of a certain fixed property. Virtues, talents, and acquirements are all that it will look for . . . And this brings me to my grand objection to monarchy, which is drawn from THE ETERNAL NATURE OF MAN. The office of king is a trial to which human virtue is not equal. Pure and universal representation, by which alone liberty can be secured, cannot, I think, exist together with monarchy. It seems madness to expect a manifestation of the *general* will, at the same time that we allow to a *particular* will that weight which it must obtain in all governments that can with any propriety be called monarchical. They must war with each other till one of them is extinguished . . .

. . . our legislators . . . have unjustly left unprotected that most important part of property, not less real because it has no material existence, that which ought to enable the labourer to provide food for himself and his family. I appeal to innumerable statutes, whose constant and professed object it is to lower the price of labour, to compel the workman to be *content* with arbitrary wages, evidently too small from the necessity of legal enforcement of the acceptance of them . . . I am not an advocate for the agrarian law [to redistribute land among the people] nor for sumptuary regulations, but I contend that the people amongst whom the law of primogeniture exists, and among whom corporate bodies are encouraged, and immense salaries annexed to useless and indeed hereditary offices, is oppressed by an inequality in the distribution of wealth which does not necessarily attend men in a state of civil society . . .

371

You ask with triumphant confidence, to what other law are the people of England subject than the general will of the society to which they belong? Is your Lordship to be told that acquiescence is not choice, and that obedience is not freedom? If there is a single man in Great Britain who has no suffrage in the election of a representative, the will of the society of which he is a member is not generally expressed; he is a Helot in that society . . .

WILLIAM BLAKE (1757–1827) 1794

From *Songs of Experience*, in *Complete Writings*, p. 217

THE HUMAN ABSTRACT

Pity would be no more
If we did not make somebody poor;
And Mercy no more could be
If all were as happy as we.

And mutual fear brings peace,
Till the selfish loves increase:
Then Cruelty knits a snare,
And spreads his baits with care.

He sits down with holy fears,
And waters the ground with tears;
Then Humility takes its root
Underneath his foot.

Soon spreads the dismal shade
Of Mystery over his head;
And the Caterpillar and Fly
Feed on the Mystery.

And it bears the fruit of Deceit,
Ruddy and sweet to eat;
And the Raven his nest has made
In its thickest shade.

The Gods of earth and sea
Sought thro' Nature to find this Tree;

But their search was all in vain:
There grows one in the Human Brain.

WILLIAM WORDSWORTH
(1770–1850)

After July 1794

From *The Prelude* (1805), X, ll. 618–57

Wordsworth, who is said to have returned to Paris the previous September and to have witnessed the execution of the Girondin Gorsas under the Reign of Terror, welcomed the fall of the Jacobins, though still it seemed to him that 'every thing was wanting that might give /Courage to those who looked for good by light /Of rational experience'; not least because the tyranny that now ruled England had set itself so obdurately against the French and the struggle for liberty that was being fought in Europe.

ENGLISH TYRANNY

                    I could see
How Babel-like the employment was of those
Who, by the recent deluge stupefied,
With their whole souls went culling from the day
Its petty promises, to build a tower
For their own safety; laughed at gravest heads,
Who, watching in their hate of France for signs
Of her disasters, if the stream of rumour
Brought with it one green branch, conceited thence
That not a single tree was left alive
In all her forests. How could I believe
That wisdom could, in any shape, come near
Men clinging to delusions so insane?
And thus, experience proving that no few
Of my opinions had been just, I took
Like credit to myself where less was due,
And thought that other notions were as sound,
Yea, could not but be right, because I saw
That foolish men opposed them.
                    To a strain
More animated I might here give way,

373

And tell, since juvenile errors are my theme,
What in those days, through Britain, was performed
To turn *all* judgements out of their right course . . .

Our Shepherds, this say merely, at that time
Thirsted to make the guardian crook of law
A tool of murder; they who ruled the State,
Though with such awful proof before their eyes
That he, who would sow death, reaps death, or worse,
And can reap nothing better, child-like longed
To imitate, not wise enough to avoid,
Giants in their impiety alone,
But, in their weapons and their warfare base
As vermin working out of reach, they leagued
Their strength perfidiously, to undermine
Justice, and make an end of Liberty . . .

WILLIAM BLAKE (1757–1827)   1794

From *Europe*, in *Complete Writings*, p. 243

SLAVERY

Every house a den, every man bound: the shadows are fill'd
With spectres, and the windows wove over with curses of iron:
Over the doors 'Thou shalt not,' and over the chimneys 'Fear' is
   written:
With bands of iron round their necks fasten'd into the walls
The citizens, in leaden gyves the inhabitants of suburbs
Walk heavy; soft and bent are the bones of villagers.

HENRY 'REDHEAD' YORKE   July 1795
(1772–1813)

From his testimony at his trial, in Howell, ed., *State Trials*, pp. 1083–5

Yorke had been arrested in May 1794 on the suspension of Habeas Corpus and
kept in prison. He decided to defend himself, with disastrous results, after
Thomas Muir (August 1793) and Maurice Margarot (1794) had been sentenced

to fourteen years by Lord Braxfield in Edinburgh, and Thomas Hardy, Horne Tooke and Thelwall (defended skilfully by Thomas Erskine) had been acquitted late in 1794. Sentenced to two years, this 'eloquent and unstable' young man emerged from Dorchester a changed and repentant man, having 'deeply and severely suffered' in prison. But his fiery speech at Sheffield in April 1794, immediately published as *Thoughts on Civil Government*, which helped to convict him, and the passage from his testimony, catch the revolutionary spirit of the time.

THE STANDARD OF LIBERTY

Sheffield Speech

. . . We desire to see wisdom demanding of miserable millions their wants, and humanity at hand to supply them. We desire to see the sanctuary of virtue erected, and the standard of Liberty planted in our land, around which the people may rally as to a Holy of Holies. In short, we desire to see the altar of Equality blazing in Britain, whose streams of fire, whilst they shock, convulse, and tear down the rotten pillars of prejudices; whilst they shall consume tyrants, and terrify public delinquents; shall pierce into the hearts of the whole people, and confirm the wide empire of morals on the wreck of superstition and vice . . . Let revolution of sentiment precede reformation in government and manners . . .

TO SPEAK IN A JUST CAUSE

Yorke's Testimony

A man feels an energy about him when embarked in a just cause . . . that which is engendered by virtue, that which enables a man to kindle in the common blaze of liberty, and impels him in a time of danger, from an enlightened love of country, to be foremost, and to share its various fate, whether of destruction or of glory . . .

The public safety is not injured by those who assemble in public squares and meetings, and advance doctrines, couched in the spirit of error, but from those who never show their faces among the people, who never publicly avow any opinions, who temporize always between truths and falsehoods, or who undulate from one side to the other, as the tempest of opinions blows them . . .

375

It may be replied that these observations have a direct tendency to ferment the public mind, and to promote sedition; but to have right thoughts of things, and to communicate those thoughts to others, is the whole part we have to act on this stage of the world.

WILLIAM BLAKE (1757–1827)   1795

From *The Song of Los* in *Complete Writings*, p. 247

THAT THE REMNANT MAY LEARN TO OBEY

Shall not the King call for Famine from the heath,
Nor the Priest for Pestilence from the fen,
To restrain, to dismay, to thin
The inhabitants of mountain and plain,
In the day of full-feeding prosperity
And the night of delicious songs?

Shall not the Counsellor throw his curb
Of Poverty on the laborious,
To fix the price of labour,
To invent allegoric riches?

And the privy admonishers of men
Call for fires in the City,
For heaps of smoking ruins,
In the night of prosperity and wantonness?

To turn man from his path,
To restrain the child from the womb,
To cut off the bread from the city,
That the remnant may learn to obey,
That the pride of the heart may fail,
That the lust of the eyes may be quench'd,
That the delicate ear in its infancy
May be dull'd, and the nostrils clos'd up,
To teach mortal worms the path
That leads from the gates of the Grave?

SAMUEL TAYLOR COLERIDGE
(1772–1834)   1795

From *The Plot Discovered; or an Address to the People, against Ministerial Treason*, in *Collected Works*, I, pp. 285–313

Though by the time he met Wordsworth in 1797, Coleridge had already (like his friend, and like Southey) begun to move to the right, and to snap, as he put it, his 'squeaking baby-trumpet of sedition', in the early 1790s he had been a passionate supporter of the French Revolution and of radical republicanism in England, as poems, articles and lectures, and the ten issues of his journal *The Watchman* demonstrate. This lecture, delivered at Bristol, attacks the Treason Bill (restricting liberty of the press) and the Convention of Seditious Meetings Bill (against liberty of speech) introduced by Pitt to muzzle the radicals.

THE DUNGHILL OF DESPOTISM

. . . 'The mass of the people have nothing to do with the laws, but to obey them!' – Ere yet this foul treason against the majesty of man, ere yet this blasphemy against the goodness of God be registered among our statutes, I enter my protest! Ere yet our laws as well as our religion be muffled up in mysteries, as a CHRISTIAN I protest against this worse than Pagan darkness! Ere yet the sword descends, the two-edged sword that is now waving over the head of Freedom, as a BRITON, I protest against slavery! Ere yet it be made legal for Ministers to act with vigour beyond law, as a CHILD OF PEACE, I protest against civil war! This is the brief moment, in which Freedom pleads on her knees: we will join her pleadings, ere yet she rises terrible to wrench the sword from the hand of her merciless enemy! We will join the still small voice of reason, ere yet it be overwhelmed in the great and strong wind, in the earthquake, and in the fire! These detestable Bills I shall examine in their undiminished proportions, as they first dared show themselves to the light, disregarding and despising all subsequent palliatives and modifications. From their first state it is made evident beyond all power of doubt, what are the wishes and intentions of the present Ministers; and their wishes and intentions having been so evidenced, if the legislature authorize, if the people endure one sentence of such Bills from such manifest conspirators against the Constitution, that legislature will by degrees authorize the whole, and the people endure the whole, yea, that legislature will be capable of authorizing even worse, and the people will be unworthy of better.

The first of these Bills is an attempt to assassinate the Liberty of the Press, the second, to smother the Liberty of Speech . . . [They] were conceived and laid in the dunghill of despotism among the other yet unhatched eggs of the old Serpent. In due time and in fit opportunity they crawled into light. Genius of Britain! crush them! . . .

Hitherto nothing has been adduced that truly distinguishes our Government from Despotism: it seems to be a Government *over*, not *by*, or *with* the people. But this conclusion we disavow. The Liberty of the Press, (a power resident in the people) gives us an *influential* sovereignty. By books necessary information may be dispersed; and by information the public will may be formed; and by the right of petitioning that will may be expressed; first, perhaps, in low and distant tones such as beseem the children of peace; but if corruption deafen power, gradually increasing till they swell into a deep and awful thunder, the VOICE OF GOD, which his viceregents must hear, and hearing dare not disobey. This unrestricted right of over-awing the Oligarchy of Parliament by constitutional expression of the general will forms our liberty; it is the sole boundary that divides us from Despotism . . . By the almost winged communication of the Press, the whole nation become one grand Senate, fervent yet untumultuous. By the right of meeting together to petition (which, Milton says, is good old English for *requiring*) the determinations of this Senate are embodied into legal form, and conveyed to the *executive* branch of Government, the Parliament. The present Bills annihilate this right. The *forms* of it indeed will remain; (the *forms* of the Roman republic were preserved under Tiberius and Nero) but the reality will have flown . . .

ROBERT BURNS (1759–96)   1795

'A Man's a Man for a' That'

MAN TO MAN . . . SHALL BROTHERS BE

Is there for honest Poverty
    That hings his head, an' a' that:
The coward slave – wa pass him by,
    We dare be poor for a' that!
For a' that, an' a' that,
    Our toils obscure an' a' that,

The rank is but the guinea's stamp,
 The Man's the gowd for a' that.

What though on hamely fare we dine,
 Wear hoddin grey, an' a' that:
Gie fools their silks, and knaves their wine,
 A Man's a Man for a' that:
For a' that, an' a' that,
 Their tinsel show, an' a' that:
The honest man, tho' e'er sae poor,
 Is king o' men for a' that.

Ye see yon birkie ca'd a lord,
 Wha struts, an' stares, an' a' that:
Tho' hundreds worship at his word,
 He's but a coof for a' that:
For a' that, an' a' that,
 His ribband, star, an' a' that:
The man o' independent mind
 He looks an' laughs at a' that.

A prince can mak a belted knight,
 A marquis, duke, an' a' that:
But an honest man's aboon his might,
 Gude faith, he mauna fa' that!
For a' that, an' a' that,
 Their dignities, an' a' that:
The pith o' sense, an' pride o' worth,
 Are higher rank than a' that.

Then let us pray that come it may
 (As come it will for a' that),
That Sense and Worth o'er a' the earth,
 Shall bear the gree, an a' that.
For a' that, an' a' that,
 It's comin' yet for a' that,
That Man to Man, the world o'er,
 Shall brothers be for a' that.

JOHN THELWALL (1764–1834) 1796

From *The Rights of Nature*, pp. 18, 28–9

Thelwall was one of the most important figures in the Jacobin opposition during the crucial years of struggle (1793–6) against an increasingly reactionary government. He ranks with Paine and Hardy, and his gifts as an orator and as a theorist made him an outstanding leader of the movement at meetings all over the country, and especially in London. In May 1794, on the suspension of Habeas Corpus, Thelwall was arrested with Hardy, Tooke and others for high treason and locked up in the Tower for months before standing trial and being acquitted. Even after this, up to and beyond the period of Pitt's two Acts of late 1795, he continued his agitation for liberty and social justice. In *The Rights of Nature*, together with the three volumes of *The Tribune*, Thelwall extends the great Painite debate, and these books became texts for radicals throughout the nineteenth century.

THE RESTORATION OF EQUAL RIGHTS

The fact is that the hideous accumulation of capital in a few hands, like all diseases not absolutely mortal, carries, in its own enormity, the seeds of cure. Man is, by his very nature, social and communicative – proud to display the little knowledge he possesses, and eager, as opportunity pretends, to increase his store. Whatever presses men together, therefore, though it may generate some vices, is favourable to the diffusion of knowledge, and ultimately promotive of human liberty. Hence every large workshop and manufactory is a sort of political society, which no act of parliament can silence, and no magistrate disperse.

. . . Lift up your voices, ye artificers, ye mechanics, ye manufacturers of the land! ye genuine props and pillars of the nation! Be not amused with pretended treaties: for what is peace but war to you, while ye drudge in servile misery for inadequate rewards, and your families pine in want and ignorance? Wear not your lungs with sighs and sullen murmurs – let not only the nocturnal phantom, but the living body of your complaints appear before your oppressors. Exert once more the manly energies of reason; and tell them, with a clear and decided tone, that 'peace is not peace without reform': and 'your discontents can never be allayed without the restoration of equal rights and equal laws, and the adoption of a pure and independent organ, through which the opinions, not of a tenth part, but of the whole nation, can be freely delivered, and distinctly heard'.

But no: we are told the nation wants no such organ. The opinions of

380

the *menial*, *dependent mass* must be taken for granted from those of their *betters*. In those more reputable orders, in that privileged four hundred thousand, who, by virtue of their situation, have an exclusive licence to enquire and discuss, the people have already 'a natural representative'. Natural representative! – Of what excellent use, in the science of confusing mankind, is the prerogative of coining new phrases! Natural representative of the people!

WILLIAM BLAKE (1757–1827) 1797

From *Vala or the Four Zoas*, 'Night the Second', in *Complete Writings*, pp. 290–91

Vala embodies the struggles of separated beings thrust into an alien divided world where man has lost his sense of organic community; the collisions and conflicts engendered by the division. The poem reflects the terrible struggles of Blake's own world, where tyranny and intolerance ruled. Enion, as the Emanation of Maternal Instinct, has been separated from Tharmas, her complement (together, first man and woman) to become a Spectre or shadow of the true self; and here she laments the loss and the destructive antagonism she is involved in.

THE PRICE OF EXPERIENCE

I am made to sow the thistle for wheat, the nettle for a nourishing
    dainty.
I have planted a false oath in the earth; it has brought forth a poison
    tree.
I have chosen the serpent for a counsellor, and the dog
For a schoolmaster to my children.
I have blotted out from light and living the dove and nightingale,
And I have caused the earthworm to beg from door to door.

I have taught the thief a secret path into the house of the just.
I have taught pale artifice to spread his nets upon the morning.
My heavens are brass, my earth is iron, my moon a clod of clay,
My sun a pestilence burning at noon and a vapour of death in night.

What is the price of experience? do men buy it for a song?
Or wisdom for a dance in the street? No, it is bought with the price
Of all a man hath, his house, his wife, his children.

Wisdom is sold in the desolate market where none come to buy,
And in the wither'd field where the farmer plows for bread in vain.

It is an easy thing to triumph in the summer's sun
And in the vintage and to sing on the waggon loaded with corn.
It is an easy thing to talk of patience to the afflicted,
To speak the laws of prudence to the houseless wanderer,
To listen to the hungry raven's cry in wintry season
When the red blood is fill'd with wine and with the marrow of lambs.

It is an easy thing to laugh at wrathful elements,
To hear the dog howl at the wintry door, the ox in the slaughterhouse
    moan;
To see a god on every wind and a blessing on every blast;
To hear sounds of love in the thunder-storm that destroys our
    enemies' house;
To rejoice in the blight that covers his field, and the sickness that cuts
    off his children,
While our olive and vine sing and laugh round our door, and our
    children bring fruits and flowers.

Then the groan and the dolour are quite forgotten, and the slave
    grinding at the mill,
And the captive in chains, and the poor in the prison, and the soldier
    in the field
When the shatter'd bone hath laid him groaning among the happier
    dead.

It is an easy thing to rejoice in the tents of prosperity:
Thus could I sing and thus rejoice: but it is not so with me.

THE NAVAL MUTINIES   1797

Manifesto, in Postgate, ed., *Revolution from 1789 to 1906*, pp. 73–4

16 April–16 May: The Two Spithead mutinies.
12 May: Outbreak at the Nore.
24 May: Refusal to accept demands after the granting of the Spithead demands.
29 May: Arrival of revolted ships of North Sea Fleet revives mutiny.
2–5 June: Thames blockaded by the Nore Fleet.
9 June: Mutiny collapses.
16 June: Last ship surrenders.

MANIFESTO OF THE DELEGATES TO THEIR COUNTRYMEN: HANDED TO LORD NORTHESK ON 6 JUNE

The delegates of the different ships at the Nore assembled in Council, to their Fellow-subjects:

Countrymen,

It is to you particularly that we owe an explanation of our conduct. His Majesty's Ministers too well know our intentions, which are founded on the laws of humanity, honour and national safety – long since trampled underfoot by those who ought to have been friends to us – the sole protectors of your laws and property. The public prints teem with falsehoods and misrepresentations to induce you to credit things as far from our design as the conduct of those at the helm of national affairs is from honesty or common decorum.

Shall we who have endured the toils of a tedious, disgraceful war, be the victims of tyranny and oppression which vile, gilded, pampered knaves, wallowing in the lap of luxury, choose to load us with? Shall we, who amid the rage of the tempest and the war of jarring elements, undaunted climb the unsteady cordage and totter on the topmast's dreadful height, suffer ourselves to be treated worse than the dogs of London streets? Shall we, who in the battle's sanguinary rage, confound, terrify and subdue your proudest foe, guard your coasts from invasion, your children from slaughter, and your lands from pillage – be the footballs and shuttlecocks of a set of tyrants who derive from us alone their honours, their titles and their fortunes? No, the Age of Reason has at length revolved. Long have we been endeavouring to find ourselves men. We now find ourselves so. We will be treated as such. Far, very far, from us is the idea of subverting the government of our beloved country. We have the highest opinion of our Most Gracious Sovereign, and we hope none of those measures taken to deprive us of the common rights of men have been instigated by him.

You cannot, countrymen, form the most distant idea of the slavery under which we have for many years laboured. Rome had her Neros and Caligulas, but how many characters of their description might we not mention in the British Fleet – men without the least tincture of humanity, without the faintest spark of virtue, education or abilities, exercising the most wanton acts of cruelty over those whom dire misfortune or patriotic zeal may have placed in their power – basking in the sunshine of prosperity, whilst we (need we repeat who we are?) labour under every distress which the breast of inhumanity can suggest. The

British seaman has often with justice been compared to the lion – gentle, generous and humane – no one would certainly wish to hurt such an animal. Hitherto we have laboured for our sovereign and you. We are now obliged to think for ourselves, for there are many (nay, most of us) in the Fleet who have been prisoners since the commencement of the War, without receiving a single farthing. Have we not a right to complain? Let His Majesty but order us to be paid and the little grievances we have made known redressed, we shall enter with alacrity upon any employment for the defence of our country; but until that is complied with we are determined to stop all commerce and intercept all provisions, for our own subsistence. The military have had their pay augmented, to insult as well as to enslave you. Be not appalled. We will adopt the words of a celebrated motto and defy all attempts to deceive us. We do not wish to adopt the plan of a neighbouring nation, however it may have been suggested; but we sell our lives dearly to maintain what we have demanded. Nay, countrymen, more: We have already discovered the tricks of Government in supplying our enemies with different commodities, and a few days will probably lead to something more. In the meantime,

> We remain, Dear Countrymen,
>   Yours affectionately, [the text for printing]
>   Your Loving Brothers, Red for Ever [Lord Northesk]

The leader of the Mutiny, Richard Parker, was hanged from the yardarm of his ship.

WILLIAM BLAKE (1757–1827)   1797

From *Vala or the Four Zoas*, in *Complete Writings*, p. 323

Urizen, the 'Eternal Mind', god of Reason and Law, a cold and ruthless tyrant, because separated from Ahania, his wife (who in Blake's terminology is his Emanation, embodying Energy, 'Eternal Delight'), reads from his 'book of brass'.

THE LAWS OF THE OPPRESSOR

Listen, O Daughters, to my voice. Listen to the Words of Wisdom,
So shall you govern over all; let Moral Duty tune your tongue.
But be your hearts harder than the nether millstone . . .

Compel the poor to live upon a Crust of bread, by soft mild arts.
Smile when they frown, frown when they smile; and when a man
   looks pale
With labour and abstinence, say he looks healthy and happy;
And when his children sicken, let them die; there are enough
Born, even too many, and our Earth will be overrun
Without these arts. If you would make the poor live with temper,
With pomp give every crust of bread you give; with gracious cunning
Magnify small gifts; reduce the man to want a gift, and then give with
   pomp.
Say he smiles if you hear him sigh. If pale, say he is ruddy.
Preach temperance: say he is overgorg'd and drowns his wit
In strong drink, tho' you know that bread and water are all
He can afford. Flatter his wife, pity his children, till we can
Reduce all to our will, as spaniels are taught with art.

ALEXANDER ALEXANDER

From *The Life of Alexander Alexander*, quoted in Barker, ed., *Long March of Everyman*, p. 42

ARMY CRUELTY: CHATHAM, 1801

A poor fellow of the 9th regiment, said to be a farmer's son in Suffolk, had the misfortune to be found asleep on his post. General Sir John Moore had the command of the Chatham division at the time; he was a severe disciplinarian. The soldier was tried by a court-martial, and sentenced to be flogged; all the troops were paraded to witness the punishment. It was a very stormy morning; the frost, which had continued for some days, gave way during the night, and the wind and sleet drove most piteously: it was a severe punishment to stand clothed looking on, how much more to be stripped to the waist and tied up to the halberts. The soldier was a fine-looking lad, and bore an excellent character in his regiment; his officers were much interested in his behalf, and made great intercession for him to the General. But all their pleading was in vain, the General remained inflexible and made a very long speech after the punishment, in which he reflected in very severe terms on the conduct of the officers and non-commissioned officers present, observing, that if they did their duty as strictly as they had any regard for their men, they ought never to report them to him, for he would pardon no man when found guilty. The poor fellow got two hundred and twenty-nine lashes, but they were uncommonly severe. I saw the drum-major strike a drummer to the ground for not using his strength sufficiently. General Sir John Moore was present all the time. At length, the surgeon interfered, the poor fellow's back was black as the darkest mahogany, and dreadfully swelled. The cats were too thick, they did not cut, which made the punishment more severe. He was instantly taken down and carried to the hospital, where he died in eight days, his back having mortified. It was the cold I think that killed him; for I have often seen seven hundred lashes inflicted, but I never saw a man's back so horrible to look upon.

WILLIAM BLAKE (1757–1827)   1802

From 'Auguries of Innocence', in *Complete Writings*, pp. 432–3

BLAKE'S WITNESS

The Babe that weeps the Rod beneath
Writes Revenge in realms of death.
The Beggar's Rags, fluttering in Air,
Does to Rags the Heavens tear.
The Soldier, arm'd with Sword and Gun,
Palsied strikes the Summer's Sun.
The poor Man's Farthing is worth more
Than all the Gold on Afric's Shore.
One Mite wrung from the Lab'rer's hands
Shall buy and sell the Miser's Lands:
Or, if protected from on high,
Does that whole Nation sell and buy . . .

WILLIAM WORDSWORTH (1770–1850)   1805

The Prelude (1805), XII, ll. 69–105

In this noble passage, Wordsworth signals the resolution of that conflict from which – 'sick, wearied out with contrarieties' – he had recoiled in horror and dismay. His withdrawal from the revolutionary events of his time was to lead him in the end to accept the injustices and wholesale mutilations that were disfiguring the life of England – a retreat which distanced him from the struggles of 'bodily labour' and left him to the deepening orthodoxy of 'Duty' and 'Faith'. But here the agitation of the challenge has not yet been resolved, and the intensity of application thus remains charged with significance.

THE WEALTH OF NATIONS

With settling judgements now of what would last
And what would disappear; prepared to find
Ambition, folly, madness, in the men
Who thrust themselves upon this passive world
As Rulers of the world; to see in these,
Even when the public welfare is their aim,
Plans without thought, or bottomed on false thought
And false philosophy; having brought to test
Of solid life and true result the books
Of modern statists, and thereby perceived
The utter hollowness of what we name
'The Wealth of Nations', where alone that wealth
Is lodged, and how increased; and having gained
A more judicious knowledge of what makes
The dignity of individual man,
Of man, no composition of the thought,
Abstraction, shadow, image, but the man
Of whom we read, the man whom we behold
With our own eyes – I could not but inquire –
Not with less interest than heretofore,
But greater, though in spirit more subdued –
Why is this glorious creature to be found
One only in ten thousand? What one is,
Why may not many be? What bars are thrown
By Nature in the way of such a hope?
Our animal wants and the necessities
Which they impose, are these the obstacles?
If not, then others vanish into air.
Such meditations bred an anxious wish
To ascertain how much of real worth
And genuine knowledge, and true power of mind
Did at this day exist in those who lived
By bodily labour, labour far exceeding

Their due proportion, under all the weight
Of that injustice which upon ourselves
By composition of society
Ourselves entail . . .

WILLIAM BLAKE (1757–1827)   1804

From *Milton*, in *Complete Writings*, pp. 480–81, 507–8

MENTAL WAR

Rouse up, O Young Men of the New Age! set your foreheads against the
ignorant Hirelings! For we have Hirelings in the Camp, the Court and
the University, who would, if they could, for ever depress Mental and
prolong Corporeal War. Painters! on you I call. Sculptors! Architects!
Suffer not the fashionable Fools to depress your powers by the prices
they pretend to give for contemptible works, or the expensive advertising
boasts that they make of such works; believe Christ and his Apostles that
there is a Class of Men whose whole delight is in Destroying. We do not
want either Greek or Roman Models if we are but just and true to our
own Imaginations, those Worlds of Eternity in which we shall live for
ever in Jesus our Lord.

And did those feet in ancient time
Walk upon England's mountains green?
And was the holy Lamb of God
On England's pleasant pastures seen?

And did the Countenance Divine
Shine forth upon our clouded hills?
And was Jerusalem builded here
Among these dark Satanic Mills?

Bring me my Bow of burning gold!
Bring me my Arrows of desire:
Bring me my Spear: O clouds unfold!
Bring me my Chariot of fire.

I will not cease from Mental Fight,
Nor shall my Sword sleep in my hand
Till we have built Jerusalem
In England's green and pleasant land.

Would to God that all the Lord's people were Prophets. Numbers xi, 29.

FOR BROTHERHOOD AND MERCY

O when shall we tread our Wine-presses in heaven and Reap
Our wheat with shoutings of joy, and leave the Earth in peace?
Remember how Calvin and Luther in fury premature
Sow'd War and stern division between Papists and Protestants.
Let it not be so now! O go not forth in Martyrdoms and Wars!
We were plac'd here by the Universal Brotherhood and Mercy
With powers fitted to circumscribe this dark Satanic death,
And that the Seven Eyes of God may have space for Redemption.
But how this is as yet we know not, and we cannot know
Till Albion is arisen; then patient wait a little while.

WILLIAM BLAKE (1757–1827)   1810

From *A Vision of the Last Judgement*, in *Complete Writings*, p. 612

POVERTY IS THE FOOL'S ROD

A Last Judgement is Necessary because Fools flourish. Nations Flourish under Wise Rulers and are depress'd under foolish Rulers; it is the same with Individuals as Nations; works of Art can only be produc'd in Perfection where the Man is either in Affluence or is Above the Care of it. Poverty is the Fool's Rod, which at last is turn'd on his own back; that is a Last Judgement – when Men of Real Art Govern and Pretenders Fall. Some People and not a few Artists have asserted that the Painter of this Picture would not have done so well if he had been properly Encourag'd. Let those who think so, reflect on the State of Nations under Poverty and their incapability of Art; tho' Art is Above Either, the Argument is better for Affluence than Poverty; and tho' he would not have been a greater Artist, yet he would have produc'd Greater works of Art in proportion to his means. A Last Judgement is not for the purpose of making Bad Men better, but for the Purpose of hindering them from oppressing the Good with Poverty and Pain by means of Such Vile Arguments and Insinuations.

THE LUDDITE RIOTS

In Barker, ed., *Long March of Everyman*, pp. 70, 94

The introduction of machinery for textile production caused great distress in the north, bringing about mass unemployment and worsening conditions even for those still working. Organized bands of men, under a real or imaginary leader named King Ludd, operated at night smashing the machines and burning down factories to draw attention to their plight. They did not attack people till a band was shot down in 1812 at the request of an employer, Horsfall, who was afterwards murdered. Severe repression followed the spread of the riots, and at a mass trial in 1813 at York there were many hangings and transportations

NED LUDD

From a piece of paper left in Chesterfield Market (Home Office Papers)

I ham going to inform you that there is Six Thousand men coming to you in Apral and then We will go and Blow Parlement house up and Blow up all afour hus labring Peple Cant Stand it No longer dam all Such Roges as England governes but Never mind Ned lud when general nody and his harmy Comes We Will soon bring about the greate Revelution then all these greate mens heads gose of.

COME ALL YE CROPPERS

Yorkshire croppers' song

Come all ye croppers stout and bold,
Let your faith grow stronger still,
Oh, the cropper lads in the county of York
Broke the shears at Forster's mill.
    The wind it blew
    The sparks they flew
Which alarmed the town full soon.

Around and around we all will stand,
And sternly swear we will,
We'll break the shears and windows too,
And set fire to the Tazzling mill.

LORD BYRON (1788–1824)

27 February 1812

From his first speech in the House of Lords, during the debate on the second reading of the Framework Bill, in Byron, *Letters and Journals*, VI, pp. 314–21

Byron spoke against the Frame-breaking Bill, by which the government intended to apply savage penalties, including hanging, to those hand-workers who were being thrown out of work by the introduction of frames, and who had spent the winter smashing the machines all over the north, calling themselves Luddites. The unrest had been brought on by a massive slump in trade in 1811 caused by the combined effects of continental war, commercial blockade, bad harvests and 'paper-money' speculation; and this had struck hard at the working population. For it was they who had to pay the price of military successes and failures abroad in terms of unemployment, mass hunger and repression. Indeed, with the blockade soon to lead to war with the US, the situation of the workers in Britain was to worsen in the next few years, sharpening the social unrest, particularly after 1815, a time of mass unemployment and industrial dislocation.

Byron directs his ridicule against the militarist policies of the government in this superb defence of the workers' rights and needs.

DEFENCE OF THE FRAME-BREAKERS

During the short time I recently passed in Nottinghamshire, not twelve hours elapsed without some fresh act of violence; and on the day I left the county I was informed that forty Frames had been broken the preceding evening, as usual, without resistance and without detection.

Such was the state of that county, and such I have reason to believe it to be at this moment. But whilst these outrages must be admitted to exist to an alarming extent, it cannot be denied that they have arisen from circumstances of the most unparalleled distress: the perseverance of these miserable men in their proceedings, tends to prove that nothing but absolute want could have driven a large, and once honest and industrious, body of the people, into the commission of excesses so hazardous to themselves, their families, and the community. At the time to which I allude, the town and country were burdened with large detachments of the military; the police was in motion, the magistrates assembled, yet all the movements, civil and military, had led to – nothing. Not a single instance had occurred of the apprehension of any real delinquent actually taken in the fact, against whom there existed legal evidence sufficient for conviction. But the police, however useless, were by no means idle: several notorious delinquents had been detected; men, liable to conviction,

391

on the clearest evidence, of the capital crime of poverty; men, who had been nefariously guilty of lawfully begetting several children, whom, thanks to the times! they were unable to maintain. Considerable injury has been done to the proprietors of the improved Frames. These machines were to them an advantage, inasmuch as they superseded the necessity of employing a number of workmen, who were left in consequence to starve. By the adoption of one species of frame in particular, one man performed the work of many, and the superfluous labourers were thrown out of employment. Yet it is to be observed, that the work thus executed was inferior in quality; not marketable at home, and merely hurried over with a view to exportation. It was called, in the cant of the trade, by the name of 'Spider work'. The rejected workmen, in the blindness of their ignorance, instead of rejoicing at these improvements in arts so beneficial to mankind, conceived themselves to be sacrificed to improvements in mechanism. In the foolishness of their hearts they imagined, that the maintenance and well doing of the industrious poor, were objects of greater consequence than the enrichment of a few individuals by any improvement in the implements of trade, which threw the workmen out of employment, and rendered the labourer unworthy of his hire . . . But the real cause of these distresses and consequent disturbances lies deeper. When we are told that these men are leagued together not only for the destruction of their own comfort, but of their very means of subsistence, can we forget that it is the bitter policy, the destructive warfare of the last eighteen years, which has destroyed their comfort, your comfort, all men's comfort? That policy, which, originating with 'great statesmen now no more', has survived the dead to become a curse on the living, unto the third and fourth generation! These men never destroyed their looms till they were become useless, worse than useless; till they were become actual impediments to their exertions in obtaining their daily bread. Can you, then, wonder that in times like these, when bankruptcy, convicted fraud, and imputed felony, are found in a station not far beneath that of your Lordships, the lowest, though once most useful portion of the people, should forget their duty in their distresses, and become only less guilty than one of their representatives? But while the exalted offender can find means to baffle the law, new capital punishments must be devised, new snares of death must be spread for the wretched mechanic, who is famished into guilt. These men were willing to dig, but the spade was in other hands: they were not ashamed to beg, but there was none to relieve them: their own means of subsistence were cut off, all other employment preoccupied; and their excesses, however to be deplored and condemned, can hardly be subject of surprise.

. . . But, admitting that these men had no cause of complaint; that the grievances of them and their employers were alike groundless; that they deserved the worst; what inefficiency, what imbecility has been evinced in the method chosen to reduce them! Why were the military called out to be made a mockery of, if they were to be called out at all? . . . As the sword is the worst argument that can be used, so should it be the last. In this instance it has been the first; but providentially as yet only in the scabbard. The present measure will, indeed, pluck it from the sheath; yet had proper meetings been held in the earlier stages of these riots, had the grievances of these men and their masters (for they also had their grievances) been fairly weighed and justly examined, I do think that means might have been devised to restore these workmen to their avocations, and tranquillity to the country. At present the country suffers from the double infliction of an idle military and a starving population. In what state of apathy have we been plunged so long, that now for the first time the house has been officially apprised of these disturbances? All this has been transacting within 130 miles of London, and yet we, 'good easy men, have deemed full sure our greatness was a ripening', and have sat down to enjoy our foreign triumphs in the midst of domestic calamity. But all the cities you have taken, all the armies which have retreated before your leaders, are but paltry subjects of self-congratulation, if your land divides against itself, and your dragoons and your executioners must be let loose against your fellow-citizens. – You call these men a mob, desperate, dangerous, and ignorant; and seem to think that the only way to quiet the *Bellum multorum capitum* is to lop off a few of its superfluous heads. But even a mob may be better reduced to reason by a mixture of conciliation and firmness, than by additional irritation and redoubled penalties. Are we aware of our obligations to a mob? It is the mob that labour in your fields and serve in your houses, – that man your navy, and recruit your army, – that have enabled you to defy the world, and can also defy you when neglect and calamity have driven them to despair! You may call the people a mob; but do not forget, that a mob too often speaks the sentiments of the people. And here I must remark, with what alacrity you are accustomed to fly to the succour of your distressed allies, leaving the distressed of your own country to the care of Providence or – the parish. When the Portuguese suffered under the retreat of the French, every arm was stretched out, every hand was opened, from the rich man's largess to the widow's mite, all was bestowed, to enable them to rebuild their villages and replenish their granaries. And at this moment, when thousands of misguided but most unfortunate fellow-countrymen are struggling with the extremes of hardship and hunger, as your charity began abroad it should end at home. A much less sum, a tithe of the bounty bestowed on Portugal, even if these men (which I cannot admit without inquiry) could not have been restored to their employments, would have rendered unnecessary the tender mercies of the bayonet and the gibbet. But doubtless our friends have too many foreign claims to admit a prospect of domestic relief; though never did such objects demand it. I have traversed the seat of war in the Peninsula, I have been in some of the most oppressed provinces of Turkey, but never under the most despotic of infidel governments did I behold such squalid wretchedness as I have seen since my return in the very heart of a Christian country. And what are your remedies? After months of inaction, and months of action worse than inactivity, at length comes forth the grand specific, the never-failing nostrum of all state physicians, from the days of Draco to the present time. After feeling the pulse and shaking the head over the patient, prescribing the usual course of warm water and bleeding, the warm water of your mawkish police, and the lancets of your military, these convulsions must terminate in death, the sure consummation of the prescriptions of all political Sangrados. Setting aside the palpable injustice and the certain inefficiency of the bill, are there not capital punishments sufficient in your statutes? Is there not blood enough upon your penal code, that more must be poured forth to ascend to Heaven and testify against you? How will you carry the bill into effect? Can you commit a whole country to their own prisons? Will you erect a gibbet in every field, and hang up men like scarecrows? or will you proceed (as you must to bring this measure into effect) by decimation? place the country under martial law? depopulate and lay waste all around you? and restore Sherwood Forest as an acceptable gift to the crown, in its former condition of a royal chase and an asylum for outlaws? Are these the remedies for a starving and desperate populace? Will the famished wretch who has braved your bayonets be appalled by your gibbets? When death is a relief, and the only relief it appears that you will afford him, will he be dragooned into tranquillity? Will that which could not be effected by your grenadiers, be accomplished by your executioners? If you proceed by the forms of law, where is your evidence? Those who have refused to impeach their accomplices, when transportation only was the punishment, will hardly be tempted to witness against them when death is the penalty. With all due deference to the noble Lords opposite, I think a little investigation, some previous inquiry would induce even them to change their purpose. That most favourite state measure, so marvellously efficacious in many and recent instances, temporizing, would not be without its advantages in this. When a proposal is made to emancipate or relieve, you hesitate, you deliberate for years, you temporize and tamper with the minds of men; but a death-bill must be passed off hand, without a thought of the consequences. Sure I am, from what I have heard, and from what I have seen, that to pass the bill under all the existing circumstances, without inquiry, without deliberation, would only be to add injustice to irritation, and barbarity to neglect. The framers of such a bill must be content to inherit the honours of that Athenian lawgiver whose edicts were said to be written not in ink but in blood. But suppose it passed; suppose one of these men, as I have seen them, – meagre with famine, sullen with despair, careless of a life which your Lordships are perhaps about to value at something less than the price of a stocking-frame; – suppose this man surrounded by the children for whom he is unable to procure bread at the hazard of his existence, about to be torn for ever from a family which he lately supported in peaceful industry, and which it is not his fault that he can no longer so support; – suppose this man, and there are ten thousand such from whom you may select your victims, dragged into court, to be tried for this new offence, by this new law; still, there are two things wanting to convict and condemn him; and these are, in my opinion, – twelve butchers for a jury, and a Jeffreys for a judge!

SHELLEY (1792–1822)   1812

From *Queen Mab*, III, ll. 118–38, IV, note to ll. 178–9; V, ll. 64–94 and note, 177–89, in *Complete Poetical Works*, pp. 772, 801, 780, 804–5, 782

KINGS AND PARASITES

Whence, think'st thou, kings and parasites arose?
Whence that unnatural line of drones, who heap
Toil and unvanquishable penury
On those who build their palaces, and bring
Their daily bread? – From vice, black loathsome vice;
From rapine, madness, treachery, and wrong;
From all that 'genders misery, and makes
Of earth this thorny wilderness; from lust,
Revenge and murder . . . And when Reason's voice,

Loud as the voice of Nature, shall have waked
The nations; and mankind perceive that vice
Is discord, war, and misery; that virtue
Is peace, and happiness and harmony;
When man's maturer nature shall disdain
The playthings of its childhood; – kingly glare
Will lose its power to dazzle; its authority
Will silently pass by; the gorgeous throne
Shall stand unnoticed in the regal hall,
Fast falling to decay; whilst falsehood's trade
Shall be as hateful and unprofitable
As that of truth is now.

WAR: THE STATESMAN'S GAME

To employ murder as a means of justice is an idea which a man of an
enlightened mind will not dwell upon with pleasure. To march forth in
rank and file, and all the pomp of streamers and trumpets, for the purpose of shooting at our fellow-men as a mark; to inflict upon them all the
variety of wound and anguish; to leave them weltering in their blood;
to wander over the field of desolation, and count the number of the dying
and the dead, – are employments which in thesis we may maintain to be
necessary, but which no good man will contemplate with gratulation and
delight. A battle we suppose is won: – thus truth is established, thus the
cause of justice is confirmed! It surely requires no common sagacity to
discern the connection between this immense heap of calamities and the
assertion of truth or the maintenance of justice.

  'Kings, and ministers of state, the real authors of the calamity, sit
unmolested in their cabinet, while those against whom the fury of the
storm is directed are, for the most part, persons who have been tre-
panned into the service, or who are dragged unwillingly from their peaceful homes into the field of battle. A soldier is a man whose business it
is to kill those who never offended him, and who are the innocent martyrs of other men's iniquities. Whatever may become of the abstract
question of the justifiableness of war, it seems impossible that the soldier
should not be a depraved and unnatural being . . .' (Godwin's *Enquirer*,
Essay V).

THE SALE OF HUMAN LIFE

Since tyrants, by the sale of human life,
Heap luxuries to their sensualism, and fame
To their wide-wasting and insatiate pride,
Success has sanctioned to a credulous world
The ruin, the disgrace, the woe of war.
His hosts of blind and unresisting dupes
The despot numbers; from his cabinet
These puppets of his schemes he moves at will,
Even as the slaves by force or famine driven,
Beneath a vulgar master, to perform
A task of cold and brutal drudgery; –
Hardened to hope, insensible to fear,
Scarce living pulleys of a dead machine,
Mere wheels of work and articles of trade,
That grace the proud and noisy pomp of wealth!

The harmony and happiness of man
Yields to the wealth of nations; that which lifts
His nature to the heaven of its pride,
Is bartered for the poison of his soul;
The weight that drags to earth his towering hopes,
Blighting all prospect but of selfish gain,
Withering all passion but of slavish fear,
Extinguishing all free and generous love
Of enterprise and daring, even the pulse
That fancy kindles in the beating heart
To mingle with sensation, it destroys, –
Leaves nothing but the sordid lust of self,
The grovelling hope of interest and gold,
Unqualified, unmingled, unredeemed
Even by hypocrisy. And statesmen boast
Of wealth!

WEALTH: A POWER USURPED BY THE FEW

There is no real wealth but the labour of man. Were the mountains of
gold and the valleys of silver, the world would not be one grain of corn
the richer; no one comfort would be added to the human race. In con-

397

sequence of our consideration for the precious metals, one man is enabled to heap to himself luxuries at the expense of the necessaries of his neighbour; a system admirably fitted to produce all the varieties of disease and crime, which never fail to characterize the two extremes of opulence and penury. A speculator takes pride to himself as the promoter of his country's prosperity, who employs a number of hands in the manufacture of articles avowedly destitute of use, or subservient only to the unhallowed cravings of luxury and ostentation . . . The poor are set to labour, – for what? Not the food for which they famish: not the blankets for want of which their babes are frozen by the cold of their miserable hovels: not those comforts of civilization without which civilized man is far more miserable than the meanest savage; oppressed as he is by all its insidious evils, within the daily and taunting prospect of its innumerable benefits assiduously exhibited before him: no; for the pride of power, for the miserable isolation of pride, for the false pleasures of the hundredth part of society. No greater evidence is afforded of the wide extended and radical mistakes of civilized man than this fact: those arts which are essential to his very being are held in the greatest contempt; employments are lucrative in an inverse ratio to their usefulness: the jeweller, the toyman, the actor gains fame and wealth by the exercise of his useless and ridiculous art; whilst the cultivator of the earth, he without whom society must cease to subsist, struggles through contempt and penury, and perishes by that famine which but for his unceasing exertions would annihilate the rest of mankind.

I will not insult common sense by insisting on the doctrine of the natural equality of man. The question is not concerning its desirableness, but its practicability: so far as it is practicable, it is desirable. That state of human society which approaches nearer to an equal partition of its benefits and evils should . . . be preferred: but so long as we conceive that a wanton expenditure of human labour, not for the necessities, not even for the luxuries of the mass of society, but for the egotism and ostentation of a few of its members, is defensible on the ground of public justice, so long we neglect to approximate to the redemption of the human race.

Labour is required for physical, and leisure for moral improvement: from the former of these advantages the rich, and from the latter the poor, by the inevitable conditions of their respective situations, are precluded. A state which should combine the advantages of both would be subjected to the evils of neither. He that is deficient in firm health, or vigorous intellect, is but half a man: hence it follows that to subject the labouring classes to unnecessary labour is wantonly depriving them of any opportunities of intellectual improvement; and that the rich are heaping up for their own mischief the disease, lassitude, and ennui by which their existence is rendered an intolerable burden.

English reformers exclaim against sinecures, – but the true pension-list is the rent-roll of the landed proprietors: wealth is a power usurped by the few, to compel the many to labour for their benefit. The laws which support this system derive their force from the ignorance and cred-ulity of its victims: they are the result of a conspiracy of the few against the many, who are themselves obliged to purchase this pre-eminence by the loss of all real comfort . . .

ALL THINGS ARE SOLD

All things are sold: the very light of heaven
Is venal; earth's unsparing gifts of love,
The smallest and most despicable things
That lurk in the abysses of the deep,
All objects of our life, even life itself,
And the poor pittance which the laws allow
Of liberty, the fellowship of man,
Those duties which his heart of human love
Should urge him to perform instinctively,
Are bought and sold as in a public mart
Of undisguising selfishness, that sets
On each its price, the stamp-mark of her reign.
Even love is sold . . .

LORD BYRON (1788–1824)   1814

'Windsor Poetics'

WINDSOR POETICS

Lines composed on the occasion of His Royal Highness the Prince Regent being seen standing between the coffins of Henry VIII and Charles I in the Royal Vault at Windsor.

Famed for contemptuous breach of sacred ties,
By headless Charles see heartless Henry lies;

Between them stands another sceptred thing –
It moves, it reigns – in all but name, a king:

Charles to his people, Henry to his wife, –
In him the double tyrant starts to life:
Justice and death have mix'd their dust in vain,
Each royal vampire wakes to life again.
Ah, what can tombs avail! – since these disgorge
The blood and dust of both – to mould a George.

LORD BYRON (1788–1824)   1815 (written 1819)

From *Don Juan*, Canto IX, stanzas 3–6, 9

WELLINGTON: 'THE BEST OF CUT-THROATS'

Though Britain owes (and pays you too) so much,
   Yet Europe doubtless owes you greatly more:
You have repair'd Legitimacy's crutch,
   A prop not quite so certain as before:
The Spaniard, and the French, as well as Dutch,
   Have seen, and felt, how strongly you *restore*;
And Waterloo has made the world your debtor
(I wish your bards would sing it rather better).

You are 'the best of cut-throats': – do not start;
   The phrase is Shakespeare's, and not misapplied:
War's a brain-spattering, wind-pipe-slitting art,
   Unless her cause by right be sanctified.
If you have acted *once* a generous part,
   The world, not the world's masters, will decide,
And I shall be delighted to learn who,
Save you and yours, have gain'd by Waterloo?

I am no flatterer – you've supp'd full of flattery:
   They say you like it too – 'tis no great wonder.
He whose whole life has been assault and battery,
   At last may get a little tired of thunder;
And swallowing eulogy much more than satire, he
   May like being praised for every lucky blunder,

400

Call'd 'Saviour of the Nations' – not yet saved,
And 'Europe's Liberator' – still enslaved.[1]

I've done. Now go and dine from off the plate
  Presented by the Prince of the Brazils,
And send the sentinel before your gate
  A slice or two from your luxurious meals:
He fought, but has not fed so well of late.[2]
  Some hunger, too, they say the people feels: –
There is no doubt that you deserve your ration,
But pray give back a little to the nation.

*

Never had mortal man had such opportunity
  Except Napoleon, or abused it more:
You might have freed fallen Europe from the unity
  Of tyrants, and been blest from shore to shore:
And *now* – what *is* your fame? Shall the Muse tune it ye?
  Now – that the rabble's first vain shouts are o'er?
Go! hear it in your famish'd country's cries!
Behold the world! and curse your victories!

ROBERT OWEN (1771–1858)   1815

From *Observations on the Effect of the Manufacturing System*, in Postgate, ed., *Revolutions from 1789 to 1906*

THE MANUFACTURING SYSTEM

The manufacturing system has already so far extended its influence over the British Empire, as to effect an essential change in the general character of the mass of the people. This alteration is still in rapid progress; and ere long, the comparatively happy simplicity of the agricultural peas-

---

1. Wellington was declared so in Parliament after the battle of Waterloo.
2. *Journal of a Soldier of the 71st Regiment during the War in Spain*: 'I at this time got a post, being for fatigue, with four others. We were sent to break biscuit, and make a mess for Lord Wellington's hounds. I was very hungry, and thought it a good job at the time, as we got our own fill while we broke the biscuit, – a thing I had not got for some days. When thus engaged, the Prodigal Son was never once out of my mind; and I sighed, as I fed the dogs, over my humble situation and my ruined hopes.'

ant will be wholly lost amongst us. It is even now scarcely anywhere to be found without a mixture of those habits which are the offspring of trade, manufactures, and commerce . . .

The inhabitants of every country are trained and formed by its great leading existing circumstances, and the character of the lower orders in Britain is now formed chiefly by circumstances arising from trade, manufactures, and commerce; and the governing principle of trade, manufactures, and commerce is immediate pecuniary gain, to which on the great scale every other is made to give way. All are sedulously trained to buy cheap and to sell dear; and to succeed in this art, the parties must be taught to acquire strong powers of deception; and thus a spirit is generated through every class of traders, destructive of that open, honest sincerity, without which man cannot make others happy, nor enjoy happiness himself . . .

But the effects of this principle of gain, unrestrained, are still more lamentable on the working classes, those who are employed in the operative parts of the manufactures; for most of these branches are more or less unfavourable to the health and morals of adults. Yet parents do not hesitate to sacrifice the well-being of their children by putting them to occupations by which the constitution of their minds and bodies is rendered greatly inferior to what it might and ought to be under a system of common foresight and humanity . . .

In the manufacturing districts it is common for parents to send their children of both sexes at seven or eight years of age, in winter as well as summer, at six o'clock in the morning, sometimes of course in the dark, and occasionally amidst frost and snow, to enter the manufactories, which are often heated to a high temperature, and contain an atmosphere far from being the most favourable to human life, and in which all those employed in them very frequently continue until twelve o'clock at noon, when an hour is allowed for dinner, after which they return to remain, in a majority of cases, till eight o'clock at night . . .

Sonnet, 'Feelings of a Republican on the Fall of Bonaparte', in *Complete Poetical Works*, pp. 526–7

FEELINGS OF A REPUBLICAN ON THE FALL OF BONAPARTE

I hated thee, fallen tyrant! I did groan
To think that a most unambitious slave,
Like thou, shouldst dance and revel on the grave
Of Liberty. Thou mightst have built thy throne
Where it had stood even now: thou didst prefer
A frail and bloody pomp which Time has swept
In fragments towards Oblivion. Massacre,
For this I prayed, would on thy sleep have crept,
Treason and Slavery, Rapine, Fear, and Lust,
And stifled thee, their minister. I know
Too late, since thou and France are in the dust,
That Virtue owns a more eternal foe
Than Force or Fraud: old Custom, legal Crime,
And bloody Faith the foulest birth of Time.

WILLIAM COBBETT (1762–1835)   2 November 1816

From *The Political Register*, in Hollis, ed., *Class and Conflict*, pp. 8–9

TO AN INSULTED WORKING CLASS

Friends and Fellow Countrymen,

Whatever the pride of rank, of riches or of scholarship may have induced some men to believe, or to affect to believe, the real strength and all the resources of a country, ever have sprung and ever must spring, from the *labour* of its people . . . Elegant dresses, superb furniture, stately buildings, fine roads and canals, fleet horses and carriages, numerous and stout ships, warehouses teeming with goods; all these, and many other objects that fall under our view, are so many marks of national wealth and resources. But all these spring from *labour*. Without the Journeyman and the labourer none of them could exist; without the assistance of their hands, the country would be a wilderness, hardly worth the notice of an invader.

As it is the labour of those who toil which makes a country abound in resources, so it is the same class of men, who must, by their arms, secure its safety and uphold its fame . . .

With this correct idea of your own worth in your minds, with what indignation must you hear yourselves called the Populace, the Rabble, the Mob, the Swinish Multitude; and, with what greater indignation, if possible, must you hear the projects of those cool and cruel and insolent men, who, now that you have been, without any fault of your own, brought into a state of misery, propose to narrow the limits of parish relief, to prevent you from marrying in the days of your youth, or to thrust you out to seek your bread in foreign lands, never more to behold your parents or friends? But suppress your indignation until . . . after we have considered the *cause* of your present misery and the measures which have produced that cause.

. . . It is the *enormous amount of the taxes*, which the government compels us to pay for the support of its army, its placemen, its pensioners, etc. and for the payment of the interest of its debt. That this is the *real* cause has been a thousand times proved; and it is now so acknowledged by the creatures of the government themselves . . . The tax-gatherers, do not, indeed, come to *you* and demand money of you; but, there are few articles which you use, in the purchase of which you do not pay a *tax*.

The *remedy* is what we have now to look to, and that remedy consists wholly and solely of such a reform in the Commons', or People's, House of Parliament, as shall give to every payer of *direct taxes* a vote at elections, and as shall cause the Members to be *elected annually* . . .

But this and *all other things*, must be done by a *reformed parliament*. – We must have that *first*, or we shall have nothing good . . .

LORD BYRON (1788–1824)   December 1816

'Song for the Luddites', in *Poetical and Dramatic Works*, I

SONG FOR THE LUDDITES

I

As the Liberty lads o'er the sea
Bought their freedom, and cheaply, with blood,
So we, boys, we

Will *die* fighting, or *live* free,
And down with all kings by King Ludd!

II

When the web that we weave is complete,
And the shuttle exchanged for the sword,
We will fling the winding sheet
O'er the despot at our feet,
And dye it deep in the gore he has pour'd.

III

Though black as his heart its hue,
Since his veins are corrupted to mud,
Yet this is the dew
Which the tree shall renew
Of Liberty, planted by Ludd!

BLACK DWARF   20 August 1817
(ed. Thomas J. Wooler, 1786–1853)

In Hollis, ed., *Class and Conflict*, pp. 32–3

THE MORALITY OF OWENISM

The principal justification of Mr Owen's pretensions are that he has succeeded in *changing*, as he calls it, the moral habits of the persons under
his employment in a manufactory at Lanark, in Scotland. For all the
good he has done in that respect, he deserves the highest thanks. It is
much to be wished, that all who live by the labour of the poor would
pay as much attention to their wants and to their interests as Mr Owen
did to those under his care at Lanark . . .

But it is very amusing to hear Mr Owen talk of *re-moralizing* the *poor*.
Does he not think that the *rich* are a little more in want of re-moralizing;
and particularly that class of them that has contributed to de-moralize
the poor, if they are de-moralized, by supporting measures which have
made them poor, and which now continue them poor and wretched?
. . . Talk of the poor being de-moralized! It is their would-be masters
that create all the evils that afflict the poor, and all the depravity that
pretended philanthropists pretend to regret.

In one point of view Mr Owen's scheme might be productive of some good. Let him abandon the labourer to his own protection; *cease to oppress him*, and the poor man would scorn to hold any fictitious dependence upon the rich. Give him a fair price for his labour, and do not take two-thirds of a depreciated remuneration back from him again in the shape of taxes. Lower the extravagance of the great. Tax those *real luxuries*, enormous fortunes obtained without merit. Reduce the herd of locusts that prey upon the honey of the hive, and think they do the bees a most essential service by robbing them. LET THE POOR ALONE. The working bee can always find a hive: LET THE POOR ALONE. Do not take from them what they can earn, to supply the wants of those who will earn nothing. Do this; and the poor will not want your splendid erections for the cultivation of misery and the subjugation of the mind.

WILLIAM BLAKE (1757–1827)   1804–20

From *Jerusalem*, in *Complete Writings*, pp. 622–3

Blake was writing *Jerusalem*, we have to remember, against the context of the Napoleonic Wars, an era of total European war, enriching the rich and impoverishing the common people. And England (Albion) was suffering under one of the most repressive systems in its history, with laws of the most barbaric kind to protect the privileged and their property and to force the poor off the land and into the factories. This Prophetic Book takes the Theme of the struggle of Contrary States already defined in *Vala* and *Milton* further still, and concerns the quest of Man in the recovery of his lost soul. Los hears the lamentations of Vala for the sons and daughters of Albion, given over to strife and war, with Abstract Philosophy in enmity against Imagination, and begins his great struggle to rebuild Jerusalem, and to regenerate Albion, to keep 'the Divine Vision in time of trouble'.

THE DIVINE VISION IS DARKEND

'Awake! awake O sleeper of the land of shadows, wake! expand!
I am in you and you in me, mutual in love divine:
Fibres of love from man to man thro' Albion's pleasant land.
In all the dark Atlantic vale down from the hills of Surrey
A black water accumulates; return Albion! return!
Thy brethren call thee, and thy fathers and thy sons,
Thy nurses and thy mothers, thy sisters and thy daughters

Weep at thy soul's disease, and the Divine Vision is darkend,
Thy Emanation that was wont to play before thy face,
Beaming forth with her daughters into the Divine bosom:
Where hast thou hidden thy Emanation, lovely Jerusalem,
From the vision and fruition of the Holy one?
I am not a God afar off, I am a brother and friend;
Within your bosoms I reside, and you reside in me:
Lo! we are One, forgiving all Evil, Not seeking recompense.
Ye are my members, O ye sleepers of Beulah, land of shades!'

But the perturbed Man away turns down the valleys dark:
Saying: '*We are not One: we are Many*, thou most simulative
Phantom of the over-heated brain! shadow of immortality!
Seeking to keep my soul a victim to thy Love! which binds
Man, the enemy of man, into deceitful friendships,
Jerusalem is not! her daughters are indefinite:
By demonstration man alone can live, and not by faith.
My mountains are my own, and I will keep them to myself:
The Malvern and the Cheviot, the Wolds, Plinlimmon and
    Snowdon
Are mine: here will I build my Laws of Moral Virtue.
Humanity shall be no more, but war and princedom and victory!'

So spoke Albion in jealous fears, hiding his Emanation
Upon the Thames and Medway, rivers of Beulah, dissembling
His jealousy before the throne divine, darkening, cold!
The banks of the Thames are clouded! the ancient porches of Albion
    are
Darkened! they are drawn thro' unbounded space, scattered upon
The Void in incoherent despair! Cambridge and Oxford and London
Are driven among the starry Wheels, rent away and dissipated
In Chasms and abysses of sorrow, enlarg'd without dimension,
    terrible.
Albion's mountains run with blood, the cries of war and of tumult
Resound into the unbounded night, every Human perfection
Of mountain and river and city are small and wither'd and
    darken'd . . .

SAMUEL BAMFORD (1788–1872)

From *Passages in the Life of a Radical* (1841), in Hollis, ed., *Class and Conflict*, pp. 96–7

As economic unrest grew in the aftermath of the European wars with their crippling cost to the people, and in the context of the oppressive measures taken against factory-workers which brought reports of arming and drilling in the north, the government (already alarmed by the Spa riots in London) suspended Habeas Corpus, and introduced the Gagging Acts, which prohibited all unlicensed public meetings. Bagguley and Drummond were the leaders of the Manchester unemployed who had organized a great 'hunger' march on London, arrested at the send-off meeting in St Peter's Fields, Manchester.

THE PEOPLE DRIVEN UNDERGROUND

Personal liberty not being now secure from one hour to another, many of the leading reformers were induced to quit their homes, and seek concealment where they could obtain it. Those who could muster a few pounds, or had friends to give them a frugal welcome, or had trades with which they could travel, disappeared like swallows at the close of summer, no one knew whither. The single men stayed away altogether; the married ones would steal back at night to their wan-cheeked families, perhaps to divide with them some trifle they had saved during their absence – perhaps to obtain a change of linen or other garment for future concealment – but most of all, as would naturally be the case, to console, and to be consoled by their wives and little ones . . .

But with all precautions, it did sometimes happen that in such moments of mournful joy the father would be seized, chained, and torn from his family before he had time to bless them or to receive their blessings and tears. Such scenes were of frequent occurrence, and have thrown a melancholy retrospection over those days. Private revenge or political differences were gratified by secret and often false information handed to the police. The country was distracted by rumours of treasonable discoveries and apprehensions of the traitors, whose fate was generally predicted to be death or perpetual imprisonment. Bagguley, Johnson, Drummond, and Benbow were already in prison at London; and it was frequently intimated to me, through some very kind relations in law, that I and some of my acquaintances would soon be arrested . . . It seemed as if the sun of freedom were gone down, and a rayless expanse of oppression had finally closed over us. Cobbett, in terror of imprisonment, had fled to America . . . John Knight had disappeared; Pilkington was out of the way somewhere, Bradbury had not yet been heard of; Mitchell moved in a sphere of his own, the extent of which no man knew save himself; and Kay and Fitton were seldom visible beyond the circle of their own village; – whilst to complete our misfortunes, our chapel keeper, in the very tremor of fear, turned the key upon us and declared we should no longer meet in the place.

Our Society, thus homeless, became divided and dismayed; hundreds slunk home to their looms, nor dared to come out, save like owls at nightfall, when they could perhaps steal through bye-paths or behind hedges, or down some clough, to hear the news at the next cottage. Some might be seen chatting with and making themselves agreeable to our declared enemies; but these were few, and always of worthless character. Open meetings thus being suspended, secret ones ensued; they were originated at Manchester, and assembled under various pretexts. Sometimes they were termed 'benefit societies'; sometimes 'botanical meetings'; 'meeting for the relief of the families of imprisoned reformers', or 'of those who had fled the country'; but their real purpose, divulged only to the initiated, was to carry into effect the night attack on Manchester, the attempt at which had before failed for want of arrangement and cooperation.

WILLIAM BLAKE (1757–1827)   1804–20

From *Jerusalem*, in *Complete Writings*, p. 656

Blake's dialectic works on many levels throughout the prophetic books. For him man lives divided in a divided world – 'a little grovelling Root outside of Himself', a divided shadow or Spectre separated from its complement, its Emanation, as Blake calls it; and the task of Los in *Jerusalem* is to rebuild the divided universe, as symbolized in his search for Enitharmon, the shadowy female. And Jerusalem (Albion) is the ultimate embodiment of this quest – which, awakened, celebrates 'the lineaments of Man', the 'Great Harvest and Vintage of the Nations'.

THE OPPRESSORS OF ALBION

The Cities of Albion seek thy face: London groans in pain
From Hill to Hill, and the Thames laments along the Valleys:

The little Villages of Middlesex and Surrey hunger and thirst:
The Twenty-eight Cities of Albion stretch their hands to thee
Because of the Oppressors of Albion in every City and Village.
They mock at the Labourer's limbs: they mock at his starv'd
  Children:
They buy his Daughters that they may have power to sell his Sons:
They compel the Poor to live upon a crust of bread by mild soft arts:
They reduce the Man to want, then give with pomp and ceremony:
The praise of Jehovah is chaunted from lips of hunger and thirst.

SHELLEY (1792–1822)   1817

From *Death of Princess Charlotte*, in *Selected Poetry*, pp. 1012–16

At the time when Shelley wrote this piece, the frustration and anger of the
unemployed and exploited working people of the north against the oppressive
forces of 'law and order' were being encouraged by Oliver, a government spy
posing as a member of the London 'Physical Force Party'. Attempting to provoke
the radicals to take up arms, he succeeded only in the two main centres, Nottingham and the West Riding, where revolutionary feeling had been mounting,
and where there were many secret meetings, meticulously reported by Oliver,
who set traps for the men of Dewsbury (all arrested) and Pentridge. The government was clearly intent on bringing revolt to a head rather than preventing an
armed rising. The Pentridge band, believing they were but one contingent among
many, though in fact virtually alone, were easily suppressed and captured. Thirty-
five were tried for high treason; and of the twenty-three found guilty, eleven were
transported for life, three for fourteen years, and Brandreth, Turner, Ludlam and
Weightman were hanged.

Shelley's indignation in setting the death of a royal princess and the luxury of
her peers against the deaths of these poor working men needs no comment.

MURDERED LIBERTY: THE PENTRIDGE RISING

. . . IX In the manufacturing districts of England discontent and disaf-
fection had prevailed for many years; this was the consequence of that
system of double aristocracy produced by the causes before mentioned.
The manufacturers, the helots of our luxury, are left by this system famished, without affections, without health, without leisure or opportunity
for such instruction as might counteract those habits of turbulence and
dissipation, produced by the precariousness and insecurity of poverty.

410

Here was a ready field for any adventurer who should wish for whatever purpose to incite a few ignorant men to acts of illegal outrage. So soon as it was plainly seen that the demands of the people for a free representation must be conceded if some intimidation and prejudice were not conjured up, a conspiracy of the most horrible atrocity was laid in train. It is impossible to know how far the higher members of the government are involved in the guilt of their infernal agents. It is impossible to know how numerous or how active they have been, or by what false hopes they are yet inflaming the untutored multitude to put their necks under the axe and into the halter. But thus much is known, that so soon as the whole nation lifted up its voice for parliamentary reform, spies were sent forth. These were selected from the most worthless and infamous of mankind, and dispersed among the multitude of famished and illiterate labourers. It was their business if they found no discontent to create it. It was their business to find victims, no matter whether right or wrong. It was their business to produce upon the public an impression, that if any attempt to attain national freedom, or to diminish the burdens of debt and taxation under which we groan, were successful, the starving multitude would rush in, and confound all orders and distinctions, and institutions and laws, in common ruin. The inference with which they were required to arm the ministers was, that despotic power ought to be eternal. To produce this salutary impression, they betrayed some innocent and unsuspecting rustics into a crime whose penalty is a hideous death. A few hungry and ignorant manufacturers seduced by the splendid promises of these remorseless blood-conspirators, collected together in what is called rebellion against the state. All was prepared, and the eighteen dragoons assembled in readiness, no doubt, conducted their astonished victims to that dungeon which they left only to be mangled by the executioner's hand. The cruel instigators of their ruin retired to enjoy the great revenues which they had earned by a life of villainy. The public voice was overpowered by the timid and the selfish, who threw the weight of fear into the scale of public opinion, and parliament confided anew to the executive government those extraordinary powers which may never be laid down, or which may be laid down in blood, or which the regularly constituted assembly of the nation must wrest out of their hands. Our alternatives are a despotism, a revolution, or reform.

x On the 7th of November, Brandreth, Turner, and Ludlam ascended the scaffold. We feel for Brandreth the less, because it seems he killed a man. But recollect who instigated him to the proceedings which led to murder. On the word of a dying man, Brandreth tells us, that 'OLIVER brought him to this' – that, 'but for OLIVER, he would not have been there.'

See, too, Ludlam and Turner, with their sons and brothers, and sisters, how they kneel together in a dreadful agony of prayer. Hell is before their eyes, and they shudder and feel sick with fear, lest some unrepented or some wilful sin should seal their doom in everlasting fire. With that dreadful penalty before their eyes – with that tremendous sanction for the truth of all he spoke, Turner exclaimed loudly and distinctly, *while the executioner was putting the rope round his neck*, 'THIS IS ALL OLIVER AND THE GOVERNMENT.' What more he might have said we know not, because the chaplain prevented any further observations. Troops of horse, with keen and glittering swords, hemmed in the multitudes collected to witness this abominable exhibition. 'When the stroke of the axe was heard, there was a burst of horror from the crowd. The instant the head was exhibited, there was a tremendous shriek set up, and the multitude ran violently in all directions, as if under the impulse of sudden frenzy. Those who resumed their stations, groaned and hooted.'[1] It is a national calamity, that we endure men to rule over us, who sanction for whatever ends a conspiracy which is to arrive at its purpose through such a frightful pouring forth of human blood and agony. But when that purpose is to trample upon our rights and liberties for ever, to present to us the alternatives of anarchy and oppression, and triumph when the astonished nation accepts the latter at their hands, to maintain a vast standing army, and add, year by year, to a public debt, which, already, they know, cannot be discharged; and which, when the delusion that supports it fails, will produce as much misery and confusion through all classes of society as it has continued to produce of famine and degradation to the undefended poor; to imprison and calumniate those who may offend them, at will; when this, if not the purpose, is the effect of that conspiracy, how ought we not to mourn?

XI Mourn then People of England. Clothe yourselves in solemn black. Let the bells be tolled. Think of mortality and change. Shroud yourselves in solitude and the gloom of sacred sorrow. Spare no symbol of universal grief. Weep – mourn – lament. Fill the great City – fill the boundless fields, with lamentation and the echo of groans. A beautiful Princess is dead: – she who should have been the Queen of her beloved nation, and whose posterity should have ruled it for ever. She loved the domestic affections, and cherished arts which adorn, and valour which defends. She was amiable and would have become wise, but she was young, and in the flower of youth the despoiler came. LIBERTY is dead. Slave! I charge thee disturb not the depth and solemnity of our grief by any

1. *The Examiner*, 9 November 1817.

412

meaner sorrow. If One has died who was like her that should have ruled over this land, like Liberty, young, innocent, and lovely, know that the power through which that one perished was God, and that it was a private grief. But *man* has murdered Liberty, and whilst the life was ebbing from its wound, there descended on the heads and on the hearts of every human thing, the sympathy of an universal blast and curse. Fetters heavier than iron weigh upon us, because they bind our souls. We move about in a dungeon more pestilential than damp and narrow walls, because the earth is its floor and the heavens are its roof. Let us follow the corpse of British Liberty slowly and reverentially to its tomb: and if some glorious Phantom should appear, and make its throne of broken swords and sceptres and royal crowns trampled in the dust, let us say that the Spirit of Liberty has arisen from its grave and left all that was gross and mortal there, and kneel down and worship it as our Queen.

WILLIAM BLAKE (1757–1827) 1804–20

From *Jerusalem*, in *Complete Writings*, pp. 699–700, 714

THE ARTS OF DEATH IN ALBION

Then left the Sons of Urizen the plow and harrow, the loom,
The hammer and the chisel and the rule and compasses; from London
  fleeing,
They forg'd the sword on Cheviot, the chariot of war and the battle-
  ax,
The trumpet fitted to mortal battle, and the flute of summer in
  Annandale;
And all the Arts of Life they chang'd into the Arts of Death in
  Albion.
The hour-glass contemn'd because its simple workmanship
Was like the workmanship of the plowman, and the water wheel
That raises water into cisterns, broken and burn'd with fire
Because its workmanship was like the workmanship of the shepherd;
And in their stead, intricate wheels invented, wheel without wheel,
To perplex youth in their outgoings and to bind to labours in Albion
Of day and night the myriads of eternity: that they may grind
And polish brass and iron hour after hour, laborious task,
Kept ignorant of its use: that they might spend the days of wisdom
In sorrowful drudgery to obtain a scanty pittance of bread,

In ignorance to view a small portion and think that All,
And call it Demonstration, blind to all the simple rules of life.

ESTRANGEMENT

The Spectre is the Reasoning Power in Man, and when separated
From Imagination and closing itself as in steel in a Ratio
Of the Things of Memory, It thence frames Laws and Moralities
To destroy Imagination, the Divine Body, by Martyrdoms and Wars.

SHELLEY (1792–1822)   Published 10 January 1818

From the Preface to *The Revolt of Islam*, in *Complete Poetical Works*,
pp. 33–4

THE NECESSITY OF HOPE

The panic which, like an epidemic transport, seized upon all classes of
men during the excesses consequent upon the French Revolution, is
gradually giving place to sanity. It has ceased to be believed that whole
generations of mankind ought to consign themselves to a hopeless inheritance of ignorance and misery, because a nation of men who had been
dupes and slaves for centuries were incapable of conducting themselves
with the wisdom and tranquillity of freemen so soon as some of their
fetters were partially loosened. That their conduct could not have been
marked by any other characters than ferocity and thoughtlessness is the
historical fact from which liberty derives all its recommendations, and
falsehood the worst features of its deformity. There is a reflux in the tide
of human things which bears the shipwrecked hopes of men into a secure
haven after the storms are past. Methinks, those who now live have survived an age of despair.

The French Revolution may be considered as one of those manifestations of a general state of feeling among civilized mankind produced
by a defect of correspondence between the knowledge existing in society
and the improvement or gradual abolition of political institutions. The
year 1788 may be assumed as the epoch of one of the most important
crises produced by this feeling. The sympathies connected with that
event extended to every bosom. The most generous and amiable natures
were those which participated the most extensively in these sympathies.

414

But such a degree of unmingled good was expected as it was impossible to realize. If the Revolution had been in every respect prosperous, then misrule and superstition would lose half their claims to our abhorrence, as fetters which the captive can unlock with the slightest motion of his fingers, and which do not eat with poisonous rust into the soul. The revulsion occasioned by the atrocities of the demagogues, and the re-establishment of successive tyrannies in France, was terrible, and felt in the remotest corners of the civilized world. Could they listen to the plea of reason who had groaned under the calamities of a social state according to the provisions of which one man riots in luxury whilst another famishes for want of bread? Can he who the day before was a trampled slave suddenly become liberal-minded, forbearing, and independent? This is the consequence of the habits of a state of society to be produced by resolute perseverance and indefatigable hope, and long-suffering and long-believing courage, and the systematic efforts of generations of men of intellect and virtue. Such is the lesson which experience teaches now. But, on the first reverses of hope in the progress of French liberty, the sanguine eagerness for good overleaped the solution of these questions, and for a time extinguished itself in the unexpectedness of their result. Thus, many of the most ardent and tender-hearted of the worshippers of public good have been morally ruined by what a partial glimpse of the events they deplored appeared to show as the melancholy desolation of all their cherished hopes. Hence gloom and misanthropy have become the characteristics of the age in which we live, the solace of a disappointment that unconsciously finds relief only in the wilful exaggeration of its own despair. This influence has tainted the literature of the age with the hopelessness of the minds from which it flows. Metaphysics, and inquiries into moral and political science, have become little else than vain attempts to revive exploded superstitions, or sophisms like those of Mr Malthus, calculated to lull the oppressors of mankind into a security of everlasting triumph. Our works of fiction and poetry have been overshadowed by the same infectious gloom. But mankind appear to me to be emerging from their trance. I am aware, methinks, of a slow, gradual, silent change . . .

LORD BYRON
(1788–1824)

19 September 1818
(Dedication and
First Canto completed)

Don Juan, Dedication (Stanzas 10–15)

THE TYRANT-HATER MILTON; THE INTELLECTUAL
EUNUCH CASTLEREAGH

If fallen in evil days on evil tongues,
    Milton appealed to the avenger, Time,
If Time, the avenger, execrates his wrongs
    And makes the word *Miltonic* mean *sublime*,
He deigned not to belie his soul in songs,
    Nor turn his very talent to a crime.
He did not loathe the sire to laud the son,
But closed the tyrant-hater he begun.

Think'st thou, could he, the blind old man, arise
    Like Samuel from the grave to freeze once more
The blood of monarchs with his prophecies,
    Or be alive again – again all hoar
With time and trials, and those helpless eyes
    And heartless daughters – worn and pale and poor,
Would he adore a sultan? He obey
The intellectual eunuch Castlereagh?

Cold-blooded, smooth-faced, placid miscreant!
    Dabbling its sleek young hands in Erin's gore,
And thus for wider carnage taught to pant,
    Transferred to gorge upon a sister shore,
The vulgarest tool that tyranny could want,
    With just enough of talent and no more,
To lengthen fetters by another fixed
And offer poison long already mixed.

An orator of such set trash of phrase,
    Ineffably, legitimately vile,
That even its grossest flatterers dare not praise,
    Nor foes – all nations – condescend to smile.
Not even a sprightly blunder's spark can blaze
    From that Ixion's grindstone's ceaseless toil,

That turns and turns to give the world a notion
Of endless torments and perpetual motion.

A bungler even in its disgusting trade,
　　And botching, patching, leaving still behind
Something of which its masters are afraid,
　　States to be curbed and thoughts to be confined,
Conspiracy or congress to be made,
　　Cobbling at manacles for all mankind,
A tinkering slave-maker, who mends old chains,
With God and man's abhorrence for its gains.

JAMES NORRIS, JP, TO VISCOUNT SIDMOUTH
Manchester, 29 July 1818

In Aspinall, ed., *Early English Trade Unions*, p. 257

THE POLITICIZATION OF DISTRESS

I am very sorry to inform your Lordship that from all I can learn, Messrs Drummond, Bagguley, Ogden, Knight, and in short, all the men who disturbed the public peace last year, have been most active for several months past in disseminating amongst the lower orders at meetings convened for the purpose in the different lesser towns in the neighbourhood the most poisonous and alarming sentiments with respect to the government of the country, and have continually inculcated the idea of a general rising, and although I do not by any means think that the system of turning out in the different trades is connected with this idea, or that the sentiment itself has taken root in the minds of the mass of the population, yet I am disposed to think that this idea gains ground and that in consequence the working classes have become not only more pertinacious but more insolent in their demands and demeanour, particularly with reference to the spinners who have no reason on earth to ask an advance of wages except that they think it is one way of coming at the property of their employers. Several inflammatory handbills have been addressed to the public from the press of Ogden . . .

They are certainly much bolder grown than they were last year, and if they can avail themselves of the present temper of the working people to throw this populous district into disorder, and I might, I think, truly add, rebellion, they certainly will attempt it. The opportunity is but too favourable, but I am not prepared to add that I think their plan is at all organized at present. The impression on the minds of a number of our most respectable merchants, etc., is that an attempt of this sort will certainly ultimately take place, and I trust whenever it does, we shall be prepared to meet it. Most undoubtedly, if these people continue to travel about the country and disseminate the principle alluded to, it must in the end gain considerable strength in the public mind and feeling . . .

WILLIAM BLAKE (1757–1827)   1804–20

From *Jerusalem*, in *Complete Writings*, pp. 737–8

THESE FIENDS OF RIGHTEOUSNESS

These beautiful Witchcrafts of Albion are gratified by Cruelty.
It is easier to forgive an Enemy than to forgive a Friend.
The man who permits you to injure him deserves your vengeance:
He also will receive it; go Spectre! obey my most secret desire
Which thou knowest without my speaking. Go to these Fiends of
   Righteousness,
Tell them to obey their Humanities and not pretend Holiness
When they are murderers: as far as my Hammer and Anvil permit.
Go, tell them that the worship of God is honouring his gifts
In other men: and loving the greatest men best, each according
To his Genius: which is the Holy Ghost in Man; there is no other
God than that God who is the Intellectual fountain of Humanity.
He who envies or calumniates, which is murder and cruelty,
Murders the Holy-one. Go, tell them this, and overthrow their cup,
Their bread, their altar-table, their incense and their oath,
Their marriage and their baptism, their burial and consecration.
I have tried to make friends by corporeal gifts but have only
Made enemies. I never made friends but by spiritual gifts,
By severe contentions of friendship and the burning fire of thought.
He who would see the Divinity must see him in his Children,
One first, in friendship and love, then a Divine Family, and in the
   midst
Jesus will appear; so he who wishes to see a Vision, a perfect Whole,
Must see it in its Minute Particulars, Organized, and not as thou,
O Fiend of Righteousness, pretendest; thine is a Disorganized

And snowy cloud, brooder of tempests and destructive War.
You smile with pomp and rigour, you talk of benevolence and virtue;
I act with benevolence and Virtue and get murdered time after time.
You accumulate Particulars and murder by analysing, that you
May take the aggregate, and you call the aggregate Moral Law,
And you call that swelled and bloated Form a Minute Particular;
But General Forms have their vitality in Particulars, and every
Particular is a Man, a Divine Member of the Divine Jesus.

BLACK DWARF
Hull, 20 July 1818
(ed. Thomas J. Wooler, 1786–1853)

The Political Protestants, in Hollis, ed., *Class and Conflict*, pp. 97–8

OUR PLUNDERED AND INSULTED COUNTRY

We, the Members of this Institution, wishing not to invade the rights of any man, or set of men, are at the same time determined not to consent to the invasion of our own rights. Therefore, we do most solemnly protest against the scandalous, wicked, and treasonable influence which the Borough Merchants have established in the People's House of Commons. Being firmly convinced, that if such corrupt and hateful influence had not existed, which has operated to the total subjugation of our rights in that House, and converted it into a perfect mockery of representation, our unfortunate country would not have been cursed with a twenty-five years' war – with a thousand millions of debt – with seventy millions of annual taxes – with ruined manufactories and commerce – with a standing army of one hundred and forty thousand men kept up in time of peace – with two millions of paupers, and twelve millions of annual Poor Rates – a Corn Bill, to prevent the people of England eating cheap bread; and thousands of British subjects perishing by hunger, and many thousands more escaping to America, to avoid such horrid misery! – A troop of Spies and Informers sent out to persuade a set of poor men who were but half fed, half clad, and consequently half mad, to commit acts of outrage, that they might have the advantage of hanging them! – With Gagging Bills – Dungeon Bills – Imprisonment without trial; – and lastly, an infamous Bill of Indemnity, to protect our seat-selling tyrants from being brought to justice for all their satanic deeds, these are the fruits of the Borough Mongering influence!

We, bitterly lamenting the condition of our plundered and insulted

Country, have resolved to unite ourselves under the denomination of POLITICAL PROTESTANTS; for the purpose of sincerely protesting against the mockery of our indisputable right to a real Representation; and to use every means in our power, which are just and lawful, to rescue the House of Commons from the all-devouring influence of the Borough Merchants, and restore it to the people, agreeable to Magna Charta, and the spirit of the Constitution; and that nothing shall ever cause us to cease in our exertions, until we are fully and fairly represented in the People's House . . .

SAMUEL BAMFORD (1788–1872)   16 August 1819

From *Passages in the Life of a Radical* (1841), pp. 149–54 passim

THE MORNING OF PETERLOO

By eight o'clock on the morning of Monday, the 16th of August 1819, the whole town of Middleton might be said to be on the alert . . . First were selected twelve of the most comely and decent-looking youths, who were placed in two rows of six each, with each a branch of laurel held presented in his hand as a token of amity and peace; then followed the men of several districts in fives, then the band of music, an excellent one . . . Our whole column, with the Rochdale people, would probably consist of six thousand men. At our head were a hundred or two of women, mostly young wives and mine own was amongst them. A hundred or so of our handsomest girls, sweethearts to the lads who were with us, danced to the music or sung snatches of popular songs . . .

At Newtown we were welcomed with open arms by the poor Irish weavers who came out in their best drapery . . . We thanked them by the band striking up 'St Patrick's Day in the Morning' . . . we wheeled quickly and steadily into Peter Street and soon approached a wide unbuilt space occupied by an immense multitude which opened and received us with loud cheers. We walked into that chasm of human beings . . .

EVIDENCE OF J.B. SMITH AND OF REV. E. STANLEY

16 August 1819

In Bruton, ed., *Three Accounts of Peterloo*; quoted in Hollis, ed., *Class and Conflict*, pp. 99–100

As soon as Henry Hunt (1773–1835) rose to address an orderly crowd of some 80,000 people at a political reform meeting in St Peter's Fields, Manchester, on 16 August 1819, local magistrates sent in the yeomanry to arrest him. These yeoman troops also attempted to seize 'revolutionary' banners carried by the crowd. Cavalry were sent into the ensuing mêlée with drawn swords, and 11 people were killed, 400 injured, including a hundred women and children. And with 161 sabre wounds among the injuries, it really was a massacre. Hunt was sentenced to two years' imprisonment; the Manchester magistrates received a letter of congratulation from the Home Secretary, Viscount Sidmouth.

THE PETERLOO MASSACRE

It seemed to be a gala day with the country people who were mostly dressed in their best and brought with them their wives, and I saw boys and girls taking their father's hand in the procession . . . At length Hunt made his appearance in an open barouche drawn by two horses, and a woman dressed in white sitting on the box. On their reaching the hustings which were prepared for the orator, he was received with enthusiastic applause; the waving of hats and flags; the blowing of trumpets; and the playing of music. Hunt stepped on to the hustings, and was again cheered by the vast assemblage. He began to address them . . . About this time there was an alarm among the women and children near the place where I stood, and I could also see a part of the crowd in motion towards the Deansgate side, but I thought it a false alarm, as many returned again and joined in the huzzas of the crowd. A second alarm arose, and I heard the sound of a horn, and immediately the Manchester Yeomanry appeared . . . I heard the order to form three deep, and then the order to march. The trumpeter led the way and galloped towards the hustings, followed by the yeomanry . . .

. . . Their sabres glistened in the air, and on they went, direct for the hustings . . . As the cavalry approached the dense mass of people, they used their utmost efforts to escape, but so closely were they pressed in opposite directions by the soldiers, the special constables, the position of the hustings, and their own immense numbers, that immediate escape was impossible . . .

On their arrival at the hustings a scene of dreadful confusion ensued. The orators fell or were forced off the scaffold in quick succession; fortunately for them, the stage being rather elevated, they were in great degree beyond the reach of the many swords which gleamed around them. Hunt fell – or threw himself – among the constables, and was driven or dragged, as fast as possible, down the avenue which communicated with the magistrate's house; his associates were hurried after him in a similar manner. By this time so much dust had arisen that no accurate account can be given of what further took place at that particular spot. The square was not covered with the flying multitude; though still in parts the banners and caps of liberty were surrounded by groups. The Manchester Yeomanry had already taken possession of the hustings, when the Cheshire Yeomanry entered on my left in excellent order, and formed in the rear of the hustings.

The Fifteenth Dragoons appeared nearly at the same moment, and paused rather than halted on our left, parallel to the row of houses. They then pressed forward, crossing the avenue of constables, which opened to let them through, and bent their course towards the Manchester Yeomanry. The people were now in a state of utter rout and confusion, leaving the ground strewed with hats and shoes, and hundreds were thrown down in the attempt to escape. The cavalry were hurrying about in all directions, completing the work of dispersion . . . I saw nothing that gave me an idea of resistance, except in one or two spots where they showed some disinclination to abandon the banners; these impulses, however, were but momentary, and banner after banner fell into the hands of the military power . . .

During the whole of this confusion, heightened at its close by the rattle of some artillery crossing the square, shrieks were heard in all directions, and as the crowd of people dispersed, the effects of the conflict became visible. Some were seen bleeding on the ground and unable to rise; others, less seriously injured but faint with the loss of blood, were retiring slowly or leaning on others for support . . . The whole of this extraordinary scene was the work of a few minutes.

SHELLEY (1792–1822)

The Mask of Anarchy, ll. 1–37, 213–302, 368–76, in *Complete Poetical Works*, pp. 338–44

This poem was written in Italy as an immediate and passionate response to the Peterloo Massacre (16 August 1819); and it is significant that here (as in *The Revolt of Islam*) its central voice, speaking of Hope and Freedom for mankind, is a woman's. At a time when half the human race had no public voice, Shelley believed that women were the true source of creative change in society, and that so long as 'Woman as the bond-slave dwells/ Of man, a slave', life must remain 'poisoned in its wells'.

THE TRIUMPH OF ANARCHY

As I lay asleep in Italy
There came a voice from over the Sea,
And with great power it forth led me
To walk in the visions of Poesy.

I met Murder on the way –
He had a mask like Castlereagh –
Very smooth he looked, yet grim;
Seven blood-hounds followed him;

All were fat; and well they might
Be in admirable plight,
For one by one, and two by two,
He tossed them human hearts to chew
Which from his wide cloak he drew.

Next came Fraud, and he had on,
Like Eldon, an ermined gown;
His big tears, for he wept well,
Turned to millstones as they fell.

And the little children, who
Round his feet played to and fro,
Thinking every tear a gem,
Had their brains knocked out by them.

Clothed with the Bible, as with light,
And the shadows of the night,

Like Sidmouth, next, Hypocrisy
On a crocodile rode by.

And many more Destructions played
In this ghastly masquerade,
All disguised, even to the eyes,
Like Bishops, lawyers, peers, and spies.

Last came Anarchy: he rode
On a white horse, splashed with blood;
He was pale even to the lips,
Like Death in the Apocalypse.

And he wore a kingly crown;
And in his grasp a sceptre shone;
On his brow this mark I saw –
'I AM GOD, AND KING, AND LAW!'

★

THE CALL TO FREEDOM

What art thou Freedom? O! could slaves
Answer from their living graves
This demand – tyrants would flee
Like a dream's dim imagery:

Thou art not, as imposters say,
A shadow soon to pass away,
A superstition and a name
Echoing from the cave of Fame.

For the labourer thou art bread,
And a comely table spread
From his daily labour come
In a neat and happy home.

Thou art clothes, and fire, and food
For the trampled multitude –
No – in countries that are free
Such starvation cannot be
As in England now we see.

To the rich thou art a check,
When his foot is on the neck

Of his victim, thou dost make
That he treads upon a snake.

Thou art Justice – ne'er for gold
May thy righteous laws be sold
As laws are in England – thou
Shield'st alike the high and low.

Thou art Wisdom – Freemen never
Dream that God will damn for ever
All who think those things untrue
Of which Priests make such ado.

Thou art Peace – never by thee
Would blood and treasure wasted be
As tyrants wasted them, when all
Leagued to quench thy flame in Gaul.

What if English toil and blood
Was poured forth, even as a flood?
It availed, Oh, Liberty,
To dim, but not extinguish thee.

Thou art Love – the rich have kissed
Thy feet, and like him following Christ,
Give their substance to the free
And through the rough world follow thee.

Or turn their wealth to arms, and make
War for thy beloved sake
On wealth, and war, and fraud – whence they
Drew the power which is their prey.

Science, Poetry, and Thought
Are thy lamps; they make the lot
Of the dwellers in a cot
So serene, they curse it not.

Spirit, Patience, Gentleness,
All that can adorn and bless
Art thou – let deeds, not words, express
Thine exceeding loveliness.

Let a great Assembly be
Of the fearless and the free

On some spot of English ground
Where the plains stretch wide around.

Let the blue sky overhead,
The green earth on which ye tread,
All that must eternal be
Witness the solemnity.

From the corners uttermost
Of the bounds of English coast;
From every hut, village, and town
Where those who live and suffer moan
For others' misery or their own,

From the workhouse and the prison
Where pale as corpses newly risen,
Women, children, young and old
Groan for pain, and weep for cold –

From the haunts of daily life
Where is waged the daily strife
With common wants and common cares
Which sows the human heart with tares –

Lastly from the palaces
Where the murmur of distress
Echoes, like the distant sound
Of a wind alive around

Those prison halls of wealth and fashion,
Where some few feel such compassion
For those who groan, and toil, and wail
As must make their brethren pale –

Ye who suffer woes untold,
Or to feel, or to behold
Your lost country bought and sold
With a price of blood and gold –

Let a vast assembly be,
And with great solemnity
Declare with measured words that ye
Are, as God has made ye, free –

*

And these words shall then become

Like Oppression's thundered doom
Ringing through each heart and brain,
Heard again – again – again –

Rise like Lions after slumber
In unvanquishable number –
Shake your chains to earth like dew
Which in sleep had fallen on you –
Ye are many – they are few.

WILLIAM HAZLITT (1778–1830)   1819

From *The Spirit of the Age* (1825), pp. 240–42

Lords Liverpool, Sidmouth, Castlereagh and Eldon were the executives of a ruling class at once contemptuous of constitutional rights and cruelly determined to stamp out all signs of dissent. For Eldon, Peterloo 'was an overt act of treason', and he saw ahead 'a shocking choice between military government and anarchy'; though many would have agreed with Shelley that these men were themselves the perpetrators of disorder, the anarchy of the rich.

FOR GOD AND KING AND LAW: LORD CHANCELLOR ELDON

There has been no stretch of power attempted in his time that he has not seconded: no existing abuse so odious or absurd, that he has not sanctioned it. He has gone the whole length of the most unpopular designs of Ministers. When the heavy artillery of interest, power, and prejudice is brought into the field, the paper pellets of the brain go for nothing; his labyrinth of nice, lady-like doubts explodes like a mine of gunpowder. The Chancellor may weigh and palter; the courtier is decided, the politician is firm, and riveted to his place in the Cabinet.

On all the great questions that have divided party opinion or agitated the public mind, the Chancellor has been found uniformly and without a single exception on the side of prerogative and power, and against every proposal for the advancement of freedom. He was a strenuous supporter of the wars and coalitions against the principles of liberty abroad; he has been equally zealous in urging or defending every act and infringement of the Constitution for abridging it at home. He at the same time opposes every amelioration of the penal laws, on the alleged ground of his abhor-

427

rence of even the shadow of innovation: he has studiously set his face against Catholic emancipation; he laboured hard in his vocation to prevent the abolition of the Slave Trade; he was Attorney-General in the trials for High Treason in 1794, and the other day, in giving his opinion on the Queen's Trial, shed tears and protested his innocence before God!

This was natural and to be expected; but on all occasions he is to be found at his post, true to the call of prejudice, of power, to the will of others and to his own interest. In the whole of his public career, and with all the goodness of his disposition, he has not shown 'so small a drop of pity as a wren's eye'. He seems to be on his guard against every thing liberal and humane as his weak side. Others relax in their obsequiousness either from satiety or disgust, or a hankering after popularity, or a wish to be thought above narrow prejudices. The Lord Chancellor alone is fixed and immovable. Is it want of understanding or of principle? No, it is want of imagination, a phlegmatic habit, an excess of false complaisance and good-nature. He signs a warrant in Council, devoting ten thousand men to an untimely death with steady nerves. Is it that he is cruel and unfeeling? No; but he thinks neither of their sufferings nor their cries; he sees only the gracious smile, the ready hand stretched out to thank him for his compliance with the dictates of rooted hate. He dooms a Continent to slavery. Is it that he is a tyrant or an enemy to the human race? No! but he cannot find in his heart to resist the commands or to give pain to a kind and generous benefactor.

Common sense and justice are little better than vague terms to him; he acts upon his immediate feelings and least irksome impulses. The King's hand is velvet to the touch; the Woolsack is a seat of honour and profit! That is all he knows about the matter. As to abstract metaphysical calculations, the ox that stands staring at the corner of the street troubles his head as much about them as he does: yet this last is a very good sort of animal with no harm or malice in him, unless he is goaded on to mischief; and then it is necessary to keep out of his way, or warn others against him!

SHELLEY (1792–1822)

England in 1819, in *Complete Poetical Works*, pp. 574–5

ENGLAND IN 1819

An old, mad, blind, despised, and dying king, –
Princes, the dregs of their dull race, who flow
Through public scorn – mud from a muddy spring –
Rulers who neither see, nor feel, nor know,
But leech-like to their fainting country cling,
Till they drop, blind in blood, without a blow, –
A people starved and stabbed in the untilled field, –
An army, which liberticide and prey
Make as a two-edged sword to all who wield, –
Golden and sanguine laws which tempt and slay;
Religion Christless, Godless – a book sealed;
A Senate, – Time's worst statute unrepealed, –
Are graves, from which a glorious Phantom may
Burn, to illumine our tempestuous day.

SHELLEY (1792–1822)   Florence, October 1819

From *Peter Bell the Third*, in *Complete Poetical Works*, pp. 350–52

A skit by John Hamilton Reynolds called 'Peter Bell, a Lyrical Ballad', appeared
a few days before Wordsworth's 'Peter Bell, a Tale'; and Shelley wrote his poem
after reading reviews in Leigh Hunt's *Examiner* of these two works. Without
intending any personal criticism of Wordsworth, a poet he greatly admired, Shelley nevertheless conceived his satire in terms of an imaginary 'great poet' quitting,
as his wife Mary put it in her Note, 'the glorious calling of discovering and
announcing the beautiful and good, to support and propagate ignorant prejudices
and pernicious errors; imparting to the unenlightened, not that ardour for truth
and spirit of toleration which Shelley looked on as the sources of the moral
improvement and happiness of mankind, but false and injurious opinions, that
evil was good, and that ignorance and force were the best allies of purity and
virtue'. The poem, in other words, is an attack upon the reactionary social conventions of his age and the repressive powers of the English government, bent on
crushing the people and depriving them of their rights by force, those 'institutes
and laws hallowed by time' which imposed the Factory Laws, the Corn Laws, the
Acts of Sedition and the Poor Laws, and had turned even poets like Wordsworth
into supporters of the system.

HELL IS A CITY MUCH LIKE LONDON

Hell is a city much like London –
    A populous and smoky city;
There are all sorts of people undone;
And there is little or no fun done;
    Small justice shown, and still less pity.

There is a Castles, and a Canning,
    A Cobbett, and a Castlereagh;
All sorts of caitiff corpses planning
All sorts of cozening for trepanning
    Corpses less corrupt than they.

There is a : : :, who has lost
    His wits, or sold them, none knows which;
He walks about a double ghost,
And though as thin as Fraud almost –
    Ever grows more grim and rich.

There is a Chancery Court; a King;
    A manufacturing mob; a set
Of thieves who by themselves are sent
Similar thieves to represent;
    An army; and a public debt.

Which last is a scheme of paper money,
    And means, being interpreted,
'Bees, keep your wax – give us the honey,
And we will plant, while skies are sunny,
    Flowers, which in winter serve instead.'

There is a great talk of revolution –
    And a great chance of despotism –
German soldiers – camps – confusion –
Tumults – lotteries – rage – delusion –
    Gin – suicide – and methodism;

Taxes too, on wine and bread,
    And meat, and beer, and tea, and cheese,
From which those patriots pure are fed,
Who gorge before they reel to bed
    The tenfold essence of all these.

There are mincing women, mewing,
   (Like cats, who *amant miseri*,)
Of their own virtue, and pursuing
Their gentler sisters to that ruin,
   Without which – what were chastity?

Lawyers – judges – old hobnobbers
   Are there – bailiffs – chancellors –
Bishops – great and little robbers –
Rhymsters – pamphleteers – stock-jobbers –
   Men of glory in the wars, –

Things whose trade is, over ladies
   To lean, and flirt, and stare, and simper,
Till all that is divine in woman
Grows cruel, courteous, smooth, inhuman,
   Crucified 'twixt a smile and whimper.

Thrusting, toiling, wailing, moiling,
   Frowning, preaching – such a riot!
Each with never-ceasing labour,
Whilst he thinks he cheats his neighbour,
   Cheating his own heart of quiet.

And all these meet at levees; –
   Dinners convivial and political; –
Suppers of epic poets; – teas,
Where small talk dies in agonies; –
   Breakfasts professional and critical;

Lunches and snacks so aldermanic
   That one would furnish forth ten dinners,
Where reigns a Cretan-tongued panic,
Lest news Russ, Dutch, or Alemannic
   Should make some losers, and some winners; –

At conversazioni – balls –
   Conventicles – and drawing rooms –
Courts of law – committees – calls
Of a morning – clubs – bookstalls –
   Churches – masquerades – and tombs.

And this is Hell – and in this smother
   All are damnable and damned;

Each one damning, damns the other;
They are damned by one another,
　By none other are they damned.

WILLIAM HONE (1780–1842)　　　December 1819

From *The Political House That Jack Built*, in Rickword, ed., *Radical Squibs*, pp. 46–7

From the moment he began publishing in 1815, Hone 'proclaimed a political stance of unqualified hostility to the measures, policies and principles of the Government', as Edgell Rickword observes. Brought up in a dissenting household, he had been early nourished on such writings as the *Pilgrim's Progress* and *The Trial of John Lilburne*, and became a member of the London Corresponding Society at sixteen. He was three times tried and acquitted of blasphemous libel, but this did not silence him, for he was at his most active afterwards, between 1819 and 1822, and *The Political House* itself ran into fifty-two editions in three months.

THE PEOPLE

'Portentous, unexampled, unexplain'd',
　　　　What man seeing this,
And having human feelings, does not blush,
And hang his head, to think himself a man?
　　　　I cannot rest
A silent witness of the headlong rage,
Or heedless folly, by which thousands die –
Bleed gold for ministers to sport away.
　　　　　　　William Cowper, 'The Task'

These are THE PEOPLE
　　　　all tatter'd and torn,
Who curse the day
　　　　wherein they were born,
On account of Taxation
　　　　too great to be borne,
And pray for relief,
　　　　from night to morn;

432

Who, in vain, Petition
                    in every form,
Who, peaceably Meeting
                    to ask for Reform,
Were sabred by Yeomanry Cavalry,
                    who,
Were thank'd by THE MAN,
                    all shaven and shorn,
All cover'd with Orders –
                    and all forlorn;
THE DANDY OF SIXTY,
                    who bows with a grace,
And has *taste* in wigs, collars,
                    cuirasses, and lace;
Who, to tricksters, and fools,
                    leaves the State and its treasure,
And when Britain's in tears,
                    sails about at his pleasure;
Who spurn'd from his presence
                    the Friends of his youth,
And now has not one
                    who will tell him the truth;
Who took to his counsels, in evil hour,
The Friends to the Reasons of lawless Power,
That back the Public Informer, who
Would put down the *Thing*, that, in spite of new Acts,
And attempts to restrain it, by Soldiers or Tax,
Will *poison* the Vermin, that plunder the Wealth,
That lay in the House, that Jack built.

SHELLEY (1792–1822)   Autumn 1821

From *Hellas*, The Preface, in *Complete Poetical Works*, p. 448

Shelley wrote *Hellas* in response to the beginnings of the Greek War of Independence – an unsuccessful revolt against the Turks in the Danubian Principalities and a later insurrection in the Morea. 'It is unquestionable,' Shelley observes in his Preface, 'that actions of the most exalted courage have been performed by the Greeks', and his sympathy for their cause is quickened by a deep sense of community with Greek culture and Greek history. 'The modern Greek,' as he says, 'is the descendant of those glorious beings whom the imagination almost refuses to figure to itself as belonging to our kind, and he inherits much of their sensibility, their rapidity of conception, their enthusiasm, and their courage.'

THE OPPRESSED AGAINST THE OPPRESSORS

Should the English people ever become free, they will reflect upon the part which those who presume to represent their will have played in the great drama of the revival of liberty, with feelings which it would become them to anticipate. This is the age of the war of the oppressed against the oppressors, and every one of those ringleaders of the privileged gangs of murderers and swindlers, called Sovereigns, look to each other for aid against the common enemy, and suspend their mutual jealousies in the presence of a mightier fear. Of this holy alliance all the despots of the earth are virtual members. But a new race has arisen throughout Europe, nursed in the abhorrence of the opinions which are its chains, and she will continue to produce fresh generations to accomplish that destiny which tyrants foresee and dread.

The Spanish Peninsula is already free. France is tranquil in the enjoyment of a partial exemption from the abuses which its unnatural and feeble government are vainly attempting to revive. The seed of blood and misery has been sown in Italy, and a more vigorous race is arising to go forth to the harvest. The world waits only the news of a revolution of Germany to see the tyrants who have pinnacled themselves on its supineness precipitated into the ruin from which they shall never arise. Well do these destroyers of mankind know their enemy, when they impute the insurrection in Greece to the same spirit before which they tremble throughout the rest of Europe, and that enemy knows well the power and the cunning of its opponents and watches the moment of their approaching weakness and inevitable division to wrest the bloody sceptres from their grasp.

———

(The first of these two paragraphs was suppressed in the first edition of 1822, and had to wait till Buxton Forman's edition of 1892 before being restored. As for the second paragraph, this demonstrates the acuteness of Shelley's awareness of events in Europe, and how closely he was watching for those shifts of power which would make it possible for the oppressed to seize their chance to rise against their enemies. It also looks ahead, predicting the revolutionary movements which were to emerge in 1848 in Germany and France and Italy and Austria-Hungary; and it gives us some idea of the part that Shelley himself might have played (had he lived) in the great struggle of the working classes in England over the issues of 1832 and the Chartist years that followed.)

WILLIAM COBBETT (1762–1835) 1822

From Sermon IV, 'Oppression', in *Thirteen Sermons*, pp. 89–96

LABOUR PRODUCES EVERY THING

. . . All property has its origin in labour. Labour itself is property; the root of all other property; and unhappy is that community, where labourer and poor man are synonymous terms. No man is *essentially* poor: poor and rich are relative terms; and if the labourer have his due, and be in good health, in the vigour of life, and willing to labour, to make him a poor man there must be some defect in the government of the community in which he lives. Because the produce of his labour would of itself produce a sufficiency of every thing needful for himself and family. The labouring classes must always form nine-tenths of a people; and what a shame it must be, what an imputation on the rulers, if nine-tenths of the people be worthy of the name of poor! It is impossible that such a thing can be, unless there be an unfair and an unjust distribution of the profits of labour. Labour produces every thing that is good upon the earth; it is the cause of every thing that men enjoy of worldly possessions; when, therefore, the strong and the young engage in labour and cannot obtain from it a sufficiency to keep them out of the ranks of the poor, there must be something greatly amiss in the management of the community; something that gives to the few an unjust and cruel advantage over the many; and surely, unless we assume the character of beasts of prey, casting aside all feelings of humanity, all love of country, and all regard for the ordinances of God, we must sincerely regret, and anxiously endeavour to remove, such an evil, whenever we may find it to exist . . . The man who can talk about the honour of his country, at a time when its millions are in a state little short of famine; and when that is, too, apparently their permanent state, must be an oppressor in his heart; must be destitute of all the feelings of shame and remorse; must be fashioned for a despot, and can only want the power to act the character in its most tragical scenes . . .

. . . Every man, who is not actually a labourer himself, has someone whom he has to employ to labour for him; and, therefore, if every such man were to take and lay before him the great precept of the gospel, and were thereupon to do as he would be done unto, there would be very little of that poverty and misery, which are now to be seen in almost every country, and at almost every step. To steal, to defraud, to purloin in any manner of way, to appropriate to one's own use the goods of another: these are all crimes, well known to the laws of God and man.

And is it not to steal; is it not to commit fraud; is it not to purloin; is it not, in short, to rob, if you take from the labourer more than the fair worth of the wages you pay him? Even to overreach, to outwit your equals in point of wealth, though in transactions illegal in themselves, are deemed worthy of expulsion from society; and yet to defraud the labourer, to defraud him who is the maker of your riches, who gives you ease and abundance, the profit of whose labour (and that alone) places you above him in the estimation of the world: to defraud him, to cheat him by the means of false measures and deceitful calculations, is thought nothing of, or if thought of, only as a matter of exultation, the criterion of cleverness being the greatest quantity of labour obtained in exchange for the smallest quantity of food!

In order to disguise from ourselves our own meanness, ingratitude and cruelty, we put the thing on a different footing: we consider labour as an article of *merchandise*, and then proceed upon the maxim, that we have a right to purchase as cheap as we can . . .

It is, however, nothing more than shuffling and equivocating with our consciences to attempt to justify by such arguments the withholding from the labourer his fair share of the profits of his labour. The man who wholly disregards every moral and religious consideration; who tells you at once that he regards the labourers as cattle, and that he has a right to treat them in that way which shall be most conducive to his own advantage, is consistent enough: he is a brute in human shape; like a brute he acts, with the additional malignity of human refinement. But what are we to say of the pretended friend of religion; of the circulator of the Bible; of the propagator of the gospel, who, with brotherly love on his lips, sweats down to a skeleton, and sends nightly home to his starving children, the labourer out of whose bones he extracts even the means of his ostentatious display of piety? What are we to say of the bitter persecutor of 'infidels', who, while he says grace over his sumptuous meals, can hear, without the smallest emotion, the hectic coughs of the squalid crowds whose half-famished bodies pine away in the pestiferous air of that prison which he calls a factory? . . .

. . . To attempt persuasion, to reason, to expostulate, with such a man is vain. Give him the thing in kind: cut up the carcase and serve it him in a charger: he remains unmoved. Nothing short of the vengeance of God can touch his heart of flint: he has lowered the measure and heightened the price; he has made the Ephah small and the Shekel great; he has falsified the balance by deceit; he has robbed the hired servant of his hire; he has bought the poor for silver and the needy for a pair of shoes; he has fattened on the gain of oppressions; he has 'eaten the flesh and

drunk the blood of his poorer brother'; 'his feasting shall be turned into
mourning, saith the Lord God, and his songs into lamentations'.

LORD BYRON (1788–1824) 1823

The Age of Bronze, XIV, ll. 1–64

APPETITE
THE LANDLORDS' INTEREST: 'RENT, RENT, RENT!'

Alas, the country! how shall tongue or pen
Bewail her now *un*country gentlemen?
The last to bid the cry of warfare cease,
The first to make a malady of peace.
For what were all these country patriots born?
To hunt, and vote, and raise the price of corn?
But corn, like every mortal thing, must fall,
Kings, conquerors, and markets most of all.
And must ye fall with every ear of grain?
Why would you trouble Buonaparte's reign?
He was your great Triptolemus; his vices
Destroy'd but realms, and still maintain'd your prices;
He amplified to every lord's content
The grand agrarian alchymy, high *rent*.
Why did the tyrant stumble on the Tartars,
And lower wheat to such desponding quarters?
Why did you chain him on yon isle so lone?
The man was worth much more upon his throne.
True, blood and treasure boundlessly were spilt,
But what of that? the Gaul may bear the guilt;
But bread was high, the farmer paid his way,
And acres told upon the appointed day.
But where is now the goodly audit ale?
The purse-proud tenant, never known to fail?
The farm which never yet was left on hand?
The marsh reclaim'd to most improving land?
The impatient hope of the expiring lease?
The doubling rental? What an evil's peace!
In vain the prize excites the ploughman's skill,
In vain the Commons pass their patriot bill;

437

The *landed interest* – (you may understand
The phrase much better leaving out the *land*) –
The land self-interest groans from shore to shore,
For fear that plenty should attain the poor.
Up, up again, ye rents! exalt your notes,
Or else the ministry will lose their votes,
And patriotism, so delicately nice,
Her loaves will lower to the market price;
For ah! 'the loaves and fishes,' once so high,
Are gone – their oven closed, their ocean dry,
And nought remains of all the millions spent,
Excepting to grow moderate and content.
Those who are not so, *had* their turn – and turn
About still flows from Fortune's equal urn;
Now let their virtue be its own reward,
And share the blessings which themselves prepared.
See these inglorious Cincinnati swarm,
Farmers, of war, dictators of the farm;
Their ploughshare was the sword in hireling hands,
Their fields manured by gore of other lands;
Safe in their barns, these Sabine tillers sent
Their brethren out to battle – why? for rent!
Year after year they voted cent per cent,
Blood, sweat, and tear-wrung millions, – why? for rent!
They roar'd, they dined, they drank, they swore they meant
To die for England – why then live? – for rent!
The peace has made one general malcontent
Of these high-market patriots; war was rent!
Their love of country, millions all misspent,
How reconcile? by reconciling rent!
And will they not repay the treasures lent?
No: down with everything, and up with rent!
Their good, ill, health, wealth, joy, or discontent,
Being, end, aim, religion – rent, rent, rent!

JOHN CLARE (1793–1864)

'The Moors', in *Selected Poems and Prose*, pp. 169–71

Clare lived almost his entire life in Northamptonshire, for thirty-nine years in his native Helpstone. He wrote intimately and freely of his world, but had little success, though for a short time 'fashionable'; and his sense of isolation, in the context of the general poverty of the rural people, no doubt contributed to the increasing distress which took him to an Epping asylum in 1837. After four years he left this place and returned to Northamptonshire, but a few months later was committed to Northampton General Asylum, where he remained till his death, and continued to write. Clare's strength lies in his rooted sense of place, and he speaks as a unique witness, 'since his is almost the only voice that can still be heard from that otherwise silent peasantry of the enclosure years'.

ENCLOSURES

From An Act for Inclosing Lands in the Parishes of Maxey . . . and Helpstone in the County of Northamptonshire, 49 Geo.III, Sess. 1809:
'And be it further Enacted, That no Horses, Beasts, Asses, Sheep, Lambs, or other Cattle, shall at any time within the first Ten Years after the said Allotments shall be directed to be entered upon by the respective Proprietors thereof, be kept in any of the public Carriage Roads or Ways to be set out and fenced off on both sides, or Laned out in pursuance of this Act.'

Far spread the moory ground, a level scene
Bespread with rush and one eternal green,
That never felt the rage of blundering plough,
Though centuries wreathed spring blossoms on its brow.
Autumn met plains that stretched them far away
In unchecked shadows of green, brown, and grey.
Unbounded freedom ruled the wandering scene;
No fence of ownership crept in between
To hide the prospect from the gazing eye;
Its only bondage was the circling sky.
A mighty flat, undwarfed by bush and tree,
Spread its faint shadow of immensity,
And lost itself, which seemed to eke its bounds
In the blue mist the horizon's edge surrounds.

Now this sweet vision of my boyish hours,
Free as spring clouds and wild as forest flowers,
Is faded all – a hope that blossomed free,

And hath been once as it no more shall be.
Enclosure came, and trampled on the grave
Of labour's rights, and left the poor a slave;
And memory's pride, ere want to wealth did bow,
Is both the shadow and the substance now.
The sheep and cows were free to range as then
Where change might prompt, nor felt the bonds of men.
Cows went and came with every morn and night
To the wild pasture as their common right;
And sheep, unfolded with the rising sun,
Heard the swains shout and felt their freedom won,
Tracked the red fallow field and heath and plain,
Or sought the brook to drink, and roamed again;
While the glad shepherd traced their tracks along,
Free as the lark and happy as her song.
But now all's fled, and flats of many a dye
That seemed to lengthen with the following eye,
Moors loosing from the sight, far, smooth, and blea,
Where swoopt the plover in its pleasure free,
Are banished now with heaths once wild and gay
As poet's visions of life's early day.
Like mighty giants of their limbs bereft,
The skybound wastes in mangled garbs are left,
Fence meeting fence in owner's little bounds
Of field and meadow, large as garden-grounds,
In little parcels little minds to please,
With men and flocks imprisoned, ill at ease.
  (Each little tyrant with his little sign
  Shows where man claims, earth glows no more divine;
  But paths to freedom and to childhood dear
  A board sticks up to notice 'no road here.')
This with the poor scared freedom bade farewell,
And fortune-hunters totter where they fell;
They dreamed of riches in the rebel scheme
And find too truly that they did but dream.

WILLIAM HAZLITT (1778–1830)   1825

From *The Spirit of the Age*, pp. 170–73

The Rev. Robert Malthus (1766–1834) published *An Essay on the Principle of Population* in 1798 (6th ed., 1826), arguing that the increase of the 'lower orders' would soon outstrip the food supply and that therefore checks on breeding were necessary. This work was to become an economic textbook for the ruling class and to be accepted as a scientific justification for the terrible poverty of the working classes, thus giving spurious legitimacy to the status quo. But Hazlitt wasn't taken in; with passionate indignation and merciless logic he demolishes the argument decades before others reached the same verdict.

THE GOSPEL ACCORDING TO MALTHUS

Mr Malthus's 'gospel is preached to the poor'. He lectures them on economy, on morality, the regulation of their passions (which, he says at other times, are amenable to no restraint), and on the ungracious topic, that 'the laws of nature, which are the laws of God, have doomed them and their families to starve for want of a right to the smallest portion of food beyond what their labour will supply, or some charitable hand may hold out in compassion'. This is illiberal, and it is not philosophical. The laws of nature or of God, to which the author appeals, are no other than a limited fertility and a limited earth. Within those bounds the rest is regulated by the laws of man. The division of the produce of the soil, the price of labour, the relief afforded to the poor, are matters of human arrangement: while any charitable hand can extend relief, it is a proof that the means of subsistence are not exhausted in themselves, that 'the tables are not full'! Mr Malthus says that the laws of nature, which are the laws of God, have rendered that relief physically impossible; and yet he would abrogate the poor-laws by an act of the legislature, in order to take away that *impossible* relief, which the laws of God deny, and which the laws of man *actually* afford. We cannot think that this view of his subject, which is prominent and dwelt on at great length and with great pertinacity, is dictated either by rigid logic or melting charity! A labouring man is not allowed to knock down a hare or a partridge that spoils his garden: a country-squire keeps a pack of hounds: a lady of quality rides out with a footman behind her on two sleek, well-fed horses.

We have not a word to say against all this as exemplifying the spirit of the English Constitution, as a part of the law of the land, or as an artful distribution of light and shade in the social picture; but if any one insists at the same time that 'the laws of nature, which are the laws of God, have doomed the poor and their families to starve', because the principle of population has encroached upon and swallowed up the means of subsistence, so that not a mouthful of food is left *by the grinding law of necessity* for the poor, we beg leave to deny both fact and inference; and we put it to Mr Malthus whether we are not, in strictness, justified in doing so?

We have, perhaps, said enough to explain our feeling on the subject of Mr Malthus's merits and defects. We think he had the opportunity and the means in his hands of producing a great work on the principle of population; but we believe he has let it slip from his having an eye to other things besides that broad and unexplored question. He wished not merely to advance to the discovery of certain great and valuable truths, but at the same time to overthrow certain unfashionable paradoxes by exaggerated statements – to curry favour with existing prejudices and interests by garbled representations. He has, in a word, as it appears to us on a candid retrospect and without any feelings of controversial asperity rankling in our minds, sunk the philosopher and the friend of his species (a character to which he might have aspired) in the sophist and party-writer. The period at which Mr Malthus came forward teemed with answers to Modern Philosophy, with antidotes to liberty and humanity, with abusive Histories of the Greek and Roman republics, with fulsome panegyrics on the Roman Emperors (at the very time when we were reviling Buonaparte for his strides to universal empire) with the slime and offal of desperate servility; and we cannot but consider the Essay as one of the poisonous ingredients thrown into the cauldron of Legitimacy 'to make it thick and slab'. Our author has indeed so far done service to the cause of truth, that he has counteracted many capital errors formerly prevailing as to the universal and indiscriminate encouragement of population under all circumstances; but he has countenanced opposite errors which, if adopted in theory and practice, would be even more mischievous, and has left it to future philosophers to follow up the principle, that some check must be provided for the unrestrained progress of population, into a set of wiser and more humane consequences.

WILLIAM HAZLITT (1778–1830)   1825

From *The Spirit of the Age*, pp. 204–6

The *Quarterly Review* was founded in 1809 as Tory rival to the *Edinburgh Review*, its first editor being William Gifford, who (as a hater of all radicals) had previously run *The Anti-Jacobin*. Among its contributors at the time of Hazlitt's attack were Canning, Disraeli and Southey.

THE QUARTERLY REVIEW: PATCHING UP A ROTTEN SYSTEM

. . . This journal . . . is a depository for every species of political sophistry and personal calumny. There is no abuse or corruption that does not there find a jesuitical palliation or a bare-faced vindication. There we meet the slime of hypocrisy, the varnish of courts, the cant of pedantry, the cobwebs of the law, the iron hand of power. Its object is as mischievous as the means by which it is pursued are odious. The intention is to poison the sources of public opinion and of individual fame, to pervert literature from being the natural ally of freedom and humanity into an engine of priestcraft and despotism, and to undermine the spirit of the English constitution and the independence of the English character. The Editor and his friends systematically explode every principle of liberty, laugh patriotism and public spirit to scorn, resent every pretence to integrity as a piece of singularity or insolence, and strike at the root of all free inquiry or discussion by running down every writer as a vile scribbler and a bad member of society, who is not a hireling and a slave. No means are stuck at in accomplishing this laudable end. Strong in patronage, they trample on truth, justice and decency. They claim the privilege of court-favourites. They keep as little faith with the public as with their opponents.

No statement in the *Quarterly Review* is to be trusted: there is no fact that is not misrepresented in it, no quotation that is not garbled, no character that is not slandered, if it can answer the purposes of a party to do so. The weight of power, of wealth, of rank is thrown into the scale, gives its impulse to the machine; and the whole is under the guidance of Mr Gifford's instinctive genius – of the inborn hatred of servility for independence, of dullness for talent, of cunning and impudence for truth and honesty. It costs him no effort to execute his disreputable task; in being the tool of a crooked policy, he but labours in his natural vocation. He patches up a rotten system, as he would supply the chasms in a worm-eaten manuscript, from a grovelling incapacity to do any thing better: thinks that if a single iota in the claims of prerogative and power were lost, the whole fabric of society would fall upon his head and crush him: and calculates that his best chance for literary reputation is by *blackballing* one half of the competitors as Jacobins and levellers, and securing the suffrages of the other half in his favour as a loyal subject and trusty partisan!

WILLIAM COBBETT (1762–1835)   28 August 1826

From *Rural Rides*, 'Down the Valley of the Avon in Wiltshire', pp. 298, 309–10, 315–16, 350–51

GETTING RID OF THE POOR

It seemed to me, that one way, and that not, perhaps, the least striking, of exposing the folly, the stupidity, the inanity, the presumption, the insufferable emptiness and insolence and barbarity, of those numerous wretches, who have now the audacity to propose to *transport* the people of England, upon the principle of the monster MALTHUS, who has furnished the unfeeling oligarchs and their toad-eaters with the pretence, that *man has a natural propensity to breed faster than food can be raised for the increase*; it seemed to me, that one way of exposing this mixture of madness and of blasphemy was, to take a look, now that the harvest is in, at the *produce*, the *mouths*, the *condition*, and *the changes that have taken place*, in a spot like this, which God has favoured with every good that he has had to bestow upon man . . .

  The parish of MILTON does, as we have seen, produce food, drink, clothing, and all other things, enough for 502 families, or 2510 persons upon *my allowance*, which is a great deal more than *three times* the present allowance, because the present allowance includes clothing, fuel, tools and every thing. Now, then, according to the 'POPULATION RETURN', laid before Parliament, this parish contains 500 persons, or, according to my division, *one hundred families*. So that here are about *one hundred* families to raise food and drink enough, and to raise wool and other things to pay for all other necessaries, for *five hundred and two* families! Aye, and five hundred and two families fed and lodged, too, *on my liberal scale*. Fed and lodged according to *the present scale*, this one hundred families raise enough to supply more, and many more, than *fifteen hundred* families; or *seven thousand five hundred* persons! And yet *those who do the work are half starved*! In the 100 families there are, we will suppose, 80 able working men, and as many boys, sometimes assisted by the women and stout girls. What a handful of people to raise such a quantity of food! What injustice, what a hellish system it must be to make those who raise it *skin and bone and nakedness*, while the food and drink and wool are almost all carried away to be heaped on the fund-holders, pensioners, soldiers, dead-weight, and other swarms of tax-eaters! If such an operation do not need putting an end to, then the devil himself is a saint . . .

And yet there is an '*Emigration Committee*' sitting to devise the means of getting *rid*, not of the *idlers*, not of the *pensioners*, not of the *dead-weight*, not of the *parsons* (to '*relieve*' whom we have seen the poor labourers taxed to the tune of a million and a half of money), not of the soldiers; but to devise means of getting rid of these working people, who are grudged even the miserable morsel that they get!

NATIONAL WEALTH 30 August 1826

I have never been able clearly to understand what the beastly Scotch *feelosofers* mean by their '*national wealth*'; but, so far as I can understand them, this is their meaning: that national wealth means, that which is *left* of the products of the country over and above what is *consumed*, or *used*, by those whose labour causes the products to be. This being the notion, it follows, of course, that the *fewer* poor devils you can screw the products out of, the *richer* the nation is . . . What, then, is to be done with this *over-produce*? Who is to have it? Is it to go to pensioners, place-men, tax-gatherers, dead-weight people, soldiers, gendarmerie, police-people, and, in short, to whole millions *who do no work at all*? Is this a cause of '*national wealth*'? Is a nation made *rich* by taking the food and clothing from those who create them, and giving them to those who do nothing of any use? . . . If the over-produce of this Valley of Avon were given, by the farmers, to the weavers in Lancashire, to the iron and steel chaps of Warwickshire, and to other makers or sellers of useful things, there would come an abundance of all these useful things into this valley from Lancashire and other parts; but if, as is the case, the over-produce goes to the fundholders, the dead-weight, the soldiers, the lord and lady and master and miss pensioners and sinecure people; if the over-produce go to them, as a very great part of it does, nothing, not even the parings of one's nails, *can come back to the valley in exchange*. And, can this operation, then, add to the '*national wealth*'? It adds to the '*wealth*' of those who carry on the affairs of state; it fills their pockets, those of their relatives and dependants; it fattens all tax-eaters; but, it can give no *wealth* to the '*nation*', which means, *the whole of the people*. National Wealth means, the *Commonwealth* or *Commonweal*; and these mean, the general *good*, or *happiness*, of the people, and the *safety* and *honour* of *the state*; and, these are not to be secured by robbing those who labour, in order to support a large part of the community in *idleness* . . .

LIBERTY TO STARVE QUIETLY   4 September 1826

In quitting DEVIZES yesterday morning, I saw, just on the outside of the town, a monstrous building, which I took for a *barrack*; but, upon asking what it was, I found it was one of those other marks of the JUBILEE REIGN; namely *a most magnificent* gaol! It seemed to me sufficient to hold *one-half of the able-bodied men in the county*! And it would do it too, and do it well! Such a system must come to an end, and the end must be dreadful. As I came on the road, for the first three or four miles, I saw great numbers of labourers either digging potatoes for their Sunday's dinner, or coming home with them, or going out to dig them. The land-owners, or occupiers, *let small pieces of land to the labourers*, and these they cultivate with the spade for their own use. They pay, in all cases, a *high rent*, and, in most cases, an enormous one. The practice prevails all the way from Warminster to Devizes, and from Devizes to nearly this place [Highworth]. The rent is, in some places, *a shilling a rod*, which is, mind, 160s. or £8 an acre! Still the poor creatures like to have the land: they work at it in their spare hours; and on Sunday mornings early: and the overseers, sharp as they may be, cannot *ascertain precisely* how much they get out of their plat of land. But, good God! what a life to live! What a life to see people live; to see this sight in our own country, and to have the base vanity to *boast* of that country, and to talk of our 'constitution' and our '*liberties*', and to affect to *pity* the Spaniards, whose working people live like gentlemen, compared with our miserable crea-tures. Again I say, give me the Inquisition and well-heeled cheeks and ribs, rather than 'civil and religious liberty', and skin and bone. But, the fact is, that, where honest and laborious men can be *compelled to starve quietly*, whether all at once or by inches, with old wheat ricks and fat cattle under their eye, it is a mockery to talk of their '*liberty*', of any sort; for, the sum total of their state is this, they have '*liberty*' to choose between death by starvation (quick or slow) and death by the halter!

446

WILLIAM BLAKE (1757–1827)

From *Annotations to Dr Thornton's 'New Translation of the Lord's Prayer'*
in *Complete Writings*, pp. 787–9

In this last year of his life, Blake's anger and indignation at the inhumanities and injustices of his age remain undiminished, as his devastating commentary on Dr Thornton's translation demonstrates. 'I look upon this,' he says, 'as a Most Malignant and Artful attack upon the Kingdom of Jesus by the Classical and Learned, thro' the instrumentality of Dr Thornton . . .' Here are three of his Annotations.

MONEY BOUGHT BREAD

From Page One

Lawful Bread, Bought with Lawful Money, and a Lawful Heaven, seen thro' a Lawful Telescope, by means of Lawful Window Light! The Holy Ghost, and whatever cannot be Taxed, is Unlawful and Witchcraft. Spirits are Lawful, but not Ghosts; especially Royal Gin is Lawful Spirit. No Smuggling real British Spirit and Truth!

Page Two

Give us the Bread that is our due and Right, by taking away Money, or a Price, or Tax upon what is Common to all in thy Kingdom.

From the Fly-leaf

Doctor Thornton's Tory Translation, Translated out of its disguise in the Classical and Scotch languages into the vulgar English.
Our Father Augustus Caesar, who art in these thy Substantial Astronomical Telescopic Heavens, Holiness to thy Name or Title, and reverence to thy Shadow. Thy Kingship come upon Earth first and thence in Heaven. Give us day by day our Real Taxed Substantial Money bought Bread; deliver from the Holy Ghost so we call nature whatever cannot be Taxed; for all is debts and Taxes between Caesar and us and one another; lead us not to read the Bible, but let our Bible be Virgil and Shakespeare; and deliver us from Poverty in Jesus, that Evil One. For thine is the Kingship, or Allegoric Godship, and the Power, or War, and

the Glory, or Law, Ages after Ages in thy descendants; for God is only an Allegory of Kings and nothing else.

Amen.

WALTER SAVAGE LANDOR (1775–1864)   1830

'The Georges'

THE GEORGES

George the First was always reckoned
Vile, but viler George the Second;
And what mortal ever heard
Any good of George the Third?
When from earth the Fourth descended
(God be praised!) the Georges ended.

RICHARD OASTLER   16 October 1830

From the *Leeds Mercury*, in Hollis, ed., *Class and Conflict*, p. 194

YORKSHIRE SLAVERY

Let truth speak out . . . Thousands of our fellow-creatures and fellow-subjects, both male and female, are this very moment existing in a state of slavery more horrid than are the victims of that hellish system '*colonial slavery*'. These innocent creatures draw out, unpitied, their short but miserable existence, in a place famed for its profession of religious zeal . . . The very streets which receive the droppings of an 'Anti-Slavery Society' are every morning wet by the tears of innocent victims at the accursed shrine of avarice, who are *compelled* – not by the cart-whip of the negro slave driver but by the dread of the equally appalling thong or strap of the over-looker, to hasten, half-dressed, *but not half-fed*, to those magazines of British infantile slavery – *the worsted mills* in the town and neighbourhood of Bradford!!

Thousands of little children, both male and female, but principally female, from seven to fourteen years of age, are daily compelled to labour from six in the morning to seven in the evening, with only – Britons, blush while you read it – *with only thirty minutes allowed for eating and recreation*. Poor infants! ye are indeed sacrificed at the shrine of avarice, without even the solace of the negro slave . . . He knows it is his sordid, mercenary master's interest that he should *live*, be *strong* and *healthy*. Not so with you. You are doomed to labour from morning to night for one who cares not how soon your weak and tender frames are stretched to breaking! When your joints can act no longer, your emaciated frames are cast aside, the boards on which you lately toiled and wasted life away are instantly supplied with other victims, who in this boasted land of liberty are hired – not sold – as slaves and daily forced to hear that they are free.

JOHN CLARE (1793–1864)   1830

'England, 1830', in *Selected Poems*, p. 194

FORGING NEW BONDS

These vague allusions to a country's wrongs,
    Where one says 'Ay' and others answer 'No'
In contradiction from a thousand tongues,
    Till like to prison-cells her freedoms grow
Becobwebbed with these oft-repeated songs
    Of peace and plenty in the midst of woe –
And is it thus they mock her year by year,
    Telling poor truth unto her face she lies,
Declaiming of her wealth with gibe severe,
    So long as taxes drain their wished supplies?
And will these jailors rivet every chain
    Anew, yet loudest in their mockery be,
To damn her into madness with disdain,
    Forging new bonds and bidding her be free?

WILLIAM COBBETT (1762–1835) 27 November 1830

From *The Political Register*, in Hollis, ed., *Class and Conflict*, pp. 120–22

In November and December 1830 the rural proletariat of south and east England rose against low wages and the threshing machines that put them out of work, reinforcing their demands by burning the ricks, sending threatening letters (often signed with the name 'Captain Swing') to magistrates and landowners, poaching their game, and smashing the machines. The Swing riots spread quickly, but were suppressed with ease. Nine men were hanged and close on 500 from thirteen counties transported. Cobbett himself was put on trial for standing up for these people, but acquitted.

RURAL WAR

[With regard to this war, Lord Grey said] . . . I can only promise that the state of the country shall be made the object of our immediate, our diligent and unceasing attention . . . To relieve the distress which now so unhappily exists in different parts will be the first and most anxious end of our deliberations; but here I declare . . . that it is my determined resolution, wherever outrages are perpetrated, or excess committed, to suppress them with severity and vigour. [Cheers.] Severity is, in the first instance, the only remedy which can be applied to such disorders with success; and, therefore, although we are most anxious to relieve the distress of the people who are suffering, let them be well assured they shall find no want of firm resolution upon our part. [Hear, hear] . . . Their first object would be to examine into the nature of the existing distress, and, as there was every reason to believe, upon the instigation of persons whom that distress did not affect . . . The danger with which the country was threatened was to be the first subject of consideration, and must be met with a prompt and determined hand. [Hear, hear, hear.]

This must certainly be an assembly of the bravest men in the whole world! Observe how they cheered every time the word *resolution*, *determination*, *severity* or *vigour*, occurred! And the '*prompt and determined hand*' seems to have fairly *entranced* their Lordships. But, now, let us inquire *coolly* into this matter. Let us fairly state the case of those who are carrying on this war. Lord Grey proposes to inquire into the '*nature of the existing distress*'. These words are enough to make one despair of him and his measures. Just as if the distress was *temporary*, and had now arisen from some *special cause*! . . . One would as soon expect them to propose an inquiry into the cause of the dirt in London streets. The one just as notorious and as obvious as the other . . .

Forty-five years ago, the labourers all brewed their own beer, and that now none of them do it; that formerly they ate meat, cheese, and bread, and they now live almost wholly on potatoes; that formerly it was a rare thing for a girl to be with child before she was married, and that now it is as rare that she is not, the parties being so poor that they are compelled to throw the expense of the wedding on the parish; that the felons

450

in the jails and hulks live better than the honest labouring people, and that these latter commit thefts and robbery, in order to get into the jails and hulks, or to be transported; that men are set to draw waggons and carts like beasts of burden; that they are shut up in pounds like cattle; that they are put up at auction like Negroes in Jamaica; that married men are forcibly separated from their wives to prevent them from breeding . . . It is no *temporary cause*, it is no new feeling of discontent that is at work; it is a deep sense of grievous wrongs; it is long harboured resentment; it is an accumulation of revenge for unmerited punishment . . . it is a natural effect of a cause which is as obvious as that ricks are consumed by fire, when fire is put to them . . .

But if this excite our astonishment, what are we to say of that part of Lord Grey's speech in which he speaks of 'Instigators'? . . . What! can these men look at the facts before their eyes; can they see the millions of labourers everywhere rising up, and hear them saying that they will '*no longer starve on potatoes*'; can they see them breaking threshing-machines; can they see them gathering together and demanding an increase of wages; can they see all this, and can they believe that the *fires* do not proceed from the same persons; but that these are the work of some invisible and almost incorporeal agency! . . .

The *motive* of it is, however, evident enough to men who reflect that every tax-eater and tithe-eater, no matter of what sort or size he or she is, is afraid to believe, and wishes the nation not to believe, that *the fires are the work of the labourers*. And *why* are they so reluctant to believe this, and so anxious that it should be believed by nobody? Because the labourers are *the millions* (for, mind, *smiths*, *wheelwrights*, *collarmakers*, *carpenters*, *bricklayers*, all are of one mind); and because, if *the millions be bent upon this work*, who is to stop it? Then to believe that the labourers are the burners, is to believe that they must have been urged to the deeds by desperation, proceeding from *some grievous wrong*, real or imaginary; and to believe this is to believe that the burnings will continue, until the *wrong be redressed*. To believe this is to believe that there must be such a change of system as will take *from the tax and tithe-eaters a large portion of what they receive, and give it back to the labourers*, and believe this the tax and tithe-eaters never will until the political Noah *shall enter into the ark*! . . . [The labourers] look upon themselves as engaged in a *war*, with a *just object* . . . Is this destructive war to go on till all law and all personal safety are at an end? . . . The truth is that, for many years past, about *forty-five millions a year* have been *withheld from the working people of England*; about five or six millions have been doled back to them in *poor-rates*; and the forty millions have gone to keep up *military academies*,

EBENEZER ELLIOTT (1781–1849)

1831

From *Corn-Law Rhymes*

DRONE V. WORKER

How God speeds the tax-bribed plough,
   Fen and moor declare, man;
Where once fed the poor man's cow,
   ACRES drives his share, man.
But he did not *steal* the fen,
   Did not *steal* the moor, man;
If he feeds on starving men,
   Still he loves the poor, man.
Hush! he bullies State and Throne,
   Quids them in his jaw, man;
Thine and mine he calls *his own*;
   Acres' lie is law, man.
Acres eats his tax on bread,
   Acres loves the plough, man;
Acres' dogs are better fed,
   Beggar's slave! than thou, man.
Acres' feeder pays his debts,
   Waxes thin and pale, man,
Harder works and poorer gets,
   Pays his debts in jail, man.
Acres in a palace lives,
   While his feeder pines, man;
Palace beggar ne'er forgives
   Dog on whom he dines, man.
Acres' feeder, beggared, begs,
   Treadmilled rogue is he, man;
Scamp! he deals in pheasants' eggs;
   Hangs on gallows-tree, man!
Who would be a useful man?
   Who sell cloth or hats, man?
Who make boiler or mend pan?
   Who keep Acres' brats, man?
Better ride, and represent;
   Better borough tools, man;
Better sit in pauperment;
   Better Corn-Law fools, man.

Why not fight the plundered poor?
　Why not use our *own*, man?
Plough the seas and *not* the moor?
　Why not pick a bone, man!
Lo! the merchant builds huge mills;
　Bread-taxed thinks and sighs, man!
Thousand mouths and bellies fills;
　Bread-taxed breaks and dies, man!
Thousand mouths and bellies then,
　Bread-taxed, writhe and swear, man:
England once bred honest men –
　Bread-taxed, Burke and Hare, man!
Hark ye! millions soon may pine,
　Starving millions curse, man!
Desperate millions long to dine
　A-la-Burke, and worse, man!
What will then remain to eat?
　Who be eaten then, man?
'Few may part, though many meet,'
　At Famine's Feast, ye ken, man.

POOR MAN'S GUARDIAN　　　12 November 1831

Report of a trial, in Thompson, *Making of the English Working Class*,
pp. 803–4

The *Poor Man's Guardian*, as the leading working-class newspaper of the 1830s,
itself illegal and unstamped, dealt with many such issues as this – the trial of
Joseph Swann, hatter, of Macclesfield, for selling unstamped newspapers. Swann
had already spent four and a half years in prison for his refusal to comply with
the authorities.

DEFIANCE

BENCH　What have you to say in your defence?

DEFENDANT　Well, sir, I have been out of employment for some time;
　neither can I obtain work; my family are all starving . . . And for
　another reason, the weightiest of all; I sell them for the good of my
　fellow countrymen; to let them see how they are misrepresented in

parliament . . . I wish to let the people know how they are being hum-
bugged . . .

BENCH Hold your tongue a moment.

DEFENDANT I shall not! for I wish every man to read these publications.

BENCH You are very insolent, therefore you are committed to three
months' imprisonment in Knutsford House of Correction, to hard
labour.

DEFENDANT I've nothing to thank you for; and whenever I come out
I'll hawk them again. And *mind you*, the first that I hawk shall be to
your house . . .

RICHARD CARLILE (1790–1843)   18 June 1831

From *Prompter*, in Hollis, ed., *Class and Conflict*, pp. 16–17

Carlile, journalist and printer of the complete works of Paine, for which he was
imprisoned, was in the great libertarian tradition, and nothing it seemed could
silence him, because even from gaol he continued to edit *The Republican* and to
expose any case of persecution that came his way; and he had the backing of the
determined people, mostly artisans, who responded to his own unequivocal
defence of liberty and justice against authority, and were willing to risk prison
themselves to help with his work.

PROFLIGATE CONSUMERS OF A NATION'S WEALTH

I charge upon the existence of kings, and priests, and lords, those useless
classes, the common poverty of the labouring classes of mankind.
I charge upon them the common warfare and slaughter of mankind. I
charge upon their wicked usurpations, their false pretentions, and their
general tyrannical dishonesty, all the social evils that afflict mankind
. . . The man is a social villain, a thief, a pickpocket, a cheat, a liar, who
preaches to another man in the name of God . . . *Down with the priests.*
There can be no general human welfare, where they are allowed to hold
influence. The lords of the two islands are like the aristocrats of every
other country, pursuing their family aggrandizement at the risk of the
peace, the lives and the health of the labouring people. They have
monopolized, hitherto, the legislative power, and have made laws pursuant to their own desires, and not pursuant to the general welfare
. . . *We must put down those lords.* Neither kings, nor priests, nor lords,

are useful to a people. We can work without them, eat without them, be skilful without them, be happy without them, make good laws without them, administer well those good laws without them, govern the country without them, communicate with other countries without them, and protect ourselves as a nation without them. They are the profligate consumers of a nation's wealth, a prey upon her strength, a chain to her neck, so many mill stones tied to her heels, clogs to her ankles, gyves to her limbs, vultures to her liver, and bad examples to her manners . . . Either in war or in peace, kingcraft, priestcraft, and lordcraft, is a system of plunder, murder and spoliation. THEN DOWN WITH KINGS, PRIESTS AND LORDS . . .

'ONE OF THE KNOW-NOTHINGS'
7 January 1832

From *Poor Man's Guardian*, in Hollis, ed., *Class and Conflict*, p. 50

WAGES AND PROFITS

Wages should form the price of goods;
Yes, wages should be all,
Then we who work to make the goods,
Should justly have them all;
But if their price be made of rent,
Tithes, taxes, profits all,
Then we who work to make the goods,
Shall have just none at all.

'ONE OF THE OPPRESSED'   14 April 1832

From *Poor Man's Guardian*, in Hollis, ed., *Class and Conflict*, pp. 74–5

Though the new Whig government which had come to power in 1830 seemed to define a clear break with the repressive regimes that had dominated England since the age of Pitt, its attitude to reform remained cautious and conservative. What is known as 'the great Reform Bill of 1832', which become law in June of that year, did not represent any advance for democracy. The ruling Whig minority was simply responding to the demands of a new and confident moneyed class and providing an acceptable alternative to what Macaulay envisaged as threatening 'the wreck of laws, the confusion of ranks, the spoliation of property and the dissolution of the social order'. The Bill was pushed through, that is, against a background of profound unrest, using the fear of anarchy and radicalism to achieve a settlement which many Whigs considered 'final'. Its main effect of course was to strengthen the powers of middle-class property-holders and (leaving the mass of the artisan and working classes legally powerless) to provide constitutional grounds for the expansion of capitalist enterprise and an even greater exploitation of the working class; and thus was to mark the real beginnings of the struggle for social reform and economic equality.

WARNING AGAINST THE REFORM BILL OF 1832

Fellow Countrymen,   Manchester, 19 March 1832
I have given you my opinion in several letters, at various times, on the present measure of *Reform* . . . That measure, if carried into effect, will do you an incalculable deal of harm . . .

As soon as the land-stealers, merchants, manufacturers and tradesmen acquire the privilege of law-making, they begin to legislate for their own individual interest; that is, to increase their rents and profits, by which they deprive you of the produce of your industry; and in proportion as their influence in law-making is increased, so are these rents and profits increased, and so likewise is your poverty increased . . . The influence of these men who live by these impositions is to be increased in making the laws, by this Bill more than ten-fold!! Will you believe now that you have any interest in the passing of this Bill, or that your interest does not consist in its being kicked out, as it was before? . . . [For] you will be starved to death by thousands, if this Bill pass, and thrown on to the dunghill, or on to the ground, naked, like dogs . . .

Of all the Bills, or *plots* (for it is nothing else) that ever was proposed on earth, this is the most deceptive and the most mischievous. This Bill proposes to extend the number of electors to about five times the present amount. This on the face of the measure appears, at first sight, a most liberal alteration. What! extend the number of voters from one hundred and fifty thousand, to six or seven hundred thousand? *Most liberal indeed*!!! But now, when we come to see that the liberality is all on one side, and none on the other – when we come to see that those whose influence is already ten-fold too great, are to have that influence ten-fold increased, while you whose influence is already ten-fold too little, are to have that influence (through the great influence of the other) incalculably diminished, it is the most *illiberal*, the most *tyrannical*, the most *abom-*

457

inable, the most *infamous*, the most *hellish* measure that ever could, or can, be proposed. Your number is four-fifths of the whole population. Your influence, therefore, at elections (in addition to your right of being elected yourselves) ought to be four times as great as all the rest of the community. Yet your influence will not be more than *one twentieth part* of that which will be exercised by those who live on the fruits of your labour. You will in reality therefore, from fear and fewness of number, have no influence at all.

ARTHUR S. WADE   17 November 1832

From *Poor Man's Guardian*, in Hollis, ed., *Class and Conflict*, pp. 134–5

SEPARATE WORKING-CLASS UNIONS

To Thomas Attwood, Esq., On the conduct of the Birmingham Political Council respecting the formation of a Midland Union of the Working Classes.

Sir –

In a newspaper report of the recent proceedings of the Council of the Birmingham Political Union, I perceive that some member of the Council asserted that . . . no sufficient reasons had been adduced for the formation of a Union of the Working Classes. It appeared to me that the reverse was the case; but that such a remark may not be urged in future, I will submit the five following reasons for the necessity of a Working Class Union –

1. Because the leaders of other Unions, being men of property living upon the rental of land, the interest of money, or the profits of trade, have separate and distinct interests from the working man: for example, he who lives on the rental of land has an interest opposed to the abolition of the corn laws, and the abolition of every other monopoly that would diminish his income; he who lives on the interest of money has a great predilection for paper schemes, bubble speculations, cheap production, and depreciated labour; he who lives on the profits of trade has an interest in obtaining labour as cheap as possible and selling it at the dearest rate; and, as all of these individual interests are opposed to the best interests of the productive classes, I ask you are those persons so fit and proper to represent them as the working classes themselves?

2. That as the majority of those who have taken an active part in these unions are men of property, they have an interest in securing the rep-

resentation of property rather than of human beings. As a proof of this, men of property, from time immemorial, have always secured the power to make laws, and always protected their own interests, reckless of the consequences; the effects of which you may this day behold in the extreme wealth on the one hand, and the destitution and starvation of the artisans of your own town on the other.

3. Believing that the wretched condition of the working classes, especially in the manufacturing districts, is principally to be ascribed to the improvement and inventions which have superseded manual labour, and thereby forced the unemployed into competition for employment; and knowing that masters and capitalists have an interest in still further increasing the powers of wood and iron, if they can procure them cheaper than human labour, I think that they are not the most proper persons, either in or out of Parliament, to take into consideration a question with reference to the proper disposal of these powers so as to benefit the working classes.

4. Because they who move in a sphere above the working classes, or who consider themselves independent of useful labour, have an interest in securing for themselves, families, and connections, places and situations in the army, navy, church and excise, and thus become identified with the aristocracy in increasing the public burdens, and, consequently, such persons are not fit to represent the interests of the working man.

5. Since there is sufficient intelligence amongst the working classes to discuss, too, questions connected with their best interests, and a growing disposition to acquire further knowledge, they ought to be free to communicate with their brethren on their rights and liberties, without being subject to the dictation or control of those persons whose interests are the reverse of their own . . .

WILLIAM COBBETT (1762–1835)   18 July 1833

Speech in the House of Commons, in Hollis, ed., *Class and Conflict*, p. 198

CHILD LABOUR THE BACKBONE OF ENGLAND

We have, Sir, this night made one of the greatest discoveries ever made by a House of Commons, a discovery which will be hailed by the constituents of the Hon. Gentlemen behind me with singular pleasure. Hitherto, we have been told that our navy was the glory of the country, and that our maritime commerce and extensive manufactures were the mainstays of the realm. We have also been told that the land has its share in our greatness, and should justly be considered as the pride and glory of England. The Bank, also, has put in its claim to share in this praise, and has stated that public credit is due to it; but now, a most startling discovery has been made, namely, that all our greatness and prosperity, that our superiority over other nations, is owing to 300,000 little girls in Lancashire. We have made the notable discovery that, if these little girls work two hours less in a day than they do now, it would occasion the ruin of the country; that it would enable other nations to compete with us; and thus make an end to our boasted wealth, and bring us to beggary!

'SENEX'   14 June 1834

From *Pioneer*

WAGES

I would banish the word *wages* from the language, and consign it, with the word slavery, to histories and dictionaries. *Wages* is a term of purchase; it means the piecemeal purchase of your blood, and bones, and brains, at weekly payments; it is the present name for the *Saturday's market price of man, woman, and child*!

ROBERT OWEN (1771–1858)   29 March 1834

'To the Population of the World', in Postgate, ed., *Revolution from 1789 to 1906*, pp. 95–6

THE CAPITALIST SYSTEM

This great truth which I have now to declare to you, is, that 'the system on which all the nations of the world are acting is founded in gross deception, in the deepest ignorance or in a mixture of both. That, under no possible modifications of the principles on which it is based, can it ever produce good to man; but that, on the contrary, its practical results must ever be to produce evil continually' – and, consequently, that no really intelligent and honest individual can any longer support it; for, by the constitution of this system, it unavoidably encourages and upholds, as it ever has encouraged and upheld, hypocrisy and deception of every description, and discouraged and opposed truth and sincerity, whenever truth and sincerity were applied permanently to improve the condition of the human race. It encourages and upholds national vice and corruption to an unlimited extent; whilst to an equal degree it discourages national virtue and honesty. The whole system has not one redeeming quality; its very virtues, as they are termed, are vices of great magnitude. Its charities, so called, are gross acts of injustice and deception. Its instructions are to rivet ignorance in the mind and, if possible, render it perpetual. It supports, in all manner of extravagance, idleness, presumption, and uselessness; and oppresses, in almost every mode which ingenuity can devise, industry, integrity and usefulness. It encourages superstition, bigotry and fanaticism; and discourages truth, commonsense and rationality. It generates and cultivates every inferior quality and base passion that human nature can be made to receive; and has so disordered all the human intellects, that they have become universally perplexed and confused, so that man has no just title to be called a reasonable and rational being. It generates violence, robbery and murder, and extols and rewards these vices as the highest of all virtues. Its laws are founded in gross ignorance of individual man and of human society; they are cruel and unjust in the extreme, and, united with all the superstitions in the world, are calculated only to teach men to call that which is pre-eminently true and good, false and bad; and that which is glaringly false and bad, true and good. In short, to cultivate with great care all that leads to vice and misery in the mass, and to exclude from them, with equal care, all that would direct them to true knowledge and real happiness, which alone, combined, deserve the name of virtue.

In consequence of the dire effects of this wretched system upon the whole of the human race, the population of Great Britain – the most advanced of modern nations in the acquirement of riches, power and happiness – has created and supports a theory and practice of government which is directly opposed to the real well-being and true interests of every individual member of the empire, whatever may be his station, rank or condition – whether subject or sovereign. And so enormous are the increasing errors of this system now become, that, to uphold it the government is compelled, day by day, to commit acts of the grossest cruelty and injustice, and to call such proceedings laws of justice and of Christian mercy.

Under this system, the idle, the useless and the vicious govern the population of the world; whilst the useful and the truly virtuous, as far

461

as such a system will permit men to be virtuous, are by them degraded and oppressed . . .

Men of industry, and of good and virtuous habits! This is the last state to which you ought to submit; nor would I advise you to allow the ignorant, the idle, the presumptuous and the vicious, any longer to lord it over the well-being, the lives and happiness, of yourselves and families, when, by *three days* of such idleness as constitutes the whole of their lives, you would for ever convince each one of these mistaken individuals that you now possess the power to compel *them* at once to become the abject slaves, and the oppressed portion of society which they have hitherto made *you*.

'SENEX'   22 March 1834

Letter in *Pioneer*, in Postgate, ed., *Revolution from 1789 to 1906*, p. 93

LABOUR AND CAPITAL

The Trades Unions would have come into being and would have combined as they are now combining, into one universal union, if the Whigs had never risen from that abject state in which they lay so long overwhelmed under Tory power, until Tory tyranny had absolutely worn itself out. They have stepped into Tory places and would be as great as Tories, but ministerial greatness is dead and gone. It was paralysed with Lord Liverpool, and, after struggling through a few uneasy administrations, expired for ever under the Duke of Wellington.

To us, brethren, it matters little who or what may be the men that direct the crazy machine called *the state*. We have little to do with them. They are so hampered by the evils of a long course of misrule, that, positively, they can do us no good if they would.

The practical object at which we aim is, the securing to every human being a fair share of the produce of his labour . . . We know that the operative manufacturer and, in fact, the labourer of every description, requires sustenance, raw material and tools. These are derived from the reserved produce of former labour, which is termed *capital*. The amount of capital in this country is very great, but, brethren, it was you that gave it existence. What hours out of every twenty-four have you not employed in building it up! And what is it now it is reared? What but a vain pretence, unless you animate it: unless you give it thought and activity, the pyramids of Egypt (those monuments of a dreadful sacrifice of human labour to pride and superstition), are not more useless, while they may boast of being more durable. Reflect, though in the reflection, brethren, I know there is much anguish, how many of your fellow labourers, how many with whom you have communed in friendship, how many connected with you by the respected and the endeared ties of relationship, have sunk in toil and want; pale, sickening, and starving; while all the energies of their bodies and of their minds was given to the rearing of this mighty mass, this boasted *capital*! 'It is reserved labour,' cries McCulloch. 'Ay, reserved,' shout a hundred bloated capitalists over their French and Spanish wines, 'reserved for our present and future prosperity!' From whom and out of whom was it reserved? From the clothing and food of the wretched – from the refreshment of the weary – from the wages of those who sink exhausted on their hard pallets after sixteen hours of almost ceaseless labour . . .

GEORGE LOVELESS   1834

From *The Victims of Whiggery*

In 1834, Loveless and a group of Dorchester labourers (the Tolpuddle Martyrs) were sentenced to seven years' transportation for daring to join a union to protect themselves against exploitation and the progressive reduction of their wages, since they found 'it was impossible to live honestly on such scanty means'. The Whig government confirmed the sentence, in spite of petitions from the people and large-scale demonstrations, and it was not until 1836 that remission was granted. Loveless tells us he wrote this poem after the passing of the sentence, and that it too was used against him. On his return, he became a delegate to the 1839 Chartist convention.

THE TOLPUDDLE MARTYRS

God is our guide! from field, from wave,
From plough, from anvil, and from loom;
We come, our country's rights to save,
And speak a tyrant faction's doom:
We raise the watch-word liberty;
We will, we will, we will be free!

God is our guide! no swords we draw,
We kindle not war's battle fires;
By reason, union, justice, law,
We claim the birth-right of our sires:
We raise the watch-word liberty;
We will, we will, we will be free!!!

FRIEDRICH ENGELS (1820–95)

From *Condition of the Working Class in England in 1844*, p. 287

THE OPERATION OF THE NEW POOR LAW (1834)

All relief in money and provisions was abolished: the only relief allowed was admission to the workhouses immediately built. The regulations for these workhouses, or, as people call them, Poor Law Bastiles, is such as to frighten away everyone who has the slightest prospect in life without this form of public charity. To make sure that relief be applied for in only the most extreme cases, and after every other effort had failed, the workhouse has been made the most repulsive residence which the refined ingenuity of a Malthusian can invent. The food is worse than that of the most ill-paid working-man, while employed, and the work harder, or they might prefer the workhouse to their wretched existence outside. Meat, especially fresh meat, is rarely furnished, chiefly potatoes, the worst possible bread and oatmeal porridge, little or no beer. The food of criminal prisoners is better, as a rule, so that the paupers frequently commit some offence for the purpose of getting into jail. For the workhouse is a jail, too; he who does not finish his task gets nothing to eat; he who wishes to go out must ask permission, which is granted or not, according to his behaviour or the inspector's whim; tobacco is forbidden, also the receipt of gifts from relatives or friends outside the house; the paupers wear a workhouse uniform, and are handed over helpless and without redress, to the caprice of the inspectors. To prevent their labour from competing with that of outside concerns, they are set to rather useless tasks: the men break stones, 'as much as the strong man can accomplish with effort in a day'; the women, children and aged men pick oakum, for I know not what insignificant use. To prevent the 'superfluous' from multiplying, and 'demoralized' parents from influencing their children, families are broken up; the husband is placed in one wing, the wife in another, the children in a third, and they are permitted to see one another only at stated times after long intervals, and then only when they have, in the opinion of the officials, behaved well. And in order to shut off the external world from contamination by pauperism from within these bastiles, the inmates are permitted to receive visits only with the consent of the officials, and in the reception-rooms; to communicate in general with the world outside only by leave and under supervision.

JOHN CLARE (1793–1864)   1835 (?)

Letter to a weekly paper, in *Selected Poems and Prose*, pp. 171–3

In rural England the Corn Laws, taxation and tithes, not to mention the Poor Law of 1834, bore down heavily upon the poor, who always seemed to suffer, whatever the politicians promised.

THE THERMOMETER OF DISTRESS

Mr Editor

In this surprising stir of patriotism and wonderful change in the ways and opinions of men when your paper is weekly loaded with the free speeches of county meetings, can you find room for mine? or will you hear the voice of a poor man? – I only wish to ask you a few plain questions.

   Amidst all this stir about taxation and tithes and agricultural distress, are the poor to receive corresponding benefits [?] They have been told so I know but it is not the first time they have heard that and been disappointed. When the tax was taken from leather they was told they should have shoes almost for nothing and they heard the parliament speeches of patriots as the forthcoming prophecies of a political millennium but their hopes were soon frost-bitten for the tax has long since vanished and the price of shoes remains just where it did. Nay I believe they are a trifle dearer than they was then – that's the only difference. Then there was a hue and cry about taking off the duty of Spiritous liquors and the best Gin was to be little more in price than small beer. The poor man shook his head over such speeches and looking at his shoes had no faith to believe any more of these cheap wonders so he was not disappointed at finding gin as dear as ever – for which he had little to regret for he preferred good ale to any spirits. And now the Malt and beer tax is in full cry what is the poor man to expect? It may benefit the farmers a little and the common brewers a good deal and there no doubt the matter will end. The poor man will not find the refuse of any more use to him than a dry bone to a hungry dog – excuse the simile reader for the poor have been likened unto dogs before now. And many other of these time-serving hue and cries might be noticed in which the poor man was promised as much benefit as the stork was in the fable for pulling out the bone from the Wolf's throat and who got just as much at last as the stork did for his pains.

Some of the patriots of these meetings seem to consider the corn law as a bone sticking in the throat of the country's distress but I am sure that the poor man will be no better off in such a matter – he will only be 'burning his fingers' and not filling his belly, by harbouring any notions of benefit from that quarter for he is so many degrees lower in the Thermometer of distress that such benefits to others will not reach him and though the Farmers should again be in the summer splendour of 'high prices' and 'better markets' as they phrase it the poor man would still be found very little above freezing point – at least I very much fear so for I speak from experience and not from hearsay and hopes as some do. Some years back when grain sold at 5 and 6 guineas a quarter I can point out a many villages where the Farmers under a combination for each others' interests would give no more in winter than 10 shillings per Week. I will not say that all did so for in a many places and at that very time Farmers whose good intentions was 'to live and let live' gave from 12 to 15 shillings per week and these men would again do the same thing but they could not compel others and there it is where the poor man loses the benefit that ought to fall to him from the farmers' 'better markets' and 'high prices' for corn. I hope Mr Editor that I do not offend by my plain speaking for I wish only to be satisfied about these few particulars and I am so little of a politician that I would rather keep out of the crowd than that my hobnails should trample on the gouty toes of anyone. Though I cannot help thinking when I read your paper that there is a vast number of taxable advocates wearing barrack shoes or they would certainly not leave the advocates for reform to achieve their triumphs without a struggle. I wish the good of the people may be found at the end and that in the general triumph the poor man may not be forgotten. For the poor have many oppressors and no voice to be heard above them. He is a dumb burthen in the scorn of the world's prosperity yet in its adversity they are found ever ready to aid and assist and though that be but as the widow's mite yet his honest feelings in the cause are as worthy as the orator's proudest orations. Being a poor man myself I am naturally wishing to see some one become the advocate and champion for the poor not in his speeches but his actions. For speeches are nothing nowadays but words and sound. Politicians are known to be exceedingly wise as far as regards themselves and we have heard of one who though his whole thoughts seemed constantly professing the good of his country yet he was cunning enough to keep one thought to himself in the hour of danger when he luckily hit upon the thought of standing upon his hat to keep himself from catching cold not to die for the good of the country as some others did and to be alive as he is at this moment. Now if the poor man's chance at these meetings is anything better than being a sort of foot-cushion for the benefit of others I shall be exceedingly happy but as it is I much fear it as the poor man's lot seems to have been so long remembered as to be entirely forgotten.

I am sir your humble Servant

A Poor Man

ANONYMOUS 1837

Address from the *London Working Men's Association*, in Hollis, ed., *Class and Conflict*, pp. 141–2

Economic distress deepened for the working class in the 1830s. In 1831 a National Union of the Working Classes (Painite and Owenite in its demands) was formed in London, and lasted till 1833, giving way to the rise of the trades unions. But in 1836, former NUWC members organized the London Working Men's Association to agitate for universal suffrage, and it was the LWMA, together with the Birmingham Political Union, which initiated Chartism, by drafting the six points which were to form the basis of the People's Charter.

THE ROTTEN HOUSE OF COMMONS

Fellow-Countrymen – Have you ever inquired how far a just and economical system of government, a code of wise and just laws, and the abolition of the useless persons and appendages of State, would affect the interests of the present 658 members of the House of Commons?

Is the *Landholder*, whose interests lead him to keep up his rents by unjust and exclusive laws, a fit representative for working men?

Are the whole host of *Money-makers*, *Speculators*, and *Usurers*, who live on the corruptions of the system, fit representatives for the sons of labour?

Are the immense number of *Lords*, *Earls*, *Marquises*, *Knights*, *Baronets*, *Honourables* and *Right Honourables*, who have seats in that house, fit to represent our interests? many of whom have the certainty before them of being the *hereditary legislators* of the other house; or are the craving expectants of place or emolument; persons who cringe in the gilded circle of a court, flutter among the gaieties of the ball, oom, to court the passing smile of Royalty, or whine at the Ministers of the day; and when the interests of the people are at stake, in the Commons, are often found the revelling debauchees of fashion, or the duelling wranglers of a gambling-house.

Are the multitude of *Military* and *Naval Officers* in the present House of Commons, whose interest it is to support that system which secures them their pay and promotion, and whose only utility, at any time, is to direct one portion of our brethren to keep the other in subjection, fit to represent our grievances?

Have we fit representatives in the multitude of *Barristers*, *Attorneys* and *Solicitors*, most of them seeking places, and all of them having interests depending on the dissensions and corruptions of the people? . . .

Is the *Manufacturer* and *Capitalist*, whose exclusive monopoly of the combined powers of wood, iron and steam enables them to cause the destitution of thousands, and who have an interest in forcing labour down to the minimum reward, fit to represent the interests of working men?

Is the *Master*, whose interest it is to purchase labour at the cheapest rate, a fit representative of the *Workman*, whose interest it is to get the most he can for his labour?

Yet such is the only description of persons composing that house, and such the interests represented, to whom we, session after session, address *our humble petitions*, and whom we in our ignorant simplicity imagine will generously sacrifice their hopes and interests by beginning the great work of political and social reformation.

Working men, inquire if this be not true, and then if you feel with us, stand apart from all projects, and refuse to be the tools of any party, who will not, as a *first and essential measure*, give to the working classes *equal political and social rights*, so that they may send their own representatives from the ranks of those who live by labour into that house, to deliberate and to determine along with *all other interests*, that the interests of the labouring classes – of those who are the foundation of the social edifice – shall not be daily sacrificed to glut the extravagance of the pampered few. If you feel with us, then you will proclaim it in the workshop, preach it in your societies, publish it from town to village, from county to county, and from nation to nation, that there is no hope for the sons of toil, till those who feel with them, who sympathize with them, and whose interests are identified with theirs, have *an equal right to determine what laws shall be enacted or plans adopted for justly governing this country.*

HARRIET MARTINEAU (1802–1876)   1837

From *Society in America*, III, p. 108–9, 151

Born in Norwich, delicate and highly-strung, Harriet Martineau was early aware of the intolerable injustices done to her sex and spent much of her long and prolific life as a writer defending women's rights and campaigning for their liberation from enslavement, both in England and in America.

THE SUBJECTION OF WOMEN

How fearfully the morals of woman are crushed, appears from the prevalent persuasion that there are virtues which are peculiarly masculine, and others which are peculiarly feminine. It is amazing that a society which makes a most emphatic profession of its Christianity, should almost universally entertain such a fallacy: and not see that, in the case they suppose, instead of the character of Christ being the meeting point of all virtues, there would have been a separate gospel for women, and a second company of agents for its diffusion. It is not only that masculine and feminine employments are supposed to be properly different. No one in the world, I believe, questions this. But it is actually supposed that what are called the hardy virtues are more appropriate to men, and the gentler to women . . .

. . . The consequences are what might be looked for. Men are ungentle, tyrannical. They abuse the right of the strongest, however they may veil the abuse with indulgence. They want the magnanimity to discern woman's human rights; and they crush her morals rather than allow them. Women are, as might be anticipated, weak, ignorant and subservient, in as far as they exchange self-reliance for reliance on anything out of themselves. Those who will not submit to such a suspension of their moral functions, (for the work of self-perfection remains to be done, sooner or later,) have to suffer for their allegiance to duty. They have all the need of bravery that the few heroic men who assert the highest rights of women have of gentleness, to guard them from the encroachment to which power, custom, and education, incessantly conduce . . .

. . . The progression or emancipation of any class usually, if not always, takes place through the efforts of individuals of that class: and so it must be here. All women should inform themselves of the condition of their sex, and of their own position. It must necessarily follow that the noblest of them will, sooner or later, put forth a moral power which shall prostrate cant, and burst asunder the bonds, (silken to some, but cold iron to others,) of feudal prejudices and usages. In the meantime, is it to be understood that the principles of the Declaration of Independence bear no relation to half of the human race? If so, what is the ground of the limitation? If not so, how is the restricted and dependent state of women to be reconciled with the proclamation that 'all are endowed by their Creator with certain inalienable rights; that among these are life, liberty, and the pursuit of happiness'?

GEORGE LOVELESS   August 1837

From *The Victims of Whiggery*, p. 31

After his return from transportation in Australia, Loveless recounted the story of the Tolpuddle labourers and their persecution, and urged working men to act in defence of their rights.

LABOUR IS THE POOR MAN'S PROPERTY

England has for many years been lifting her voice against the abominable practice of negro slavery; numbers of her great men have talked, have laboured, have struggled, until at length emancipation has been granted to her black slaves in the West Indies. When will they dream of advocating the cause of England's white slaves? . . . Never – no never, will (with a few honourable exceptions) the rich and the great devise means to alleviate the distress, and remove the misery felt by the working men of England. What then is to be done? Why, the labouring classes must do it themselves, or it will be for ever left undone: the laws of reason and justice demand their doing it. Labour is the poor man's property, from which all protection is withheld. Has not then the working man as much right to preserve and protect his labour as the rich man has his capital?

But I am told that the working men ought to remain still and let their cause work its way – 'that God in his good time will bring it about for him'. However, this is not my creed; I believe that God works – by means and men . . . Under this such an impression . . . Let every working man come forward, from east to west, and from north to south, unite firmly but peaceably together as the heart of one man; let them be determined to have a voice in, and form a part of, the British nation; then no longer would the interest of the millions be sacrificed for the gain of a few, but the blessings resulting from such a change would be felt by us, our posterity, even to generations yet unborn. Such a measure I am well aware, would be dreaded, reviled, and reprobated by the monied part of the nation; they would devise all those schemes, stratagems and policy that the art and cunning of man can invent to thwart and retard it. But let the working classes of Britain . . . listen to nothing that might be presented before them to draw their attention from the subject . . . and they will accomplish their own salvation and that of the world. Arise, men of Britain, and take your stand! rally round the standard of Liberty, or for ever lay prostrate under the iron hand of your land and money-mongering taskmasters!

J. R. STEPHENS   10 November 1838

From the *Northern Star*, in Hollis, ed., *Class and Conflict*, p. 208

DEMAND FOR REPEAL OF THE NEW POOR LAW

. . . If this damnable law, which violated all the laws of God, was continued, and all means of peaceably putting an end to it had been made in vain, then, in the words of their banner, 'For children and wife we'll war to the knife.' If the people who produce all wealth could not be allowed, according to God's word, to have the kindly fruits of the earth which they had, in obedience to God's word, raised by the sweat of their brow, then war to the knife with their enemies, who were the enemies of God. If the musket and the pistol, the sword and the pike, were of no avail, let the women take the scissors, the child the pin or needle. If all failed, then the firebrand – aye, the firebrand – the firebrand, I repeat. The palace shall be in flames. I pause, my friends. If the cottage is not permitted to be the abode of man and wife, and if the smiling infant is to be dragged from a father's arms and a mother's bosom, it is because these hell-hounds of commissioners have set up the command of their master the devil, against our God.

FEMALE POLITICAL UNION
OF NEWCASTLE

In the *Northern Star*, in Hollis, ed., *Women in Public*, pp. 288–9

WOMEN AGAINST BONDAGE

Fellow Countrywomen,

We call upon you to join us and help our fathers, husbands and brothers, to free themselves and us from political, physical and mental bondage . . .

We have been told that the province of woman is her home, and that the field of politics should be left to men; this we deny . . . Is it not true that the interests of our fathers, husbands, and brothers, ought to be ours? If they are oppressed and impoverished, do we not share those evils with them? If so, ought we not to resent the infliction of those wrongs upon us? . . .

We have seen that because the husband's earnings could not support his family, the wife has been compelled to leave her home neglected and, with her infant children, work at a soul and body degrading toil . . . We have seen the poor robbed of their inheritance, and a law enacted to treat poverty as a crime . . . – this law was passed by men and supported by men, who avow the doctrine that the poor have no right to live . . .

For years we have struggled to maintain our homes in comfort, such as our hearts told us should greet our husbands after their fatiguing labour. Year after year has passed away, and even now our wishes have no prospect of being realized, our husbands are over-wrought, our houses half-furnished, our families ill-fed, and our children uneducated – the fear of want hangs over our heads; the scorn of the rich is pointed towards us; the brand of slavery is on our kindred, and we feel the degradation . . .

We have searched and found that the cause of these evils is the Government of the country being in the hands of a few of the upper and middle classes, while the working men who form the millions, the strength and wealth of the country, are left without the pale of the Constitution, their wishes never consulted, and their interests sacrificed by the ruling factions . . . For these evils there is no remedy but the just measure of allowing every citizen of the United Kingdom, the right of voting in the election of the members of Parliaments, who have to make the laws that he has to be governed by, and grant the taxes he has to pay; or, in other words, to pass the people's Charter into a law and emancipate the white slaves of England . . .

We tell the wealthy, the high and mighty ones of the land, our kindred shall be free. We tell their lordly dames that we love our husbands as well as they love theirs, that our homes shall be no longer destitute of comfort . . . we call on all persons to assist us in this good work, but especially those shopkeepers which the Reform bill enfranchised . . . They ought to remember that our pennies make their pounds . . .

MRS GASKELL (1810–65)   1839

From *Mary Barton: A Tale of Manchester Life*, pp. 126–7, 143–5

The formal constitution of Chartism was ratified during a meeting at Newhall Hill on 6 August 1838. The movement had grown out of the terrible sufferings of the 1830s, particularly after the Reform Act of 1832, and gathered momentum with the campaigns against the factory system and the new Poor Law. Both extreme radicals (men like Ernest Jones, Feargus O'Connor, Bronterre O'Brien, John Frost) and Tories or middle-class reformers (such as Richard Oastler, J. R. Stephens, William Lovett and Francis Place) were caught up in the movement, which split into two groups – the 'Moral Force' and the 'Physical Force' Chartists – the one working for reform, the other for revolution. Physical force Chartism led to bloody riots in Birmingham and other cities and to the tragic isolation of the Newport rising, after which there were many arrests. In the meantime, the first national petition, signed by 1,280,000 people, had been organized and rejected.

WORKING-CLASS POVERTY AND THE FIRST CHARTIST PETITION, 1839

From Chapter 8

. . . The most deplorable and enduring evil that arose out of the period of commercial depression to which I refer, was this feeling of alienation between the different classes of society. It is so impossible to describe, or even faintly to picture, the state of distress which prevailed in the town at that time, that I will not attempt it; and yet I think again that surely, in a Christian land, it was not known even so feebly as words could tell it, or the more happy and fortunate would have thronged with their sympathy and their aid. In many instances the sufferers wept first, and then they cursed. Their vindictive feelings exhibited themselves in rabid politics. And when I hear, as I have heard, of the sufferings and privations of the poor, of provision shops where ha-porths of tea, sugar,

473

butter, and even flour, were sold to accommodate the indigent, – of parents sitting in their clothes by the fire-side during the whole night for seven weeks together, in order that their only bed and bedding might be reserved for the use of their large family, – of others sleeping upon the cold hearthstone for weeks in succession, without adequate means of providing themselves with food or fuel (and this in the depth of winter), – of others being compelled to fast for days together, uncheered by any hope of better fortune, living, moreover, or rather starving, in a crowded garret, or damp cellar, and gradually sinking under the pressure of want and despair into a premature grave; and when this has been confirmed by the evidence of their care-worn looks, their excited feelings, and their desolate homes, – can I wonder that many of them, in such times of misery and destitution, spoke and acted with ferocious precipitation?

An idea was now springing up among the operatives, that originated with the Chartists, but which came at last to be cherished as a darling child by many and many a one. They could not believe that the government knew of their misery; they rather chose to think it possible that men could voluntarily assume the office of legislators for a nation, ignorant of its real state; as who should make domestic rules for the pretty behaviour of children, without caring to know that those children had been kept for days without food. Besides, the starving multitudes had heard, that the very existence of their distress had been denied in Parliament; and though they felt this strange and inexplicable, yet the idea that their misery had still to be revealed in all its depths, and that then some remedy would be found, soothed their aching hearts, and kept down their rising fury.

So a petition was framed, and signed by thousands in the bright spring days of 1839, imploring Parliament to hear witnesses who could testify to the unparalleled destitution of the manufacturing districts. Nottingham, Sheffield, Glasgow, Manchester, and many other towns, were busy appointing delegates to convey this petition, who might speak, not merely of what they had seen, and had heard, but from what they had borne and suffered. Life-worn, gaunt, anxious, hunger-stamped men, were those delegates.

JOHN BARTON DESCRIBES THE CHARTISTS' MARCH TO PARLIAMENT

From Chapter 9

'. . . Well, after breakfast, we were all set to walk in procession, and a time it took to put us in order, two and two, and the petition as was yards long, carried by th' foremost pairs. The men looked grave enough, yo may be sure; and such a set of thin, wan, wretched-looking chaps as they were!'

'Yourself is none to boast on.'

'Ay, but I were fat and rosy to many a one. Well, we walked on and on through many a street, much the same as Deansgate. We had to walk slowly, slowly, for th' carriages and cabs as thronged th' streets. I thought by-and-by we should may be get clear on 'em, but as th' streets grew wider they grew worse, and at last we were fairly blocked up in Oxford Street. We getten across at last though, and my eyes! the grand streets we were in then! . . . By this it were dinner-time, or better, as we could tell by th' sun, right above our heads, and we were dusty and tired, going a step now and a step then. Well, at last we getten into a street grander nor all, leading to th' Queen's palace, and there it were I thought I saw th' Queen. Yo've seen th' hearses wi' white plumes, Job?'

Job assented.

'Well, them undertaker folk are driving a pretty trade in London. Wellnigh every lady we saw in a carriage had hired one o' them plumes for the day, and had it niddle noddling on her head. It were the Queen's drawing-room, they said, and th' carriages went bowling along toward her house, some wi' dressed up gentlemen like circus folk in 'em, and rucks o' ladies in others. Carriages themselves were great shakes too. Some o' th' gentlemen as couldn't get inside hung on behind, wi' nose-gays to smell at, and sticks to keep off folk as might splash their silk stockings. I wondered why they didn't hire a cab rather than hang on like a whip-behind boy; but I suppose they wished to keep wi' their wives, Darby and Joan like. Coachmen were little squat men, wi' wigs like th' oud fashioned parsons. Well, we could na get on for these car-riages, though we waited and waited. Th' horses were too fat to move quick; they'n never known want o' food, one might tell by their sleek coats; and police pushed us back when we tried to cross. One or two on 'em struck wi' their sticks, and coachmen laughed, and some officers as stood nigh put their spy-glasses in their eye, and left 'em sticking there like mountebanks. One o' th' police struck me. 'Whatten business have yo to do that?' said I.

'"You're frightening them horses," says he in his mincing way (for Londoners are mostly all tongue-tied, and can't say their a's and i's properly), "and it's our business to keep you from molesting the ladies and gentlemen going to her Majesty's drawing-room."

'"And why are we to be molested," asked I, "going decently about our business, which is life and death to us, and many a little one clemming at home in Lancashire? Which business is of most consequence i' the sight o' God, think yo, ou'n or them gran' ladies and gentlemen as yo think so much on?"

'But I might as well ha' held my peace, for he only laughed.'

John ceased. After waiting a little to see if he would go on of himself, Job said,

'Well, but that's not a' your story, man. Tell us what happened when yo got to th' Parliament House.'

After a little pause John answered,

'If yo please, neighbour, I'd rather say nought about that. It's not to be forgotten or forgiven either by me or many another; but I canna tell of our downcasting just as a piece of London news. As long as I live, our rejection that day will bide in my heart; and as long as I live I shall curse them as so cruelly refused to hear us; but I'll not speak of it no more.'

FIRST CHARTIST PETITION
Rejected 12 July 1839

The People's Charter, in Postgate, ed., *Revolution from 1789 to 1906*, pp. 127–9

UNIVERSAL SUFFRAGE

Unto the Honourable the Commons of the United Kingdom of Great Britain and Ireland in Parliament assembled, the Petition of the undersigned, their suffering countrymen,

HUMBLY SHOWETH

That we, your petitioners, dwell in a land where merchants are noted for enterprise, whose manufactures are very skilful, and whose workmen are proverbial for their industry.

The land itself is goodly, the soil rich, and the temperature wholesome; it is abundantly furnished with the materials of commerce and

476

trade; it has numerous and convenient harbours; in facility of internal communication it exceeds all others.

For three-and-twenty years we have enjoyed a profound peace.

Yet, with all these elements of national prosperity, and with every disposition and capacity to take advantage of them, we find ourselves overwhelmed with public and private suffering.

We are bowed down under a load of taxes; which, notwithstanding, fall greatly short of the wants of our rulers; our traders are trembling on the verge of bankruptcy; our workmen are starving; capital brings no profit and labour no renumeration; the home of the artificer is desolate, and the warehouse of the pawnbroker is full; the workhouse is crowded and the manufactory is deserted.

We have looked on every side, we have searched diligently in order to find out the causes of a distress so sore and so long continued.

We can find none in nature, or in Providence.

Heaven has dealt graciously by the people; but the foolishness of our rulers has made the goodness of God of none effect.

The energies of a mighty kingdom have been wasted in building up the power of selfish and ignorant men, and its resources squandered for their aggrandizement.

The good of a party has been advanced to the sacrifice of the good of the nation; the few have governed for the interests of the few, while the interest of the many has been neglected or insolently and tyrannously trampled upon.

It was the fond expectation of the people that a remedy for the greater part, if not for the whole, of their grievances, would be found in the Reform Act of 1832.

They were taught to regard that Act as a wise means to a worthy end; as the machinery of an improved legislation, when the will of the masses would be at length potential.

They have been bitterly and basely deceived.

The fruit which looked so fair to the eye has turned to dust and ashes when gathered.

The Reform Act has effected a transfer of power from one dominating faction to another, and left the people as helpless as before.

Our slavery has been exchanged for an apprenticeship to liberty, which has aggravated the painful feeling of our social degradation, by adding to it the sickening of still deferred hope.

We come before your Honourable House to tell you, with all humility, that this state of things must not be permitted to continue; that it cannot very long continue without very seriously endangering the stability of

477

the throne and the peace of the kingdom; and that if by God's help and all lawful and constitutional appliances, an end can be put to it, we are fully resolved that it shall speedily come to an end.

We tell your Honourable House that the capital of the master must no longer be deprived of its due reward; that the laws which make food dear, and those which, by making money scarce, make labour cheap, must be abolished; that taxation must be made to fall on property, not on industry; that the good of the many, as it is the only legitimate end, so it must be the sole study of the government.

As a preliminary essential to these and other requisite changes, as means by which alone the interests of the people can be effectually vindicated and secured we demand that those interests be confided to the keeping of the people.

When the state calls for defenders, when it calls for money, no consideration of poverty or ignorance can be pleaded in refusal or delay of the call.

Required, as we are, universally, to support and obey the laws, nature and reason entitle us to demand, that in the making of the laws, the universal voice shall be implicitly listened to.

We perform the duties of freemen; we must have the privileges of freemen.

WE DEMAND UNIVERSAL SUFRAGE

The suffrage to be exempt from the corruption of the wealthy, and the violence of the powerful, must be secret.

The assertion of our right necessarily involves the power of its uncontrolled exercise.

WE DEMAND THE BALLOT

The connection between the representatives and the people, to be beneficial must be intimate.

The legislative and constituent powers, for correction and for instruction, ought to be brought into frequent contact.

Errors, which are comparatively light when susceptible of a speedy popular remedy, may produce the most disastrous effects when permitted to grow inveterate through years of compulsory endurance.

To public safety as well as public confidence, frequent elections are essential.

With power to choose, and freedom in choosing, the range of our choice must be unrestricted.

We are compelled, by the existing laws, to take for our representatives, men who are incapable of appreciating our difficulties, or who have little sympathy with them; merchants who have retired from trade, and no longer feel its harrassings; proprietors of land who are alike ignorant of its evils and their cure; lawyers, by whom the honours of the senate are sought after only as a means of obtaining notice in the courts.

The labours of a representative, who is sedulous in the discharge of his duty, are numerous and burdensome.

It is neither just, nor reasonable, nor safe, that they should continue to be gratuitously rendered.

We demand that in the future election of members of your Honourable House, the approbation of the constituency shall be the sole qualification; and that to every representative so chosen shall be assigned, out of the public taxes, a fair and adequate remuneration for the time which he is called upon to devote to the public service.

Finally, we would most earnestly impress upon your Honourable House, that this petition has not been dictated by any idle love of change; that it springs out of no inconsiderate attachment to fanciful theories; but that it is the result of much and long deliberation, and of convictions, which the events of each succeeding year tend more and more to strengthen.

The management of this mighty kingdom has hitherto been a subject for contending factions to try their selfish experiments upon.

We have felt the consequences in our sorrowful experience – short glimmerings of uncertain enjoyment swallowed up by long and dark seasons of suffering.

If the self-government of the people should not remove their distresses, it will at least remove their repinings.

Universal suffrage will, and it alone can, bring true and lasting peace to the nation; we firmly believe that it will also bring prosperity.

May it therefore please your Honourable House to take this our petition into your most serious consideration; and to use your utmost endeavours, by all constitutional means, to have a law passed, granting to every male of lawful age, sane mind and unconvicted of crime, the right of voting for members of Parliament; and directing all future elections of members of Parliament to be in the way of secret ballot; and ordaining that the duration of Parliaments so chosen shall in no case exceed one year; and abolishing all property qualifications in the members; and providing for their due remuneration while in attendance on their Parliamentary duties.

MRS GASKELL (1810–65)   1839

From *Mary Barton*, pp. 157–8

AFTER THE REJECTED PETITION

From Chapter 10

Despair settled down like a heavy cloud; and now and then, through the dead calm of sufferings, came pipings of stormy winds, foretelling the end of these dark prognostics. In times of sorrowful or fierce endurance, we are often soothed by the mere repetition of old proverbs which tell the experience of our forefathers; but now, 'it's a long lane that has no turning', 'the weariest day draws to an end', etc., seemed false and vain sayings, so long and so weary was the pressure of the terrible times. Deeper and deeper still sank the poor; it showed how much lingering suffering it takes to kill men, that so few (in comparison) died during those times. But remember! we only miss those who do men's work in their humble sphere; the aged, the feeble, the children, when they die, are hardly noted by the world; and yet to many hearts, their deaths make a blank which long years will never fill up. Remember, too, that though it may take much suffering to kill the able-bodied and effective members of society, it does not take much to reduce them to worn, listless, diseased creatures, who thenceforward crawl through life with moody hearts and pain-stricken bodies.

The people had thought the poverty of the preceding years hard to bear, and had found its yoke heavy; but this year added sorely to its weight. Former times had chastised them with whips, but this chastised them with scorpions.

Of course, Barton had his share of mere bodily sufferings. Before he had gone up to London on his vain errand, he had been working short time. But in the hopes of speedy redress by means of the interference of Parliament, he had thrown up his place; and now, when he asked leave to resume work, he was told they were diminishing their number of hands every week, and he was made aware by the remarks of fellow workmen, that a Chartist delegate, and a leading member of a Trades' Union, was not likely to be favoured in his search after employment . . .

480

JOHN WARDEN AND GEORGE LLOYD   1839

From the *Northern Star* 11 April 1840, reporting on their trial at
Liverpool Assizes, in Hollis, ed., *Class and Conflicts*, pp. 238; 241–2

On 12 August 1839 there was a great Chartist strike (or 'National Holiday' as it
was called) in Bolton, as in other places, when the people came out against what
the Charter called 'the murderous majority of the upper and middle classes, who
prey upon their labour'. Warden and Lloyd were arrested as agitators. They were
found not guilty.

WE, THE CHARTISTS

John Warden

. . . if you once destroy the aspirations of the great mass of the people
for political privileges, or debar them from the exercise of rights which
they feel they ought to possess, you crush them into an abyss of slavery,
and, having degraded them into slaves, you must expect from them nothing but the vices of slaves; immorality in all its multiplied forms; social
misery with social degradation; political hatred with political wrong.
Once bestow upon the men who produce all your wealth – who build
your houses – who fill your granaries – who make your table groan
beneath the accumulated luxuries of every clime – who provide for your
wants in peace, and who protect you in the hour of danger – who man
your fleets, and who fight your battles; – once bestow upon these men
the power of exercising those privileges which none have a right to
deprive them of, and which all ought to possess, and you will put a stop
to those political animosities which always disturb, and often destroy
those social relations, without which no community can long exist, and
without which no nation can be powerful and happy. We, the Chartists,
have asked no more than this, and depend upon it, the great and growing
wants of the people can never be satisfied with less.

Gentlemen, we live in new times – the labourer is no longer content
to live as a mere passive serf, created only to minister to the wants of
some feudal lord, or some rich commercial speculators. He has nobler
aims and higher aspirations. He feels that he was not made for the purpose of conforming to institutions which he has not the power of mod-
ifying, according to his wants, and which, instead of multiplying his
pleasures, tend in their general effects to extend the number of his miseries . . . he feels that the welfare of the people can only be promoted

481

and secured when the laws, so potent in their influences over the happiness of the community, are made by all and for the interest of all . . .

George Lloyd

My Lord, what have I suffered? I was arrested early on the morning of the day after 12 August – a day on which there had been no disturbance – no riot – no breach of the peace; I was hurried away after my examination before the magistrates, who committed me without anything like evidence, and who have instituted this prosecution rather to screen themselves from their own negligence and imprudence that to punish me for any supposed crime – I was carried away and denied the constitutional privilege of bail – I was hurried away from my home and from my family, guarded by two troops of dragoons, one on each side of the carriage which brought me to prison, as though I had been guilty of some enormous offence – I was hurried away to Kirkdale, there to remain without the privilege of putting in bail, which could have procured bail of sufficient responsibility, I was hurried along to the prison, where I remained for six weeks, and had afterwards to sit in a dark cell, under this Court, during the whole of the proceedings of the last Assizes; and all this I had to suffer, simply for asserting the rights of my fellow-creatures. And my Lord and Gentlemen of the Jury, when I tell you that I have suffered this much, and that while I was in this confinement news was brought to me that my wife and two children had died in consequence of the illegal and sudden arrest made upon my person, then I say, my Lord and the Gentlemen of the Jury, knowing that you are not without the feelings of men, and of Englishmen, will admit that I have suffered more than enough, even supposing the worst charges in that indictment should be fully proved against me. I will not, however, deceive your Lordships and the Jury. The report to which I have just alluded, although calculated to induce, in the mind of any man, the most painful sensations, and to render under such circumstances an illegal imprisonment more dreadful than death in its worst forms, did not turn out to be true. My wife did not die in consequence of my imprisonment, although she had had a premature confinement brought on by it. When I came out of prison, the first thing I had to do was to endeavour to tranquillize a dear and affectionate child, who, in consequence of the arrest of her father, had been deprived of reason. I succoured that child, but in vain – she died in my arms; and when dead, my circumstances were such, that I had to beg the price of materials to make her a coffin, and even had with my own hands to make that coffin, before her remains could be committed to the dust . . .

These things, my Lord, and Gentlemen of the Jury I have suffered simply for asserting the rights of my fellow-creatures – [Here Mr Lloyd himself seemed to be much affected, and overpowered for a moment, but with a nerve that few men have been known to possess he resumed his address in a tone of manly dignity, and proceeded] – My Lord, and Gentlemen of the Jury, afflicting as those circumstances are to me – afflicting as they must have been to any man placed in my situation, I am prepared for the sake of those principles, to part with everything which is dear to me – with everything which can be called sacred in the enjoyment of domestic society and domestic peace, and to suffer ten times more than I have suffered, or more than I can imagine myself capable of suffering, rather than give up that which I am persuaded it is the right of every Englishman to enjoy. My Lord, and Gentlemen of the Jury, I will not trouble you with any further observations. I leave my case in your hands with confidence, knowing that I shall receive justice. My Lord, justice is all I ask; mercy I do not need.

'REFORMATOR'   17 November 1839

From *Charter* (a working-class Chartist newspaper), in Hollis, ed., *Class and Conflict*, pp. 243–4

There was widespread arming in the north in 1839 against the terrible conditions that prevailed, and the Physical Force Chartists organized in London for a general rising, which failed because the movement was split and only south Wales responded, its miners led by John Frost being defeated after thirty of his men were shot. The threat to execute Frost led to other risings at Dewsbury, Sheffield and Bradford. Frost was eventually transported, and five hundred leading Chartists imprisoned, putting an end to such direct action.

THE NEWPORT RISING

. . . At least eight thousand men, mostly miners employed in the neighbourhood (which is very densely populated) were engaged in the attack upon the town of Newport and that many of them were armed. Their design seems to have been to wreak their vengeance upon the Newport magistrates, for the prosecution of Vincent and others, now lying in

Monmouth gaol, and after securing the town, to advance to Monmouth, and liberate these prisoners. The ultimate design of the leaders does not appear; but it probably was to rear the standard of rebellion throughout Wales, in hopes of being able to hold the royal forces at bay, in that mountainous district, until the people of England, assured by successes, should rise, *en masse*, for the same objects. According to the evidence now before the world, Mr Frost, the late member of the Convention, led the rioters, and he, with others, has been committed for high treason. On entering Newport, the people marched straight to the Westgate Hotel, where the magistrates, with about forty soldiers were assembled, being fully apprised of the intended outbreak. The Riot Act was read, and the soldiers fired down, with ease and security, upon the people who had first broken and fired into the windows. The people in a few minutes found their position untenable, and retired to the outside of the town, to concert a different plan of attack, but ultimately returned home, without attempting anything more. The soldiers did not leave their place of shelter to follow them. About thirty of the people are known to have been killed, and several to have been wounded . . . It is fortunate that the people did not think of setting fire to the buildings adjoining the Westgate Hotel, which would have compelled the soldiers to quit their stronghold, and surrender themselves prisoners . . . but it is far better for the sacred cause of liberty that this foolish rising was so ill-conducted as to be checked at the outset. The rioters did not disgrace themselves by any wanton destruction of property nor by plunder. The Chartists, as a body, are too well-informed to offer any countenance or encouragement to any such resorts to violence, for the attainment of their just rights.

JOSEPH ARCH (1826–1919)   Winter 1840

The Life of Joseph Arch by Himself, pp. 10, 12, 17, 25, 34–5

VILLAGE TYRANNY

Because my father had refused to sign for 'a small loaf and a dear one', he could not get any work whatever for eighteen weeks. He tried hard to get a job, but it was useless; he was a marked man, and we should have starved if my mother had not kept us all by her laundry work.

It was a terrible winter . . . Those who owned and held the land believed, and acted up to their belief as far as they were able, that the land belonged to the rich man only, that the poor man had no part or lot in it, and had no sort of claim on society. If the poor man dared to marry and have children, they thought he had no *right* to claim the necessary food wherewith to keep himself and his family alive. They thought, too, every mother's son of them, that, when a labourer could no longer work, he had lost the right to live. Work was all they wanted from him; he was to work and hold his tongue, year in and year out, early and late, and if he could not work, why, what was the use of him? It was what he was made for, to labour and toil for his betters, without complaint on a starvation wage. When no more work could be squeezed out of him he was no better than a cumberer of other folk's ground, and the proper place for such as he was the churchyard, where he would be sure to lie quiet under a few feet of earth, and want neither food nor wages any more. A quick death and a cheap burying – that was the motto of those extortioners for the poor man past work . . .

I remember a thing which made my mother very angry. The parson's wife issued a decree, that the labourers should sit on one side of the church and their wives on the other. When my mother heard of it she said, 'No, "those whom God hath joined together let no man put asunder", and certainly no woman shall!'

The teaching in most of the village schools, then, was bad almost beyond belief. 'Much knowledge of the right sort is a dangerous thing for the poor', might have been the motto put up over the door of the village school in my day. The less book-learning the labourer's lad got stuffed into him, the better for him, and the safer for those above him, was what those in authority believed and acted up to . . . These gentry did not want him to know; they did not want him to think; they only wanted him to work. To toil with the hand was what he was born into the world for, and they took precious good care to see that he did it from his youth upwards. Of course he might learn his catechism; that, and things similar to it, was the right, proper, and suitable knowledge for such as he; he would be the more likely to stay contentedly in his place to the end of his working days . . .

We labourers had no lack of lords and masters. There were the parson and his wife at the rectory. There was the squire, with his hand of iron overshadowing us all. There was no velvet glove on that hard hand, as many a poor man found to his hurt. He brought it down on my father because he would not sign for a small loaf and a dear one; and if it had not been for my mother, that hand would have crushed him to the earth, maybe crushed the life right out of him. At the sight of the squire the people trembled. He lorded it right feudally over his tenants, the farmers; the farmers in their turn tyrannized over the labourers; the labourers were no better than toads under a harrow. Most of the farmers were oppressors of the poor; they put on the iron wage-screw, and screwed the labourers' wages down, down below living point; they stretched him on the rack of life-long abject poverty.

CHARLES DICKENS (1812–70)   1840–41

From *The Old Curiosity Shop*, pp. 424–6, 427–8

BLACK COUNTRY NIGHTMARE

From Chapter 45

. . . Before, behind, and to the right and left, was the same interminable perspective of brick towers, never ceasing in their black vomit, blasting all things living or inanimate, shutting out the face of day, and closing in on all these horrors with a dense dark cloud.

But night-time in this dreadful spot! – night, when the smoke was changed to fire, when every chimney spitted up its flame; and places, that had been dark vaults all day, now shone red-hot, with figures moving to and fro within their blazing jaws, and calling to one another with hoarse cries – night, when the noise of every strange machine was aggravated by the darkness; when the people near them looked wilder and more savage; when bands of unemployed labourers paraded the roads, or clustered by torchlight round their leaders, who told them, in stern language, of their wrongs, and urged them on to frightful cries and threats; when maddened men, armed with sword and fire-brand, spurning the tears and prayers of women who would restrain them, rushed forth on errands of terror and destruction, to work no ruin half so surely as their own – night, when carts came rumbling by, filled with rude coffins (for contagious disease and death had been busy with the living crops); when orphans cried, and distracted women shrieked and followed in their wake – night, when some called for bread, and some for drink to drown their cares, and some with tears and some with staggering feet, and some with bloodshot eyes, went brooding home – night, which, unlike the night that Heaven sends on earth, brought with it no peace, nor quiet, nor signs of blessed sleep – who shall tell the terrors of the night to the young wandering child?

THE OPPRESSED PEOPLE: A WOMAN'S DESPAIR

From Chapter 45

Towards the afternoon her grandfather complained bitterly of hunger. She approached one of the wretched hovels by the wayside, and knocked with her hand upon the door.

'What would you have here?' said a gaunt man, opening it.

'Charity. A morsel of bread.'

'Do you see that?' returned the man hoarsely, pointing to a kind of bundle on the ground. 'That's a dead child. I and five hundred other men were thrown out of work three months ago. That is my third dead child, and last. Do you think *I* have charity to bestow, or a morsel of bread to spare?'

The child recoiled from the door, and it closed upon her. Impelled by strong necessity, she knocked at another, a neighbouring one, which, yielding to the slight pressure of her hand, flew open.

It seemed that a couple of poor families lived in this hovel, for two women, each among children of her own, occupied different portions of the room. In the centre stood a grave gentleman in black, who appeared to have just entered, and who held by the arm a boy.

'Here, woman,' he said, 'here's your deaf and dumb son. You may thank me for restoring him to you. He was brought before me this morning, charged with theft; and with any other boy it would have gone hard, I assure you. But, as I had compassion on his infirmities, and thought he might have learned no better, I have managed to bring him back to you. Take more care of him for the future.'

'And won't you give me back *my* son?' said the other woman, hastily rising and confronting him. 'Won't you give me back *my* son, sir; who was transported for the same offence?'

'Was *he* deaf and dumb, woman?' asked the gentleman sternly.

'Was he not, sir?'

'You know he was not.'

'He was,' cried the woman. 'He was deaf, dumb and blind to all that was good and right, from his cradle. Her boy may have learned no better! where did mine learn better? where could he? who was there to teach him better, or where was it to be learned?'

'Peace, woman,' said the gentleman; 'your boy was in possession of all his senses.'

'He was,' cried the mother; 'and he was the more easy to be led astray because he had them. If you save this boy because he may not know right

487

from wrong, why did you not save mine, who was never taught the difference? You gentlemen have as good a right to punish her boy, that God has kept in ignorance of sound and speech, as you have to punish mine, that you kept in ignorance yourselves. How many of the girls and boys – ah, men and women, too – that are brought before you and you don't pity, are deaf and dumb in their minds, and go wrong in that state, and are punished in that state, body and soul, while you gentlemen are quarrelling among yourselves whether they ought to learn this or that? Be a just man, sir, and give me back my son.'

'You are desperate,' said the gentleman, taking out his snuff-box, 'and I am sorry for you.'

'I *am* desperate,' returned the woman, 'and you have made me so. Give me back my son, to work for these helpless children. Be a just man, sir, and as you have mercy on this boy, give me back my son!'

The child had seen and heard enough to know that this was not a place at which to ask for alms. She led the old man softly from the door, and they pursued their journey.

BRONTERRE O'BRIEN (1805–64)   24 April 1841

In the *Northern Star*, in Hollis, ed., *Class and Conflict*, pp. 270–71

O'Brien and Feargus O'Connor, Chartist leaders, believed that any alliance with the middle class, particularly after 1832 and the new Poor Law, would turn working men into fodder for middle-class causes and thus weaken the Charter. Later, both modified their views on this question.

THE CHARTER: NO ALLIANCE

We have a perfect right to hold them responsible for those evils – seeing they will neither remove them themselves, nor suffer us to do so – and that as no sane person would think of uniting for any purpose with known enemies, our proper business as Chartists, is to combine together as one man, not *with* the middle class, but *against* them, in order to put an end to their usurpations.

But, it is said, some of them are friendly to us, would you exclude them? Certainly not; if they be really friendly, they will unite with us to get *the Charter* – if they be not, they will exclude themselves. We cannot reject any man, of any class, who *bona fide* admits our principles;

nor have we ever spurned the cooperation of middle-class Chartists. On the contrary we have always received them with open arms, and will do so again . . . The People's Charter excludes no one from the rights of citizenship; neither will the Chartists exclude anyone from their 'Unions', who does not exclude the Charter. But we can form no alliance – we can enter into no compact with men who require from us, as the conditions of their joining us, that we renounce the Charter. To renounce the Charter would be either to renounce our own rights – which would be madness – or to barter away the rights of others, which would be wickedness . . . It is asking us either to degrade ourselves, or betray one another . . . Once admit the infamous policy of setting off 'cheap bread' against invaluable principles, of placing men in the same category as bricks and mortar, and sacrificing each other's rights to the guilty fears and cupidity of our enemies – once, I say, admit that infamous policy, and away goes everything which now helps to bind us together in the strength of unity, power, character, self respect, mutual confidence, the consciousness of growing power, the terror we have struck into the enemy, the certainty of ultimate success – in short, we become morally and politically defunct.

'But without the aid of the middle classes, how is Universal Suffrage to be got?' This means – 'How are the unrepresented people to get the franchise without the consent of the middle classes, expressed by their representatives in Parliament?' I answer the question by putting another – 'How did the middle classes get the franchise?'

If you answer this question honestly, your answer will be – 'Why, by taking it to be sure.' Or, which amounts to the same thing, 'by letting the Government see that they would take it, if not freely and promptly conceded'. This is the only way that any people have ever got enfranchised; and whenever the working people shall be united and resolute as were the middle classes in 1831, they will get enfranchised in the same way . . .

That the middle classes will not unite with us for the Charter is manifest. 'Tis equally clear that nothing short of Universal Suffrage or the Charter will accomplish the changes we require; why waste breath, then, arguing, 'whether we ought or ought not to unite with the middle classes'?

ANONYMOUS

23 April 1842

Report in the *Northern Star*, in Hollis, ed., *Class and Conflict*, p. 211

DESTITUTION AND DEFIANCE IN NORTH LANCASHIRE

. . . Mr Beesley then detailed the alarming destitution and misery which prevailed in North Lancashire. They were compelled to lie on shavings; they had no covering for the night save the rags which they wore during the day, and were compelled to have their shirts washed on a Saturday night to appear decent on Sunday; and were destitute of food during a considerable portion of the week. In some places the authorities had done all that laid in their power to put Chartism down; they had threatened to stop the relief of all who were Chartists; one individual who was in the receipt of 3s. 6d. per week from the authorities, was informed by them that they had heard he had subscribed to the Chartist fund; if he continued this they would give him no more relief; but he boldly told them that he would support the Charter until they had gained their rights as Englishmen, and if they stopped his relief, they should take him and wife and five children into the workhouse. This showed the determined spirit evinced by the men of North Lancashire.

THE 1842 CHARTIST PETITION

3 May 1842

From *Parliamentary Debates (Hansard)*, 3rd series

The Second Petition was rejected by the House. Macaulay saw it as an attack on property, and thus 'utterly incompatible with the very existence of civilization'. It marks the end of the second period of Chartist activity. It was signed by 3,315,752 people.

THE PEOPLE'S CHARTER: FUNDAMENTAL CHANGE

TO THE HONOURABLE THE COMMONS OF GREAT BRITAIN AND IRELAND, IN PARLIAMENT ASSEMBLED

The Petition of the undersigned people of the United Kingdom, Showeth
– That Government originated from, was designed to protect the freedom

490

and promote the happiness of, and ought to be responsible to, the whole people . . .

That the only authority on which any body of men can make laws and govern society, is delegation from the people.

That as Government was designed for the benefit and protection of, and must be obeyed and supported by all, therefore all should be equally represented . . .

That your honourable House, as at present constituted, has not been elected by, and acts irresponsibly of, the people; and hitherto has only represented parties, and benefited the few, regardless of the miseries, grievances, and petitions of the many. Your honourable House has enacted laws contrary to the expressed wishes of the people, and by unconstitutional means enforced obedience to them, thereby creating an unbearable despotism on the one hand, and degrading slavery on the other . . .

That your petitioners instance, in proof of their assertion, that your honourable House has not been elected by the people; that the population of Great Britain and Ireland is at the present time about twenty-six millions of persons; and that yet, out of this number, little more than nine hundred thousand have been permitted to vote in the recent election of representatives to make laws to govern the whole.

That the existing state of representation is not only extremely limited and unjust, but unequally divided, and gives preponderating influence to the landed and monied interests to the utter ruin of small-trading and labouring classes.

That the borough of Guildford, with a population of 3,920 returns to Parliament as many members as the Tower Hamlets, with a population of 300,000; Evesham, with a population of 3,998, elects as many representatives as Manchester, with a population of 200,000 . . .

That bribery, intimidation, corruption, perjury, and riot, prevail at all parliamentary elections, to an extent best understood by the Members of your honourable House.

That your petitioners complain that they are enormously taxed to pay the interest of what is termed the national debt, a debt amounting at present to £800,000,000, being only a portion of the enormous amount expended in cruel and expensive wars for the suppression of all liberty, by men not authorized by the people, and who, consequently, had no right to tax posterity for the outrages committed by them upon mankind. And your petitioners loudly complain of the augmentation of that debt, after twenty-six years of almost uninterrupted peace, and whilst poverty and discontent rage over the land.

That taxation, both general and local, is at this time too enormous to be borne; and in the opinion of your petitioners is contrary to the spirit of the Bill of Rights, wherein it is clearly expressed that no subject shall be compelled to contribute to any tax, tallage, or aid, unless imposed by common consent in Parliament.

That in England, Ireland, Scotland, and Wales, thousands of people are dying from actual want; and your petitioners, whilst sensible that poverty is the great exciting cause of crime, view with mingled astonishment and alarm the ill provision made for the poor, the aged, and infirm; and likewise perceive, with feelings of indignation, the determination of your honourable House to continue the Poor-law Bill in operation, notwithstanding the many proofs which have been afforded by sad experience of the unconstitutional principle of that bill, of its unchristian character, and of the cruel and murderous effects produced upon the wages of working men, and the lives of the subjects of this realm.

That your petitioners conceive that bill to be contrary to all previous statutes, opposed to the spirit of the constitution, and an actual violation of the precepts of the Christian religion; and, therefore, your petitioners look with apprehension to the results which may flow from its continuance.

That your petitioners would direct the attention of your honourable House to the great disparity existing between the wages of the producing millions, and the salaries of those whose comparative usefulness ought to be questioned, where riches and luxury prevail amongst the rulers, and poverty and starvation amongst the ruled.

That your petitioners, with all due respect and loyalty, would compare the daily income of the Sovereign Majesty with that of thousands of the working men of this nation; and whilst your petitioners have learned that her Majesty receives daily for her private use the sum of £164 17s. 10d. they have also ascertained that many thousands of the families of the labourers are only in the receipt of 3¾d. per head per day . . .

That notwithstanding the wretched and unparalleled condition of the people, your honourable House has manifested no disposition to curtail the expenses of the State, to diminish taxation, or promote general prosperity.

That unless immediate remedial measures be adopted, your petitioners fear the increasing distress of the people will lead to results fearful to contemplate; because your petitioners can produce evidence of the gradual decline of wages, at the same time that the constant increase of the national burdens must be apparent to all.

492

That your petitioners know that it is the undoubted constitutional right of the people, to meet freely, when, how and where they choose, in public places, peaceably, in the day, to discuss their grievances, and political or other subjects, or for the purpose of framing, discussing, or passing any vote, petition, or remonstrance upon any subject whatsoever.

That your petitioners complain that the right has unconstitutionally been infringed; and five hundred well disposed persons have been arrested, excessive bail demanded, tried by packed juries, sentenced to imprisonment, and treated as felons of the worst description.

That an unconstitutional police force is distributed all over the country, at enormous cost, to prevent the due exercise of the people's rights. And your petitioners are of opinion that the Poor-law Bastiles and the police stations, being co-existent, have originated from the same curse, viz., the increased desire on the part of the irresponsible few to oppress and starve the many.

That a vast and unconstitutional army is upheld at the public expense, for the purpose of repressing public opinion in the three kingdoms, and likewise to intimidate the millions in the due exercise of those rights and privileges which ought to belong to them.

That your petitioners complain that the hours of labour, particularly of the factory workers, are protracted beyond the limits of human endurance, and that the wages earned, after unnatural application to toil in heated and unhealthy workshops, are inadequate to sustain the bodily strength, and supply those comforts which are so imperative after an excessive waste of physical energy.

That your petitioners also direct the attention of your honourable House to the starvation wages of the agricultural labourer, and view with horror and indignation the paltry income of those whose toil gives being to the staple food of this people.

That your petitioners deeply deplore the existence of any kind of monopoly in this nation, and whilst they unequivocally condemn the levying of any tax upon the necessaries of life, and upon those articles principally required by the labouring classes, they are also sensible that the abolition of any one monopoly will never unshackle labour from its misery until the people possess that power under which all monopoly and oppression must cease; and your petitioners respectfully mention the existing monopolies of the suffrage, of paper money, of machinery, of land, of the public press, of religious privileges, of the means of travelling and transit, and of a host of other evils too numerous to mention, all arising from class legislation, but which your honourable House has always consistently endeavoured to increase instead of diminish.

That your petitioners are sensible, from the numerous petitions presented to your honourable House, that your honourable House is fully acquainted with the grievances of the working men; and your petitioners pray that the rights and wrongs of labour may be considered, with a view to the protection of the one, and to the removal of the other; because your petitioners are of opinion that it is the worst species of legislation which leaves the grievances of society to be removed only by violence or revolution, both of which may be apprehended if complaints are unattended to and petitions despised.

That your petitioners complain that upwards of nine millions of pounds per annum are unjustly abstracted from them to maintain a church establishment, from which they principally dissent . . . Your petitioners complain that it is unjust, and not in accordance with the Christian religion, to enforce compulsory support of religious creeds, and expensive church establishments, with which the people do not agree.

That your petitioners believe all men have a right to worship God as may appear best to their consciences, and that no legislative enactments should interfere between man and his Creator.

That your petitioners direct the attention of your honourable House to the enormous revenue annually swallowed up by the bishops and the clergy, and entreat you to contrast their deeds with the conduct of the founder of the Christian religion, who denounced worshippers of Mammon, and taught charity, meekness, and brotherly love . . .

That your petitioners maintain that it is the inherent, indubitable, and constitutional right, founded upon the ancient practice of the realm of England, and supported by well approved statutes, of every male inhabitant of the United Kingdom, he being of age and of sound mind, non-convict of crime, and not confined under any judicial process, to exercise the elective franchise in the choice of Members to serve in the Commons House of Parliament.

That your petitioners can prove, that by the ancient customs and statutes of this realm, Parliament should be held once in each year.

That your petitioners maintain that Members elected to serve in Parliament ought to be the servants of the people, and should, at short and stated intervals, return to their constituencies, to ascertain if their conduct is approved of, and to give the people power to reject all who have not acted honestly and justly.

That your petitioners complain that possession of property is made the test of men's qualification to sit in Parliament.

That your petitioners can give proof that such qualification is irrational, unnecessary, and not in accordance with the ancient usages of England.

That your petitioners complain, that by influence, patronage, and intimidation, there is at present no purity of election; and your petitioners contend for the right of voting by ballot.

That your petitioners complain that seats in your honourable House are sought for at a most extravagant rate of expense; which proves an enormous degree of fraud and corruption.

That your petitioners, therefore, contend, that to put an end to secret political traffic, all representatives should be paid a limited amount for their services.

That your petitioners complain of the many grievances borne by the people of Ireland, and contend that they are fully entitled to a repeal of the legislative union.

That your petitioners have viewed with great indignation the partiality shown to the aristocracy in the courts of justice, and the cruelty of that system of law which deprived Frost, Williams, and Jones, of the benefit of their objections offered by Sir Frederick Pollock during the trial at Monmouth, and which was approved of by a large majority of the judges.

That your petitioners beg to assure your honourable House that they cannot, within the limits of this their petition, set forth even a tithe of the many grievances of which they may justly complain; but should your honourable House be pleased to grant your petitioners a hearing by representatives at the Bar of your honourable House, your petitioners will be enabled to unfold a tale of wrong and suffering – of intolerable injustice – which will create utter astonishment in the minds of all benevolent and good men, that the people of Great Britain and Ireland have so long quietly endured their wretched condition, brought upon them as it has been by unjust exclusion from political authority, and by the manifold corruption of class-legislation.

That your petitioners, therefore, exercising their just constitutional right, demand that your honourable House do remedy the many gross and manifest evils of which your petitioners complain, do immediately, without alteration, deduction, or addition, pass into a law the document entitled 'The People's Charter' . . .

And that your petitioners, desiring to promote the peace of the United Kingdom, security of property, and prosperity of commerce, seriously and earnestly press this, their petition, on the attention of your honourable House.

And your petitioners, etc.

PLACARD ISSUED BY TRADE UNION DELEGATES

15 August 1842

In Postgate, ed., *Revolution from 1789 to 1906*, p. 133

This notice was issued by trade union delegates in Manchester, following a resolution calling for a strike which spread through Lancashire over wages at the mills. What began at Ashton-under-Lyne turned into a general strike for the Charter in the north of England, and lasted from August till September. It was broken partly by the use of soldiers, and there were many arrests.

LIBERTY

Liberty to the trades of Manchester and the surrounding districts – Fellow-workmen, we hasten to lay before you the paramount importance of this day's proceedings. The delegates from the surrounding districts have been more numerous at this day's meeting than they were at yesterday's, and the spirit and determination manifested for the people's rights have increased every hour. In consequence of the unjust and unconstitutional interference of the magistrates our proceedings were abruptly brought to a close by their dispersing the meeting; but not until, in their very teeth, we passed the following resolution: 'Resolved – that the delegates in public meeting assembled, do recommend to the various constituencies which we represent, to adopt all legal means to carry into effect the People's Charter; and further we recommend that delegates be sent through the whole of the country to endeavour to obtain the cooperation of the middle and working classes in carrying out the resolution of ceasing labour until the Charter become the law of the land.'

Englishmen, legally determine to maintain the peace and well-being of Society; and show, by your strict adherence to our resolution, that we are your true representatives. Do your duty. We will do ours. We meet again tomorrow: and the result of our deliberations will be fully laid before you.

THOMAS COOPER

August 1842

From *Life Written by Himself*, pp. 206–8

After the strikes of the summer resolved upon here fifty-nine men were charged with seditious conspiracy. 'These unhappy men,' declared the outraged Lord Abinger to the jury, 'do not consider that the first object of civilized society is the establishment and preservation of property . . .' All the men were, however, acquitted.

FOR A GENERAL STRIKE

When I entered the railway carriage at Crewe, some who were going to the Convention recognized me – and, among the rest, Campbell, secretary of the 'National Charter Association'. He had left London on purpose to join the Conference; and, like myself, was anxious to know the *real* state of Manchester. So soon as the City of Long Chimneys came in sight, and every chimney was beheld smokeless, Campbell's face changed, and with an oath he said, 'Not a single mill at work! something must come out of this, and something serious too!'

In Manchester, I soon found McDouall, Leach, and Bairstow, who, together with Campbell, formed what was called the 'Executive Council of the National Charter Association' . . . In the streets, there were unmistakable signs of alarm on the part of the authorities. Troops of cavalry were going up and down the principal thoroughfares, accompanied by pieces of artillery, drawn by horses . . . We met . . . the next morning, Wednesday, the 17th of August, when James Arthur of Carlisle was elected President. There were nearly sixty delegates present; and as they rose, in quick succession, to describe the state of their districts, it was evident they were, each and all, filled with the desire of keeping the people from returning to their labour. They believed the time had come for trying, successfully, to paralyse the Government. I caught their spirit – for the working of my mind had prepared me for it . . . When the executive, and a few others, had spoken, all in favour of the universal strike, I told the Conference I should vote for the resolution because it meant fighting, and I saw it must come to that. The spread of the strike would and must be followed by a general outbreak. The authorities of the land would try to quell it; but we must resist them. There was nothing now but a physical force struggle to be looked for. We must get the people out to fight; and they must be irresistible, if they were united.

497

CHARTIST DECLARATIONS

Manchester,
17 August 1842

In Hollis, ed., *Class and Conflict*, pp. 290–91

This was the address of the executive committee of the NCA, adopted by delegates to the National Charter Association conference.

CALL FOR SUPPORT

Brother Chartists – The great political truths which have been agitated during the last half-century have at length aroused the degraded and insulted white slaves of England to a sense of their duty to themselves, their children, and their country. Tens of thousands have flung down their implements of labour. Your taskmasters tremble at your energy, and expecting masses eagerly watch this great crisis of our cause. Labour must no longer be the common prey of masters and rulers . . .

We do now universally resolve never to resume labour, until labour's grievances are destroyed, and protection secured to ourselves, our suffering wives, and helpless children, by the enactment of the People's Charter. Englishmen! the blood of your brethren reddens the streets of Preston and Blackburn and the murderers thirst for more. Be firm, be courageous, be men! Peace, law and order have prevailed on our side – let them be revered until your brethren in Scotland, Wales and Ireland are informed of your resolution; and when a universal holiday prevails, which will be the case in eight days, then of what use will bayonets be against public opinion? – The trades, a noble, patriotic band, have taken the lead in declaring for the Charter, and drawing their gold from the keeping of tyrants. Follow their example. Lend no whip to rulers therewith to scourge you.

Intelligence has reached us of the widespreading of the strike; and now, within fifty miles of Manchester, every engine is at rest, and all is still, save the miller's useful wheels and friendly sickle in the fields . . .

Our machinery is all arranged, and your cause will, in three days, be impelled onward by all the intellect we can summon to its aid: therefore, whilst you are peaceful, be firm; whilst you are orderly, make all be so likewise; and whilst you look to the law, remember that you had no voice in making it, and are therefore slaves to the will, the law, and the price of your masters. All officers of the association are called upon to aid and assist in the peaceful extension of the movement, and to forward all moneys for the use of delegates who may be expressed over the country.

498

Strengthen our hands at this crisis. Support your leaders. Rally round our sacred cause, and leave the decision to the God of justice and of battle.

Mr O'Connor, at the Manchester Conference

He stated that it was the duty of the Chartists to take advantage of passing events. Not that he anticipated so much from the present strike, but after we had expended so much money and time in inducing the trades to join us, we would never get them to join again unless we passed some such resolution.

EBENEZER JONES (1820–60)   1843

From *Ways of Regard*, in *Studies of Sensation and Event*, pp. 165–7

Jones lived through a period of great upheaval which saw the decisive formulation of British capitalism and the crushing of popular resistance (which, after the breakdown of Chartism in 1848, did not revive until the 1880s). He was himself a supporter of the Chartists, and believed the wage-system a form of slavery which 'demoralizes the entire people'. *Ways of Regard* defines various levels of consciousness, and in its presentation of a ruthless master class and its slaves the poem registers the terrible conditions of the working class in England.

Seeing these slaves and hearing their leader speak, a young man speaks out against their oppressors:

MUTILATION

All their boasted order,
Their laws unbroken, all the deep submission
Of their whipp'd slaves, – is terrible disorder;
Disorder of the universe and of the heart.
They shall know anarchy is abroad, more dread
That her wild step is noiseless, that her form
Is undistinguishable, save at times
By the red fires that in the yards of law
Curl round rebellious serfs; while then her bearing
Hath not the noble fierceness of a storm-god,
But with assassin calmness her cold smile
Measures a secret dagger. They outcry,

'The nation flourishes, its power is vast,
Its wealth supreme.' Oh idiot knaves and liars!
Say, is a flag a nation? is an army?
Do half a million traders make a nation?
A thousand lords? The people is the nation;
If they be slaves, if they be suffering,
The power, the majesty, the wealth you boast,
Is tinsel hiding the rottenness you ordain!
And much they prate of station. Much they say
Touching God-order'd ranks. Me they accuse
Of rendering slaves superior to that state,
In which, they say, it has pleased God to place them!
They counsel – if your slave seem fond of freedom,
Starve him, till he be glad to lick your foot
And then get crumbs; if he would fain be wise,
Work him, until the writhing of his body
Shall suffocate his mind; if he would love,
And husband womanhood, let famish'd children
Of others terrify; even from his birth
Palsy his heart with fear, darken his soul,
Defile his body. Yea! this mutilation
They do advise, when smilingly they say,
Be slaves so educate, that to their stations,
Their natures may be fitted. 'Educate!'
Ye villains sacrilegious, who would rob
God's human temple of its majesty,
That ye may stable there in barbarous pomp!
Misname not thus your murderous reduction
Of beauty into baseness, man to brute.
Man has no station; he must upward soar
Towards bright-wing'd deities, or sink down towards fiends;
Man cannot pause. –
Go! bid the sun to rot within its heavens!
Arrest the marching melodies of stars!
Chill every river into stagnancy!
Deracinate the fruitful earth of growth!
Though infinite space grow dark, the soul of man
Shall soar triumphantly. Within this cavern
Are thousands, sworn to rise from out the mire,
Whereto you damn them; they will rise, – will rise,
Though war may hew their pathway, though their march

Be in blood to the armpits! Oh that it were mine
To lead them bloodless conquerors! They will rise, –
But with the chains they shatter from their limbs,
Must they do hellishly. A vessel, laden
With captives fetter'd unto famine and plague,
Now is this land; the slaves force-freed, will make it
A burning wreck; themselves amidst the flames,
Maniacs, wild dancing. Oh who, who can know,
How to redeem this people?

EBENEZER JONES (1820–1860)   1843

A Coming Cry, in *Studies of Sensation and Event*

A COMING CRY

The few to whom the law hath given the earth God gives to all
Do tell us that for them alone its fruits increase and fall;
They tell us that by labour we may earn our daily bread,
But they take the labour for their engines that work on unfed;
And so we starve; and now the few have publish'd a decree, –
Starve on, or eat in workhouses, the crumbs of charity;
Perhaps it's better than starvation, – once we'll pray, and then
We'll all go building workhouses, million, million men!

We'll all go building workhouses, – million, million hands,
So jointed wondrously by God, to work love's wise commands;
We'll all go building workhouses, – million, million minds,
By great God charter'd to condemn whatever harms or binds;
The God-given mind shall image, the God-given hand shall build
The prisons for God's children by the earth-lords will'd;
Perhaps it's better than starvation, once we'll pray, and then
We'll all go building workhouses, – million, million men.

What'll we do with the workhouses? million, million men!
Shall we all lie down, and madden, each in his lonely den?
What! we whose sires made Cressy! we, men of Nelson's mould!
We, of the Russell's country, – God's Englishmen the bold!
Will we, at earth's lords' bidding, build ourselves dishonour'd graves?
Will we who've made this England, endure to be its slaves?
Thrones totter before the answer! – once we'll pray, and then
We'll all go building workhouses, – million, million men.

BENJAMIN DISRAELI (1804–81)   The mid-1840s

From *Sybil: or the Two Nations*

By the mid-1840s the ruthless exploitation of the propertyless majority that followed the 1832 Reform Act had further sharpened the divisions between the rich and the poor. With its two great petitions already contemptuously rejected by Parliament and the collapse of the 1842 General Strike in the north, the Chartist movement seemed finished. It was to remain quiescent till the onset of new crises from 1846 onward revived Chartism for its final 1848 appeal, doomed to defeat like the others. And it is significant that it was not the workers' movement that succeeded during this period but its rival, the Anti-Corn-Law League, organized by middle-class radicals with the support of the manufacturers, and linking the repeal of the Corn Laws (achieved in 1846) with the economic principle of Free Trade, which entailed, in Marx's words, 'the open, official subjection of society to the laws of modern bourgeois production'. But perhaps the most devastating symptom of the capitalist system at work at this time was the terrible famine that struck Ireland in 1845 – its impoverished people forced to feed themselves on potatoes because they had to sell all the wheat they grew to pay the rising rents imposed by absentee landlords exacting their corn profits. As A. L. Morton puts it (in *A People's History of England*, p. 456): 'The facts about the Famine have been grossly distorted by all orthodox historians. There was really no famine in any ordinary sense of the word, but only the failure of one crop, the potatoes. "Providence sent the potato blight, but England made the famine" was a saying current at the time. In 1847, when hundreds of thousands of people died of starvation and hunger typhus, food to the value of £17,000,000 was actually exported from the country under the protection of English troops. The million and a half people who died in these years did not die of famine but were killed by rent and profit.'

In this context, there is an irony and trenchancy about the following passage, from the second of Disraeli's 'Young England' condition-of-the-people novels, which needs no comment.

THE TWO NATIONS

From Book 2, Chapter 5

'Well, society may be in its infancy,' said Egremont, slightly smiling; 'but, say what you like, our queen reigns over the greatest nation that ever existed.'

'Which nation?' asked the young stranger, 'for she reigns over two.'

'Yes,' resumed the young stranger after a moment's interval. 'Two nations; between whom there is no intercourse, and no sympathy; who are as ignorant of each other's habits, thoughts, and feelings, as if they were dwellers in different zones, or inhabitants of different planets; who are formed by a different breeding, are fed by a different food, are ordered by different manners, and are governed by the same laws.'

'You speak of –', said Egremont, hesitatingly.

'The rich and the poor.'

CHARLOTTE BRONTË (1816–55)   1847

From *Jane Eyre*, pp. 141, 344

MILLIONS ARE IN SILENT REVOLT

From Chapter 12

It is in vain to say human beings ought to be satisfied with tranquillity: they must have action; and they will make it if they cannot find it. Millions are condemned to a stiller doom than mine, and millions are in silent revolt against their lot. Nobody knows how many rebellions besides political rebellions ferment in the masses of life which people earth. Women are supposed to be very calm generally: but women feel just as men feel; they need exercise for their faculties, and a field for their efforts as much as their brothers do; they suffer from too rigid a restraint, too absolute a stagnation, precisely as men would suffer; and it is narrow-minded in their more privileged fellow-creatures to say that they ought to confine themselves to making puddings and knitting stockings, to playing on the piano and embroidering bags. It is thoughtless to condemn them, or laugh at them, if they seek to do more or learn more than custom has pronounced necessary for their sex.

AT ONCE SO FRAIL AND SO INDOMITABLE

From Chapter 27

. . . While he spoke my very conscience and reason turned traitors against me, and charged me with crime in resisting him. They spoke almost as loud as Feeling: and that clamoured wildly. 'Oh, comply!' it said. 'Think of his misery; think of his danger; look at his state when left alone; remember his headlong nature; consider the recklessness following on despair – soothe him; save him; love him; tell him you love him and will be his. Who in the word cares for *you*? or who will be injured by what you do?'

Still indomitable was the reply: '*I* care for myself. The more solitary, the more friendless, the more unsustained I am, the more I will respect myself. I will keep the law given by God; sanctioned by man. I will hold to the principles received by me when I was sane, and not mad – as I am now. Laws and principles are not for times when there is no temptation: they are for such moments as this, when body and soul rise in mutiny against their rigour; stringent are they; inviolate they shall be. If at my individual convenience I might break them, what would be their worth? They have a worth – so I have always believed; and if I cannot believe it now, it is because I am insane – quite insane, with my veins running fire, and my heart beating faster than I can count its throbs. Preconceived opinions, foregone determinations are all I have at this hour to stand by; there I plant my foot.'

I did. Mr Rochester, reading my countenance, saw I had done so . . .

KARL MARX (1818–83)   29 November 1847

Speech in London to the Fraternal Democrats, in *Revolutions of 1848*, pp. 99–100

The Fraternal Democrats served as an international link for the Chartists with the oppressed nations of Europe, and both Marx and Engels spoke at this meeting. They had come to London to attend the secret second congress of the Communist League, and Marx directly addressed the Chartists in his speech, on the seventeenth anniversary of the Polish revolution of 1830.

DEFEAT YOUR ENEMIES AT HOME

The unification and brotherhood of nations is a phrase which is nowadays on the lips of all parties, particularly of the bourgeois free traders. A kind of brotherhood does indeed exist between the bourgeois classes of all nations. It is the brotherhood of the oppressors against the oppressed, of the exploiters against the exploited. Just as the bourgeois class of one country is united in brotherhood against the proletarians of that country, despite the competition and struggle of its members among themselves, so the bourgeoisie of all countries is united in brotherhood against the proletarians of all countries, despite their struggling and competing with each other on the world market. In order for peoples to become really united their interests must be common. For their interests to be common the existing property relations must be abolished, since the exploitation of one nation by another is caused by the existing property relations. And it is only in the interests of the working class to abolish existing property relations; only they have the means to achieve it. The victory of the proletariat over the bourgeoisie represents at the same time the victory over national and industrial conflicts, which at present create hostility between the different peoples. Therefore, the victory of the proletariat over the bourgeoisie also signifies the emancipation of all downtrodden nations.

The old Poland is certainly lost, and we should be the last to wish for its restoration. But not only is the old Poland lost. The old Germany, the old France, the old England, the old social order in general is lost. The loss of the old social order, however, is not a loss for those who have nothing to lose in the old society, and at the same time this is the case for the large majority of people in all countries. They have, in fact, everything to gain from the destruction of the old society, for it is a precondition for the formation of a new society no longer based on class antagonisms.

Of all countries it is England where the opposition between the proletariat and the bourgeoisie is most highly developed. Thus the victory of the English proletariat over the English bourgeoisie is of decisive importance for the victory of all oppressed peoples over their oppressors. Poland, therefore, must be freed, not in Poland, but in England. You Chartists should not express pious wishes for the liberation of nations. Defeat your own enemies at home and then you may be proudly conscious of having defeated the old social order in its entirety.

Part Six

THE TRIUMPH OF CAPITALISM 1848–1914

The accumulation of wealth at one pole of society involves a simultaneous accumulation of poverty, labour torment, slavery, ignorance, brutalization, and moral degradation at the opposite pole – where dwells the class that produces its own product in the form of capital.

Karl Marx, *Capital*

. . . true political freedom is impossible to people who are economically enslaved: there is no first and second in these matters, the two must go hand in hand together: we cannot live as we will, and as we should, as long as we allow people to *govern* us whose interest it is that we should live as *they* will, and by no means as we should.

William Morris, *The Hopes of Civilisation*

. . . the emancipation of labour is neither a local nor a national, but a social problem, embracing all countries in which modern societies exist, and depending for its solution on the concurrence, practical and theoretical, of the most advanced countries.

Karl Marx, *Rules of the International Working Men's Association*

KARL MARX (1818–83) AND FRIEDRICH ENGELS (1820–95)

February 1848

From *The Communist Manifesto*, in Marx, *Revolutions of 1848*, pp. 70–71, 79, 82–3, 85

Though the Manifesto was not translated into English until 1850, when it appeared in George Harney's *Red Republican*, it nevertheless properly belongs to the year 1848; and, printed in London a few weeks before the revolution in France, registers 1848 as a decisive turning-point in European and English history in terms of the challenge of the struggle between the forces of capitalism and the newly-defined (proletarian) working class created by the capitalist system. It spells out the conditions of development which were to characterize the structure of European society and its contradictions in the second half of the nineteenth century, and which the continental revolutions were shortly to confirm, based upon the triumph of bourgeois capitalism.

CAPITAL AND WAGE-LABOUR: THE CASH NEXUS

The bourgeoisie, wherever it has got the upper hand, has put an end to all feudal, patriarchal, idyllic relations. It has pitilessly torn asunder the motley feudal ties that bound man to his 'natural superiors', and has left remaining no other nexus between man and man than naked self-interest, than callous 'cash-payment'. It has drowned the most heavenly ecstasies of religious fervour, of chivalrous enthusiasm, of philistine sentimentalism, in the icy water of egotistical calculation. It has resolved personal worth into exchange value, and in place of the numberless, indefeasible chartered freedoms, has set up that single, unconscionable freedom – free trade. In one word, for exploitation, veiled by religious and political illusions, it has substituted naked, shameless, direct, brutal exploitation . . .

The bourgeoisie cannot exist without constantly revolutionizing the instruments of production, and thereby the relations of production, and with them the whole relations of society. Conservation of the old modes of production in unaltered form, was, on the contrary, the first condition of existence for all earlier industrial classes. Constant revolutionizing of production, uninterrupted disturbance of all social conditions, everlasting uncertainty and agitation distinguish the bourgeois epoch from all earlier ones. All fixed, fast-frozen relations, with their train of ancient and venerable prejudices and opinions, are swept away, all new-formed ones become antiquated before they can ossify. All that is solid melts into air, all that is holy is profaned, and man is at last compelled to face with sober senses, his real conditions of life, and his relations with his kind.

The need of a constantly expanding market for its products chases the bourgeoisie over the whole surface of the globe. It must nestle everywhere, settle everywhere, establish connections everywhere . . .

The essential condition for the existence, and for the sway of the bourgeois class, is the formation and augmentation of capital; the condition for capital is wage-labour. Wage-labour rests exclusively on competition between the labourers. The advance of industry, whose involuntary promoter is the bourgeoisie, replaces the isolation of the labourers, due to competition, by their revolutionary combination, due to association. The development of modern industry, therefore, cuts from under its feet the very foundation on which the bourgeoisie produces and appropriates products. What the bourgeoisie therefore produces, above all, are its own gravediggers. Its fall and the victory of the proletariat are equally inevitable . . .

CLASS PROPERTY: THE PRODUCTS OF SOCIETY

You are horrified at our intending to do away with private property. But in your existing society, private property is already done away with for nine tenths of the population; its existence for the few is solely due to its non-existence in the hands of those nine tenths. You reproach us, therefore, with intending to do away with a form of property, the necessary condition of whose existence is the non-existence of any property for the immense majority of society.

In one word, you reproach us with intending to do away with your property. Precisely so; that is just what we intend.

From the moment when labour can no longer be converted into capital, money, or rent, into a social power capable of being monopolized, i.e., from the moment when individual property can no longer be transformed into bourgeois property, into capital, from that moment, you say, individuality vanishes.

You must, therefore, confess that by 'individual' you mean no other person than the bourgeois, than the middle-class owner of property. This person must, indeed, be swept out of the way, and made impossible.

Communism deprives no man of the power to appropriate the products of society; all that it does is to deprive him of the power to subjugate the labour of others by means of such appropriation . . .

CLASS CULTURE

All objections urged against the communistic mode of producing and appropriating material products have, in the same way, been urged against the communistic mode of producing and appropriating intellectual products. Just as, to the bourgeois, the disappearance of class property is the disappearance of production itself, so the disappearance of class culture is to him identical with the disappearance of all culture.

That culture whose loss he laments is, for the enormous majority, a mere training to act as a machine.

But don't wrangle with us so long as you apply, to our intended abolition of bourgeois property, the standard of your bourgeois notions of freedom, culture, law, etc. Your very ideas are but the outgrowth of the conditions of your bourgeois production and bourgeois property, just as your jurisprudence is but the will of your class made into a law for all, a will whose essential character and direction are determined by the economic conditions of existence of your class.

The selfish misconception that induces you to transform into eternal laws of nature and of reason the social forms springing from your present mode of production and form of property – historical relations that rise and disappear in the progress of production – this misconception you share with every ruling class that has preceded you. What you see clearly in the case of ancient property, what you admit in the case of feudal property, you are of course forbidden to admit in the case of your own bourgeois form of property . . .

Does it require deep intuition to comprehend that man's ideas, views and conceptions, in one word, man's consciousness, changes with every change in the conditions of his material existence, in his social relations and in his social life?

What else does the history of ideas prove, than that intellectual production changes its character in proportion as material production is changed? The ruling ideas of each age have ever been the ideas of its ruling class . . .

HENRY HETHERINGTON
(1793–1849)

21 August 1849

His Testament, in Holyoake, *Life and Character of Henry Hetherington*

Hetherington was a printer and Chartist; he died of cholera.

HIS TESTAMENT

As life is uncertain, it behoves everyone to make preparations for death; I deem it therefore a duty incumbent on me, ere I quit this life, to express in writing, for the satisfaction and guidance of esteemed friends, my feelings and opinions in reference to our common principles . . .

In the first place, then – I calmly and deliberately declare that I do not believe in the popular notion of an Almighty, All-wise and Benevolent God – possessing intelligence, and conscious of his own operations; because these attributes involve such a mass of absurdities and contradictions, so much cruelty and injustice on His part to the poor and destitute portion of His creatures – that, in my opinion, no rational reflecting mind can, after disinterested investigation, give credence to the existence of such a Being.

Second, I believe death to be an eternal sleep – that I shall never live again in this world, or another, with a consciousness that I am the same identical person that once lived, performed the duties, and exercised the functions of a human being.

Third, I consider priestcraft and superstition the greatest obstacle to human improvement and happiness. During my life I have, to the best of my ability, sincerely and strenuously exposed and opposed them, and die with a firm conviction that Truth, Justice, and Liberty will never be permanently established on earth till every vestige of priestcraft and superstition be utterly destroyed.

Fourth, I have ever considered that the only religion useful to man consists exclusively of the practice of morality, and in the mutual interchange of kind actions. In such a religion there is no room for priests and when I see them interfering at our births, marriages and deaths pretending to conduct us safely through this state of being to another and happier world, any disinterested person of the least shrewdness and discernment must perceive that their sole aim is to stultify the minds of the people by their incomprehensible doctrines that they may the more effectively fleece the poor deluded sheep who listen to their empty babblings and mystifications.

512

Fifth, as I have lived so I die, a determined opponent to the nefarious and plundering system. I wish my friends, therefore, to deposit my remains in unconsecrated ground, and trust they will allow no priest, or clergyman of any denomination, to interfere in any way whatsoever at my funeral . . .

These are my views and principles in quitting an existence that has been chequered with the plagues and pleasures of a competitive, scrambling, selfish system; a system by which the moral and social aspirations of the noblest human being are nullified by incessant toil and physical deprivations; by which, indeed, all men are trained to be either slaves, hypocrites or criminals. Hence my ardent attachment to the principles of that great and good man Robert Owen. I quit this world with a firm conviction that his system is the only true road to human emancipation . . .

ARTHUR HUGH CLOUGH (1819–61) 3 June 1849

'Say not the Struggle Nought Availeth'

Clough in Rome, watching with some detachment but with mounting indignation the French assault upon the city and the death-agonies of Mazzini's Republic, observes in a letter to Tom Arnold: 'This, my dear Tom, is being written while guns are going off – there – there – there! For these blackguard French are attacking us again . . .' He sent the version of 'Say not the Struggle' printed here to his friend about this time, so it might even have been written while watching the struggle outside the Porta San Pancrazio that sealed the fate of Rome.

SAY NOT THE STRUGGLE NOUGHT AVAILETH

Say not the struggle nought availeth,
  The labour and the wounds are vain,
The enemy faints not, nor faileth,
  And as things have been, things remain.

If hopes were dupes, fears may be liars;
  It may be, in yon smoke concealed,
Your comrades chase e'en now the fliers,
  And, but for you, possess the field.

For while the tired waves, vainly breaking,

513

Seem here no painful inch to gain,
Far back, through creeks and inlets making,
    Came silent, flooding in, the main.

And not by eastern windows only,
    When daylight comes, comes in the light;
In front, the sun climbs slow, how slowly,
    But westward, look, the land is bright!

ERNEST JONES (1819–69)   14 July 1852

From the *People's Paper*, in Marx, *Surveys from Exile*, pp. 267–8

This speech was made by Jones, the Chartist candidate, on election day at Halifax in 1852. Apparently, after the speeches, the procedure was (in the first instance) to invite *all* the people present – including those (the majority) who were not on the register – to elect candidates by a show of hands. This, however, was no more than a gesture of formal politeness to the populace; for if the show of hands did not return those candidates preferred by the minority of electors, a poll would then be demanded in which only registered electors could vote. On this occasion, Jones (securing a nomination of 20,000 votes) and Henry Edwards (Tory) were elected by the show of hands against the Whig Sir Charles Wood and the Manchester man Crossley, choice of the minority of electors. Wood and Crossley then demanded a poll, with the result that the two losers in the popular vote were duly elected by 500 votes as the official representatives for Halifax. Marx, in his article on the Chartists (*New York Tribune*, 25 August 1852, reprinted in *Surveys from Exile*, p. 266), described Jones as 'the most talented, consistent and energetic representative of Chartism'.

THE BUY-CHEAP-AND-SELL-DEAR SYSTEM

Electors and non-electors, you have met upon a great and solemn festival. Today the constitution recognizes universal suffrage in theory, though it may perhaps deny it in practice on the morrow . . . Today the representatives of two systems stand before you, and you have to decide beneath which you shall be ruled for seven years. Seven years – a little life! . . . I summon you to pause upon the threshold of those seven years: today they shall pass slowly and calmly in review before you: today decide, you 20,000 men, that perhaps five hundred may undo your will tomorrow. I say the representatives of two systems stand before you.

Whig, Tory, and money-monger are on my left, it is true, but they are all as one. The money-monger says, buy cheap and sell dear. The Tory says, buy dear, sell dearer. Both are the same for labour. But the former system is in the ascendant, and pauperism rankles at its root. That system is based on foreign competition. Now I assert that under the buy-cheap-and-sell-dear principle, brought to bear on foreign competition, the ruin of the working and small trading classes must go on. Why? Labour is the creator of all wealth. A man must work before a grain is grown, or a yard is woven. But there is no self-employment for the working man in this country. Labour is a hired commodity – labour is a thing in the market that is bought and sold; consequently, as labour creates all wealth, labour is the first thing bought – 'Buy cheap! Buy cheap!' Labour is bought in the cheapest market. But now comes the next: 'Sell dear! Sell dear!' Sell what? *Labour's produce*. To whom? To the foreigner – aye! and to the *labourer himself* – for labour, not being self-employed, the labourer is *not* the partaker of the first fruits of his toil. 'Buy cheap, sell dear.' How do you like it? 'Buy cheap, sell dear.' Buy the working man's labour cheaply, and sell back to that very working man the produce of his own labour dear! The principle of inherent loss is in the bargain. The employer buys the labour cheap – he sells, and on the sale he must make a profit; he sells to the working man himself – and thus every bargain between employer and employed is a deliberate cheat on the part of the employer. Thus labour has to sink through eternal loss, that capital may rise through lasting fraud. But the system stops not here. This is brought to bear on foreign competition – which means, we must ruin the trade of other countries, as we have ruined the labour of our own. How does it work? The high-taxed country has to undersell the low-taxed. Competition abroad is constantly increasing – consequently cheapness must increase constantly also. Therefore, wages in England must keep constantly falling. And how do they effect the fall? By *surplus labour*. How do they obtain the surplus labour? By monopoly of the land, which drives more hands than are wanted into the factory. By monopoly of machinery, which drives those hands into the street – by woman labour which drives the man from the shuttle – by child labour, which drives the woman from the loom. Then planting their foot upon that living base of surplus, they press its aching heart beneath their heel, and cry 'Starvation! Who'll work? A half loaf is better than no bread at all' – and the writhing mass grasps greedily at their terms. Such is the system for the working man . . .

KARL MARX (1818–83)   4 September 1852

From the *New York Daily Tribune*, in *Surveys from Exile*, pp. 276–7

Arriving in London as a refugee in 1849 and remaining there till his death, Marx had to come to terms with the failure of the 1848 revolutions and (in November 1852) the collapse of the Communist League, which left him for the next twelve years (till the formation of the International Working Men's Association) in more or less complete political isolation. But though in the 1850s, in this deadly city of his exile, he and his family were faced with grinding poverty, alleviated to some extent by help from Engels, Marx's confidence in the future – sustained by the rigour and strength of the intellectual foundations he had already laid – never wavered. For this was a decade of astonishing activity. He filled twenty-four note-books with reading notes on every kind of subject (1850–53), wrote *The Eighteenth Brumaire* (1852), the *Grundrisse* (1857–8) – a series of seven notebooks which laid the groundwork for *Theories of Surplus Value* (1861–3) and *Capital* itself – and *A Contribution to the Critique of Political Economy* (1859). All this time intensely at work in the British Museum, he still found the energy (because in desperate need of money) to write a series of badly paid articles for the *New York Daily Tribune* (1852–61) on contemporary developments in Europe, which included a number of pieces on conditions in Britain.

Marx at first drafted his *Tribune* articles in German, which Engels then translated and sent off; but within a few months he was able to write fluently in English.

THE MAKING OF PARLIAMENT: THE GENERAL ELECTION, 1852

In order to comprehend the character of bribery, corruption and intimidation, such as they have been practised in the late election, it is necessary to call attention to a fact which operated in a parallel direction.

If you refer to the general elections since 1831, you will find that, in the same measure as the pressure of the voteless majority of the country upon the privileged body of electors was increasing; as the demand was heard louder from the middle classes for an extension of the circle of constituencies; and from the working class to extinguish every trace of a similar privileged circle – that in the same measure the number of electors who actually voted grew less and less, and the constituencies thus more and more contracted themselves. Never was this fact more striking than in the late election.

Let us take, for instance, London. In the City the constituency numbers 26,728; only 10,000 voted. The Tower Hamlets number 23,534 registered electors; only 12,000 voted. In Finsbury, of 20,025, not one half voted. In Liverpool, the scene of one of the most animated contests, of 17,433 registered electors, only 13,000 came to the polls.

These examples will suffice. What do they prove? The apathy of the privileged constituencies. And this apathy, what does it prove? That they have outlived themselves – that they have lost every interest in their own political existence. This is in no wise apathy against politics in general, but against a species of politics, the result of which, for the most part, can only consist in helping the Tories to oust the Whigs, or the Whigs to conquer the Tories. The constituencies feel instinctively that the decision lies no longer with Parliament, or with the making of Parliament. Who repealed the Corn Laws? Assuredly not the voters who had elected a Protectionist Parliament, still less the Protectionist Parliament itself, but only and exclusively the pressure from without. In this pressure from without, by other means of influencing Parliament than by voting, a great portion even of electors now believe. They consider the hitherto lawful mode of voting as an antiquated formality, but from the moment Parliament should make front against the pressure from without, and dictate laws to the nation in the sense of its narrow constituencies, they would join the general assault against the whole antiquated system of machinery.

The bribery and intimidation practised by the Tories were, then, merely violent experiments for bringing back to life dying electoral bodies which have become incapable of production, and which can no longer create decisive electoral results and really national Parliaments. And the result? The old Parliament was dissolved, because at the end of its career it had dissolved into sections which brought each other to a complete standstill. The new Parliament begins where the old one ended; it is paralytic from the hour of its birth.

CHARLES DICKENS (1812–1870)   1852

From *Bleak House*, pp. 50–51, 267–8, 272–5, 619, 683, 696–7, 900–901

Bleak House gives concrete embodiment to the ponderous mechanisms of a class-ridden social system rotten from top to bottom. With its pervasive and devastating metaphorical power, it attacks the very structure of mid-Victorian society itself as a system of inexorable blind force in the fog and dust and confusion of which men and women (and children) are worn down, broken, crushed. And it is no accident that serial publication of the novel began in the same year as the Great

Exhibition of 1851, which celebrated the technological and mercantile triumphs of English capitalism and its immense riches augmenting the wealth of the propertied classes from markets all over the world.

FOG EVERYWHERE

From Chapter 1

The raw afternoon is rawest, and the dense fog is densest, and the muddy streets are muddiest, near that leaden-headed old obstruction, appropriate ornament for the threshold of a leaden-headed old corporation – Temple Bar. And hard by Temple Bar, in Lincoln's Inn Hall, at the very heart of the fog, sits the Lord High Chancellor in his High Court of Chancery.

Never can there come fog too thick, never can there come mud and mire too deep, to assort with the groping and floundering condition which this High Court of Chancery, most pestilent of hoary sinners, holds, this day, in the sight of heaven and earth.

On such an afternoon, if ever, the Lord High Chancellor ought to be sitting here – as here he is – with a foggy glory round his head, softly fenced in with crimson cloth and curtains, addressed by a large advocate with great whiskers, a little voice, and an interminable brief, and outwardly directing his contemplation to the lantern in the roof, where he can see nothing but fog. On such an afternoon, some score of members of the High Court of Chancery bar ought to be – as here they are – mistily engaged in one of the ten thousand stages of an endless cause, tripping one another up on slippery precedents, groping knee-deep in technicalities, running their goat-hair and horse-hair warded heads against walls of words, and making a pretence of equity with serious faces, as players might. On such an afternoon, the various solicitors in the cause, some two or three of whom have inherited it from their fathers, who made a fortune by it, ought to be – as are they not? – ranged in a line, in a long matted well (but you might look in vain for Truth at the bottom of it), between the registrar's red table and the silk gowns, with bills, cross-bills, answers, rejoinders, injunctions, affidavits, issues, references to masters, masters' reports, mountains of costly nonsense, piled before them. Well may the court be dim, with wasting candles here and there; well may the fog hang heavy in it, as if it would never get out; well may the stained glass windows lose their colour, and admit no light of day into the place; well may the uninitiated from the streets, who peep in through the glass panes in the door, be deterred from entrance by its owlish aspect, and by the drawl languidly echoing to the roof from the padded dais where the Lord High Chancellor looks into the lantern that has no light in it, and where the attendant wigs are all stuck in a fog-bank! This is the Court of Chancery; which has its decaying houses and its blighted lands in every shire; which has its worn-out lunatic in every madhouse, and its dead in every churchyard; which has its ruined suitor, with his slipshod heels and threadbare dress, borrowing and begging through the round of every man's acquaintance; which gives to monied might the means abundantly of wearying out the right; which so exhausts finances, patience, courage, hope; so overthrows the brain and breaks the heart; that there is not an honourable man among its practitioners who would not give – who does not often give – the warning, 'Suffer any wrong that can be done you, rather than come here!'

THIS MONSTROUS SYSTEM

From Chapter 15 [Mr Gridley describes his long dispute in Chancery over a legacy of £300.]

'. . . My whole estate, left to me in that will of my father's, has gone in costs. The suit, still undecided, has fallen into rack, and ruin, and despair, with everything else – and here I stand, this day! Now, Mr Jarndyce, in your suit there are thousands and thousands involved where in mine there are hundreds. Is mine less hard to bear, or is it harder to bear, when my whole living was in it, and has been thus shamefully sucked away?'

Mr Jarndyce said that he condoled with him with all his heart, and that he set up no monopoly, himself, in being unjustly treated by this monstrous system.

'There again!' said Mr Gridley, with no diminution of his rage. 'The system! I am told, on all hands, it's the system. I mustn't look to individuals. It's the system. I mustn't go into Court, and say, "My Lord, I beg to know this from you – is this right or wrong? Have you the face to tell me I have received justice, and therefore am dismissed?" My Lord knows nothing of it. He sits there, to administer the system. I mustn't go to Mr Tulkinghorn, the solicitor in Lincoln's Inn Fields, and say to him when he makes me furious, by being so cool and satisfied – as they all do; for I know they gain by it while I lose, don't I? – I mustn't say to him, I will have something out of someone for my ruin, by fair means or foul! *He* is not responsible. It's the system. But, if I do no violence to any of them, here – I may! I don't know what may happen if I am carried beyond myself at last! – I will accuse the individual workers of that system against me, face to face, before the great eternal bar!'

THE ROTTING FOUNDATIONS OF THE PILLARS OF SOCIETY

From Chapter 16

Jo lives – that is to say, Jo has not yet died – in a ruinous place, known to the like of him by the name of Tom-all-Alone's. It is a black, dilapidated street, avoided by all decent people; where the crazy houses were seized upon, when their decay was far advanced, by some bold vagrants, who, after establishing their own possession, took to letting them out in lodgings. Now, these tumbling tenements contain, by night, a swarm of misery. As, on the ruined human wretch, vermin parasites appear, so, these ruined shelters have bred a crowd of foul existence that crawls in and out of gaps in walls and boards; and coils itself to sleep, in maggot numbers, where the rain drips in; and comes and goes, fetching and carrying fever, and sowing more evil in its every footprint than Lord Coodle, and Sir Thomas Doodle, and the Duke of Foodle, and all the fine gentlemen in office, down to Zoodle, shall set right in five hundred years – though born expressly to do it.

Twice, lately, there has been a crash and a cloud of dust, like the springing of a mine, in Tom-all-Alone's; and, each time, a house has fallen. These accidents have made a paragraph in the newspapers, and have filled a bed or two in the nearest hospital. The gaps remain, and there are not unpopular lodgings among the rubbish. As several more houses are nearly ready to go, the next crash in Tom-all-Alone's may be expected to be a good one.

This desirable property is in Chancery, of course. It would be an insult to the discernment of any man with half an eye to tell him so. Whether 'Tom' is the popular representative of the original plaintiff or defendant in Jarndyce and Jarndyce; or, whether Tom lived here when the suit had laid the street waste, all alone, until other settlers came to join him; or, whether the traditional title is a comprehensive name for a retreat cut off from honest company and put out of the pale of hope; perhaps nobody knows. Certainly, Jo don't know.

'For *I* don't,' says Jo; '*I* don't know nothink.'

It must be a strange state to be like Jo! To shuffle through the streets, unfamiliar with the shapes, and in utter darkness as to the meaning, of those mysterious symbols, so abundant over the shops, and at the corners of streets, and on the doors, and in the windows! To see people read, and to see people write, and to see the postman deliver letters, and not to have the least idea of all that language – to be, to every scrap of it, stone blind and dumb! It must be very puzzling to see the good company going to the churches on Sundays, with their books in their hands, and to think (for perhaps Jo *does* think, at odd times) what does it all mean, and if it means anything to anybody, how comes it that it means nothing to me? To be hustled, and jostled, and moved on; and really to feel that it would appear to be perfectly true that I have no business, here, or there, or anywhere; and yet to be perplexed by the consideration that I *am* here somehow, too, and everybody overlooked me until I became the creature that I am! It must be a strange state, not merely to be told that I am scarcely human . . . but to feel it of my own knowledge all my life! To see the horses, dogs, and cattle, go by me, and to know that in ignorance I belong to them, and not to the superior beings in my shape, whose delicacy I offend! Jo's ideas of a Criminal Trial, or a Judge, or a Bishop, or a Government, or that inestimable jewel to him (if he only knew) the Constitution, should be strange! His whole material and immaterial life is wonderfully strange; his death, the strangest thing of all.

Jo comes out of Tom-all-Alone's . . . he sits down to breakfast on the doorstep of the Society for the Propagation of the Gospel in Foreign Parts, and gives it a brush when he has finished, as an acknowledgement of the accommodation. He admires the size of the edifice, and wonders what it's all about. He has no idea, poor wretch, of the spiritual destitution of a coral reef in the Pacific, or what it costs to look up the precious souls among the cocoa-nuts and bread-fruit.

He goes to his crossing, and begins to lay it out for the day. The town awakes; the great tee-totum is set up for its daily spin and whirl; all that unaccountable reading and writing, which has been suspended for a few hours, recommences. Jo, and the other lower animals, get on in the unintelligible mess as they can . . .

THE GOVERNMENT FALLS: ENGLAND WITHOUT A PILOT

From Chapter 40

England has been in a dreadful state for some weeks. Lord Coodle would go out, Sir Thomas Doodle wouldn't come in, and there being nobody in Great Britain (to speak of) except Coodle and Doodle, there has been no Government. It is a mercy that the hostile meeting between these two great men, which at one time seemed inevitable, did not come off; because if both pistols had taken effect, and Coodle and Doodle had killed each other, it is presumed that England must have waited to be governed until young Coodle and young Doodle, now in frocks and long stockings, were grown up. The stupendous national calamity, however, was averted by Lord Coodle's making the timely discovery, that if in the heat of debate he had said that he scorned and despised the whole ignoble career of Sir Thomas Doodle, he had merely meant to say that party differences should never induce him to withhold from it the tribute of his warmest admiration; while it as opportunely turned out, on the other hand, that Sir Thomas Doodle had in his own bosom expressly booked Lord Coodle to go down to posterity as the mirror of virtue and honour. Still England has been some weeks in the dismal strait of having no pilot . . . to weather the storm; and the marvellous part of the matter is that England has not appeared to care very much about it, but has gone on eating and drinking and marrying and giving in marriage, as the old world did in the days before the flood. But Coodle knew the danger, and Doodle knew the danger, and all their followers and hangers-on had the clearest possible perception of the danger. At last Sir Thomas Doodle has not only condescended to come in, but has done it handsomely, bringing in with him all his nephews, all his male cousins, and all his brothers-in-law. So there is hope for the old ship yet . . .

THE SOCIAL DISEASE OF THE SLUMS

From Chapter 46

Much mighty speech-making has there been, both in and out of Parliament, concerning Tom, and much wrathful disputation how Tom shall be got right. Whether he shall be put into the main road by constables, or by beadles, or by bell-ringing, or by force of figures, or by correct

522

principles of taste, or by high church, or by low church, or by no church; whether he will be set to splitting trusses of polemical straws with the crooked knife of his mind, or whether he shall be put to stone-breaking instead. In the midst of which dust and noise, there is but one thing perfectly clear, to wit, that Tom only may and can, or shall and will, be reclaimed according to somebody's theory but nobody's practice. And in the hopeful meantime, Tom goes to perdition head foremost in his old determined spirit.

But he has his revenge. Even the winds are his messengers, and they serve him in these hours of darkness. There is not a drop of Tom's corrupted blood but propagates infection and contagion somewhere. It shall pollute, this very night, the choice stream (in which chemists on analysis would find the genuine nobility) of a Norman house, and his Grace shall not be able to say Nay to the infamous alliance. There is not an atom of Tom's slime, not a cubic inch of any pestilential gas in which he lives, not one obscenity or degradation about him, not an ignorance, not a wickedness, not a brutality of his committing, but shall work its retribution, through every order of society, up to the proudest of the proud, and to the highest of the high. Verily, what with tainting, plundering, and spoiling, Tom has his revenge.

JO, A COMMON CREATURE OF THE COMMON STREETS

From Chapter 47

. . . Jo is brought in. He is not one of Mrs Pardiggle's Tockahoopo Indians; he is not one of Mrs Jellyby's lambs, being wholly unconnected with Borrioboola-Gha; he is not softened by distance and unfamiliarity; he is not a genuine foreign-grown savage; he is the ordinary home-grown article. Dirty, ugly, disagreeable to all the senses, in body a common creature of the common streets, only in soul a heathen. Homely filth begrimes him, homely parasites devour him, homely sores are in him, homely rags are on him: native ignorance, the growth of English soil and climate, sinks his immortal nature lower than the beasts that perish. Stand forth, Jo, in uncompromising colours! From the sole of thy foot to the crown of thy head, there is nothing interesting about thee.

He shuffles slowly into Mr George's gallery, and stands huddled together in a bundle, looking all about the floor. He seems to know that they have an inclination to shrink from him, partly for what he is, and partly for what he has caused. He, too, shrinks from them. He is not of the same order of things, not of the same place in creation. He is of no order and no place; neither of the beasts, nor of humanity . . .

'You are quite safe here. All you have to do at present is to be obedient, and to get strong. And mind you tell us the truth here, whatever you do, Jo.'

'Wishermaydie if I don't sir,' says Jo, reverting to his favourite declaration 'I never done nothink yit, but wot you knows on, to get myself into no trouble. I never was in no other trouble at all, sir – 'sept not knowin' nothink and starwation.'

A VERY GREAT SYSTEM

From Chapter 62

'. . . We are a very prosperous community, Mr Jarndyce, a very prosperous community. We are a great country, Mr Jarndyce, we are a very great country. This is a great system, Mr Jarndyce, and would you wish a great country to have a little system? Now, really, really!'

He said this at the stair-head, gently moving his right hand as if it were a silver trowel, with which to spread the cement of his words on the structure of the system, and consolidate it for a thousand ages.

ELIZABETH BARRETT BROWNING (1806–61)

'The Cry of the Children', stanzas 6–8, 13

CHILD SLAVERY

Alas, alas, the children! They are seeking
    Death in life, as best to have:
They are binding up their hearts away from breaking,
    With a cerement from the grave.
Go out, children, from the mine and from the city,
    Sing out, children, as the little thrushes do;
Pluck you handfuls of the meadow-cowslips pretty,
    Laugh aloud, to feel your fingers let them through!
But they answer, 'Are your cowslips of the meadows
    Like our weeds anear the mine?

Leave us quiet in the dark of the coal-shadows,
    From your pleasures fair and fine!

'For oh,' say the children, 'we are weary
    And we cannot run or leap;
If we cared for any meadows, it were merely
    To drop down in them and sleep.
Our knees tremble sorely in the stooping,
    We fall upon our faces, trying to go;
And underneath our heavy eyelids drooping
    The reddest flower would look as pale as snow.
For, all day, we drag our burden tiring
    Through the coal-dark, underground;
Or, all day, we drive the wheels of iron
    In the factories, round and round.

For all day the wheels are droning, turning;
    Their wind comes in our faces,
Till our hearts turn, our heads with pulses burning,
    And the walls turn in their places:
Turns the sky in the high window, blank and reeling,
    Turns the long light that drops adown the wall,
Turn the black flies that crawl along the ceiling:
    All are turning, all the day, and we with all.
And all day, the iron wheels are droning,
    And sometimes we could pray,
'O ye wheels' (breaking out in a mad moaning)
    'Stop! be silent for to-day!'
                    ★
And well may the children weep before you!
    They are weary ere they run;
They have never seen the sunshine, nor the glory
    Which is brighter than the sun.
They know the grief of man, without its wisdom;
    They sink in man's despair, without its calm;
Are slaves, without the liberty of Christdom,
    Are martyrs, by the pang without the palm:
Are worn as if with age, yet unretrievingly
    The harvest of its memories cannot reap, –
Are orphans of the earthly love and heavenly.
    Let them weep! let them weep! . . .

KARL MARX (1818–83)   18 March 1854

Letter to the Labour Parliament, in the *People's Paper*, in *Surveys from Exile*, pp. 277–8

Marx was elected as an honorary delegate, perhaps on the proposal of Ernest Jones, to the Labour Parliament, which was held in Manchester from 6 to 18 March 1854 as 'part of an unsuccessful attempt by the Chartist left wing to create a broad workers' organization' following the wave of strikes in 1853–4. Marx's letter was read to the 'Parliament' on 10 March.

TOWARDS THE EMANCIPATION OF LABOUR

I regret deeply to be unable, for the moment at least, to leave London, and thus to be prevented from expressing verbally my feelings of pride and gratitude on receiving the invitation to sit as Honorary Delegate at the Labour Parliament. The mere assembling of such a Parliament marks a new epoch in the history of the world. The news of this great fact will arouse the hopes of the working classes throughout Europe and America.

Great Britain, of all other countries, has seen developed on the greatest scale the despotism of capital and the slavery of labour. In no other country have the intermediate stations between the millionaire commanding whole industrial armies and the wage slave living only from hand to mouth so gradually been swept away from the soil. There exist here no longer, as in continental countries, large classes of peasants and artisans almost equally dependent on their own property and their own labour. A complete divorce of property from labour has been effected in Great Britain. In no other country, therefore, has the war between the two classes that constitute modern society assumed such colossal dimensions and features so distinct and palpable.

But it is precisely from these facts that the working classes of Great Britain, before all others, are competent and called for to act as leaders in the great movement that must finally result in the absolute emancipation of labour. Such they are from the conscious clearness of their position, the vast majority of their numbers, the disastrous struggles of their past, and the moral strength of their present.

It is the working millions of Great Britain who first have laid down the real basis of a new society – modern industry, which transformed the destructive agencies of nature into the productive power of man. The English working classes, with invincible energies, by the sweat of their brows and brains, have called into life the material means of ennobling labour itself, and of multiplying its fruits to such a degree as to make general abundance possible.

By creating the inexhaustible productive powers of modern industry they have fulfilled the first condition of the emancipation of labour. They have now to realize its other condition. They have to free those wealth-producing powers from the infamous shackles of monopoly, and subject them to the joint control of the producers, who, till now, allowed the very products of their hands to turn against them and be transformed into as many instruments of their own subjugation.

The labouring classes have conquered nature; they have now to conquer man. To succeed in this attempt they do not want strength, but the organization of their common strength, organization of the labouring classes on a national scale – such, I suppose, is the great and glorious end aimed at by the Labour Parliament.

If the Labour Parliament proves true to the idea that called it into life, some future historian will have to record that there existed in the year 1854 two parliaments in England, a parliament at London and a parliament at Manchester – a parliament of the rich, and a parliament of the poor – but that men sat only in the parliament of the men and not in the parliament of the masters.

Yours truly,

CHARLES DICKENS (1812–70)   1854

From *Hard Times*

MACHINES AND MEN

From Book I, Chapter 11

So many hundred Hands in this Mill; so many hundred horse Steam Power. It is known, to the force of a single pound weight, what the engine will do; but not all the calculators of the National Debt can tell me the capacity for good or evil, for love or hatred, for patriotism or discontent, for the decomposition of virtue into vice, or the reverse, at any single moment in the soul of one of these its quiet servants, with the composed faces and the regulated actions. There is no mystery in it; there is an unfathomable mystery in the meanest of them, for ever. – Supposing we were to reverse our arithmetic for material objects, and to govern these awful unknown qualities by other means!

A BLACK IMPASSABLE WORLD

From Book II, Chapter 5

[Stephen Blackpool (the factory-worker) answering Mr Bounderby (the self-made man).]

'Sir, I canna, wi' my little learning an' my common way, tell the genelman what will better aw this – though some working men o' this town could, above my powers – but I can tell him what I know will never do't. The strong hand will never do't. Agreeing fur to mak one side unnat'rally awlus and for ever right, and toother side unnat'rally awlus and for ever wrong, will never, never do't. Nor yet lettin alone will never do't. Let thousands upon thousands alone, aw leading the like lives and aw faw'en into the like muddle, and they will be as one, and yo will be as anoother, wi' a black impassable world betwixt yo, just as long or short a time as sitch-like misery can last. Not drawin nigh to fok, wi' kindness and patience and cheery ways, that so draws nigh to one another in the monny troubles, and so cherishes one another in their distresses wi' what they need themseln – like, I humbly believe, as no people the genelman has seen in aw his travels can beat – will never do't till th' Sun turns t' ice. Most o' aw, rating 'em as so much Power, and reg'latin 'em as if they was figures in a soom, or machines, wi'out souls to weary and souls to hope – when aw goes quiet, draggin on wi' 'em as if they'd nowt o' th' kind, and when aw goes onquiet, reproachin 'em for their want o' sitch humanly feelins in their dealins wi' yo – this will never do't, Sir, till God's work is onmade.'

A WARNING

From Book II, Chapter 6

Utilitarian economists, skeletons of schoolmasters, Commissioners of Fact, genteel and used-up infidels, gabblers of many little dog's-eared creeds, the poor you will have always with you. Cultivate in them, while there is yet time, the utmost graces of the fancies and affections, to adorn their lives so much in need of adornment; or, in the day of your triumph, when romance is utterly driven out of their souls, and they and a bare existence stand face to face, Reality will take a wolfish turn, and make an end of you.

WORK AS MURDER

From Book III, Chapter 6

[Stephen, having fallen down a mine-shaft, is dying. He speaks of the lethal nature of the pits, and of himself and others trapped and enslaved by the system.]

'I ha' fell into th' pit, me dear, as have cost wi'in the knowledge o' old fok now livin, hundreds and hundreds o' men's lives – fathers, sons, brothers, dear to thousands an thousands, an' keepin 'em fro' want and hunger. I ha' fell into a pit that ha' been wi' th' Fire-damp crueller than battle. I ha' read on't in the public petition, as onny one may read, fro' the men that works in pits, in which they ha' pray'n and pray'n the lawmakers for Christ's sake not to let their work be murder to 'em, but to spare 'em for the wives and children that they loves as well as gentlefok loves theirs. When it were in work, it killed wi'out need; when 'tis let alone, it kills wi'out need. See how we die an' no need, one way an' another – in a muddle – every day!'

ARTHUR HUGH CLOUGH (1819–1861)

'The Latest Decalogue'

TEN MIDDLE-CLASS COMMANDMENTS

Thou shalt have one God only; who
Would be at the expense of two?
No graven images may be
Worshipped, except the currency:
Swear not at all; for, by thy curse
Thine enemy is none the worse:
At church on Sunday to attend
Will serve to keep the world thy friend:
Honour thy parents; that is, all
From whom advancement may befall:
Thou shalt not kill; but needst not strive
Officiously to keep alive:
Do not adultery commit;
Advantage rarely comes of it:

Thou shalt not steal; an empty feat,
When it's so lucrative to cheat:
Bear not false witness; let the lie
Have time on its own wings to fly:
Thou shalt not covet; but tradition
Approves all forms of competition.
The sum of all is, thou shalt love,
If any body, God above:
At any rate shall never labour
More than thyself to love thy neighbour.

KARL MARX (1818–83)   6 March 1855

From an article in the *Neue Oder-Zeitung*, in *Surveys from Exile*,
pp. 281–3

The terrible sufferings of the Crimean War (1854–6) added immeasurably to the
economic crises in Britain and to the incompetence of the 'Indifferents and Incapables' who governed.

THE BRITISH CONSTITUTION

While the British Constitution has failed all along the line wherever the
war has put it to the test, on the home front the Coalition ministry – the
most constitutional in English history – has disintegrated. Forty thousand British soldiers have died on the shores of the Black Sea, victims
of the British Constitution! Officers, Command Headquarters, Commissariat, Medical Corps, Transport Corps, Admiralty, Horse Guards, Ordnance Department, the Army and Navy – all have collapsed. They have
completely ruined their reputation in the eyes of the world; but all have
the satisfaction of knowing that they were only doing their duty in the
eyes of the British Constitution! *The Times* spoke truer than it knew when
it declared that it was the British Constitution itself that was on trial. It
has stood trial and has been found guilty.

But what is this British Constitution? Are its essential features to be
found in the laws governing representation and the limitations imposed
on the executive power? These characteristics distinguish it neither from
the Constitution of the United States nor from the constitutions of the
countless joint-stock companies in England which know 'their business'.

The British Constitution is, in fact, only an antiquated and obsolete compromise made between the bourgeoisie, which rules in actual practice, although *not officially*, in all the decisive spheres of bourgeois society, and the landed aristocracy, which forms the *official government*. After the 'Glorious Revolution' of 1688 only one section of the bourgeoisie, the *financial aristocracy*, was originally included in the compromise. The Reform Bill of 1831 opened the door to another group – the *millocracy*, as they are called in England: the high dignitaries of the *industrial* bourgeoisie. Legislative history since 1831 is the history of concessions made to the industrial bourgeoisie, from the Poor Law Amendment Act to the repeal of the Corn Laws, and from the repeal of the Corn Laws to the Succession Duty on landed property.

Although the bourgeoisie – itself only the highest social stratum of the middle classes – thus also gained general *political* recognition as the *ruling class*, this only happened on one condition; namely that the whole business of government in all its details – including even the executive branch of the legislature, that is, the actual making of laws in both Houses of Parliament – remained the guaranteed domain of the landed aristocracy. In 1830 the bourgeoisie preferred a renewal of the compromise with the landed aristocracy to a compromise with the mass of the English people. Now, subjected to certain principles laid down by the bourgeoisie, the aristocracy (which enjoys exclusive power in the Cabinet, in Parliament, in the Civil Service, in the Army and Navy and which is thus one half, and comparatively the most important one, of the British nation) is being forced at this very moment to sign its own death warrant and to admit before the whole world that it is no longer destined to govern England. Observe the attempts being made to galvanize the corpses of the aristocracy into life! Ministry after ministry is formed, only to dissolve itself after governing for a few weeks. The crisis is permanent; the government only provisional. All political action has been suspended, and everyone admits that his only concern is to keep the political machine adequately oiled so that it does not come to a complete standstill. Not even the House of Commons recognizes itself in the ministries which are created in its image.

In this general state of helplessness there is not only a war to be waged but an enemy even more dangerous than Tsar Nicholas to be fought. This enemy is the *commercial* and *industrial* crisis, which since last September has been increasing in force and scope with every day that passes. Its iron hand has stopped the mouths of the superficial apostles of free trade who have been preaching for years that, since the repeal of the Corn Laws, saturated markets and social crises have been banished forever into the shadowy realm of the past. The markets are saturated again, and no one is decrying the lack of caution which has prevented manufacturers from curbing production louder than the same economists who were lecturing us five months ago, with dogmatic infallibility, that it was impossible to produce too much.

CHARLES DICKENS (1812–70)   April 1855

From a letter to Layard, in *Letters*, II, pp. 651–2

The mismanagement and misconduct of the Crimean War, the inefficiency, indifference and cruelty of the administration, led Dickens to take part in demands for reform. Considering Palmerston 'the emptiest impostor and the most dangerous delusion ever known', he makes his own bleak analysis of the situation.

OVERTURNING

. . . There is nothing in the present age at once so galling and so alarming to me as the alienation of the people from their own public affairs . . . They have had so little to do with the game through all these years of Parliamentary Reform, that they have sullenly laid down their cards, and taken to looking on. The players who are left at the table do not see beyond it, conceive that the gain and loss and all the interest of the play are in their hands, and will never be wiser until they and the table and the lights and the money are all overturned together. And I believe . . . that it is extremely like the general mind of France before the breaking out of the first Revolution, and is in danger of being turned by any one of a throng of accidents – a bad harvest – the last strain of too much aristocratical insolence or incapacity – a defeat abroad – into such a devil of a conflagration as has never been beheld since. Meanwhile all our English tufthunting, toadeating, and other manifestations of accursed gentility . . . are expressing themselves every day . . . It seems to me an absolute impossibility to direct the spirit of the people at this pass until it shows itself . . . You can no more help a people who do not help themselves, than you can help a man who does not help himself . . . I know of nothing that can be done beyond keeping their wrongs continually before them.

KARL MARX (1818–83)   28 June 1855

From the *Neue Oder-Zeitung*, in *Surveys from Exile*, pp. 290–94

The Sunday Trading Bill had already passed its third reading. It called for the closure of all shops on Sunday. As Marx points out: 'The working class receives its wages late on Saturday; Sunday trading, therefore, exists solely for them. They are the only section of the population forced to make their small purchases on Sundays, and the bill is directed against them alone.'

AGITATION AGAINST THE SUNDAY TRADING BILL

London, 25 June
The instigator of the Sunday Trading Bill, Lord Robert Grosvenor, had answered the objection that his bill was directed only against the poor and not against the rich classes by saying that the aristocracy was largely refraining from employing its servants and horses on Sundays. At the end of the week the following poster issued by the Chartists could be seen on all the walls in London announcing in large print:

> *New Sunday Bill* prohibiting newspapers, shaving, smoking, eating and drinking and all other kinds of recreation and nourishment both corporal and spiritual, which the *poor people* still enjoy at the present time. *An open-air meeting* of artisans, workers and '*the lower orders*' generally of the capital will take place in Hyde Park on Sunday afternoon to see how religiously the aristocracy is observing the Sabbath and how anxious it is not to employ its servants and horses on that day . . . Come and bring your wives and children in order that they may profit by the example their 'betters' set them!

It should be realized that what Longchamps means to the Parisians, the road along the Serpentine means to English high society: it is the place where in the afternoons, particularly on Sundays, they parade their magnificent carriages with all their trappings and exercise their horses followed by swarms of lackeys. It will be evident from the poster quoted above that the struggle against clericalism, like every serious struggle in England, is assuming the character of a *class struggle* waged by the poor against the rich, by the people against the aristocracy, by the 'lower orders' against their 'betters'.

At 3 o'clock about 50,000 people had gathered at the appointed spot on the right bank of the Serpentine in the huge meadows of Hyde Park. Gradually the numbers swelled to at least 200,000 as people came from the left bank too. Small knots of people could be seen being jostled from one spot to another. A large contingent of police was evidently attempting to deprive the organizers of the meeting of what Archimedes had demanded in order to move the earth: a fixed place to stand on. Finally, a large crowd made a firm stand and the Chartist [James] Bligh constituted himself chairman on a small rise in the middle of the crowd. No sooner had he begun his harangue than Police Inspector Banks at the head of forty truncheon-swinging constables explained to him that the Park was the private property of the Crown and that they were not allowed to hold a meeting in it . . . After some preliminary exchanges, in the course of which Bligh tried to demonstrate that the Park was public property and Banks replied that he had strict orders to arrest him if he persisted in his intention, Bligh shouted amidst the tremendous roar of the masses around him: 'Her Majesty's police declare that Hyde Park is the private property of the Crown and that Her Majesty is not inclined to lend her land to the people for their meetings. So let us adjourn to Oxford Market.'

With the ironic cry of '*God save the Queen!*' the throng dispersed in the direction of Oxford Market. But meanwhile, [James] Finlen, a member of the Chartist leadership, had rushed to a tree some distance away. A crowd followed him and surrounded him instantly in such a tight and compact circle that the police abandoned their attempts to force their way through to him. 'We are enslaved for six days a week,' he said, 'and Parliament wants to rob us of our bit of freedom on the seventh. These oligarchs and capitalists and their allies, the sanctimonious clerics, want to do *penance* – not by mortifying themselves but by mortifying us – for the unconscionable murder committed against the sons of the people sacrificed in the Crimea' . . .

The spectacle lasted for three hours . . . Zealous Chartist men and women battled their way through the crowds throughout these three hours, distributing leaflets . . .

Today's London papers carry on average only a short account of the events in Hyde Park. There have been no leading articles yet with the exception of Lord Palmerston's *Morning Post*. This paper writes:

A scene, in the highest degree disgraceful and dangerous, was enacted yesterday in Hyde Park . . . [an] outrage on law and decency . . . It was distinctly illegal to interfere, by physical force, in the free action of the legislature . . . We must have no repetition of violence on Sunday next, as has been threatened.

But at the same time it declares that the 'fanatical' Lord Grosvenor is solely 'responsible' for the trouble and that he has provoked the 'just indignation of the people'! As if Parliament has not given Lord Grosvenor's Bill its three readings! Has he perhaps also exerted pressure 'by physical force in the free action of the legislature'?

KARL MARX (1818–83)   London, 14 April 1856

Speech at the fourth anniversary of the *People's Paper*, in *Surveys from Exile*, pp. 299–300

A REVOLUTIONARY AGE

In our days everything seems pregnant with its contrary. Machinery, gifted with the wonderful power of shortening and fructifying human labour, we behold starving and overworking it. The new-fangled sources of wealth, by some strange weird spell, are turned into sources of want. The victories of art seem bought by the loss of character. At the same pace that mankind masters nature, man seems to become enslaved to other men or to his own infamy. Even the pure light of science seems unable to shine but on the dark background of ignorance. All our invention and progress seem to result in endowing material forces with intellectual life, and in stultifying human life into a material force. This antagonism between modern industry and science on the one hand, modern misery and dissolution on the other; this antagonism between the productive powers and the social relations of our epoch is a fact palpable, overwhelming, and not to be controverted. Some parties may wail over it; others may wish to get rid of modern arts, in order to get rid of modern conflicts. Or they may imagine that so signal a progress in industry wants to be completed by as signal a regress in politics. On our part, we do not mistake the shape of the shrewd spirit that continues to mark all these contradictions. We know that to work well the new-fangled forces of society, they only want to be mastered by new-fangled men – and such are the working men. They are as much the invention of modern time as machinery itself. In the signs that bewilder the middle class, the aristocracy and the poor prophets of regression, we do recognize our brave friend, Robin Goodfellow, the old mole that can work in the earth so fast, that worthy pioneer – the Revolution. The English working men are the first-born sons of modern industry. They will then, certainly, not be the last in aiding the social revolution produced by that industry, a revolution which means the emancipation of their own class all over the world, which is as universal as capital-rule and wages-slavery. I know the heroic struggles the English working class have gone through since the middle of the last century – struggles no less glorious because they are shrouded in obscurity, and burked by the middle-class historian. To revenge the misdeeds of the ruling class, there existed in the Middle Ages, in Germany, a secret tribunal called the 'Vehmgericht'. If a red cross was seen marked on a house, people knew that its owner was

535

doomed by the 'Vehm'. All the houses of Europe are marked with the mysterious red cross. History is the judge – its executioner, the proletarian.

JOHN RUSKIN (1819–1900)   1860

From *Unto This Last*

RICHES AND POVERTY

From Essay 2, p. 28

Political economy (the economy of a State, or its citizens) consists simply in the production, preservation, and distribution, at fittest time and place, of useful or pleasurable things. The farmer who cuts his hay at the right time; the shipwright who drives his bolts well home in sound wood; the builder who lays good bricks in well-tempered mortar; the housewife who takes care of her furniture in the parlour, and guards against all waste in her kitchen; and the singer who rightly disciplines, and never overstrains her voice, are all political economists in the true and final sense: adding continually to the riches and well-being of the nation to which they belong.

But mercantile economy, the economy of 'merces' or of 'pay,' signifies the accumulation, in the hands of individuals, of legal or moral claims upon, or power over, the labour of others; every such claim implying precisely as much poverty and debt on one side, as it implies riches or right on the other.

From Essay 4, p. 66

If, in the exchange, one man is able to give what cost him little labour for what has cost the other much, he 'acquires' a certain quantity of the produce of the other's labour. And precisely what he acquires, the other loses. In mercantile language, the person who thus acquires is commonly said to have 'made a profit'; and I believe that many of our merchants are seriously under the impression that it is possible for everybody, somehow, to make a profit in this manner. Whereas, by the unfortunate constitution of the world we live in, the laws both of matter and motion have quite rigorously forbidden universal acquisition of this kind. Profit, or material gain, is attainable only by construction or by discovery; not by exchange. Whenever material gain follows exchange, for every *plus* there is a precisely equal *minus*.

Unhappily for the progress of the science of Political Economy, the plus quantities, or – if I may be allowed to coin an awkward plural – the pluses, make a very positive and venerable appearance in the world, so that everyone is eager to learn the science which produces results so magnificent; whereas the minuses have, on the other hand, a tendency to retire into back streets, and other places of shade, – or even to get themselves wholly and finally put out of sight in graves: which renders the algebra of this science peculiar, and difficultly legible; a large number of its negative signs being written by the account-keeper in a kind of red ink, which starvation thins, and makes strangely pale, or even quite invisible ink, for the present.

CHILD LABOUR   1862

STITCHING GLOVES

Mary Thorpe of Bulwell, Nottingham, giving evidence to the Children's Employment Commission, in Barker, ed., *Long March of Everyman*, p. 106

Little children here begin to work at stitching gloves when very young. My little sister, now 5½ years years old, can stitch a good many little fingers and is very clever, having been at it for two years . . . She used to stand on a stool so as to be able to see up to the candle on the table. I have seen so many begin as young as that, and they do so still, because it makes them cleverer if they begin young. Parents are not particular about the age if they have work as they must do it.

Little children are kept up shamefully late if there is work, especially on Thursday and Friday nights when it is often till 11 and 12. Children younger than 7 but not younger than 6, are kept up as late as that. Mothers will pin them to their knee to keep them to their work, and if they are sleepy give them a slap on the head to keep them awake. If the children are pinned up so, they cannot fall when they are slapped, or if they go to sleep. I have often seen the children slapped in this way and cry. The child has so many fingers set for it to stitch before it goes to bed and it must do them.

What makes the work come so heavy at the end of the week is that the men are slacking at the beginning. On St Monday they will go pigeoning or on some other amusement, and do but little of Tuesday beyond setting the winders to work and much do not begin regularly till Wednesday . . . It would be much better for all to make Monday like any other day. As it is, the work is always behind, and comes into the stitchers at all times on Friday night up to 12, and 1 and 2. They must sit up to do the work then as the gloves have to be finished and taken into Nottingham in the morning.

A LONDON WATERCRESS GIRL

From Henry Mayhew, *London Labour and the London Poor*

. . . I go about the streets with water-creases, crying, 'Four bunches a penny, water-creases.' I am just eight years old – that's all and I've a big sister and a brother and sister younger than I am. On and off I've been near a twelvemonth in the streets. Before that I had to take care of a baby for my aunt . . . Before I had the baby I used to help my mother, who was in the fur trade; and if there were any slits in the fur, I'd sew them up. My mother learned me to needle-work and to knit when I was about five. I used to go to school, too, but I wasn't there long . . . It's very cold before winter comes on reg'lar – specially getting up of a morning. I gets up in the dark by the light of the lamp in the court . . . I bears the cold – you must; so I puts my hands under my shawl, though it hurts 'em to take hold of the creases, especially when we take 'em to the pump to wash 'em. No; I never see any children crying – it's no use.

KARL MARX (1818–83)   October 1864

From *The First International*, pp. 73, 75–6, 77–8, 80–81, 82–3

Marx established the First International in London for the purpose of coordinating the activities of the working classes of 'all countries in which modern society exists' toward the achievement of socialism. The first meeting of the International took place on 28 September in St Martin's Hall, without Marx, who then drew up for the General Council his Inaugural Address and Provisional Rules, and immediately set to work to build up the organization, thus bringing to an end his twelve-year period of isolation from active politics. From now on, until the split in 1872, he was to work hard to develop and expand the movement, in spite of continual disputes with the Anarchists. The First International was dissolved in

1876, and it was not until after Marx's death that the Second International was formed, in Paris, in 1889.

ENGLAND'S WEALTH AND THE WORKING CLASSES

From *The Inaugural Address to the International Working Men's Association*

Fellow working men,

It is a great fact that the misery of the working masses has not diminished from 1848 to 1864, and yet this period is unrivalled for the development of its industry and the growth of its commerce. In 1850, a moderate organ of the British middle class, of more than average information, predicted that if the exports and imports of England were to rise fifty per cent, English pauperism would sink to zero. Alas! On 7 April 1864 the Chancellor of the Exchequer delighted his parliamentary audience by the statement that the total import and export trade of England had grown in 1863 'to £443,955,000, that astonishing sum about three times the trade of the comparatively recent epoch of 1843'. With all that, he was eloquent upon 'poverty'. 'Think,' he exclaimed, 'of those who are on the border of that region', upon 'wages . . . not increased'; upon 'human life . . . in nine cases out of ten but a struggle of existence'. He did not speak of the people of Ireland, gradually replaced by machinery in the north, and by sheep-walks in the south, though even the sheep in that unhappy country are decreasing, it is true, not at so rapid a rate as the men . . .

Dazzled by the 'Progress of the Nation' statistics dancing before his eyes, the Chancellor of the Exchequer exclaims in wild ecstasy: 'From 1842 to 1852 the taxable income of the country increased by 6 per cent; in the eight years from 1853 to 1861, it has increased from the basis taken in 1853 20 per cent. The fact is so astonishing as to be almost incredible . . . This intoxicating augmentation of wealth and power,' adds Mr Gladstone, 'is entirely confined to classes of property.'

If you want to know under what conditions of broken health, tainted morals, and mental ruin, that 'intoxicating augmentation of wealth and power entirely confined to classes of property' was, and is being, produced by the classes of labour, look to the picture hung up in the last *Public Health Report* of the workshops of tailors, printers, and dressmakers! Compare the *Report of the Children's Employment Commission* of 1863, where it is stated, for instance, that:

539

The potters as a class, both men and women, represent a much degenerated population, both physically and mentally . . . The unhealthy child is an unhealthy parent in his turn . . . A progressive deterioration of the race must go on . . . The degenerescence of the population of Staffordshire would be even greater were it not for the constant recruiting from the adjacent country, and the inter-marriages with more healthy races.

Glance at Mr Tremenheere's blue book on *The Grievances complained of by the Journeyman Bakers!* . . .

Everywhere the great mass of the working classes were sinking down to a lower depth, at the same rate, at least, that those above them were rising in the social scale. In all countries of Europe it has now become a truth demonstrable to every unprejudiced mind . . . that no improvement of machinery, no application of science to production, no contrivances of communication, no new colonies, no emigration, no opening of markets, no free trade, nor all these things put together, will do away with the miseries of the industrious masses; but that, on the present false bases, every fresh development of the productive powers of labour must tend to deepen social contrasts and point social antagonisms. Death by starvation rose almost to the rank of an institution, during the intoxicating epoch of economic progress, in the metropolis of the British empire . . .

To conquer political power has therefore become the great duty of the working classes. They seem to have comprehended this, for in England, Germany, Italy and France there have taken place simultaneous revivals, and simultaneous efforts are being made at the political reorganization of the working men's party.

One element of success they possess – numbers; but numbers weigh only in the balance if united by combination and led by knowledge. Past experience has shown how disregard of that bond of brotherhood which ought to exist between the workmen of different countries, and incite them to stand firmly by each other in all their struggles for emancipation, will be chastised by the common discomfiture of their incoherent efforts. This thought prompted the working men of different countries assembled on 28 September 1864, in public meeting at St Martin's Hall, to found the International Association.

Another conviction swayed that meeting.

If the emancipation of the working classes requires their fraternal concurrence, how are they to fulfil that great mission with a foreign policy in pursuit of criminal designs, playing upon national prejudices, and squandering in piratical wars the people's blood and treasure? It was not the wisdom of the ruling classes, but the heroic resistance to their criminal folly by the working classes of England, that saved the west of Europe from plunging headlong into an infamous crusade for the perpetuation and propagation of slavery on the other side of the Atlantic. The shameless approval, mock sympathy, or idiotic indifference, with which the upper classes of Europe have witnessed the mountain fortress of the Caucasus falling a prey to, and heroic Poland being assassinated by, Russia; the immense and unresisted encroachments of that barbarous power, whose head is at St Petersburg, and whose hands are in every cabinet of Europe, have taught the working classes the duty to master themselves the mysteries of international politics; to watch the diplomatic acts of their respective governments; to counteract them, if necessary, by all means in their power; when unable to prevent, to combine in simultaneous denunciations, and to vindicate the simple laws of morals and justice, which ought to govern the relations of private individuals as the paramount rules of the intercourse of nations.

The fight for such a foreign policy forms part of the general struggle for the emancipation of the working classes.

Proletarians of all countries, unite!

RIGHTS AND DUTIES

Introduction to *Provisional Rules*

Considering,

That the emancipation of the working classes must be achieved by the working classes themselves; that the struggle for the emancipation of the working classes means not a struggle for class privileges and monopolies, but for equal rights and duties, and the abolition of all class rule;

That the economic subjection of the man of labour to the monopolizer of the means of labour – that is, the sources of life – lies behind servitude in all its forms, all social misery, mental degradation, and political dependence;

That the economic emancipation of the working classes is therefore the great end to which every political movement ought to be subordinate as a means;

That all efforts directed towards that great end have hitherto failed for want of solidarity between the manifold divisions of labour in each country, and from the absence of a fraternal bond of union between the working classes of different countries;

That the emancipation of labour is neither a local nor a national but a social problem, embracing all countries in which modern society exists, and depending for its solution on the concurrence, practical and theoretical, of the most advanced countries;

That the present revival of the working classes in the most industrious countries of Europe, even while it raises new hope, gives solemn warning against a relapse into the old errors, and calls for the immediate combination of the unconnected movements;

For these reasons –

The undersigned members of the committee, holding its powers by resolution of the public meeting held on 28 September 1864, at St Martin's Hall, London, have taken the steps necessary for founding the Working Men's International Association;

They declare that this International Association and all societies and individuals adhering to it, will acknowledge truth, justice, and morality, as the basis of their conduct towards each other, and towards all men, without regard to colour, creed, or nationality;

They hold it the duty of a man to claim the rights of a man and a citizen, not only for himself, but for every man who does his duty. No rights without duties, no duties without rights . . .

CHARLES DICKENS (1812–70)   1865

From *Our Mutual Friend*, pp. 159–60, 187–8, 565–6, 893–4

In *Our Mutual Friend*, Dickens conceives of money (and property) as an elemental source of corruption, corroding, perverting and undermining the pattern of individual and social relationships. It is a river of filth, a mound of dust, a falsifying standard; it turns people into objects and twists feelings out of all proportion; it creates boredom and disillusionment and voids of class discrimination; it eats away at the personality or distorts it into such crippling and inhibiting forms as to poison the whole being of a man or woman. In one way or another all the characters in the novel are contaminated by it – Lizzie and Eugene, Bella and John Harmon, Mr and Mrs Boffin, Headstone, Wegg and Riderhood, Betty Higden, Jenny, the Wilfers, the Podsnaps, the Veneerings and the Lammles.

TRAFFIC IN SHARES

From Book I, Chapter 10

[The mature young lady, Sophronia Akershem, it about to be married to the mature young gentleman, Alfred Lammle, each, as it turns out, under the false impression that the other has 'shares'.]

The mature young lady is a lady of property. The mature young gentleman is a gentleman of property. He invests his property. He goes, in a condescending amateurish way, into the City, attends meetings of Directors, and has to do with traffic in Shares. As is well known to the wise in their generation, traffic in Shares is the one thing to have to do with in this world. Have no antecedents, no established character, no cultivation, no ideas, no manners; have Shares. Have Shares enough to be on Boards of Direction in capital letters, oscillate on mysterious business between London and Paris, and be great. Where does he come from? Shares. Where is he going to? Shares. What are his tastes? Shares. Has he any principles? Shares. What squeezes him into Parliament? Shares. Perhaps he never of himself achieved success in anything, never originated anything, never produced anything! Sufficient answer to all; Shares. O mighty Shares! To set those blaring images so high, and to cause us smaller vermin, as under the influence of henbane or opium, to cry out night and day, 'Relieve us of our money, scatter it for us, buy us and sell us, ruin us, only we beseech ye take rank among the powers of the earth, and fatten on us!'

MR PODSNAP: PROVIDENCE AND THE POOR

From Book I, Chapter 11

[On Mr Podsnap's hearthrug, 'a stray personage of meek demeanour' has made a reference 'to the circumstance that some half-dozen people had lately died in the streets of starvation . . . clearly ill-timed, after dinner . . . not in good taste'.]

'I don't believe it,' said Mr Podsnap, putting it behind him.

The meek man was afraid we must take it as proved, because there were the Inquests and the Registrar's returns.

'Then it was their own fault,' said Mr Podsnap.

Veneering and other elders of the tribes commended this way out of it. At once a short cut and a broad road.

The man of meek demeanour intimated that truly it would seem from the facts as if starvation had been forced upon the culprits in question – as if, in their wretched manner, they had made their weak protests against it – as if they would have taken the liberty of staving it off if they could – as if they would rather not have been starved upon the whole, if perfectly agreeable to all parties.

'There is not,' said Mr Podsnap, flushing angrily, 'there is not a country in the world, sir, where so noble a provision is made for the poor as in this country.'

The meek man was quite willing to concede that, but perhaps it rendered the matter even worse, as showing that there must be something appallingly wrong somewhere.

'Where?' said Mr Podsnap.

The meek man hinted, Wouldn't it be well to try, very seriously, to find out where?

'Ah!' said Mr Podsnap. 'Easy to say somewhere; not so easy to say where! But I see what you are driving at. I knew it from the first. Centralization. No. Never with my consent. Not English.'

An approving murmur arose from the heads of tribes; as saying, 'There you have him! Hold him!'

He was not aware (the meek man submitted of himself) that he was driving at any ization. He had no favourite ization that he knew of. But he certainly was more staggered by these terrible occurrences than he was by names, of howsoever so many syllables. Might he ask, was dying of destitution and neglect necessarily English?

'You know what the population of London is, I suppose,' said Mr Podsnap.

The meek man supposed he did, but supposed that had absolutely nothing to do with it, if its laws were well administered.

'And you know; at least I hope you know,' said Mr Podsnap, with severity, 'that Providence has declared that you shall have the poor always with you?'

The meek man also hoped he knew that.

'I am glad to hear it,' said Mr Podsnap, with a portentous air. 'I am glad to hear it. It will render you cautious how you fly in the face of Providence.'

In reference to that absurd and irreverent conventional phrase, the meek man said, for which Mr Podsnap was not responsible, he the meek man had no fear of doing anything so impossible; but –

But Mr Podsnap felt that the time had come for flushing and flourishing this meek man down for good. So he said:

'I must decline to pursue this painful discussion. It is not pleasant to my feelings. It is repugnant to my feelings. I have said that I do not admit these things. I have also said that if they do occur (not that I admit it), the fault lies with the sufferers themselves. It is not for *me*' – Mr Podsnap pointed 'me' forcibly, as adding by implication, though it may be all very well for *you* – 'it is not for me to impugn the workings of Providence. I know better than that, I trust, and I have mentioned what the intentions of Providence are. Besides,' said Mr Podsnap, flushing high up among his hair-brushes, with a strong consciousness of personal affront, 'the subject is a very disagreeable one. I will go so far as to say it is an odious one. It is not one to be introduced among our wives and young persons, and I –' He finished with that flourish of his arm which added more expressively than any words, And I remove it from the face of the earth.

THIS BOASTFUL HANDIWORK OF OURS – A MOUNTAIN OF PRETENTIOUS FAILURE

From Book III, Chapter 8

. . . My lords and gentlemen and honourable boards, when you in the course of your dust-shovelling and cinder-raking have piled up a mountain of pretentious failure, you must off with your honourable coats for the removal of it, and fall to the work with the power of all the queen's horses and all the queen's men, or it will come rushing down and bury us alive.

Yes, verily, my lords and gentlemen and honourable boards, adapting your Catechism to the occasion, and by God's help so you must. For when we have got things to the pass that with an enormous treasure at disposal to relieve the poor, the best of the poor detest our mercies, hide their heads from us, and shame us by starving to death in the midst of us, it is a pass impossible of prosperity, impossible of continuance. It may not be so written in the Gospel according to Podsnappery; you may not 'find these words' for the text of a sermon, in the Returns of the Board of Trade; but they have been the truth since the foundations of the universe were laid, and they will be the truth till the foundations of the universe are shaken by the Builder. This boastful handiwork of ours, which fails in its terrors for the professional pauper, the sturdy breaker of windows and the rampant tearer of clothes, strikes with a cruel and a wicked stab at the stricken sufferer, and is a horror to the deserving

545

and unfortunate. We must mend it, lords and gentlemen and honourable boards, or in its own evil hour it will mar every one of us.

THE LAWS AND THE POOR
From the Postscript

In my social experiences since Mrs Betty Higden came upon the scene and left it, I have found Circumlocutional champions disposed to be warm with me on the subject of my view of the Poor Law. My friend Mr Bounderby could never see any difference between leaving the Coketown 'hands' exactly as they were, and requiring them to be fed with turtle soup and venison out of gold spoons. Idiotic propositions of a parallel nature have been freely offered for my acceptance, and I have been called upon to admit that I would give Poor Law relief to anybody, anywhere, anyhow. Putting this nonsense aside, I have observed a suspicious tendency in the champions to divide into two parties; the one contending that there are no deserving Poor who prefer death by slow starvation and bitter weather, to the mercies of some Relieving Officers and some Union Houses; the other admitting that there are such Poor, but denying that they have any cause or reason for what they do. The records in our newspapers, the late exposure by the *Lancet*, and the common sense and senses of common people, furnish too abundant evidence against both defences. But, that my view of the Poor Law may not be mistaken or misrepresented, I will state it. I believe there has been in England, since the days of the STUARTS, no law so often infamously administered, no law so often openly violated, no law habitually so ill-supervised. In the majority of the shameful cases of disease and death from destitution that shock the Public and disgrace the country, the illegality is quite equal to the inhumanity – and known language could say no more of their lawlessness.

THE SECOND REFORM BILL   1866–7

The oligarchy of the Palmerston years formed a sort of 'board of control' (Bagehot) for the advancement of unfettered self-interest at home; but in the early sixties 'the meddle and muddle' of its policies, against the background of the American Civil War (a struggle supported in England along class lines), the continuing scandal of landlordism in Ireland, and the rise of Bismarck in Germany, was to change the whole balance of the power-structure. And with Gladstone and Disraeli taking over after 1865, the question of extending the franchise in a context of renewed working-class agitation was to become the basis at once for keeping the people quiet and for recruiting personnel (as it turned out) to support the competitive war of imperialist influence which was to dominate Europe after 1871. (This world expansion of aggressive nation states was to lead inexorably down the narrowing paths of ruling-class rivalry to the holocaust of the First World War.) But in 1866–7 the agitation round the Reform Bill (Disraeli's 'leap in the dark') was also to re-awaken the working-class movement for the first time since 1848, with the trade unions inspired by the socialist principles of Marx's International. The ruling class was startled by the sudden outburst of demonstrations and riots which occurred all over the country; and for writers like Ruskin, Arnold, Carlyle, George Eliot and Trollope, drawing back in alarm, cultural anarchy and chaos even seemed a real threat. But though on the whole both George Eliot and Trollope support the received views of the establishment about the 'ignorance' and 'mob-rule' of the working class, they do also manage to catch something of the mood of the time.

A FREEMAN'S SHARE

From George Eliot, *Felix Holt* (1866), Chapter 30, pp. 396–7

On the Nomination-day for an election at Duffield, Felix listens to a working-class speaker in whom he recognizes 'the fluency and the method of a habitual preacher or lecturer', whose argument for suffrage he himself later speaks against, reflecting George Eliot's own radical-conservative views. The novel is itself set symbolically in the period of the *First* Reform Bill.

'. . . Well, they say – you've got the Reform Bill; what more can you want? . . . But I say, the Reform Bill is a trick – it's nothing but swearing-in special constables to keep the aristocrats safe in their monopoly; it's bribing some of the people with votes to make them hold their tongues about giving votes to the rest. I say, if a man doesn't beg or steal, but works for his bread, the poorer and the more miserable he is, the more he'd need have a vote to send an inspector to parliament – else the man who is worst off is likely to be forgotten; and I say, he's the man who ought to be first remembered. Else what does their religion mean? Why do they build churches and endow them that their sons may get well paid for preaching a Saviour, and making themselves as little like Him as can be? . . . If the poor man had a vote in the matter, I think he'd choose a different sort of a church to what that is. But do you think the aristocrats will ever alter it, if the belly doesn't pinch them?

547

Not they. It's part of their monopoly. They'll supply us with our religion like everything else, and get a profit on it. They'll give us plenty of heaven. We may have land *there*. That's the sort of religion they like – a religion that gives us working men heaven, and nothing else. But we'll offer to change with 'em. We'll give them back some of their heaven, and take it out in something for us and our children in this world. They don't seem to care so much about heaven themselves till they feel the gout very bad; but you won't get them to give up anything else, if you don't pinch 'em for it. And to pinch them enough, we must get the suffrage, we must get votes, that we may send the men to parliament who will do our work for us; and we must have parliament dissolved every year, that we may change our man if he doesn't do what we want him to do; and we must have the country divided so that the little kings of the counties can't do as they like, but must be shaken up in one bag with us. I say, if we working men are ever to get a man's share, we must have universal suffrage, and annual parliaments, and the vote by ballot, and electoral districts.'

DEMONSTRATION

From Anthony Trollope, *Phineas Finn* (1866–7), chapter 25, pp. 262–3

The setting for this scene was the working-class unrest following Robert Lowe's insolent opposition to reform on the grounds that workers were unfit for the franchise. There were huge demonstrations in Hyde Park and Trafalgar Square, with rioting by what Arnold called 'Hyde Park roughs', when railings were pulled up and windows smashed. Trollope is of course for 'law and order', but he isn't frightened into conservative retreat, like Arnold and Carlyle. Here the people are supporting a Petition for the Ballot.

———

The petition was to be presented at six o'clock, but the crowd, who collected to see it carried into Westminster Hall, began to form itself by noon. It was said afterwards that many of the houses in the neighbourhood of Palace Yard and the Bridge were filled with soldiers; but if so, the men did not show themselves. In the course of the evening three or four companies of the Guards in St James's Park did show themselves, and had some rough work to do, for many of the people took themselves away from Westminster by that route. The police, who were very numerous in Palace Yard, had a hard time of it all afternoon . . . The petition, which was said to fill fifteen cabs . . . was being dragged about half the day, and it certainly would have been impossible for a member to have made his way into the House through Westminster Hall between the hours of four and six . . . as all the spaces round St Margaret's Church and Canning's monument were filled with the crowd. Parliament Street was quite impassable at five o'clock, and there was no traffic across the Bridge from that hour till after eight. As the evening went on, the mob extended itself to Downing Street and the front of the Treasury Chambers, and before the night was over all the hoardings around the new Government offices had been pulled down. The windows also of certain obnoxious members of Parliament were broken, when those obnoxious members lived within reach. One gentleman who unfortunately held a house in Richmond Terrace, and who was said to have said that the ballot was the resort of cowards, fared very badly; – for his windows were not only broken, but his furniture and mirrors were destroyed by the stones that were thrown. . . .

KARL MARX (1818–83)   1867

From *Capital*, pp. 273–5

In his chapter on 'The Working Day' Marx accumulates massive evidence of the exploitation of labour, child and adult, in British industry – in lace-making, pottery, matches, wallpapering, baking, ploughing, the railways – and it is this which makes the following indictment unanswerable.

SURPLUS POPULATION FOR SURPLUS VALUE

From Vol. I, chapter 8

The general experience of capitalists is that overpopulation is persistent – this meaning overpopulation in relation to the momentary requirements of capital in the matter of labour to promote its self-expansion. But such an excess of population is made up of generations of human beings who are stunted, short-lived, replacing one another swiftly, plucked so to say before they are ripe. On the other hand, no intelligent observer can fail to see that capitalist production (though, historically considered, it dates but from yesterday) has already sapped the vital energy of the people at the root; that the degeneration of the industrial population is only kept in check by the continuous absorption of fresh and vigorous elements from the rural districts; and that even the agricultural workers, though they live in the open air, and though the formidable and universally operative principle of natural selection is at work among them to maintain their stock out of the most powerful specimens, are already passing into a phase of incipient decay. The capitalists have such good reason for denying the suffering of the legions of workers who surround them, that in practice they are no more moved by the prospect of the coming degeneration and final disappearance of the human race than they are disturbed by the prospect that the earth may one day fall into the sun. When there is a boom on the stock exchange, every one who takes part in the swindle knows that sooner or later the crash will come, but each man hopes that the disaster will involve his neighbours, after he himself has taken safe shelter with a goodly share of loot. 'After me, the deluge!' is the watchword of every capitalist and of every capitalist nation. Capital, therefore, is reckless as regards illness or premature death of the workers, unless forced to pay heed to these matters, forced by social compulsion. When complaints are voiced regarding physical and mental degeneration, early death, and the tortures of overwork, the capitalists answer: 'Why should these things trouble us, since they increase our profits?' From a broad outlook, however, such matters do not depend upon the good will or the evil will of individual capitalists. Owing to free competition, the imminent laws of capitalist production hold sway irresistibly over every individual capitalist.

LYDIA ERNESTINE BECKER (1827–1890)
17 July 1868

From a letter to Dr Pankhurst, in Pankhurst, *Suffragette Movement*, pp. 36–7

The original committee that launched the long campaign for women's suffrage met in Manchester in 1866, with Jacob and Ursula Bright and Dr Pankhurst present, and Elizabeth Wostonholme (later Mrs Elmy) as secretary. Lydia Becker joined the movement in 1867, and then took over as secretary of what had become the Manchester National Society for Women's Suffrage. She was to work unstintingly for the cause during the next twenty years. She is here referring to an article on women in a journal. Mrs Butler is Josephine Butler, very much a part of the movement at the time.

. . . I wonder if the writer who coolly analyses the question, as if it were one of abstract right, understands that women really feel it as a matter of political life or death. I believe men think women do not feel at all, at least that women do not feel as men would if they were similarly treated. Whenever men propose to women to pass their lives under conditions which men would not like for their own lives, they may be sure that women do not like it either and would not submit if they could help themselves.

Miss Bancroft of St Anne's Manor is intensely indignant at having no vote. Three of her employees – men who live in small cottages – have votes, and she who pays so large a rent and rates and keeps the three men at work cannot have one. 'It is infamous!' she says.

I shall be very glad if you can draft a feasible scheme for a cooperative store or warehouse. There is nothing like buying and selling for making money; and women can buy and sell very well. There is nothing either laborious or 'unfeminine' in either process. Most of the plans for promoting 'employment for women' seem to contemplate pursuits requiring bodily labour – handicrafts – the most irksome and least remunerative of all occupations.

I sent you Mrs Butler's pamphlet. Tell me what you think of it. The statistics are startling. Nearly 1,000,000 *wives* working for their bread! How many of their husbands live off their wives' earnings, I wonder! The census does not give *that*.

I wonder whether you can trace in Mrs Butler's page something of that vivid and far-reaching sympathy with all forms of human suffering which is the great secret of her influence. The circumstances of her life are such as would cause an ordinary woman to limit her *life* to her home. She is most happily married, has three children, and is in such weak health that if she were to make alleviation of her own bodily sufferings her chief care no one could wonder or blame her. But she maintains that it is not the disappointed and the personally unlucky women who feel most keenly the disadvantageous position of their sex; it is the happiest who are most induced to exert themselves for the benefit of others less fortunate, and she is an example of her own theory . . .

JOHN STUART MILL (1806–1873)   1869

From *The Subjection of Women*, pp. 24–5, 26–8, 91–2, 187–8

Mill wrote his classic of feminist writing in 1861, three years after the death of his wife, Harriet Taylor; and her influence upon its formulation was profound. Indeed, the essay should properly be seen as a collaboration, for it is a fruit of their twenty-eight years of intimacy and intellectual debate.

WOMEN: AN ENSLAVED CLASS

. . . Ever since there have been women able to make their sentiments known by their writings (the only mode of publicity which society permits to them), an increasing number of them have recorded protests against their present social condition: and recently many thousands of them, headed by the most eminent women known to the public, have petitioned Parliament for their admission to the Parliamentary Suffrage. The claim of women to be educated as solidly, and in the same branches of knowledge, as men, is urged with growing intensity, and with a great prospect of success; while the demand for their admission into the professions and occupations hitherto closed against them, becomes every year more urgent. Though there are not in this country, as there are in the United States, periodical Conventions and an organized party to agitate for the Rights of Women, there is a numerous and active Society organized and managed by women for the more limited object of obtaining the political franchise. . . . How many more women there are who silently cherish similar aspirations, no one can possibly know; but there are abundant tokens how many *would* cherish them, were they not so strenuously taught to repress them as contrary to the proprieties of their sex. It must be remembered, also, that no enslaved class ever asked for complete liberty at once . . .

All causes, social and natural, combine to make it unlikely that women should be collectively rebellious to the power of men. They are so far in a position different from all other subject classes, that their masters require something more from them than actual service. Men do not want solely the obedience of women, they want their sentiments. All men, except the most brutish, desire to have, in the woman most nearly connected with them, not a forced slave but a willing one, not a slave merely, but a favourite. They have therefore put everything in practice to enslave their minds. The masters of all other slaves rely, for maintaining obedience, on fear; either fear of themselves, or religious fears. The masters of women wanted more than simple obedience, and they turned the whole force of education to effect their purpose. All women are brought up from the very earliest years in the belief that their ideal of character is the very opposite to that of men; not self-will, and government by self-control, but submission, and yielding to the control of others . . . When we put together three things . . . first, the natural attraction between opposite sexes; secondly, the wife's entire dependence on the husband, every privilege or pleasure she has being either his gift, or depending entirely on his will; and lastly, that the principal object of human pursuit, consideration, and all objects of social ambition, can in general be sought or obtained by her only through him, it would be a miracle if the object of being attractive to men had not become the polar star of feminine education and formation of character. And, this great means of influence over the minds of women having been acquired, an instinct of selfishness made men avail themselves of it to the utmost as a means of holding women in subjection, by representing to them meekness, submissiveness, and resignation of all individual will into the hands of a man, as an essential part of sexual attractiveness. Can it be doubted that any of the other yokes which mankind have succeeded in breaking, would have subsisted till now if the same means had existed, and had been as sedulously used, to bow down their minds to it? . . .

. . . The generality of the male sex cannot yet tolerate the idea of living with an equal. Were it not for that, I think that almost everyone, in the existing state of opinion in politics and political economy, would admit the injustice of excluding half the human race from the greater number of lucrative occupations, and from almost all high social functions; ordaining from their birth either that they are not, and cannot by any possibility become, fit for employments which are legally open to the stupidest and basest of the other sex, or else that however fit they may be, those employments shall be interdicted to them, in order to be preserved for the exclusive benefit of males. In the last two centuries, when (which was seldom the case) any reason beyond the mere existence of the fact was thought to be required to justify the disabilities of women, people seldom assigned as a reason their inferior mental capacity; which . . . no one really believed in. The reason given in those days was not women's unfitness, but the interest of society, by which was meant the interest of men . . .

When we consider the positive evil caused to the disqualified half of the human race by their disqualification – first in the loss of the most inspiriting and elevating kind of personal enjoyment, and next in the weariness, disappointment, and profound dissatisfaction with life, which are so often the substitute for it; one feels that among all the lessons which men require for carrying on the struggle against the inevitable imperfections of their lot on earth, there is no lesson which they more need, than not to add to the evils which nature inflicts, by their jealous and prejudiced restrictions on one another. Their vain fears only substitute other and worse evils for those which they are idly apprehensive of: while every restraint on the freedom of conduct of any of their human fellow creatures . . . dries up *pro tanto* the principal fountain of human happiness, and leaves the species less rich, to an inappreciable degree, in all that makes life valuable to the individual human being.

FRANCES POWER COBBE (1822–1904)   1869

From Josephine Butler, ed., *Woman's Work and Woman's Culture*, quoted in Hollis. ed., *Women in Public*, p. 23

THE CAUSE OF WOMAN

To admit that Woman has affections, a moral nature, a religious sentiment, an immortal soul, and yet to treat her for a moment as a mere animal link in the chain of life, is monstrous; I had almost said, blasphemous. If her existence be of no value in itself, then no man's existence is of value; for a moral nature, a religious sentiment, and an immortal soul are the highest things a man can have, and the woman has them as well as he. If the links be valueless then the chain is valueless too; and the history of Humanity is but a long procession of spectres for whose existence no reason can be assigned . . . Believing that the same woman, a million ages hence, will be a glorious spirit before the throne of God, filled with unutterable love, and light, and joy, we cannot satisfactorily trace the beginning of that eternal and seraphic existence to Mr Smith's want of a wife for a score of years here upon earth; or to the necessity Mr Jones was under to find somebody to cook his food and repair his clothes. If these ideas be absurd, then it follows that we are not arrogating too much in seeking elsewhere than in the interests of Man the ultimate *raison d'être* of Woman.

KARL MARX (1818–83)   9 April 1870

From a letter to Siefried Meyer and August Vogt, in *First International*, pp. 168–70

The long and terrible history of the oppression of Ireland by the English, beginning with the Overlordship of the twelfth century, was merely extended by Pitt's manipulative Act of Union of 1800, which laid the foundations of the economic exploitation of the absentee landlords and ruthless extortion during the Napoleonic Wars. This economic tyranny further deepened the decline of the peasantry and the tenant-farmers, reducing the people to penury which, in the great famine of the 1840s, led to the death of nearly one million and the emigration of two million. Hence Marx's argument (letter to Kugelmann, November 1869) that the English working class 'can never do anything decisive here in England until it makes a decisive break with the ruling class in its policy on Ireland'. For, as 'the English republic under Cromwell came to grief in Ireland', so (under the divisive conditions of ruling-class tyranny that prevailed now) would the struggle for the emancipation of labour.

THE NATIONAL EMANCIPATION OF IRELAND

. . . Ireland is the bulwark of the *English landed aristocracy*. The exploitation of this country is not only one of the main sources of their material wealth; it is their greatest *moral* strength. They represent in fact *England's domination over Ireland*. Ireland is, therefore the great means by which the English aristocracy maintains *its rule in England* itself . . .

As far as the English *bourgeoisie* is concerned, it has first of all a common interest with the English aristocracy in transforming Ireland into mere pasture land, to supply the English market with meat and wool at the cheapest possible prices. It has the same interest in reducing the Irish population to such a small number, by eviction and forcible emigration, that *English capital* (invested in leasehold farmland) can operate in this country with 'security'. It has the same interest in clearing the estate of Ireland that it had in the clearing of the agricultural districts of England and Scotland. The £6,000–£10,000 absentee and other Irish revenues which at present flow annually to London must also be taken into account.

But the English bourgeoisie has other, much more important interests in the present structure of the Irish economy. As a result of the steadily increasing concentration of farms, Ireland supplies the English labour market with its surplus (labour) and thus lowers the wages and the material and moral position of the English working class.

And most important of all! All English industrial and commercial centres now possess a working class *split* into two *hostile* camps: English proletarians and Irish proletarians. The ordinary English worker hates the Irish worker because he sees in him a competitor who lowers his standard of life. Compared with the Irish worker he feels himself a member of the *ruling nation* and for this very reason he makes himself into a tool of the aristocrats and capitalists *against Ireland*, and thus strengthens their domination *over himself*. He cherishes religious, social and national prejudices against the Irish worker. His attitude is much the same as that of the 'poor whites' towards the 'niggers' in the former slave states of the American Union. The Irishman pays him back with interest in his own coin. He sees in the English worker both the accomplice and the stupid tool of *English rule in Ireland*.

This antagonism is artificially sustained and intensified by the press, the pulpit, the comic papers, in short, by all the means at the disposal of the ruling classes. It is the *secret of the impotence of the English working class*, despite its organization. It is the secret which enables the capitalist class to maintain its power, as this class is perfectly aware . . .

England, as the metropolis of capital, as the power which has up to now ruled the world market, is for the time being the most important country for the workers' revolution; moreover it is the *only* country where the material conditions for this revolution have developed to a certain degree of maturity. To accelerate the social revolution in England is therefore the most important object of the International Working Men's Association. The only means of accelerating it is to bring about the independence of Ireland. It is therefore the task of the 'International' to bring the conflict between England and Ireland into the foreground and everywhere to side openly with Ireland. It is the special task of the General Council in London to arouse the consciousness in the English working class that *for them* the *national emancipation of Ireland* is not a question of abstract justice or humanitarian sentiment but the first condition of their own social emancipation . . .

JOSEPHINE BUTLER (1828–1906)   1870

From *Personal Reminiscences of a Great Crusade* (1896), pp. 17–19

The Contagious Diseases Acts of 1864, 1866 and 1869 (against prostitution) permitting the arrest of suspected women by special police and compulsory medical examination, were attacked by Josephine Butler as depriving women as a class of their constitutional rights and agitated against till they were (in 1886) repealed. The protest, drawn up by Harriet Martineau, was signed by 2000 women, including Florence Nightingale and Mary Carpenter.

VICTIMS OF MALE VICE

On the 1st January 1870 was published the famous Women's Protest, as follows: We, the undersigned, enter our solemn protest against these Acts.

1st. – Because, involving as they do such a momentous change in the legal safeguards hitherto enjoyed by women in common with men, they have been passed, not only without the knowledge of the country, but unknown, in a great measure, to Parliament itself; and we hold that neither the Representatives of the People, nor the Press, fulfil the duties which are expected of them, when they allow such legislation to take place without the fullest discussion.

2nd. – Because, so far as women are concerned, they remove every guarantee of personal security which the law has established and held sacred, and put their reputation, their freedom, and their persons absolutely in the power of the police.

3rd. – Because the law is bound, in any country professing to give civil liberty to its subjects, to define clearly an offence which it punishes.

4th. – Because it is unjust to punish the sex who are the victims of a vice, and leave unpunished the sex who are the main cause, both of the vice and its dreaded consequences; and we consider that liability to arrest, forced medical treatment, and (where this is resisted) imprisonment with hard labour, to which these Acts subject women, are punishments of the most degrading kind.

5th. – Because, by such a system, the path of evil is made more easy to our sons, and to the whole of the youth of England; inasmuch as a moral restraint is withdrawn the moment the State recognizes, and provides convenience for, the practice of a vice which it thereby declares to be necessary and venial.

6th. – Because these measures are cruel to the women who come under their action – violating the feelings of those whose sense of shame is not wholly lost, and further brutalizing even the most abandoned.

7th. – Because the disease which these Acts seek to remove has never been removed by any such legislation. The advocates of the system have utterly failed to show, by statistics or otherwise, that these regulations have in any case, after several years' trial, and when applied to one sex

557

only, diminished disease, reclaimed the fallen, or improved the general morality of the country. We have, on the contrary, the strongest evidence to show that in Paris and other Continental cities where women have long been outraged by this system, the public health and morals are worse than at home.

8th. – Because the conditions of this disease, in the first instance, are moral, not physical. The moral evil through which the disease makes its way separates the case entirely from that of the plague, or other scourges ... We hold that we are bound, before rushing into experiments of legalizing a revolting vice, to try to deal with the *causes* of the evil, and we dare to believe that with wiser teaching and more capable legislation, those causes would not be beyond control.

... I never myself viewed this question as fundamentally any more a woman's question than it is a man's. The legislation we opposed secured the enslavement of women and the increased immorality of men; and history and experience alike teach us that these two results are never separated ...

... The fact that this new legislation *directly* and shamefully attacked the dignity and liberties of women, became a powerful means ... of awakening a deeper sympathy amongst favoured women for their poorer and less fortunate sisters than had probably ever been felt before. It consolidated the women of our country, and gradually of the world, by the infliction on them of a double wrong, an outrage on free citizenship, and an outrage on the sacred rights of womanhood. It helped to conjure up also a great army of good and honourable men through the length and breadth of the land, who, in taking up the cause of the deeply injured class, soon became aware that they were fighting also for themselves, their own liberties, and their own honour.

Thus the peculiar horror and audacity of this legislative movement for the creation of a slave class of women for the supposed benefit of licentious men forced women into a new position. Many, who were formerly timid or bound by conventional ideas to a prescribed sphere of action, faced right round upon the men whose materialism had been embodied in such a ghastly form, and upon the Government which had set its seal upon that iniquity; and so, long before we had approached near to attaining to any political equality with men, a new light was brought by the force of our righteous wrath and aroused sense of justice into the judgement of Society and the Councils of Nations, which encouraged us to hope that we should be able to hand down to our successors a regenerated public spirit concerning the most vital questions of human life, upon which alone, and not upon any expert or opportunist handling of them, the hopes of the future must rest.

GERARD MANLEY HOPKINS 2 August 1871
(1844–89)

Letter to Robert Bridges, in *Poems and Prose*, pp. 170–71

An alienated but deeply caring man, Hopkins's peculiar intensity comes from the conflict in him between the imaginative needs of the artist and the discipline imposed upon him by the demands of the priesthood – what Bridges called 'the naked encounter of sensualism and asceticism'. As a Jesuit, he felt he ought to give up writing, but didn't; and though set apart, he was deeply aware of the ruthless industrialism of his age, and clearly concerned about social conditions. His own quest for equilibrium, his sensate delight in the living beauty of the world, coupled with the anguish of vocation, took him deep, to where 'the just man justices', in respecting the self that each thing speaks, the self that 'flashes off frame and face'. And he knew, 'pitched past pitch of grief', the meaning of struggle: 'the mind, the mind has mountains; cliffs of fall /Frightful, sheer, no-man-fathomed'.

COMMUNISM

My Dear Bridges,

Our holidays have begun, so I will write again. I feel inclined to begin by asking whether you are secretary to the International as you seem to mean me to think nothing too bad for you but then I remember that you never relished 'the intelligent artisan'. I must tell you I am always thinking of the Communist future. The too intelligent artisan is master of the situation I believe. Perhaps it is what everyone believes, I do not see the papers or hear strangers often enough to know. It is what Carlyle has long threatened and foretold. But his writings are, as he might himself say, 'most inefficacious-strenuous heaven-protestations, caterwaul, and Cassandra-wailings'. He preaches obedience but I do not think he has done much except to ridicule instead of strengthening the hands of the powers that be. Some years ago when he published his *Shooting Niagara* he did make some practical suggestions but so vague that they should rather be called '*too* dubious moonstone-grindings and on the whole impracticable-practical unveracities'. However I am afraid some great

559

revolution is not far off. Horrible to say, in a manner I am a Communist. Their ideal bating some things is nobler than that professed by any secular statesman I know of (I must own I live in bat-light and shoot at a venture). Besides it is just. – I do not mean the means of getting to it are. But it is a dreadful thing for the greatest and most necessary part of a very rich nation to live a hard life without dignity, knowledge, comforts, delight, or hopes in the midst of plenty – which plenty they make. They profess that they do not care what they wreck and burn, the old civilization and order must be destroyed. This is a dreadful look out but what has the old civilization done for them? As it at present stands in England it is itself in great measure founded on wrecking. But they got none of the spoils, they came in for nothing but harm from it then and thereafter. England has grown hugely wealthy but this wealth has not reached the working classes; I expect it has made their condition worse. Besides this iniquitous order the old civilization embodies another order mostly old and what is new in direct entail from the old, the old religion, learning, law, art, etc. and all the history that is preserved in standing monuments. But as the working classes have not been educated they know next to nothing of all this and cannot be expected to care if they destroy it. The more I look the more black and deservedly black the future looks, so I will write no more . . .

RICHARD PANKHURST (1839–97)   13 May 1873

Speech at the Manchester Republican Club, in Pankhurst, *Suffragette Movement*, p. 20

In the wake of the Franco-German war and the resistance of the Paris Commune, a wave of republicanism swept the country. It was fuelled by knowledge of the Queen's declared opposition to all movements of reform and to European liberation, and her attempt to force the British government to support Austria; as also by the growing cost to the nation of the royal family, and her complaint that she could not maintain her children on the £385,000 granted to her by the nation. Dr Pankhurst presided at the inaugural meeting of the Manchester club.

REPUBLICANISM

It is not so much the direct power of the Crown which is so injurious, as its indirect influence. It is the shelter of privilege, the centre of vested and sinister influences. It is the excuse for receiving large emoluments without rendering any service . . .

It was necessary in the days of the Commonwealth to get the liberties of the people by the people armed; it is now necessary to change an aristocratic into a democratic republic only by the people enfranchised . . .

We want, first of all, the complete enfranchisement of the people; having got that the obvious and necessary consequence is the creation of a representative assembly – the organ of the national will . . . This representative assembly will nominate the great chiefs of the Executive, and being nominated by the assembly, they will be the servants of the assembly.

The Executive the lesser, the Parliament the greater; the Executive the learner, the Parliament the teacher; the Legislature supreme, the Executive subordinate . . .

The lineal descendants of the despotic sovereign and the tyrannic nobility are the Crown, as held under the Act of Settlement, and the hereditary peerage sitting in the House of Lords. The lineal descendants of the serfs are the English working men and labourers, as their status is prescribed by the class legislation of the Master and Servant Act 1867, and the Criminal Law Amendment Act 1871 . . .

SAMUEL BUTLER (1835–1902)   1876

'The Righteous Man', in *Essential Samuel Butler*, pp. 408–9

THE RIGHTEOUS MAN

The righteous man will rob none but the defenceless,
Whatsoever can reckon with him he will neither plunder nor kill;
He will steal an egg from a hen or a lamb from an ewe,
For his sheep and his hens cannot reckon with him hereafter –
They live not in any odour of defencefulness:
Therefore right is with the righteous man, and he taketh advantage
   righteously,
Praising God and plundering.

The righteous man will enslave his horse and his dog,
Making them serve him for their bare keep and for nothing further,
Shooting them, selling them for vivisection when they can no longer
   profit him,

Backbiting them and beating them if they fail to please him;
For his horse and his dog can bring no action for damages,
Wherefore, then, should he not enslave them, shoot them, sell them
   for vivisection?

But the righteous man will not plunder the defenceful –
Not if he be alone and unarmed – for his conscience will smite him;
He will not rob a she-bear of her cubs, nor an eagle of her eaglets –
Unless he have a rifle to purge him from the fear of sin:
Then may he shoot rejoicing in innocency – from ambush or a safe
   distance;
Or he will beguile them, lay poison for them, keep no faith with
   them;
For what faith is there with that which cannot reckon hereafter,
Neither by itself, nor by another, nor by any residuum of ill
   consequences?
Surely, where weakness is utter, honour ceaseth.

Nay, I will do what is right in the eyes of him who can harm me,
And not in those of him who cannot call me to account.
Therefore yield me up thy pretty wings, O humming-bird!
Sing for me in a prison, O lark!
Pay me thy rent, O widow! for it is mine.
Where there is reckoning there is sin,
And where there is no reckoning sin is not.

ANONYMOUS MANIFESTO   No date

In Rickword and Lindsay, eds., *Handbook of Freedom*, pp. 349–50

THE CROFTERS' WAR

The enemy is the landlord, the agent, the capitalist, and the Parliament
which makes and maintains inhuman and iniquitous laws.

   Cut down the telegraph-wires and posts, carry away the wires and
instruments! Stop the mail-carts, destroy the letters.

   Burn the property of all obnoxious landlords, agents, etc. Set fire to
the heather to destroy the game; disturb the deer; poison game-dogs!

   The oppressed toilers of England and the millions of disinherited people are watching your actions. Their hearts are with you in your battle
for right and liberty.

   God save the People!

ANDREW MEARNS 1883

From *The Bitter Cry of Outcast London, An Enquiry into the Condition of the Abject Poor*, in Keating, ed., *Into Unknown England*, pp. 99–102

This inquiry was published anonymously as a penny pamphlet, and widely distributed, no doubt among the virtuous middle classes. It encouraged the writing of similar pamphlets on cities throughout Britain, and influenced the setting up of a Royal Commission on the Housing of the Working Classes (1884–5), a typically condescending organ of the social system whose ruthless pursuit of wealth and profit had brought about these very conditions. Mearns was Secretary of the London Congregational Union, and was helped in his study by James Munro and W. C. Preston.

POVERTY: THE OTHER SIDE OF THE COIN

. . . The cause of what we have described is the POVERTY of these miserable outcasts. The poverty, we mean, of those who try to live honestly; for notwithstanding the sickening revelations of immorality which have been disclosed to us, those who endeavour to earn their bread by honest work far outnumber the dishonest. And it is to their infinite credit that it should be so, considering that they are daily face to face with the contrast between their wretched earnings and those which are the produce of sin. A child seven years old is known easily to make 10s. 6d. a week by thieving, but what can he earn by such work as match-box making, for which 2¼d. a gross is paid, the maker having to find his own fire for drying the boxes, and his own paste and string? Before he can gain as much as the young thief he must make 56 gross of match-boxes a week, or 1296 a day. It is needless to say that this is impossible, for even adults can rarely make more than an average of half that number. How long then must the little hands toil before they can earn the price of the scantiest meal! Women, for the work of trousers finishing (i.e. sewing in linings, making button-holes, and stitching on the buttons) receive 2½d. a pair, and have to find their own thread. We ask a woman who is making tweed trousers how much she can earn in a day, and are told one shilling. But what does a day mean to this poor soul? *Seventeen hours*! From five in the morning to ten at night – no pause for meals. She eats her crust and drinks a little tea as she works, making in very truth, with her needle and thread, not her living only, but her shroud. For making men's shirts these women are paid 10d. a dozen; lawn tennis aprons, 3d. a dozen; and babies' hoods from 1s. 6d. to 2s. 6d. a dozen. In St George's-in-the-East large numbers of women and children, some of the latter only seven years

563

old, are employed in sack-making, for which they get a farthing each . . . With men it is comparatively speaking no better. 'My master,' says one man visited by a recent writer in the *Fortnightly Review*, 'gets a pound for what he gives me 3*s*. for making.' And this it is easy to believe, when we know that for a pair of fishing boots which will be sold at three guineas, the poor workman receives 5*s*. 3*d*. if they are made to order, or 4*s*. 6*d*. if made for stock. An old tailor and his wife are employed in making policemen's overcoats. They have to make, finish, hot-press, put on the buttons, and find their own thread, and for all this they receive 2*s*. 10*d*. for each coat. This old couple work from half-past six in the morning till ten at night, and between them can just manage to make a coat in two days. Here is a mother who has taken away whatever articles of clothing she can strip from her four little children without leaving them absolutely naked. She has pawned them, not for drink, but for coals and food. A shilling is all she can procure, and with this she has bought seven pounds of coals and a loaf of bread. We might fill page after page with these dreary details, but they would become sadly monotonous, for it is the same everywhere. And then it should not be forgotten how hardly upon poverty like this must press the exorbitant demand for rent. Even the rack-renting of Ireland, which so stirred our indignation a little while ago, was merciful by comparison. If by any chance a reluctant landlord can be induced to execute or pay for some long-needed repairs, they become the occasion for new exactions. Going through these rooms we come to one in which a hole, as big as a man's head, has been roughly covered, and how? A piece of board, from an old soap-box, has been fixed over the opening by one nail, and to the tenant has been given a yard and a half of paper with which to cover it; and for this expenditure – perhaps 4*d*. at the outside – *threepence a week has been put upon the rent*. If this is enough to arouse our indignation, what must be thought of the following? The two old people just mentioned have lived in one room for fourteen years, during which time it has only once been partially cleansed. The landlord has undertaken that it shall be done shortly, and for the past three months has been taking 6*d*. a week extra for rent for what he is thus *going to do*. This is what the helpless have to submit to; they are charged for these pestilential dens a rent which consumes half the earnings of a family, and leaves them no more than 4*d*. to 6*d*. a day for food, clothing and fire; a grinding of the faces of the poor which could scarcely be paralleled in lands of slavery and of notorious oppression. This, however, is not all; for even these depths of poverty and degradation are reached by the Education Act, and however beneficent its purpose, it bears with cruel weight upon the class we have described, to whom twopence or a penny a week for the school fees of each of three or four children, means so much lack of bread.

WILLIAM MORRIS (1834–96)   23 January 1884

From *Art and Socialism* (published as a pamphlet, 1884), in *Political Writings*, pp. 123–4, 126–7

A SYSTEM OF WAR

Nothing should be made by man's labour which is not worth making; or which must be made by labour degrading to the makers

Simple as that proposition is, and obviously right as I am sure it must seem to you, you will find, when you come to consider the matter, that it is a direct challenge to the death to the present system of labour in civilized countries. That system, which I have called competitive Commerce, is distinctly a system of war; that is of waste and destruction: or you may call it gambling if you will, the point of it being that under it whatever a man gains he gains at the expense of some other man's loss. Such a system does not and cannot heed whether the matters it makes are worth making; it does not and cannot heed whether those who make them are degraded by their work: it heeds one thing and only one, namely, what it calls making a profit; which word has got to be used so conventionally that I must explain to you what it really means, to wit the plunder of the weak by the strong! Now I say of this system, that it is of its very nature destructive of Art, that is to say of the happiness of life. Whatever consideration is shown for the life of the people in these days, whatever is done which is worth doing, is done in spite of the system and in the teeth of its maxims; and most true it is that we do, all of us, tacitly at least, admit that it is opposed to all the highest aspirations of mankind.

Do we not know, for instance, how those men of genius work who are the salt of the earth, without whom the corruption of society would long ago have become unendurable? The poet, the artist, the man of science, is it not true that in their fresh and glorious days, when they are in the heyday of their faith and enthusiasm, they are thwarted at every turn by Commercial war, with its sneering question 'Will it pay?' Is it not true that when they begin to win worldly success, when they become comparatively rich, in spite of ourselves they seem to us tainted by the contact with the commercial world?

Need I speak of great schemes that hang about neglected; of things most necessary to be done, and so confessed by all men, that no one can seriously set a hand to because of the lack of money; while if it be a question of creating or stimulating some foolish whim in the public mind, the satisfaction of which will breed a profit, the money will come in by the ton? Nay, you know what an old story it is of the wars bred by Commerce in search of new markets, which not even the most peaceable of statesmen can resist; an old story and still it seems for ever new, and now become a kind of grim joke, at which I would rather not laugh if I could help it, but am even forced to laugh from a soul laden with anger . . .

THE DAY-SPRING OF A NEW HOPE

That is what three centuries of Commerce have brought that hope to which sprang up when feudalism began to fall to pieces. What can give us the day-spring of a new hope? What, save general revolt against the tyranny of Commercial war? The palliatives over which many worthy people are busying themselves now are useless: because they are but unorganized partial revolts against a vast widespreading grasping organization which will, with the unconscious instinct of a plant, meet every attempt at bettering the condition of the people with an attack on a fresh side; new machines, new markets, wholesale emigration, the revival of grovelling superstitions, preachments of thrift to lack-alls, of temperance to the wretched; such things as these will baffle at every turn all partial revolts against the monster we of the middle classes have created for our own undoing.

WILLIAM MORRIS (1834–96)   30 November 1884

From *How We Live and How We Might Live* (printed in *commonweal*, 1887), in *Political Writings*, pp. 157–8

EQUALITY OF CONDITION

. . . Rather . . . take courage, and believe that we of this age, in spite of all its torment and disorder, have been born to a wonderful heritage fashioned of the work of those that have gone before us; and that the day of the organization of man is dawning. It is not we who can build up the new social order; the past ages have done the most of that work for us; but we can clear our eyes to the signs of the times, and we shall then see that the attainment of a good condition of life is being made possible for us, and that it is now our business to stretch out our hands and take it.

And how? Chiefly, I think, by educating people to a sense of their real capacities as men, so that they may be able to use to their own good the political power which is rapidly being thrust upon them; to get them to see that the old system of organizing labour for *individual profit* is becoming unmanageable, and that the whole people have now got to choose between the confusion resulting from the break-up of that system and the determination to take in hand the labour now organized for profit, and use its organization for the livelihood of the community: to get people to see that individual profit-makers are not a necessity for labour but an obstruction to it, and that not only or chiefly because they are the perpetual pensioners of labour, as they are, but rather because of the waste which their existence as a class necessitates. All this we have to teach people, when we have taught ourselves; and I admit that the work is long and burdensome; as I began by saying, people have been made so timorous of change by the terror of starvation that even the unluckiest of them are stolid and hard to move. Hard as the work is, however, its reward is not doubtful. The mere fact that a body of men, however small, are banded together as Socialist missionaries shows that the change is going on. As the working classes, the real organic part of society, take in these ideas, hope will arise in them, and they will claim changes in society, many of which doubtless will not tend directly towards their emancipation, because they will be claimed without due knowledge of the one thing necessary to claim, *equality of condition*; but which indirectly will help to break up our rotten sham society, while that claim for equality of condition will be made constantly and with growing loudness till it *must* be listened to, and then at last it will only be a step over the border, and the civilized world will be socialized; and, looking back on what has been, we shall be astonished to think of how long we submitted to live as we live now.

BLOODY SUNDAY, TRAFALGAR SQUARE

13 November 1887

Throughout October 1887 repeated assaults and arrests were made against the unemployed demonstrating in Trafalgar Square, and on 8 November Sir Charles Warren, Commissioner of Police, banned all meetings. Nevertheless, a demonstration was arranged for the 13th to protest against coercion in Ireland and to assert the right to freedom of speech at home, and thousands (Irish and English) turned out.

LONDON IN A STATE OF SIEGE

R. B. Cunninghame Graham, Radical-Socialist MP for North-West Lanark, in *The Commonweal* (19 November), quoted in Rickword and Lindsay, eds., *Handbook of Freedom*, p. 361

What happened is known to all: how no procession reached the Square; how they were all illegally attacked and broken up, some of them several miles from the Square . . . It is still, I think, fresh in the memory of all, how, with the help of all the professional perjurers in London, all the arms collected from that vast crowd amounted to three pokers, one piece of wood, and an oyster knife. How I failed to join the procession, and having met Messrs Burns and Hyndman by accident, proceeded to the Square; how we were assaulted and knocked about and sent to prison, is matter of notoriety in London . . .

I saw that the police were afraid; I saw on more than one occasion that the officials had to strike their free British men to make them obey orders; I saw that the horses were clumsy and badly bitted, and of no use whatever in a stone street . . . I saw much, too, to moralize on. The tops of the houses and hotels were crowded with well-dressed women, who clapped their hands and cheered with delight when some miserable and half-starved working-man was knocked down and trodden under foot.

This, then, is all I can tell you of the great riots [sic] in Trafalgar Square, where three men were killed, three hundred kicked, wounded and arrested . . . All honour to the Socialists for being the first body of Englishmen in the metropolis to have determined that the death of three Englishmen, killed by the folly of Sir Charles Dogberry and worthy Mr Verges, the Home Secretary, shall not go unregarded, nor I hope unpunished.

A PAINFUL LESSON

William Morris, *The Commonweal* (19 November), from Morris, *Political Writings*, pp. 208–9

We Socialists should thank our master for his lesson . . . Warren has won a victory, but on what terms! It is clear . . . that he would not have been thoroughly successful if he had not had a free hand given him: if he had not attacked citizens marching peaceably through the streets in just such a way as Banditti might do, destroying and stealing their property, they would have been able to claim their right of meeting in Trafalgar Square in such a way that nothing but sharp shot and cold steel could have dealt with them. London has been put under martial law, nominally for behoof of a party, but really on behoof of a class, and *war* (for it is no less, whatever the consequences may be) has been forced upon us. The mask is off now, and the real meaning of all the petty persecution of our open-air meetings is as clear as may be. No more humbug need be talked about obstruction and the convenience of the public: it is obvious that those meetings were attacked because we displeased the dominant class and were weak. Last Sunday explains all, and the bourgeois now goes about boasting that he is the master and will do what he likes with his slaves. Again, the humbug is exposed of the political condemnation of coercion by Act of Parliament in Ireland when here in London we have coercion without Act of Parliament; and the feeble twitterings of the *Daily News* will be received with jeers by the triumphant Tories.

And the greatest humbug which Sunday's events have laid bare is 'the protection afforded by law to the humblest citizen'. Some simple people will be thinking that Warren can be attacked legally for his murderous and cowardly assaults of Sunday.

I say Warren, because it is no use beating the *stick* that beats you. Some perhaps will think that there may be a chance of his getting a few years' penal servitude for inciting to riot and murder. But these persons forget that he has been *ordered* to act as he did just as he *ordered* his brigands, and that Salisbury & Co. who *ordered* him have done so at the *orders* of the class which they represent. They have made the laws, but have never intended to keep them when inconvenient. It has now become inconvenient to keep them – and in consequence we must think ourselves lucky to be *only* beaten by the policemen's baton if the bourgeois don't like us – lucky to get off the six months' or twelve months' imprisonment which is likely to accompany such an *accident*. In short, the very Radicals

569

have been taught that slaves have no rights. The lesson is a painful one, but surely useful to us boastful Englishmen: nay, in the long run it is necessary.

A DEATH SONG

Written by Morris for the funeral of one of the demonstrators, Alfred Linnel, killed by the police, at which tens of thousands were present, including Morris, Annie Besant, W. T. Stead, and other Radical-Socialist leaders.

What cometh here from west to east awending?
   And who are these, the marchers stern and slow?
We bear the message that the rich are sending
   Aback to those who bade them wake and know.
Not one, not one, nor thousands must they slay,
But one and all if they would dusk the day.

We asked them for a life of toilsome earning,
   They bade us bide their leisure for our bread;
We craved to speak to tell our woeful learning:
   We come back speechless, bearing back our dead.
Not one, not one, nor thousands must they slay,
But one and all if they would dusk the day.

They will not learn; they have no ears to hearken.
   They turn their faces from the eyes of fate;
Their gay-lit halls shut out the skies that darken.
   But, lo! this dead man knocking at the gate.
Not one, not one, nor thousands must they slay,
But one and all if they would dusk the day.

Here lies the sign that we shall break our prison;
   Amidst the storm he won a prisoner's rest;
But in the cloudy dawn the sun arisen
   Brings us our day of work to win the best.
Not one, not one, nor thousands must they slay,
But one and all if they would dusk the day.

FREDERICK HARRISON (1831–1923)   1888

Declaration, in Rickword and Lindsay, eds., *Handbook of Freedom*, pp. 362–3

CAPITALISM CONDEMNED

To me, at least, it would be enough to condemn modern society as hardly an advance on slavery or serfdom, if the permanent condition of industry were to be that which we behold, that ninety per cent of the actual producers of wealth have no home that they can call their own beyond the end of the week; have no bit of soil, or so much as a room that belongs to them; have nothing of value of any kind, except as much old furniture as will go into a cart; have the precarious chance of weekly wages, which barely suffice to keep them in health; are housed, for the most part, in places that no man thinks fit for his horse; are separated by so narrow a margin from destitution that a month of bad trade, sickness, or unexpected loss brings them face to face with hunger and pauperism.

But below this normal state of the average workman in town and country, there is found the great band of destitute outcasts – the camp-followers of the army of industry – at least one-tenth of the whole proletarian population, whose normal condition is one of sickening wretchedness. If this is to be the permanent arrangement of modern society, civilization must be held to bring a curse on the great majority of mankind.

BEATRICE WEBB (1858–1943)   8 March 1889

From her diary, quoted in Hollis, ed., *Women in Public*, pp. 21–2

MEN AND WOMEN

Interesting talk with Professor Marshall, first at dinner at the Creightons, and afterwards at lunch at his own house. It opened with chaff about men and women: he holding that woman was a subordinate being, and that, if she ceased to be subordinate, there would be no object for a man to marry. That marriage was a sacrifice of masculine freedom, and would only be tolerated by male creatures so long as it meant the devotion, body and soul, of the female to the male. Hence the woman must not develop her faculties in a way unpleasant to the man: that strength, courage, independence were not attractive in women; that rivalry in men's

571

pursuits was positively unpleasant. Hence masculine strength and masculine ability in women must be firmly trampled on and boycotted by men. *Contrast* was the essence of the matrimonial relation: feminine weakness contrasted with masculine strength: masculine egotism with feminine self-devotion.

'If you compete with us we shan't marry you', he summed up with a laugh.

I maintained the opposite argument: that there was an ideal of character in which strength, courage, sympathy, self-devotion, persistent purpose were united to a clear and far-seeing intellect; that the ideal was common to the man and to the woman; that these qualities might manifest themselves in different ways in the man's and the woman's life; that what you needed was not different qualities and different defects, but the same virtues working in different directions, and dedicated to the service of the community in different ways.

THE DOCKERS' STRIKE   August 1889

'The Red Flag', a song written by Jim Connell, a docker, in Rickword and Lindsay, eds., *Handbook of Freedom*, p. 363

The great Dock Strike of 1889 came as a climax to a sudden quickening determination among the exploited workers of the East End of London. The upsurge of resistance began when seven hundred match-girls went on strike after reading Mrs Besant's denunciation of their conditions at work. This courageous act was followed by the organization of a Gas-workers Union, which (spurred on by Tom Mann, John Burns and Will Thorne) succeeded a few months later in getting concessions from the companies. Then suddenly a small dispute in the docks exploded into a massive total strike, coordinated by Mann, Burns and Ben Tillett, and for three weeks or more they held out, marching in procession day after day with their banners through the City, helped in the end by large donations for their dwindling strike-fund from Australian workers, so that they were able to achieve almost all their demands. This strike was to be the basis for the victories of other workers, and to encourage the growth of unions all over the country.

THE RED FLAG

The people's flag is deepest red;
It shrouded oft our martyred dead;

And ere their limbs grew stiff or cold
Their heart's blood dyed its every fold.

Then raise the scarlet banner high
Within its shade we'll live and die.
Though cowards flinch and traitors sneer,
We'll keep the Red Flag flying here.

It waved above our infant might
When all ahead seemed dark as night;
It witnessed many a deed and vow –
We must not change its colour now.

It well recalls the triumphs past;
It gives the hope of peace at last.
The banner bright, the symbol plain
Of human right and human gain.

With heads uncovered swear we all
To bear it onward till we fall.
Come dungeon dark or gallows grim,
This song shall be our parting hymn.

WILLIAM BOOTH (1829–1919)   1890

From *In Darkest England and the Way Out* in Keating, ed., *Into Unknown England*, pp. 146–8

THE FRUITS OF CAPITALISM: AFRICA IN ENGLAND

The Equatorial Forest traversed by Stanley resembles that Darkest England of which I have to speak, alike in its vast extent – both stretch, in Stanley's phrases, 'as far as from Plymouth to Peterhead'; its monotonous darkness, its malaria and its gloom, its dwarfish, de-humanized inhabitants, the slavery to which they are subjected, their privations and their misery . . . Hard it is, no doubt, to read in Stanley's pages of the slave-traders coldly arranging for the surprise of a village, the capture of the inhabitants, the massacre of those who resist, and the violation of all the women; but the stony streets of London, if they could but speak, would tell of tragedies as awful, of ruin as complete, of ravishments as horrible, as if it were in Central Africa; only the ghastly devastation is covered, corpse-like, with the artificialities and hypocrisies of modern civilization.

The lot of a Negress in the Equatorial Forest is not, perhaps, a very happy one, but is it so very much worse than that of many a pretty orphan girl in our Christian capital? We talk about the brutalities of the Dark Age, and we profess to shudder as we read in books of the shameful exaction of the right of feudal superior. And yet here, beneath our very eyes, in our theatres, in our restaurants, and in many other places, unspeakable though it is but to name it, the same hideous abuse flourishes unchecked. A young penniless girl, if she be pretty, is often hunted from pillar to post by her employers, confronted always by the alternative – Starve or Sin. And when once the poor girl has consented to buy the right to earn her living by the sacrifice of her virtue, then she is treated as a slave and an outcast by the very men who have ruined her. Her word becomes unbelievable, her life an ignominy, and she is swept downward, ever downward, into the bottomless perdition of prostitution. But there, even in the lowest depths, excommunicated by Humanity and outcast from God, she is far nearer the pitying heart of the One true Saviour than all the men who forced her down, aye, and than all the Pharisees and Scribes who stand silently by while these fiendish wrongs are perpetrated before their very eyes.

The blood boils with impotent rage at the sight of these enormities, callously inflicted, and silently borne by these miserable victims. Nor is it only women who are the victims, although their fate is the most tragic. Those firms which reduce sweating to a fine art, who systematically and deliberately defraud the workman of his pay, who grind the faces of the poor, and who rob the widow and the orphan, and who for a pretence make great professions of public-spirit and philanthropy, these men nowadays are sent to Parliament to make laws for the people. The old prophets sent them to Hell – but we have changed all that. They send their victims to Hell, and are rewarded by all that wealth can do to make their lives comfortable. Read the House of Lords Report on the Sweating System, and ask if any African slave system, making due allowance for the superior civilization, and therefore sensitiveness, of the victims, reveals more misery.

WILLIAM MORRIS (1834–96) January–October 1890

From *News from Nowhere*, in *Three Works*, pp. 288, 316–17

After *A Dream of John Ball* (1886–7), in which he projects his socialist vision back into the past, Morris now reaches forward into the as yet unrealized future. He envisages 'the change beyond the change', dreaming ahead to a world in which the new society of 'pure Communism' has already become a reality beyond the revolutionary struggle without which it could not have been achieved. Morris defines the stages of this struggle with precise concern for detail in 'How the Change Came' (Chapter 17), and it is this attention to the logic of a developing revolutionary situation that gives the book its anchored perspective.

BITTER WAR

[Hammond speaks:] 'Does anything especially puzzle you about our way of living, now you have heard a good deal and seen a little of it?'

Said I: 'I think what puzzles me most is how it all came about.'

'It well may,' said he, 'so great as the change is. It would be difficult indeed to tell you the whole story, perhaps impossible: knowledge, discontent, treachery, disappointment, ruin, misery, despair – those who worked for the change because they could see no further than other people went through all these phases of suffering; and doubtless all the time the most of men looked on, not knowing what was doing, thinking it all a matter of course, like the rising and setting of the sun – and indeed it was so.'

'Tell me one thing, if you can,' said I. 'Did the change, the "revolution" it used to be called, come peacefully?'

'Peacefully?' said he; 'what peace was there amongst those poor confused wretches of the nineteenth century? It was war from beginning to end: bitter war, till hope and pleasure put an end to it.'

'Do you mean actual fighting with weapons?' said I, 'or the strikes and lock-outs and starvation of which we have heard?'

'Both, both,' he said. 'As a matter of fact, the history of the terrible period of transition from commercial slavery to freedom may thus be summarized. When the hope of realizing a communal condition of life for all men arose, quite late in the nineteenth century, the power of the middle classes, the then tyrants of society, was so enormous and crushing, that to almost all men, even those who had, you may say despite themselves, their reason and judgement, conceived such hopes, it seemed a dream. So much was this the case that some of those more enlightened

575

men who were then called Socialists, although they well knew, and even stated in public, that the only reasonable condition of Society was that of pure Communism (such as you now see around you), yet shrunk from what seemed to them the barren task of preaching the realization of a happy dream. Looking back now, we can see that the great motive-power of the change was a longing for freedom and equality, akin if you like to the unreasonable passion of the lover; a sickness of heart that rejected with loathing the aimless solitary life of the well-to-do educated men of that time: phrases, my dear friend, which have lost their meaning to us of the present day; so far removed we are from the dreadful facts which they represent . . .'

HOW THE CONFLICT CAME TO AN END

Hammond goes on to recount, stage by stage, the drift towards open civil war.

'When the conflict was once really begun, it was seen how little of any value there was in the old world of slavery and inequality. Don't you see what it means? In the times which you are thinking of, and of which you seem to know so much, there was no hope; nothing but the dull jog of the mill-horse under compulsion of collar and whip; but in that fighting-time that followed, all was hope: 'the rebels' at least felt themselves strong enough to build up the world again from its dry bones – and they did it, too!' said the old man, his eyes glittering under his beetling brows. He went on: 'And their opponents at least and at last learned something about the reality of life, and its sorrows, which they – their class, I mean – had known nothing of. In short, the two combatants, the work-man and the gentleman, between them –'

'Between them,' said I, quickly, 'they destroyed commercialism!'

'Yes, yes, *yes*,' said he; 'that is it. Nor could it have been destroyed otherwise; except, perhaps, by the whole of society gradually falling into lower depths, till it should at last reach a condition as rude as barbarism, but lacking both the hope and the pleasures of barbarism. Surely the sharper, shorter remedy was the happiest?'

'Most surely,' said I.

'Yes,' said the old man, 'the world was being brought to its second birth; how could that take place without a tragedy? Moreover, think of it. The spirit of the new days, of our days, was to be delight in the life of the world; intense and overweening love of the very skin and surface of the earth on which man dwells, such as a lover has in the fair flesh of the woman he loves; this, I say, was to be the new spirit of the time.

576

All other moods save this had been exhausted: the unceasing criticism, the boundless curiosity in the ways and thoughts of man, which was the mood of the ancient Greek, to whom these things were not so much a means, as an end, was gone past recovery; nor had there been really any shadow of it in the so-called science of the nineteenth century, which, as you must know, was in the main an appendage to the commercial system. In spite of appearances, it was limited and cowardly, because it did not really believe in itself. It was the outcome, as it was the sole relief, of the unhappiness of the period which made life so bitter even to the rich, and which, as you may see with your bodily eyes, the great change has swept away – '

GEORGE BERNARD SHAW (1856–1950)   1891

From 'The Quintessence of Ibsenism', in *Major Critical Essays*, p. 40

FREEDOM FOR WOMEN: SWEEPING THE WORLD CLEAR OF LIES

The sum of the matter is that unless Woman repudiates her womanliness, her duty to her husband, to her children, to society, to the law, and to everyone but herself, she cannot emancipate herself. But her duty to herself is no duty at all, since a debt is cancelled when the debtor and creditor are the same person. Its payment is simply a fulfilment of the individual will, upon which all duty is a restriction, founded on the conception of the will as naturally malign and devilish. Therefore Woman has to repudiate duty altogether. In that repudiation lies her freedom; for it is false to say that Woman is now directly the slave of Man: she is the immediate slave of duty; and as man's path to freedom is strewn with the wreckage of the duties and ideals he has trampled on, so must hers be. She may indeed mask her iconoclasm by proving in rationalist fashion, as Man has often done for the sake of a quiet life, that all these discarded idealist conceptions will be fortified instead of shattered by her emancipation. To a person with a turn for logic, such proofs are as easy as playing the piano is to Paderewski. But it will not be true. A whole basketful of ideals of the most sacred quality will be smashed by the achievement of equality for women and men. Those who shrink from such a clatter and breakage may comfort themselves with the reflection that the replacement of the broken goods will be prompt and certain. It is always a case of 'The ideal is dead: long live the ideal!' And the advantage of the work of destruction is that every new ideal is less of an illusion than the one it has supplanted; so that the destroyer of ideals, though denounced as an enemy of society, is in fact sweeping the world clear of lies.

FRIEDRICH ENGELS (1820–95) April 1892

From the Introduction to *Socialism: Utopian and Scientific*, in Marx and Engels, *Selected Works*, pp. 391–3

THE ENGLISH WORKING CLASS IS MOVING

. . . The English bourgeoisie are, up to the present day, so deeply penetrated by a sense of their social inferiority that they keep up, at their own expense and that of the nation, an ornamental caste of drones to represent the nation worthily at all state functions; and they consider themselves highly honoured whenever one of themselves is found worthy of admission into this select and privileged body, manufactured, after all, by themselves.

The industrial and commercial middle class had, therefore, not yet succeeded in driving the landed aristocracy completely from political power when another competitor, the working class, appeared on the stage. The reaction after the Chartist movement and the Continental revolutions, as well as the unparalleled extension of English trade from 1848 to 1866 (ascribed vulgarly to Free Trade alone, but due far more to the colossal development of railways, ocean steamers and means of intercourse generally), had again driven the working class into the dependency of the Liberal Party, of which they formed, as in pre-Chartist times, the Radical wing. Their claims to the franchise, however, gradually became irresistible; while the 'Whig' leaders of the Liberals 'funked', Disraeli showed his superiority by making the Tories seize the favourable moment and introduce household suffrage in the boroughs, along with a redistribution of seats. Then followed the ballot; then in 1884 the extension of household suffrage to the counties and a fresh redistribution of seats, by which electoral districts were to some extent equalized. All these measures considerably increased the electoral power of the working class, so much so that in 150 to 200 constituencies that class now furnishes the majority of voters. But parliamentary government is a capital school for teaching respect for tradition; if the middle class look with awe and veneration upon what Lord John Manners playfully called 'our old nobility', the mass of the working people then looked up with respect and deference to what used to be designated as 'their betters', the middle class. Indeed, the British workman, some fifteen years ago, was the model workman . . .

. . . But for all that the English working class is moving . . . It moves, like all things in England, with a slow and measured step, with hesitation here, with more or less unfruitful, tentative attempts there; it moves now and then with an over-cautious mistrust of the name of socialism, while it gradually absorbs the substance; and the movement spreads and seizes one layer of the workers after another. It has now shaken out of their torpor the unskilled labourers of the East End of London, and we all know what a splendid impulse these fresh forces have given it in return. And if the patience of the movement is not up to the impatience of some people, let them not forget that it is the working class which keeps alive the finest qualities of the English character, and that, if a step in advance is once gained in England, it is, as a rule, never lost afterwards. If the sons of the old Chartists . . . were not quite up to the mark, the grand-sons bid fair to be worthy of their forefathers . . .

CHARLES CHAPLIN (1889–1977)   1894–5

From *My Autobiography* (1966), quoted in Barker, ed., *Long March of Everyman*, p. 157

Charlie Chaplin was born at Walworth and grew up in various districts of south London.

WOMAN AND CHILDREN IN THE WORKHOUSE

Mother had now sold most of her belongings. The last thing to go was her trunk of theatrical costumes . . . Like sand in an hour-glass our finances ran out, and hard times again pursued us. Mother sought other employment, but there was little to be found. Problems began mounting. Instalment payments were behind; consequently Mother's sewing machine was taken away. And Father's payments of ten shillings a week had completely stopped . . . There was no alternative: she was burdened with two children, and in poor health; and so she decided that the three of us should enter the Lambeth workhouse, [and] there we were made to separate, Mother going in one direction to the women's ward and we in another to the children's. How well I remember the poignant sadness of that first visiting day: the shock of seeing Mother enter the visiting-room garbed in workhouse clothes. How forlorn and embarrassed she looked! In one week she had aged and grown thin, but her face lit up when she saw us . . . She smiled at our cropped heads and stroked them consolingly, telling us that we would soon all be together again. From her apron she produced a bag of coconut candy which she had bought at the workhouse store with her earnings from crocheting lace cuffs for one of the nurses . . .

OSCAR WILDE (1854–1900)   1896

The Ballad of Reading Gaol (1898), V, stanzas 1–7

PRISON LAW

I know not whether Laws be right,
  Or whether Laws be wrong;
All that we know who lie in gaol
  Is that the wall is strong;
And that each day is like a year,
  A year whose days are long.

But this I know, that every Law
  That men have made for Man,
Since first Man took his brother's life,
  And the sad world began,
But straws the wheat and saves the chaff
  With a most evil fan.

This too I know – and wise it were
  If each could know the same –
That every prison that men build
  Is built with bricks of shame,
And bound with bars lest Christ should see
  How men their brothers maim.

With bars they blur the gracious moon,
  And blind the goodly sun:
And they do well to hide their Hell,
  For in it things are done

580

That Son of God nor son of Man
  Ever should look upon!

The vilest deeds, like poison weeds,
  Bloom well in prison air;
It is only what is good in Man
  That wastes and withers there:
Pale Anguish keeps the heavy gate,
  And the Warder is Despair.

For they starve the little frightened child
  Till it weeps both night and day:
And they scourge the weak, and flog the fool,
  And gibe the old and grey,
And some grow mad, and all grow bad,
  And none a word may say.

Each narrow cell in which we dwell
  Is a foul and dark latrine,
And the fetid breath of living Death
  Chokes up each grated screen,
And all, but Lust, is turned to dust
  In Humanity's machine.

WILLIAM MORRIS (1834–96)   May Day, 1896

From *Justice* (a pamphlet)

The imperialist powers had been slowly expanding their territories abroad for decades. But in the eighties the process began to quicken; and after the Berlin Conference of 1884, which met to 'legitimize' the carving up of Africa into 'spheres of influence', there was an explosion of activity, with new markets opened up to the predatory enterprise of European capitalism, in contemptuous indifference to its subject peoples. The imperialists had now engaged in a relentless game of power which, played for the highest stakes, could only end in confrontation. This Morris had long warned against, and in his last public statement he returns to the subject, offering at the same time a confirmation of the movement he had done so much to promote. He was already ill, and died on 3 October 1896.

THE HUNGER FOR FREEDOM

The capitalist classes are doubtless alarmed at the spread of Socialism all over the civilized world. They have at least an instinct of danger; but with that instinct comes the other one of self-defence. Look how the whole capitalist world is stretching out long arms towards the barbarous world and grabbing and clutching in eager competition at countries whose inhabitants don't want them; nay, in many cases, would rather die in battle, like the valiant men they are, than have them. So perverse are these wild men before the blessings of civilization which would do nothing worse for them (and also nothing better) than reduce them to a propertyless proletariat.

And what is all this for? For the spread of abstract ideas of civilization, for pure benevolence, for the honour and glory of conquest? Not at all. It is for the opening of fresh markets to take in all the fresh profit-producing wealth which is growing greater and greater every day; in other words, to make fresh opportunities for *waste*; the waste of our labour and our lives.

And I say this is an irresistible instinct on the part of the capitalists, an impulse like hunger, and I believe that it can only be met by another hunger, the hunger for freedom and fair play for all, both people and peoples. Anything less than that the capitalist powers will brush aside. But that they cannot; for what will it mean? The most important part of their machinery, the 'hands' becoming MEN, and saying, 'Now at last we will it; we will produce no more for profit but for *use*, for *happiness*, for LIFE.'

HILAIRE BELLOC (1870–1953)   1896

'The Justice of the Peace', From *Verses and Sonnets*, in *Verse*, p. 147

THE JUSTICE OF THE PEACE

Distinguish carefully between these two,
  This thing is yours, that other thing is mine.
You have a shirt, a brimless hat, a shoe
  And half a coat. I am the Lord benign
Of fifty hundred acres of fat land
To which I have a right. You understand?

I have a right because I have, because,
    Because I have – because I have a right.
Now be quite calm and good, obey the laws,
    Remember your low station, do not fight
Against the goad, you know, it pricks
Whenever the uncleanly demos kicks.

I do not envy you your hat, your shoe.
    Why should you envy me my small estate?
It's fearfully illogical in you
    To fight with economic force and fate.
Moreover, I have got the upper hand,
And mean to keep it. Do you understand?

JACK LONDON (1876–1916)   1903

From *The People of the Abyss*, in Keating, ed., *Into Unknown England*,
p. 266

London spent seven weeks living in the East End of London as one of the poor,
with the intention of writing a 'study of the economic degradation of the poor'
that would speak directly of their plight.

THE LONDON SLUMS

Nowhere in the streets of London may one escape the sight of abject
poverty, while five minutes walk from almost any point will bring one
to a slum: but the region my hansom was now penetrating was one
unending slum. The streets were filled with a new and different race of
people, short of stature, and of wretched or beer-sodden appearance. We
rolled along through miles of bricks and squalor, and from each cross
street and alley flashed long vistas of bricks and misery. Here and there
lurched a drunken man or woman, and the air was obscene with sounds
of jangling and squabbling. At a market, tottery old men and women
were searching in the garbage thrown in the mud for rotten potatoes,
beans, and vegetables, while little children clustered like flies around a
festering mass of fruit, thrusting their arms to the shoulders into the
squalid corruption, and drawing forth morsels but partially decayed,
which they devoured on the spot.

Not a hansom did I meet with in all my drive, while mine was like an apparition from another and better world, the way the children ran after it and alongside. And as far as I could see were the solid walls of brick, the slimy pavements, and the screaming streets; and for the first time in my life the fear of the crowd smote me. It was like the fear of the sea; and the miserable multitudes, street upon street, seemed so many waves of a vast and malodorous sea, lapping about me and threatening to well up and over me.

'Stepney, sir; Stepney Station,' the cabby called down.

ROBERT TRESSELL (?–1911)

From *The Ragged Trousered Philanthropists*, pp. 163–4

Frank Owen, the central character in the book, a worker in the building trade and a committed socialist, is involved in many discussions with his comrades, 'political' talks at meal-times, attempting to convince them of the need for socialism. He is here talking about poverty and how to do away with it.

POVERTY

Poverty is not caused by men and women getting married; it's not caused by machinery; it's not caused by 'over-production'; it's not caused by drink or laziness; and it's not caused by 'over-population'. It's caused by Private Monopoly. That is the present system. They have monopolized everything that it is possible to monopolize; they have got the whole earth, the minerals in the earth and the streams that water the earth. The only reason they have not monopolized the daylight and the air is that is is not possible to do it. If it were possible to construct huge gasometers and to draw together and compress within them the whole of the atmosphere, it would have been done long ago, and we should have been compelled to work for them in order to get money to buy air to breathe. And if that seemingly impossible thing were accomplished tomorrow, you would see thousands of people dying for want of air – or of the money to buy it – even as now thousands are dying for want of the other necessaries of life. You would see people going about gasping for breath, and telling each other that the likes of them could not expect to have air to breathe unless they had the money to pay for it. Most of you here, for instance, would think so and say so. Even as you think at present that it's right for a few people to own the Earth, the Minerals and the Water, which are all just as necessary as is the air. In exactly the same spirit you now say: 'It's Their Land', 'It's Their Water', 'It's Their Coal', 'It's Their Iron', so you would say 'It's Their Air', 'These are Their gasometers, and what right have the likes of us to expect them to allow us to breathe for nothing?' And even while he is doing this the air monopolist will be preaching sermons on the Brotherhood of Man; he will be dispensing advice on 'Christian Duty' in the Sunday magazines; he will give utterance to numerous more or less moral maxims for the guidance of the young. And meantime, all around, people will be dying for want of some of the air that he will have bottled up in his gasometers . . .

SYLVIA PANKHURST (1882–1960) 13 October 1905

From *The Suffragette Movement* pp. 189–90

Three years after the formation of the Women's Social and Political Union by her mother, during which Christabel and Sylvia and all the women involved in the campaign for women's suffrage sought to promote the cause through committees, meetings, the formation of branches and the lobbying of Parliament, with little effect upon the institutionalized male club-world of politics except for a small minority led by Keir Hardie, it became clear that more aggressive methods would have to be pursued. And it was at an election meeting by the Liberal, Sir Edward Grey, at the Manchester Free Trade Hall, that the militancy began which was to be marked by government repression and such sadistic measures as the notorious 'Cat and Mouse' Act. Annie Kenney, thin and haggard, a former textile worker from Oldham, where the women had formed strong trade unions, was courageous, impulsive and determined.

MILITANT ACTION

Sir Edward Grey was making his appeal for the return of a Liberal Government when a little white 'Votes for Women' banner shot up. 'Labour Representation' was the cry of the hour. Christabel thrust Annie Kenney forward, as one of the organized textile workers, and a member of a trade union committee, to ask: 'Will the Liberal Government give women the vote?' Other questions were answered; that question was ignored. When it was persisted in, Annie Kenney was dragged down by the men sitting near her, and one of the stewards put a hat over her face. Christabel

585

repeated the question. The hall was filled with conflicting cries: 'Be quiet!' 'Let the lady speak.' In the midst of the hubbub the Chief Constable of Manchester, William Peacock, came to the women and told them that if they would put the question in writing, he would take it himself to Sir Edward Grey, but it went the round of chairman and speakers, and none of them vouchsafed a reply. When Sir Edward Grey rose to acknowledge a vote of thanks, Annie stood on a chair to ask again, whilst Christabel strove to prevent her removal; but Liberal stewards and policemen in plain clothes soon dragged both from the hall. Determined to secure imprisonment, Christabel fought against ejection. When detectives thrust her into an ante-room she cried to her captors: 'I shall assault you!'; and retorted, when they pinioned her: 'I shall spit at you!' Her threat was not carried out in a very realistic manner, but she made as though to accomplish it, and also managed to get a blow at the inspector as she and Annie Kenney were flung out of the building. Yet still she was not arrested. Outside in South Street she declared they must hold a meeting, and when they attempted to address the crowd now flocking out of the hall, her desire was attained: they were arrested and taken to the town hall.

Meanwhile in the Free Trade Hall cries of protest had been raised against the ejection of the two women. Sir Edward Grey, feeling that some explanation was expected of him, expressed regret for what had happened: 'I am not sure that, unwittingly, and in innocence, I have not been a contributing cause . . .'

Christabel was charged next day with spitting in the face of a police superintendent and an inspector . . . She was surprised by the horrified astonishment expressed that a young lady could so behave . . . 'I knew that anything of that kind would be technically an assault, and I couldn't get at them in any other way.' One question to the police witnesses was the only explanation she vouchsafed to the Court: 'Were not my arms held at the time?' She was ordered to pay a fine of 10*s.* or go to prison for seven days, and Annie Kenney 5*s.* or three days. They were placed in the Third Division, the lowest class, to which the majority of prisoners are sent; they wore the prison dress and ate the prison food.

The Press, almost without exception, adopted a hostile tone . . .

Keir Hardie at once telegraphed: 'The thing is a dastardly outrage, but do not worry, it will do immense good to the Cause. Can I do anything?'

SYLVIA PANKHURST (1882–1960)   1909?

From *The Suffragette Movement*, pp. 316–19

After the return of the Liberals, suffrage Bills were persistently defeated, and the militant suffragette policy of stone-throwing and damage to private property led to many arrests following brutal treatment by the police, and a series of hunger-strikes.

FORCIBLE FEEDING

The Government was not slow to take advantage of the new tactics to inflict harsher punishments upon their instruments. These women should not be permitted to terminate their imprisonment by the hunger strike, as thirty-seven women had already done, four of them twice in succession. The Birmingham prisoners commenced their fast on 18 September. The Home Secretary ordered the medical officer of the prison to feed them forcibly by means of a rubber tube passed through the mouth or nose into the stomach. The fact appeared in the Press on 24 September. It was received with horrified consternation by everyone connected with the militant movement; by no one more than by Keir Hardie, in whom emotional distress now invariably caused the reaction of physical illness. He immediately tabled a Parliamentary question. Masterman, replying for the Home Secretary, described the forcible feeding as 'hospital treatment'. Hardie, white with wrath, retorted: 'A horrible, beastly outrage.' Philip Snowden cried: 'Russian barbarism!' The supporters of the Government shouted with laughter. Keir Hardie wrote to the Press:

. . . Women, worn and weak with hunger, are seized upon, held down by brute force, gagged, a tube inserted down the throat, and food poured or pumped into the stomach. Let British men think over the spectacle . . .

I was horrified at the levity displayed by a large section of Members of the House when the question was being answered. Had I not heard it, I could not have believed that a body of gentlemen could have found reason for mirth and applause in a scene which I venture to say has no parallel in the recent history of our country. One of these days we shall learn that Mrs Leigh, or some other of her brave fellow prisoners, has succumbed to the 'hospital treatment', as a man did in 1870.

. . . Only when an action at law, against the Home Secretary and the governor and doctor of Birmingham prison, was commenced on behalf of Mary Leigh, could direct testimony be obtained from the prisoners.

587

It now transpired that Mrs Leigh had been handcuffed for upwards of thirty hours, the hands fastened behind during the day and in front with the palms outward at night. Only when the wrists had become intensely painful and swollen were the irons removed. On the fourth day of her fast, the doctor had told her that she must either abandon the hunger strike or be fed by force. She protested that forcible feeding was an operation, and as such could not be performed without a sane patient's consent; but she was seized by the wardresses and the doctor administered food by the nasal tube. This was done twice daily, from 22 September till 30 October. All her companions were forcibly fed, one being released before her, and the others, save one, shortly afterwards . . .

SYLVIA PANKHURST (1882–1960)   May, 1910

From *The Suffragette Movement*, pp. 396–7

IMPERIALISM VERSUS INTERNATIONALISM

At Parten Kirchen we had learnt of King Edward's death. Behind the clamant domestic controversies of his reign, looming as an ominous shadow, in wait to cloud all other issues, reared Foreign Policy. Two ideals strove for mastery: imperialism and aggressive armaments, *versus* arbitration and conciliation, with the ultimate goal of international citizenship in the United States of the World. Between these poles a multitude of rival policies contended: the neutrality of Britain, a moderate navy and a small army, *versus* participation in alliances which would make this country the decisive factor in a world balance of power, a policy entailing a great navy and an army organized for expansion in case of war. This last was the policy of the Liberal Cabinet. Insatiable Conservative hot-bloods demanded more battleships. A section of the Liberals – Brailsford, Ponsonby, Trevelyan and others – strove to turn the Government towards internationalism, or neutrality at least; and thereby found themselves, willy nilly, in frequent alliance with Keir Hardie and the pacifist section of the Labour Party, which most of them were eventually to join. As a constitutional sovereign, and perhaps with somewhat more of personal impulse than was indispensable to his office, King Edward had borne the ceremonial part in cementing the French and Russian alliances, which were to counter German expansion in industry, commerce, territory, and raw materials. Victoria had differed vehemently with the foreign policies of her Ministers; Edward, for his agreement with the Governments preceding the greatest war in history, was termed 'the peacemaker'.

At his death Parliamentary controversies were for the moment suspended. We learnt this in Oberammergau, and news presently reached us from Clements Inn that all WSPU propaganda had been stopped until after the Royal funeral; a great procession had been postponed for a month. *Votes for Women*, black bordered, displayed the portrait of Queen Alexandra as its cover, and the following week that of Queen Mary. Christabel, daughter of Republican Dr Pankhurst, vied with the Conservative organs in her expressions of devotion to the throne. In her repetition of the legend of the peacemaking achieved in the reign of Edward, it was as though she knew nothing of the struggle convulsing the groups of political thinkers through which she had passed; had heard no protests against the race of naval armaments, no cries of alarm at the division of Europe into two armed camps. She had been untouched by Keir Hardie's impassioned protests against British aid in stabilizing the Tsarist Government, which had exterminated the popular uprising of 1905–6 with torture and massacre, and in two years had executed upwards of 3,000 political prisoners, and butchered 19,000 people by its 'Black Hundreds'. The struggle for freedom in Russia she dismissed as a 'men's movement'. The representatives of the suppressed Duma who came to London appealing for the support of British Democrats, were to her merely 'old Liberals'. She made no effort to see beyond them . . .

SYLVIA PANKHURST   18 November 1910
(1882–1960)

From *The Suffragette Movement*, pp. 343–4

The Conciliation Bill, promising a limited franchise for women, was suppressed after passing its Second Reading, and the suffragettes were told it would not be granted in 1910. This put an end to the truce that had been earlier declared, and at a mass demonstration outside the Houses of Parliament on 18 November, there were scenes of 'unexampled violence'.

BLACK FRIDAY

I saw Ada Wright knocked down a dozen times in succession. A tall man with a silk hat fought to protect her as she lay on the ground, but a group of policemen thrust him away, seized her again, hurled her into the crowd and felled her again as she turned. Later I saw her lying against the wall of the House of Lords, with a group of anxious women kneeling round her. Two girls with linked arms were being dragged about by two uniformed policemen. One of a group of officers in plain clothes ran up and kicked one of the girls, whilst the others laughed and jeered at her. Again and again we saw the small deputations struggling through the crowd with their little purple bannerettes: 'Asquith has vetoed our Bill.' The police snatched the flags, tore them to shreds, and smashed the sticks, struck the women with fists and knees, knocked them down, some even kicked them, then dragged them up, carried them a few paces and flung them into the crowd of sightseers. For six hours this continued. From time to time we returned to the Caxton Hall, where doctors and nurses were attending to women who had been hurt. We saw the women go out and return exhausted, with black eyes, bleeding noses, bruises, sprains and dislocations. The cry went round: 'Be careful; they are dragging women down the side streets!' We knew this always meant greater ill-usage. I saw Cecilia Haig go out with the rest; a tall, strongly built, reserved woman, comfortably situated, who in ordinary circumstances might have gone through life without ever receiving an insult, much less a blow. She was assaulted with violence and indecency, and died in December 1911, after a painful illness arising from her injuries. Henria Williams, already suffering from a weak heart, did not recover from the treatment she received that night in the Square, and died on 1 January . . .

H. N. Brailsford and Dr Jessie Murray collected evidence from witnesses and sufferers, who testified to deliberate acts of cruelty, such as twisting and wrenching of arms, wrists, and thumbs; gripping the throat and forcing back the head; pinching the arms; striking the face with fists, sticks, helmets; throwing women down and kicking them; rubbing a woman's face against the railings; pinching the breasts; squeezing the ribs. A girl under arrest was marched to the police station with her skirts over her head. An old woman of seventy was knocked down by a blow in the face, receiving a black eye and a wound on the back of the head. The Conciliation Committee requested a Government inquiry into the conduct of the police, but Churchill refused. He said that instead of dispersing the women by a baton charge, or permitting the disorders to continue for a long time, it had been his desire to have them arrested as soon as they gave lawful occasion. It was his predecessor, not he, who had given orders to make as few arrests as possible. His own directions had not been 'fully understood or carried out' (House of Commons, 8

590

March). This explanation was received with derision by those who had witnessed the scenes. It was contradicted by its author's own subsequent statement (House of Commons, 13 March): 'No orders, verbal or written, directly or indirectly emanating from me, were given to the police.'

One hundred and fifteen women and two men had been arrested on 'Black Friday'.

KEIR HARDIE (1856–1915)   28 November 1910

From his Address to the Merthyr Labour Representation Association for the General Election

The miners of south Wales were among the most militant of the organized working-class movements, and Keir Hardie represented their interests as MP for Merthyr Tydfil both in and outside Parliament from 1900 till his death. An important strike in 1905 against monopoly ownership and its exploitation was followed by strikes in other parts of the country. This was the beginning of combined activity by the biggest unions, and when the General Election of late 1910 was called the miners of the Cambrian Combine were already involved in a great strike, which lasted from November till August 1911, was marked by bloody skirmishes with the police, and prepared the way for the dockers' strikes and the national coal strike of 1912. The unofficial strike in the Aberdare and Rhondda Valleys referred to by Hardie met with harsh brutality from the soldiers and special police drafted in to crush it, which involved punitive beatings of women and old people.

MEN ON STRIKE

Comrades,
. . . The events of the past few weeks in the Aberdare and Rhondda Valleys must have shown you anew that a Liberal Government is first and foremost a Capitalist Government. If the bloodshed and riotous Conduct of which the Police have been guilty had taken place under a Conservative Government every Liberal Platform would have rung with denunciation of the wicked Tories; but, because it is the Liberals who are responsible there is a conspiracy of silence in the Press, and every Liberal speaker is dumb.

The Home Secretary not only defends the actions of the Police and refuses an inquiry into the charges against them but also eulogizes the hooligans in uniform, whilst Liberal MPs, with few exceptions, back him up by their votes in the Division Lobby.

As a consequence of this the men on strike are believed by millions of people who know nothing of the facts to be wild, riotous, drunken, worthless scamps, whereas the very opposite is the truth. The Military and Police have been sent to help the masters to crush the men.

The trick won't succeed.

During the Contest I shall be a good deal in other Constituencies where Labour men are being opposed. Both Parties fear the presence in Parliament of Labour men whom they can neither silence nor control. I want to see the number of such men increased, so that political hypocrites of the Churchill type may be unmasked, and the Health, Comfort, Safety, and general Well-being of the Working Class promoted. I know you will hold the fort for Labour in my absence.

Fraternally Yours

THE LIVERPOOL DOCK STRIKE   1911

In a period of increasing prosperity and rising prices, profits rose steeply, more or less in proportion to the decrease in real wages, which continued till 1914. It was the realization of this that brought about the bitter struggles of the pre-war period. The Liverpool strike was preceded by strikes at Southampton and Hull in June, and Manchester in July. It was organized unofficially soon after the outbreak of the great London dock strike.

AN ARMED CAMP

From Mann, *Single Tax to Syndicalism*, p. 80

The whole of Liverpool looked like an armed camp. The 80,000 strikers continued successfully in spite of all the parading of the military. The soldiers were compelled to do the disgraceful work of helping the few blacklegs present. Thus, for example, when the authorities decided to open a railway goods yard and fetch out a few hundredweight of freight, they requisitioned mounted police, foot police, cavalry, infantry with fixed bayonets – altogether some hundreds of men to escort a couple of lorries.

On the other hand, goods that were intended for the hospitals and public institutions were brought out by Union drivers unaccompanied by anyone other than a couple of Committee men. On each lorry was a

592

large placard bearing the words, 'By Authorization of the Strike Committee', and these carried milk and flour, and each as it appeared was cheered by thousands.

Backed by over 7,000 military and special police, the local authorities were determined to provoke disorder. Mounted and foot police were sent out in large numbers to the centre of the city, and these made uncalled-for attacks upon peaceful pedestrians, riding them down and clubbing any young men who happened to be near. Naturally people resented this and retaliated, and this is how riots were caused.

REPRESSION

From Torr, *Tom Mann*, pp. 41–2

On 13 August, Bloody Sunday, a brutal attack was made by the police on the mass demonstration on St George's Hall Plateau, addressed by Tom, who there gave the call for the general transport strike of the whole city. Although the demonstration had been authorized, a trivial disturbance on its outskirts was made the excuse for beating-up hundreds of demonstrators, who were left lying helpless on the ground.

The *Manchester Guardian* remarked that the police used their truncheons like flails: 'a display of violence that horrified those that saw it'. The strike committee had arranged to have a film taken of the demonstration, and this film showed the whole action of the police. At the picture theatre where it was to be exhibited next day, however, the police ordered every section of it which told against them to be cut out . . .

On 14 August fierce battles took place between strikers and police and the Riot Act was read. The city was in a state of siege and practically under martial law. On the same day the troops fired into a group of workers who had tried to stop a prison van; two were killed.

Favourable settlements had been reached for most sections of the strikers when the City Corporation refused to reinstate the tramwaymen. The other strikers thereupon refused to go back, and after Tom Mann and the Committee had threatened to call a national sympathetic strike, the Corporation gave way. The membership of the Dockers' Union increased from 8,000 to 32,000 and conditions were substantially improved. Immediately arising from this strike was the national strike of 145,000 railwaymen which began on 17 August and itself led to the amalgamation of the three sectional unions into the National Union of Railwaymen.

REFUSAL

From Torr, *Tom Mann*, p. 42

Let Churchill do his utmost. Let him order ten times more military to Liverpool and let every street be paraded by them, not all the king's forces with all the king's men can take the vessels out of the docks to sea. The workers decide the ships shall not go, what government can say they shall go and make the carters take the freight and the dockers load same, and the seamen man the steamers?

Tell us that, gentlemen, is there really a stronger power than that of the workers in properly organized relationship? If so, trot it out. Demonstrate your power to prevent the liners being held up, prove your capacity to get them loaded and out again in time and safely manned, to destination!

You affect to be so superior to the mere labourer, very well, get on without him – if you can – if you can. Bring in your military, still further demonstrate your power – to get nothing done; meanwhile the workers' demands had better receive attention at your hands.

FORCE

From Mann, *Single Tax to Syndicalism*, p. 82

No man could have gone through the Liverpool strike without having his eyes opened to the real existence of the military and police. True to its traditions, the 'Liberal' Government slaughtered the people here as they had at Featherstone, Llanelly and elsewhere.

ROBERT TRESSELL (?–1911)

From *The Ragged Trousered Philanthropists*, pp. 511–12, 522–3

If Owen dominates Tressell's novel as the propagandist of socialism among his fellow workers at Rushtons, builder and decorator, it is his friend George Barrington who, in his 'Great Oration' towards the end of the book, most fully defines both the evils of 'the present System' and the concept of a socialist society such as had been prefigured by the struggles of the Chartists and articulated for the working class of Britain and the continent by Marx, Engels and Morris among others, thus laying the foundations (against the misery, apathy and disillusionment induced by capitalist exploitation) for the progressive movements of the turn of the century, and Tressell's own vision as a socialist realist.

THE GREAT CHANGE

It is an admitted fact that about thirteen millions of our people are always on the verge of starvation. The significant results of this poverty face us on every side. The alarming and persistent increase of insanity. The large number of would-be recruits for the army who have to be rejected because they are physically unfit; and the shameful condition of the children of the poor. More than one-third of the children of the working classes in London have some sort of mental or physical defect; defects in development; defects of eyesight; abnormal nervousness; rickets, and mental dullness. The difference in height and weight and general condition of the children in poor schools and the children of the so-called better classes, constitutes a crime that calls aloud to Heaven for vengeance upon those who are responsible for it.

It is childish to imagine that any measure of Tariff Reform or Political Reform such as a paltry tax on foreign-made goods or abolishing the House of Lords, or disestablishing the Church – or miserable Old Age Pensions, or a contemptible tax on land, can deal with such a state of affairs as this. They have no House of Lords in America or France, and yet their condition is not materially different from ours. You may be deceived into thinking that such measures as those are great things. You may fight for them and vote for them, but after you have got them you will find that they will make no appreciable improvement in your condition. You will still have to slave and drudge to gain a bare sufficiency of the necessaries of life. You will still have to eat the same kind of food and wear the same kind of clothes and boots as now. Your masters will still have you in their power to insult and sweat and drive. Your general condition will be just the same as at present because such measures as those are not remedies but red herrings, intended by those who trail them to draw us away from the only remedy, which is to be found only in the Public Ownership of the Machinery, and the National Organization of Industry for the production and distribution of the necessaries of life, not for the profit of a few but for the benefit of all!

That is the next great change; not merely desirable, but imperatively necessary and inevitable! That is Socialism! . . .

THE CHALLENGE

Such are the days that shall be! but
    what are the deeds of today,
In the days of the years we dwell in,
    that wear our lives away?
Why, then, and for what are we waiting?
    There are but three words to speak:
We will it. And what is the foeman
    but the dream strong wakened and weak?

Oh why and for what are we waiting, while
    our brothers droop and die,
And on every wind of the heavens, a
    wasted life goes by?
How long shall they reproach us, where
    crowd on crowd they dwell,
Poor ghosts of the wicked city,
    gold-crushed, hungry hell?

Through squalid life they laboured,
    in sordid grief they died,
Those sons of a mighty mother, those
    props of England's pride.
They are gone, there is none can undo it
    nor save our souls from the curse;
But many a million cometh, and shall
    they be better or worse?

It is We must answer and hasten and open wide the door,
For the rich man's hurrying terror and the slow-foot hope of the poor.
Yea, the voiceless wrath of the wretched and their unlearned
    discontent,
We must give it voice and wisdom, till the waiting tide be spent.
Come then since all things call us, the living and the dead,
And o'er the weltering tangle a glimmering light is shed.

THE 'DON'T SHOOT' LEAFLET   1912

The year 1912 brought the first national miners' strike and a further London dock
strike against the victimization of trade unionists. And it was against this back-

ground that five people, among them Tom Mann and two others prosecuted as the printers, were sentenced to prison terms of up to nine months for circulating a leaflet appealing to the soldiers during the Liverpool strike, after two men had been shot dead.

DON'T SHOOT!

Men! Comrades! Brothers! You are in the army. So are we. You, in the army of Destruction. We, in the Industrial or army of Construction.

We work at mine, mill, forge, factory, or dock, etc., producing and transporting all the goods, clothing stuffs, etc., which make it possible for people to live.

You are Workingmen's Sons.

When We go on Strike to better Our lot, which is the lot also of your Fathers, Mothers, Brothers, and Sisters, you are called upon by your Officers to MURDER US. Don't do it.

Don't you know that when you are out of the Colours, and become a 'Civvy' again, that You, like us, may be on strike, and You, like us, liable to be murdered by other soldiers.

Boys, Don't Do It.

'Thou shalt not kill,' says the Book.

Don't forget that!

It does not say, 'unless you have a uniform on'.

No! Murder is Murder . . .

Think things out and refuse any longer to murder your Kindred. Help us to win back Britain for the British and the World for the Workers.

H. N. BRAILSFORD (1873–1958) 1914

From *The War of Steel and Gold*, pp. 308–9

In the months immediately preceding the outbreak of war, Britain was in the grip of serious unrest. Following the wave of strikes of the previous three years, a Triple Alliance was formed between the miners, railwaymen and transport workers, pledging mutual support in readiness for a general strike. At the same time the campaign for women's suffrage, with 107 buildings set fire to, 141 acts of destruction reported in the press and many women arrested, was continuously in action. And in March the British army officers stationed at the Curragh near Dublin threatened to resign rather than move against Carson's Ulster Volunteers, formed to prevent the application of Home Rule, and themselves challenged by a volunteer force gathered in the south. Such internal disorders were everywhere sharpening against Westminster, and were only diverted by the international crisis brought about by the imperialist powers, and the war itself.

AN INDIGNANT SCEPTICISM

There is in all of us an uneasy sense that this international struggle is distracting the mind of society, which ought to be bent on the civilization of our own barbarous way of life, while it dissipates on the engines of strife the resources that would suffice to raise the casual labourer and the sweated woman worker to a human level of comfort and freedom. That vague distress, if it is to help us forward, must be translated into a searching curiosity, and developed into an indignant scepticism. It is not enough to desire peace. The generation which attains peace will have won it by an intellectual passion. It must feel the waste and the degradation of our present fears so deeply, that it will think its way through the subtleties and the secrecies which render plausible the present misconduct of international affairs. It will find, when it has faced its problem, that it is not natural necessities but class-interests which condemn us to the armed peace. It will realize that in the vast competitive process, by which capital is spreading itself over the globe, there is no motive which can require, no reason which can excuse, the hostility of nations. Let a people once perceive for what purposes its patriotism is constituted, and its resources misused, and the end is already in sight. When that illumination comes to the masses of the three Western Powers, the fears which fill their barracks and build their warships will have lost the power to drive. A clear-sighted generation will scan the horizon and find no enemy. It will drop its armour, and walk the world's highways safe.

THE FIRST WORLD WAR   1914

Editorial, *Daily Herald*, 29 July 1914

German absolutism and European nationalism; imperialistic rivalry for the possession of world markets; ruling-class groups locked in deadly battle for economic and military supremacy and manipulating their own interests in supreme indifference to the rights and interests of their subject peoples everywhere, at home and abroad: these are the underlying conditions which brought Europe to the obscenities of the First World War. No doubt the policies of the European powers that led to 1914 had different aims; and no doubt the war itself was conceived as a legitimate extension of the economic war that had been going on for decades. But that is the measure of the anti-social nature of such policies. Geared to ruthless competition, and warped beyond imagination by the conditions of the arms race, they made war inevitable. 'After me, the deluge!' There were those who tried to organize the people of Europe – people like Keir Hardie, Liebknecht and Rosa Luxembourg; but they were defeated by the massive propaganda campaign that drowned the call to reason and international solidarity.

THE WORKERS' RESPONSIBILITY

The present European crisis throws a grave responsibility on the Trade Unions. At any moment the working classes of Europe may be called upon to defend interests in which they are not concerned, for a cause that tends in no way to uplift them. Theirs will be the loss and the burden, whatever side may be victorious. As the guardians of their welfare, it is the duty of the Trade Unions to declare that this thing shall not be.

There has been much talk of recent years about the international solidarity of labour. A bureau has been established to deal with questions of European concern. Resolution after resolution has been passed by congress after congress, protesting against the iniquity of war, and calling upon the workers to take steps to ensure its prevention.

It is possible to ensure its prevention if the workers show the right spirit. In the first place let them understand that the nasal jingoism which cries out in the market place for war is the antithesis of patriotism. In the second place let them remember that it is their brothers who will be shot down. The capitalists for whose benefit the war will be waged lose nothing save in the sphere of finance . . .

The labour leaders must act at once. We have had enough of resolutions. It is time for action. There is given to the worker the opportunity to strike a blow at the very heart of the capitalist system. If he declares that he has no concern with any conflict save the industrial conflict; if he thus makes clear the solidarity of working-class interests throughout Europe, he can ensure the commencement of a new era in history. He will make it plain that henceforward the Army is not a tool in the hands of the aristocracies. He will make it plain that the workers will decide the problems for the decision of which they must bear the cost.

599

SYLVIA PANKHURST
(1882–1960)

29 July–2 August 1914

From *The Home Front*, pp. 31–2

STAND TOGETHER FOR PEACE!

On 29 July 1914, the International Socialist Bureau convened in Brussels, had resolved on a special conference in Paris, on 9 August; a conference which never met; for war had sealed the frontiers, and the international Socialist movement had been rent in twain, its principles of fraternity vanquished by the trump of war. This débâcle still unforeseen, on 30 July the Bureau participated in a great peace demonstration. Keir Hardie, Jaures, Haase of Germany and the rest, marched under white banners bearing the inscription: 'Guerre à la Guerre' . . . Haase . . . warned the Governments in the event of war: 'The peoples, tired out by such manifold misery and oppression, may wake up and establish a Socialist society.'

On 31 July Keir Hardie as chairman, Arthur Henderson as secretary of the British section of the International Socialist Bureau, had issued an appeal to the workers against the War . . .

Stand together for peace! Combine and conquer the militarist enemy and the self-seeking imperialists, today, once and for all . . . Proclaim that for you the days of plunder and butchery have gone by . . .

Down with class rule! Down with brute force! Down with war! Up with the peaceful rule of the people!!

On 2 August a Trafalgar Square anti-war demonstration was held by the Bureau, with as many speakers of prominence who could claim to speak for Labour and Socialism as the brief notice allowed. Keir Hardie was there, and Arthur Henderson, H. M. Hyndman, Will Thorne, Ben Tillett and many others who presently were cheering for the War.

In every belligerent country such demonstrations were held, organized by the Socialists, responded to by the populace . . . The cry went forth: 'War on War!! Long Live the International Brotherhood of the Peoples!' Greetings were sent from Britain to Germany; from Germany to France and Russia. Yet when the great conflict had actually been joined, only a small fraction of those who had cried for peace and brotherhood maintained their stand . . .

DAILY HERALD EDITORIAL   5 August 1914

ENGLAND AND GERMANY AT WAR
THE DIE IS CAST

The die is cast. Without the consent of the British people, and against the feeling of the overwhelming mass of the nation, we are plunged into a European war, the extent and the horrors of which no man can foresee.

We cannot forbear from saying that the whole thing is a calamity and a disaster, both from the point of view of the nation and of humanity. It is imperative upon us to make this final protest.

We urge upon all those who retain their reason to act together in this time of grave peril; not to be elated by victories nor cast down by defeats. To insist on no aggrandisement if British arms are successful, but still to work for the bringing back of peace as speedily as possible, so that this horror may pass away from us.

Misery will course through the land. Starving children and women will need our assistance.

It is the duty of all now to insist that the poor shall be protected against the machinations of the plunderers, who, taking advantage of the necessities of the people, will force up food prices.

Meanwhile let us do all in our power to bring a saner vision to Europe, so that this madness may pass away . . .

CHRISTABEL PANKHURST   7 August 1914
(1880–1958)

The Suffragette (periodical)

A CIVILIZATION MADE BY MEN

As I write a dreadful war-cloud seems about to burst and deluge the peoples of Europe with fire, slaughter, ruin – this then is the World as men have made it, life as men have ordered it.

A man-made civilization, hideous and cruel enough in time of peace, is to be destroyed.

A civilization made by men only is a civilization which defies the law of nature, which defies the law of right Government.

This great war, whether it comes now, or by some miracle is deferred till later, is Nature's vengeance – is God's vengeance upon the people who held women in subjection, and by doing that have destroyed the perfect human balance. Just as when the laws governing the human body are defied we have disease, so when the law of right government is defied – the law that men and women shall cooperate in managing their affairs – we have a civilization imperfect, unjust, savage at its best and foredoomed to destruction.

Had women been equal partners with men from the beginning, human civilization would have been wholly different from what it is. The whole march of humanity would have been to a point other than we have reached at this moment of horrible calamity.

There are men who have a glimmering idea of something better, but only by the help of women could civilization have been made other than cruel, predatory, destructive. Only by the help of women as citizens can the World be saved after the holocaust is ended . . .

Let us in everything strive unceasingly that the World may learn from the tragedy by which it is menaced, that for the sake of the human race, for the sake of the divinity that is in the human race, women must be free.

DAILY HERALD EDITORIAL   10 August 1914

THE BLOOD DELUGE

The democratic elements in these islands seem helpless at the moment – their time is not yet. They were unable or unwilling to prevent or check the rush to war, and the utter set-back to civilization, such as it is or was, that must ensue. They can do little or nothing to mitigate the great horrors, or to hasten their end. The spirit of democracy, in fact, plays as slight a part today in the general life of Europe as practical Christianity. Madness, murder, fever, illusion are rampant in a hundred fields and centres. Culture, progress, the graces and amenities of life are in danger of being relegated for disastrous days, or even years, to the region of fads and dreams. Thousands who thought they were proceeding, howsoever slowly, towards social sanity and cooperation are shaking their heads or maintaining a disgusted and humiliating silence.

They feel that at the best they can only wait resignedly for the cessation of the shocks and death-dealing, the ebb of passion and slaughter, the painful return to sobriety and rebuilding. They have been deceived even by some that they thought were of their own household; Mr Ramsay MacDonald has felt called upon to resign the chairmanship of the Labour Party (a fact for which he is to be applauded and honoured) apparently on account of – indescribable irony! – a spirit of Labour Jingoism. Thousands of wage-slaves themselves are being hurriedly decked out or disguised as soldiers and headed to a charnel-house.

The whole situation shows in fearsome wise how little the millions are free: physically, socially, intellectually, mentally, or otherwise. It is a stupendous illustration of slavery, exterior and interior. A few war-lords and diplomats, dwelling with abstraction and working in the dark, have disagreed or lost their heads, and forthwith they are able to disorganize all Europe and set the greater part of it crashing towards chaos. And now we are told that momentous causes are at stake, that rights and privileges we have never enjoyed in practice are in jeopardy. Hosts of poor wage-slaves believe it all! The sad serf with his pound or twenty-five shillings a week and his struggling family, in the mean street or slum, imagines that his joyous existence, his artistic and intellectual possessions, are threatened from Potsdam. The pity and the fatuity of it all!

The nations, the peoples, are *not* at war, and they have no cause for war. Little minorities of bosses and formalists are ordering vast masses of enslaved soldiers to destruction, and hosts of civil onlookers to penury and distraction. That is the position in a sentence . . .

[And] the painful reality is this: every death on every field and wave is more or less a loss to democracy and Trade Unionism in Europe, and to the workers as a whole, whether the victim be Belgian, German, French, British, Austrian, Servian or Russian . . .

MARY WEBB (1881–1927)   1914

'Autumn 1914', in *Scars upon My Heart*

AUTUMN 1914

He's gone, her man, so good with his hands
In the harvest-field and the lambing shed.
Straight ran his share in the deep ploughlands –
And now he marches among the dead.

O children, come in from your soldier-play
In the black bean tents! The night is falling;
Owls with their shuddering cry are calling;
A dog howls, lonely, far away.

His son comes in like a ghost through the door.
He'll be ready, maybe, for the next big war.

EPILOGUE

TOWARDS THE FUTURE

Intelligence enough to conceive, courage enough to will, power enough to compel. If our ideas of a new society are anything more than a dream, these three qualities must animate the due effective majority of the working people; and then, I say, the thing will be done.

William Morris, *Communism* (1893)

Therefore we dare not despair, but will look for, wait for, and hope for deliverance still.

John Bunyan, *The Holy War* (1682)

Looking back on the world of 1914 and all that had been put at risk, it seems that nothing could have prevented the ruthless development of industrial and commercial capitalism after 1848 or the imperialist rivalry of Britain, France and Germany at the end of the century from moving down the narrowing paths of competition towards confrontation and catastrophe. The war that was the culmination of this predatory nationalism unleashed upon the defenceless masses of Europe a fury of destructiveness that demonstrated the innate cruelty and barbarism of the capitalist system at work and the incubus-like power of its rulers to manipulate their people into a state of patriotic fervour, battening upon them, sapping them of all will to resist, and inspiring in them the zeal of a sleep-walking mob to kill and be killed. Not that it was envisaged as such by those who had brought it about. For them, from their remote positions of command, it seemed rather to have the flavour of heroic adventure, judging from Churchill's comments in *The Gathering Storm*. 'Apart from the excesses of the Russian Revolution,' he declares, 'the main fabric of European civilization remained erect at the close of the struggle.' In the rhetoric of this public-school view of war, it is as if it had all been nothing but a huge gentlemanly misunderstanding; for 'when the storm and dust of the cannonade passed suddenly away, the nations, despite their enmities, could still recognize each other as historic racial personalities'. Which is to confirm that afterwards, in spite of Russia's refusal to play the game, the ruling classes still retained control, and to demonstrate how totally the war had failed to solve any of the basic problems, even if it did destroy the German Empire.

As for the fighting itself – the unspeakable carnage of Verdun, Ypres, the Somme, Arras, Passchendaele, where millions died in futile obedience to the inefficiency, bankruptcy and obtuseness of their generals – in ruling-class terms 'the laws of war had on the whole been respected', since it didn't seem to matter what had happened to the ordinary soldiers. There was, after all, 'a common professional meeting-ground between military men who had fought one another'! And it was of course they – the generals, the statesmen, the diplomats, the businessmen, the profiteers of war, 'vanquished and victors alike' – who (ignoring the disillusionment and the stunned silence of the millions) 'preserved the semblance of civilized states' and made their 'solemn peace' under 'the reign of law' – if only to assert once again the authority and power of a morally discredited system.

The war, in other words, had taught these people almost nothing. For between Versailles and Munich they pursued policies which, in their ineptitude, hypocrisy and equivocation, and their opposition to socialism in Europe, let alone the Soviet Union, were to encourage the growth of fascism, and thus to lead inexorably to 1939. It was this, indeed, that the Russian Revolution had stood out against and emerged as a challenge to – the tyranny of privilege and property, the devious pursuit of class interest and class exploitation, with its cynical indifference (masked by the civilities of class authority) to the needs of the working masses. The fact that 'the greatest and most necessary part of a very rich nation', as Hopkins had written of England long before, was once again to be forced by the cruelties of the market 'to live a hard life without dignity, knowledge, comforts, delight or hopes in the midst of plenty' did not count. It was the inalienable rights of the rich that counted, the laws and institutions of an economic and social order controlled by those who, from behind their sham facades of civility and rectitude, had already dragged the peoples of Europe into the murderous degradation of war.

'The past has deceived us,' Yeats was to write in the disillusionment of 1918. 'Let us accept the worthless present.' But this was a pessimism only the privileged could afford. And for working-class men returning from the battlefields, or the working-class men and women who (throughout the war, against oppressive odds) had carried on the struggle at home for their fundamental rights, such pessimism would have meant the end of hope, and a blank betrayal of all that had been fought for inch by inch at such great cost through so many generations.

But it must have been clear to them that the world was going to have to fight, as Lenin declared in 1920, a slow and painful battle to create social-ism from 'the mass of human material twisted by centuries of slavery, serfdom, petty nationalist economies, and the war of all against all'. Caught in the devastating trap of a capitalist war, forced to work and to die for a creed which served to strengthen their enemies and to weaken their own powers of resistance, ordinary men and women had been laun-ched on a new and difficult period in their long struggle 'against poverty and the intellectual privation it entails, and against war, which is bred from poverty'.

It is a struggle which is still going on, and has yet to be won, directed towards the making of a world in which economic inequality, social de-privation and injustice will have been replaced by a system which embo-dies the communal responsibilities and rights of men and women work-ing without fear, in equality of comradeship, for common ends and the fulfilment of their highest needs.

FURTHER READING

General

Arber, E., ed., *An English Garner*, 8 vols., London, 1895–7

Arendt, Hannah, *On Revolution*, London, 1964

Barker, Theo. ed., *The Long March of Everyman 1750–1960*, London 1975

Barraclough, Geoffrey, *An Introduction to Contemporary History*, London, 1964
   History in a Changing World, Oxford, 1957

Calendar of the Close Rolls, London (British Library)

Carr, E. H., *What is History?*, London, 1961

Cohn, Norman, *The Pursuit of the Millennium*, London, 1970

Cole, G. D. H., *Social Theory*, London, 1920
   The Common People 1746–1938 (with Raymond Postgate), London, 1938; 5th edition, 1961
   Introduction to Economic History 1750–1950, London, 1952
   A History of Socialist Thought, 1789–1939, 5 vols., London, 1953–60

Collingwood, R. G., *The Idea of History*, Oxford, 1946

Coulton, G. G., ed., *Social Life in Britain from the Conquest to the Reformation*, Cambridge, 1918

Deane, P., and Cole, W. A., *British Economic Growth 1688–1959*, Cambridge, 1962

Engels, Friedrich, 'Socialism, Utopian and Scientific'; 'Origin of Family, Private Property and State'; in *Selected Works of Marx and Engels*, London, 1968

Fischer, Ernst, *The Necessity of Art*, Harmondsworth, 1963

Foot, Michael, *Debts of Honour*, London, 1980

Ford, Boris, ed., *The New Pelican Guide to English Literature: 2, The Age of Shakespeare*, Harmondsworth, 1982

Haller, William, *The Rise of Puritanism 1570–1643*, Columbia, 1938

Hammond, J. L. and B., *The Village Labourer*, London, 1911
   The Town Labourer, London, 1917

Hampton, Christopher, *Socialism in a Crippled World*, Harmondsworth, 1981

Harleian Miscellany, ed. Oldys and Park, 10 vols., London, 1808–13

Hauser, Arnold, *The Social History of Art*, 4 vols., London, 1962

Hill, Christopher, *Society and Puritanism in Pre-Revolutionary England*, London, 1964
   Reformation to Industrial Revolution 1530–1780, London, 1967

Hobsbawm, E. J., *The Age of Revolution*, London, 1962

Huizinga, J., *The Waning of the Middle Ages*, London, 1924, reprinted Harmondsworth, 1955

Lukacs, Georg, *The Historical Novel*, 1969
   History and Class Consciousness, London, 1971 (first published 1922)

Marx, Karl, *Grundrisse*, ed. Martin Nicolaus, Harmondsworth, 1973
   Capital, 3 vols., Harmondsworth, 1975–81

Morton, A. L., *A People's History of England*, London, 1979 (first published 1938)
   The English Utopia, London, 1952

Pelling, H. M., ed., *The Challenge of Socialism* (documents), London, 1954

Postgate, Raymond, *Revolution from 1789 to 1906*, Gloucester, Mass., 1962

Rickword, Edgell, *Literature in Society*, London, 1978

Rickword, Edgell, and Lindsay, Jack, *A Handbook of Freedom 700–1918*, reprinted as *Spokesmen for Liberty*, London, 1939, 1941

Rushworth, J., *Historical Collections*, 8 vols., London, 1721

Russell, Bertrand, *Freedom and Organisation 1814–1914*, London, 1934

Shaw, G. B., *Selected Prose*, ed. Dora Russell, London, 1950

Stent, Doris May, *The English Woman in History*, London, 1957

Stone, L., ed., *Social Change and Revolution in England 1540–1640*, London, 1965

Tawney, R. H., *The Acquisitive Society*, London, 1921
  Religion and the Rise of Capitalism, London, 1926
  The Radical Tradition, London, 1964

Taylor, A. J. P., *The Troublemakers: Dissent 1792–1939*, London, 1956

Thompson, E. P., *The Making of the English Working Class*, London, 1963
  The Poverty of Theory, London, 1978

Trevelyan, G. M., *English Social History*, London, 1944

Weber, Max, *The Protestant Ethic and the Spirit of Capitalism*, London, 1930 (first published in German 1904–5)

Williams, Raymond, *Culture and Society 1780–1950*, London, 1958
  The Long Revolution, London, 1961
  The Country and the City, London, 1973

1 The Middle Ages, 1381–1453

Anonimalle Chronicle, see Oman, below

Calendar of the Close Rolls, covering the years 1381–1453, 17 vols., London, 1921–41 (British Library)

Chronicles and Memorials of Great Britain and Ireland during the Middle Ages, 91 vols., London, 1858–69 (Rolls Series)

Cole, H., ed., *Documents Illustrative of English History in the Thirteenth and Fourteenth Centuries*, London, 1844

Coulton, G. G., *The Black Death*, London, 1929

English Chronical 1378–1471, An, ed. J. S. Davies, London, 1856 (Camden Society, LXIV)

Froissart, Jean, *The Chronicles*, translated by John Bourchier (Baron Berners), reprinted in 2 vols., London, 1812 (first published 1523–5)

Gregory, William, *Chronicle*, in *Historical Collections of a London Citizen*, ed. J. Gairdner, London, 1876 (Camden Society NS XVII)

Knighton, Henry, *Chronicon*, edited J. R. Lumby, 2 vols., London, 1889–95 (Rolls Series)

Langland, William, *A Vision concerning Piers Plowman*, rendered into modern English by A. Burrell, London, 1912 (Everyman Library)

Oman, Charles, *The Great Revolt of 1381*, Oxford, 1906 (contains translation of the *Anonimalle Chronicle*, pp. 186–205)

Owst, G. R., *Literature and Pulpit in Mediaeval England*, Cambridge, 1933

Pollard, A. W., ed., *Fifteenth Century Prose and Verse*, London, 1903

Rolls of Parliament, vols. 3–6 (including the Lollard Petition of 1394), London, n.d. (Rolls Series)

Statutes of the Realm, 1381–1450, I, i, London, 1810; II, ii, London, 1816

Three Fifteenth Century Chronicles, ed. J. Gairdner, London, 1880 (Camden Society, NS XXVIII)

Trevelyan, G. M., 'The Peasants' Rising and the Lollards', in *English Historical Review*, XIII, 1898, pp. 509–22
  England in the Age of Wycliffe, London, 1899

Walsingham, Thomas, *Chronicle of England (1328–1388)*, ed. E. M. Thompson, London, 1874

Historia Anglicana 1272–1422, ed. H. T. Riley, 2 vols., London, 1862–4 (Rolls Series)

Wright, T., ed., *Political Song and Poems to Richard III*, London, 1861 (Rolls Series)

Wycliffe, John, *Apology for Lollard Doctrines* (attributed to Wycliffe), London, 1842 (Camden Society, XX)

    Selected English Works, ed. T. Arnold, 2 vols., London, 1871

    Three Treatises, ed. J. H. Todd, Dublin, 1851

2 The Break-up of the Feudal System, 1453–1603

Barrow, Henry, *Supplication to Parliament* (1593), in *Harleian Miscellany*, 4, London, 1744

Brook, Benjamin, *Thomas Cartwright: Memoir of his Life and Writings*, London, 1845

Browne, Robert, *Treatise of Reformation without Tarrying for Any*, ed. T. G. Crippen, London, 1903 (first published 1582)

    The Writings of Robert Harrison and Robert Browne, ed. A. Peel and L. H. Carlson, London, 1953

Burghley Papers, from 1542 to 1596, 2 vols., London, 1740–59

Collinson, P., *The Elizabethan Puritan Movement*, London, 1967

Crowley, Robert, *Select Works*, ed. J. M. Cowper, London, 1872 (EETS)

Dickens, A. G., *The English Reformation*, London, 1964

    Reformation and Society in Sixteenth-Century Europe, London, 1966

Dudley, Edmund, *The Tree of Commonwealth*, ed. D. M. Brodie, Cambridge, 1948

Forrest, William, *Life and Letters*, ed. T. Starkey, London, 1878

Fryde, Edmund, and Miller, Edward, eds., *Historical Studies of the English Parliament*, II, Cambridge, 1970

Furnivall, F. J., ed., *Ballads from Manuscripts*, London, 1868

Hall, Edward, *Chronicle: A History of England from Henry IV to Henry VIII*, ed. Sir Henry Ellis, London, 1809

Haller, William, *Elect Nation: the Meaning and Relevance of Foxe's Book of Martyrs*, Evanston, Ill., 1964

Latimer, Hugh, *Writings*, ed. G. E. Corrie, London, 1844

Marprelate, Martin, *The Marprelate Tracts*, ed. W. Pierce, London, 1911 (see also under Pierce)

Massinger, Philip, *Plays*, ed. F. Cunningham, London, 1868 (particularly *The Bondman*)

More, Sir Thomas, *Utopia*, translated from the Latin by Ralph Robinson (1551), ed. Churton Collins, Oxford, 1904

Mozley, J. F., *John Foxe and his Book*, London, 1940

Neale, J. E., *Queen Elizabeth*, London, 1934

Neville, Alexander, *Norfolk's Furies, or a View of Kett's Camp*, ed. Richard Woods, London, 1615 (first published 1549)

Penry, John, *The Notebook of John Penry 1593*, ed. A. Peel, London, 1944

    Three Treatises Concerning Wales, ed. D. Williams, London, 1960

Pierce, W., ed., *Historical Introduction to the Marprelate Tracts*, London, 1909

Pollard, A. W., ed., *Fifteenth Century Prose and Verse*, London, 1903 (Rolls Series)

Skelton, John, *The Complete Poems*, ed. Philip Henderson, London, 1931

Stow, John, *The Annales of England*, to 1605; continued by E. Howes up to 1631, London, 1632 (first published 1580 as *The Chronicles of England*)

Stubbs, Philip, *The Anatomie of Abuses*, ed. F. J. Furnivall, London, 1877 (first published 1583)

Tawney, R. H., *The Agrarian Problem in the Sixteenth Century*, London, 1912

Tyndale, William, *Parable of the Wicked Mammon*, London, 1842 (first published 1528)

    Works, London, 1848–50 (including *Obedience of a Christian Man* (1528), *Answer to Sir Thomas More* (1530) and translations of the Bible)

Waddington, J., *Penry: The Pilgrim Martyr, 1559–1593*, London, 1854
Wilson, Derek, *England in the Age of Thomas More*, London, 1978

3 The Rise of Capitalism, 1603–88

Arraignment and Tryall, with a Declaration of the Ranters, The, London, 1650
Bacon, Sir Francis, *Works* (including *Novum Organum, Essays Civil and Moral, The Advancement of Learning, New Atlantis*), ed. J. Spedding, R. L. Ellis, D. D. Heath, 14 vols., London, 1857–72
Baxter, Richard, *Reliquiae Baxterianae*, ed. Matthew Sylvester, London, 1696. As *Autobiography*, ed., J. M. Lloyd Thomas, London 1925 (Everyman)
Berens, L. H., *The Digger Movement*, London, 1906
Brailsford, H. N., *The Levellers and the English Revolution*, London, 1961
Bunyan, John, *Works*, ed. G. Offer, 3 vols., London, 1862
Burton, Robert, *The Anatomy of Melancholy*, ed. H. Jackson, 3 vols., London, 1932 (Everyman)
Butler, Samuel, *Hudibras*, ed. J. S. Wilders, London, 1961 (first published 1663)
Calendar of State Papers, Domestic, 1620–60
Carlyle, Thomas, *Oliver Cromwell's Letters and Speeches*, ed. S. C. Lomas, London, 1904
Clarendon, Lord, *History of the Rebellion and Civil Wars in England*, ed. W. D. Macray, 6 vols., Oxford, 1888
Clarke Papers, The, ed. C. H. Firth, 2 vols., *1647–49* (including the Putney Debates) and *1651–60*, London, 1891 and 1901 (Camden Society, NS XLIX and LIV)
Firth, C. H., *Oliver Cromwell*, London, 1900 (World's Classics)
Fox, George, *Journal*, 2 vols., London, 1694, 1698; London, 1924 (Everyman)
Gardiner, S. R., ed., *Cases in the Courts of Star Chamber and High Commission*, London, 1886 (Camden Society NS XXXIX)
Haller, William, ed., *Tracts on Liberty in the Puritan Revolution*, 3 vols., New York, 1933
Haller, William, and Davies, G., eds., *The Leveller Tracts 1647–1653*, Gloucester, Mass., 1964
Harrington, James, *The Commonwealth of Oceana*, ed. H. Morley, London, 1883 (first published 1656)
Hill, Christopher, *Intellectual Origins of the English Revolution*, Oxford, 1965
God's Englishman, London, 1970
The World Turned Upside Down, Harmondsworth, 1975
Milton and the English Revolution, London, 1977
Hobbes, Thomas, *Leviathan*, ed. C. B. Macpherson, Harmondsworth, 1968 (first published 1651)
Hutchinson, Lucy, *Memoirs of the Life of Colonel Hutchinson*, ed. J. Sutherland, Oxford, 1973
Manning, Brian, *The English People and the English Revolution*, London, 1976
Marvell, Andrew, *The Complete Works*, ed. A. B. Grosart, 4 vols., London, 1872–5
The Poems and Letters, ed. H. M. Margoliouth, 2 vols., Oxford, 1927
Selected Poetry and Prose, ed. D. Davison, London, 1952
Milton, John, *Complete Prose Works*, gen. ed. D. M. Wolfe, New Haven, Conn., 1953 (7 vols. published)
The English Poems of John Milton, London, 1940 (World's Classics)
Prose Writings, ed. C. E. Vaughan, London, 1927 (Everyman)
The Works, gen. ed. F. A. Patterson, 20 vols., New York, 1931–40 (Columbia Milton)
Morton, A. L., *The World of the Ranters*, London, 1970
Freedom in Arms, London, 1975
Nayler, James, *A Collection of Sundry Books* . . . London, 1716
Petegorsky, D. W., *Left-Wing Democracy in the English Civil War*, London, 1940
Sabine, G. H., see Winstanley

Sidney, Algernon, *Discourses Concerning Government*, London, 1751 (first published 1680)

Thornbury, G. W., *Songs of the Cavaliers and Roundheads*, London, 1857

Thurloe, J., *Collection of State Papers, 1638–1660*, 7 vols., London, 1742

Whitelocke, Bulstrode, *Memorials of the English Affairs*, London, 1682

Willey, Basil, *The Seventeenth-Century Background*, London, 1934

Winstanley, G., *The Law of Freedom and Other Writings*, ed. C. Hill, Harmondsworth, 1973
The Works, ed. G. H. Sabine, Ithica, NY, 1941

Wolfe, D. M., ed., *Leveller Manifestoes of the Puritan Revolution*, New York, 1944

Woodhouse, A. S. P., ed., *Puritanism and Liberty*, London, 1938 (includes the Putney Debates)

Wright, T., *Political Ballads Published in England during the Commonwealth*, London, 1841 (Percy Society)
Songs and Ballads, London, 1861 (Percy Society)

*

British Library, Thomason Collection, (pamphlets, books, newspapers, etc. of the period 1640–60 collected by George Thomason); catalogue by G. K. Fortescue, 1908

4 The Expansion of Empire, 1689–1788

Addison, Joseph, *The Spectator*, ed. G. Gregory Smith, London, 1907 (Everyman)

Astell, Mary, *An Essay in Defence of the Female Sex*, London, 1721

Burns, Robert, *Complete Poetical Works*, ed. J. L. Robertson, Oxford, 1931

Churchill, Charles, *Poetical Works*, ed. W. Tooke, revised J. L. Hannay, London, 1892

Crabbe, George, *Poems*, ed. Sir A. W. Ward, London, 1905–7

Defoe, Daniel, *Novels and Selected Writings*, 14 vols., Oxford, 1927–8

Dickinson, H. T., ed., *Politics and Literature in the Eighteenth Century*, London, 1974

Fielding, Henry, Novels, particularly *Joseph Andrews*, *Jonathan Wilde*, *Tom Jones*

Gibbon, Edward, *The Decline and Fall of the Roman Empire*, 7 vols., Oxford, 1903–6 (World's Classics)
Memoirs, ed. G. Birkbeck Hill, London, 1900

Goldsmith, Oliver, *Selected Works*, ed. Richard Garnett, London, 1950

Johnson, Samuel, *Prose and Poetry*, ed. Mona Wilson, London, 1950

Junius, *The Letters of Junius*, ed. C. W. Everett, London, 1927

Locke, John, *An Essay Concerning Human Understanding*, ed. J. W. Yolton, London, 1961
Two Treatises of Government, ed. P. Laslett, London, 1960

Mandeville, Bernard de, *The Fable of the Bees*, ed. F. B. Kaye, 2 vols., London, 1924

Marshall, E., *English People in the Eighteenth Century*, London, 1956

Namier, Sir Lewis, *The Structure of Politics at the Accession of George III*, London, 1957

Plumb, J. H., *England in the Eighteenth Century*, Harmondsworth, 1950

Priestley, Joseph, *On the First Principles of Government*, London, 1768

Pope, Alexander, *Poetical Works*, ed. Herbert Davis, Oxford, 1966

Rude, G., *Wilkes and Liberty*, Oxford, 1962

Sutherland, L. S., *The East India Company in Eighteenth Century Politics*, Oxford, 1952

Swift, Jonathan, *Gulliver's Travels*, ed. J. Hayward, London, 1934
Prose Works, ed. Herbert Davis, 14 vols., Oxford, 1939–68

Willey, Basil, *The Eighteenth-Century Background*, London, 1940

5 The Age of Revolution and Total War, 1789–1848

Bamford, Samuel, *Early Days and Passages in the Life of a Radical*, ed. H. Dunckley, London, 1893

Blake, William, *Complete Writings*, ed. Sir Geoffrey Keynes, London, 1966

Brailsford, H. N., *Shelley, Godwin and their Circle*, London, 1913

Bronowski, J., *William Blake and the Age of Revolution*, London, 1972

Burke, Edmund, *Reflections on the Revolution in France*, Harmondsworth, 1969

Byron, Lord, *Letters and Journals*, ed. Thomas Moore, London, 1832
   Poetical and Dramatic Works, revised ed., 3 vols., London, 1963 (Everyman)

Clare, John, *Selected Poems*, ed. J. W. and A. Tibble, London, 1965 (Everyman)
   Selected Poems and Prose, ed. Eric Robinson and Geoffrey Summerfield, London, 1966

Cobbett, William, *Rural Rides*, ed. George Woodcock, Harmondsworth, 1967 (first published 1830)
   Thirteen Sermons, London, 1828

Cole, G. D. H., *The Life of William Cobbett*, London, 1924
   The Life of Robert Owen, London, 1930

Dickens, Charles, *The Old Curiosity Shop* (1840–41), *Barnaby Rudge* (1841), *Dombey and Son* (1848) and other early novels

Elliott, Ebenezer, *Corn-Law Rhymes*, London, 1831

Engels, Friedrich, *Condition of the Working Class in England in 1844*, London, 1892

Erdmann, David V., *Blake: Prophet against Empire*, Princeton, New Jersey, 1954

Godwin, William, *Enquiry Concerning Political Justice*, 3rd ed., London, 1798 (first published 1793)

Hall, W. P., *British Radicalism 1791–97*, New York, 1912

Hazlitt, William, *The Spirit of the Age*, London, 1954 (World's Classics)

Hobsbawm, E. J., *The Age of Revolution – Europe 1789–1848*, London, 1962

Hollis, Patricia, *Class and Conflict in Nineteenth-Century England*, London, 1973

Jones, Ebenezer, *Studies of Sensation and Event*, London, 1879

Lincoln, Anthony, *Social and Political Ideas of English Dissent 1763–1830*, Cambridge, 1938

Loveless, George, *The Victims of Whiggery*, 1837 (pamphlet)

Martineau, Harriet, *Poor Law and Paupers*, London, 1833
   Society in America, 3 vols., London, 1837

Marx, Karl, *Early Writings*, introduced by Lucio Colletti, Harmondsworth, 1975
   The Revolutions of 1848, ed. David Fernbach, Harmondsworth, 1975

O'Connor, Feargus, *The Employer and the Employed*, London, 1844

Paine, Thomas, *Rights of Man*, ed. Henry Collins, Harmondsworth, 1969
   The Complete Writings of Thomas Paine, ed. P. S. Foner, New York, 1945

Pinchbeck, Ivy, *Women Workers and the Industrial Revolution*, London, 1930

Rickword, Edgell, ed., *Radical Squibs and Loyal Ripostes*, London, 1971 (particularly William Hone's pamphlets)

Rudkin, O. D., *Thomas Spence and his Connections*, London, 1927

Shelley, Percy Bysshe, *The Complete Poetical Works*, ed. T. Hutchinson, revised B. P. Kurtz, Oxford, 1934
   Selected Poetry, Prose and Letters, ed. A. S. B. Glover, London, 1951

Thelwall, John, *The Rights of Nature*, London, 1796

Thompson, E. P., *The Making of the English Working Class*, London, 1963

Thompson, William, *Appeal of One Half of the Human Race, Women, Against the Pretensions of the Other Half, Men*, New York, 1970 (first published 1825)

Wickwar, W. D., *The Struggle for the Freedom of the Press*, London, 1928

Wollstonecraft, Mary, *Vindication of the Rights of Woman*, ed. Miriam Kramnick, Harmondsworth, 1975

Wordsworth, William, *The Prelude: A Parallel Text*, ed. J. C. Maxwell, Harmondsworth, 1971
   The Prose Works, ed. Alexander Grosart, 3 vols., London, 1876

6 The Triumph of Capitalism, 1848–1914

Bebel, August, *Women and Socialism*, New York, 1910
Booth, William, *In Darkest England and the Way Out*, London, 1890
Brailsford, H. N., *The War of Steel and Gold*, London, 1914
Briggs, Asa, *Victorian People: 1851–67*, Harmondsworth, 1965
Butler, Josephine, *The Education and Employment of Women*, London, 1868
　Personal Reminiscences of a Great Crusade, London, 1896
Butler, Samuel, *Erewhon*, London, 1872
　The Essential Samuel Butler, ed. G. D. H. Cole, London, 1950
Clough, Arthur Hugh, *Poems*, Oxford, 1951
Cole, G. D. H., *The World of Labour*, London, 1913
Dickens, Charles, *Bleak House* (1852), *Hard Times* (1854), *Little Dorrit* (1857), *Our Mutual Friend* (1865) and other later novels
　The Letters, II, ed. W. Dexter, London, 1938 (Nonesuch Dickens)
Eliot, George, *Felix Holt, the Radical*, Harmondsworth, 1972 (first published 1866)
Fawcett, Millicent, *Women's Suffrage: A Short History*, London, 1912
Gaskell, Mrs, *Mary Barton*, Harmondsworth, 1970 (first published 1848)
　North and South, Harmondsworth, 1970 (first published 1854–5)
Hollis, Patricia, *Women in Public – The Women's Movement 1850–1900*, London, 1979
Keating, Peter, ed., *Into Unknown England: 1866–1913*, London, 1976
Lansbury, George, *My Life*, London, 1931
London, Jack, *The People of the Abyss*, London, 1903
Lucas, John, and Goode John, eds., *Literature and Politics in the Nineteenth Century*, London, 1971
Mann, Tom, *Memoirs*, London, 1923
Marx, Karl, *Capital*, London, 1974 (Everyman)
　The First International and After, ed. David Fernbach, Harmondsworth, 1974
　The Revolutions of 1848, ed. David Fernbach, Harmondsworth, 1973
　Surveys from Exile, ed. David Fernbach, Harmondsworth, 1973
Mayhew, Henry, *London Labour and the London Poor*, London, 1861
　The Unknown Mayhew, ed. E. P. Thompson and E. Yeo, London, 1971
Mill, J. S., *The Subjection of Women*, London, 1869
Morris, William, *Three Works by William Morris – The Pilgrims of Hope, A Dream of John Ball, News from Nowhere*, ed. A. L. Morton, London, 1973
　Political Writings, ed. A. L. Morton, London, 1973
Morton, A. L., *The English Utopia*, London, 1952
Pankhurst, Sylvia, *The Home Front*, London, 1932
　The Suffragette Movement, London, 1977 (first published 1931)
Rubel, Maximilian, and Manall, Margaret, *Marx without Myth – a Chronological Study of his Life and Work*, London, 1975
Ruskin, John, *Unto This Last – the First Principles of Political Economy*, London, 1860
　Fors Clavigera – Letters to the Workmen & Labourers of Great Britain, 8 vols., London, 1871–84
Shaw, G. B., 'The Quintessence of Ibsenism', in *Major Critical Essays*, London, 1932
Thompson, E. P., *William Morris, Romantic to Revolutionary*, London, 1955, 1976
Trollope, Anthony, *Phineas Finn* (1869) and the other Palliser novels
　The Way We Live Now (1875)
Wells, H. G., *New Worlds for Old*, London, 1908
Wilson, Edmund, *To the Finland Station*, New York, 1953

Additional Sources

Arbor, Edward, ed., *The English Scholar's Library of Old and New Works*, no. 4, London, 1878

Arch, Joseph, *The Life of Joseph Arch by Himself*, London, 1898

Aspinall, A., ed., *Early English Trade Unions*, London, 1949

Aubrey, W. H. S., *History of England*, London, 1870

Beer, M., ed., *The Pioneers of Land Reform*, London, 1920

Belloc, Hilaire, *Verse*, London, 1954

Bolingbroke, Henry St John, Lord, *Works*, 4 vols., London, 1967

Brodie, D. M., ed., *A Collection of Three Manuscripts*, Cambridge, 1948

Brontë, Charlotte, *Jane Eyre*, ed. Q. D. Leavis, Harmondsworth, 1966

Burgh, James, *Political Dissertations*, 3 vols., London, 1774–5

Cobbett, William, *The Progress of a Ploughboy to a Seat in Parliament*, ed. W. Reitzel, London, 1933

Coleridge, S. T., *Collected Works*, I, ed. Patton, Mann, Princeton, NJ, 1971

Cooper, Thomas, *The Life of Thomas Cooper Written by Himself*, London, 1872

Davenant, Charles, *The True Picture of a Modern Whig*, London, 1701

Dickens, Charles, *Bleak House*, ed. Norman Page, Harmondsworth, 1971
    Hard Times, ed. David Craig, Harmondsworth, 1969
    The Old Curiosity Shop, ed. Angus Easton, Harmondsworth, 1972
    Our Mutual Friend, ed. Stephen Gill, Harmondsworth, 1971

Herritage, S. J., ed., *England in the Reign of Henry VIII*, London, 1878

Holyoake, G. J., *Life and Character of Henry Hetherington*, London, 1849

Hopkins, G. M., *Poems and Prose*, ed. W. H. Gardner, Harmondsworth, 1953

Howell, T. B. and T. J., *State Trials*, London, 1818

Mann, Tom, *Single Tax to Syndicalism*, 1911 (pamphlet)

Morris, William, *A Dream of John Ball*, London, 1888

Oldys, W., ed., *The Harleian Miscellany*, III, London, 1745

Peacock, W., ed., *English Prose*, Oxford, 1921

Torr, Dona, *Tom Mann*, London, 1936

Tressell, Robert, *The Ragged Trousered Philanthropists*, London, 1955 (first published in an abridged edition in 1914)

Trollope, Anthony, *Phineas Finn*, ed. John Sutherland, Harmondsworth, 1972

Vox Populi, Vox Dei (A Complaint of the Commons against Taxes), London, 1821 (reprinted from Harleian MS 367)

Webb, Mary, *Scars upon My Heart*, ed. C. W. Reilly, London, 1981

Wyatt, Sir Thomas, *The Poems*, ed. A. K. Foxwell, 2 vols., London, 1913

INDEX

Act of Settlement (1701), 35

Adam, 16, 18, 47, 51, 83, 199, 273, 339, 355, 357, 361

Addison, Joseph, 296–7

Africa, 21, 573–4, 581

agitators (New Model Army), 19, 32, 184, 188, 223–4

Agreement of the People (1647), 32, 184, 188

agriculture, 17, 86, 87–90, 109, 144, 145–6, 332–3, 336, 351, 363, 398, 401, 437, 444–6, 453–4

Alexander, A., 385–6

alienation, 362, 381–2, 398–9, 414, 461, 473, 532, 559

America, 21, 37, 284, 326–8, 341, 342, 343, 345, 348, 349, 357, 364, 409, 419, 449, 526

American Civil War, 43, 546

American War of Independence, 37, 326–8, 329, 345, 357

Anabaptists, 171, 178, 203, 261

Anonimalle Chronicle, 24, 47, 50, 53–6, 57–63

Anti-Corn-Law League, 41, 502

Arch, Joseph, 44, 484–6

Archbishop of Canterbury, 27, 29, 31, 50, 56, 58, 61, 71, 107, 122, 123, 125, 126, 127, 129, 130–32, 133, 135, 136, 137, 204

Areopagitica (Milton), 31, 172–5

arms race, 588, 589, 599

army (state): conditions, 334, 358–6; used against the people, 112, 117, 391, 393, 394, 411, 421–2, 483–4, 493, 548, 592–4, 593, 594, 596–7; *see also* New Model

Arnold, Matthew, 547, 548

Asquith, Herbert, 590

Astell, Mary, 297–8

atheism, 241, 293, 403, 455–6, 512–13

Australia, 37, 470, 572

Austria, 560, 603

Austrian Succession, War of (1740–48), 36

Austro-Prussian war, 43

Bacon, Sir Francis, 28, 141, 144, 151, 158–9

Bagehot, Walter, 546

Ball, John, 15, 18, 47, 50–52, 53, 56, 67, 68, 72

ballot, 478, 495, 548, 549, 578

Bamford, Samuel, 408–9, 420

Bank of England, 35, 41, 460

Baptists, 19, 261, 276–82

Barrow, Henry, 28, 135

Becker, Lydia E., 550–51

Belloc, Hilaire, 582–3

Berlin Conference (1884), 44, 581

Besant, Annie, 570, 572

Bill of Rights, 35, 289–90, 492

Bilney, Thomas, 107

Birmingham Political Union, 458–9

Bismarck, 44, 547

Black Death, 17, 25, 49

Black Dwarf (newspaper), 405, 419–20

Blackheath, 56, 78, 80, 109

Blake, William, 13, 15, 16, 339, 344–5, 349–51, 364, 369–70, 372–3, 374, 376, 381–2, 384–5, 388–9, 406–7, 409–10, 413–14, 418–19, 447–8

Bleak House (Dickens), 17, 42, 517–21

Bligh, James, 534

'Bloody Assize' (1685), 35, 284

'Bloody Sunday' (1887), 45, 568–70

Boer War, 45

Bolingbroke, Lord, 310–11

Booth, William, 573–4

Bottomley, Jacob, 238–9

bourgeoisie, 504–5, 509–11, 531, 555, 578; *see also* Middle Class

Boyne, Battle of the, 35
Brailsford, H. N., 588, 590, 597–8
Braxfield, Lord, 21, 37, 375
Brecht, Bertolt, 12
Bridges, Robert, 559
Bright, John, 41
Bright, Ursula and Jacob, 550
British Empire, 27, 28, 33, 34, 35, 36, 37, 38, 39, 40, 44, 45, 287, 327–8, 357, 401, 540, 547, 573–4, 581, 588
Bromyard, John, 73–4
Brontë, Charlotte, 503–4
Browne, Robert, 123–4, 135, 136, 171, 203
Browning, Elizabeth Barrett, 524–5
Bunyan, John, 20, 276–82, 432, 604
Burford (revolt), 206, 223–4
Burgh, James, 325–6
Burke, Edmund, 37, 332, 341, 345, 346–7
Burns, John, 45, 568, 572
Burns, Robert, 333, 334–6, 337–8, 378–9
Burton, Robert, 160–61
Butler, Josephine, 550, 551, 556–9
Butler Samuel, 561–2
Byron, Lord, 15, 16, 17, 391–5, 399–401, 404–5, 416–17, 437–8

Cade, Jack (rebellion), 24, 26, 27, 77–82, 169
Canning, George, 430, 443, 549
Capital (Marx), 22, 43, 507, 516, 549–50
capitalist system, *passim*; described, 20–24; More, 92–3; Crowley, 199–20, 121; Bacon, 144–5; Shakespeare, 153–5; Winstanley, 248–50; Swift, 304; Pope, 307–10; Spence, 361–2; Byron, 391–5; Shelley, 397–9; Owen, 401–2, 460–62; Cobbett, 445–6; Marx, 509–11, 549–50; Ernest Jones, 514–15; Dickens, 518–24; Hopkins, 560; Morris, 565–6; Tressell, 584–5
Captain Pouch Rising, 28, 155–7
Carlile, Richard, 455–6
Carlyle, Thomas, 179, 182, 547, 548, 559
Carson, Sir Edward, 597–8
Cartwright, Thomas, 122–3, 135
Castlereagh, Viscount, 21, 416–17, 423, 427, 430–32
'Cat and Mouse' Act, 585
Cavalier Parliament, 34
Caxton, William, 26

censorship, 16, 28, 34, 39, 96, 125, 132, 145, 172–5, 178, 179, 183–4, 186, 192, 204, 218, 298, 366–7, 377, 378, 345–6, 533
Chaplin, Charles, 579–80
Charles I, 20, 28–32, 159, 163, 164, 168–9, 176, 177, 179, 183, 185, 186, 188, 192, 194, 197, 219, 229, 230, 234, 242, 243, 257, 284, 399, 400; execution, 196, 200–202, 203, 204
Charles II, 34, 265, 272, 276, 277, 284
Charter (Chartist newspaper), 483–4
Chartism, 15, 17, 21, 23, 41, 42, 434, 463, 467, 473–6, 480, 481–2, 488–9, 496, 502, 503–4, 514, 526, 533–4, 578, 579, 594
Chartist petitions: of 1839, 41, 473, 475, 476–80; of 1842, 41, 490–95; of 1848, 42, 502
child labour, 402, 448–9, 459–60, 515, 524–5, 537–8, 549, 563–4
Churchill, Charles, 316–17
Churchill, Winston, 590–91, 592, 594, 604–5
Civil Wars (1642–51), 19, 20, 30, 31, 32–3, 152, 168–247, 262–3, 266, 267, 268, 298
Chronicles, 13, 24, 189; *see also* Anonimalle, Froissart, Gregory, Hall, Knighton, Walsingham
Clare, John, 16, 439–40, 449, 465–7
Clarkson, Lawrence, 178, 239–41
class culture, 511
class war, 451, 471, 497, 500, 526, 560, 562, 569
Clonmell (Ireland), 33, 263
Clough, Arthur Hugh, 513–14, 529–30
Coalition, Wars of (1792–1815), 21, 37–9, 355, 365, 366, 368, 383–4, 393, 419, 427, 431
Cobbe, Frances Power, 554
Cobbett, William, 22, 38, 39, 334, 403–4, 408–9, 430, 435–7, 446–6, 449–52, 459–60
Colchester (battle), 194, 196
Coleridge, S. T., 377–8
common land, 20, 88, 90, 106–7, 112, 113, 145–6, 156–7, 158, 163–4, 188, 198, 199, 200, 212, 213–14, 225–7, 229–30, 231–3, 234, 236, 240, 249–52, 323, 361, 361, 362–3, 439–40

616

commonwealth, 92, 95, 113, 114, 116, 124, 126, 129, 138, 158, 162, 306, 310; seventeenth century, 16, 19, 20, 32, 33, 165–200; as republic, 200–69, 326, 561

Communism, 22, 198, 199, 200, 231, 232, 247, 254, 504, 510–11, 516, 559, 560, 575–7

Communist Manifesto (Marx and Engels), 22, 42, 509–11

Congregationalists, 123, 135, 136

Connel, Jim (docker), 572–3

Conservatives, 588, 589, 591; *see also* Tories

Cooper, Thomas (Chartist), 497

Copernicus, 27

Coppe, Abiezer, 218–21

Corn Laws, 38, 39, 41, 42, 419, 429, 437, 453, 458, 465, 466, 502

Council of State, 20, 32, 201, 203, 204, 205, 206, 208, 211, 213, 223, 224, 235, 242

Council of Trent (1545), 27, 176

Court of High Commission, 27, 30, 35, 133, 135, 136, 137, 163, 289

covenants, 29, 30, 181, 229, 230, 232, 233, 236, 317

Cowper, William, 432

Crabbe, George, 332–3

Cranmer, Thomas, 27

Crimean war, 43, 430–31, 532, 534

Cromwell, Oliver, 19, 20, 30, 31, 32, 33, 34, 163, 169, 179–80, 188, 190, 196, 206, 212, 222, 223, 247–51, 255, 256–7, 258–9, 260, 261–3, 284, 555

Cromwell, Richard, 34

Crowley, Robert, 118–22

Cunningham Grahame, R. B., 568

Daily Herald, 598–9, 601, 602–3

Darwin, Charles, 43

Davenant, Charles, 292–4

Declaration of Independence, 37, 326–8, 470

Declaration of the Rights of Man, 37, 341–2

Defoe, Daniel, 287, 291–2, 295–6

demonstrations, 30, 375, 420–27, 433, 463, 533–4, 547, 548, 568–70, 572–3, 589–90, 593

Derby Turn-out, 40

Dickens, Charles, 15, 17, 42, 486–8, 517–21, 527–9, 532, 542–6

Diggers, 15, 19–20, 32, 198, 212–14, 225–7, 229–38, 240, 247–55

Disraeli, Benjamin, 443, 502–3, 547, 578

dockers, 15, 572–3, 591, 592–4, 596

Don Juan (Byron), 17, 400–401, 416–17

Donne, John, 140

Drogheda (1649), 33

Dudley, Edmund, 85–6

Dunbar (battle, 1650), 20, 33, 255, 256

East India Company, 28, 36

economic conditions, 14, 17, 18, 19, 21, 23, 50, 77, 80, 86, 119, 121, 141, 144, 186, 198, 199, 248–55, 306–7, 310–11, 314, 336, 391, 392, 401–2, 403–4, 406, 408, 435–6, 441–2, 444–6, 478, 509–11, 535, 536–7, 539–40, 543, 555, 592, 598–9

education, 43, 45, 109, 110, 141, 151, 172, 174, 179, 237, 296, 297, 300, 332, 348, 351, 352, 353, 355, 380, 381, 408, 452, 484, 485, 487–8, 521, 538, 552, 553, 564, 567

Edward VII, 588, 589

Edwards, Thomas, 169, 175, 176

Eldon, Lord, 21, 423, 427–8

elections, 268, 315, 325, 330, 363, 367, 404, 438, 458, 478–9, 491, 495, 514, 591

Eliot, George, 547–8

Elizabeth I, 27, 122, 123, 126, 128, 129, 130, 131, 133, 136, 137, 138, 146, 159, 246

Elliott, Ebenezer, 453–4

enclosures, 16, 17, 18, 19, 38, 86, 87–90, 106–7, 109, 110, 112, 113, 119, 120, 121, 141, 156–7, 163–4, 188, 200, 213, 214, 225, 234, 236, 322–3, 439–40, 539

Engels, Friedrich, 22, 42, 464–5, 504, 509–11, 516, 578–9, 595

Fabian Society, 44

factories, 388, 390, 401–2, 405, 406, 429, 436, 486, 527

Fairfax, Sir Thomas, 31, 184, 196, 225, 226, 233

Fielding, Henry, 314–15

Finlan, James (Chartist), 534

First International, 538, 541–2, 547, 556, 559

First World War, 21, 22, 23, 45, 547, 598–605,; protests, 599, 600, 601–2

617

Fish, Simon, 101–3
Fleet prison, 58, 128, 135, 165
forcible feeding, 587–8
Forrest, William, 110–12
Fox, Charles James, 366
Fox, George, 216–18, 241–2, 256, 258–9, 271, 272
frame-breaking, 390–95, 449–52
France, 21, 25, 26, 28, 29, 34, 35, 36, 37, 38, 40, 42, 43, 44, 106, 121, 144–5, 227, 293, 310, 329, 341–4, 349, 350, 355, 356, 358, 365, 373, 400, 403, 415, 434, 505, 509, 513, 532, 540, 588, 595, 600, 603, 604
Franco-German War, 44, 560
Free Trade, 502, 504, 509, 531, 540, 578
French Revolution, 16, 37, 341–4, 345, 348, 349–51, 354, 356, 357, 370, 377, 414–15, 532
Froissart, *Chronicles*, 24, 50–52, 57, 67
Frost, John, 473, 483–4, 495
Fulke Greville, Lord Brooke, 159–60

Gagging Acts, 39, 408, 419
Gaskell, Mrs, 473–6, 480
gas-workers, 572
General Election: of 1852, 516; of 1910, 591
General Strike (1842), 496–9, 502
George III, 317, 321, 326, 327, 367, 368, 369, 383, 384, 428, 429, 430, 448
George IV, 448
Germany, 21, 22, 42, 44, 45, 96, 368, 431, 434, 505, 535–6, 540, 547, 560, 588, 598, 600, 603, 604, 605
Gibbon, Edward, 336–7
Gifford, William, 443–4
Gladstone, William Ewart, 539, 547
'Glorious Revolution' (1688), 20, 35, 289–90, 296, 342, 347, 531
Godwin, William, 351, 355, 359–61
Goldsmith, Oliver, 16, 318–19, 322–3
Goodwin, John, 169–70
Gordon Riots, 37
Great Exhibition (1851), 517–18
Greece, 433–4, 577
Greek War of Independence, 433
Gregory, William, *Chronicle*, 76–7, 77–8, 80–82
Grey, Lord, 450, 451
Grey, Sir Edward, 585–6

Grosvenor, Lord Robert, 533, 534
Gutenberg Bible, 26

Habeas Corpus, 37, 39, 374, 380, 408
Haig, Cecilia (suffragette), 590
Hales, Sir Robert (Chancellor, 1381), 52, 53, 61
Hall, Edward, *Chronicle*, 98–100, 106–7
Hampden, John, 29
hanging, 22, 56, 67, 76, 82, 117, 118, 122, 390, 391, 394, 410, 411–12, 419, 450, 453
Hardie, Keir, 23, 45, 585, 586, 587, 588, 589, 591–2, 599, 600
Hardy, Thomas, 37, 366–9, 375, 380
Harney, George, 509
Harrison, Frederick, 571
Hazlitt, William, 355, 427–8, 441–2, 443–4
Henderson, Arthur, 600
Henry VI, 77, 78, 79, 80, 81, 82
Henry VIII, 27, 85, 86, 99, 100, 101, 103, 104, 107, 128, 140, 399, 400
Hetherington, Henry, 512–13
Hill, Christopher, 16, 198, 210, 242, 247, 262, 263, 265, 269
Hobbes, Thomas, 244–7
Holcroft, Thomas, 351
Hone, William, 432–3
Hopkins, Gerard Manley, 559–60
hours of work, 402, 449, 460, 493, 537, 538, 563–4
House of Commons, 28, 29, 30, 71, 168, 169, 176–7, 181, 191, 192, 193, 203, 206, 215, 216, 229–30, 257, 276, 283–4, 289, 293, 308, 317, 322, 323–4, 329, 330–31, 367, 404, 419–20, 437, 459–60, 467–8, 476–80, 490–95, 531, 587
House of Lords, 30, 32, 34, 176, 177, 191, 192, 194, 203, 204, 257, 268, 269, 289, 322, 330, 364, 391, 450, 468, 561, 574, 595
Hundred Years' War, 17, 18, 25–6, 77, 145
hunger, 42, 69, 73, 74, 90, 93, 94, 102, 108, 111, 112, 119, 135, 136, 160, 191, 192, 200, 230, 287, 294, 303, 307, 314, 332–3, 334, 353, 358, 391, 394, 395, 401, 408, 410, 419, 424, 435, 436, 474, 492
hunger strikes, *see* Women's suffrage
Hunt, Henry, 421

Hunt, Leigh, 429
Hyde Park demonstrations, 533–4, 548
Hyndman, H. M., 568, 600

Imperialism (after 1870), 547, 581, 588–9, 598, 604, 605
India, 28, 36
Independent Labour Party, 45
Independents (seventeenth century), 30, 31, 123, 169, 175, 178, 192, 203, 237, 246, 255, 261
Industrial Revolution, 21, 388, 390–95, 401–2, 413–14, 526, 535–6
informers, government, 410–12, 419, 424
International Socialist Bureau, 600
International Working Men's Association, 22, 43, 507, 516, 538–42
Ireland, 26, 27, 28, 32, 33, 38, 42, 44, 45, 169, 179, 181, 235, 259, 263, 315–17, 416, 420, 492, 495, 498, 502, 539, 547, 555–6, 564, 568, 569, 597–8
Ireton, General, 32, 181–2, 189, 190, 196, 206
Irish famine, 42, 502, 555

Jacobins, 37, 38, 355, 361, 373, 380, 444
Jamaica, 33, 451
James I, 28
James II, 20, 35, 289
Jaures, Jean, 600
Jefferson, Thomas, 326–8, 341
Jeffreys, Judge, 35, 284, 289, 395
Jerusalem (Blake), 16, 339, 406–7, 409–10, 413–14, 418–19
Jews, 139, 307
Johnson, Joseph, 351
Johnson, Samuel, 313, 316
Jones, Ebenezer, 499–501
Jones, Ernest, 473, 514–15, 526
Joyce, Cornet George, 31
'Junius', 321–2, 323–4

Kenney, Annie, 585–6
Kett, Robert, 24, 27, 112, 113, 115, 116, 118
Kett, William, 112, 118
Knighton, Henry, 72–3

Labour Parliament (1854), 526–7
Labour party, 23, 588, 592, 602–3

landlords, 194, 214, 225, 229–30, 231–3, 234, 237, 248, 251, 252, 253, 306, 310, 329, 362, 363, 473–8, 446, 455, 502, 547, 562, 564
Landor, W. S., 448
Langland, Willism, 69
Latimer, Hugh, 27, 107–10
Laud, Archbishop, 29, 31, 125, 166, 204
Law of Freedom (Winstanley), 247–55, 257–8
Leigh, Mary (suffragette), 587–8
Lenin, 23, 606
Levellers, 15, 19, 20, 31, 32, 33, 156, 163–4, 169, 178, 181, 184, 188, 191–3, 194, 198, 202–11, 212, 213, 214, 219, 221–3, 223–4, 256–8, 270, 345, 355, 367, 444
Liberal party, 578, 585–6, 587, 588, 591, 594; *see also* Whigs
Liebknecht, Karl, 23, 599
Lilburne, Elizabeth, 214–15
Lilburne, John, 19, 29, 31, 32, 33, 165–6, 177, 181, 184, 191–3, 194, 198, 203–7, 209–10, 214, 216, 256–8, 472
Linnel, Alfred, 570
Liverpool dock strike (1911), 592–4
Liverpool, Lord, 21, 427, 462
Lloyd, George (Chartist), 482–3
Locke, John, 290–91
Lockyer, Robert, 212, 215
Lollards, 18, 25, 74–5, 76–7, 96
London Corresponding Society, 38, 361, 366–9, 432
London, Jack, 583–4
London Working Men's Association, 467
Long Parliament (1640), 29, 33
Loveless, George, 463–4, 470–71
Lovett, William, 473
Lowe, Robert, 548
Luddite riots, 39, 390–95, 404–5
Luther, Martin, 27, 96, 140, 389
Luxembourg, Rosa, 23, 599

Macauley, Lord, 456–7, 490
MacDonald, Ramsay, 602–3
Malthus, Robert, 38, 415, 441–2, 444, 464
Manchester Guardian, 593
Mandeville, Bernard de, 294
Mann, Tom, 45, 572, 592–4, 596–7
Margarot, Maurice, 37, 367–9, 374

Marprelate, Martin: controversy, 28, 125, 136; tracts, 28, 125–35

Marshalsea prison, 87, 128

Marston Moor (battle, 1644), 31, 196, 284

Martineau, Harriet, 469–70

Marvell, Andrew, 259–61, 262–3, 276, 282–4

Marx, Karl, 13, 22, 23, 35, 42, 43, 153, 502, 504–5, 507, 509–11, 514, 516–17, 526–7, 530–32, 533–6, 538–42, 547, 549–50, 555–6, 595

Massinger, Philip, 161–2, 164–5

Master and Servant Act (1867), 561

match-girls (1889), 572

Mayhew, Henry, 538

Mazzini, Giuseppe, 513

middle class (power), 457, 488–9, 509–11, 516, 529–30, 535, 575

Mill, John Stuart, 552–4

Milton, John, 13, 15, 16, 20, 30, 31, 32, 33, 34, 133, 149, 166–8, 169, 172–6, 196, 200–202, 203, 242–4, 255, 263–70, 273–5, 355, 378, 416

miners, 15, 309, 452, 483, 524–5, 529, 591, 596, 597

monarchy: absolutist, 13, 15, 16, 17, 18, 19, 28, 32, 56, 60, 76, 78, 79, 99, 128, 142–3, 146, 159–60, 177, 196, 201, 203, 250, 253, 265–9, 284, 295, 296, 326, 327, 329, 336, 342, 348, 355, 358, 370, 399–400, 416; constitutional, 284, 289, 295, 310, 315, 321, 323, 324, 330, 353, 355, 356, 357, 360, 371, 395–6, 410, 424, 428, 429, 434, 448, 560

Monmouth rebellion, 35, 284

monopoly ownership, 21, 89, 187, 234, 309–11, 336, 357, 455, 458, 468, 493, 510, 515, 527, 547–8, 584–5, 591

More, Sir Thomas, 15, 18, 27, 86–90, 90–93

Morning Post, 534

Morris, William, 23, 44, 67–8, 507, 565–7, 575–7, 581–2, 595, 604

Morton, A. L., 502

Muggletonians, 178

Murray, Dr Jessie, 590

Napolean, 38, 39, 401, 403, 437, 442

Napoleonic Wars, 21, 406, 555; see also Coalition, Wars of

Naseby (battle, 1645), 31, 196

National Charter Association, 497, 498–9

National debt, 311, 329, 357, 368, 404, 411, 412, 419, 430, 491, 527

National Union of Railwaymen, 593, 597

Nayler, James, 256, 262, 270–71

Neville, Alexander, 24, 112–18

Newgate prison, 122, 128, 220, 257

New Model Army (1645–60), 19, 31, 176, 179–80, 181–2, 183, 184–8, 188–91, 192, 194, 195, 196, 203, 205, 212, 222, 223–4, 232, 233–4, 236, 237, 238, 250, 256, 257, 262, 265, 284

Newport Rising (1839), 41, 473, 483–4

Norfolk Revolt (1549), 15, 19, 27, 112–18

Northern Star, 41, 471, 472, 481–3, 488–9, 490

Oastler, Richard, 448–9, 473

O'Brien, Bronterre (Chartist), 473, 488–9

O'Connor, Feargus (Chartist), 473, 488, 499

Oldcastle, Sir John, 35, 76

Our Mutual Friend (Dickens), 17, 542–6

Overton, Richard, 19, 32, 176–7, 182–4, 203–5, 207–8, 209–10

Owen, Robert, 38, 40, 401–2, 405, 460–62, 467, 513

Paine, Tom, 37, 326–7, 339, 345–9, 345–9, 351, 354–7, 361, 380, 455, 467

Palmerston, Lord, 532, 534, 546

Paris Commune (1871), 44, 560

Pankhust, Christabel, 45, 585–6, 589, 601–2

Pankhurst, Emmeline, 45

Pankhurst, Dr Richard, 43, 550, 560–61, 589

Pankhurst, Sylvia, 45, 585–91, 600

Paradise Lost (Milton), 16, 263–4, 269–70, 373–5

Parker, Richard, 384

Pauper Press, 22, 41, 405, 419–20, 454–5, 455–9, 460, 462–3, 465–7, 471, 472, 481–3, 488–9, 509, 514–15, 526–7, 535–6

Peasants' Revolt (1381), 14, 15, 17–18, 25, 47, 49–68

Penn, William, 35

Penry, John, 28, 125, 133, 135, 136–8

Pentridge Rising, 39, 410–13

People's Charter, 41, 467, 472, 496, 498

People's Paper, 514–15, 526–7, 535–6

Peterloo Massacre, 21, 39, 420–27, 429, 433

Petition of Right (1628), 29, 215, 224

Pioneer, 460, 462–3

Pitt, William, 21, 37, 38, 39, 377, 380, 456

Place, Francis, 473

Plug riots, 41

Poland, 357, 504, 505, 541

police, 40, 391, 394, 408, 421, 422, 445, 476, 493, 533, 534, 548, 556, 568–9, 570, 586, 587, 590, 594

Poor Law (1834), 40, 464–5, 471, 473, 488, 492, 493, 531, 546, 579–80

Poor Laws, 21, 314–15, 404, 419, 429, 441, 451

Poor Man's Guardian, 454–5, 456–9

Pope, Alexander, 16, 287, 307–10

Prelude (Wordsworth), 343–4, 358, 365–6, 373–4, 386–8

Presbyterians, 30, 31, 32, 34, 135, 175, 176, 178, 179, 180, 181, 182, 192, 203, 222, 237, 242, 245, 246, 255, 261, 262

press, 377, 378, 443, 448–9, 493, 530, 534, 586, 587, 691, 593, 598–9, 601, 602–3; *see also* Pauper Press

Preston (battle, 1648), 32, 194, 262

Price, Richard, 342–3

prices, 69, 76, 80, 88, 89, 110–11, 119, 141, 144, 191, 306–7, 309, 334, 341, 388, 395, 436, 437, 447, 456, 465–6, 601

Pride's Purge, 32

Priestley, Joseph, 319–21, 351, 354

Prince, Thomas, 32, 203–5, 206, 208–9, 209–10

Prince Regent, 399, 400, 433

Prostitution, 370, 574; *see also* Josephine Butler

Protestants, 27, 28, 35, 107, 108, 171, 201, 235, 267, 389

Prynne, William, 29, 165

Public Health Report (1864), 539

Puritans, 19, 28, 30, 118, 122, 125, 126, 131, 132, 157, 166, 198

Putney Denates, 20, 32, 184, 188–91

Quakers, 19, 20, 216–18, 219, 238, 241–2, 256, 257, 258–9, 262, 270–72

Queen Mab (Shelley), 22, 395–9

railways, 40, 42, 44, 578

Rainborough, Thomas, 14, 188, 189, 190

Ranters, 19, 178, 218–21, 238–9, 239–41, 262

Ready and Easy Way to Establish a Free Commonwealth (Milton), 16, 20, 34, 149, 265–9

Reform Act (1832), 21, 22, 40, 456–8, 473, 477, 488, 502, 531, 547; Second Reform Act (1867), 43, 546–9, 578; Third (1884), 44, 578

Reformation, 27, 96, 103, 107, 124, 125, 127, 128, 133, 157, 166–8, 174, 234, 266

regicide, 32, 37, 152, 200–202, 204, 230, 234, 242, 243, 355, 365

rent, 60, 69, 87, 109, 110, 111, 119, 121, 194, 252, 329, 362, 363, 399, 437–8, 446, 456, 457, 458, 467, 502, 510, 551, 562, 564

Repeal of the Corn Laws, 42, 502, 517, 531

Restoration (1660), 20, 33, 34, 218, 269–85

revolution, 16, 19, 20, 29, 30–33, 37, 40, 42, 45, 133, 142, 181, 218–21, 227, 228, 232, 234, 242, 244, 247, 263, 284, 289, 296, 310, 315, 320, 324, 326–8, 339, 341–4, 345, 348, 349, 354, 355, 358–9, 361, 364, 367, 386, 388, 390, 411, 434, 473, 504, 509–11, 532, 533–4, 556, 560, 575–7, 604

Revolutions of 1848, 42, 434, 509, 513, 516, 578

Richard II, 15, 25, 54, 55, 56, 57, 59–66, 67, 142

Rickword, Edgell, 432

Ridley, Nicholas, 107

Rights of Man (Paine), 37, 339, 341–2, 345–9, 354–7

Riot Act, 484, 593

risings and riots, 161–2, 227, 319, 320, 417–18, 452; *see also* Cade, Captain Pouch Rising, Lollards, Newport Rising, Norfolk Revolt, Peasants Revolt, Pentridge Rising, Plug riots, Suffolk Rising, Swing riots

Roman Catholicism, 27, 28, 35, 37, 74, 107, 108, 135, 136, 137, 157, 161, 166, 175, 235, 237, 246–7, 267, 282, 289, 389, 428, 559

Roses, Wars of, 18, 26

621

Royalists, 28–34, 179, 181, 196, 214, 244, 247, 250, 298, 358
Rump Parliament, 32, 33, 34, 247, 257
Ruskin, John, 536–7, 547
Russia, 39, 43, 45, 357, 431, 541, 588, 589, 600, 603
Russian Revolution (1905), 589
Russian Revolution (1917), 604, 605
Rye House plot, 35, 284

St George's Hill, Surrey (1649), 198, 212, 226, 229, 231, 236
Salisbury, Marquis of, 569
Salmasius, 242
Saltmarsh, John, 178–9
Scotland, 26, 27, 29, 30, 31, 33, 36, 37, 136, 166, 175, 181, 194, 196, 247, 255, 259, 266, 326, 333, 405, 445, 447, 492, 498
Second International (1889), 539
sedition, 37, 38, 39, 120–22, 141, 183, 206, 243, 269, 345, 366, 376, 377, 429, 498
Sedition Acts, 21
Seven Years' War (1756–63), 36
Sexby, Edward, 188, 190
Shakespeare, William, 13, 15, 83, 139, 142–3, 145–7, 152–5, 157–8, 316, 400, 447
Shares, 543
Shaw, G. B., 577–8
Shelley, Mary, 351, 429
Shelley, P. B., 15, 16, 22, 351, 395–9, 403, 410–13, 414–15, 423–7, 429–32, 433–4
Shirle, John, 67
ship money, 29
Sidmouth, Viscount, 21, 39, 417, 421, 424, 427
Sidney, Algernon, 35, 284–5
Sieyès, Abbé de, 349–51
Six Acts (1819), 39
Skelton, John, 93–5
Smithfield, 15, 61–4, 77
Snowden, Philip, 587
socialism, 18, 22, 538, 547, 565, 566–7, 568–9, 575–6, 579, 581–2, 584–5, 594–6, 600, 605
Society of Friends, see Quakers
South America, 35, 40, 309
South Sea Bubble, 36, 309
Southey, Robert, 377, 443

Soviet Union, 23, 605
Spa Fields riot, 39, 408
Spain, 27, 28, 33, 35, 36, 37, 38, 106, 133, 306, 313, 329, 357, 400, 401, 434, 446
Spanish Succession, war of (1701–13), 35
Speenhamland Act, 38
Spence, Thomas, 361–3
Spithead Mutiny, 382–4
Star Chamber, Court of, 30, 163, 165, 172, 204
statutes, 13, 17, 25, 26, 49, 71–2, 80, 110, 128, 187, 371, 377, 394
Stead, W. T., 570
Stephens, J R., 471, 473
Stow, John, Annals, 155–7
Strafford, Earl of, 29–30, 125, 204
strikes, 21, 23, 36, 38, 39, 40, 41, 43, 45, 481, 496–9, 526, 572–3, 587–8, 591–4, 596–7
Stock Exchange, 431, 550
Stubbes, Philip, 124–5
Suffolk Rising (1526), 98–9
suffrage, 21, 22, 40, 41, 43, 188–9, 190, 268, 322, 325–6, 330–31, 367–9, 371–2, 380, 404, 411, 457–8, 467–9, 472, 478–80, 489, 494, 514, 547–8, 561, 578
Sunday Trading Bill (1855), 533–4
Swann, Joseph, 454–5
Swift, Jonathan, 15, 16, 287, 299–307
Swing riots, 40, 449–52

Taylor, Harriet, 552
taxes, 17, 19, 28, 29, 53–4, 77, 141, 185, 187, 191, 205, 224, 226, 229, 249, 276, 292, 293, 307, 310, 314, 326, 329, 336, 353, 356, 357, 363, 404, 406, 411, 419, 430, 432, 433, 445, 446, 447, 449, 451, 453, 456, 365–6, 477, 478, 479, 491–2, 515, 539, 595
Tenure of Kings and Magistrates (Milton), 32, 200–202
Thelwall, John, 375, 380–81
Thirty-Nine Articles (1563), 27
Thompson, William (Leveller), 223–4
Thomson, James, 312–13
Thorne, Will, 572, 600
Tickell, John, 218
Tillett, Ben, 572, 600
Times, 530

tithes, 18, 19, 102, 119, 120, 168, 186, 187, 205, 220, 234, 237, 248, 252, 451, 456, 465

Tolpuddle Martyrs, 40, 463–4, 470

Tories, 20, 35, 39, 289, 310, 443, 462, 473, 514, 515, 517, 569, 588, 589

Tower of London, 26, 31, 32, 57, 59, 60, 61, 104, 184, 191, 206, 209, 210, 215, 256, 284, 380

Trades Union Congress, 43, 44

trade unions, 40, 41, 43, 45, 458–9, 462–3, 496, 547, 572–3, 585, 591–2, 593, 596, 599, 603

Trafalgar Square demonstrations, 44–5, 548, 568–70, 600

transportation, 390, 394, 404, 410, 444, 450, 451, 463, 470, 483, 487

Triplow Heath, 31, 224

Tressell, Robert, 584–5, 594–6

Triple Alliance of Unions (1913), 597

Trollope, Anthony, 547, 548–9

'Two Nations', 502–13

Tyler, Wat, 15, 55, 60–64, 169

Tyndale, William, 96–7, 100

Ulster, 33, 597–8

unemployment, 22, 39, 42, 44–5, 87, 88, 89, 99, 335, 362, 390, 391, 392, 404, 408, 410, 449–52, 454, 457, 459, 464–5, 474, 477, 480, 484, 486, 487, 490, 515

USA, 326, 328, 329, 345, 391, 530, 552, 556, 595

Utopia (More), 18, 86–90, 90–93

Victoria, Queen, 475, 492, 502, 534, 560, 588

Wade, Arthur S., 458–9

Wales, 25, 136, 182, 183, 196, 483, 492, 498, 591

Walsingham, Thomas, *Chronicles*, 50, 52–3, 65–6

Walworth, William, 58, 61, 63, 64–5

Walwyn, William, 19, 32, 171–2, 194–6, 202–3, 206, 209–10, 210–11, 221–3

Warden, John (Chartist), 481–2

Warr, John, 227–8

Warren, Sir Charles, 568, 569 .

Washington, George, 345

Waterloo, 21, 39, 400

Watson, Richard, 370

wealth, in common: defined, 19–20; Ball, 51; More, 90–91; Kett, 113; Bacon, 141, 151; Shakespeare, 154, 157–8; Winstanley, 198–200, 213–14; 250–55; Milton, 242–4; Spence, 362–3; Wordsworth, 387–8; Cobbett, 445–6; Marx, 526–7; Morris, 566–7

weapons of destruction, 300–301, 303–4, 363

Webb, Beatrice, 571–2

Webb, Mary, 603

Wellington, Duke of, 21, 400–401, 462

West Indies, 37, 470

Wexford (massacre), 33

Whigs, 16, 20, 35, 40, 284, 289, 292–4, 310, 456–7, 462, 463, 514, 515, 517, 578

Whitelock, Bulstrode, 212, 216

Whitgift, Archbishop, 27, 122, 125, 129, 130–32, 133, 135, 136, 137

Wilde, Oscar, 580–81

Wildman, John, 184–8, 189, 191, 192–3

Wilkes, John, 36, 52–3, 317–18

William of Orange, 35, 289, 290

Williams, Henria (suffragette), 590

Winstanley, Gerrard (Digger), 12, 14, 19, 20, 149, 197–200, 212–14, 225–7, 229–38, 240, 247–55, 345

Wollstonecraft, Mary, 351–4

Wolstonholme, Elizabeth, 550

women: condition, 12, 22, 69, 72, 77, 102, 120, 157, 211, 240, 297–8, 381, 469–70, 537, 552–4, 563–4, 571–2, 601–2, 603; rights, 214–15, 216, 239–40, 351–4, 470, 485, 503–4, 554; struggle for change, 16, 60, 156, 163–4, 170, 270, 420–22, 423, 472–3, 552, 577–8; and suffrage, 43, 45, 550–51, 585–6, 587–8, 589–90, 597; as victims, 88, 135, 136, 137–8, 186, 194, 251, 297–8, 305–7, 337–8, 354, 370, 448–9, 482, 487–8, 556–9, 574, 579–80

Women's Social and Political Union, 585, 589; *see also* Women, suffrage

Wooler, Thomas J., *see* Black Dwarf

Worcester (battle, 1651), 20, 247, 255

Wordsworth, William, 15, 16, 343–4, 358–9, 365–6, 370–72, 373–4, 377, 386–8, 429 workhouse (Poor Law), 464–5, 477, 490, 501, 523, 579–80

working class (post–1789): action, 364, 390, 391–5, 404–5, 411, 417–18, 434, 449–51, 452, 454–5, 457–8, 463, 475–6, 481, 483–4, 496–9, 533–4, 548–9, 562, 568, 572–3, 575–6, 579, 591, 592–4, 599, 600; aims, 378–9, 380–81, 419–20, 424–7, 462, 468–9, 472–3, 476–80, 526–7, 541–2, 547–8, 556, 566–7; organization, 419–20, 449–50, 458–9, 462, 463, 470–71, 474, 488–9, 526–7, 540–41, 579, 591

Wright, Ada (suffragette), 589–90

Wyatt, Sir Thomas, 103–6

Wycliffe, John, 15, 18, 50, 67, 69–71, 72, 73, 74, 96, 167

Yeats, W. B., 605

Yorke, Henry 'Redhead', 374–6